Moth Busters, Dr. Prepper, and Oral Robbers

Freaky Florida Investigations

Margaret Lashley

Published by Zazzy Ideas, Inc., 2020.

Copyright

Dedication

TO MY BROTHER EARL, who exemplified all that is good and kind and true about the redneck spirit.

And to "Florida Man," who is all that is the exact opposite.

What Readers are Saying about the Series

...

"*I READ A LOT, AND KINDLE suggested your book. This book is laugh out loud funny. Is everyone in Florida crazy? I have read Tim Dorsey, Carl Hiaasen, and Randy Wayne White. Those writers are funny but they need to watch out for you.*"

"*A funny cozy, science fiction, thriller, mystery all rolled into one great story!*"

"*I read the whole book in two days, something I've never done before! I just couldn't wait to find out what was going to happen next!*"

"*Margaret Lashley has a knack for creating funny, small town strange, off the wall, but so endearing type of characters.*"

"*If you enjoy laugh-out-loud comedy, this book is for you!*"

"*Plenty of mysteries and slap stick humor with a backwoods redneck cousin thrown in the mix. I almost felt like I was reading a cross between Terry Pratchett and Piers Anthony.*"

"*The twists and turns of the story line kept me eagerly turning the pages to see what would happen next and kept me thinking as well. Loved the small town feel of the book and the very real to life characters. Great start to a new series!*"

Prologue

THE MAJORITY OF SCIENTISTS believe there's an elegant order to the universe. But then again, most of them have never spent any time in Florida.

Sometime around 1987, the oddly shaped chunk of land dangling off the southeastern corner of the United States began to be overrun by a strange creature—a hominid who, prior to the invention of Google, had remained completely unknown to the human genome.

He's identified collectively as "Florida Man."

Exactly how, when, or why this subspecies first appeared in Florida is still highly debated. However, mainstream theorists agree on one point—the creature's complex migratory behavior is typically prompted by "the forcible removal of his person" from his former place of employment and/or familial abode.

Once freed from normal societal obligations, Florida Man's primal urges, compounded by alcohol, old Jimmy Buffet songs, and/or warrants for his arrest, compel him to climb into an orange AMC Pacer with $23.46 in his wallet and keep driving south until he runs out of money, beer, gas, brain cells, land mass, or some tragically interchangeable combination thereof.

Like any invasive species, Florida Man's influence on the native population has been widespread and devastating. In fact, Florida Man has single-handedly changed both the state's reputation and its constitution.

Florida's longtime moniker, "The Sunshine State" is soon to be replaced with "The W-T-F State."

In addition, due to the exponential increase in Florida Man's bizarre behavioral tendencies, the state legislature is now considering a revision to the state motto, "Florida: In God We Trust." Current proposed alternatives include:

"Florida: Never Wear Pants Again!"

"Florida: Stupors. They're not Just for Breakfast Anymore!"

"Florida: Sure, You Can Pay for that with a Live Alligator!"

And my personal favorite, "Florida: Really, God? *Really?*"

Florida Man has been caught on video surveillance tape burglarizing cars wearing nothing but a ball cap and a bra, dancing atop a patrol car to ward off vampires, breaking into homes to suck people's toes, and shoplifting puppies with a python in his pants.

And that was just last week.

"Florida Man" is to the Sunshine State what the "People of Walmart" are to retailers—an embarrassing, unavoidable, yet morbidly fascinating source of revenue and perverse entertainment.

As a native Floridian—and somewhat decent, law-abiding citizen—I thought I would remain immune to the plague of unchecked lunacy corrupting our once-fine state.

But I was wrong.

I didn't go searching for Florida Man. But somehow, nevertheless, he found me.

Or, at least, I *think* it was him ....

Chapter One

I WISH I COULD SAY I'd been doing something glamorous or heroic when the world as I knew it skittered off its axis. You know—saving a baby, cracking a drug cartel—that kind of thing. But the truth was, I'd been working security detail at a mall.

I was *Paul Blart Mall Cop*—without even the lousy Segway.

I'd been sitting on a bench outside the mall taking a coffee break when it happened. I spotted a guy in green crocs and tiger-striped hot-pants helping himself to a bicycle with the aid of a pair of bolt cutters. After spilling my coffee down the front of my shirt, I ran after him.

Next thing I knew, I heard a bang.

Then the lights went out.

When they came back on, well, I couldn't see it at the time, but my whole life had shifted trajectory. I was about to collide head-on with fate.

Who knew it traveled around in a 1967 Winnebago?

I got shot between the eyes on a Thursday afternoon by a freak packing a Saturday-Night Special.

It wasn't the first bad joke the world had played on me.

I also had a bachelor's degree in Art Appreciation.

I WOKE UP IN AN UNFAMILIAR bed in an unfamiliar room. Everything was so ... *white*. And peaceful. And quiet.

Either I'd died, or I'd been committed to a psych ward.

I sucked in what felt like my first breath in ages. The place smelled like plastic. And disinfectant. And ....

Fritos?

Slowly, I turned my thumping head to the left. My cousin Earl was passed out on a vinyl recliner beside me. Atop his potbelly, a family-size bag of corn chips rose and fell in rhythm with his breathing.

"Earl?"

My voice sounded like it was underwater. A twinge of concern upped the volume in my throbbing head.

"Earl?"

Earl snorted himself awake, then glanced over at me.

His eyes nearly doubled. He shot up out of his chair as if it were an ejector seat. Fritos flew everywhere.

"Bobbie!" he shouted, then caught himself.

Earl wasn't one for outward displays of emotion. Not the caring kind, anyway. We'd been rivals for nearly thirty years. There was no point in him getting all sappy now.

"You're awake," he said with a bit more reserve.

"You've got a real knack for the obvious," I cracked. My words echoed weirdly inside my skull. "What happened? Where am I?"

"In the hospital. You got ... uh ... shot between the eyes."

Earl's voice caught. He winced and slapped on a snide grin. But the tears brimming in his eyes contradicted his charade of callousness.

Tears? Crap. That can't be good.

"I remember now," I said. "There was that guy at the mall—the one in hot-pants .... He *shot* me?"

"Yep."

I tried to sit up, but the IV tube in my arm protested against it. "How bad off am I?"

"The good news is, your thick skull stopped the bullet. Lord knows you don't need any more brain damage."

Either Earl's humoring my dying ass or it's not that bad.

"Right." The left side of my mouth attempted a sarcastic smirk. "So what's the *bad* news, Frito Bandito?"

My cousin wagged his eyebrows. "Well, you've done got yourself one hell of a Kentucky waterfall."

"What?" I scowled and reached toward my head, pulling the IV tube along for the ride. My fingers landed on a tender lump in the middle of my forehead, then moved higher to the swath of smooth skin atop my partially shaved head.

"Argh! Gimme a mirror!"

Earl's cheeks dimpled, but he kept his mouth shut and handed me the mirror lying on the table beside my hospital bed.

I peered at my reflection. My face went slack. The top of my head all the way to my ears had been shaved bald. The rest of my long, auburn hair clung limply to the back of my skull like a greasy clown wig. I dropped the mirror onto my chest in disgust. "Ugh!"

"Sir!" a woman's voice sounded from behind Earl. "I told you to notify a nurse as soon as he regained consciousness! Are you in pain, Mr. Drex?"

"That's *Miss* Drex," Earl said.

"Oh. Pardon me." The nurse looked down at the chart hanging at the end of my bed, apparently unconvinced.

"No worries," Earl said. "Common mistake."

As much as I hated to admit it, Earl was right. I'd never been the "girliest" of girls. My newly receding hairline wasn't helping on that score.

"How are you feeling?" the nurse asked.

"Okay, I guess." Considering the circumstances, I felt surprisingly good. Sure, my head throbbed. But it was no worse than the hangover I'd self-inflicted last weekend.

"I'll get Dr. Brown." She shot Earl a raised eyebrow. "Sir, it would be good if you gave Miss Drex some privacy when he arrives."

Earl bobbed his shaggy head at her. "Yes, ma'am."

I studied my bear of a cousin. Despite his display of bravado, his brow had more furrows in it than a freshly plowed corn field.

"It's okay," I said to the nurse. "Like it or not, he's the only family I've got."

"As you wish."

As the nurse left, Earl's cellphone chirped. He glanced at the screen and shoved it back into the pocket of his blue mechanic's coveralls.

"Who was it?" I asked. "A customer?"

"We should be so lucky."

"How long have I been here?"

"Three or four hours."

"Geez! Who's running the garage?"

"Uh ... nobody. In case you haven't noticed, we're *both* here."

Panic shot through me. "Help me up, Earl. I can't afford to be in the hospital! My health insurance from the mall job doesn't kick in until next month."

"Yeah, about that—"

I sat up and peeled the tape from the IV in my arm.

Earl objected. "Now hold up there a second."

I scowled. "No! I might *look* like hell, but I feel fine."

"Well, to tell the truth, you don't look much worse than you did on prom night. Remember? You had that monster zit on your forehead and—"

"Shut up and help me get out of here! Do you have another set of coveralls with you?"

"Down in the truck."

"Go get them. And hurry!"

EARL AND I WERE HALFWAY down the hospital corridor—two shady mechanics in shabby blue coveralls—when a doctor walked by us. I think he would have mistaken us for janitors if he hadn't recognized my fancy haircut. Or maybe it was the bandage between my eyes ....

"Roberta Drex?" he asked, turning to stare at us as our paths crossed. "I'm your attending physician, Dr. Brown."

Earl and I kept walking, pretending not to hear. The doctor called after us. "What are you doing out of bed Ms. Drex?"

I turned to face him. "Uh ... leaving. I'm sorry, but I can't afford to stay here."

The doctor appeared more annoyed than surprised. "You can't afford *not* to. You were unconscious for several hours. Don't you want to know what's wrong with you before you leave?"

I scanned the doctor's face. If I was dying, he didn't give it away. "Okay. Give it to me straight. What's wrong?"

Dr. Brown glared at me, then wilted. "Well, to be honest, we did an initial brain scan, but couldn't find anything."

I glanced over at Earl's smirking face. He opened his mouth to say something stupid, but I shut him down with a look that could wither gonads at fifty paces.

"So, in other words, there's nothing really wrong with me. Thanks, Doc. I'll be leaving now."

Dr. Brown grabbed my arm. "Hold on a moment! Yes, the initial scan indicates your brain appears undamaged. But you were struck by a ricocheting bullet, Ms. Drex. While it slowed considerably before it impacted your skull, there could be undetected residual effects."

I frowned. "Like what?"

"Any number of things. But right now, the damage appears to be contained to skin abrasions and hematomas confined to the non-subdural dermis."

Earl crinkled his nose. "That sounds bad."

I sighed. "It's just doctor talk for a scratch and a bruise. Am I right, Doc?"

"Yes," Dr. Brown admitted. "You're one lucky lady."

"Yeah. Getting shot in the head. That's my kind of luck, all right."

"A sense of humor. That's a good sign, too. Patients have been known to lose theirs as a result of head trauma."

"Too bad," Earl quipped. "So much for the power of prayer."

I shot Earl another dirty look and turned to the doctor. "Then I'm good to go? Like I said, I really can't afford to be here."

The doctor pursed his lips. "Well, I'm still concerned. You lost consciousness longer than typical. You may have suffered a concussion. Still, there appears to be no brain swelling. The MRI we took should tell us more. To be on the safe side, I'd like to keep you overnight for observation."

I winced. "Listen, I appreciate your concern and all. But a night here would cost me more than I make in a month." I poked my chin in my cousin's direction. "Can't Earl here keep an eye on me?"

The doctor glanced at our threadbare coveralls and sighed. "I can't hold you here against your will. But you'll have to sign a form saying you refused treatment. I'll have the nurse give you a list of concussion warning signs. Promise me if you have any symptoms you'll come back to the hospital immediately."

"Sure. I promise." I sighed as relief emanated from my wallet.

Earl saluted the guy. "You can count on me, Doc."

Dr. Brown's face sagged with symptoms of early-onset regret. He blew out a breath and led us to the nurses' station. I signed the waiver form while a nurse gave Earl a pamphlet on concussions and a bag of bandages. After thanking them, we headed toward the exit.

We were halfway down the hall when my head began to hum. I flinched, then did a double take.

Standing in front of the visitor's lounge was the guy in the hoodie. The man I'd caught stealing a bike outside the mall. The guy I'd chased. The same punk who'd shot me with his Saturday-Night Special.

I gasped and elbowed Earl in the ribs. "What's *he* doing here?"

"Who?"

"That guy."

"Where?"

Anger boiled up inside me. "Over *there*, Earl. By the vending machine. That's the guy who *shot* me!"

Earl shook his head like I was crazy. "That ain't him."

My eyes narrowed. "Yes it is. How many other people would be wearing tiger pants and lime-green Crocs?"

Earl patted my shoulder. "Around here? Could be anybody."

I scowled. "Dang it, Earl! I guess I'm gonna have to run him down all by myself. Geez! I always have to do *everything*. Get out of my way!"

I took a step toward the guy and blanched. He was gone.

"Where'd he go?" I took another step.

Earl caught me by the arm and spun me around. "Stop it, Bobbie."

"Let go of me!" I tugged against my cousin's bear-claw grip. "We've got to go after him!"

Earl looked me in the eye. "Hold your horses, Cuz. I'm telling you, I'm a hundred percent sure whoever you saw wasn't the kid who shot you."

I glared at my cousin. Only a *man* could be a hundred percent sure of anything.

"How can you *say* that?" I hissed.

"'Cause the punk who shot you got runned over by a monster truck heading for the mud-bugging flats. He's *dead*."

"Dead?"

"Squashed flatter'n road kill. Well, everything but his Hello Kitty backpack."

Chapter Two

ON THE HOUR-LONG DRIVE from the hospital in Gainesville to our hometown of Point Paradise, Earl wouldn't stop ribbing about me "seeing ghosties," "losing it," and my "screws coming loose."

By the time we made it back to the auto garage, I'd convinced myself that the world was full of jerks in tiger-skin hot-pants. The guy I'd seen at the hospital couldn't have been the same one who'd shot me. There'd probably been a sale on green crocs and Hello Kitty backpacks at Wal-mart, and now the town was crawling with lookalike doofuses.

The whole thing had been a figment of my imagination.

As I climbed out of the truck, I caught my reflection in the side mirror and remembered that my half-shaved head was, unfortunately, no figment.

I blew out a breath. Then I stomped across the parking lot and up the stairs leading to my apartment above the garage. I fumbled the door open, marched into the kitchen, and fished a pair of scissors from a drawer. Then I stood in front of the hall mirror and began whacking away at my remaining locks.

"Practicin' medicine without a license is illegal in Florida," Earl said, coming in behind me.

"I'm pretty sure it's illegal *everywhere*," I said sullenly. "And this *isn't* a medical procedure."

"Sure it is." He snorted. "It's a mullet-ectomy."

My eyes narrowed. I stared at my reflection in the mirror, blew out a sigh, and snipped off the last strands of hair hanging behind my left ear. The long clump fell to the floor, along with what was left of my vanity.

I turned my head to get a side view of my homemade hairdo. It was all I could do not to groan out loud.

A choppy band of inch-long auburn hair encircled the back and sides of my otherwise bald head. If that weren't bad enough, an angry red crater pulsed like a mini volcano in the center of my forehead.

If Bozo and the Cyclops had a baby, it still wouldn't be this ugly.

Earl laughed. "You know you're famous now, right?"

"Famous?" My pulse lurched. "Good grief! Please tell me you didn't talk to any reporters!"

Tiger Pants Shoots Cyclopoid Mall Cop. Good lord! I could end up on the home page of the Florida Man website!

Earl smirked and raised an eyebrow. "Just one. Turns out Third-Eye Blind's looking for a new mascot."

I bit down hard against a sudden, stinging pressure behind my nose. Crying wasn't my style. Especially not in front of Earl Shankles. But geez! How much more was I supposed to take?

"I need a wig," I hissed.

"Nah. I think you look great." Earl chuckled and rubbed his hands together. "I guess some money's gonna change hands tonight."

"What are you talking about?"

"Come on, Bobbie. Half of Point Paradise thinks you're really a guy. Now that you're going bald, people round here will be calling in their bets. You can count on it."

A vein pulsed in my left temple. "Could you cut me a break, just this *once?* I got shot in the head, for crying out loud." My reflection in the mirror made me wince afresh. "What am I gonna do? I can't go around looking like *this.*"

"Just do what we guys do when we go bald."

I braced myself for another insult. "*What?*"

"Wear a hat."

"Oh."

Earl held out his Redman chewing tobacco ball cap. I nearly choked. In the saga of our redneck family, the grubby cap was legendary.

"Lucky Red" had been handed down to Earl by his father. He'd been wearing it the day he'd caught a twelve-pound bass in a fishing tournament on Wimbly Lake. The scale-busting lunker had won my uncle a shiny trophy and a brand-new bass boat. It was the most luck our family had had in generations.

Lucky Red was one of Earl's few prized possessions. Lending me the cap was the closest thing to "I love you" my cousin had ever expressed to me.

"Thanks." I reached for the cap.

Earl yanked it away. "It's a loaner, mind you."

"Fine." I snatched the cap from Earl, stared at the dirty brim and scowled. "Great. Looks like I'll have to wash it first."

Earl burst out laughing.

Part of me longed to join in, but the rest of me snuffed out the urge.

Perfect. Here I am, borrowing "luck" from the very man who stole all of mine in the first place.

Good one, universe.

Har har har.

Chapter Three

"DOCTOR SAYS YOU SHOULD take it easy," Earl said, towering over me with his luxurious headful of shiny, black hair.

After just sheering myself like a sheep, I found myself envious of him for *that*, too.

Great. Like I need another reason.

"Yeah. I know," I said sullenly, and carried Lucky Red into the kitchen. Earl trailed along behind me, annoying me to no end with his persistent existence.

"I could've carried you up the stairs," he said.

"I'm not an *invalid*, Earl!"

"I know that! Sheesh. I'm only trying to help."

"Sorry." I gave my cousin the best smile I could muster under the circumstances, then reached into the cabinet under the sink and pulled out a spray bottle of Windex. "It's just that, well, I'm used to taking care of myself."

I spritzed the ball cap while Earl hovered over me like an incompetent, micromanaging supervisor.

"I know you are, Bobbie. But you don't *have* to. You want me to stay the night on the sofa?"

"No."

He folded his huge arms over his barrel chest. "Well, I'm staying anyway. Somebody's got to keep an eye on you."

"*Fine.*"

I scrubbed the cap with a sponge while Earl wandered around the shabby, two-bedroom apartment that had been my parent's place for thirty years. When Dad passed away six months ago, I'd come back to try and salvage the family business.

It wasn't going well.

"This place looks like a museum to your folks," Earl called out from the living room.

"Yeah. It should. It was *their* place, after all." I hadn't had the heart to change a single thing since I'd moved in. "It feels like sacrilege for me to even be here."

Earl poked his head back into the kitchen. "Why would you say *that?*"

"You know why." I kept my voice flat. "They never wanted me in the first place. I'm the prodigal son who turned out to be the pitiful daughter."

Earl opened his mouth, but shut it without saying anything.

I put Lucky Red in the sink and filled the basin with warm, soapy water. "Listen, I'm gonna let your hat soak for an hour while I go take a nap."

Earl held up a piece of paper and shook it at me. "Keep the bedroom door open. This here list from the hospital says I should check on you every fifteen minutes."

My throat tightened. "Okay. Whatever."

I stomped to my parents' old room, kicked the oversized work boots from my feet, and flopped onto the bed. I wasn't tired. I just wanted a moment's peace.

Alone.

By myself.

Without Earl.

I stared at the picture on the nightstand. Inside the cheap frame was an image of my father, Robert Drex, sitting behind the wheel of a red, 1964-1/2 Ford Mustang. He was parked in the lot in front of the shop. A shiny, new sign above the garage's service bay doors proudly proclaimed *Robert's Mechanics.* My mom, Edith, stood below the sign, her back against the wall. Her mother, my Grandma Selma, stood beside her, holding me in her arms.

Nobody was smiling.

Why the hell did I come back to Point Paradise? To help Mom out? To save Dad's mechanic shop? To show Earl who's boss once and for all?

I chewed my lip. Who was I kidding? I was no business woman. It wasn't *all* my fault, but the shop was now so far in arrears I'd had to take that job at the mall just to keep the lights on. And Earl? He wasn't even grateful! I mean, where else could a redneck jerk like him find work? Who would hire the moronic lug except my father?

The door to my bedroom creaked open. Earl stuck his head inside. "You doing okay?"

As if working as a mall cop hadn't been embarrassing enough, I'd somehow managed to make myself even *more* dependent on my idiot cousin. It was absolutely the last damned thing in the world I wanted.

"Yeah, I'm fine."

Earl eyed me skeptically. "Okay. But I'm leaving the door open wider. So it don't squeak and wake you up."

"*Fine.*"

"You need anything?"

"Only to be left alone."

Earl's dumb, pleasant face soured a notch. "Can do."

Earl disappeared behind the door. I bit down hard against my anger. I knew I should be nicer to him. He was trying, after all. But it was so much easier for him.

He had won.

I tossed and turned, my mind seething over Earl Shankles. He was my first cousin. My life-long tormentor. The usurper of my father's affections. The whole reason my life had turned out like this ....

BACK WHEN EARL AND I were kids, I'd spent every afternoon helping out around my dad's garage after school. By the time I was eight, I could do oil changes, switch out spark plugs, replace dead batteries, and fix flat tires.

But everything had changed when I turned eleven. I'd hit puberty and had the audacity to turn out to be a girl after all. My mechanic-in-training days came to a screeching halt. My father dropped me like a hot soldering gun, banishing me from his service bay forever.

With his fantasy son reduced to wearing a training bra, my father had picked Earl to be my replacement. My cousin not only took my place as flunkey at my dad's shop—he stole my father's heart and never gave it back.

As soon as high school was over, I ran off to college and found someone else to break my heart all over again.

I guess I showed them.

I blew out a sigh and stared at the ceiling.

What did Earl have that I didn't? Why did Dad give him what rightfully belonged to me?

When I'd come home for my father's funeral, I'd discovered that Earl had taken over running my father's business. I figured it had been easy pickings for him. My mother had never wanted anything to do with the garage. I'm sure she'd gladly handed over the reins to Earl.

Well, I'd set that business straight on day one. I'd taken back charge of the books and Earl Shankles' paycheck. Mom had been relieved. So relieved, in fact, that she'd taken the liberty of running away with our postman, David Applewhite, two days after Dad's funeral. A week later she'd called to let me know they'd gotten married at a drive-thru chapel in Vegas.

Mom gets married again at sixty, and I can't even get a second date ....

I glanced at the clock. Earl would be making his rounds any minute. I rolled over and sighed for the hundredth time.

For crying out loud, just go to sleep, Bobbie!

But I couldn't. Something inside me was making me madder than a wet hornet. I felt trapped. Dragged down by circumstances beyond my control.

The door creaked open. I shut my eyes and pretended to be asleep. Logically, I knew it wasn't Earl's fault that my father had chosen him over me. But I couldn't dislodge my resentment.

In the game of life, I was a dodgeball target.

And tonight, thanks to a random act of stupidity, I needed my crummy cousin to make sure I didn't lapse into a coma.

I turned over on my other side and made myself a solemn vow.

There was *no way* I was going to let myself die in this lousy, run-down, piss-hole of a place in the middle of freaking nowhere.

That fate I planned to leave to Earl Shankles.

Chapter Four

WHEN I WOKE UP, IT was daylight. The old clock radio next to my frowning family's photo read 9:38 a.m.

I stumbled to the kitchen, lured by the smell of brewing coffee. As I poured myself a cup, I noticed Earl's Lucky Red cap was in the windowsill, nearly dry.

I heard the toilet flush. Earl emerged from the bathroom looking proud of himself. I didn't want to know what for.

"Mornin'," I begrudged as a peace offering.

"Mornin', Sleeping Beauty. You feeling okay?"

"Yeah."

"You know you snore louder than Candy Vincent?"

I scowled. "How do you know how loud Candy Vincent snores?"

"Uh ... rumors."

"Yeah, right."

Earl made himself a cup of coffee as I took a seat at the kitchen table. After he'd stirred in enough sugar to induce a diabetic coma, he joined me.

"While you were out like a light last night, you got a couple of calls on your cellphone."

"My mom?"

Earl glanced away. "Uh ... no. Reporters mostly. When I told them you were gonna live, they kind of lost interest."

"Story of my life."

Earl stared into his coffee mug. "Your boss at the mall called, too. He said times are tough. Had to make some layoffs. Blah, blah, blah. Bottom line, no need for you to worry about coming back in."

"Great. Any other good news?"

"Some cop called. Said he met you at the mall last week. What's his name? Paul Newman?"

"Terry Paulson."

Earl smiled softly. "Yeah. You always *were* good with names."

Especially when the person looked better *than Paul Newman.*

"What did he want?" I asked.

"He said he wanted to marry you."

I blanched. "What?"

Earl laughed. "Well, to use his exact words, he said he 'had a proposal for you.'"

My nose crinkled. "I wonder what he meant by that?"

Earl wagged his eyebrows at me. "Maybe it's an *indecent* proposal. No, wait. Maybe this guy's opening up a new ghost-buster division. See any more *haints* last night?"

I shot him a sour face. "Only the ghost of my dearly departed hair." I ran my hand along the red stubble. "Crap. What am I gonna do? I can't go see Detective Paulson wearing an ad for chewing tobacco on my head."

Earl grinned. "Don't worry, Bobbie. While you were snoring your lungs out, I thought of something. Here. I found this in granny's place next door."

Earl held out a shoebox.

"What were you doing snooping around in Grandma Selma's apartment?" I demanded.

"Cool your jets. She was *my* granny, too."

"Gimme that!"

I yanked the shoebox from Earl's hands and lifted the lid. Inside was a short, curly wig made of blue and silver polyester fibers.

Poor Grandma. She'd worn her best Sunday wig to the grave with her.

I took the cheap wig out of the shoebox and held it up to the light.

Earl snorted. "Don't tell me you're actually thinking about wearing that thing."

"No. But seeing as how I don't have a lot of options, maybe Beth-Ann can fix it. See you later."

I got up from the table.

"Where you going?" Earl demanded.

"I'm gonna get a shower, then I'm going to see Beth-Ann. If she can work a miracle on this thing, I'll be heading over to see Detective Paulson afterward."

"Do you really think you should be driving?"

"It's either drive myself to Beth-Ann's or stay here and let you drive me crazy. I think I'll take my chances on the road."

Earl threw up his hands. "Have it your way."

"I will. You've had it your way long enough."

"What's that supposed to mean?"

"Nothing." I sucked in a deep breath and blew it out. "Earl?"

"What?"

"Thanks for lending me Lucky Red."

He shot me a suspicious look. "Yeah."

I grabbed the cap from the windowsill and headed down the hallway.

"I hope Windex kills germs," I hollered back at Earl. "I wouldn't want to catch a staph infection from this thing."

Chapter Five

"BE CAREFUL OUT THERE," Earl said as I climbed into my father's red Mustang. "Don't go getting yourself lost."

"Not much chance of that."

How could I end up any further off track than Point Paradise?

I cranked the engine. As I let the vintage muscle car idle for a minute, I stared at the flashing yellow light that marked the intersection of Norville Street and Obsidian Road. Or, as we locals called it, "The corner of nowhere and oblivion."

My father's business, Robert's Mechanics, was the only semi-viable business on the otherwise desolate crossroads. Cattycorner from it was an appliance store turned junk shop, which changed renters every six months or so. Next to that dump was another junk shop that had given up the ghost for good when it caught fire this past summer.

That fire had been the last nail in the coffin of my father's ambition to put Robert's Mechanics and Point Paradise on the map. He'd bought both junk places across the street for next to nothing, which was still more than they'd been worth. I tried to sell the properties to keep the garage afloat, but so far there'd been no takers. Not even a nibble.

In a way, I was glad Dad hadn't lived to see the junk shop across the street burn down. When I'd first come back, I'd been gung-ho on Dad's dream to reinvigorate the tiny town. But after six months of dealing with deadbeat renters and garage customers' rubber checks, my sentiments had taken a nosedive.

More and more, my ambition concerning Point Paradise was to drive away and never look back. I'd even begun to fantasize about torching the place as I fled. To me, Point Paradise had become the dreary deathtrap of my dead dad's dreams.

I sighed, shifted the Mustang into first, and pulled out of the parking lot. I headed east on Obsidian Road toward Waldo, the nearest clump of buildings big enough to be incorporated into an actual town. That's where my friend Beth-Ann's beauty shop was, and Dana's Café, where I was to meet with Detective Terry Paulson later in the afternoon—provided the wig-gig went well.

About half a mile down Obsidian Road, I passed the only other business in Point Paradise. It was an abandoned gas station converted into a drive-thru convenience store.

Owned by some guy from Waldo, the dive was run by Artie Jacobs, who'd lived up to his high school prediction of being least likely to succeed. Considering where we'd all come from, he had every right to be proud. Around here, there'd been a hell of a lot of competition for the title.

I spotted Artie sitting in his chair by the cash register. Per tradition, I honked and waved. Before he could wave back, I gunned the engine and blew past him, grinning like Jack Nicholson in *The Shining*.

Pathetic, I know. But in a town this small and this broke, you took your cheap thrills where you could find them.

At the end of the road, I hooked a right and headed south on US 301 toward Waldo. Feeling antsy, I lifted the ball cap and scratched my itchy scalp. Tiny stubbles of hair were already growing in. I wondered how long it would take for my auburn locks to reach ponytail length again.

Beth-Ann would know. She was a good friend and a miracle worker when it came to hair. I hoped she still had one doozy left in her bag of tricks for me.

I was sure as hell gonna need it.

Chapter Six

A FEW MILES OUTSIDE of Waldo, I passed a roadside billboard and hit the brakes out of habit. Besides being the butt of innumerable "Where's Waldo?" jokes, the tiny town had earned itself two national distinctions—neither of which was ever brought up in polite conversation.

Three years ago, Waldo had been designated the nation's worst speed trap by AAA. After discovering Waldo's seven police officers had written nearly twelve thousand speeding tickets that year, AAA had paid to erect the billboard I'd just blown past. It used to read, "Speed Trap Waldo 6 Miles" in black and yellow, the most readable color combination to the human eye.

The billboard was abandoned now, as was the entire Waldo police force. The incident had raised such a stink that the entire department had been disbanded and their duties turned over to the Alachua County Sheriff's Department.

Two years later, the Florida Legislature gave Waldo its other national distinction by passing a law banning traffic-ticket quotas for law officers. They named it the "Waldo Bill." As for the notoriety the town received, the rest of us were secretly jealous.

Everything exciting always seemed to happen in Waldo.

A rural-route school bus buzzed past me on US 301. It was most likely heading toward Hawthorne, the nearest town with a public school.

Poor saps.

I thought about how Beth-Ann and I had met on a bus just like it when we were sixteen. She'd climbed aboard wearing black jeans, a black T-shirt, black boots, black hair, black fingernails, black eye makeup, and black lipstick. I'd never seen anyone like her. Beth-Ann had been the first "Goth" kid at Hawthorne High—maybe the only one in all of Alachua County.

I turned the Mustang off US 301 onto Country Lane and smiled, remembering the first words Beth-Ann had ever said to me.

"Normal is for losers."

She'd given my boy's jeans, chain wallet, and close-cropped red hair the once-over, then sat in the seat next to me and delivered that line. Then she'd offered me a bottle of black nail polish. I'd been so stunned I didn't even try to stop her as she took my hand and painted my nails. It was my first-ever manicure.

I bit my lip and glanced down at my fingernails. I could use a manicure now, actually. But it would be a waste of money I didn't have. Besides, there was no point. Carburetors didn't care if you had soft cuticles.

I pulled the Mustang up to a little wooden cottage and cut the ignition. Beth-Ann worked out of her house. She'd converted the detached garage into a beautician studio. A hand-painted sign hanging over the garage door read, "Beth-Ann's Beauty Parlor. Yes, I Know It's A Garage."

I walked around the corner of the garage and down the footpath lined with pavers. The side entry door was ajar. I pushed it open the rest of the way.

A chalk-pale face looked up from sweeping the floor. Still sporting black hair, black lipstick, and thick eyeliner, Beth-Ann wasn't about to give up her Goth dream anytime soon.

"Holy crap!" Beth-Ann said as I took off the Redman cap and gave her a gander at my red monk's ring. "Did you get attacked by a psychotic clown or something?"

"No. Just shot between the eyes." I flounced onto her salon chair.

"I heard about the shooting, Bobbie. Good thing you've got a thick skull."

I whirled around in the chair. "Really? You, too? I'm fine, by the way."

She rested her hands on my shoulders and winked at me. "I know that, Bobbie. Otherwise, I wouldn't be teasing you."

I shot her a tight smile. "Speaking of teasing ...." I pulled the wig out of the shoebox. "Can you do something with this?"

Beth-Ann's face puckered like she'd smelled a fart. "Geez, Bobbie. I'm a beautician, not a magician."

I let out a sigh. "Okay. It was worth a shot." I got up out of the chair and took a step toward the door.

"Wait!" Beth-Ann said. "Let me check my wig box. I think I've got something in there you could use."

"You've got a *wig box?*"

Beth-Ann opened a cabinet and pulled out a cardboard box.

"Yeah. You know. Donations. Leave-behinds. Hey, it's a woman's prerogative to change her mind—and her hairstyle." She glanced at my head and winced. "You of all people should know that."

She rifled through an old Amazon box that appeared to be harboring the dehydrated husks of an entire generation of tribbles.

"Aha! Here it is!" Beth-Ann held up a bright-red wig. "Sit back down, sister."

With no better option springing to mind, I flopped back into the barber chair. Beth-Ann stretched the wig out like a shower cap and placed it over my semi-bald dome. She tugged it left and right, and spun me around for a gander in the mirror.

"Ta da!"

I gulped. I'd gone from Kentucky Waterfall Woman to Sharon Osborne on a bender in under thirty seconds. Combined with my garage coveralls, the look was perfect—if I wanted to masquerade as *Woody Woodpecker* working the night shift at a Texaco.

"You're kidding," I said.

"Hey, beggars can't be choosers."

I blew out a breath. "How much is it?"

"For you? Nothing. Compliments of the house."

"That's *some* compliment."

Beth-Ann shrugged. "If you'd rather go on looking like a redneck Franciscan monk, be my guest."

I sighed. "You're right. What the hell."

"I've also got a clothes box, in case you ever decide to change out of those mechanic's coveralls. I haven't seen you in anything else since you came back, Bobbie. Why are you always wearing them, anyway? Some kind of sick penance?"

"I run a mechanic's garage, in case you forgot."

"I know. But not 24-7. Your life isn't *over*, you know."

I scowled. "You sure about that?"

"Yes." Beth-Ann shot me a look. "What happened to you? You used to actually *like* other humans."

"Sorry. It's just that ... I dunno. Carl did a number on me. And that whole thing with Earl. What is it with guys? They think they run the universe."

Beth-Ann shot me a sympathetic smile. "Guys only have the power we give them. Just like everything else in life. So, when are you going to get your life out of that greasy garage and back in the sassy saddle with me?"

I smirked. "Soon." I turned to go, then hesitated. "Hey. Any chance you can do something with my face?"

Beth-Ann stared at the scabby crater between my eyes.

"Like I said, Bobbie. I'm a beautician, not a magician."

She eyed my deflated face and winked. "Aww, come on. Have a seat. Lemme see what I can do."

Chapter Seven

I GAVE MY SPIKEY RED wig a quick tug, ponied up a bit of feminine chutzpa, and sauntered into Dana's Café.

I'd come to meet Detective Terry Paulson about a proposal. Part of me hoped my cousin Earl had been right, and the proposal would be an indecent one. Pathetic as it was, this meeting was the closest thing I'd had to a date since Artie had asked me for a lift when his car broke down.

Not wanting to appear desperate or overeager, I'd turned down Beth-Ann's offer of more alluring attire and stuck with my usual outfit—my dad's fraying coveralls and oversized work boots. The problem was, the heavy boots made it impossible to pull off an actual saunter. Instead, I tripped over the threshold and stumbled into the coffee shop like a drunken hobo.

Paulson watched it all from a table for two.

Despite my cheeks burning with humiliation, my heart leaped at the sight of him in uniform, just as it had when I'd met him for the first time at the mall last week.

I shot Paulson a smile, swiped habitually at my auburn bangs, and froze for a second when I realized they were no longer there. In their place was a bandage the size of a monkey diaper.

"Well, look at you," Detective Paulson said in a voice that lilted with flirtation. "I have to say, I liked your hair longer. What'd you do? Get shot in the head or something?"

I couldn't decide whether to kiss him or kick him in the groin, so I smiled. "Very funny."

Paulson's smirk faded. His brow furrowed. "I heard the news. I'm sorry I wasn't there to help when it happened."

I pursed my lips and shrugged. "No worries. Gainesville's way out of your jurisdiction anyway."

Paulson winced. "True. But what I meant to say is that I'm glad you're okay. You're not going back to that job at the mall, are you?"

I shook my head. "No. You take one lousy bullet between the eyes, and they throw you out like last month's fryer grease. My manager called this morning. I've been laid off."

"Ouch. I *thought* you looked upset. Is that what's bugging you?"

Ugh! Every time I heard someone ask, "What's bugging you?" I thought of some flea-infested rodent ... or Carl Blanders, my ex, which, in my book, was pretty much the same thing. But at the moment, it was Detective Paulson who was getting under my skin. I wanted to slap his smug, irritatingly attractive face—then roll around in the hay with him. But not actually *roll around in the hay*. Being naked in a pile of dirty, pokey, dried-up stems of grass sounded itchy—and downright uncomfortable.

I looked up from my wandering thoughts. Paulson was studying me with a pair of laser-beam eyes the color of glacier shards.

"Uh ... no," I said. "Nothing's bugging me. I just hate that expression."

"Well, in this case, the term 'buggy' fits."

"What do you mean?"

"Have a seat." Paulson half-stood and gestured for me to sit.

"I prefer to stand." I curled my hands into fists to hide the motor oil under my fingernails. I didn't want to get too near Paulson. There was no need for him to discover my signature cologne was Quaker State.

"Have it your way." Paulson leaned back in his chair. "After Jack Barker, uh ... *left*, I found a report involving Mildred Vanderhoff. Apparently, the old gal's gone off her rocker."

"You must be new in town," I quipped, then remembered that Paulson was. In fact, it was rather miraculous there was a police officer there in Waldo at all.

Three years had passed since Waldo's infamous speed-trap debacle. Four months ago, the town had finally been reissued its first dedicated police officer, Jack Barker.

At fifty-three years of age and three-hundred pounds, it wasn't exactly surprising when Barker had suffered a heart attack. Two weeks ago, they'd hauled him out of this very café and up to Gainesville for treatment. I'd heard a rumor that Artie had been at the scene, and had finished Barker's half-eaten donut.

The official story was that Officer Barker was on sick leave, recovering. But we all knew he was at a gastric bypass clinic getting his colon resected. Detective Paulson had been assigned to fill in during the interim, while Barker whittled down his waistline.

I took a step closer and curled my fingers around the back of the chair opposite Paulson. "Of course, being new in town, you wouldn't know this, Detective Paulson. But old lady Vanderhoff's been Point Paradise's resident crazy cat lady since as long as I can remember. She's a rite of passage for kids around here." I smiled coyly. "In fact, you're nothing but a dork until you've mustered up the courage to ring her doorbell and run."

"You don't say." Paulson grinned. "So, did *you?*"

"Sure. When I was six. On Halloween. She came to the door wearing a green monster mask. Made me drop a load in my pedal pushers—along with my pillowcase full of candy."

Yes. That's the way to talk sexy to a man, Bobbie. No wonder you haven't had a date since Blanders ....

"But that's ancient history," I added hastily.

Paulson's left eyebrow arched. "Let's hope so."

I glanced down at my frayed coveralls. My cheeks burned. I wanted to crawl under a rock and drag brush up to its edge to cover up any trace of my ever having existed. But that wasn't an option. So, instead, I slapped on an expression of casual interest, toed my father's scruffy right boot, and asked, "What does the report say?"

"According to Vanderhoff, someone keeps calling her home phone. They say weird things and hang up."

I shifted onto my other foot. "Well, like I said, it's probably the neighborhood kids earning their stripes. In case you haven't noticed, they do *everything* on the phone nowadays."

Paulson shot me a salacious smile, then leaned over and removed a file from his briefcase. He opened it and read aloud from the pages within. "Vanderhoff says, and I quote, 'When I pick up the phone, I hear *beep-beep-beep,* and a robot tells me to do naughty things.'"

I bit my bottom lip. "Huh. Okay. That's weird. Even for Vanderhoff."

Paulson shot me a boyish grin. "I know, right? I mean, who uses a *landline* anymore?"

That one earned him half a genuine smile. "When did she start getting the calls?"

Paulson's blue eyes shifted back to the report. "Ever since she came back from Beth-Ann's Beauty Parlor a week ago last Wednesday, apparently."

"You're joking."

"That's what Jack's report says." Paulson tossed the file onto the table in front of him. It spun half a circle and came to rest with a corner hanging off the edge. "Read it yourself."

"Why? What's it got to do with me?"

Paulson's grin faded. "Well, I thought about what you told me last week. Are you still interested in becoming a private investigator?" He glanced up at the bandage on my forehead. "I mean, after this mall cop incident?"

My gut flopped. I'd never been less sure of something in my entire life. But if I didn't become a P.I., how else was I ever going to escape Point Paradise and motor oil under my nails—not to mention Earl's farty Frito breath?

"Yeah. I'm sure," I said, and rolled my eyes up toward my forehead. "This little thing? Nothing but a flesh wound."

Paulson shook his head. "Mall cop." He tapped a finger on the report. "I can't believe they made you risk your life for ten bucks an hour."

"That's why I took that P.I. training course on line. To get licensed as a Class CC Intern." I hung my head. "Problem is, I need two years of on-the-job training to get my real investigator's license." I looked up and smiled wryly. "Then I'll be eligible to die with the dignity of knowing I was making *twenty-four* bucks an hour."

Paulson grinned. "I take it you finished the course?"

"They tell me the diploma's in the mail."

He whistled. "Wow. You can get a certificate for anything over the internet nowadays."

"Thanks," I said sourly. "So, did you just call me in here to bust my chops or what?"

Paulson winked. "If I did, is that a crime?"

Considering how broke I am? Yes. I wasted at least a buck fifty in gas to get here. You could've asked me about the diploma over the phone.

"I guess not," I said, and turned to go.

Paulson's voice sounded behind me.

"Wait, Bobbie. You need work."

I froze in place. What I *really* needed was cash. But the word "work" was close enough. I turned back around. Paulson's face wasn't exactly serious, but it wasn't mocking, either.

"I'm listening," I said.

Paulson stood. I couldn't help but do a mental inventory.

Tall? Check. Dark? Check. Handsome? Double check.

"You still with me?" he asked.

My eyes traveled from Paulson's manly frame to his piercing blue eyes. "Yes, sir."

"Good. Because when I came across this file, I immediately thought of you. I mean, what better practice for a newly licensed CC intern?"

"What do you mean?"

"You can take on the case of the Crazy Cat lady. A CC for a CC. Get it?"

"Ugh," I groaned. "I get it. What's it pay?"

Paulson winced and made a sucking sound out of the side of his sexy mouth. "Officially? Nothing. It'll be practice. Like an apprenticeship, of sorts."

My interest disappeared along with my smile. "No thanks."

"Listen, I can't pay you on the books. But how about a wager?"

I frowned. "What do you mean?"

"You solve Vanderhoff's problem, and I'll give you twenty bucks out of my own pocket."

Given the current state of my financial affairs, his offer was disconcertingly appealing. "Why would you do that?"

"Because, with Jack on vacation, I'm busy with bigger fish to fry than an old lady who sat too long under a hairdryer." He flashed his charming smile. "Come on. Help me out with Vanderhoff."

I stared into his mesmerizing blue eyes until one of them winked.

"It'll be fun, Bobbie," Paulson coaxed. "You can be my new 'low man on the totem pole,' so to speak."

Great. Now even Paulson doesn't see me as female. My work here in Point Paradise is complete.

"How could I refuse an offer like that?" I said sourly, and reached for the file.

Paulson yanked it away.

"I'm not done," he said and grinned seductively. "I said it was a *wager*. If you don't solve the case, *you* owe *me* something."

"What?"

"Dinner."

Huh. Maybe this wasn't just a pity call after all.

I should've been happy about that. But my gut fired off a warning knot.

Don't get involved with Paulson.

The guy's charming, sky-blue eyes were like a window into my soul. If history repeated itself, the view from that window would be the last thing I'd see before I jumped through it and splattered my guts all over the sidewalk, right next to my broken heart.

Geez. When did I get to be such a romantic?

"Fine." I grabbed the file. Paulson hadn't specified what *kind* of dinner I'd owe him if I didn't solve the case. As far as I knew, a McHappy Meal still cost way less than twenty bucks.

So it was a wager I couldn't lose. At least, not financially.

"I'll solve it. You'll see," I said, and turned to go. I attempted a dramatic exit, but tripped on my oversized work boots and fell to one knee, right next to a trashcan.

Awesome.

I put a hand on the rim, hauled myself up, and willed myself not to look back.

Then I stomped out the door of Dana's Café, cursing the dead man who'd left me to fill his stupid shoes.

Chapter Eight

IT WAS A FEW MINUTES after four o'clock when I left Detective Paulson in Dana's Café and headed back toward Point Paradise. From Waldo, Robert's Mechanics was ten miles away, down rural backroads habituated mostly by hunters, lost tourists, and the flattened carcasses of animals with poor depth perception.

Being stuck in Point Paradise amongst the forgotten Florida backwoods of sawgrass and pines, to me Paulson's arrival had been the most interesting thing to happen since Earl found a two-headed turtle out in Wimbly Swamp last year.

The image of Paulson's handsome face coaxed a smile from my sullen lips as I drove south on Obsidian Road. In a better mood than I'd been in ages, I slowed down as I approached the Stop & Shoppe drive-thru. I thought about buzzing through just to give Artie something to bitch about, but decided against it.

I was working a case now. I needed to act like a professional.

Vanderhoff's house was a few blocks behind the Stop & Shoppe. It was one of a tiny cluster of modest ranch houses built in the 1950s, back when people were still gullible enough to buy swampland, and Point Paradise was still gullible enough to think it had a future. The developer had dubbed the place Cherry Manor.

Cherry Manor. Yeah, right.

No cherry trees grew in Florida, and there were certainly no manors within thirty miles of Point Paradise. In fact, I was pretty sure that, except for the size of the oak trees growing in the front yards, nothing had changed in Cherry Manor since the post WWII boon that had sparked its construction in the first place.

The Mustang's engine coughed when I switched off the ignition in front of Vanderhoff's house. From the sound of it, I needed a new air filter. I made a mental note of it. But right now, the granny who'd gone goofy was top on my priority list.

I climbed out of the car and walked up the plain concrete sidewalk leading to the plain concrete porch of her plain concrete-block house.

I rang the bell.

A lumpy green face appeared in the small window in the front door. It was the same grotesque mask that had caught me off guard that fateful Halloween three decades ago. This time, however, I didn't crap my coveralls.

Given the overall state of my life at the moment, I decided to count that as a win.

I waved to Vanderhoff.

She opened the door.

Dressed in a red turban and a faded muumuu, she looked like the love child of a ménage á trois between Zoltar, the Grinch, and any random backwoods redneck me-maw.

"Is that you, Mrs. Vanderhoff?" I knew it was, but I was working an official case now, and wanted to follow P.I. protocol: Always establish the identity of individuals before questioning them.

Vanderhoff's features shifted indistinguishably underneath the yellowish-green glop on her face. "What are you doing here, Bobbie? My car ain't broke down."

"No, Mrs. Vanderhoff. I'm here helping out Detective Paulson."

She eyed the yard behind me. "Where's Jack Barker?"

"Vacation."

"Oh yeah. How's he doing?"

"Fine. Can I come in?"

"Why?"

"Just want to ask you a few questions. About those phone calls you've been getting."

"Oh. Sure. Come on in. Let me wash my face."

She ushered me into her living room and motioned me toward a faded, flower-print couch. I sat down and glanced around. Despite being her neighbor for decades, I'd never actually been inside her house before.

I hadn't had the nerve.

After all, her house was Point Paradise's equivalent of *The Munsters'* place. I laughed to myself.

What had I been afraid of back when I was a kid? The old lady's harmless.

Then I stopped laughing.

Across the room, an ancient porcelain doll in a tattered lace dress stared at me. From her perch atop a wingback chair, she looked like a miniature corpse pissed off about being jerked out of her coffin.

I swallowed hard and glanced to my left. In a dark corner sat a curio cabinet stuffed with more dolls. Each of them glared at me from their overcrowded, glass prison.

A jolt of cold electricity shot down my back.

Geez! Are these like ... voodoo *dolls? Is this how Vanderhoff gets her revenge on the kids who bother her? Oh my lord ... has she got one of ...* me?

"So what do you want to know?" Vanderhoff asked, startling me so badly I shot up off the couch.

"Uh ... questions ...." I fumbled for words as I waited for the crawling sensation beneath my red wig to subside. "I hear you ... uh ... you told Jack you've been getting weird phone calls."

I studied Vanderhoff's face and decided she'd looked better with the avocado mask.

She sucked her teeth. "Yeah, they're weird, all right."

Suddenly, she jabbed a hand in the pocket of her faded muumuu. In P.I. mode, I braced myself in the event evasive action would be required. The old lady was crazy. For all I knew, she could've been packing a Colt 45—and I didn't mean malt liquor.

Her hand emerged holding a TV remote. An odd mixture of relief and disappointment echoed through my gut.

"Bobbie, you remember that show, *The Jetsons?*"

"Yeah." I straightened my slouching shoulders and shook off the willies. "I mean, yes, ma'am." I pulled a notepad and pencil from my purse to record the account.

"Well, the guy who keeps calling me sounds like that robot, Rosie. Only if she was a man, you know what I mean?"

Not really.

"Sure, Mrs. Vanderhoff. What did the robot say, exactly?"

The old lady leaned in closer to divulge her confidential information. "*Beep-beep-beep,*" she whispered into my face.

My fingers relaxed around my pencil. I waved away the cloud of stale smoker's breath that came along with her confession and said, "I see. Did you say anything back?"

Vanderhoff shook her turbaned head. "Well, no. I hung up on him. I mean, who knows what 'beep' means in robot language? He could've been making an obscene phone call for all I know."

Right. Robocop's taken up a new career making perverted robo-calls. Case solved.

I bit my lip and tried to appear professional. I figured maybe flattery would loosen up the witness. "Yes. Well, that's certainly one interpretation, Mrs. Vanderhoff. And, might I say, you took a very smart approach, hanging up on him."

The old woman smiled, causing her dentures to slip. "Thanks, Bobbie."

"So, how many times did Robo ... I mean, *the robot* call?"

"Three or four times. I wasn't gonna bother the police, Bobbie. But when he told me to commit a crime, that's when I called Jack."

"A crime?"

"Yep. After he quit all that dad-blamed beeping business, that deviant demanded I get over to the A&P and steal six bananas."

Something inside me went slack. It might've been my will to live. "Well, that's quite specific. And ... did you?"

"Did I what?"

"Steal the bananas."

Vanderhoff's eyes doubled in size. "No way! I'm not a dad-burned thief!"

"Of course not." I dialed my tone to conciliatory. "I'm sorry. Tell me, why do you think the robot called *you*, Mrs. Vanderhoff?"

She scratched her head with a yellowed fingernail. "I don't know. Maybe he thought I was easy. There ain't a lot of eligible bachelorettes here in Point Paradise, as you well know."

Okaaaay....

I doodled a cross-eyed lunatic in my notebook. "Is there anything else you can remember that I should know?"

Vanderhoff studied me for a moment. "Yes. For the record, I think it was pretty low what that scoundrel, Carl Blanders done to you, honey."

"Thanks, Mrs. Vanderhoff."

"I mean, dumping you for Candy Vincent after all them years. It ain't right. After all, you still got some of your looks left."

I eyed her sourly. "Thanks."

"Candy Vincent's a tramp, if you ask me," Vanderhoff rambled on. "Who names a kid Candy and expects her to be anything but a tramp? Am I right?"

"Yes. You're right. Thanks. And I'm sorry about what's happened to your niece Mandy."

The old woman winced. "You know, that new haircut of yours kind of reminds me of her."

Really? Poor Mandy.

Vanderhoff sighed and reached into the other pocket of her muumuu. My back stiffened. What would she pull out this time? A butcher knife? A doll head? A tub of guacamole?

Before I could grab her arm to stop her, Vanderhoff pulled out a fist and thrust it at my face. I flinched. When I opened my eyes, she unfurled her gnarled fingers to reveal a handful of green pills.

"You want a Paxil, honey?" she asked. "It helps. And you sure look like you could use one. I heard you got shot, but your skull was too thick for it to do any real damage."

My jaw clamped tight enough to straighten bent metal.

I have got to get the hell out of this stupid town!

"No thanks, Mrs. Vanderhoff. I have to go. But here, let me give you my number in case this robot guy calls again, or if you think of anything else that might be relevant."

I handed her one of my cards. Besides the online course and the fee for the state exam, a set of cheap business cards was the only investment I'd made in my budding P.I. career. I didn't even have a gun. Nobody I knew offered a lay-a-way program for a Glock, and slingshots were *so* third century.

Vanderhoff took the card. "Okay, Bobbie. I'll stick it on the fridge with one of the magnets Mandy sent me."

"Good plan." As I turned to leave, my footstep caused an oak floorboard in her living room to squeak.

Vanderhoff grabbed my arm. "Did you hear that?"

"Hear what?"

"The floor. It just said my name. *Mil-dred. Mil-dred*. Didn't you hear it?"

I shot Vanderhoff the kind of hope-against-hope smile people in movies offer serial killers on the off chance it'll persuade them not to chop them into cat food. I modeled it after the doomed smile I'd seen on the faces of all of those dead-eyed dolls camping out in her living room.

"Yes, I heard it," I said. "*Mil-dred*. Plain as day. You have a good night, now, Mrs. Vanderhoff."

I hurried out the front door, slamming it behind me. When I stepped off the porch and glanced back, Vanderhoff's turban-topped face was staring at me through that small windowpane in the door like Norman Bates in *Arabian Nights*.

A chill squirmed through my spine. I sprinted to my car, my nerves half shot. I'd just interviewed my first P.I. subject, and I'd just committed my first P.I. mistake.

I'd lied to the client.

As I tumbled into the driver's seat of the Mustang, I rationalized that I hadn't *really* lied to Vanderhoff. Not completely.

It was true that I hadn't heard the floorboard squeak "Mil," but I'd definitely heard it say "dread." In fact, like a spider with icicles for legs, dread had crawled all the way up my spine and was spinning a frosty web in my brain.

Is this what it's like to be a P.I.? Geez!

The only reason I even signed up for that stupid course was so I could keep tabs on my dates—if I ever got another one. Never again was I going to be the last one to know someone was cheating on me—and with Candy Vincent, no less!

I reached into my stash of Tootsie Pops and pulled out the last sucker in the bag. It was green. I hated green. What kind of flavor was *green*?

I unwrapped the sucker and popped it into my mouth anyway—for the same reasons I'd taken this bizarre, hand-me-down assignment from Paulson in the first place.

I was broke. I was angry. And I was out of options.

I snorted out a jaded laugh.

Those three traits seemed to come with the territory for anyone un-lucky enough to be trapped in Point Paradise.

A sudden flash of light to my right caught my attention. I looked over to see the lights had gone out in Vanderhoff's living room. There was nothing more I could do there tonight, so I cranked the engine and tossed the nasty green Tootsie Pop in the Mustang's ashtray.

Then a weird feeling came over me.

I'd just had my most interesting night in months. The strange en-counter with Vanderhoff had left me invigorated, oddly spooked, and feeling a bit in over my head.

Oh my word. Is this what it feels like to be ... alive?

I'd almost forgotten.

I rolled up the car window and pictured the rugged, charming face of Detective Terry Paulson. He'd been the first person in a long time to cut me a break.

With only an intern's CC license, I wasn't supposed to work a case without a full-fledged P.I. alongside me. Florida required I obtain two years of on-the-job training before I could I call myself a *real* private in-vestigator.

I smiled. Paulson's arrival had been like manna from heaven. I mean, where the hell else was I going to find someone willing to give me a shot?

Paulson had bent the rules by letting me interview Vanderhoff on my own. But in a tiny, nowhere kind of place like Point Paradise, the rules tended to slide when you knew everyone on a first-name basis.

Besides, what could be the harm in me poking around? The worst that could happen was I'd end up having to buy Paulson a cheeseburg-er—and maybe get myself laid.

But neither of those things were going to happen tonight.

So, with nothing else to go on and nothing else to do, I shifted into drive and pointed the Mustang in the direction of Waldo and the A&P.

Somebody was going bananas. Whether it was me or old lady Vanderhoff was still up for debate. As I headed down the road, I had no illusions about my prospects. I was still a pawn in the game of life. But for the first time in ages, I actually felt like playing.

Chapter Nine

THE A&P TURNED OUT to be a bust. No weirdos lurking around, at least not by Florida standards. Everyone had on the right amount of clothing and no one was holding a sign reading "Will Work for Beer."

I made the most of the trip by picking up a loaf of Wonder bread for toast in the morning, then headed for home.

As I got near the Stop & Shoppe, I thought it might be fun to buzz through, just to make Artie haul his humongous butt off his chair and wait on me. But after scrounging the bottom of my purse to pay for the bread, I didn't have enough money for a lousy Tootsie Pop. So instead, I settled for flipping him the bird as I cruised past.

In the fading light, I leaned out the window to see if Artie had seen my single-digit salutation. I'd expected to see his familiar scowl hovering above his scraggly soul patch and double chin. Instead, my eyes landed on something even more disturbing.

I blinked.

No. That can't be.

I slammed on the brakes. And, after executing the fastest three-point turn on record, I zoomed back to the Stop & Shoppe. It was still there.

I hit the brakes, rubbed my eyes, and took another look.

Still there.

Against all logic, a pair of red, glowing orbs hovered in the darkness about six feet above the roof of the run-down convenience store. I grabbed my cellphone to take a picture. When I looked up again, they were gone.

What the—?

I figured they must've been some kind of reflection, so I pulled up under the sagging awning that served as the Stop & Shoppe's low-rent drive-thru. Artie was busy sawing logs in his executive armchair, his feet up on the counter by the cash register.

The fat bastard had slept through the entire thing.

That figures.

I revved the engine, startling a loud fart out of Artie.

"What?" he grumbled, rubbing his beady eyes. It was uncanny. Artie possessed the same basic body shape and face of a middle-aged manatee.

"You see anything funny this evening?" I asked.

"Funny?" Artie leaned sideways, causing his chair to creak in a way that sounded both painful and precarious.

"Yeah. You know, *unusual.*"

He scowled. "No."

I shifted the Mustang into reverse and set the brake. The engine sputtered out.

Damn air filter.

I wrapped my fingers around the key and was about to re-restart the ignition when I heard scratching coming from the awning overhead.

"What's that?" I asked.

"Probably rats." Artie gave a disinterested shrug. "Or tree limbs, maybe. The skinflint owner don't spend a dime to keep this place up. Just last week I had to—"

"Hush!" I cocked my head toward the ceiling.

"What?" Artie shot me a scowl. "You doing pest control now, Bobbie?"

"Shut up, Artie! *Listen!*"

The scratching sound continued, traversing the length of the roof awning from the roadside toward the back, where the Stop & Shoppe butted up against the woods.

I got out of the Mustang and sprinted past the end of the awning, then strained to see the rooftop. I couldn't make out squat in the darkness.

"You got a flashlight?" I yelled at Artie.

His chair squealed. "Sure," he hollered back. "For six-fifty. You want batteries it's another four bucks."

"Ugh." I shook my head and walked back to the Mustang. As I peeled out of the Stop & Shoppe, I glanced back. No red orbs.

Hospital shooters? Robot phone calls? Now these stupid glowing orbs? What next? Sasquatch in a tutu?

As the Stop & Shoppe disappeared in my rearview mirror, I made a mental note to add a flashlight to my P.I. kit—once I *had* a P.I. kit.

From the looks of it, I was going to need one.

Either that, or I needed to seriously consider making an appointment with a psychiatrist.

Chapter Ten

MY CELLPHONE RANG. I cracked open an eye and searched around in the tangled bedsheets for it.

"Hello?"

"I've got one for you."

My brain cramped. "What do you want, Earl? I'm still half asleep."

"It's nine-thirty."

"It's my day off, okay?"

"True mechanics never take a day off."

"Ugh. I got shot in the head, remember?"

He snorted. "How long you gonna ride *that* gravy train?"

"Earl, I'm only gonna ask one more time. What do you want?"

"Like I said, Bobbie. I've got one for you."

"Listen. I'm in *no* mood for one of your dumb jokes."

"It's a *customer*, you dingdong. Unless you don't want one."

My brain perked to life at the prospect of a paycheck. I bolted upright in bed. "Oh. What are we looking at?"

"Right now? A guy with a moustache that could win a Groucho Marx contest. And for the record, it's only *me* who's looking at him, Sleeping Beauty."

"I *meant* what are we looking at for *work*, smartass. Flat tire? Oil change? Please say it's major mechanical failure."

"I dunno. He walked here."

I squeezed my cellphone so hard it chirped. "Are you saying he doesn't have a vehicle? If this is another one of your stupid pranks, Earl, I'm gonna fire you."

"No prank. The guy needs a tow. I'm thinking it could be worth a few bucks. Should I tell him to get lost? You've got better things to do?"

I heard the *ka-ching* of a cash register—as it tumbled off a cliff. "Don't let him go anywhere! I'll be down in three minutes."

Earl laughed. "I'll do my best to keep him entertained."

"No jokes, Earl. Especially that stupid one about the gear shaft. You hear me?"

My phone went dead. I jumped out of bed and peeked through the blinds. From the dusty window of my apartment above the mechanic shop, I could see Earl talking to some guy dressed in black. He hadn't been kidding after all.

I let go of the blinds and made a mad dash for the bathroom. I figured I had no more than three minutes before Earl told that gear-shaft joke and we lost the only customer we'd had in a week. I pulled a T-shirt on over my head, wriggled into my father's coveralls and humongous work boots, and clomped down the stairs.

I bet the guy's onboard computer's on the fritz. They mess up everything.

I considered computers—especially *onboard* computers—to be the ruination of life as I knew it.

About the same time cars became equipped with them, I'd become equipped with boobs. Dad had given me the boot, and my cousin Earl had gotten the benefit of sopping up all my father's knowledge—*and* his time.

With all Dad's attention on Earl, my mother had finally gotten her chance to make me into a girl. It hadn't gone well. I guess by then I was too far off the grid.

Mom and Grandma Selma didn't know what to do with a girl who refused to wear a dress and who tied dolls to fence posts and shot out their eyes for BB-gun practice. After a while, they'd given up on the whole idea of domesticating me. "Don't bother me and I won't bother you," became a routine which lasted until I took off for college.

Even so, when Dad died and Mom up and ran off with Mr. Applewhite, it really threw me for a loop. Given her submissive nature, I didn't think she had it in her to go rogue.

Mom had left me all alone to run the garage with Earl. I'd have fired the jerk on day one, but I didn't know anything about those blasted onboard computers.

So my cousin and I had formed our own sort of weird alliance. He'd remained head mechanic at my dad's shop, and I'd become "the boss"—in other words, the person responsible for dealing with the bills, the customers, and the paperwork. But it was no "don't bother me and I won't bother you" relationship.

Just the opposite.

Earl and I bothered the hell out of each other—for sport.

I stumbled to the bottom of the stairs and caught sight of my reflection in the mirror by the door. Nothing like forgetting you're a bald cyclops to give you a friendly jolt in the morning. Better than a double espresso.

I gasped, fumbled back upstairs, and grabbed my wig. There was no time to fix my face. But, thankfully, nobody expected much in the way of appearance from a mechanic.

Secretly, I considered it one of the best perks of this whole lousy job.

Chapter Eleven

THE DOOR LEADING TO the parking lot squeaked as I pushed it open. An orange streak of late-morning sun hit me across the face, making me wince like a three-eyed vampire.

"This here's the boss man, Bobbie Drex," Earl said as I tumbled out the door and shuffled over to them. "Or, as we like to call her, 'the boy with boobs.'"

So much for establishing myself as the authority figure.

I sneered at Earl. "Did I mention that you're fired?"

Earl grinned, confident in his irreplaceability. He nodded and deadpanned, "Yeah. Just let me go collect my severance package."

"It's hard to find good help nowadays," I said to the guy with the moustache, extending my hand for a shake.

Anywhere but Florida, the guy would've been considered an odd duck. He wore a vintage fedora, which he tipped at me in an old-fashioned gesture of courtesy. As he did, I noticed he also had a knot on his forehead. Unlike mine, however, his was big enough to smuggle a boiled egg inside. His lip was busted as well. I figured he must've been in one hell of a bar fight recently.

"Name's William Knickerbocker," he said. He winced slightly when he raised his hand to shake mine. "Or as some folks like to call me, 'the boy *without* boobs.'"

Everybody's a smartass.

"How about I call you Bill?" I said dryly.

"That works, too. My vehicle's about two and a half miles down the road that way." Bill winced again as he raised his arm to point south down Obsidian Road. "I need a tow and repairs."

"What are you driving?"

"An RV."

Ka-ching!

"I think we can help you out with that, Bill. But I'm not sure about *you*." I took a furtive glance at his bulging forehead. "What are you? Some kind of professional barroom brawler?"

He grinned. "No. But it's amazing how often I end up looking like one." He touched his forehead. "This is just your typical head-against-the-windshield goose egg."

My eyebrows ticked up a notch. "You were in an accident?"

"Yeah. I think I hit a deer or something."

"A deer, you say." I exchanged a knowing glance with Earl. Venison beat an empty stomach any day of the week, even if it *was* road kill. It was fine, as long as you got there quick enough.

"What about *you*?" Knickerbocker asked, his eyes on the red knot between my eyes. "Where'd you get *that* beaut?"

"Oh. I, uh ...."

"She just had her demons exorcized," Earl quipped.

Knickerbocker's left eyebrow shot up. I looked past him at Earl. He was behind Knickerbocker, his face twisted into an idiotic expression aimed at making me lose my composure. I clenched my jaw to squelch the burning desire to kick Earl where the sun don't shine.

"Earl, darling?" I said between my teeth, "When you're done having a seizure, could you please give Bill here a lift back to his vehicle? Hook it up to Bessie and tow it back."

Earl's face switched to his normal, easy-going grin. I hated how easily he could shift gears.

"Yes, boss man." He moseyed toward the garage's only working service bay.

Bill blanched. "*Bessie?* You're going to pull my RV with a *cow?*"

I smirked. "Not exactly."

The sound of an angry diesel engine thundered from inside the service bay.

I nodded toward the garage. "*That's* Bessie."

Knickerbocker turned around just as a huge, black, four-wheel-drive monster truck emerged from the bay. Equipped with a 540-horsepower Hemi engine and tractor tires taller than me, Bessie could yank Godzilla out of Tokyo.

Earl steered the massive truck out of the garage and idled it next to Bill and me. "Hop in," he said to Knickerbocker.

"You wouldn't happen to have a stepladder, would you?" Bill asked.

"Fresh out." I patted my pockets. "Earl, Bill here said he hit a deer. Be sure and check that out."

Earl winked. "Yes, boss man."

Knickerbocker reached over his head to open Bessie's passenger door. He grunted as he hauled his tall, lanky body inside the cab. The effort made him wince and lick the seam on his busted lip.

He closed the door and Earl hit the gas, tearing another pothole in the crumbling asphalt parking lot. The pair disappeared past the flashing yellow light and down Obsidian Road.

Once they were out of sight, I slipped into the garage, unfastened the padlock on the electrical box, and flipped over a few breakers. A couple of overhead lights blinked on, and an air compressor began to hum.

I smiled to myself. I didn't care if Knickerbocker was a tourist, a weirdo, or even an escapee from nearby Stark Prison.

We were flat broke.

With any luck, the repairs on his busted vehicle would generate enough money to pay last month's light bill before they cut off the juice.

Chapter Twelve

FROM MY APARTMENT ABOVE the garage, I spotted Bessie passing underneath the flashing yellow light at the intersection. Hitched to the monster truck's rear was the most dilapidated hunk of junk I'd seen since my last trip to the Waldo antiques center.

Crap. So much for hitting the motherlode. I guess I'm gonna need Detective Paulson's twenty bucks after all.

As I watched Earl ease the rusty, algae-covered hulk of an RV into the service bay, I punched a number into my cell phone.

"Paulson? It's Bobbie Drex here with a case update."

"Well, don't *you* sound all official-like?" he crooned. "Let me guess. Vanderhoff's got early-onset Alzheimer's?"

"Good one. No. I think there may be more to it than that. I drove by the A&P last night. There was some weird guy hanging out in the parking lot in a yellow Volkswagen Beetle."

It was a lie. There hadn't been so much as an alley cat roaming the parking lot. But if my mother had taught me anything, it was that if you gave someone enough detail, you could make *anything* sound plausible. Besides, it was for a good cause. I was so broke twenty bucks would've doubled my net worth.

"Really? A yellow Volkswagen?" Paulson asked. The news seemed to catch him off guard. "Did you get a license plate number?"

My throat tightened. "No."

"So what's the possible connection between the Volkswagen and the calls Vanderhoff's getting?"

I cringed. "Well, I don't know. I didn't say I'd cracked the case. I just have a gut feeling there's more to Vanderhoff's story than your theory that a beauty parlor hairdryer cooked her brains."

"Right. Speaking of which, have you gone by Beth-Ann's to check out the dryer?"

Crap. I should have thought of that when I was at her place yesterday.

"It's on my follow-up list for today."

"Good. Just do me a favor."

"What?"

"Don't go chasing strange vehicles around in the dark. At least, not without me."

I grinned. "No worries there, I promise." That *wasn't* a lie. I didn't have money to waste on gas. The Mustang only got fifteen miles to a gallon. On a good day. Downhill.

"Okay. Call me when you've got something," Paulson said.

"Roger that."

I clicked off the phone and tromped down the stairs and over to the service bay. When I got there, Earl was deep under the hood of the RV, giving Knickerbocker the diagnosis on his raggedy-ass old Minnie Winnie.

"Threw a rod," Earl was saying. "Right through the gear shaft."

I wasn't sure if Earl was being serious or had just delivered the punchline to the joke I'd expressly banned him from telling. I checked Knickerbocker's face. He seemed unconcerned either way.

"Can you fix it?" Knickerbocker asked.

Earl shrugged. "Sure. But do you really think it's worth spending the money on this old hunk—"

I kicked Earl in the shin. Hard.

His surprised eyes met mine, and I shot him a look that could curdle an enamel paint job. He winced and rubbed his leg.

"What a classic," I said, beaming at Knickerbocker.

"Uh ...," Earl fumbled. "I mean, I have to say, sir, she's a real beauty."

Knickerbocker's battered face sagged a little more. He let out a sigh. "Listen. I know she's no looker, but she's got sentimental value. Do what you can for her, would you?"

"Don't you want to know the cost first?" Earl asked. He glanced over at me and withered again under my angry glare.

Bill shook his head. "No. Whatever it costs, it's okay." He turned to me. "As long as you take cash, that is."

"We definitely take cash," I blurted before Earl had a chance to say anything else idiotic. He might've been a mechanical genius, but he was the crappiest salesperson in the known Milky Way Galaxy.

"We'll get to work on it right away," I said. "Earl will figure out the parts you need. You put down a deposit that pays for the parts, and we'll get them ordered right away."

Knickerbocker smiled absently. "That sounds good. How long will it take to fix?"

"I'd say not more than three to six days," Earl said, "depending on availability of parts."

"You have someplace to stay?" I asked Knickerbocker.

"I can't stay in the RV?"

I shook my head. "No. It'll be up on the lift."

"And maybe in a few pieces, I suspect," Earl said.

Knickerbocker shrugged and smiled in a vague, pained kind of way. "Then I guess I'm going to need a place to stay."

"I've got a small in-law apartment upstairs," I blurted. "I could rent it to you for say, eighty-nine dollars a night?"

Knickerbocker looked at me strangely, then let out a groan. His eyes rolled up into his head, and he collapsed backward, right into Earl's waiting arms. My cousin caught him by the torso, then laid him out on the floor of the service bay like a side of beef.

"I'd a passed out, too," Earl said. "You shouldn't a gone over fifty-nine bucks, tops."

"This isn't funny, Earl. The guy may have a concussion or something. Help me get him up the stairs."

"Shouldn't we call a doctor?"

"Who? Dr. Greenblatt? He moved away two months ago."

"Oh, yeah." He looked me in the eyes. "Good thing you and me can't afford to get sick."

I didn't try to argue with Earl's logic. It made more sense than anything else going on at the moment. I grabbed Knickerbocker's legs, Earl hooked his arms under his shoulders, and we toted him toward the stairwell.

As I wrangled the door open with an elbow, Earl's stomach growled.

"Oh," he said. "I almost forgot. I searched around, but couldn't find no signs of a deer. This feller here must'a hit something else."

I sighed.

So much for free venison stew tonight.

Chapter Thirteen

I STARED AT THE STRANGER sprawled out in Grandma Selma's old bed.

Earl and I had carried Knickerbocker upstairs to her tiny in-law apartment. It was attached to my parent's place by a short breezeway. I hadn't been inside it for months. The air inside smelled faintly of dust and her perfume.

We'd laid Knickerbocker on the bed and pulled his shirt off to assess him for injuries. Between his neck and left shoulder, we'd discovered a large bruise ringed with broken skin. It was sort of oval-shaped, and as big as the bottom of a plastic jug of Castrol Motor Oil.

I'd figured the injury must've come from the shoulder strap on his seatbelt. Knickerbocker's RV was too old to have airbags to soften the impact.

Earl, on the other hand, had insisted the injury was a Sasquatch bite. I'd shot him another choice selection from my repertoire of scathing looks, handed him my life savings, and sent him off to the A&P to fetch some aspirin, rubbing alcohol, and two cans of chicken soup, whatever was cheapest.

While Earl was away, I'd stayed behind to keep an eye on our unanticipated patient. Equipped with the hospital's handy-dandy concussion watch list, I sat on an old wicker settee and intermittently glanced over at Knickerbocker, biding my time by scanning articles from a selection of outdated magazines I'd filched from the recycle bin at Beth-Ann's.

I was engrossed in a fascinating article on new and exciting ways to reinvent green bean casserole when Knickerbocker groaned. I jumped up and sprinted to his side.

"Are you okay, Mr. Knickerbocker?"

He opened his eyes. Either his irises were black, or his pupils had swallowed them whole.

"Mr. Knickerbocker?" I repeated.

His eyes pointed in my direction, but whether he could see me or not, I couldn't tell. He muttered something that sounded like a foreign language, then shifted his dazed eyes to his left, as if he was searching for something.

"It's okay," I said soothingly. "You're okay." I touched his arm. He jerked away.

"Mr. Knickerbocker!" I said louder. "You're okay. Can you hear me?"

"Huh?" He grunted, and turned back toward me. His dilated pupils were now rimmed with green.

"You're safe with me," I said.

"Where am I?" he asked.

"My grandmother's apartment. You passed out."

"Oh."

"I sent Earl for supplies," I said, then heard a rumble. I went to the window. Earl was pulling Bessie into the parking lot, having spent, literally, my last dime.

I walked back over to the bedside. "I don't mean to be crass, but I'll need money before we can go any further."

Knickerbocker's head lolled on the pillow. He glanced down at his naked chest. "Go any further? Are we ... uh ... did we just—?"

My back bristled with Southern indignation. "Before we can order parts. For your RV."

"My RV?"

"Yes. You said you hit a deer."

"Oh. Deer. Right. Did it survive?"

My eyebrows inched closer together. "I don't know. We didn't see any signs of it around the accident site."

"Why am I here ... in this bed?"

"You fainted. You hit your head in an accident. You walked here. We towed your RV? You don't remember?"

"Uh ... sure. But why am I half naked?" Knickerbocker lifted the sheet and took a peek under it. "You didn't see my ... uh ... *lizard*, did you?"

A snort of laughter erupted from behind me. I turned to see Earl standing there holding a paper grocery sack, grinning like a lottery winner.

Earl smirked at me, then eyed Knickerbocker. "Been a long time since *that one there's* seen a lizard."

Knickerbocker reached up and touched the goose egg on his forehead. His brow furrowed. "So you *didn't* see it?"

"*I* didn't," Earl said. "But having just freshly arrived, I can only speak for myself."

I punched Earl's arm. "Stop it. He's delirious."

I turned to Knickerbocker. "Now you lay back and let me disinfect your wounds."

"You remember what bit you?" Earl asked as I took the bag, opened the bottle of alcohol, and poured some onto a wad of toilet paper.

"Bit me?" Knickerbocker asked.

"He's talking about the wound on your shoulder," I said.

I shot Earl some side-eye, then sat on the edge of the bed beside Knickerbocker. I dabbed at the half-circle of bruised, slightly broken flesh.

Knickerbocker winced. "Feels like a cracked clavicle," he said. "Must've been the seatbelt."

I turned and sneered at Earl. He crinkled his nose at me.

"I hate to bring this up," Earl said, "but it'd be good to get some money down on them parts before the supply stores close for the day."

"Parts?" Knickerbocker asked.

"Your RV broke down, remember?" I asked.

"Sure." Knickerbocker tried to sit up, but fell back onto the pillows. "Sorry. I feel ... uh ...."

"Should I call a doctor?" I asked. "You don't look so good."

"No doctors!" Knickerbocker said with more energy than I thought he had left in him. He tried to sit up again, but gave up and leaned back on the pillows. "I hate doctors."

Earl's eyebrows raised to his shaggy hairline. "I hear *that.*"

"Look. In the glove compartment," Knickerbocker said. "I keep money in there. Take whatever you need."

My right eyebrow arched. "Aren't you worried we might ... you know ... cheat you?"

"Yeah. Or rob you blind or something?" Earl added.

Knickerbocker studied us both through a pair of half-dilated, blood-shot eyes.

"Don't take this personally," he said. "But from the looks of you two, I don't think you've got enough ambition for anything like that."

Chapter Fourteen

I CLOSED THE DOOR TO the bedroom, leaving Knickerbocker propped up on pillows with a glass of tap water and a selection of *Southern Living* magazines circa 1997.

"What do you think we should do?" I whispered to Earl as we walked down the hall toward the kitchen. "He seems confused. Do you know anything about treating a cracked clavicle?"

"Not a thing," Earl said. "But if I'm right and that fella got hisself bit up by Bigfoot, he's probably got some kind of poison fever, you know, causing him to be all delusional and whatnot."

I closed my eyes and blew out a breath. Talking to Earl was like trying to have a conversation with Jethro on the *Beverly Hillbillies*. He had the same country twang, the same dumb luck, and the same irritating happy-go-lucky attitude. He also had an uncanny knack for calling things accurately, despite having no intellectual pursuits beyond *Auto Trader* and *Pimp My Ride*. It was downright infuriating.

"It's not a Bigfoot bite!" I hissed at Earl. "It's from his seatbelt. He said so himself."

"What about all that lizard mumbo-jumbo? That don't make him a very reliable witness, if you ask me."

"He's probably confused. From the accident."

Earl shrugged. "Or he's some nut-job fresh outta the looney bin."

I glared at Earl. I wanted to dismiss his comment out of hand. But doubt threaded its way across my mind like one of my Grandma Selma's cross-stitches. And that spider with icicle legs crawled out from under my wig again and made a beeline for where my bra hooked in the back.

"I don't want to be alone with him," I blurted. "Earl, you make the soup. I'll go check out the glove compartment."

"Yeah. Let's see if his cash is just a delusion too." Earl crinkled his nose. "Uh ... how do I make it?"

I looked up at the six-foot-four lump of uselessness. "Soup? You're kidding. You open the can, Earl. You pour it in a pan. Then you cook it till it boils."

"What kind of pan?"

I groaned, shook my head, and stomped down the stairs.

Halfway down, I turned around and stomped back up the stairwell. "Where are the keys?"

Earl grinned, pulled them out of the breast pocket of his coveralls, and dangled them in front of me like a cat toy. I swiped them from his hand and blew him a raspberry.

What a jerk!

I UNLOCKED THE DRIVER'S door of Knickerbocker's crappy old RV. It had a built-in cab, and I figured it measured around twenty-four feet long. Despite the exterior looking as if it were ready for the junkyard, I was surprised to discover the interior was almost mint.

One glance at the shiny chrome controls jutting from the aqua-painted metal dashboard and I was eight years old again—a kid in a candy store.

Sweet.

From the looks of it, the Minnie Winnie had to have been manufactured in the late 1960s, back when groovy was still a thing worth striving for.

Of course, the windshield was a total loss. It was shattered into an opaque hodgepodge of tiny ice cubes. The driver's seat also had a gash on the left side, near the headrest. Nicotine-hued foam rubber spewed out from the gaping slit in the aquamarine vinyl like raw chicken fat.

I glanced around the floorboards and passenger seat. No receipts. No junk food wrappers. Not even a roadmap or a coffee ring. If this guy was living in his RV, you'd never have known it. I laughed to myself.

He must be totally OCD.

I tried the glove compartment. It was locked. I fumbled with the key ring and tried the smallest key. It didn't work. I tried the next one. The key slipped in. I turned it, and the metal glovebox fell open like a slack jaw.

My own jaw followed suit.

Inside the glove compartment sat row upon row of neatly bundled cash—the kind of money you'd expect to nab from a successful bank heist.

I closed my mouth and cautiously picked up a packet. I fanned through the bills with my thumb.

Twenties. Fifty of them. A cool grand.

I picked up two more paper-banded packs and noticed a silver glint behind them. I shoved aside a few stacks. A 9mm Glock came into view.

I gasped.

I'd wanted a Glock since I was eight years old.

As I reached for the gun, a thought made me recoil as if I'd been attacked by a rattlesnake.

Who is this guy? Black clothes. Wads of cash. Driving in the middle of nowhere—in the middle of the night. There's no way he can be good news.

I should call Officer Paulson!

I patted down my coveralls. Five heavy-duty utility pockets and not one of them contained my cellphone. I mentally kicked myself in the ass, then stuffed three bundles of bills into my right hip pocket. I stacked the others back neatly, locked the glovebox, and was about to leave when curiosity got the better of me.

I swiveled the seat around, got up, and crept into the main cabin of the RV.

Beyond the reach of the overhead service bay lights, the RV's interior grew dim and veiled in a grayish gloom. As my eyes adjusted to the faint light, a modest kitchen, a small banquette, and a fold out couch built into the wall came into view.

Typical, old retro-style RV.

Beyond the main cabin, I could see a small hallway. At the end of it was a metal door. I walked to the edge of the hallway for a closer inspection.

The door looked like something from a lock-up unit. Four deadbolts secured the door above the doorknob. Four more below. Definitely not original equipment.

The hair on the back of my neck bristled.

Why would anyone do that?

A noise in the garage sent me whirling around on my thick, rubber heels.

Crap! Knickerbocker's coming!

My upper torso twisted toward the front of the RV. The bottom half wasn't quite so quick. I tried to take a step, tripped on my boots, and did a belly flop onto the floor of the main cabin.

"Oof!" I grunted as I hit the floor, the wind knocked out of me.

I lay there a second, taking inventory of my body parts, then hiked myself up on one elbow. As I waited for my breath to catch and the stars to clear from my corneas, I caught a movement from the corner of my eye.

I turned my head and found myself face-to-face with a pair of yellow-green, reptilian eyes.

Chapter Fifteen

THE REPTILE'S BULBOUS eyes stared blankly at me from inside a ten-gallon terrarium. It had been tucked beneath the banquette in Knickerbocker's RV.

I grunted and hauled myself to sitting on the linoleum floor.

Well, what do you know? Knickerbocker really does have a lizard.

"LOOK WHAT I FOUND," I said to Earl as I walked into the kitchen of Grandma Selma's apartment toting the terrarium.

"Well, I'll be. That looks like a lizard, all right." Earl shook his head. "Too bad, Cuz." He winked at me. "For a minute there, I thought you'd done got lucky."

"Hardy har har." I set the terrarium on the counter and pursed my lips to stifle a grin.

"Earl, that's not all I found." I pulled the stacks of twenties out of my pocket and fanned them in front of Earl's face. "I guess you can go ahead and order those parts now."

Earl's eyes grew as big as boiled eggs. "Lord a'mighty! How much you got there?"

"Three grand. But there's more if you need it."

Joy and avarice mud-wrestled on Earl's face, providing me with some much-relished sadistic pleasure.

"You got that soup ready?" I asked.

"Yeah." Earl took an iron skillet off the burner and poured its contents into a bowl. The whole while, he kept one eye trained on the money, until I shoved the bills back in my pocket.

"I'll carry the soup," I said. "You carry the lizard."

"What about the saltines?" Earl held up a waxy paper sleeve of crackers. "You can't have soup without saltines."

"You spent my last bit of my money on ... ugh!" Then I remembered the money in my pocket and lightened my mood. "Fine." I set the bowl on a plate and tossed a handful of crackers around the edges. "Happy now?"

Earl eyed my bulging money pocket. "I guess."

"Grab the lizard and follow me."

We crept down the hall, both of us quiet for a change. I balanced the plate and bowl precariously on one set of fingertips, like a French waiter, and tapped on the bedroom door with my free hand.

No reply.

I pushed the door open. The bed was empty.

"Mr. Knickerbocker?" I called out.

The floor-length curtains moved. Knickerbocker peeked out from behind them.

"Uh ... I brought you some soup. And Earl here has your ... uh ... lizard."

Knickerbocker's bloodshot eyes lit up at the sight of the terrarium. "Gizzard!"

Earl shot me the look he usually reserved for customers who pull into our garage and ask if we have clean restrooms.

"I'll set her down right here on the bureau," Earl said, and gingerly placed the glass terrarium on top of granny's ancient oak chest of drawers.

Knickerbocker took a step toward us, then loomed sideways, as if he'd just gotten off a Tilt-a-Whirl. His hand landed on the bed, catching his fall.

"Get back in bed right now," I said. "Eat your soup. You need to build your strength."

Knickerbocker smiled weakly and complied. He crawled into bed and took the bowl of soup I offered with two shaky hands.

"Saltines. Nice touch," he said, and slurped the soup as if he hadn't eaten in weeks.

Earl ogled the small, lime-green lizard through the glass of the terrarium. "If you don't mind me asking, Mr. K, why're you traveling around with a lizard of the reptilian persuasion?"

Knickerbocker looked up from his soup and shrugged. "No barking. No walking. No litter box. Gizzard only needs one thing. Crickets and fresh water."

"That's two things," I said.

"Oh. Right," Knickerbocker said absently. "Do you think you could get her some?"

"Crickets or water?" I asked.

"Both."

I looked over at my cousin. "Sounds like a job for you, Earl."

He pouted. "Why me?"

"Because I'm heading back over to Beth-Ann's."

Earl grinned. "Aw, come on, Bobbie. That wig looks fine. Besides, you don't have to get yourself all dolled up on my account. Or is it on account of *someone else*?" He shot Knickerbocker a wink.

I sneered. "It's not about either of you."

I hadn't told Earl about the case I was working with Officer Paulson, or about getting my private investigator intern certificate. I wasn't in the mood to live either one of those personal gems down just yet.

"Can I bring you back anything?" I asked as I walked toward the bedroom door.

"How about a comb?" Knickerbocker said. He ran his hand over the top of his head and seemed genuinely surprised to discover he was as bald as a cue ball.

I turned away so neither man could see my eyes roll around in their sockets.

Great. Another weirdo man to take care of.

Thanks, universe. That's all I need.

Chapter Sixteen

ON MY WAY TO BETH-ANN'S beauty shop, I noticed four or five buzzards circling above the woods a few miles south of Point Paradise. In this rural area, lots of people dumped their trash instead of paying for pickup, so I didn't think much of it. I drove on, intent on nailing my second interview as a P.I. intern.

No mistakes this time, I chided myself. *Beth-Ann's a friend, but I can't let that influence my professionalism.*

"HEY, YOU," BETH-ANN said as she swept up a heap of black, wavy hair. "Just gave myself a trim. You need one?"

"Ha ha. You're a riot." I glanced at my wig in the mirror, frowned, and gave it a quick adjustment.

"What's up, then?" she asked.

"Not much." Taking a note from my training course, I tried to act casual, in order to put the interviewee at ease. "Just searching for intelligent life. You seen any lately?"

Beth-Ann grinned. "In Waldo? Not even a molecule. You?"

"Nope. But I *did* meet a man."

Beth-Ann's face shifted from studied indifference to juicy-gossip intrigue. "Really?" She leaned on her broom handle. "Spill it, girl!"

I shrugged. "Not much to tell yet. He came into town today with a busted RV. He's boarding in Grandma's apartment for a few days."

"What's his name?"

"William Knickerbocker."

Beth-Ann rolled her huge, violet eyes. "Ugh! I hope he's cuter than he sounds."

"Meh. Not really. Kind of skinny. Bald. Not my type."

Beth-Ann's shoulders slumped. "Figures. Not even potential as a new client." She bent over and scooped the hair up into a dustpan. "So what else is up?"

I puffed out my chest a little. It went unnoticed due to my oversized coveralls. "Paulson gave me a case to work on."

Beth-Ann's eyes twinkled with interest. "The sexy detexy? He gave you a *real* case? Tell me every juicy detail!"

"Well, that's kind of why I'm here. The case involves old lady Vanderhoff. She says she's been getting weird phone calls. "

"Vanderhoff?" Beth-Ann crinkled her nose. "Oh, geez, Bobbie. Paulson's playing you! Can't you see that? He probably wants to get you somewhere dark and secluded so he can get in your pants."

I grinned. "Jealous?"

Beth-Ann sneered. "Damned straight." She sighed, then laughed. "Vanderhoff's crazy. Remember that time she saw Jesus' face in a potato chip?"

I pursed my lips to a bloodless line. "Ruffles, no less. Don't remind me. Earl grabbed it out of her hand and ate it."

We locked eyes and both said, "Ruffles have religion."

We laughed a moment, then Beth-Ann shook her head. "Ruined that poor woman's chance at a *National Enquirer* spotlight. You know she still talks about it?"

"No!"

"Yep. Every time she comes in, near about."

I grinned, then cleared my throat, straightened my shoulders, and shifted into professional P.I. mode. "Seriously, Beth-Ann. What would Paulson have to gain by sending me on a wild goose chase with Vanderhoff?"

"What does any guy get out of torturing a woman?" Beth-Ann scowled for a second, then smirked at me. "I can't believe you're gonna be a detective! Tell me. How much is he paying you for the case?"

I bit my lip. "If I figure out who's behind the calls, I get twenty bucks."

"Twenty bucks? Geez. What a tightwad. And if you *don't?*"

"I have to take Paulson to dinner."

Beth-Ann shook her head. "And you don't think *that's* you getting played? Sorry girl, but license or not, you're no *Magnum P.I.*"

I sighed and drummed my grease-stained nails on a washbasin. "I went to her house last night."

"Whose house?"

"Old lady Vanderhoff's."

Beth-Ann's face went paler, if that was possible. "Wait a minute. You went *inside?*"

"Yeah."

She grabbed my forearm. "What was it like? Were there balls of tinfoil as big as beanbag chairs? Empty Cool Whip containers stacked to the ceiling? Real children's skeletons in her closet?"

"No. Actually, it looked relatively normal. Except for the dolls."

"Dolls?" Beth-Ann recoiled and dropped my arm. "Yuck!"

"I know. There were tons of them. Totally creepy."

"Did you find out anything?"

"Only that she's even crazier than I thought. She told me a robot told her to steal bananas."

Beth-Ann's eyes narrowed. "That's got your cousin Earl's name written all over it, Bobbie. I bet he put her up to it. To get back at you for leaving that rotten can of sardines under Bessie's driver's seat on his birthday."

My lips twisted over to one side of my face. "I hadn't thought of that."

Beth-Ann laughed. "Maybe you should have, detective."

"Okay. Maybe you're right. Still, just in case, do you mind if I ask you a few questions?"

"Sure."

I pulled a notepad and pen from my coveralls. Beth-Ann smirked, but only for a flash, then slapped on a semi-serious expression.

"When did Vanderhoff come in here last?" I asked.

"On Wednesday a week ago. Her bi-weekly wash and set."

I scribbled it down. "Did you use any new dyes or shampoos on her that might have caused a reaction?"

"Nope. Normal stuff. And no color that week. Just the wash and set."

"So she was here for how long?"

"From two in the afternoon to quarter past three."

I looked up at Beth-Ann. "That's pretty precise."

"I've been doing her hair for fifteen years, Bobbie. I've got that baby down to a science."

"Okay. Did she happen to sit under a hairdryer?"

"Of course. With a headful of curlers. You know the routine."

"I mean ... for maybe *longer* than usual?"

"Nope. I had another appointment right after. Nosy Nellie Parker at three-thirty. I had to keep on schedule or Nellie'd blab all over Alachua County about how my standards were slipping."

"That's the hairdryer, right?" I pointed to a chrome and purple chair that appeared to have been transported straight from the set of a low-budget, sci-fi movie.

Beth-Ann eyed me like I'd lost it. "Yes. It's the only one I've got. You and Carl sold it to me, remember?"

"Of course." I walked over to check it out. Of all the things in Beth-Ann's kitschy 1950s-vibe shop, her hair-drying chair was my favorite.

Sleek, low-slung, and boxy, the chair was upholstered in a light-lavender vinyl with a starburst pattern. Tubular chrome pipes served as its spindly-looking arms and legs.

But the part I liked best was the dryer head itself. The conical-shaped dome of stainless steel was the size and shape of the business end of a ballistic missile. It always made me think of a helmet left behind by an egg-headed alien.

I looked around for a manufacturer's tag. "What's the chair called again?"

"The Atomic Purple Salon Chair," Beth-Ann said. "Circa 1950-something. But I call her 'Girlie.'"

I grunted and scribbled it down on a notepad. I was about to leave when I noticed an earwig crawl out of one of the holes in the chrome dryer head.

"Anything else?" Beth-Ann asked. "Hate to give you the bum's rush, Bobbie, but I've got a perm coming in any second."

"No, that's it for now." I walked toward the door. "Thanks. You might want to spray for bugs. See you next week?"

"Bugs?" Beth-Ann scowled, then she zeroed in on a spot above my eyes. "Hey, you could use a brow wax."

"I think I'll hold onto all the hair I have left for right now." I opened the side door, hesitated, then turned around. Beth-Ann was bending over her dustpan.

"Hey, Beth-Ann?"

She looked up. I bit my lip, then blurted out what I wanted to ask before I lost my nerve.

"Do you believe in Sasquatch?"

Beth-Ann grinned slyly. "Did Earl put you up to this?"

When I didn't grin back, she straightened up to standing. "Wait. Are you serious?"

I shrugged and chewed my bottom lip. Then decided to laugh it off.

"Naw. I was just kidding around."

Chapter Seventeen

ON THE WAY BACK TO the garage, I wondered whether Beth-Ann was the most reliable source to confer with about the existence of hairy, ape-like creatures. Sure, she was non-judgmental. And a great hairstylist. People came from all over to get their hair done by her. But thinking about it now, maybe she was a little *too* open-minded.

A few weeks ago, after attending some kind of New-Age meetup, she'd advised me not to pray using negative words. She'd said that God couldn't hear "no" or "don't." So if someone prayed, "I don't want to be poor," all God heard was "I want to be poor," and so he granted their wish.

I was actually beginning to think there was something to it.

Ever since Carl Blanders dumped me, I'd been praying, "I don't want another no-good man in my life." Perhaps that double negative had been too confusing for the Creator of the Known Universe to figure out. Why else would another oddball loser wash up on my doorstep after I'd distinctly prayed for the exact opposite?

But then again, God had made up for it by delivering Terry Paulson to Point Paradise. The thought of his blue eyes and boyish grin made me want to call him up and flirt with him over the phone.

What the heck.

I pulled out my cellphone to call him. I figured I'd use the pretense of giving him a case update. But what did I have to report? That the brain-scrambling hairdryer in question turned out to be Atomic Purple? I frowned, nixed the idea, shoved my phone in my pocket, and turned the radio up.

I was a couple miles away from Point Paradise when I saw the buzzards again. I realized they were circling the same area where Knickerbocker had his accident. Curious, I pulled over. As soon as I opened the door, I could smell the unmistakable odor of rotting meat.

Too late for venison barbeque. But no doubt about it. Knickerbocker most certainly hit something....

With no obvious trail in the sawgrass, I followed my nose into the woods. About fifty feet into the pines, I saw a whitish-yellow lump in the leaves, up next to a pile of brush. As I got closer, I could see it was the corpse of a hog about the size of an Igloo cooler. Its body was intact. Its jaws appeared to be covered in coagulated blood. Flies buzzed around it in noisy clouds.

Gross. Well, that solves that mystery.

I turned around to head back to the car.

My knees went wobbly. I nearly fell down.

Leaning up against a pine tree was another dead body. Only this one was human. Dressed in a pair of orange prison overalls, I couldn't tell if it was a man or woman. The person's throat and face had been pretty much ripped to shreds.

Paranoia swept over me like an arctic blast. *Is the killer still here? Watching me?*

My body began to shake uncontrollably.

I have to get out of here!

But my legs didn't seem to get the magnitude of the situation. They were stuck, frozen in place.

A fly buzzed around my face, then lit on my cheek. I swatted it away, horrified at the thought of where it had last landed. Nausea and dizziness flooded my senses, as if I'd suddenly become aware of the Earth spinning on its axis.

Get. The. Hell. Out. Of. Here!

With every ounce of willpower I could muster, I got my stiff, paralytic legs take a step toward the road. The second step wasn't any easier. As I attempted a third, a tree branch cracked behind me.

A hot surge of adrenaline raced through my veins, startling me out of my stupor. My legs unlocked, finally joining the rescue team.

I took off, pounding my way through the underbrush on coltish, half-numb legs. As I came to the road clearing, my father's red Mustang shone like a blazing beacon in a raging sea. I jumped in, rolled up the windows, and locked both doors—three times.

Shivering with shock, rational thought eluded me. I knew a corpse couldn't chase me. Still, I kept waiting for it to appear out of the scrub. Every molecule inside me was screaming for me to get the hell out of there and never look back.

But running wasn't an option.

I swallowed hard and took a deep breath. If I was going to do this P.I. thing, I had to suck it up and grow a pair. Besides, my shaking hands were shaking so badly I couldn't get the key in the ignition anyway.

I sat in the car trembling like a wet Chihuahua in the snow for a full ten minutes. Finally, my hands calmed down to a jitter. I reached into a pocket for my cellphone.

"Paulson? It's Drex."

"How's my favorite P.I. in training?" he joked.

"I found a dead body."

"What! Where?"

"On Obsidian Road. About two and a half miles south of the intersection."

I waited for a response. None came.

"What should I do?" I asked.

"Hold on. I'm thinking. Don't tell anyone. I'll be there as soon as I can."

Chapter Eighteen

OFFICER PAULSON ARRIVED nearly an hour later. I was kind of grateful it took him that long. I was still a bit shaky when he pulled up beside me on the side of the road. My legs felt wobbly as I climbed out of the Mustang. I leaned against it for support.

"Sorry. I was out on a case on the other side of Waldo," he said as he got out of his car. "You okay?"

"No. It was horrible. Whoever it is ... they're all mangled up. Probably by the hog."

"There's a hog?"

"Yes. It's dead, too."

"Show me."

I hesitated. "Do I have to?"

"No. But do you want to be a detective or not?"

I shook my head. "I dunno."

His expression softened. "Wait here, then. Where is it?"

"Straight ahead. You can't miss it. Follow the trail I made in the sawgrass." *As I ran like a headless chicken-shit through the woods.*

"Got it." Paulson disappeared into the pines. He returned about fifteen minutes later.

"Sorry, Drex. But I can't find anything. I'm going to need your help after all."

I nodded. "Follow me."

RELUCTANTLY, I LED Paulson through the tangled undergrowth of wiregrass and palmettos to the horrific scene. I pointed a finger at the animal's corpse about twenty feet away. "There's the hog over there."

"Yes. I see it," he said. "But where's the body?"

"Behind us."

I turned slowly, eyes half shut, not wanting to see it again.

"Where?" Paulson asked.

I cracked open a flinching eye. The corpse in the orange overalls was nowhere to be seen. My mouth fell open.

"It was right over there." I pointed to a stand of pines.

"Are you sure whoever it is was dead? Maybe they got up and—"

I shook my head numbly. "No. They were dead all right."

"Uh-huh. Well, Bobbie, I hate to say it, but you *did* just experience a head trauma. And I heard a rumor you saw a phantom shooter at the hospital. Maybe you should go talk to your doctor or something. You might be having hallucinations."

My gut flopped. "I could have sworn it was real."

Paulson put an arm around my shoulder. In other circumstances, I might have liked it. But at the moment, all I could see and smell around me was death. At least I knew then I wasn't into necrophilia.

"You want me to drive you back to your shop?" Paulson asked.

"No. I'll be okay."

"Then I'll follow you. To make sure you get back all right. It's my fault. I shouldn't have put you through this so soon after your accident. You should get some rest."

I sighed. "You're right. Do me a favor, Paulson?"

"Sure."

"Don't tell anybody about this. The last thing I need is Earl finding out. He'll be on the phone turning me over to some UFO network or something."

"Okay. It's just a dead hog. Mum's the word. As long as you promise you'll take it easy. And go see a doctor."

I crossed my fingers behind my back. "I promise."

Right. Like I'm gonna spill my guts to a shrink and end up in the looney bin like poor Aunt Clara. No thanks.

Chapter Nineteen

THE SUN WAS DIPPING below the tree line when I pulled the Mustang onto the crumbling asphalt parking lot in front of the mechanic shop. In the runoff ditch between the road and weedy yard, Earl was squatting in the grass, hopping around on his heels like a giant frog in a black wig and overalls.

Any other time, the scene would've provided me sadistic, comic relief. Tonight, it was just relief, pure and simple.

I blew out a big breath, hoping some of the lingering horror would exit with it. I slapped on a trembling smirk and climbed out of the Mustang.

"Someone finally turn you into a toad?" I half-heartedly yelled at my cousin.

He stood up. His face bore an odd mixture of trepidation and indignation.

"Near 'bouts." He nodded toward the garage and glanced up at the second story. "That weirdo up there. He passed out in his soup blabbering something about a rubber octopus."

My trembling smirk collapsed. "What? He must be in worse shape than I thought."

Earl shot me an *I-told-you-so* look. "Sasquatch bite. I'm telling you."

"Can it, Earl."

Earl shrugged. "You're the boss."

I scowled. "I don't get it, Earl. If Knickerbocker's so bad off, how in the world did he manage to walk here this morning?"

"Shock, maybe? Or maybe he got one of them adrenaline surges. You know. Like them stories you hear about where some tiny little gal lifts up a Mack Truck to get her baby out from underneath it."

I shook my head. "Earl, I'm not in the mood to hear any more of your stupid crap tonight."

His face puckered. "It ain't stupid crap. Look it up yourself. It's on the Internet."

"I would, if I could afford to get the cable hooked up again. But all the money we earn goes to pay *your* salary." I shot him an angry scowl. "Just gimme the crickets and go on home."

Earl scowled. "Happy to oblige." His face softened. "Sure you don't need any help with that guy upstairs?"

"No. I can manage. If he's not better in the morning, I'll call 9-1-1."

"Alrighty then. Call me if you need me." Earl opened his huge, meaty palm and offered up a couple of half-squashed crickets.

"Thanks," I said as the bugs tumbled into my hand. I closed my fingers around them and felt the insects wriggle in my palm. They weren't the only things on their last legs.

The sapphire ring on my hand was the only thing of value I hadn't yet pawned to make ends meet. A gift from Grandma Selma, I hoped I wouldn't have to part with it.

"Watch yourself, you hear?" Earl said as he walked away. He turned back and shot me a look he'd stolen from my father—an odd expression between worry and pity.

My fear evaporated into anger. "Don't tell me you're actually *worried* about me," I said.

"Naw," Earl said. "It's *him* I'm a-feared for. I wouldn't want to be left alone with you for all the money in China." Earl brushed his hands off on the seat of his coveralls, turned his back to me, and headed toward Bessie.

"Yeah?" I called after him. "Well ... I hope Bigfoot gets *you* next."

Earl spun around. "Ha! So you *do* believe that fella got bit by the Sasquatch!"

"I do not!"

"Well, don't you worry about me, little Cuz. No dumb ol' skunk ape's gonna get me. Not in Bessie, he won't. I'll flatten him under my tires. Make him into a primate pancake."

I scowled. "Sounds delicious."

Chapter Twenty

AFTER LETTING MYSELF into Grandma Selma's apartment, I crept down the hall and tapped lightly on the bedroom door. Knickerbocker didn't answer. I peeked inside to find him sleeping soundlessly in bed. I tiptoed in and dropped the two mangled crickets into the terrarium. The lizard eyed them, then stared at me blankly.

"Sorry," I whispered. "They're a bit squished."

Knickerbocker moaned. I whipped around, startled.

He was still asleep, so I snuck over for a closer look. His brow was sweaty. I touched his forehead. It felt feverish. He writhed in his sleep and mumbled something. I leaned in closer. He repeated the same two words over and over. They sounded like "rubber octopi."

Geez. Earl hadn't been kidding after all.

I was no doctor, but I was pretty sure a bump on the head shouldn't cause a fever. I checked the mark on Knickerbocker's shoulder. It was swollen and red. Had he really suffered some kind of animal bite? I thought about the padlocked room in the back of his RV. Had something—or *someone*—escaped from there and attacked him?

My mind flashed back to the dead hog in the woods.

That hog could have bit him! What if it had rabies? Oh my lord! The hog died of rabies, and now Knickerbocker's turning into a human Hogzilla!

AFTER CALMING MYSELF with a couple of shots of gin, I rethought my earlier man-Hogzilla theory. I decided to check on Knickerbocker one more time before I called animal control. Whether he was a nut or a saint, I couldn't tell. But one thing I knew for sure. Right now, that man needed my help.

I fetched a clean washcloth from the bathroom, ran some cool water over it, and wiped Knickerbocker's brow, careful to avoid putting pressure on the knot on his forehead. The bump looked smaller. And I was surprised to see tiny stubs of hair growing back all over his head.

Knickerbocker wasn't bald, after all. Just shaved. Like me.

No wonder he wore that dumb fedora.

Then I noticed something that made my spine shiver. Faint, circular marks dotted his entire scalp. About the size of quarters, they reminded me of tentacle marks.

Rubber octopi.

Good grief! Is Knickerbocker a scuba diver? Has he been attacked by a giant squid? What the hell is going on here?

He moaned again. I felt his forehead. The poor guy was burning up. I'd have to wait until morning to get any answers out of him.

I rinsed the washcloth and placed it, clean and cool, against his forehead, covering his eyes. Then I took a moment to study the odd stranger before me.

Knickerbocker was lean and muscular. Not a workout body—more of a wiry, forgets-to-eat kind of physique. He was around six feet tall. Unremarkable in looks, save for the cheesy moustache and tentacle marks. He didn't have any tattoos that I could see, so he probably hadn't done any jail time.

I doused a paper towel with alcohol and dabbed at the angry red circle of broken skin between his neck and left shoulder. He was definitely unconscious. If he'd been awake, he'd have reacted to the sting.

As I leaned closer, I could smell the muskiness of him—a kind of nervous perspiration mixed with honest sweat. I wondered how long it had been since he'd bathed. His clothes could do with a wash. So could mine, for that matter.

I left the alcohol-soaked paper towel on his wound and reached down to unbutton his pants to throw them in the laundry. As I touched the metal button on the fly of his black jeans, a surge of electricity tingled throughout my body.

Unlike the other jolts I'd experienced of late, this one wasn't entirely unpleasant. I sat up in surprise.

I know it's been a long time since I've seen a man in his skivvies, but am I really that pathetic?

I set my jaw to clinical nurse mode and finished undoing the button of his jeans. I began to unzip his fly, but my fingers froze. In the exact spot previously covered by his pants button was what appeared to be a second navel.

I sucked in a breath.

Two bellybuttons? Who is this guy?

I blinked in disbelief.

No, no, no! That doesn't make any sense.

I looked again. It was still there.

Scar tissue. From an operation. Or a gunshot wound. It had to be.

I reached out to touch it ... to put my finger in the hole ....

Knickerbocker groaned. I jumped about three inches. I quickly re-buttoned his jeans and covered him up with the sheet.

Should I call 9-1-1? Detective Paulson? The FBI? The Mutual UFO Network, for crying out loud?

I looked over at the terrarium.

I need to think this through. If he was a criminal, would he be traveling with a pet lizard? And what kind of psycho would trust me and Earl with all his cash?

There was only one thing I knew for sure. Knickerbocker was a pay-ing customer. Didn't I owe it to him to at least give him the opportunity to explain himself?

I snorted out a jaded laugh.

That's rich, Bobbie. You owe it to him. You owe a lot of people, but this guy isn't one of them.

The cold, hard truth of it was, the guy had money. And I was in dire straits. Knickerbocker himself might not have been a godsend, but his cash sure was. Besides, there was no need to make any hasty decisions just yet.

I refilled his water glass, set out a couple of Tylenol tablets, and turned off the lamp by his bedside. Then I tiptoed over to my apartment and got the afghan my Grandma Selma had knitted for me right before she died. I made myself a nest on the living room couch and lay there, wide-eyed for ten minutes or so, thinking about phantom shooters and ripped-faced corpses and psycho killers with twin navels.

A sudden flash of lightning turned the long, flowy curtains into floating spirits of the undead. Distant thunder rumbled through the darkness like gravelly voices from the grave.

Sometimes I really hated my stupid imagination.

I got up and dragged a dining room chair up to the bedroom door where Knickerbocker was sleeping. I wedged it tight against the door-knob and went back to the couch.

As Grandma Selma always said, "Better safe than sorghum."

She always was one to mix her metaphors.

Chapter Twenty-One

BRANCHES TORE AT MY *face as I fled through the woods. Something was after me. Stalking me. Something big. Something evil.*

Its pounding footsteps grew louder. It was gaining on me! I didn't dare look back. I might trip and fall.

But I simply had *to see ....*

I turned my head.

In an instant, I felt myself falling.

My palms hit the dirt. I tumbled headfirst onto the moist ground. As I skittered across a thick blanket of pine needles, their pointy ends stabbed my flesh like tiny daggers. Then I slammed into a pine tree.

The rough bark gouged my skin like a cheese grater. But there was no time to assess my wounds. I pushed myself up and turned around.

Two glowing red eyes leered at me from the darkness.

A guttural growl reverberated through the thick air. The creature lunged at me, jaws snapping.

Hot spittle splatted against my forehead. I smelled the heat, the foulness of its breath, as its long, yellow claws ripped into the side of my head, tearing out my left eye. It fell to the ground and rolled into a hole a few feet away.

Oddly, I could only see through my detached *eye. From its vantage in the dirt, I made out a hairy, man-like beast wearing a black fedora.*

Its bear-like claws ripped into my throat. I tried to scream, but my larynx was already shredded. My howl fluttered out like a low, staccato moan.

Suddenly, the beast froze as if a director had yelled, "Cut!" It looked at me, confused.

"Wait a minute," it said to my detached eye. "Smelled the heat*?"*

I woke with a start, half-paralyzed with sleep. My heart thumped in my chest like a grounded boat motor. I turned my head a fraction of an inch and yelped in pain. My neck had gotten wedged against the armrest of the couch, and was now stiff as an roller-derby hairdo.

I sat up and rubbed it, making a mental note to never eat Vienna sausages after ten p.m. again. I heaved a sigh, then hauled myself off the couch to check on Knickerbocker.

I un-stuck the chair from under the bedroom doorknob and cracked the door open for a peek. He was still in bed, asleep. The clock radio on the nightstand read 6:18 am.

Good.

After checking on Knickerbocker around midnight, he'd settled down and slept peacefully through the rest of the night.

I started to go, but noticed fresh blood on his lip. A vague memory flashed across my mind. I'd thought it had been another one of my crazy, meat-byproduct-induced dreams.

Maybe not ....

I'd been changing the washcloth on Knickerbocker's forehead when it happened. He'd grabbed my arm and pulled me to him. He'd kissed me hard on the mouth. The force had reopened his split lip. I'd been caught so off guard that it'd been over with before I could protest.

Afterward, Knickerbocker had slumped back into a fitful slumber. I'd snuck out of the room and wedged the chair under the doorknob again.

Had that all been a dream? Another odd delusion?

His bloody lip said otherwise. So did the smear of blood I discovered on my chin when I looked in the bureau mirror. I was washing it away when my phone rang. I ran down the hall to catch it before it woke up Knickerbocker.

"Hello?" I whispered into my cellphone.

"You're still alive. Thank God!" It was Beth-Ann.

"Uh ... is there a reason I shouldn't be? Look, I haven't had any coffee yet and—"

"I Google-searched Knickerbocker," she said. "Obviously, you didn't."

"No. Why would I?"

"I thought you wanted to be a detective."

"Private Investigator," I said sourly. "And *unlike you, I* believe in a person's right to privacy."

I didn't see any reason to mention to Beth-Ann that my cable had been cut off months ago. Or that I had a smartphone that was way smarter than me. I mean, who could see anything on that tiny screen anyway?

"So I guess you don't want to hear what I found out, then," she teased.

I nearly choked on a wayward yawn. "I didn't say *that*."

"Get this, Bobbie. There's *no such guy* as William Knickerbocker. At least, nobody alive in the US."

She suddenly had my full attention. "You're kidding."

"Nope. Just some guy who invented some lightbulb thing back in the Dark Ages. He died, like, a million years ago."

I suddenly understood why Beth-Ann had failed both high school history *and* math. "You could've gotten the spelling wrong," I said, trying to assuage the niggling sense of unease creeping up my spine.

"I guess. But I doubt it."

"Listen. Thanks for the info, but I gotta go. I need coffee." What I *really* needed was a weapon, in case Knickerbocker was a psycho from planet Kill'emall.

"Okay. But be careful, Bobbie."

"I will." I hung up and sprinted out of my grandma's apartment and into my own. I got a pot of coffee brewing and called Earl. He answered on the sixth ring.

"What?" he growled.

"I was just wondering when you're coming in." I didn't want to tell him I was scared. In our family thesaurus, vulnerability was synonymous with weakness.

"It's Sunday, dingdong," Earl groused. "My day off. Parts won't be here till tomorrow anyway. What's your problem?"

I've got a twin-naveled space-alien, psycho-killer hiding out in my grandma's bed like the big, bald wolf.

"Nothing, Earl. Have a nice day." I clicked off the phone, made two cups of coffee, then went down to the service bay and retrieved Knickerbocker's Glock from the RV's glove compartment.

It was time for Mr. William Knickerbocker to come clean.

Chapter Twenty-Two

KNICKERBOCKER, IF THAT *was* his real name, wasn't in bed when I pried the chair free again and opened the bedroom door. He was in the shower. I could hear the water running, and I could see his black jeans laid out on the bed.

Right next to his wallet.

I set the coffee cups on the nightstand and patted my right hip pocket to reassure myself the Glock was still there. Then I did something totally against my nature.

I rifled through his stuff.

It didn't take long. The wallet was nearly empty except for a few credit cards with the name Nick Grayson. Had he stolen another man's wallet? Inside the billfold were five hundred-dollar bills so crisp and new they looked like Monopoly money.

I unsnapped the flap to a pocket in the wallet. It fell open to reveal a tin-colored badge that could've come from a Cracker Jack box. The words Private Investigator ran along the top edge of a circle in the badge's center. Inside the circle was a strange emblem made of three triangles, kind of like a 3-D Star of David.

I re-snapped the flap, folded the wallet, and carefully placed it back in the same exact spot by the jeans on the bed.

When I turned around, a naked man was staring at me.

"Do you usually pilfer through your guests' belongings?"

Knickerbocker's voice was strangely devoid of any distinguishable tone. Or maybe I was too distracted by his other assets to notice. He was stark naked.

"Who *are* you?" I demanded.

"Who are *you?*" he volleyed.

Something indiscernible flickered across his green eyes, then they hardened to what appeared to be quiet resolve. He took the towel he was drying his head with and wrapped it high around his waist. I got the feeling he was keener to cover his twin navels than his privates. He glanced to his left, licked his bottom lip, and took a step toward me.

I stumbled backward and fumbled for the Glock in my pocket. I yanked it out and pointed the gun at him. "Tell me who you are. *Now.*"

He considered me thoughtfully. "Does anyone every truly know who they are?"

"What do you mean?"

"Nothing. Who do you *think* I am?"

"You said you're William Knickerbocker. But there's no such person. The name in the wallet says Nick Grayson."

"So why are you asking?"

I wasn't expecting a philosophical rebuttal. "I ... I want to know why you're using an alias. Are you on the run or something?"

"Sort of." He sighed. "No. Not really. I only give my real name out on a need-to-know basis. You didn't need to know. By the way, is that my gun?"

"Shut up! I'm the one asking the questions!"

"How am I supposed to answer them if you order me to shut up?"

I blew out an exasperated breath. This was not going to plan.

"I'm a detective," I lied. "Working undercover. What are you doing here? What's with the rubber octopus? And the tentacle marks all over your head?" I thought about asking about his twin navels too, but I was afraid it might land me in one of those, "Now I'll have to kill you," kind of scenarios.

"Hold on," he said. "Rubber octopus? That's a new one."

"You kept saying it in your sleep. Octopi rubber. Something like that."

A glint of recognition flashed across his eyes. "Oh. *Oculi rubere.* It's Latin. It means red eyes."

I relaxed my grip on the Glock a notch. "Why would you keep saying *that?*"

He hesitated for a moment as he studied me. "Uh ... because my eyes were red."

I shook my head. "Over an over? I don't think so. You were delirious. That term *means* something to you."

His expression softened slightly. "Wait a second ... you took care of me last night, didn't you."

"Yes."

He reached a hand toward me. I stiffened my stance and braced the Glock in both hands.

Knickerbocker stepped back and held up his hands. "Sorry. I just wanted to say thank you."

I shifted uncomfortably. "Uh ... you're welcome."

His eyes shifted over toward the nightstand. "You won't shoot me if I reach for that coffee, will you? It smells great."

"No. Go ahead."

As he reached for a cup, a warning signal pinged in my brain.

He could throw hot coffee in my face!

"Stop!" I shouted. "I need a few answers first."

He eyed the coffee longingly, then looked back at me. "Okay, I guess I owe you that. Shoot." His eyes widened. "I mean—don't *shoot*, shoot. Just ask your questions."

"So who are you? Knickerbocker or Grayson?"

"Grayson. Nick Grayson."

"How can I be sure?"

He smiled charmingly. "Why would I lie to you? You've already seen my lizard."

He winked a green eye at me. I blushed. Then he glanced over at the terrarium. I blushed some more. Was it possible he remembered kissing me last night? Or maybe he didn't. He *had* been delirious, after all.

"May I ask *your* name?"

"Bobbie ... I mean *Roberta* Drex."

"Nice to meet—"

"What do you do for a living, Grayson?"

He winced. "That one's a bit tricky."

I snorted. "You're a private investigator. Like me."

He nodded. "True. I am a P.I. But I'm nothing like you."

My jaw flexed. *What a jerk!*

"No, you're *not*," I said sourly.

Grayson winced. "I didn't mean it like *that*. What I meant was ... I kind of investigate more ... uh ... *esoteric* things."

"What do you mean?"

"In layman's terms? The unexplained."

"Unexplained?"

"Yes. Things that can't be explained by normal, rational, sensible logic."

"You mean like ghosts and stuff?"

Grayson smirked ever so slightly. "Well, not exactly. I'm investigate unusual events that leave physical evidence."

"Like bigfoot?"

"If compelling evidence is found, yes."

I pursed my lips. "I don't believe in all that."

Grayson smiled. "That's okay. They still believe in *you*."

I adjusted my stance, a bit angry at being teased. "You're full of crap, aren't you?"

"Yes. And so are you, Roberta Drex. In fact, the average person walks around with over twenty-five pounds of feces clogging up their colon."

I grimaced with disgust. "Why would you know that? Why would you *want* to know that?"

Grayson eyed me curiously, as if I were a fun, new toy. "As I said, I have unusual interests."

"I think you have an unusual head injury."

Greyson glanced upward, as if to get a look at the bump on his forehead. "Yeah, that too. Look, I'm sorry if I've been a bother. Let me pay you for your troubles, and I'll be on my way."

"I don't think so." I gripped the gun tighter. "I think I should call the cops. Or the FBI."

"Go ahead. But might I suggest Homeland Security? Be sure to tell them you're holding a gun on a man for babbling about a rubber octopus. Don't forget I've got a Bigfoot bite, a shaved head, two navels, and I'm traveling in an RV with an accomplice—a lizard named Gizzard. Just don't be surprised when they haul *you* away instead of me."

He had a point. *What am I supposed to do now?*

Grayson must've read my expression like an open comic book.

"Right now, lady, the only person who'd believe your story is *me*. Listen, you can either let me go or shoot me. But if you choose option B, I would highly recommend taking the safety off my Glock first."

I looked down at the gun. Like a viper striking, Grayson snatched it from my hand. As I looked up, I heard a click. I winced, closed my eyes, and waited for the second bullet in less than a week to strike me between the eyes.

Chapter Twenty-Three

THE BULLET NEVER CAME.

I hazarded a peek out of one eye.

Grayson was standing less than two feet away from me, holding the butt-end of the Glock toward me. He'd undone the safety and was offering me back his lethal weapon.

I took it. He didn't resist.

"Why did you do that?" I asked, stunned.

"Because I want you to trust me."

"Why?"

"Because if we can't trust each other, we can never be friends."

I swallowed against the dry knot in my throat. "Friends?"

"I'd hate to part as enemies after you've been so kind."

I suddenly felt undone with confusion. Was *I* the bad guy in all of this? My face flushed with heat. Southern guilt could do that to a person. Then I remembered that if he left, he'd take his wallet with him.

"Part?" I asked, my voice a notch nicer. "Why do you have to go? I mean, what's the rush?"

"It's not safe to be around me. I try not to put my friends in harm's way."

I looked at him sideways. "That sounds noble and all, but it smells like buffalo chips to me."

Grayson looked taken aback. "What do you mean?"

"Around here, friends stick together through thick and thin."

Grayson cocked his head and smiled wistfully. "You have no idea how thin the ice can get when you skate near me."

"I was born and raised in Florida," I quipped. "I don't know how to ice skate. But I do recognize a cold shoulder when I see one."

Grayson laughed. "You're an interesting woman, Bobbie Drex. If that *is* your real name."

"It is. Believe me. I wish it wasn't."

I nodded toward the nightstand and the two steaming mugs atop it. "Now drink your coffee, Nick, before it gets cold."

I SAT DOWN AT THE ROUND, oak dining table where my parents had eaten three square meals a day for the past thirty years. Along the walls, pictures of relatives glared disapprovingly at me as I shared a meager breakfast of toast and coffee with the stranger who'd arrived yesterday in almost as bad shape as his RV.

Emboldened by a shot of caffeine, I braved a question I'd been itching to ask Grayson since he'd said the word *unexplained*. It wasn't exactly a question I could've asked Earl, for cripes' sake. Or even Beth-Ann. But given my two recent run-ins with odd visions, I was dying for a little perspective from someone who perhaps knew something more about the topic.

"Do you believe in ghosts?" I asked casually as I topped off his cup of coffee.

"Me?" Grayson's brow furrowed. "Depends on what you mean by *ghosts.*"

"The spirits of dead people." I sat down and pulled my chair closer to the table. "Do you think they're real, or simply hallucinations?"

Grayson shrugged. "What's the difference?"

My back stiffened. "Well, one is *real* and the other's ...." I trailed off, uncertain how to continue my argument.

"My point exactly," Grayson said with a light laugh. "Who could know for sure? Every person's reality is different, Drex. We believe what we *decide* to believe, against all known intelligence to the contrary."

"What do you mean?" I frowned, unhappy with his answer, and took a giant, ripping bite from my slice of buttered toast.

"Let's face it. The so-called 'facts' are irrelevant to most people. Unless, of course, they happen to support their opinions."

"What are you saying? That people are blind to the truth?"

He slathered butter on his toast. "Well, that depends on what you call the *truth*."

I jabbed a knife into a jar of fig preserves. "I think I should warn you. I'm armed and you're getting on my last nerve."

Grayson smiled. "It's human nature to seek *validation*, Drex, not *in*validation. A person's point of view, no matter how soundly laid out, is still merely an opinion. It's not an absolute."

My nose crinkled with annoyance and skepticism. "I'm still not following you. Give me an example."

"Okay. Let's see ... how about *everything* you've ever read, said, or witnessed in this lifetime?"

I nearly spewed my coffee. "What?"

"*Every* book ... even history books, science books, the great philosophers ... they're nothing more than limited interpretations of personal experiences. They're simply the musings and opinions of their authors."

"Huh?"

"Think about it. How many times has science declared something as absolute fact, then had to retract it? How many times has 'recorded history' proven to be nothing more than a self-flattering account from the winning side?"

My lip jerked upward as if yanked with a fishhook. "Lots of times, I guess."

Grayson seemed to take my concession with easy indifference. "Then again, maybe they weren't wrong after all."

"What?" My mind screeched like a needle across a record. "If you're trying to confuse me, Grayson, congratulations. You win."

Grayson sighed. "I'm not trying to be ambiguous. It's just that I believe truth is merely a temporary construct."

I blew out a breath. "Okay, if I'm going to wrap my head around this, I'm going to need more coffee. *Lots* more coffee." I got up to fetch the pot.

Grayson drained his cup and held it up for a refill. "Some philosophers believe that at any given time, we're only evolved enough as a species to embrace a certain level of social and scientific principle. So we decide what truth is, what *reality* is, based on a sort of bell curve of the *intellectual collective*."

I frowned. "What are you saying? That *nothing* is ever absolute? That nothing is ever really *true?*"

"Not exactly. What I'm saying is that truth is a *fluid* thing, Drex. Every individual has their own truth, and who's to say whether it's right or wrong?"

"That's pretty deep down the rabbit hole for a vagabond conspiracy-chaser living in a ratty RV."

Grayson's chin lifted slightly. His eyebrows knitted together, giving him a look of mock pretentiousness. "I'm *not* a vagabond. I prefer the term 'non-localized, alternative solutions investigator.'"

I smirked. "Well, I suppose you *are* entitled to *your* opinion of reality."

Grayson grinned. "Touché."

I refilled his coffee cup. "So tell me, no bull this time. What's up with the red octopus thing?"

"*Oculi rubere*. It's Latin for red eyes."

"You said that. But why were you repeating it over and over in your sleep?"

Grayson glanced around, as if to ensure no one else was listening. He leaned in toward me. "Because I came out here on a case. I'm investigating rumors of a red-eyed creature that's been roaming the pine forests and swamps around Waldo."

I nearly dropped the coffee pot. "And I thought you were full of it *before*."

"I'm not joking."

"You're really chasing a monster? Gimme a break, Grayson!"

"My alternative P.I. services happen to include the occasional tracking of cryptids," he said defensively.

"Cryptids?"

"Yes. As yet undiscovered or unexplained creatures."

"Like ghosts?"

"More substantial than that. Creatures who leave behind footprints."

"And dead bodies?"

Grayson's eyebrow shot up. "Perhaps. Why do you ask?"

I shrugged, uncertain of how much to reveal to him. "Have you, you know, actually *seen* this red-eyed thing you're chasing?"

"Yes. At least, I think so. On the road the night before last. Right after my RV broke down. The whole incident—or accident—whatever it was, was *odd*."

"What do you mean?"

"My RV came slamming to a halt ... as if I'd hit something." Grayson absently felt the tender knot on his forehead. "After getting up close and personal with the windshield, I looked over to my left. I would swear I saw a pair of red eyes staring at me from the woods."

Ice spider made another beer run down my spine. "Maybe it was your own reflection in the window."

"No. Couldn't've been. The driver's side window was down."

I grimaced. "Did you get a picture of it or anything?"

"No. I remember reaching over to roll up the window ... then this stabbing pain suddenly shot through my shoulder."

"It *bit* you?"

"I don't know." Grayson slowly rotated his shoulder. "It could've been the seatbelt harness. I think I cracked my clavicle. Anyway, the next thing I knew, it was daybreak. I was still sitting upright in the driver's seat. I remembered seeing the flashing yellow light up the road. I thought it was close, so I got out and walked it."

"The flatlands around here can be deceiving."

Grayson's eyebrow shot up. "You're telling me. I kept walking and walking, but the light wasn't getting any closer. I was beginning to think it was a mirage. Then, finally, two and a half miles later, I ended up at your garage."

I thought about the bite-shaped wound on Grayson's left shoulder. What if it really *was* a bite? Should I tell him about the two glowing red spheres I'd seen atop the Stop & Shoppe drive-thru? Were those the red eyes he was chasing? They certainly couldn't have belonged to deer—not unless Rudolph was doing a pre-Christmas test flight.

I decided against saying anything. Especially after all the gobbledy-gook he'd just spilled. If Grayson wasn't going to give me any straight answers, then he wouldn't be getting any from *me*.

But I really wanted some straight answers.

I chewed my lip. Maybe if I took Grayson to the place I'd seen the dead body, he'd stop this esoteric bull-crap philosophizing and give me some useful information. According to my P.I. training course, I shouldn't lead the witness. If I was going to do this, it would be better to take him there without telling him anything, then let him conjure up his own version of reality.

The man certainly seemed up to the task.

"I went back to the scene of your accident," I said. "I don't think what you hit was a deer."

Grayson's eyebrows rose slightly. "No? What do you think it was?"

"Not sure. You up for a ride? I'll show you."

Grayson glanced quickly at his mug. "Can I take my coffee with me?"

"Yeah."

"Okay, then. Let's go."

Chapter Twenty-Four

"IS THIS A SIXTY-FOUR?" Grayson asked as he climbed into the Mustang.

"Sixty-four and a half."

"Candy-apple red. Goes well with your auburn hair."

"Actually, it's Rangoon Red. And this is a wig."

Grayson cocked his head at me and smiled. "Really? Wh—"

"Don't ask."

"Okay." He looked down at my boots. "So what's with the clodhoppers, Red?"

"Don't call me Red. They're my father's work boots."

"He doesn't need them?"

"Not where he is at the moment."

"Where's that?"

"You tell me, Mr. Philosopher. He's dead."

Grayson nodded. "Oh. The old Heaven-or-Hell paradox. If you're into that sort of thing."

"You're not?"

"No. But I'm quite certain there's an intelligence at work behind all that exists. Does that work for you?"

I shot him some side-eye. "Not really."

Grayson glanced to his right for a moment, as if he were consulting someone sitting beside him. He turned to face me again. "That's okay. The universal intelligence says *you* don't actually work for *it*, either."

Red flags began to wave like a NASCAR pileup. So I did what I usually did when that happened with a guy.

I ignored them.

I shifted into first and headed out of the parking lot.

"Tell me something," I said as we buzzed down Obsidian Road. "What's with the fedora?"

Grayson touched the vintage hat on his head. "This old thing? Keeps my head warm."

"It's a Dobb's Fifth Avenue from the 1950s."

Grayson shot me an appreciative smile. "That it is. Impressive."

"I worked in antiques after college."

"Smart move. I worked in entomology."

My foot nearly slipped off the accelerator. "Really? Can I ask you something?"

"Sure."

"Can earwigs really drive a person crazy?"

Grayson laughed. "I have to hand it to you. You do pose some interesting topics of conversation."

I winced. "Sorry. I've never been much for small talk."

"Me neither. To answer your question, I suppose anything could drive a person crazy if they gave it enough power."

I groaned. "Not philosophy again. Come on. I'm talking about real life. Like ... what if an earwig crawled inside somebody's ear?"

"Ah. *Anisolabis maritima*. The poor, maligned little earwig. That's an urban myth. Sure, once in a while one finds its way into someone's ear. But it's just looking for a dark, moist place to hide out. There's never been a case of one damaging anyone's brain or driving them crazy. In fact, they're one of the few insects that display maternal instincts. But then again, they also eat guano. Why do you ask?"

I shrugged. "No particular reason. We're here."

I pulled the Mustang off the road where Grayson's RV had come to a standstill two nights ago. It wasn't hard to find. A few straggling scavengers still circled in the sky above, marking the spot like Mother Nature's own GPS death drones.

"Ugh. Buzzards," I said, looking up as I climbed out of the car.

"Vultures," Grayson corrected.

"Po-*tay*-to, po-*tah*-to," I said. "Follow me."

Grayson kept close, just a step or two behind me as I searched for the trail I'd trampled into the sawgrass yesterday. The overnight rains had plumped the grass and washed the sand, making the trail barely discernable.

"Only Americans call members of the genus *Cathartes* buzzards," Grayson said behind me as I fumbled my way through the thigh-high grass. "To everyone else on the planet, a buzzard is a hawk, a bird of prey."

"Does it matter?" I asked, slightly annoyed.

"In detective work, getting the details correct is critical. Buzzards are actually turkey vultures."

"Okay, okay," I said. "They're *vultures*. But that over *there* is a dead hog."

I pointed to the carcass lying about fifteen feet ahead in a clearing just beyond a stand of pines. The animal appeared to have lost its bloat and collapsed inward. It looked like a moth-eaten fur coat.

Grayson walked up to the carcass. He squatted down close enough to disturb a swarm of flies. "It's a hog, all right. Gave somebody hell, too. The fur around its jaws is black with encrusted blood."

"What do you mean some*body?* Couldn't another animal have attacked it?"

"Sure. As long as the other animal knew how to wield a knife. See those straight, inch-long wounds in its side?"

I stepped closer and tried not to breathe. Grayson took a stick and poked at a few holes, making my stomach twist. "Knife punctures," he said, as matter-of-factly as if he were giving someone his lunch order.

I'll have a homicidal stab wound and a side of fries.

I grimaced. "You sure you didn't hit it with your RV?"

"Yes. I don't see any crushing injuries. No broken bones."

"Could the hog be the source of the red eyes you saw the other night?"

"Well, I think we can rule that out, too."

"How?"

Grayson lifted the hog's head up with a stick. The eye socket on the other side of its head had been sewn shut.

"That would be hard to pull off with only one eye," Grayson said almost merrily. "Yes. Those are knife punctures, all right. This hog put up one hell of a fight. I'm surprised the guy who tangled with it made it out of here alive."

"Uh ... maybe he didn't."

Grayson looked up at me. "Why do you say that?" He rose to his feet like a shot, then glanced all around him. "Do you see a body?"

"No. But yesterday, I *thought* I did. I must've imagined it, because when I came back an hour later with Paulson, it wasn't here."

Grayson studied me. "Are you in the habit of seeing imaginary dead bodies?"

When I didn't dignify his question with an answer, Grayson's face softened. "Look. It may be important. What did this body you thought you saw look like? Was it male? Female?"

"I don't know. The face was ... gone. Ripped off or something. Its head was a bloody pulp."

Grayson nodded. I studied him for signs of skepticism, but couldn't detect anything but earnest interest.

"What else can you tell me about it?" he asked.

"It was wearing an orange jumpsuit."

"Hmmm. Must have been an escaped convict."

"That's what I thought, too. But now I'm not so sure."

"Why not?"

"Ever since I was a kid playing in the woods, I always worried I'd come across an escapee from Starke Prison. Maybe I really *did* just imagine it."

"But you're not a kid anymore," Grayson said.

I looked away and studied the ground at his feet.

"Something tells me there's more to this, Drex. Something you're not telling me."

Ahh crap. What the hell.

"This isn't the first dead guy I've seen lately who turned out to be a mirage."

Grayson took a step toward me. "What do you mean?"

I sighed. I was in this deep. Might as well go all the way.

"The guy who shot me on Thursday? I saw him in the hospital as I was leaving. I'd *swear* it was him. But then Earl told me it couldn't have been, because he was dead. Hit by a bus."

Grayson nodded. "Time to cue the *Twilight Zone* music, huh?"

Dammit. I shouldn't have told him.

"So where was this guy you saw yesterday?" Grayson asked.

I pointed to a stand of trees. "Up against that pine over there."

I followed Grayson over to the tree. He examined the bed of rust-colored pine needles surrounding the trunk, then used a stick to clear a spot in the sand below. The normally light-gray sand was tinged pinkish-red.

"Could be your guy was no ghost."

I peered at the pink sand. "Is that blood?"

"Possibly. Hard to be sure after all the rain last night."

I glanced around the woods, suddenly horrified. "So what happened to the body? He was dead, I'm sure of it. He couldn't have gotten up or crawled away."

I wanted to ask Grayson if he believed in zombies, but then again, I didn't want to know the answer.

"See these marks and scuffs in the sand?" Grayson pointed to a set of half washed away canine-looking tracks and slash lines in the sand. "He could've been dragged off by predators. Or eaten down to nothing by your friendly neighborhood vultures."

I shook my head. "Not possible."

"Why not?"

"After I saw the body ... or mirage, or whatever the hell it was, I ran back to my car and called Paulson. It took him about an hour to arrive. When we came back here, the hog was still over there, but the body was gone. I *had* to have imagined it. Vultures couldn't have eaten it in an hour."

"Don't be so sure," Grayson countered. "A few years ago, a woman fell to her death hiking in the French Pyrenees. Before the rescue helicopter could get there, she'd been totally devoured by vultures in under forty-five minutes."

"Are you serious?"

"Yes. Nothing left but shoes and clothes and a few bones."

"Gross! How do you know that?"

"A good private investigator keeps up with those kinds of things. That, and I happen to have a subscription to the *Huffington Post*."

"Ugh! Even if you're right, and I'm not saying you are, shouldn't there be something left of the body? Or at least the orange jumpsuit? It should be easy to spot in the grass around here."

Grayson smiled like a proud professor. "*Now* you're thinking like a private investigator."

"Save your praise. I'm not really a P.I. At least, not yet. I've only got my intern license."

Grayson smiled. "I know."

My eyebrows shot up in surprise. "How?"

Grayson's smirk evaporated. He cocked his head to one side. "I'm a private investigator. I thought I'd mentioned that."

"Argh! You're exasperating!"

"Okay, okay. Ever heard of a thing called Google?"

"Of course."

"You should try it sometime."

"Ha ha. I would, but I don't have internet at home at the moment."

"At *home?* Don't you have a smartphone?"

"Yes."

"Drex, if you're serious about becoming a P.I., I suggest you learn how to use your phone. Now, let's do a little beating around the bush and see if we can find some trace of this orange jumpsuit person, shall we? He or she might turn out to be our red-eyed monster after all."

"Fine."

"And while we're at it, tell me all about this getting shot business," he said. "And the other dead guy you think you saw."

Chapter Twenty-Five

DESPITE SEARCHING FOR nearly an hour, Grayson and I couldn't find a trace of the dead person in the orange jumpsuit. Grayson thought the pinkish stain in the sand could've been blood or a layer of microbial fungus. He collected a sample for testing. If it *was* blood, it could've come from the hog. So the jury was still out on whether my concussion was causing hallucinations, or I'd simply lost my freaking mind.

"Well, that was fun," Grayson said as we climbed back into the Mustang. "I thought we were going to see a dead deer, but we ended up with a one-eyed hog who, tragically, found himself on the wrong end of Jack the Knife."

"I should call Officer Paulson," I said, sticking the key into the ignition. "Let him know about the knife wounds and all."

Grayson buckled his seatbelt, wincing at the effort. "Who is he again?"

"He's the cop assigned to Point Paradise. We're too small to have our own police department. So Paulson acts as kind of a liaison, covering our area from his office in Waldo."

"Well, you picked an interesting first case, I'll give you that. Sure beats tracking down deadbeat dads and cheating spouses."

"This isn't *my* case. I only told Paulson about it."

"Sure," Grayson said. "That's right. You can't work cases by yourself with an intern license."

"Yeah, *technically*. But I already *am* working another case for Paulson, kind of."

Grayson shot me a devious grin. "*Really?*"

I shrugged. "It's just a stupid little thing. He didn't want to be bothered with it."

Grayson wagged his eyebrows and spoke in faux Groucho Marx. "Tell me, Gracie. How stupid is it?"

I laughed. "Our village kook keeps getting weird phone calls. Beeping. Robot voices. Stuff like that. It's nothing, really. But I guess, like you said, you've gotta start somewhere."

"You're kidding," Grayson said.

"I *wish*."

Grayson touched my arm. "No. I'm serious. You ever heard of a place called Point Pleasant, West Virginia?"

"No."

"It was the site of some weird happenings back in the 1960s. People in that little town started getting weird phone calls."

I shrugged. "Yeah? Well, who doesn't every now and again?"

Grayson nodded. "Fair enough. But quite a few of them also reported being chased by a flying, red-eyed monster."

The hair on the back of my neck bristled. I turned the key in the ignition and shook my head. Could that really have been what I saw—what I tried to chase down—at the Stop & Shoppe?

"They called him the Mothman," Grayson said.

I willed myself not to say a word about my encounter. I was already halfway to crazy. I didn't need to give Grayson any more fuel to drive me the rest of the way to nutsville.

"You and Earl are gonna love each other," I said as sarcastically as I could muster. "He's a freaking conspiracy theorist, too."

"You're not?"

"Nope," I said, and mashed the accelerator. "Life itself is enough of a conspiracy for me."

Chapter Twenty-Six

"WELL, THERE GOES MY getaway plan," Grayson said as he surveyed the carnage inside the service bay of my dad's garage. The engine to his RV had been thoroughly disassembled by Earl, who'd spread its innards all over the place like he was getting ready for a jumble sale.

I winced. "Sorry. But I tried to warn you. The engine was shot, anyway. Earl's a great mechanic. He'll have it back together for you in a jiff. Three days, tops."

Grayson licked his busted lip as he digested the news. "Well, I guess I should make the best of it. Hold on a second."

He climbed inside the RV. A moment later, I heard bottles clinking around. I thought he was going to haul out a couple of beers, but he came back holding a Q-Tip. One end of it was fluorescent pink.

"What do you think?" he asked, showing it to me.

I eyed it dubiously. "Not my shade of lipstick. But I think it'd go great with your green eyes."

Grayson laughed. "I did a Kastle-Meyer on the soil sample."

"A castle what?"

"Kastle-Meyer. A drop of phenolphthalein here, a drop of hydrogen peroxide there, and voilá. Pink means positive for blood."

I crinkled my nose at the swab. "Is it human?"

"Indeterminate. I'd need to do a precipitin test to find out. And for that, I'd need more blood, a lab, and perhaps an unlucky rabbit."

"Oh."

Grayson tossed the swab into a trashcan. "Do you have lunch plans? My treat."

If I was hungry, I couldn't tell. I was still too grossed out by the whole dead hog thing.

"Tell you what," I said, "given the state of our foreheads, I think we could both use a rest. I'll make us some soup. We'll get a nap, and then head out later to an early supper. I'm not that hungry right now. Besides, I need to call Paulson and catch him up on what we found."

Grayson nodded. "Actually, that sounds good. I could use a rest. What did you have in mind for dinner?"

"There's a little Mexican restaurant in Waldo. El Molino's."

He waggled his eyebrows at me. "You had me at *Mexican*."

"Good. But, just so you know, I'm not interested."

"You're not interested in eating?"

I frowned. "No. I meant .... Look, you're not trying to ask me out, are you? I hope there's no ... you know ... *ulterior motive*."

Grayson shot me a look. "Oh. Well, make no mistake, Drex. There's an ulterior motive, all right. I didn't see a restaurant for twenty miles before my RV broke down. And I've heard the Uber service in this area sucks."

I smiled. "Give me a few minutes and I'll bring you a bowl of chicken noodle."

"Could you do me a favor?" Grayson asked.

"What?"

"Would you change your shoes for dinner? Or if you don't have any, go barefoot?"

I crinkled my nose. "Why?"

"Call me a softie, but I hate to see you dragging around in a dead man's past."

My throat grew tight. I gave him the once-over. He gave me a friendly smile.

"Okay," I said. "I'll see what I can do."

I STUDIED MY REFLECTION in the mirror and readjusted my wig. Then I fished my cellphone from the pocket of my coveralls and spent ten minutes trying to figure out how to add Paulson's number to my list of phone contacts.

Damned computers! Carl used to do all this crap for me. Why did I let myself get so dependent on him?

I gave up and punched Paulson's number into the phone. "Paulson? It's me, Bobbie Drex."

"Hello, there. Anything new with Vanderhoff?"

"No. But listen. I went back out to the site where we found the hog."

"You did? Why?"

"I dunno. Curiosity? Anyway, I found something we missed yesterday. On the hog's body. Its fur had puncture wounds all over it. Like it had been stabbed by someone."

"Stabbed? Huh. What did you do with the carcass?"

"Nothing. It's still there."

"This may be a case of animal cruelty."

"Or worse. Paulson, you know that body I thought I saw? It may have been real after all. I was thinking the hog could've been killed by an escaped con."

"Did you find the body?"

"No. But the ground by the tree? You know, where I thought I saw it? The sand had a pinkish hue. It's blood."

"That could be critical evidence, Bobbie. I'll get out there and collect samples."

"But I—"

"Listen, Bobbie. Don't worry. You did good. I'll double-check the police reports for any mention of escaped prisoners. And I'll run back over to the scene right now and bag some soil samples for evidence. Don't go back there. We don't want more contamination of the scene, in case this turns out to be something bigger than a dead hog."

"Okay. But I'd hurry if I were you. There were vultures circling."

Paulson sniggered. "Buzzards don't bother me. I've had to fight off more than a few in my day."

"Grayson says they're vultures."

"Who's Grayson?"

"A guy staying here while his RV gets fixed. He's a private investigator."

"You don't say. Was he there with you at the scene?"

"Yes. He said last night's rain washed away a lot of trace evidence."

"That's not good. Listen, be careful with this guy. He may say he's a P.I., but you never know about strangers. And with your recent concussion, you might not have the best judgment right now."

That niggling feeling of unease returned. "Okay. You're right. But I already told him we'd go to dinner at El Molino's tonight. Do you want me to ask him anything?"

"Not that I can think of at the moment. But tell him to keep his hands to himself, okay?"

I smiled. "I'll do my best."

I clicked off the phone. I was no detective, but I was pretty sure I noted a hint of jealousy in Paulson's voice. I kicked off my father's boots and adjusted my wig. Hair or no hair, it was time to give that weirdo Grayson something to boggle his already warped little mind.

Chapter Twenty-Seven

"SO THERE REALLY *is* a woman underneath those coveralls."

I stared Grayson down across a sticky, brown laminate table. We were sitting in a duct-taped-together vinyl booth inside El Molino Mexican restaurant in beautiful, downtown Waldo.

I was sporting my sexiest top that didn't have a grease stain on the front, and I'd slurped down just enough of a frozen margarita to have the guts to ask him some probing questions. I fired them off in rapid succession, before I lost my nerve.

"Okay, what gives with the octopus circles on your head? That lizard in the terrarium? The dumpy RV? All that cash in your glove compartment? Your obsession with a red-eyed monster called Mothman?"

Grayson eyed me curiously, then fired back with his own volley.

"What's with the woodpecker wig? Daddy's boots? Dressing like a man? Wanting to be a P.I.?" He sat up in the booth. "I thought you were a small-town mechanic, Drex. Turns out you're a freaking KGB interrogator!"

I shrunk back in my seat. "Sorry." I hiccupped. "But you have to admit, there's a lot of really odd things about you."

Grayson twisted one side of his mouth and blew out a breath. "Maybe you're right. But it's not good to tell someone all your secrets at once. Not when you're holding as many as I am."

His face changed from serious to playful as if he'd flipped a switch. He waggled his bushy eyebrows at me. "If we both spill our entire guts tonight, what will we have left to talk about on our second date?"

I rolled my eyes. "Date? I wouldn't bring a cockroach here on a date."

"Huh." Grayson nodded thoughtfully. "I wouldn't have taken you for someone into arthropods."

I shot Grayson a look, but got distracted when the waitress arrived with a stack of tacos big enough to feed a Free-Will Baptist hootenanny.

The smell of cumin and ground beef made me salivate. I grabbed a taco off the top of the heap. Grayson followed suit right behind mine.

"You took quite a chance, handing me back your Glock," I said and shoved half the taco into my mouth.

Grayson watched me like a lazy cat watches a mouse. "You might see it that way. But my whole life is about taking calculated risks ... on the right people, that is."

"*Calculated* risks?"

He shrugged and shot me a sly grin. "While you were wincing in terror, I took the magazine out of the Glock."

I nearly choked on my mouthful of taco. "That's not fair!"

"Why? You *still* could've beaten me over the head with it."

"Anyone ever tell you you've got serious trust issues?"

Grayson burst out laughing. "All the time. How about you?"

I suppressed a smirk and looked at the corner of the ceiling. "Maybe once. Twice ...."

"How about a toast, then?" Grayson said. "To paranoia. Mother Nature's bodyguard."

I reached for my margarita. Grayson raised his mug of beer and winced.

I flinched in empathy. "Does your shoulder still hurt?"

"A bit. But that's to be expected. I *should* be dead. What did you do to stop the poison?"

"Poison?"

Grayson's eyes lost their playful edge for a millisecond. "I meant infection."

"Oh. Nothing. Just rubbed it with alcohol."

"Huh. Who would have thought something that simple could cure a Mothman bite?"

I studied his twinkling eyes and smirking face. It was impossible to tell if Grayson was teasing me or not. I really hated that I couldn't read him. After all those years sizing people up at Blanchard's antique auctions, I thought I could read *anyone*.

There went that theory.

I raised my glass. "Like I said, you and Earl are gonna get along like gangbusters. Cheers."

Our glasses clinked together, and our eyes remained locked as we each took a sip. I looked away first, and set my margarita on the table.

"Are you ever going to answer my questions?" I asked.

Grayson's left eyebrow shot up like Spock's. "Sure. Pick one. I'll answer *one*. Fair enough?"

"Better than nothing, I guess." I thought about it for a moment. "So, all that money in your glove compartment. Did you make it as a private investigator?"

"Yes."

"How?"

Grayson shook his head. "Nope. That's another question."

"Argh!"

He smirked. "My turn. Why are you wearing that wig?"

"They shaved my head in the hospital."

Grayson took off his fedora, revealing his pale scalp. His bald dome appeared dark gray from the short stubble covering it like a five o'clock shadow.

"Finally. A point of commonality," he said.

"Commonality? You mean the hospital or the head shave?"

Grayson put his hat back on. "No more questions."

I frowned. "What are we gonna talk about then?"

Grayson smiled sinisterly. "Tell you what. How about a dare?"

"A dare?" I took another slurp of margarita to prepare myself.

"Yes. You show me your bald head, and I'll tell you about my lizard."

I nearly spewed my drink. "Your flirting skills suck, you know that?"

Grayson half grinned, half grimaced. "Sorry. I meant it as a joke."

"Whatever," I said. "Still, no deal. You're not seeing my bald head."

"Okay. Tell me why you dress like a man."

"Nope." I shot him a smug look. "*That's* another question."

Grayson studied me for a moment. "Answer it, and I'll tell you about how I earn my money."

Finally, there was a man in front of me with an offer I actually didn't want to refuse. I took another slug of margarita—this time for courage.

"I was supposed to be a boy."

Grayson blanched. "What?"

I blew out a sigh 37 years in the making. "I was supposed to be Robert Drex, Jr. But somewhere in transit, I got my wires crossed and the plumbing wrong. My sonogram 'penis' turned out to be the extended middle finger of my left hand."

Grayson sat back, his eyes dancing with intrigue. "No way."

"No. No *penis*. My parents had to add an "A" to the name they'd planned to put on my birth certificate. That sonogram was the end of dear Robert and beginning of me, Roberta—a very poor substitute, indeed."

I took another slurp of margarita and shrugged with resignation. "But hey, what kid hasn't disappointed their parents, right? I just decided to get it over with extra early."

Grayson shook his head. "Did they make you pretend to be a guy, too?"

I scowled. "No. But as a kid, I hung out in the service bay with my Dad, mostly. Until I hit puberty, that is. Then my father made me get out and stay out. Mom and Grandma Selma tried to make me into a girl, but by then, I was eleven. It was too late."

"Huh," Grayson said.

I fortified myself with another slug of margarita. "You wanna know something?"

"What?"

I glanced around, then flinched. "I've never actually worn a dress. My poor mother couldn't make me. Not even on prom night. It just felt ... *weird*, you know?"

Grayson's face took on a studios appearance, like a doctor handing out a diagnosis. "Perhaps you'd already passed some critical stage of development, beyond which you couldn't embrace pantyhose."

I laughed, relieved he hadn't judged me as some kind of freak. "Yeah. Maybe. Now, I guess I'm doomed to live out the rest of my life in jeans."

Grayson smiled. "Well, at least you didn't say mechanic's coveralls."

"Oh, hell no!" I shook my tipsy head and sloshed my drink all over the table. "This whole situation is ... is ... well. Crap. I don't know what it is."

"I don't get it," he said. "What's stopping you from just ditching this place and leaving?"

I sighed and slumped further into the booth. "Look. When my father died, I had to take over his auto repair shop. I wanted to save his legacy,"

"His legacy?"

I scowled. "Okay, I wanted to prove I was every bit as good a mechanic as Earl, okay? I sunk my life savings into that god-forsaken garage. And what did I get in return? *Broke!* That's what!" I shook my head. "That place is a freaking money pit. Earl won."

Grayson eyed me curiously. "Earl won?"

"He gets a paycheck, and I'm stuck paying the bills. You want to know why I tromp around in my dead father's shoes?"

I didn't wait for Grayson to answer.

"Because I can't afford to buy my own stupid pair of steel-toed boots! That's why!"

Grayson nodded solemnly. Then he smirked mischievously. "So, tell me Drex. What were you doing before you became the world's surliest mechanic?"

For some reason I couldn't explain, I burst out laughing and I couldn't stop.

I laughed until I snorted. Then, I laughed at my snorting. I laughed at my pain. I laughed at my stupidity. I laughed at the utter absurdity of my life. I laughed at the utter absurdity of Nick Grayson, the bald, fedora-wearing P.I. with two navels.

God, it feels good to laugh.

The waitress came over with another round of drinks.

"Ah," Grayson said. "Just what we need. Reinforcements."

He grabbed his bottle of beer, then gently placed my margarita on the table in front of me.

"Please, go on," he said, and smiled at me encouragingly. "Tell me all about your life before becoming a grease monkey."

He raised his beer bottle. I met it with my margarita.

"I was an antiques dealer," I said, then took a sip. "With my fiancé. Correction ... *ex*-fiancé. Carl Blanders." I set the drink down and shrugged. "It was a good gig, actually. Until he went and traded me in for someone with a higher Blue Book value."

"Ouch."

I sighed. "Yeah. But that's another story. Let's just say that for now, I'm stuck doing what I'm doing until I can come up with something better."

"Like becoming a private investigator?"

I studied Grayson a moment to see if he was mocking me. He wasn't. "Yeah."

"You know, I think you may have the makings of a good one, Red."

My back bristled. "Listen, Grayson. Call me a boy if you want. Call me a jackass. Call me crazy, for all I care. But like I told you before, *don't* call me Red. Do it again and I just might take a socket wrench to your carburetor ... if you catch my drift."

"I get it," Grayson said, holding up his hands. "Deal."

"Deal?" a familiar voice sounded to my right. "What kind of *deal* are you two making?"

I looked over to see Officer Paulson stomping up to the end of the booth. He glared at us, his ice-blue eyes nearly hidden behind angry, narrow slits.

"There's no deal, Paulson," I said. "We're just exchanging information."

Paulson eyed me, then Grayson. "I thought I told you not to discuss the case, Bobbie."

Grayson met his stare. "I assure you, we weren't talking about any *case*. You must be Detective Paulson. I'm Nick Grayson."

Grayson stood and held his hand out. Paulson shook it, but only after waiting a beat.

"What are you doing in Point Paradise, Mr. Grayson?" Paulson asked.

"Just a little sightseeing." Grayson looked at me and winked. "You have to admit she's quite a sight. Am I right?"

Paulson's face flushed. The tendons in his neck tightened. "Ms. Drex here is a treasure, Mr. Grayson. And folks around here ... well, we like to keep a close eye on our valuables."

Grayson nodded. "Well, I can—"

"You two have a nice evening," Paulson said, cutting Grayson off. He turned to me. "Bobbie, give me a call tomorrow. I want a full report on *you-know-who*."

Paulson turned on his heels and marched out of the restaurant.

"Is 'you-know-who' perhaps 'little-old-me'?" Grayson asked, batting his eyelashes.

I didn't answer, because I really didn't know.

Chapter Twenty-Eight

AT MIDNIGHT, THE OLD landline to my parent's business started ringing.

It'd been in continuous service since they'd opened Robert's Mechanics three decades ago. I hadn't had the heart to disconnect the number, since their old-time customers still used it from time to time. It hadn't rung in weeks. But now that I only had two hours sleep on a three-margarita hangover, it wouldn't shut the hell up.

The fourth time it started ringing, I was too boiling mad to stop myself from answering it.

"What?" I yelled into the phone.

"*Beep-beep-beep.*"

"Who is this?"

"*Beep-beep-beep.*"

"I'm hanging up, now, jackass."

"We're watching," a robotic voice said.

"Who's watching?" I demanded.

There was no reply.

The line went dead.

Great. Mrs. Vanderhoff's somehow managed to get me on robocop's telemarketing list.

I slammed the phone down and crawled back into bed. Then that tingly ice spider crawled up my spine and made a nest in my hair.

I got back up to make sure my front door was locked. It wasn't. I set the lock, then I fumbled around for something to defend myself against a killer robot.

Gun? Don't have one. Knife? No. I can't stand the sound of metal on metal.

I spotted the flyswatter on my kitchen counter. I scowled.

Better than nothing, I guess.

I picked it up and went back to bed.

I AWOKE TO THE SOUND of someone banging around in the service bay downstairs. Even when you're expecting it, Monday morning always comes too early.

Unless, of course, you're an annoying early-bird like my cousin Earl.

I got up and fumbled around aimlessly for a minute, trying to decide whether or not to tell someone about my weird phone call last night. Lord knows I couldn't tell Earl. He'd have a field day with it. I couldn't tell Paulson, either. He was already on the verge of having me psychoanalyzed.

Not that I cared that much. But if I got labeled as crazy ... well, there'd go my P.I. gig.

I padded to the kitchen and made a pot of coffee. It was still perking when a knock sounded at my front door.

I figured Earl must've been here for hours and already gone through the coffee thermos he brought with him every day.

"Come in," I called out.

"Can't. It's locked."

Oh yeah.

I shuffled down the hall in my dad's old T-shirt and sweatpants. Not ready for a dose of Earl-style humiliation, I slapped on my Woody Woodpecker wig before I cracked open the door.

"What do you want, Earl?" I hissed.

It wasn't Earl.

"Uh ... just hoping to get a cup of that coffee I smell?" Grayson averted his eyes, but only after he'd gotten a good look at me in all my morning glory.

Great.

"Gimme a minute, for cripe's sake!" I yelled, and slammed the door.

I groaned at my reflection in the hallway mirror, then readjusted my wig and rubbed the sleep from my eyes. I stared at my saggy sweatpants and lost all hope.

I opened the door. "Sorry. You kind of caught me off guard."

Dressed neatly in his typical attire of black t-shirt, black jeans, black fedora, and black shoes, Grayson looked like a member of the wardrobe SWAT team here to bust me for non-compliance.

"Not a morning person, are we?" he asked, then smiled at me cheerfully.

My eyes narrowed. "You want some coffee or not?"

"Yes. Please. Might I add, you look dapper this morning."

I scowled. "Dapper is a masculine descriptive."

"Well, those *are* men's clothes, aren't they? I swear, do you own anything actually manufactured for the female anatomy?"

I slammed the coffee cup on the table. "Jeans. You saw 'em last night. What are you doing up so early, anyway?"

"Call me *The Princess and the Pea*, but it's hard to sleep through the whine of a pneumatic drill."

I winced. "Oh. Yeah. Sorry about that. But the good news is, that means Earl's busy fixing your RV."

"Good. So what's on the agenda for today?" Grayson asked, tapping his index finger annoyingly on his coffee mug.

My nose crinkled. "What do you mean?"

"Well, seeing as I'm kind of stuck here, I thought I'd explore the local entertainment options."

"What are you talking about? There's nothing to do here."

Grayson scratched his chin. "Remind me again. Why do you live here?"

I blew out a sigh that could've extinguished the candles on a centenarian's birthday cake.

"I *told* you. I'm working on my escape."

"Oh, yes. The P.I. gig."

"Right. Which reminds me, I've got to give Paulson a report on Vanderhoff today."

Grayson's left eyebrow raised slightly. "Vanderhoff?"

"The old lady who keeps getting the weird phone calls. Hey. You didn't call the shop last night, did you?"

"No. But I heard the phone ring four times."

"My parent's old landline. Sorry. It turned out to be a prank call. Nothing but beeps and static. Then some stupid mechanical voice said, 'We're watching you.'"

Grayson's back straightened. "Interesting."

"Nuts is more like it. Should I tell Paulson? He already thinks I'm crazy for seeing imaginary dead guys."

Grayson chewed his lip for a moment. "I tell you what. You help me, and I'll help you."

"Help me? How?"

"Let me borrow your car, and I'll teach you how to bug a phone. Deal?"

I sneered. "Whose phone? Earl's? I already hear way more out of his stupid mouth than I want to."

"No. *Vanderhoff's*. We can put a listening device in her phone, and then you'll know whether she's cuckoo for Cocoa Puffs or telling the truth."

I scowled. "In my book, that's called invasion of privacy."

Grayson shrugged and locked eyes with me. "In mine it's called on-the-job training."

Chapter Twenty-Nine

I SLIPPED INTO A PAIR of jeans and my best threadbare button-down shirt. With the woodpecker wig centered on my skull and the last dregs of Mom's dried-up eyeliner applied, I almost looked feminine. I blew out a sigh, then hobbled down the stairs in a pair of Mom's inch-high red pumps to check on Earl in the service bay.

"Well, look at you," Earl teased. "I ain't seen you out of coveralls in a year. I thought you'd done sewed yourself into 'em."

I shot him some side-eye. "Yeah. Ha ha and all that. Look, you got everything you need to keep going on the repairs to Grayson's vehicle?"

"Who's Grayson?"

Oh, crap! I don't want to get into this with Earl. Not right now.

"Knickerbocker," I said. "It's his first name."

Earl eyed me mischievously. "You two on a first-name basis now?"

"He's a private investigator, Earl. He's going to help me on the Vanderhoff case."

"The Vanderhoff case? What. You a detective now, too?"

Aww crap!

"I'm working on something for Paulson, okay? Grayson's helping me out."

Earl grinned. "I *bet* he is."

"Listen, Earl. He's a customer. Nothing more. He's paid six days rent in advance, and shelled out the entire tab for the parts. He even gave me five-hundred down toward your labor costs. That's nearly thirty-five hundred bucks. Don't blow it, okay? We need the money."

"I dunno, Bobbie. Something smells fishy to me."

"Who cares? His money's good. And you know as well as I do, we damned sure need it."

Earl put on his pondering face for a moment. Not a good portent of things to come.

"You're right, boss man." He sniggered and punched me in the arm. "If you ask me, sounds like a case of 'Don't ask, don't *smell*.'"

As my eyes returned from their orbit around their sockets, I spied Grayson coming down the stairs. His polished leather shoes were the only things gleaming in the entire garage.

"Good morning, Earl," he said after shooting me a wink. "How're the repairs going?"

Earl smirked. "Don't ask, don't sme—"

I punched Earl hard on the arm.

"Ouch!" He shot me a redneck scowl. "That hurt!"

"You ready to go, Drex?" Grayson asked.

I looked him in the eye. "Never been more ready."

Grayson grinned. "Come on, then. Let's roll."

Chapter Thirty

AS I STEERED THE MUSTANG out of the crumbling parking lot of the mechanic shop, Grayson fiddled with a weird, old-fashioned looking cellphone he'd retrieved from his RV. I smiled. Maybe he didn't embrace technology either.

"How'd you become a private investigator?" I asked.

Grayson fiddled with some buttons on the device in his hand. "I read a book when I was a kid called, *So You Want to be a Detective.*"

I shook my head and smirked. "It's never a straight answer with you, is it?"

Grayson shrugged and set the device in his lap. "Playing it straight all the time is no fun, Drex. Sometimes, a sense of humor is the only thing that gets you through the rough spots."

I rolled my eyes. "Yeah. Life can be a real riot, all right."

"Come on. Of all the career choices in the world, what made *you* want to be a private investigator?"

I steered the Mustang onto Obsidian Road and scowled. "I took one of those aptitude tests on Facebook."

"You mean the kind that tells you what kind of pizza you'd be?"

"Exactly. It said I should be a shoe store manager."

"Ouch."

"Freaking Facebook."

Grayson laughed and fiddled with the door lock like an antsy little kid. "I don't follow. How did *that* lead into you getting a P.I. intern license?"

I shifted into third. "I was so pissed off after that Facebook test that I drank half a bottle of vodka. I woke up around three in the morning, still snockered. As fate would have it, the TV was blaring this late-night infomercial on how to 'Train at home in your spare time to become a private investigator.'"

"I see." Grayson pursed his lips and tapped his fingers on the door handle.

I bit my lip. "I know it sounds totally lame, but I was only pulling in ten bucks an hour as a mall cop. Barely enough to cover the gas to Gainesville and back."

"Wait a minute." Grayson stopped tapping his finger and turned to stare at me. "You were a *mall cop?*"

I pressed my molars together, wanting to curse myself out for letting that one slip.

Grayson laughed out loud, stifled himself, then burst out laughing again. He sucked in some air and blurted, "Did you have your own Segway?" Then he doubled over in the passenger seat.

I mashed the gas pedal to the floor. "Smartass."

"Sorry," he said, trying to compose himself. "It's just that ... well, most people who go into this line of work have a background in the military or law enforcement." He snickered, then recovered himself. "Though, I suppose mall cop could count as some branch of non-government counter-intelligence."

I shot him some major side-eye. "Ha. Ha. Ha."

Grayson pursed his lips. "Okay, okay. I'm done." He took a deep breath. "Tell me, from which prestigious school did you earn your intern certificate, Detective Drex?"

I glared at him. "The Forensic Academy, okay? It was just one of those wild-hair things. Like I said, I was half-lit when I called them. I put the tuition on a credit card. It was non-refundable. When I sobered up in the morning, I figured, the money's gone, so what the hell."

"Your insatiable passion for the profession is inspiring," Grayson said soberly.

I grinned despite myself. "Thanks."

"Where did you plan on getting your two years of on-the-job training?"

I scowled. "I didn't. I thought that once I passed the test for the Class CC intern license, I was good to go."

"I guess you should've done a better job investigating it before you shelled out the money."

I blew out a breath and rolled my eyes. "I guess. But half a pint of Stolli has a way of making me lose my train of thought."

"Apparently, so does tequila."

I winced, then pulled up in front of Vanderhoff's nondescript house in Cherry Manor. "We're here."

Grayson opened the side door and tipped his fedora at me. "Well, Ms. Graduate of the Forensic Academy. Time to show me what you've got."

Chapter Thirty-One

OLD LADY VANDERHOFF took a final drag off her Marlboro and stamped out the stub in the overflowing ashtray on her kidney-shaped coffee table. She sat back in the wingback chair and eyed Grayson and me. Perched on the chair above her left shoulder, a dead-eyed doll glared back at us like a graveyard demon.

"Beth-Ann put me under the dryer and went out for a smoke," the old woman said. "I was all by myself in her garage." She glanced over at me. "I mean, you know, *beauty parlor*."

"Go on," Grayson said.

"Well, some guy all dressed up in a hat and an old-fashioned, double-breasted suit came in and asked me my name. I told him a lady don't just give out her personal details like that." She hocked a loogie and spit it in-to a napkin. "Then the fella asked for the time. I told him. But then, he said something weird."

"What?" I asked, trying not to look at her napkin.

Vanderhoff straightened her shoulders. "He said something like, 'Excuse me, but I meant to inquire after the *year*.' Just like that. Well, when I told him, he looked kind of surprised. He thanked me and then just up and left. When I got home, my phone was ringing. It was those damned beeping robots."

"You didn't mention the guy before," I said.

She shrugged. "Eh. I didn't think it was important. Well, truth is, I forgot. My memory ain't what it used to be."

"So have you gotten any more calls?" Grayson asked.

"Yeah. Last night, as a matter of fact. That robot bastard again. Now he wants me to meet him tonight at the Stop & Shoppe at nine-thirty. Well, I told him I couldn't go."

"Why not?" Grayson asked.

Vanderhoff looked surprised by his question. "Why, that's when *Matlock* is on!"

I stifled a smirk. "Was it the same voice that told you to go to A&P and steal the bananas?"

"I would assume so." Vanderhoff glanced over at Grayson and shook her head as if it were obvious I was some kind of nincompoop. "I mean, how many robots would get the idea to call *me* up? Right, Detective Grayson?"

"Good point," Grayson said. "Pardon me, but could I trouble you for a glass of water, Mrs. Vanderhoff?"

The old lady batted her gray eyelashes at him. "No trouble at all, for you, honey."

Vanderhoff heaved herself out of the chair and hobbled to the kitchen. I followed her in and stood in the doorway, serving as a lookout for Grayson's and my surreptitious plans to bug her telephone.

As Vanderhoff reached for a glass in a cabinet, I snuck a peek back into the living room. Grayson was fiddling with the phone jack on the wall. I don't know why, but I'd expected him to stick something into the receiver of the old rotary dial phone, like they always did in the black-and-white detective movies I'd seen.

I frowned and turned around. Vanderhoff had the glass in the sink, filling it from the tap. She turned off the faucet and took a step toward the living room.

"Uh ... wow," I said, sidestepping in front of her. "That's a lot of magnets." I pointed to her refrigerator.

Vanderhoff's head pivoted on her turkey neck. "Yeah. But I won't be getting no more. Mandy used to send 'em to me from all over the place."

"Oh." My eyes scanned the dozens of magnets littering the freezer door. Amongst the tacky display, I spotted my business card. It was half-covered with a round, brown magnet that looked suspiciously like a mound of dog poop.

Nice.

I glanced back into the living room. Grayson motioned he needed more time. I turned back and smiled at Vanderhoff. "I see you've stuck my card on the fridge there. That magnet ... where's it from?"

Vanderhoff hobbled closer to the refrigerator. While she squinted at the magnet, I shot a glance into the living room. Grayson was sticking the old-fashioned cell phone thingy under the sofa cushion.

"Grave Creek Mound," Vanderhoff said. She straightened up and sniffed. "That was the last one she sent, if I recall correctly."

I nodded solemnly. "I heard you reported her missing. I really am sorry."

"Thanks." Vanderhoff smiled. "Kids nowadays. Hopefully she'll turn up."

"I hope so."

Vanderhoff fetched the glass of water from the sink and took a step toward the living room. I sprinted ahead of her in an effort to warn Grayson she was coming. My gut flopped when I saw him fluffing the pillows on the sofa.

He winked at me and said, "And that, my little grasshopper, is how it's done."

"How what's done?" Vanderhoff asked.

I cringed. Grayson didn't even blink.

"Conducting an interview, ma'am," he said. "As you know, I'm here to help train our little Bobbie to become a bona fide private investigator. Don't you think she did a fine job today?"

Vanderhoff shrugged noncommittally. "I guess." She handed Grayson the glass of water. He drank it down in one, long gulp.

"We should be going," I said as he handed her back the empty glass.

"Thank you for your time. It's been lovely." Grayson kissed Mrs. Vanderhoff's hand. She beamed at him like a smitten, geriatric schoolgirl.

"Come back anytime, Detective Grayson," she said as we stepped onto the front porch. She followed us out and stood in the doorway, grinning and waving as we climbed into the Mustang.

"You seem to have a way with women," I said, and waved back at Vanderhoff. Her grin faded. Then she went inside and closed the door.

"She seemed nice enough," Grayson said.

"Sure. For a woman whose been known to spot the Virgin Mary in her French toast."

Grayson laughed. "It always pays to be polite—until it doesn't. That should be rule number one in the P.I. handbook."

I grimaced. "What does that even *mean?*"

Grayson grimaced, then burst into a grin. "Hey. I know! Let's get a picture of you standing in front of her place."

I eyed him suspiciously. "For what?"

Grayson pulled his cellphone from his pocket. "For your scrapbook, of course. *Detective's First Year.*" He snapped off a couple of shots of me with my mouth hanging open.

"I wasn't ready," I said.

"She's ready?" a woman asked excitedly. She was walking by on the sidewalk, towing a little white poodle on a leash beside her.

"What?" I asked.

The woman came over and bent down beside the driver's side window. She was Nellie Parker. I'd seen her at the beauty parlor a couple of times. Nosy Nellie was a bad tipper, according to Beth-Ann.

"Vanderhoff," Parker said. "Is she finally getting ready to sell her place?"

"No. Why would you think that?"

Parker's face collapsed with disappointment. "You're the second ones to stop and take a picture of her place today."

"Really?" I asked. "Who were the others?"

"I dunno. Just a guy I'd never seen before. I figured he was a realtor from Waldo or something." Parker glanced over at Vanderhoff's house and let out a big sigh. "Well, too bad, Doodles. We should get going." The little dog yipped. She turned back to face me. "Y'all have a nice day, now."

"You too," Grayson said.

"You thinking what I'm thinking?" I asked.

Grayson sighed. "Darn it. I guess I'm gonna miss Matlock."

I fought back a grin, turned the key in the ignition, and fired up the Mustang.

"Let's do a test call," Grayson said as we cruised out of Cherry Manor and past the Stop & Shoppe. "See if mister tele-buggy's working."

"How?"

"Give Vanderhoff a ring."

I blanched. "Who? Me? What should I say?"

"Ask her if her refrigerator's running. Or if she's got Prince Albert in a can."

I rolled my eyes. "Don't you ever take *anything* seriously?"

"A few things. Sure. But this doesn't make the short list."

I pulled over and dialed Vanderhoff. The phone rang ten times before she answered it.

Grayson kept an eye on his own cell phone. When Vanderhoff finally picked up, a text message came up on his phone display. He tapped a button and stuck a pair of earbuds in his ears while I spoke with Vanderhoff.

"Mrs. Vanderhoff?" I asked.

"Oh. It's you, Bobbie. I wasn't gonna answer. I thought it might be that robot man again."

"No. Just me. I wanted to say thank you for your hospitality."

"Oh. You're welcome, honey."

"Have a good day. Let me know if you get any more weird calls."

"I will. Tell Detective Grayson it was a pleasure to meet him. He can come by any—"

"I will. Bye." I hung up and sneered at Grayson. "I think she's got a crush on you, lady-killer."

He grinned and pulled out the earbuds. "Jealous? I heard every word."

"So it's working?"

"Like a charm."

"Good. Speaking of charm, I need to call Paulson."

Grayson's eyebrows met in the middle of his forehead. "I fail to see the connection."

I smirked. "I need to give him an update on the case. But I don't know exactly what to say."

"Tell him Mothman's in town and is performing a one-night-only gig at the Stop & Shoppe tonight at nine-thirty."

I shot him a look. "You know, you're almost as bad as Earl."

Grayson grinned. "You said *almost*. I must be making progress."

Chapter Thirty-Two

"WHERE TO NOW, DETECTIVE Drex?" Grayson joked as we drove back toward Point Paradise.

"Well, I need to stop by the A&P."

"Let me guess. To check if Mothman's flitting around *Wool*worth's? Get it?"

"Ugh. Unfortunately, yes, I get it. And no. I need groceries. I'm out of coffee, milk, and pretty much everything else. I didn't think you'd want to go."

"Sure. Why not? But before we do that, I've got another idea."

"What?"

"Seeing as how we've got a stakeout coming up tonight, I thought we might work on your P.I. training some more."

"Okay. How?"

"I think it's high time you learned how to shoot a gun."

I raised an eyebrow. "That's not a bad idea, actually. I know a place we can fire off a few rounds. Why don't we swing by the garage and get your gun?"

"No need." Grayson patted his side. "I've got my trusty Glock right here."

"You've had it on you the whole time?"

"Of course. Never leave home without it. Don't worry. I've got a concealed carry license."

That wasn't *exactly* what I was concerned about. I'd been driving around with an armed stranger.

Whether Grayson was a friend or a fiend, the jury inside my brain was still in hot deliberation. If I was going to unload rounds with this guy, I needed to let someone else know, in case the guy turned out to be Dahmer and I turned out to be his next Happy Meal.

"Sure," I said. "Just going to check in with Earl. See if he needs any-thing."

I pulled the Mustang over and punched Earl on speed dial. I pasted on a smile and tried to sound casual. "Hey. I'm going with Grayson to do some target shooting. You need anything at the A&P?"

"Target shooting?" Earl laughed. "Is that what they're calling it nowadays? I thought it was 'Netflix and chill.'"

"Earl, we're going to test-fire his Glock. That's all."

"Here I am, gunning an engine, and you're gunning to get laid."

"Earl, you're fired."

I hung up the phone and looked over at Grayson. "Did you hear any of that?"

"Not a word. But since someone's expecting a 'happy ending,' I think it's only proper to buy you lunch first. What else has Waldo got to offer besides El Molino's?"

"Why?"

Grayson thumped his chest lightly with his fist. "I haven't quite fully recovered from last night's tacos yet."

FROM A PICNIC TABLE outside a small roadside attraction known as Randy's Rib Shack, I watched Grayson lick barbeque sauce off his fin-gers. Suddenly, I had a ghastly vision of it being blood instead of tomato sauce.

"How do you like Randy's special recipe?" I asked, trying to tame my willies.

"Not bad. Why aren't you eating?"

"I kind of lost my appetite."

"Is it me?" Grayson waggled his saucy fingers and grinned at me like a deranged demon. "Still think I might be after your lucky charms?"

"No." I smirked. "I've seen inside Randy's kitchen."

Grayson stopped mid-bite, grimaced, and set the beef rib back down on his plate.

I laughed. "You know, you keep mentioning this Mothman creature. What's the deal with that?"

Grayson wiped his fingers on a paper napkin. "It's supposed to be a true story. Like I said before, I'm here investigating reports of a red-eyed creature. Granted, that could be any number of cryptids—Bigfoot, the Boggy Creek Monster, even a wayward chupacabra. But since I've hooked up with you, I'm leaning more toward Mothman."

"Why?"

Grayson shrugged. "Sightings of a red-eyed, flying creature. Strange lights in the sky. And now, thanks to you and Vanderhoff, I know people are getting the same kind of weird phone calls the folks did back in the 1960s in Point Pleasant."

My nose crinkled at the prospect of a monster lurking nearby. "Did they ever catch this Mothman guy?"

"No. And after the tragedy, reported sightings of him dwindled to nothing."

I swallowed my spit. "Tragedy?"

Grayson shot me an incredulous look. "The Silver Bridge collapse. You never heard of it? The bridge spanning the Ohio River. It collapsed on December 15, 1967. It was full of rush-hour traffic. Forty-six people died."

"And they blamed that on Mothman?"

"Not exactly. They thought Mothman was some kind of omen. A sign. Haven't you ever heard of *The Mothman Prophecies?*"

"That movie with Richard Gere?"

"Yes. But also the book. It was a *New York Times* bestseller. It gives a sort of blow-by-blow diary of what happened in the town of Point Pleasant from 1966 to '67. The year of the Garuda."

Grayson picked up a little paper cup of barbeque sauce and downed it like a shot.

I grimaced. "Garuda?"

"That's what John Keel, the author of the book called it. The Garuda's a bird-like creature from Hindu and Buddhist mythology. People in Point Pleasant reported sightings of it all over the place. To some, it looked like a winged man. Others thought it was a giant bird. Some even thought it was a monster—a demon with bat wings. But they all agreed on two things. It had glowing red eyes, and it could fly."

A chill went down my spine. Maybe that *was* what I'd seen on the roof of the Stop & Shoppe the other night. "Did it kill people?"

"No. None that got reported, anyway. But it *did* seem to have a penchant for chasing people around and scaring the daylights out of them. Its favorite M.O. was to buzz by people in their cars. But it never actually caught anybody. Not that I know of, anyway. So it's hard to say what would've happened if it had."

I crinkled my nose. "Well, I don't want to be the first one to find out."

Grayson arched an eyebrow. "No?"

"So what exactly do you hope to achieve with this investigation of yours?"

"I'm hoping to find hard evidence to substantiate the creature's existence."

"Oh. Like what? A feather?"

"I don't think Mothman has feathers. Maybe a talon. Hair sample. Blood. I'd like to catch it, actually. But at this point, I'd even settle for scat."

I grimaced. "Moth poop? Who'd want that?"

"You'd be surprised. Lots of people think there's power in cryptic relics."

"Power for what?"

"For good or evil. Buddhists think the Garuda might hold the key to levitation and enlightenment. Others, well, who knows? Maybe they think it can turn them into Batman."

My eyebrows inched closer together. "So you really think this thing's real? That it's still alive?"

"I hope so. But nobody knows. After the bridge collapse, sightings of the creature pretty much disappeared from West Virginia. The reports around Waldo are the first in over fifty years."

My mind returned to my wallet. Maybe he'd pay me for my sighting story. "Are you offering any kind of ... reward?"

Grayson threw his sticky hands up. "Whoa. I answered your questions. Now it's your turn to answer one of mine."

I sighed. "Okay. What do you want to know?"

"Are you dating Paulson?"

I nearly choked on my iced tea. "That's none of your business," I hacked.

"I know. But he seemed a bit ... hmm ... *overzealous* yesterday at El Molino's."

"He's being protective. You *are* a stranger in town, after all."

Grayson shot me a perplexed look. "We're all strangers where we aren't known."

Okaay ....

"Speaking of Paulson, I still need to stop by his office," I said. "I promised him a report on Vanderhoff, but he didn't answer his phone this morning. Are you done eating?"

Grayson nodded. "Almost." He picked up the salt shaker, shook a generous portion of salt into his palm, and licked it.

What a weirdo.

"His office is here in Waldo," I said, pretending not to notice. "We might as well get it over with while we're here."

Chapter Thirty-Three

"ACCORDING TO THE ADDRESS, Paulson's office is a few miles on the other side of town," I said as we cruised down US 301 through the tiny, crumbling heart of Waldo.

"This place looked a lot better in the dark last night," Grayson said. "Oh. I take that back. I didn't see the big white horsey before."

He pointed to the sign for the Waldo Farmer's & Flea Market. Atop it stood a life-sized replica of a white horse. The stallion's jaunty expression seemed too dignified for the hodge-podge collection of nondescript buildings that made up Waldo Antiques Village.

"Let's stop," Grayson said. "I wonder what other curiosities they might have."

"They're closed on Mondays," I said, relieved for the excuse. "Besides, there's nothing there but junk disguised as antiques. After fifteen years in the business, I know the difference."

"I'll take your word on that."

Grayson watched the tiny town click by, its buildings standing not much more than a sidewalk's breadth away from the steaming asphalt of US 301.

"They like to stick close to the road here," he commented.

"Yeah. When they widened it to four lanes, they didn't leave the town much breathing room."

As we hit the center of Waldo, we passed City Hall, a white, boxy little structure no bigger than a coffee shop. Then, in quick succession, we passed the Waldo barber shop, Dixieland Music RV park, a junky place selling cypress-wood souvenirs, an Amtrak station, the Tropix Inn motel, and a clot of dilapidated, corrugated-metal buildings tacked together with rusty nails and faded hopes.

As the scenery on both sides of the road was reclaimed by pinewoods and swamp, Grayson asked, "That's it? Where's Paulson's office?"

"He said it was out near Alto Lake Preserve. As you could see from your deluxe tour of Waldo, downtown office space is at a premium. Oh. There it is."

I shifted into second and took a left onto Alto Road. About a hundred yards up the rutted dirt lane, we came to a mailbox. A red clay driveway maybe twenty yards long led to a rustic wooden cabin tucked in among overgrown hedges.

"That must be it," I said.

The plain, metal mailbox next to the road had no name on it. It was mounted on an L-shaped post. A wooden, hand-painted sign hung below the mailbox. It read, "One nation under God."

That may have been so, but this place looked as godforsaken as any I'd ever seen.

"The place looks abandoned," Grayson said.

"Get used to it," I said. "Half the county looks that way. I don't see a car. He must be out on patrol."

"What kind of car does he drive?"

I frowned. "I dunno. A blue one?"

Grayson shook his head. "Blue? That's all you've got?"

"I don't pay much attention to that kind of thing. Today's cars all look alike to me."

"Drex, if you're going to be a P.I., you need to acquaint yourself with makes and models. You're going to spend half your time either tailing vehicles or trying to spot them. That's how people get around nowadays. You know, since that whole horse and buggy thing went by the wayside."

I blew out a breath. This whole P.I. thing was sounding like more work than I'd imagined it would be. My cellphone buzzed, saving me from having to come up with a snarky comeback. I looked at the display and groaned.

"You gonna get that?" Grayson asked.

"No. It's the hospital again. They keep calling. I don't know how I'm going to pay the bill."

"Huh." Grayson shot me a devious grin. "I've got just the thing to take your mind off thoughts of impending poverty."

"What?"

"Let's do something fun."

I frowned. "Like what?"

Grayson waggled his bushy eyebrows at me. "Let's go shoot something."

Chapter Thirty-Four

WITH NO OFFICER PAULSON to be found, we left the cabin in Lake Alto Reserve and drove back through Waldo. I turned onto Obsidian Road, then, a mile later, onto an unmarked dirt road. A quarter mile in, we reached the unofficial target-shooting spot known to gun-toting locals as Bullet Point.

I shifted into second and slowed down until I saw the fence posts. "That's it," I said, and shifted into reverse and set the brake.

Grayson pulled out his Glock. A tinge of panic surged through me. If Grayson shot me, would Earl even bother to come find me? And if he did, would the vultures beat him to my remains?

I eyed Grayson's gun and forced a smile. "It won't take long to go through that magazine."

Grayson reached under the seat and pulled out a carton of ammo. "Good thing I brought more."

My eyes met my wig-line. "When did you put those under there?"

Grayson grinned. "When you weren't looking, obviously. Do you know you have a tendency to close your eyes when you're nervous?"

"Arggh!"

I flung open the car door and stomped over to the fence. Amongst the heap of battered tin cans and broken beer bottles, I found a few cans that weren't completely shot through with bullet holes. I set them up on fence posts and marched back over to Grayson.

"You go first," I said.

"No. Ladies first," he insisted. "Here, let me show you how to hold the gun."

"I know how!" I said.

"Sorry," Grayson said, handing me the gun. "Judging by your performance in my bedroom yesterday, I thought I could give you some pointers."

My mouth ached to deliver a devastating comeback, but I had nothing. Instead, I took my stance. Grayson sidled in close behind me, his chest nearly touching my back. As I inserted the earplugs he gave me, his arms encircled my shoulders.

My back arched from the electric twinge of his body heat.

I steadied myself. His forearms paralleled mine. His hands enveloped my fingers. As I held the polymer grip of the Glock in my hands, I could smell the musky maleness of him envelop me. I trembled.

"Hold your arms steady," he whispered.

I set my jaw. "You mean like *this?*"

I fired off five rounds in rapid succession. Five rusty Green Giant vegetable cans went flying off in all directions.

Grayson let go of me and stepped back. "Whoa!"

"Beginner's luck," I quipped, and headed over to the fence to reset the cans.

Grayson followed a step behind me. He picked up a freshly shot can. "Not bad," he said, holding it out for me to see. "But you're a little off center."

"Look closer," I said. "I was aiming for the giant's face."

Grayson examined the bullet hole above the Green Giant's neck. His mouth dropped open. "How'd you learn to shoot like that?"

"You forget. I was a boy until I was eleven. I got pretty good with a Daisy BB gun." I smirked. "I don't mean to brag or anything, but I can shoot out a baby doll's eye at a hundred paces."

Grayson whistled. "With one hand tied behind your back, I bet."

I grinned. "Should we set them up for you?"

Grayson nodded. "Sure."

Smug wallowed all over my face as I handed Grayson the Glock. I bent over and reached down for a can.

My heart nearly fell into my throat.

Staring back at me from the weeds was the raw, empty eye socket of a bloody skull.

I shot to standing. My brain went haywire. My ears throbbed with a strange, underwater-pulsing sound.

Something warm trickled down my leg.

Blood?

"You okay?" Grayson asked.

His voice sounded mere inches away. The hair on the back of my neck stood up.

OMG! That psycho's gone and stabbed me! He's lured me out here to ....
Holy crap! This is Grayson's freaking killing field!

I screamed, ditched the green bean can, and made a mad scramble for the Mustang.

Grayson's footsteps crunched behind me. I could tell he was gaining on me.

Dear God! Will he rip my throat out, like he did the others?

Am I really going to die in this crappy hellhole of a place after all?

Chapter Thirty-Five

"DREX!" GRAYSON'S VOICE shouted out behind me. "Wait!"

I'd just flung myself into the Mustang, and was trying to get the key in the ignition. But my hands were shaking like I had ahold of a jackhammer.

Please, key! Please! Get in the freaking ignition!

I looked up. Grayson was ten feet from the car, his green eyes looked wild.

"What are you doing?" he yelled.

I jabbed the keys at the ignition hole. "Stay away from me!"

Grayson stopped in his tracks. "What's going on?"

The key slipped into the ignition. I turned it. The Mustang roared to life.

"I saw it. I know what you did!"

"What I did? What did I do?"

"The skull!" I screamed as I shifted into first.

Grayson blanched. "Skull? Where?"

"You know where!"

"What? Wait! Drex! You think I killed someone?" He took another step toward the car.

"Don't come any closer!" I shouted, and gunned the engine. The Mustang lurched forward, then stalled.

Damned air filter!

Grayson came a step closer and pulled out his Glock. My heart nearly stopped.

"Let me talk to you," he yelled. "Look, I'm dropping the weapon."

Suddenly, the gun fired, shooting out my left front tire.

I screamed and turned the ignition again. It caught. I slammed the Mustang into first and gently pressed the gas. The car moved forward a foot.

"Wait!" Grayson yelled.

But I didn't wait. What for? To get my brains blown out?

I shifted into second and mashed the pedal to the floor. Clouds of orange dust billowed up behind my squealing tires as the muscle car took off, fishtailing down the dirt road.

Grayson slowly disappeared in the dust behind me. I thought I was in the clear. But fifty yards out, I hit a huge pothole. The driver's side window disappeared into the door panel with a crunch of breaking glass.

Then, the tread on the blown tire peeled away like a strip of black alligator hide. The bare left front rim couldn't grip in the sand. The Mustang veered wildly to the left. It took all I had to keep it on the road as I hobbled along, the rim gouging and scraping and slinging up sand.

Without traction, the car inched along slowly—slower than I could run. I dared a glance in the rearview mirror. Grayson was about thirty feet behind me, and gaining fast.

Crap!

I scanned the car for a weapon.

Nothing.

I glanced in the rearview mirror and nearly swallowed my tongue. Grayson was almost to the car!

I grabbed the only thing I could find to defend myself—the green Tootsie Pop I'd licked once, then tossed in the ashtray. Grayson jogged up to my broken window. I hurled the sucker at him with all my might. It hit home, beaning him right below his left eye.

"Ow!" he yelled, rubbing the impact spot. "What'd you do that for? And why the hell are you running away from me?"

"You shot at me!" I screeched.

Grayson grimaced. "It was an accident. I swear!"

"No it wasn't. You're trying to kill me!"

"I am not!"

"Are too!"

"Am not!" Grayson rolled his eyes. "This is ridiculous. What are we? Three-year-olds?"

I stared at him sullenly. "How do I know you're not some serial killer living in that RV in the woods? What about that skull I saw!"

"What skull?" Grayson asked. "I don't know anything about a skull. Geez, Drex. I'm trying to *help* you!"

"*Help* me?"

"Yes. With your detective license, remember?"

My eyes narrowed. "Oh. In that case, thank you very much. I'll send Officer Paulson to pick you up."

I hit the gas. The Mustang's wheels spun in the sand.

"Come on, Drex," Grayson said, holding up his hands. "I don't want you to call the police."

I scowled. "You're in some kind of trouble with the law, aren't you? I *knew* it!"

Grayson shook his head. "No. I swear. I just ... I don't want my name in a public incident report, okay? Come on, I'm no killer. See? I'm too charming." He tried to wink his swollen eye, but only managed a flinch.

I sneered at him. "Lots of psychopaths can be charming when they need to be."

He shrugged. "Fair enough. But Drex, I could've killed you a dozen times already if that's what I wanted to do."

I jerked back in horror. "Is that supposed to be reassuring?"

He sighed. "It's the best I can come up with right now."

I stared at the strange man dressed in black. "Who are you really, Grayson?"

He touched the bruise on his cheek just below his swollen eye. "I'm a physicist."

Suddenly, the horror and fear clinching my gut evaporated. No one could make up a story like that. Not on the fly. Not with a Tootsie Pop freshly hurled into his eye.

"Prove it," I said.

Grayson smiled ingratiatingly. "Uh ... E equals MC squared?"

I laughed. I don't know why. Probably from sheer hysteria.

Grayson grinned. "Well, aren't we a pair. You think I'm Ted Bundy, and you look like John Wayne Gacy."

I shot a quick glance in the rearview mirror. My wig had flown off during the fracas, exposing my red, exceedingly receding hairline. Last night's mascara had melted into black rings around my eyes.

If that weren't bad enough, it wasn't blood that I'd felt earlier, when I'd first seen that skull.

It was urine.

I'd peed my pants.

Just when I think life can't get any crappier, it can.

I laid my hands over the steering wheel, rested my bullet-riddled forehead on my forearms, and laughed and laughed and laughed and laughed.

Chapter Thirty-Six

GRAYSON HELPED ME CHANGE the tire on the Mustang. Actually, he changed the tire while I fixed my wig and held him at gunpoint with his own Glock. This time, it wasn't so much because I didn't trust him, but because I had the upper hand. Besides, I needed the practice—for my P.I. license and all. This go around, however, I made sure the damned gun was loaded.

Changing the tire and handing over his gun to me were part of the deal Grayson had made in exchange for me giving him a ride back to civilization—and for not calling the cops.

The other part of the deal was that he had to come clean about who he was and what he was really up to out here in the middle of nowhere. He'd agreed to my terms without argument. Apparently, Grayson didn't feel like dying in a backwoods crap hole, either.

"So why'd you lie to me about being William Knickerbocker?" I asked, enjoying the weight of the Glock in my hand.

Grayson looked up from cranking the lug-nut wrench. "Because I didn't want to leave a trail. I'm kind of a big deal in some scientific circles. If the academic board found out I was chasing Mothman ... well, let's just say it could put a damper on my already fragile credibility, if you know what I mean."

"What about the whole private investigator malarkey?"

Grayson looked surprised. "That isn't malarkey. I am. A private investigator, I mean."

I sneered. "That seems highly implausible."

Grayson wagged his eyebrows. "Perhaps, yet it remains tantalizingly within the realms of theoretical possibility."

I gave him half an eye roll. "I guess being a physicist pays for your hobby hunting monsters?"

"More like the other way around. Physicists don't get paid jack. That's why I quit, kind of."

"So you really *can* make good money as a P.I.?"

Grayson shook his head. "It's always about the money with you."

I frowned. "I've got bills to pay. *Big* bills. *Hospital* bills."

"How much?"

I grimaced. "I don't know. I'm afraid to call them back."

Grayson frowned. "I detest doctors. No. I take that back. I detest the Western medical model."

"Why?"

"The whole thing is based on being dead."

My eyebrows converged below the crater in the middle of my forehead. "What?"

"Long story short, about four hundred years ago—"

"Hold on," I said, waving the gun. "You said 'short.'"

Grayson grinned and tightened the last lug nut. "Once upon a time, the Pope sanctioned this French guy named Descartes to dissect cadavers for scientific purposes. Now, thanks to his work, the entire Western medical model is based on the premise that we're nothing more than a biological machine made out of meat and bones."

"So?"

"Believe me, we're a lot more than that."

I sighed. "Are you saying that we have a soul? I thought you were a physicist, not a preacher."

"We don't *have* a soul, Drex. We *are* a soul. The body's merely a semi-material manifestation for our exploration and experimentation in third-dimension reality."

I crinkled my nose. "Okay. *Now* I believe you're a physicist. Can you repeat what you just said *in English?*"

"We need a body to maneuver this earthly plain. You can't drive a car without a foot on the gas pedal. No foot, no car, no go. See?"

"Sort of ...."

Grayson stood up and dusted off his knees. "Look, enough lessons for one day. What say we head over to the A&P, like you'd planned in the first place?"

"Okay. But I want to know more about—"

"Quantum physics?" Grayson asked hopefully.

"No. How you made your money as a P.I."

Grayson sighed. "You do have a persistently one-track mind, Drex. To the point of dogged determination, one might say."

I eyed him suspiciously. "When I'm interested in the subject, sure."

He smiled. "Good. *Your* motivation is money. *Mine* is mystery. Pursuing 'monsters' as you call them, takes persistence. And determination. And discretion. Extracting evidentiary material of the as-yet esoteric is a huge challenge."

I wasn't exactly sure what he was talking about, but didn't want to appear dumb. "Then why do it?"

"Simple. I want to be the first person to prove their existence beyond a shadow of a doubt."

I frowned. "Excuse me, but going back to that whole bell curve thingy you mentioned the other day. Do you think the *intellectual collective* is ready for the truth? About Mothman and bigfoot, I mean?"

Grayson's lip curled upward. "Well, that's just it, isn't it? I have to come up with a better version of the facts before it can become the new truth."

"Let me wrap my head around this," I said. "If your version becomes the new truth, it becomes the new reality? Or is it the other way around?"

Grayson grinned. "And I thought you were just a pretty face."

I smiled. No one had called me pretty since Grandma Selma passed away. I didn't like to think I was vain, but his compliment felt pretty damned good.

"So, should we gather some provisions before we head to your first stakeout?" Grayson asked.

I grinned. "Sure. What do you usually eat when you're tailing someone?"

"What most lovers of the unexplained eat, of course. Cheetos."

My nose crinkled. "Cheetos? Why?"

"Because no one's ever been able to scientifically prove what they're made of. Plus, they have the added bonus of glowing orange in the dark."

I shook my head. "Okay. To the A&P it is."

As I shifted into first, a thought hit me. I turned to Grayson. "What about the skull I saw in the woods? Shouldn't someone know about it?"

Grayson locked eyes with me. "I suspect *someone* already does."

I reached for my phone. "I'm going to call Paulson."

"Do what you want," Grayson said. "But if it were up to me, I'd wait until after our stakeout. It might not be safe for Paulson to go out into those woods alone. He's going to need backup."

"But shouldn't we at least warn him? We're out here goofing around looking for some Mothman freak when there could be a psycho killer on the loose."

Grayson locked eyes with me. "Who says the two things aren't inter-related?"

My mouth fell open. "You think they are?"

Grayson shrugged. "In the world of quantum physics, Drex, *everything's* interrelated."

Chapter Thirty-Seven

WHILE GRAYSON WANDERED the aisles of the A&P grocery store in Waldo, I snuck into the restroom to call Beth-Ann for a reality check.

"Hey, you got a minute?" I whispered into the phone.

"Just closing up shop. I swear I think I may be the only person on the planet still doing permanent waves."

"Listen, you were right about Knickerbocker. He *was* using that name as an alias. He said he did it to keep under the radar with his colleagues. His real name is Nick Grayson."

"Nick Grayson?" Beth-Ann's tired voice picked up a lilt. "Now *there's* a name I can work with. Still, too bad he's bald."

"He's not. His head's shaved. His hair's growing back."

"Does this mean you're calling dibs on him?"

"Geez! No. I was calling because ... well, I don't know whether to trust him or not. We went out to Bullet Point, you know, to shoot a few rounds. I found a skull in the grass—"

"What?" Beth-Ann nearly choked. "A *human* skull?"

"I don't know. I didn't get that good a look at it. I ... uh ... kind of freaked and ran. Then Grayson shot out my tire—"

"He *what?* Good grief! Are you okay?"

"Yeah. It was all a big misunderstanding. At least, I'm pretty sure it was."

"Now you listen here, Ms. Roberta Drex," Beth-Ann barked. "You stay out of the woods with that guy! He could be a madman. Like that Unabomber dude. He could have been living in the woods in that camper for years, getting crazier by the hour!"

"That's what I thought, too. At first. But if that were true, he could've killed me by now."

A toilet flushed. Nosy Nellie Parker emerged from a stall. I turned my back on her and cupped my hand over the phone.

"Maybe he's playing games," Beth-Ann said. "Building your trust."

"But why?" I whispered.

"Who knows? Blood sport? Why do psycho killers do anything they do?"

Parker washed her hands and hit the hand dryer.

"He says he's a physicist," I yelled over the noise.

"What? Like that pi-R-squared crap?"

"Yeah."

"Why are you yelling? Is this some kind of code? Has he got you at gunpoint?"

"What? No."

The hand dryer went off. Parker gave me the once-over and left the bathroom.

"Okay. Maybe you're right," Beth-Ann said. "If I were a serial killer, I'd have picked an easier cover. You know, like a restaurateur or janitor or something. Physicist seems like a weird choice for an alibi."

I bit my lip. "So maybe he's okay after all?"

"I dunno. Maybe. Either way, please tell me you'll be careful, okay?"

"I will. I'm going on a stakeout with him tonight at nine-thirty at the Stop & Shoppe."

"A stakeout at Artie's? You're kidding!"

"It's a long story. Have you ever heard of the Mothman?"

"The Mothman? Yeah. But what's that got to do—"

"I gotta go. Call me at ten tonight, would you? To make sure I'm still alive?"

"Absolutely. Be safe."

"I will," I said, then clicked off the phone, adjusted my wig in the mirror, and went off to find Grayson.

GRAYSON AND I WERE sitting in my Mustang by the side of the road in the dark, weeds up to the windows. On the opposite side of Obsidian Road, the fluorescent lights of the Stop & Shoppe gave off a bluish-white glow in the gloom, as if the place was some forlorn ghost of failed merchandising past.

"You're getting crumbs all over the seat," I grumbled at Grayson as he crunched on a handful of Cheetos. "You know, that isn't the healthiest stakeout food in the world—or the stealthiest. You're leaving a trail of orange goop all over the place."

"You're right." Grayson waggled his orange fingertips at me. "Could you imagine committing a murder with Cheetos fingers? No way to make a clean getaway."

I crinkled my nose. "Gross."

Grayson grinned. "Max Planck had it right when he said the world we perceive through our senses is only a tiny fragment of the vastness of Nature."

I rolled my eyes. "I doubt he was talking about Cheetos crumbs. Who's Max Planck, anyway?"

Grayson shot me a stunned look. "You don't know who Max—oh, how sad. Everybody knows Einstein. But poor Max Planck. Every bit as brilliant a physicist, yet cast to the second shelf of history."

I blew out a bored laugh. "Yeah, I hate when that happens. Poor Max. Was he another starving physicist, or did he become a P.I. like you, to pay the bills?"

"Neither. Max did all right for himself without a second job."

I sneered. "How nice for him. You know, you still haven't explained how you got all that cash in your glovebox."

Grayson shrugged. "Like they say, 'Do what you love and the money comes.' The pursuit of the mystical and unexplained is what makes me feel alive, Drex."

I shot him a sour look. "Yeah? Paying the rent makes *me* feel alive. Or, at least, it gives me the fleeting feeling I might survive for another month."

He laughed. "You're such a cynic. Okay. Let's just say I found something that was worth a lot of money to the right client."

I perked up. "What kind of client is the *right* client?"

"I only have one criteria. My client is always H.B."

"H.B.? You mean—*Halle Barry?*"

"No. Highest bidder."

"*Highest* bidder? You mean there's more than one nutcase out there interested in this stuff?"

Grayson sighed. "I'm glad to see you're keeping an open mind. You'd be surprised how many people want to get their hands on evidence that defies all conventional explanation. With rarity comes great value."

"So what was it you cashed in ... excuse me ... *collected evidence* on?"

Grayson glanced out the window. "Sorry. That's on a need-to-know basis."

"Come on, Grayson!"

Grayson went through the motions of locking his busted lip and throwing away the key.

I snorted. "You're such an idiot. Okay. I give. What does it take to be privy to this secret information of yours?"

"*Trusting* me, for one," Grayson said. "And being a partner."

"You have *partners?*"

He shrugged. "Had."

"What happened to them?"

"That's also on a need-to-know basis."

Jerk!

I turned and glared out the windshield, then held a pair of binoculars to my eyes so Grayson couldn't see how pissed off I was. I focused in on the Stop & Shoppe. After adjusting the viewfinder, I realized Artie was bending over the ice-cream freezer. I was staring right into his big, fat butt-crack. I groaned in disgust.

"What now?" Grayson asked.

"Nothing."

"Look, sorry about the Cheetos crumbs," he said. "But if you want to be a P.I., you're going to need a different car anyway. This one is way too conspicuous. You need some kind of gray, late-model, blend-into-the-scenery kind of vehicle."

"Oh. You mean like an old, algae-covered RV?"

"I'm on vacation."

"For how long? That thing looks like you've been camping in it since the Y2K scare."

Grayson sighed. "Okay. You have a point. But as far as RVs go, you have to admit, no one would ever suspect what I'm doing in it. Your Mustang here is the equivalent of me riding around in a shiny red bus with *Monster Hunter on Tour* emblazoned all over it."

Apparently, every single thing about my life is wrong. Even the stupid car I'm driving.

I was more than ready for a change of subject. "What time is it?" I asked.

"Nine twenty-six."

"Getting close to nine thirty. Let's concentrate on the Stop & Shoppe for now."

"Good idea."

We sat in silence, binoculars trained on the dilapidated old gas station. Not a damned thing happened—unless you counted Artie lifting up a butt cheek to fart.

I checked my phone. It was 9:57 p.m. "I think it's time we—"

Grayson's cellphone pinged. He glanced at it, then over at me. "It's Vanderhoff. She's getting a phone call."

I smirked. "Maybe it's Matlock."

Grayson grinned and put his phone on speaker.

"Penelope? Is that you?" a man's voice asked.

"Why, it sure is, tiger."

The voice was Vanderhoff's. In sexy mode.

Yuck.

"So nice of you to call," she said. "I was just thinking I'd have to go to bed all by my lonesome tonight."

The man laughed huskily. "Well, we wouldn't want that. Are you wearing those sexy little red panties of yours?"

"You know I am. And now they're getting all w—"

I reached over and clicked off the phone. "I don't want to hear any more. I already threw up in my mouth a little."

Grayson laughed. "Phone sex operators. Always the ones you'd never suspect, am I right?"

I grimaced, trying to block the vision my mind was trying to form. "Well, at least now I know how she supplements her Social Security check."

"What say we cruise through the Stop & Shoppe for a six-pack to celebrate?" Grayson said.

I frowned. "Celebrate *what?*"

"Your first stakeout."

"But it was a bust." I reached down to crank the engine.

"Yeah, but we sat in the car for over twenty minutes without killing each other. That should count for—" Grayson's eyes shifted to the Stop & Shoppe. "Hold on! What's that?"

Grayson lifted his binoculars to his eyes and trained them on something across the road.

"It's Artie," I deadpanned. "Wow. He actually got out of his chair."

"No," Grayson whispered. "Up on the roof."

I tipped my binoculars up slightly. There they were. Those red eyes again, just like two nights ago. "Oh, my—"

I never had a chance to finish my sentence.

Suddenly, the red eyes dipped, then headed right at us.

In the dim light of a quarter moon, a huge, bat-like creature swooped down over the car. As it passed over us, I stuck my head out the window and watched, slack-jawed, as it disappear over the treetops behind us.

Chapter Thirty-Eight

"WHAT WAS *that*?" I squealed.

"Mothman!" Grayson said, like a kid who just spotted Santa. "Come on! Let's see if it landed in the trees behind us!"

I winced. "Are you out of your freaking gourd?"

Grayson flung open the car door. "Depends on who you ask. Are you coming?"

I grabbed his arm. "Wait! It might've been a helicopter. You know, chasing an escaped convict."

Grayson grinned at me. "Sure. If the convict was flying."

My phone buzzed, scaring the bejeebers out of me. Grayson broke free of my grip and disappeared into the woods. I clicked on the phone.

"You still alive?" Beth-Ann whispered.

"Yes, I think so," I whispered back.

"Did you see Mothman?"

"Uh ... thanks for calling, Beth-Ann, but I gotta go."

I clicked off the phone and sat there, too stunned to move.

Had I? Had I really just seen Mothman?

Suddenly I realized I was alone. In the dark. With my car window open! I grabbed the crank and pumped it furiously. Nothing happened.

"What the—?"

Then I remembered the windowpane had broken at Bullet Point. My mind began to jump around like a squirrel on a hot stove.

Was that part of Grayson's plan all along?

I shot an arm across the passenger seat to roll up the other window. Something grabbed my shoulder from behind. I screamed, whirled around, and hurled a blind punch at whatever had a hold of me.

"Ouch!" Grayson yelled. "Drex, it's me!"

"You scared the crap out of me!" I screeched, wringing my painful knuckles.

Grayson opened his mouth to speak, but his cellphone pinged with another text alarm. He looked at the display. "Vanderhoff again," he said, and ran around the car. He jumped into the passenger seat and clicked his phone to speaker mode.

"Hello?" Vanderhoff said.

"*Beep. Beep. Beep.* You weren't there," a mechanical voice said. "Tell no one ... or you're next."

"Tell no one *what?*" Vanderhoff asked. Her voice sounded frail and shaky.

The line went dead.

"So she's not crazy after all," I whispered. I turned to Grayson. "What do you think this means?"

Grayson shook his head. "I don't know. But maybe we should do the same thing. For now, anyway."

"Do what?"

Grayson's green eyes locked onto mine.

"Don't tell anybody. You know. For Vanderhoff's sake."

Chapter Thirty-Nine

I WOKE UP THE NEXT morning shivering. I reached for Grandma Selma's afghan at the foot of my bed. It wasn't there. I sat up. In the pinkish-gray of twilight, I couldn't see it anywhere.

I crawled out of bed and looked around the room. It wasn't on the floor, either. I got on my hands and knees to look under the bed.

When I lifted the dust ruffle, two red, glowing eyes stared back at me. I nearly swallowed my tonsils.

A squeaky, ghost of a scream made it halfway up my throat, then collapsed into a disgusted groan. The eyes weren't eyes. They were the reflectors on a pair of hand weights I wore back when I used to work out.

Geez. I hope this isn't going to be one of those crappy days that lasts a freaking week.

I put a hand on the bed for leverage and hauled myself up off my knees. Shivering from the cold, I slipped out of my sleeping sweats into work sweats, then climbed into my coveralls. As I padded to the kitchen in my stockinged feet to get the coffee going, a random brain cell fired.

I'd left Grandma Selma's afghan in her apartment the night I'd slept on the couch to keep an eye on Grayson.

Duh!

I dumped coffee into a filter and was contemplating taking a shower when I heard the sound of Earl banging around in the garage's service bay below. I turned on the pot, tugged on a jacket, stuck my feet into my father's boots, and made a quick clomp downstairs for a progress report on Grayson's RV.

To be honest, my motivation was more out of self-defense that curiosity. If I was going to face Grayson this morning, my poor, addled brain needed a topic of conversation a tad lighter than his screwy metaphysical philosophy.

"How's it going?" I asked Earl's backside. He was bent over the engine compartment of the old RV, tinkering with something or another.

"Not too bad. I need a couple more parts." Earl straightened up and handed me a list scrawled on a scrap of paper. "Be good if we could get 'em ordered this morning, boss man."

I glanced over the list. "Sure. Go ahead."

"How'd your date go with Grayson last night?" Earl teased as he stuffed the list back into his pocket.

"It wasn't a date. We just ... you know ... shot stuff."

Earl grinned. "Sure you did." He turned and stuck his head back under the hood of the RV.

I should've just turned around and gone back upstairs. Earl ate up conspiracy theories like Cheerios. But I had a burning question on my mind, and my smartphone was still too smart for me to figure out how to search the internet with it. That, and the bifocal demon had finally caught up with me. I needed glasses to read the damned cellphone screen. Glasses I couldn't afford—both financially and cosmetically.

I closed my eyes, took a deep breath, and said, "Hey Earl, you ever heard of Mothman?"

He popped up from under the hood. "Mothballs? Sure. I can't stand—"

"No. Moth*man*."

Earl's eyes lit up. "That critter what scared the daylights outta them people up in West Virginia? Sure, I heard of it."

"What did it turn out to be?"

"Turn out to be? It was the *Mothman*, Bobbie."

I suppressed a groan. "I mean in the official reports. What did they say it was?"

Earl raised an eyebrow, grabbed his stubbly chin, and rubbed beneath his nose with his index finger. "They never did say for sure. Some folks thought it came from outer space. Some thought it was a giant bat, all swoll-up and deformed by radioactive crap from that abandoned military place it hung around."

I cringed, but kept going. "Why would people think it was from outer space?"

"On account of seeing all kind of strange lights in the sky. And them weird phone calls."

My back stiffened. "What kind of phone calls?"

"Clicks. Beeps. Static. Stuff like that, mostly. Then these guys in black showed up and started tellin' everybody not to say nothing about what they saw. That's *really* why people think Mothman was the real deal, Bobbie. If it was a hoax, why would these guys come around and tell them folks to keep quiet about it?"

"What guys?"

"The weird dudes in black. That's where that whole 'men in black' thing came from, I think."

I frowned. "What were they like? These men in black?"

"Folks said they looked human, mostly. But something was always off about 'em. Some had real big, googly eyes. Like a bug. Some wore clothes that was out of style."

"Earl, that describes half of Alachua County."

Earl laughed. "I'm talking *really* old stuff. Like from the '40s and '50s. Or clothes that looked like they came from the future. They also spoke kind of stiff-like. Used old-fashioned words. A few of 'em didn't know basic stuff, either. Like it was the first time they'd ever set foot on Earth."

"What do you mean?"

"Well, I remember something about this one guy who tried to drink Jell-O."

I blew out an annoyed breath. "He was probably just drunk. You're full of it, Earl."

"Am not! You know, now that I think about it, when Knickerbocker come up in here, he was all dressed in black." He made googly eyes at me. "Maybe he's one of them M-I-B's. Think about it, Bobbie. He showed up here outta nowhere. And he's always wearing that funny old hat."

I scowled. "He wears that hat because his head is cold." I blew out a frustrated sigh. "How much longer before the RV is fixed?"

Earl shrugged. "Might have it ready for a test run tomorrow. Why?"

"I need to give Grayson a progress report this morning."

"Where is he?"

"Upstairs."

Earl's face took on a mischievous look. "Well, while he's not here, let me show you something I found in his RV. Maybe you'll change your mind about your boyfriend being one of them M-I-B weirdos."

The part of me that wanted to tell Earl to mind his own business got kicked to the curb by the part of me dying to know what he'd uncovered. I followed my cousin over to the RV's side door, and then crept inside with him.

I was expecting Earl to show me a baby alien in a pickle jar. Instead, he pointed to the kitchen and said, "Look."

My nose crinkled in disappointment. "What?"

"All them cabinets is locked."

I stared at the small padlocks on the kitchen cabinets. "So?"

"Why would he lock up his cabinets?"

"So stuff doesn't fall out when he's traveling? Or so nosy jerks like you don't go through them?"

Earl shrugged. "All right. But why would he have eight deadbolts on his *bedroom door?*"

"How should I know? Same reason? To keep you out?"

"I'm telling you, Bobbie. Something ain't kosher with that feller. Why you asking me about the Mothman anyway?" Earl grinned. "Wait. Don't tell me. That's what Knickerbocker calls his little man, ain't it? Did you get a look at it last night?"

"No!" I growled. "He's a *customer*. That's all. Now get back to work."

I turned to go. Earl called after me.

"Hey Bobbie, you ever smelled mothballs?"

I turned back around. "Yeah. Why?"

"How'd you get your big nose between his tiny legs?"

"Earl, you're fired."

I turned and stomped out of the garage. My cousin had aggravated the stew out of me for the millionth time. But he'd also gotten me thinking.

Why *hadn't* Grayson mentioned anything about men in black when he told me about the Mothman case?

Chapter Forty

AS I REACHED THE TOP of the stairs, Grayson came out of Grandma Selma's apartment. I couldn't help but notice he was dressed all in black, including that old fedora.

Could he really be an MIB like Earl said?

"Good morning," Grayson said pleasantly. "Coffee ready?"

"Yeah. Sure. Come on in."

As he followed me into my apartment, my mind raced around like a rat on a greased Hot Wheels track. Earl was right. Grayson *did* come out of nowhere. He wore black clothes. Yesterday, he drank barbeque sauce like it was a shot of whisky, and licked salt like a Jersey cow. He claimed to be a physicist ....

Oh my word! A man from outer space would be well acquainted with physics, wouldn't he? It was the perfect foil!

"You call Paulson?" Grayson asked.

I whirled around. Grayson was putting a dash of salt in his coffee mug. I stared, open-mouthed.

"What?" he said. "It cuts the bitterness."

My cellphone buzzed. I looked at the display. "It's the hospital again."

"Answer it, Drex. They're not going to go away."

I groaned and picked up the phone. "Hello?"

"Roberta Drex?" a woman's voice asked.

"Yes."

"I'm calling for Dr. Brown. He'd like for you to come in for an appointment."

"What for?"

"He'd like to discuss your MRI results."

I cringed. "Can't you tell me over the phone?"

"No, I'm afraid not. Please. He says it's imperative that you come in as soon as possible."

"Tomorrow?"

"I had a cancellation. The doctor's got an opening in an hour if you can make it."

I sighed. "Okay. I'll be there." I clicked off the phone.

"What's the deal?" Grayson asked.

"I dunno. Dr. Brown wants to see me right away. It can't be good. Unless .... Maybe this whole thing is a trap to shake me down for the bill."

Grayson's lip twisted. "I wouldn't put it past them. Blasted doctors. Speaking of jerks, did you call Paulson yet?"

I shot Grayson a look. "Yes. I told him about finding the skull out at Bullet Point."

"What did he say?"

"That he'd check it out. And I should get some rest. He thinks I could've had another post-concussion hallucination."

"Huh." Grayson took a sip of coffee. "So he thinks the skull could be another false sighting? Besides the dead guy in the orange jumpsuit and the dead guy who shot you?"

"Yeah."

Greyson tapped his upper lip with an index finger. "Spooky action at a distance."

"What?"

"Quantum physics theory. You see—"

My mind glazed over. "Save it. Maybe Paulson's right. Maybe I *am* imagining things. I haven't felt like myself since the accident." I glanced at the clock. "Crap. I've got to be at the hospital in Gainesville in an hour. I better get going."

Grayson followed me toward the door. "Can I catch a ride with you into town?"

"I guess. But first, tell me where you got your physics degree."

"The University of Hard Knocks."

I turned, suddenly angry. "I'm serious, Grayson!"

Grayson held his hands up. "MIT. Geez! Don't shoot."

I scowled. "Sorry. I'm just nervous."

"Understandable. Nothing good ever came from an MRI."

"Or an MIT," I muttered to myself, then I stumbled down the stairs toward the garage, Grayson hot on my heels.

When we got to the service bay, Earl was hunched over the RV's engine again, singing along with Madonna to *Material Girl*.

I suddenly felt all alone in the world.

I turned to Grayson. "Will you come to the hospital with me to see Dr. Brown?"

Grayson's left eyebrow shot up. "*Me?* Why?"

"Who else am I going to take? *Him?*"

Grayson glanced over at Earl and blew out a breath. "You have a point. Okay. I guess I owe you one."

Chapter Forty-One

"YOU COULD BE SUFFERING from a coup contrecoup concussion," Grayson said as we climbed into the Mustang.

"A coo-coo what?"

"Coup contrecoup. It's a kind of brain injury. A coup injury happens when your head's struck by a moving object. A contrecoup injury occurs when your head is moving and hits a stationary object. You said the bullet hit you, then you hit the sidewalk. You could've sustained a kind of 'rebound' injury to both sides of your brain. Both a coup and a contrecoup."

"Oh."

"That might explain the strange visions," Grayson continued. "You may be having flashbacks, or memories mixed together."

"You mean my brain may be scrambled?" I turned the key in the ignition. The Mustang roared to life. I scowled at the dashboard.

Yeah, sure. Now *you're working just fine. Stupid car.*

"Eh ... not exactly," Grayson said. "The effects of a coup contrecoup injury are usually temporary. But, then again, they can last a long time, too."

I steered the car out onto Obsidian Road. "How do you know all this stuff?"

"Head injuries can change people. They can cause your personality to shift—your brain function to shift. In some cases, even your brain *capabilities* to shift. That's how I got my eidetic memory."

"I have an idiotic memory, too," I said. "Why is it that I can only remember totally useless stuff?"

"Not idiotic. *Eidetic.* I have total recall of stuff I've seen for just a few seconds. My memory's like a photo album. I can kind of go in and view memories like they're photographs."

"You're saying you have a photographic memory?"

"Yes and no. With a photographic memory, you can recall pages of text, lists of numbers, that kind of thing. But a true photographic memory has never been proven to exist."

I shot Grayson some sarcastic side-eye. "Tell that to anyone who's ever walked in on their parents in bed together."

Grayson laughed. "Fair enough."

"So you got your great memory from an accident," I said. "Should I believe you, or is this another cover story? Maybe you're really some super-brained alien from another planet."

Grayson's lip curled sinisterly. "I'd tell you, Drex, but then I'd have to erase your memory."

I nearly steered into the ditch. "You can *do* that?"

"Your question is irrelevant," he said in a strange, robotic tone.

I thought about punching the jerk in the arm. Instead, I decided to take the bait. "Why?" I asked.

Grayson smiled at me, then spoke in his normal voice. "Because, Drex. If I could erase your memory, how would you ever know?"

"DR. BROWN WILL SEE you now," the nurse said. The look on her face made me feel as if she'd read my charts and knew I shouldn't be buying any green bananas.

"Come in with me," I pleaded with Grayson, and took his hand. I still had serious doubts about the guy, but if some stranger in a lab coat was going to walk into a room that smelled like disinfectant and tell me I only had hours to live, I didn't want to be alone when I heard the news.

Any port in a storm.

"Ms. Drex," Dr. Brown said as I entered his office. He looked surprised when Grayson followed me in. "Who's this?"

"My fiancé," I said. I smiled and squeezed Grayson's hand. He surprised me by squeezing back. My already pounding heart thumped a beat faster.

"Have a seat," Dr. Brown said. "I'll come to the point. We found an anomaly on your MRI."

My shoulders slumped. "What kind of anomaly? Am I going to die?"

"First of all, it's not life-threatening at this point. At least, not as far as we can tell."

I stared at the stranger in the lab coat. "What do you mean? What's wrong with me?"

Dr. Brown stabbed a finger at the MRI scan on his desk. "See this mass here next to your pineal gland? It's vestigial."

"I'm going to be a vegetable?" I squeaked.

"*Vestigial*. It's the remnants of your *twin*, Ms. Drex."

My mouth fell open. "My *twin*? How is that possible? I didn't have a twin."

"But you *did*," the doctor said. "It just didn't wholly survive gestation. You see, early in your mother's pregnancy, your fetus absorbed the embryonic mass that was supposed to become your twin brother. He vanished, if you will. Except for this small mass of tissue here."

"How do you know the twin was a male?" Grayson asked.

The doctor looked up from the scan. "Well, a vestigial twin can be completely formed, or it can be a random clump of cells or body parts. An arm, teeth, that kind of thing. Given the shape and density of the mass, the vestigial twin in Ms. Drex's brain appears to be made entirely of ... ahem ... *gonadal* tissue."

"*What!*" I shot a glance at Grayson. He was pursing his lips. Whether it was from concern over my health or he was trying not to laugh, I couldn't tell. My head was too busy swimming against a tsunami of unexpected, unwanted thoughts ....

"What's the prognosis?" I heard Grayson ask.

His voice sounded dull, as if he were underwater. Too stunned to react, I sat still and passive as the two men spoke to each other about me as if I weren't there.

"The mass is at the center of her brain," Dr. Brown said. "It would be extremely difficult to remove surgically. But as long as she's not displaying adverse symptoms and the mass doesn't enlarge, I believe the best course of action is to leave it as it is and monitor it every few months."

"Keep an eye on it. Make sure it doesn't sprout limbs." Grayson said, his voice echoing in my clogged ears.

Dr. Brown's eyes widened. "Well, in a manner of speaking, yes."

"I'd like to take the scans with me," Grayson said.

"These are part of Ms. Drex's confidential medical files."

Grayson stood up. "She paid for them, didn't she?"

Dr. Brown shrunk back in his chair. "Well, technically, no. Not until she settles her bill."

"How much is it?" Grayson asked.

"I ... I don't know. I don't handle such things."

"Of course not. A doctor never sullies himself by talking about money." Grayson turned to me. "Drex, wait here. I'll be right back."

"Where's he going?" Dr. Brown asked as Grayson disappeared out the door.

"I have no idea. Am I going to be all right, doctor?"

"Ms. Drex, I'm a doctor, not God. Only *he* knows for sure."

A hot flare of indignation thawed my frozen state. "Typical," I muttered to myself. "Of course God has to be a *man*."

"What?" Dr. Brown asked.

"Nothing. Doctor, what will happen if this thing ... this twin ... *gets bigger?*"

"If it begins to exert pressure on your brain, any manner of symptoms could occur."

"Like hallucinations?"

"Well, yes. I suppose. Why? Have you had any?"

"I ... uh ...."

Grayson burst back into the office. He shoved a receipt in front of Dr. Brown's face. "Bill's paid in full." He grabbed the MRI and my file from the doctor's desk and turned to face me. I was speechless.

"Ready to go, dear fiancé?" he asked.

I bolted to my feet like a conspirator in a prison break. "Absolutely."

"She should be under the care of a physician," Dr. Brown said.

"She will be," Grayson replied. "I'm a doctor."

Dr. Brown's expression was as stunned as mine.

"I'll be sending for the rest of her records," Grayson said. "In the meantime, thank you, Doctor, and have a good day."

Grayson locked his arm around mine and led me out the door. I wanted to press him for details about paying my bill, but was distracted by an orderly pushing a patient on a gurney. Her head was wrapped like a mummy.

"I don't want that to happen to me," I whimpered.

"What?"

"The patient who just went by. She just had brain surgery or something."

"Don't worry," Grayson said. "I don't think you'll need it. I think I know what's going on here."

I looked up into his eyes. "What? It's not that coup contraband thing, is it?"

He smiled sourly. "You really should pay more attention, Drex. No. It's not that."

"What, then?"

"I'll explain on the ride home."

I winced. "Will you have to erase my memory afterward?"

Grayson kept his eyes ahead. "We'll see. But at this rate, I don't think it'll be necessary. You don't seem capable of holding a straight thought in your head."

Chapter Forty-Two

"THANK GOD I DIDN'T take Earl with me," I said, sucking in a lungful of fresh air as we headed toward the Mustang in the hospital parking lot. "He already thinks I'm half guy. Now I've got the gonad to prove it."

Grayson shot me a look. "Having a gonad doesn't make you half a guy, Drex."

"It doesn't?"

"No. It makes you a hermaphrodite."

I scowled. "If you're trying to cheer me up, you should work on your bedside manner, Dr. Grayson. What kind of doctor are you, anyway? Or was that just another lie?"

Grayson looked offended. "What do you mean *another* lie?"

"Are you a brain surgeon, or what?"

"I'm a certified holistic practitioner."

"Holistic medicine? Isn't that curing people with rocks and crystals and psychic crapola?"

"Don't forget needles and potions and poultices," Grayson said sourly.

"Oh, great." I fumbled for the keys.

"I think I should drive, Drex. You're in no shape to be behind the wheel. In your state, you might mistake a red light for a black hole."

After just finding out I had my twin's gonad kicking me in the pineal, I didn't bother to argue his point. I handed Grayson the keys. He opened the passenger door for me, waited until I was buckled in, and handed me my medical scans.

As he closed the door and walked around to the driver's seat, an odd numbness overtook me. I felt out of my element—as if I'd fallen down a hole and landed in someone else's life ... in someone else's reality.

This can't be happening. A man is actually treating me with concern and respect ....

Grayson scooted into the driver's seat. I turned to face him. "Grayson, I don't know how to thank you. I'll pay you back—"

"Forget it." He closed the driver's door and reached for the ignition. "That was a lot for you to take in. We should do an energy clearing on you when we get back to your place."

I crinkled my nose. "Energy clearing? Couldn't I just get a chocolate milkshake instead? Now that I'm gonna die, who cares about my thighs?"

Grayson shook his head. "You're not dying, Drex. Look, I know you don't believe it, but alternative healing modalities have been around for thousands of years. Why would people keep using them if they didn't work?"

I shot him a look. "Because they didn't have *real* medicine back then?"

"Oh. So sawing open your skull, digging out parts of it and hoping for the best is *real* medicine?"

I shrunk back in my seat. This wasn't happening. The scans had to be wrong. My nose grew hot. I fought back tears. I glanced over at Grayson. "You said you think you know what's wrong with me. So, what is it?"

"It's just a theory. I need to run some tests on you first." He reached to put the key in the ignition.

"Tests? What, are you going to do? Read my aura? Fix a hole in my psychic energy field?"

"No." He cranked the engine.

"Come on," I said. "Have you ever seen any of that holistic crap work?"

Grayson put his hand on the gear shaft, then stopped. "Yes. I absolutely have. I don't know why you're so skeptical, Drex. There've been at least a hundred scientifically run clinical trials demonstrating the effectiveness of all sorts of things that, according to Western medicine, shouldn't work."

I sniffed back a tear. "Like what?"

"Well, take *the placebo effect*, for one. In tons of pharmaceutical trials, people given a sugar pill got results as good as those taking the actual medicine. Stuff like *that* drives doctors nuts. But it kind of proves the whole tenet behind the holistic approach."

"What? That everything's a crapshoot?"

Grayson sighed and shook his head. "No. Just the opposite. Everything's a *placebo*, Drex. If you *believe* whatever it is you're doing will heal you, it will. Holistic medicine taps into our inner capacity to heal ourselves."

"So you think I can get rid of this twin thing by wishing it away?"

Grayson shrugged. "Maybe. But then again, why would you want to? You're unique, Drex. And I think that's why you've been seeing things."

I leaned over, closer to him. "Why?"

"You heard the doctor. The vestigial twin. The impact of the bullet must've dislodged it. Shaken it loose somehow. Now it's pushing up against your pineal gland."

"So? What's that got to do with seeing things?"

Grayson studied me for a moment, his green eyes locked on mine. "Some ancient cultures called the pineal the 'third eye.'"

"You mean, like a cyclops?"

"No. The third eye is the *spiritual* eye. The seat of enlightenment. It's the gateway to other worlds ... other *dimensions*, if you will."

"Bull crap, Grayson! We've all got pineal glands. If that were true, we'd *all* be seeing stuff."

Grayson shrugged. "Maybe we do—but mostly when we're kids, before our pineal glands calcify over."

I shot him a look. "What are you talking about?"

"Remember how you were when you were a kid? Carefree. Joyful. Full of imagination and wonder? Anything seemed possible—even creating your own special world."

I frowned. "Sort of, I guess."

"That's what it's like to have a fully-functioning pineal gland." He shifted into reverse and pulled out of the parking space.

I chewed my lip. "So what happens? Why does it quit working?"

Grayson sighed. "Lots of reasons. Adulthood, mainly. Changes in our hormones and diet cause it to calcify. Most people lose function by the time they're seven or eight. Getting it back is what the life work of most mystics and shamans is all about. Some say it's the true goal of yo-gis, and why yoga was developed in the first place."

I studied the windshield as we pulled into traffic. "I thought yoga was an exercise."

"Here in the States, maybe. Power yoga. Swing yoga. They've lost the whole point."

"If it's not to fight flab, what *is* the point of yoga?"

"To awaken the kundalini energy and experience cosmic conscious-ness and union with the divine. To reconnect with the life force that brings bliss."

I sneered. "Well, I hate to break it to you, but my pineal gland must still be calcified. I'm not feeling anything even *close* to bliss."

Grayson laughed. "Drex, you're either the luckiest person on Earth or the *un*luckiest. I guess we'll find out soon enough. Mind if we stop at that medical supply place over there?"

"Why?"

"I need some Ten20 conductive paste. I'd like to give you an elec-troencephalogram."

My eyebrows raised an inch. "Electric shock treatment? No way!"

"No," Grayson said. "An electroencephalogram. To measure your brain waves. I've got my own machine."

"What? Why?"

"Long story."

My nose crinkled. "Will it hurt?"

"Not physically, no."

I bit my lip and weighed my options. It didn't take long, given I had exactly zero. I owed Grayson big time for paying my hospital bill.

"If I let you do this, you promise you won't tell Earl a word about it?"

Grayson raised his hand in a Boy Scout pledge. "As your physician, it's my sworn pledge to maintain your confidentiality. Your medical records are on a need-to-know basis."

I grimaced. "That's what scares me about you, Grayson. Who do you think needs to know?"

WHILE GRAYSON WAS IN the medical supply store, I had just enough time to increase my paranoia to psychosis level.

Why has this strange guy paid my hospital bill? What's in it for him? Am I his human Guinea pig now?

Grayson returned to the car carrying a paper bag. "Have electrode paste, will travel," he quipped.

"So what am I? Some new lab rat for you to experiment on?"

He smiled and climbed in. "I have to admit, your case *is* most intriguing."

"What if I don't want to take your electro-polygraph thing?"

"Electroencephalogram." He handed me the paper bag. "Come on. Like I said, it won't hurt. I do it to myself all the time."

"Wait. Is that why your head's shaved, and you have those tentacle marks all over your skull?"

"Yep." Grayson turned to me and smiled. "Very nice deduction, by the way, future P.I."

Grayson glanced at a point above my eyes. "And, seeing as how your head is already shaved, now's the perfect opportunity to get an initial electroencephalogram of your alpha brain waves. We'll need a baseline for comparison. You see, with your pineal gland reactivation you—"

"Sorry, Grayson," I said, cutting him off. "I'm not so sure about this. Things with you keep getting weirder and weirder. Enough with this baloney!"

Grayson looked taken aback. "It's not *baloney*, Drex. You have a unique opportunity here. I don't want to see you waste it."

"An *opportunity?*" I grumbled. "For what? Seeing things? Going crazy?"

"No," Grayson said calmly. "For seeing things and *not* going crazy."

Chapter Forty-Three

THE MUSTANG FLEW PAST the pinewoods and wide-open pasture-lands between Gainesville and Waldo. An early autumn frost had turned the wiry grasses endless shades of gray. They echoed my mood precisely.

"So how's this electro whatever-agram going to keep me from going crazy?" I asked Grayson as he swerved to miss an already flattened armadillo.

"It's not. It's simply a measuring tool. An EEG displays your alpha brainwave activity. The more alpha waves you produce, the more relaxed your nervous system is."

"So what's the point? Will this thing tell if I'm having hallucinations?"

"No."

"Will it help me to not have them anymore?"

"Highly doubtful."

"Then what's in it for *me?*"

"Quite a lot." Grayson glanced over at me. "I'm offering you a chance to learn to control your body's subconscious reactions with your conscious mind. Think about it, Drex. Whether you're having hallucinations or what you saw was real, if you can train yourself to override your innate fight-or-flight response, you can remain calm in any situation. That's a pretty good skill for a P.I. to have."

I looked over at him. "Is that why you do it? The test, I mean?"

"Yes," Grayson said. "I can't tell you if what you're seeing is real or not. Only you can decide that. The real question is, do you want to be scared out of your wits every time you see something, or do you want to learn to control your reaction?"

I frowned. "Are those my only two options?"

Grayson grinned. "I'm afraid so. What do you say? You ready to let me run an EEG on you?"

"I dunno."

Grayson shot me a boyish grin. "It comes with free tacos from El Molino."

I blew out a breath. "*And* a chocolate shake?"

"You drive a hard bargain, Drex. But okay. Deal."

GRAYSON CRUNCHED A tortilla chip. Shards scattered over the same greasy table in the same greasy booth we'd sat at last time we were in El Molino.

Grayson wiped up the crumbs. "Just think, Drex. You could be sitting on a mountaintop that yogis work their entire lives to climb."

"What are you talking about?" I dawdled with the corn chip in my hand, unable to commit to a bite.

"Yogis practice all kinds of strange things for decades, trying to stimulate their pineal glands. But you might've done it with one shot."

I crinkled my nose. "Why would they want to stimulate their pineal glands?"

"For enlightenment. For bliss. Take the Khechari Mudra."

"The ketchup what?" I dredged the tortilla chip in the little bowl of salsa. An image of my skull being cut open turned my stomach.

"The Khechari Mudra," Grayson said. "It's a special technique master yogis use. They train their tongues to be flexible enough to access their nasal passages from inside their throats."

My stomach turned some more. "Are you saying they pick their noses from the inside with their tongues?" I glanced at my salsa-covered chip and cringed. "Gross!"

"No. The pineal gland is located—"

"Listen, Grayson," I said, cutting him off. "I'm trying to eat here. Could we stop with all this for right now?"

Grayson shrugged. "Sure. You're not into bliss. I get it."

"I didn't say *that*. It's just ... well, it's a bit too much to ask for, isn't it? I mean, what is *bliss* anyway?"

"Yogis describe the feeling of bliss as being like the climax point of orgasm."

I nearly choked on my iced tea. "Excuse me?"

Grayson laughed. "For people stuck in lower consciousness, when it comes to bliss, the best they can hope for is the fleeting sensation of orgasm. That's why sex is such a big deal to people trapped in mundane states of existence. They can only get a tiny, transitory glimpse of the never-ending cosmic bliss attained by some yogis."

"A mundane existence doesn't sound so bad to me," I said. "Sorry, but I don't think I could stand being in a never-ending state of orgasm."

Grayson stifled a grin and locked eyes with me. "Me either. But once in a while wouldn't be so bad now, would it?"

I shifted my eyes down to the bowl of salsa. "No. I suppose it wouldn't."

Chapter Forty-Four

"I HOPE YOU ENJOY THIS particular selection from my whine cellar," Grayson quipped in an attempt to lessen my nervousness. He waggled his eyebrows and said, "I call this one *Nightmare on Overwh'Elm Street*. Get it?"

I made a sour face and laid back on my bed. I blew out a breath and chewed my lip as Grayson fiddled with the controls on some weird-looking monitoring machine he'd dragged out of his RV.

The sticky electrodes pasted all over my skull itched and tugged at my scalp. I shook my head softly, chiding myself for being such a gullible doofus.

What the hell have I gotten myself into? Grayson's either a quack or a genius, and I'm either a guinea pig or a fool. Will I be able to figure out which before it's too late?

"Relax and breathe," Grayson said.

He'd taken off his fedora and rolled up his sleeves—neither of which did anything to enhance his credibility with me. He looked like a bald politician running for county pallbearer.

"I've established your resting alpha wave pattern, see?" Grayson pointed at a graph on the machine.

I gave him a tentative nod. *Whatever, you weirdo.*

"Now I'm going to show you some pictures." He set his open laptop on a TV tray at the side of my bed. "Watch the blue screen."

I did as instructed. I smiled at the first image that popped onto the display. It was a basket of basset hound puppies in a field of daisies. The second image popped up and I nearly swallowed my tongue.

It was a pile of mangled zombie corpses.

"What the hell, Grayson!" I yelled. "No wonder you keep this crap in a padlocked cabinet!"

"Hmmm," Grayson said, keeping his eyes on the machine. He pointed to the graph displayed on the monitor. "See how your activity changed here?"

"What? Whose wouldn't? Where'd you get pictures like that, anyway?"

"Lie back, breathe. A picture can't harm you, and neither can a ghost."

I sneered. "How do *you* know?"

"Well, theoretically, ectoplasmic anomalies—"

I rolled my eyes. "Never mind. I know what this *really* is. It's desensitization training."

Grayson's eyebrow shot up. "Yes, in a way, you're right. A person can get used to anything after a while. Even bombs dropping in warzones. But when it comes to other-worldly and other-dimensional beings, it requires a conscious effort to remain centered, even for seasoned professionals."

I locked eyes with him. "Can you? You know, control your *own* reactions?"

"*Now*, yes. But I couldn't at first."

I studied Grayson. He seemed sincere. "Really?"

"Really," he said. "There's some truly scary, as yet unexplainable crap out there, Drex. To do my job, I've got to rise above the fear."

He turned a knob on the machine. "I want you to look at each image and breathe. You control how you feel about each one. Remember, they have no power other than what you give them."

I breathed in deeply. The needle on the machine jumped up, indicating my alpha waves had increased. "Hey, I'm doing it," I said, surprised.

"Yes, you are." Grayson's smile took a subtle slant toward the sadistic. A new image popped on the screen. A greenish, pus-bloated face screamed at me from the black, rotten hole that used to be its mouth. Maggots tumbled out.

My alpha waves crashed. "Holy crap!"

"Breathe," Grayson coaxed. "You're in control. Find your safe space. Your grounding center."

"My grounding center?"

"Your favorite teddy bear. A pet bunny. Whatever makes you feel safe and at peace."

I grimaced. "It sure isn't pus face."

"*Practice*, Drex. It works. And if you're seeing what I think you might be seeing, you're going to need this as your first line of defense."

"What?" I nearly choked. "What do you *think* I'm seeing?"

"What you most fear, Drex. The guy who shot you. An escaped convict from Starke. A woman needing brain surgery."

Something clicked inside my mind. "Geez! You're right. I fear all of those things. The images ... they seemed so real."

Grayson nodded. "Maybe they were, maybe they weren't."

I chewed my lip. "So what's this 'first line of defense' you mentioned?"

"Breathing."

"*Breathing?* Really? Uh ... hello. I've been doing that all my life."

"And doing it wrong, I might add," Grayson said. "Use your breath to calm and center yourself, like I showed you. Now, I'm going to leave you here to complete the program on your own."

Grayson turned and walked toward my bedroom door.

"Wait!" I called out. "What's the *second* line of defense? In case they get past the first?"

Grayson laughed. "These are just images. They can't harm you. They'll come up and disappear automatically. When the program's done, it'll shut off. Your challenge is to find your calm center before each new image emerges."

I frowned. "Where are you going?"

Grayson cocked his head at me. "You said I could borrow your car."

"Yes, but—"

"You didn't say I needed to tell you where I was going. I promise I'll take good care of it. And I'll be back before dawn. Tell you what—I'll even fill the tank."

"But," I started to get up.

"Don't move. If you pull out an electrode, you'll have to start over."

I fell back onto the bed. "Ugh. How many times have you done this yourself?"

"More times than I can remember."

"By yourself?"

"Yes." Grayson grabbed his fedora off the bureau. "But don't worry. You're not alone. Your Grandma Selma's standing by your bedside. She says, 'Hi,' by the way."

I turned to look. No one was there.

I looked back. Grayson was gone.

Sneaky bastard.

Chapter Forty-Five

WHETHER IT WAS THE power of suggestion or Grandma Selma really *was* by my side, I thought I smelled White Shoulders, her signature perfume. Unsettled, I stuck with my task, and tried out different "happy places" until I found one that seemed to work somewhat consistently, no matter what vile images Grayson's horrible training program threw at me.

After exhausting its repertoire of bloated corpses, devilish beings, and alien autopsies, the program ended. The screen on Grayson's computer went blue, and a yellow smiley face emoji popped up. Under it flashed the words, "Have a Nice Day!" The computer beeped and shut itself off.

I sat up and checked the clock. It was 8:36 p.m. Grayson had left me alone with his computer, and he wouldn't be back for hours.

Perfect time to brush up on my computer skills ....

I hit the power button. The laptop's screen blinked back to life. A flashing message on the display read, "Are you sure you want to do this?"

Startled, I jerked my hand away from the screen. My face grew hot. I cautiously reached over and whacked the power button. The computer shut down again. I closed it, carried it over to the bureau, and set it down.

"No," I said aloud, in case the computer was somehow recording me. "I'm *not* sure I want to do this. I'm not sure at all."

AFTER SCRUBBING THE electrode paste from my stubbly scalp, I took a shower, pulled on some sweatpants and a T-shirt, and brushed my teeth. After all those gory test images, I was too wired to sleep. I couldn't even concentrate enough to follow the plot of *Matlock*.

I switched off the TV and slumped onto the couch.

I missed my Grandma Selma. She'd been the only person I could count on to give me a woman's perspective in the messed-up man's world we lived in. She'd passed away two years before my father. I'd lost my mother way before that—first to bourbon, then to parts unknown with Mr. Applewhite. With no one else springing to mind for a friendly chat, I called Beth-Ann.

"I still don't know if Grayson is a genius or a psycho," I said when she picked up.

"Don't tell me you went out on another date with him," she said, not missing a beat.

"No. And it wasn't a date. He hooked me up to electrodes."

"Ooooh. Kinky. What else did he do?"

"Argh! It wasn't like that. He was measuring my alpha waves. He's into all this yoga and kundalini crap."

"It's not crap, Bobbie."

"You're into it, too? Why didn't you tell me?"

"Around here, people already think I'm weird enough."

I blew out a breath. "Beth-Ann, I need to know if this guy's for real, or if he's some kind of nut job. Have you got any helpful hints on how to do that?"

"Isn't there anything in your detective handbook?"

"It doesn't cover Mothman kooks."

"Then do a Google search on Grayson. Check out his Facebook profile."

"I don't want to be a busybody, Beth-Ann. This town's got enough of them already."

"Oh. So *that's* why you wanted to become a private investigator. So you could *stay out of* other peoples' business. *Now* I get it."

"Ugh. You're right. But there's so much more to being a P.I. than I thought."

"Like what?"

"Like *this*. I mean, how can you tell the good guys from the bad guys?"

"Uh ... you never saw that problem coming?"

My gut sunk four inches. "I'm an idiot."

"No, you're not, Bobbie. You're just naïve when it comes to men. Give me his full name and everything you've got on him, and I'll do the search. That way, you can keep your hands clean."

"Thanks, Beth-Ann. You're a lifesaver."

Beth-Ann laughed. "I hope you don't mean that literally."

Geez. So do I.

Chapter Forty-Six

I WAS COZIED UP ON the couch with a vodka cocktail. Okay, it was a glass of vodka. But it was a small glass.

It was nearly midnight, and Grayson still hadn't returned. I'd switched on the TV half an hour ago. A beautiful woman in a cocktail dress and diamond earrings was busy convincing me to buy a contraption that could clean my drapes and give me a facial.

But not at the same time.

I was reaching for my cellphone to order the blasted thing when the landline for Robert's Mechanics rang. It was exactly midnight. I picked up the receiver, thinking it might be Grayson with a flat tire or something.

"Hello?"

"*Beep beep beep.*"

The hair on the back of my neck stood up.

"Who are you?" I demanded. I was pretty sure the faltering squeak in my voice did nothing to persuade these robots that I meant business.

"*Beep beep beep.*"

"What do you want?" I hissed, barely able to squeeze the words from my tight lungs.

A mechanical voice buzzed over the line. "Bring a large pepperoni pizza to 387 Obsidian Road. Pronto."

Air whooshed back into my lungs.

"Earl, you're fired," I screeched.

I heard him howl with laughter as I clicked off the phone. I flopped back onto the couch, totally pissed. Then a thought made my back straighten.

Crap! I forgot to check on Vanderhoff today!

I couldn't now. It was too late. Besides, Grayson had my car. I'd have to wait until morning. I sighed and turned my attention back to the TV.

Just my luck. I'd missed the limited-time offer to order one VaccuFacial and get a second one free.

I scowled and clicked the "off" button on the TV remote.

After draining my vodka glass, I hauled myself off the couch and padded down the hall to my bedroom. Pulling back the curtains, I stared out at the thin slice of silvery moon, wondering where Grayson was. I didn't want to be a nag by calling him. He was a grown man, after all.

As I pulled down the bedcovers, I shivered.

Crap.

I'd left Grandma's afghan in Grayson's apartment. I couldn't go get it now. Not without invading his privacy. I climbed into bed and lay down. A beam of moonlight shone in my eye. I'd forgotten to close the curtains.

Double crap.

I hauled myself out of bed, grabbed a handful of curtain, and totally freaked.

Inches from the windowpane, two glowing, red orbs hovered at eye level with me. I closed my eyes, shook my head, and took a deep, calming breath.

It's just my imagination.

I opened my eyes.

The glowing red orbs were still there.

But now they weren't orbs.

They were *eyes.*

Burning, ember-like eyes—set deep inside the skull of a hideous, insect-like face!

As a blood-curdling scream ripped from my lungs, I caught a glimpse of something on its back. It was a cape.

No.

It was Grandma Selma's afghan.

Icy spiders crawled up my back.

That horrible thing's been inside my house!

My knees gave out.

I crumpled to the floor.

The safe little world I once knew went bye-bye.

Chapter Forty-Seven

I WAS IN A TUG OF WAR with Mothman over Grandma Selma's afghan. Through my bedroom window, I slapped his ugly insect face with a flyswatter and grabbed the corner of the blanket. I gave it a huge tug, but bug-man held on with his spindly, lobster-claw hands.

He wasn't letting go.

Well, neither was I.

I dug my heels into the shag carpet and tugged for all I was worth. But a sudden, swift yank by Mothman pulled me out the second-story window.

I was dangling in midair!

As I hung onto the tail-end of Grandma Selma's blanket for dear life, Mothman buzzed above the pathetically small metropolis of Point Paradise, trying to shake me loose.

I saw the roof over my parent's garage ... the flashing light at the intersection of nowhere and oblivion ... the sagging awning of the Stop & Shoppe. As we flew over Cherry Manor, I spotted old lady Vanderhoff's house. I took my chance and let go of Grandma's afghan. I tumbled, butt-first, into old lady Vanderhoff's swimming pool.

She heard my cannonball splash and came running out of the house. Vanderhoff was naked except for a pair of red, lace panties and that green avocado mask. My poor eyes didn't know where to look.

"You're going to electrocute yourself!" she yelled, and handed me a mirror. My bald head was covered in electrodes.

She shook her avocado-smeared head at me. "Drex! What's wrong with you?"

Wait a minute. This has to be a dream. Mrs. Vanderhoff always called me Bobbie. Never Drex.

I snorted myself awake.

I was on the floor of my bedroom, my right cheek stuck to the pages of a *Good Housekeeping* magazine. A beam of morning sun filtered its way through the dust circling in the air. I blinked against the glare, then I nearly peed my pants.

Mothman was standing right over me.

I jolted awake like Frankenstein in a nuclear reactor.

I screamed, scooted backward across the floor on my butt, and kicked at the creature like a deranged donkey.

"I know I have morning breath," Mothman said, "but I think that's a bit of an overreaction."

I blinked again, then blushed. With the light no longer stabbing my eyes, Mothman had melted into Grayson.

"What are you doing in my bedroom?" I yelled.

"Checking on you. Your front door was open, so I came in. Why are you on the floor?" He wagged a shaming finger at me. "Don't tell me you got into the vodka again."

"Shut up! Where were you last night?"

"Excuse me? I wasn't aware I owed you an explanation. Or are you my warden now?"

"You should've been here!" I screeched. "Mothman was here! He tried to get in my bedroom window!"

Grayson's eyes nearly doubled in size. "What? Damn! Did you get a good look at it?"

"Yes," I grumbled. "And I'm okay, in case you're interested."

Grayson grimaced. "Oh. Yes. Good. I'm glad." He smiled at me for a moment, then said, "So? What did it look like?"

"Like a moth ... man. Sort of." I hesitated as I tried to read Grayson's expression. He had the best poker face I'd ever seen. "And he—" I began, then changed my mind.

"He what?" Grayson coaxed.

"He...." I stopped and shook my head. "No. You'll laugh at me."

He slapped on a solemn face. "I won't. I promise."

"He ... he stole Grandma Selma's afghan."

I had to hand it to him. Grayson's effort to suppress a grin was truly valiant. He nearly swallowed his lips.

"This afghan," he asked with one raised eyebrow, "it wasn't made of *wool*, was it?"

"You're such a jerk!" I yelled. I picked up a pillow from the floor and threw it at him.

"Come on, Drex. I'm just trying to get you to lighten up."

"How can you joke about *this* of all things?"

"Because it helps. Especially when you know the things I know."

I stared at him, red-faced, unable to decide if I was angry, mortified, or just plain embarrassed. "What do you know?"

Grayson bent down and offered me a hand. "How about *I* fix the coffee this morning? You get cleaned up. And when you're ready, we can talk."

Chapter Forty-Eight

IF I'D LEARNED ONE thing in life, it was that caffeine could solve a myriad of problems. Abject terror over Mothman, however, wasn't one of them.

On that score, Grayson was no help, either.

"Hope you don't mind. I put some clothes in the wash," he said as I hobbled into the kitchen. My knees were still wobbly from my encounter with the insectoid peeping Tom, whether it was real or I'd just imagined it.

"Sure. No worries." I shuffled to the counter and made myself a cup of coffee. "Why in the world would Mothman be after *me?*" I grumbled, and took a giant gulp.

Grayson was sitting at the round oak table. He glanced over at the portrait of Jesus my parents had hanging on the wall. "God doesn't send you anything that you're not ready for, Drex. That which does not kill us makes us stronger."

I sneered. "Thank you, oh great Pez dispenser full of stupid clichés."

"Come on, Drex. You didn't get a degree in Art Appreciation to end up managing a grease pit in the middle of nowhere. You're ready for something bigger."

I looked down at my coffee. A fly was doing the backstroke in it. "Sure I am," I said as I poured the coffee down the sink. "Because I'm smart, I'm pretty, and gosh-darn it, people like me."

Grayson snickered. "You've already told me more than once that you want out of this place. So, here it is, your big break, and you act all surprised. *Hurt*, even. I'm telling you now, you might as well embrace the situation like you personally ordered it, and dive in. Because you did. And you can."

Anger flared up inside me like a Duraflame starter packet. "*Ordered* this? Are you talking about Mothman, or *you*? Right now, if I had to choose, I'd pick Mothman. He's a whole hell of a lot less irritating."

Grayson smirked. "Be careful what you wish for. You just might get it."

"Pez hack," I spat.

Grayson shot me a grin I wanted to erase with an Uzi. "When the student is ready, the teacher appears, Drex. And I do believe it's time for another lesson for the unruly pupil."

"What lesson?"

I glared at him, then rolled my eyes. Did it matter? What else did I have going on?

"I need more coffee first," I growled.

Grayson nodded. "Then pour yourself a gallon and come with me."

GRAYSON'S LATEST P.I. "lesson" had me kicking around outside in the cold mist of morning, checking the ground under my bedroom window for evidence of Mothman's visitation last night.

"What are we looking for?" I grumbled. "There's no footprints. I told you, the thing was flying."

"Look for hairs. Detritus. Anything that looks out of place."

"Like what?"

"Like *that*."

Grayson pointed upward to the boughs of a small crepe myrtle tree. Hanging about ten feet off the ground was a piece of yarn.

My heart soared. I wasn't crazy. "Grandma's afghan! See? I *didn't* imagine it!"

"Hold your horses. It's a piece of yarn in a tree, Drex. It could've gotten there a hundred different ways. *You* could have put it there, for all I know."

"Me?" I said with righteous indignation.

"Sure. You could've tossed the blanket out the window last night in the middle of some weird, somnambulistic dream."

"Dirty mind!"

"That means *sleepwalking*, gutter girl."

I scowled, folded my arms across my chest, and festered in self-re-crimination. Meanwhile, Grayson found a hook-shaped stick and used it to bend the crepe myrtle branch downward to retrieve the evidence. He stuck the foot-long piece of blue yarn in a plastic baggie. Then, to my surprise, he held the baggie open, stuck his nose in, and sniffed.

What a sicko.

"It's wool, all right," Grayson said. "I can smell the difference."

I marched over to him and grabbed for the baggie. "Give me that!"

"No can do." He raised the baggie up and out of my reach. "I need to test it for DNA. Does it look like it might have come from your granny's blanket?"

"Maybe," I grumbled. "It's a bunch of colors. Now what?"

Grayson didn't answer. He was looking right at me, but his eyes were far away. I hoped he was pondering a solution to this whole crazy mess. Or, even better, how to get his ass out of town.

"Interesting," he said at last.

"Interesting? That's all you've got to say?"

"I thought maybe this was all a coincidence. But now, well, let's just say I've never been a big believer in coincidences."

I shot him a sour look. "What are you talking about?"

"What's your safe space, Drex? You know, from the test yesterday. What do you envision to keep the monsters at bay?"

My back stiffened. "None of your business."

"I disagree. I wouldn't be asking if it wasn't important."

I'd envisioned myself balled up in my grandma's lap, sucking my thumb. Thinking about it now, my cheeks flared with heat. "It's personal."

"*Fine.*" Grayson blew out an aggravated breath. "I think I know, anyway. I'd like to test you again. To hone your skills some more."

"You might think you know me, Grayson, but you don't know sh—" My phone rang. It was Paulson. "I better get this."

I turned my back to Grayson. "Hello? Paulson? Listen, I'm sorry I didn't get by Vanderhoff's yesterday. I was—"

"Save it, Bobbie," Paulson said curtly. "There's no need for you to give me a case update. Vanderhoff's dead."

"Oh, my word! What happened?"

"Someone broke in through a window. Ripped her throat out in the middle of the night."

I glanced at Grayson. He was looking away, but I got the feeling he'd been listening in. He'd been gone all night. His clothes were in the washing machine. A knife-blade of fear stabbed me in the back.

"Bobbie? Are you there?" Paulson asked.

I took a step away from Grayson and whispered, "Yes. Should I come by?"

"No. The FBI's been called. Stay where you are. Is that lodger of yours still around?"

Cold wind swept down my spine. "Yes."

"Be careful, Bobbie."

"I will." I hung up the phone.

"What's up?" Grayson asked.

I turned to face him and tried to smile, but it wouldn't stick. "Nothing. Beth-Ann's cat had kittens is all. I'm going to go over there to, you know, help out with the delivery."

"I love kittens. Can I come?"

Grayson took a step toward me. I took a step back.

"Well," I fumbled, "I'm gonna get my eyebrows tweezed, too. So why don't you hang around here? Talk to Earl. He told me your RV should be ready soon. Maybe today, even."

Grayson eyed me like he wasn't buying it. "What's really going on?"

I looked away. "Nothing. I just need some girl time, okay?"

Grayson shot me a dubious look. "Okay."

I wanted to run, to get the hell away from Grayson. But I willed myself not to. Instead, I channeled my fear into enough energy to march back up the stairs to my apartment without falling on my face.

As I headed down the hall to my bedroom, the sound of the washing machine made me stop in my tracks. I looked around to make sure Grayson wasn't behind me, then I carefully opened the bi-fold doors to the closet housing the washer and dryer. I lifted the lid on the washing machine and peeked inside. The water around the clothes in the drum was tinged dark pink.

"What are you doing?" Grayson's voice rang out behind me. I dropped the lid on my finger.

"Ah ... uh ... nothing," I said, my finger pulsing with pain. I tried the lame smile again, but even *I* wasn't buying it. "I just wanted to see if there was room in the washer for, you know, a few of my unmentionables."

Grayson smiled. "Sure."

"Thanks."

"Don't *mention* it," he quipped. "Get it?"

I laughed, but this time his humor was totally lost on me.

Chapter Forty-Nine

AS I PULLED OUT OF the parking lot, I caught Grayson eyeing me from the upstairs window of my grandmother's apartment. Something creepy crawled down my neck and over my shoulders.

Great. Thanks to him, not even my own home feels safe anymore.

I hit the gas and headed in the direction of Cherry Manor. Despite Officer Paulson's instructions to stay clear, I felt compelled to check on Mrs. Vanderhoff. I'd known her since I was a kid.

Suddenly, I had an epiphany. I was driving my dead father's car, wearing his coveralls and boots, and atop my head was some random stranger's wig Beth-Ann had fished out of an Amazon box.

Is any part of my life something I actually chose for myself?

I did a mental inventory and couldn't come up with a single thing. I was working a hand-me-down job, living a hand-me-down life. My grandmother was gone. My father was gone. My mother was gone. And now, Mrs. Vanderhoff was gone. Point Paradise was slipping away, despite my attempt to resurrect it.

Maybe it's time to just let it go ....

The pine trees ticked by on either side of the road. Never again would I be a little tomboy stalking dolls in the woods with a BB gun. Never again would I get another warm, White Shoulders-scented hug from my Grandma Selma. Never again would I help my dad change an oil filter. Or hear my mother chide me about how dirty I'd gotten my clothes.

Clothes.

Grayson's bloody laundry was churning in my washing machine. Was he getting rid of evidence, or just skid marks?

He might be a murderer. He might be a saint. But either way, Grayson had been right. I *had* wished for change. *Big* change. A *whole new life* kind of change.

I'd yearned for something more interesting—more exciting than changing dead spark plugs. But tracking down Mothman? Had someone upstairs heard my prayers wrong?

Again?

I blew out a sigh. As aggravating as he was, at least I still had Earl.

Yippee.

I hit the gas, wishing I could outrun a past I no longer wanted. But what else was out there? Only a future I couldn't see. Still, one thing was for sure. Wherever I ended up, that stupid twin inside my head was along for the ride.

Thanks to it, my life was never going to be the same.

Grayson was right. I should've been a lot more careful about what I'd wished for.

Chapter Fifty

I PULLED UP IN FRONT of Vanderhoff's modest little block home. It had been plain before. But somehow, today it seemed even plainer, now that her life had gone out of it.

Paulson's car was out front. A blue Toyota Corolla. I made a mental note of it, then walked up to the front door and rapped my knuckles on the wood paneling. Paulson's face appeared in the small window.

"What are you doing here?" he asked as he opened the front door a crack.

"I thought I might be able to help."

"It's pretty gruesome."

"Where is she?"

"In her bed."

Paulson opened the door wider. His hands had blood on them. He noticed that I noticed.

"It's awful, Bobbie." He turned, and I followed him into Vanderhoff's kitchen. "I covered her with the bedsheets. I couldn't bear for someone to see her like that...all exposed and everything."

Paulson's voice cracked as he washed his hands in the sink. I noticed my business card on the refrigerator. My heart pinged.

Poor Mrs. Vanderhoff. Oh, geez! Poor ME! If the FBI finds my bogus P.I. card, I'm toast!

While Paulson had his back to me, I peeled my business card from the fridge. The magnet came to, glued to the card by some sticky substance I didn't have the time or desire to discern at the moment. I jammed them both in my pocket right before Paulson turned around.

He reached for the dishtowel hanging off the refrigerator door. His eyes were filled with tears. I patted him on the back. He nearly broke down. "How could something like this happen?" he asked.

"I don't know."

"Maybe you were right about seeing that convict in the woods after all." Paulson sniffed back tears. "Thanks for coming by, but you should go now. This may be the work of a serial killer. Like I told you before. The FBI's been notified. They should be here any minute now. I don't want you to get hung up in all this. I had no idea it would turn out like ...." His voice trailed off.

I winced. He looked devastated. "Okay," I said, and patted him on the shoulder. "You sure you're all right?"

"Yes." Paulson looked me in the eyes, an apologetic expression twisting his handsome face. "I know it's unprofessional to cry. But I've just never seen anything like this."

"I understand. Nobody expects much to happen here in Point Paradise."

As Paulson ushered me to the door, a thought crossed my mind. Should I retrieve the tele-bug device Grayson had stashed under Vanderhoff's couch cushion? For a second, I considered telling Paulson about it. But with Vanderhoff dead in the next room and the FBI on their way, every fiber of my being wanted to get the hell out of there. This whole thing was way out of my league. Besides, who was *I* to point the finger at Grayson? What if it really *was* the Mothman who did it?

Mothman? Cripes! I really do *need a shrink.*

I decided to keep my trap shut and let the FBI do their own investigation. They'd find the tele-bug soon enough. And if Grayson was guilty, he'd be found out. To borrow one of Grayson's pez-hack clichés, let the chips fall where they may.

Paulson ushered me out the front door. "I guess that means our little wager is off."

"Wager?" I asked.

"Twenty bucks or dinner. For figuring out the phone calls."

"Oh. Right," I said absently. "Yes. You're off the hook."

"That's too bad." Paulson gave me a sad smile and closed the door.

I walked to the Mustang and climbed in. As I turned the ignition, something about Paulson and men in general got under my skin like a swarm of chiggers.

Guys. Do they ever *stop thinking about sex?*

A tap on the passenger door window made me flinch. It was Nellie Parker, the dog-walking neighbor lady I'd seen last time I was here with Grayson.

"What's happening at Mrs. Vanderhoff's?" she asked. "Did she find a buyer?"

"I don't think she's looking for one, Mrs. Parker. She's dead."

"Dead?" Parker's face registered delight for a second, then shifted into the furrowed-brow concern of a decent, law-abiding citizen. "That's too bad." She looked down at her dog. "Well, Doodles, I guess we won't be seeing any more of Popeye."

"Who's Popeye?" I asked.

Parker made a sour face. "Vanderhoff's mangy, one-eyed pig. He's the terror of the neighborhood. Always digging out from under the fence and trying to do his business with my poor Doodles. I can't say I'll miss him."

"*Or* poor Mrs. Vanderhoff?" I asked sarcastically.

"Well, to be honest, no."

For the umpteenth time, I tried to roll up my broken driver's side window, and for the umpteenth time, I grimaced at my own stupidity. I shifted into first, and, just to prove I was honest as well, I did what I told Grayson I was going to do.

I headed to Waldo to see Beth-Ann.

"IF GRAYSON ASKS, YOUR cat had kittens," I said as I walked into Beth-Ann's converted beauty-shop garage.

"I don't have a cat. And why would Grayson call *me?*"

"I don't know. But I want to have a plan, just in case he does."

"You sound paranoid, Bobbie."

"Maybe I am. Vanderhoff died last night."

"Dang it!" Beth-Ann hollered. "I just ordered a whole case of that blue rinse she uses."

I shot her some side-eye. "Somebody *murdered* her, Beth-Ann."

Beth-Ann did a double take. "What?"

"They ripped her throat out. Just like the corpse I saw in the woods."

"What corpse? Don't tell me there's a serial killer on the loose and you didn't even bother to tell me!"

"I'm telling you now."

"And you think Grayson's the killer?"

I studied her face. "Maybe. Why would you say that?"

"I did that Google search, like you asked. He's got kind of a shady past."

"And *you* didn't bother to tell *me?* He could have killed me, for crying out loud, Beth-Ann! Do you know he was gone all last night? And this morning ... his laundry ... it was all bloody."

"Criminy!"

I winced. "What did you find out about him?"

"That he was telling the truth, mostly. Grayson *was* a physicist, like he said. But he got discredited and lost his position at MIT."

"Why?"

"The grounds were kind of vague. Unethical behavior."

"That could mean anything from stealing paperclips to creating mutants in a lab." I wrung my hands. "What are we going to do?"

"I know what *I'm* gonna do."

Beth-Ann marched over to a cabinet and opened a drawer. She pulled out a pistol and pointed the barrel toward the sky. "Watch out Mothman, and any other kind of man who gets in my way."

I eyed her enviously. "You wouldn't happen to have another one of those, would you?"

Beth-Ann bit her lip. "Well, I was saving it for your birthday, but I think I'd rather give it to you now, so you live to turn thirty-seven." She reached into the drawer and pulled out a wrapped gift.

"Here, Detective Drex. Happy Birthday."

Chapter Fifty-One

I RETURNED TO ROBERT'S Mechanics feeling like a new woman. I was invigorated, supercharged, and packing heat.

With my very own, no-hand-me-down Glock tucked away in the right hip pocket of my coveralls, I was prepared to handle whatever Grayson threw at me. And I figured he wouldn't cross me. He knew firsthand what a good shot I was.

I pulled into the parking lot. Grayson's RV was out of the service bay. Earl's coverall-covered butt was bent over the open hood.

"How much longer?" I asked as I shut off the Mustang's coughing engine.

"Just took it for a test drive." Earl wiped a socket wrench with an oily rag. "Needs a few adjustments and she's ready to roll."

"Good, because I'm ready for Grayson to leave."

Earl's eyebrows disappeared under his shaggy bangs. "Lover's quarrel?"

"Har har har. I think he's outstayed his welcome. And what gives? I thought you said you'd have that thing ready by now."

"I would've," he argued, "but these two fellas stopped by asking for directions to Alto Lake. I told 'em to find Waldo and—"

My eyebrows shot up. "What did they look like?"

"Like them men-in-black fellas. Only they was men in *blue*. Probably FBI." Earl looked up to the sky and scratched his stubbly chin. "I wonder if a UFO crashed somewheres around here."

"What makes you think they were FBI? Did they say so?"

"No. But I watch *The X-Files*, Bobbie. I know the difference."

"Earl, they *were* the FBI. Paulson called them. Vanderhoff's been killed."

"Kilt? As in dead?"

"Yes. Murdered."

"How? Who done it?"

"I don't know. Where's Grayson?"

"Upstairs packing."

For his getaway, no doubt.

"Okay. Listen, Earl. If he tries to leave, don't let him."

Earl smiled slyly. "Lookin' for one more roll in the hay first?"

"No!" I hissed. "He owes us a hundred and eighty-eight dollars."

I turned and stomped up the stairs, my bravado fading with each step.

Should I call Paulson? Should I confront Grayson on my own? Should I just get the money from him and let him go?

I tapped on the door to Grandma Selma's apartment. Grayson called out, "Come in."

I crept in cautiously, my pistol drawn at my side. Grayson was sitting at the kitchen table. He looked up from his laptop and smiled. Beside him on the table were two stacks of pink T-shirts and boxers, neatly folded and stacked with the kind of precision that made me further question his mental state.

Yep. Totally OCD.

I eyed him suspiciously. "Funny. I pictured you as the tidy-whitey type."

Grayson shrugged. "That's what I get for buying cheap red handkerchiefs. I tried out that biker, do-rag look. But I think the fedora is more me." He held a red kerchief to his forehead. "What do you think?"

You've got a sketchy answer for everything, that's what I think.

I tightened my grip on the Glock hidden from his view. "You going somewhere?"

Grayson shrugged. "Thought I'd rob a liquor store and go to Disneyland. You in?"

"Cut the crap, Grayson. You're a liar. You told me you're a physicist."

Grayson's brow furrowed. "I *am*."

"You were discredited."

"So? Once a physicist, always a physicist. How did you find that out, anyway? Did you use my computer?" Grayson smiled in a way that made me squirm inside.

"No."

"Why not? Couldn't get past the question on the screen?"

I frowned. "I didn't try. I guess I really *didn't* want to find out what would happen if I tried to use it. What do you do to people who mess with your computer anyway? Rip their throats out?"

"It's a *joke*, Drex." Grayson laughed and shook his head. "You really *are* uptight. Look." He turned the laptop around on the table until the screen faced me. The same question from last night was flashing on the display: "Are you sure you want to do this?"

He pressed the button. The computer opened to a menu. "See? It's not even locked. The only password required is a conscience. Looks like you've got one. Congratulations."

"My personal integrity is important to me," I said in a way I hoped implied that I didn't think *his* was.

Grayson eyed me silently for a moment. "I want to show you something."

I hesitated. "If it's your lizard, I'm not interested."

Grayson laughed. "Keep Gizzard out of this."

He got up and walked past me, out of my grandmother's apartment, down the breezeway, and into my apartment.

Flabbergasted, I tagged along after him. "Where are we going?" I asked.

"To your bed."

"Forget it!" I yelled. He turned around. I hid the gun behind my back.

"I want to show you some important evidence I found, Drex. And I want you to be hooked up to the alpha wave monitor when you see it. I need to see how you react subconsciously."

"Why?" I asked angrily. "What difference does it make?"

"It makes *all* the difference, Drex. Trust me on this."

"*Trust* you? Why *should* I?"

Grayson shrugged. "I guess that's a valid question. But good grief? If you don't by now, will you ever?"

I stared at Grayson until he sighed.

"Would it help if I asked nicely?" he said.

I didn't answer.

"Would you *please* do this for me, Drex? Cherry on top? People's lives could be at stake. Including yours."

I know. That's what I'm afraid of.

Chapter Fifty-Two

I WAS LYING IN MY BED, my hand tucked inside the pocket of my coveralls. Unbeknownst to Grayson, my fingers were wrapped tightly around the grip of my sleek, new subcompact Glock. The barrel was pointed at Grayson's heart as he leaned over me and stuck electrodes on my stubbly scalp.

"Calm your mind," he said softly.

Clearing my head was oddly difficult to do with him so near. Just inches from me, I found the animal warmth of his body teasing me in places long left unteased. Grayson was a man of mystery. Dangerous. Provocative. Strangely alluring. Possibly insane.

If I wasn't careful, he could be the death of me.

"Try to keep your concentration," he said, "Find your inner balance."

His eyes were bright with excitement—the sparkling, wide-open, intense eyes of a madman. Was he going to shock me senseless and try to rip my throat out? I didn't know. But I'd found myself too curious to refuse him. He'd promised to show me something that would change my world as I knew it.

For better or worse, I was ready for the change.

And, thanks to Beth Ann, I was also ready with my Glock.

"Brace yourself," Grayson said, and took a step back. He began to fiddle with the controls on the machine. "What I'm about to show you isn't for sissies."

"Okay. I'm ready."

"Here goes." Grayson pushed a button. An image came on his laptop screen. But this time, it wasn't a series of static pictures. It was a video.

Shaky and amateurish, it appeared to have been made with someone's cellphone as they walked around inside a small ship or submarine. Everything was gray and slick. The hand holding the camera was trembling so badly that after a few seconds of watching, I began to feel nause-ated.

I swallowed against the bile rising in my throat. On the screen, the cameraman entered a small, black, oval doorway. What happened next made me forget all about being sick.

I was too astounded.

Beyond the doorway, three gray, human-like alien creatures looked up from what appeared to be control panels. Despite having no eyelids, no discernable nose, and only a slit for a mouth, I could still clearly read the panic on their faces.

Suddenly, a cacophony of human voices rang out in confusion, like the drug raids I'd seen on detective shows. A man in military fatigues ran in front of the camera. He yelled at the creatures. "Stop what you're do-ing. *Now!* Release them!"

The shaky camera panned to the right. Three columnar, aquarium-like tubes glowed eerily in the dim light. Inside each one was a human child no older than ten.

I gasped.

"Steady," Grayson said. "Think of your happy place."

In my mind, I climbed into Grandma's lap as the man with the au-tomatic weapon fired at the top of the first glass tube. It shattered. The child inside tumbled out and cried, "Daddy!"

I wrapped Grandma's imaginary afghan around me as the guy in fa-tigues fired at the other tubes. They blew apart. The children held captive inside screamed and cried out for their parents.

The camera panned left. The three gray aliens were in a state of sheer horror, clumped together in a corner like frightened rats.

Then a man screamed.

It was a horrific, unforgettable howl. Off camera, the automatic weapon fired repeatedly. The phone taking the video fell to the ground.

Screams and shrieks and unearthly wails echoed into each other, but whatever was emitting them wasn't captured by the phone. The device lay still on the floor, its camera focused on the ceiling of what surely must have been some kind of alien spacecraft.

I hugged Grandma and started sucking my thumb. Hard.

Suddenly, the decapitated head of a gray alien flew into view. It hit the ceiling above the camera, then fell on top of the cellphone with a sickening thump. The image went black.

"Excellent," Grayson said.

"Excellent?" I screeched. "You think *that's* excellent?"

"Not the video. *You.* Drex, you were able to maintain your alpha waves better than anyone I've ever seen."

He showed me the graph. My alpha waves looked like a roller-coaster ride that fell into a ravine. "That doesn't look that impressive to me."

"Believe me, compared to the others, this is phenomenal."

"What others?"

Grayson shrugged.

"Is this just another made-up test, Grayson?" I wished and hoped and prayed he'd say yes.

"Depends." Grayson stared at me with the least readable expression I'd ever seen on a human face. "Do you want it to be fake?"

"Hell, yes!" I bellowed.

Grayson nodded.

I bit my lip. "But it's not, is it?"

"That information is on a need-to-know basis, Drex."

Aggravation climbed up my neck and clenched my jaws like a vise. "Why are you showing me this, Grayson?"

"Because I think you've got a gift."

I scowled. "This pineal twin thing?"

"That's part of it."

I locked eyes with him. "What do you want to use my so-called *gift* for?"

"I can't tell you—unless you're all in."

"What do you mean?"

"I was discredited by MIT because of my pursuit of unexplained phenomena. I believe there's more out there than what we currently understand, Drex."

"Like what?"

"Mothman. Bigfoot. Skin Walkers. Who knows? There's a whole gamut of things that exist beyond the ability for the rational mind to accept. I'm obsessed with proving that they're real. And I want you to help me."

"*Me?* Help *you?*"

"Yes. Be my partner."

"Partner?" I muttered, too stunned to do anything but parrot Grayson's words back at him.

Grayson nodded. "It's dangerous. But it's also the adventure of a lifetime. But Drex, if you take this step, there's no going back to life as you now know it."

I think I've already crossed that threshold.

Someone banged on the front door, making me jump off the bed and rip half my electrodes out.

"Hey boss man," Earl called out. "We're almost out of Fritos!"

I pressed my molars together and looked Grayson square in the face. "So how much does this partner thing pay?"

Chapter Fifty-Three

"WHERE'D YOU GET THE film?" I asked Grayson as I pulled the rest of the pasty electrodes off my scalp.

He smiled thoughtfully. "I have friends in low places. *Now* do you believe me? At least about the *possibility* of Mothman being real?"

I shook my head. "I don't know. To me, the two don't seem related."

Grayson frowned. "What would it take to convince you? I've *seen* him, Drex. You saw him yourself last night."

"I saw something fly over my head, and I saw something at my window. In both instances, it was dark. I'm not exactly prepared to say there's a mutant cryptid on the loose."

"Your skepticism is appreciated ... up to a point," Grayson said. "As for me, the only question remaining is why Mothman would choose to turn up *here*, in Point Paradise."

"I think I might know the answer to that."

Grayson looked at me, surprised. "You do?"

I pulled the dog-poo shaped magnet from my pocket. "I got this off Vanderhoff's refrigerator. She said it was the last thing her niece Mandy sent her from her travels."

"So?"

"Mandy's been missing for two weeks."

Grayson studied the magnet. "Grave Creek Mound?"

"Yeah. I Google searched it."

Grayson looked up at me and smiled. "You did, did you?"

I shot him a sour look. "Save it." I nodded at the magnet. "The place is an old Indian burial mound. It's in West Virginia, not that far from that Point Pleasant place where they had—"

"The original sightings of Mothman," Grayson said, finishing my sentence. He set the magnet down and flipped open his laptop. "Interesting."

"It's just a burial mound of a chief or something."

Grayson shook his head. "Then why would it warrant an entry by Lewis & Clarke in 1803?" He stared at the screen. "Drex, this is the biggest burial mound in the United States."

"Okay. So it's big. I only brought it up because I think it might've been possible for—"

"This mound is over two thousand years old," Grayson said, paying me no mind. His eyes were glued to the screen. "Good grief. It's over sixty feet tall and as big around as a football field."

"So?"

"Says here it was excavated in 1838. They found two burial chambers and three bodies inside."

"And let me guess. You think one of them was Mothman?"

"Drex, why would Stone Age people bust their butts moving sixty thousand tons of dirt just to cover three bodies? They didn't have backhoes back then, remember."

"I know that."

"They didn't even have horses or the wheel." Grayson studied the screen again. "Huh. It says the original structure had a forty-foot-wide moat around it, too."

I blew out a breath. "Okay. It had a moat. What's that got to do with Mothman?"

"It seems to me like these people wanted to make damned sure those bodies didn't get unburied. But why?"

I shrugged. "I dunno. Why did *any* ancient culture build monuments?"

Grayson shot me a knowing glance. "Precisely."

I rolled my eyes. "Argh!"

Ignoring me, Grayson returned to his computer screen. "Huh. It says during the excavation, they noticed the soil around the bodies had turned blue."

"Blue? What could cause that?"

"Copper. Toxins. Radioactivity."

Radioactivity?

"Okay, Grayson. Suppose you're right. What if they *did* bury Moth-man monsters in there? How could they have gotten out of the mound?"

"Any number of ways. Through excavations. Earthquakes. Coal mining. Injection of industrial waste. Any of those could have unsettled the soil and created an escape pathway. Look."

I glanced at the computer screen. The giant earthen heap comprising Grave Creek Mound was dotted with huge trees that appeared to be a hundred years old or better.

"These trees growing on the mound could've disturbed a protective talisman or penetrated a protective barrier," Grayson said. "Even time itself could've done the deed. It's had a couple of thousand years to crack it."

I shrugged. "I guess."

Grayson punched a few keys on his computer. A map of the town of Moundsville, West Virginia appeared. "Huh. Take a look at this."

"What?"

"Look what's just a few blocks away from the burial mound."

I glanced at the map. "The Roller Derby?"

"No."

"Dairy Queen?"

"No. The West Virginia State Penitentiary."

"Aha! That's what I've been trying to tell you, Grayson. About how Mothman got here, I mean."

"What? You think Mandy gave Mothman a lift on her way home to Point Paradise?"

"Well ... not exactly. Maybe Mandy got involved with a conman in Moundsville. Or maybe he spotted her in town and marked her as a target. It's the last place she's been seen in weeks."

"Hmm," Grayson said, rubbing his chin.

"I mean, it's plausible, isn't it?" I asked. "Maybe a criminal type followed Mandy back here to Point Paradise. You said yourself that everything's interrelated."

Grayson's lip twitched. "Sure. But why would Mothman need a ride when he can fly?"

I groaned. "Not Mothman. A *convict*."

Grayson shot me a *why don't you believe* look.

"Okay," I said. "For the sake of argument, let's say it's Mothman. You said Mothman liked to chase cars. Maybe he followed her car here. Or maybe he likes to chase women, too, and the combo was irresistible."

Grayson appeared to be mulling over my idea. "Well, it's the best theory we've got to work with right now. Speaking of work, will you give my partner offer a serious think?"

I smiled. "Yes. I will."

"Good. No pressure or anything, but I'm considering leaving in the morning, so I'll need an answer then. With the Feds around, I don't want to tangle you up in anything you don't want to be part of. I can continue my investigation alone from the RV, no worries."

I let out a bitter laugh. "That's rich. I'm already tangled up in this, Grayson. And what about the wiretap contraption you left at Vanderhoff's? You going to take that with you, too?"

"No. I bought the tele-bug on the black market. No one can trace it back to me. Besides, she won't be getting any more calls."

My internal alarm began clanging again. I hadn't mentioned Vanderhoff's death to Grayson. "How do you know?"

"Because I—"

The phone rang. Grayson clammed up mid-confession. Somehow, he knew Vanderhoff was dead without me telling him. Had he killed her after all? I grabbed the phone like it was the governor offering a stay of execution.

"Hello?"

"Bobbie, it's Paulson."

"Hi—"

"Listen very carefully," he whispered. "I'm trapped in my office out at Alto Lake. I didn't want to tell you, but two convicts escaped from Starke Prison ten days ago. Two FBI agents came out to help me apprehend them, but something in the woods out here killed them." His voice cracked. "Bobbie, whatever it is, it's after *me* now! I need help—"

The line went dead.

I looked at Grayson. "Paulson's in trouble. The nearest help is all the way in Gainesville. I gotta go."

Grayson stood. "Not without me."

I shook my head. "No. You need to stay here."

"Not happening."

Whoever or whatever was after Paulson, I knew it wasn't Grayson. He had an airtight alibi. He was standing right beside me, pointing his Glock in my ribs.

Chapter Fifty-Four

I WAS DRIVING MY FATHER'S Mustang like a hostage on a desperate, life-or-death mission.

Mainly because I *was*.

Grayson was in the passenger seat beside me, his Glock pointed at my vital organs.

"What are you doing?" I hissed at him. "You ask me to be your partner, then you pull a gun on me? Are you working undercover? FBI? CIA? MIB?"

I was too afraid to say what I really thought. It might set Grayson off enough to pull the trigger. Was he a deranged physicist? A throat-ripping serial killer? A crazy UFO chaser? An alien with two navels? A real-life *Dr. Jekyll, Mr. Hyde*?

Or maybe it was even worse than that. Maybe he was telling the truth.

"No offense, but I just didn't have time to argue with you," Grayson said. "Is this the fastest this thing will go?"

I stomped the gas pedal. "Vanderhoff's throat was ripped out. Did you do it?"

"No."

I eyed him angrily. "But you practically *confessed*. You said she wouldn't be getting any more calls. You *knew* she was dead!"

Grayson eyed the road ahead. "I didn't know she was dead. And I didn't know her throat had been ripped out."

"Then how did you know she wouldn't get any more calls? Wait. *You* made all those weird calls, didn't you?"

"Geez! No, I didn't make those calls, Drex. I know because when I tried to test the battery on the tele-bug, it told me her phone line had been disconnected."

"Oh." My gut flopped. I slunk back in my seat, more confused than ever. Grayson stared straight ahead, unnerving me. At this point, I had nothing left to lose. I went for broke.

"How do I know *you're* not the killer, Grayson?" I asked. "How can I be sure you're not some kind of monster trying to save yourself?"

Grayson turned and looked me in the eye. He shook his head softly and said, "Aren't we *all*, Drex?"

We drove along in the fading daylight until the darkness and tension were both thick enough to cut with a hacksaw. I blew through Waldo without another word to Grayson. Only when I pulled onto the road leading to Paulson's office cabin by Lake Alto Preserve did Grayson break the silence between us.

"Listen, Drex. I didn't mean to scare you. But I wasn't going to let you come out here alone, and I knew you'd put up a fight. We would've wasted time pissing and moaning at each other while this Mothman creature ripped Paulson's throat out."

"Fine," I said, and got out of the car. I was too angry and scared to say anything more. Grayson had a point. Still, lots of serial killers came across as rational people, didn't they?

As Grayson and I approached the driveway to Paulson's cabin, we saw a gray sedan blocking the dirt road.

"I had a feeling," Grayson said. "Good thing you've got a gun."

What? How did he know about my Glock?

"Had a feeling about what?" I asked.

"Things not being what they seem. They rarely are. Is that Paulson's car?"

"No."

"Then he's got company."

"Mothman?" I asked.

Grayson shook his head. "No. Most likely the FBI. Like I said before, Mothman prefers to fly."

Chapter Fifty-Five

GRAYSON CAUTIOUSLY climbed out of the Mustang, his Glock firmly in his grasp. He waved it slightly, motioning for me to follow his lead.

We skirted past the gray sedan and stalked, hunch-backed, the twenty yards to Paulson's cabin. Our only cover was the darkness of a crescent moon. As we approached the front door, the yellowish light on the front porch flickered.

The shower-scene music from *Psycho* jarred through my head.

"What's the plan?" I asked, hoping it didn't include me getting killed.

"We'll have to play it by ear," Grayson whispered. "Keep your voice down."

He pulled me next to him, our backs against the outside wall of the cabin. Then he leaned over, reached out, and turned the knob on the front door. He waited a beat, then pushed it open with a kick of his heel.

After about thirty seconds of listening to crickets, Grayson took a cautious peek inside. He waved me in.

Paulson's place was a sty. It was literally covered in spider webs, pizza boxes, and crushed beer cans.

"Geez," I whispered. "This guy's a pig."

"Help," a weak voice called out from behind a ratty sofa. It didn't sound like Paulson.

I gripped my Glock and inched over until I saw a pair of legs. Nice dress pants and Gucci loafers. Definitely not Paulson. Not on a cop's salary.

I whipped around the sofa and pointed my Glock at the guy. "Who are you?" I demanded with a harsh whisper. "What's going on here?"

A second later, Grayson was at my side.

"FBI," the man gurgled. Only then did I see the blood oozing out from beneath his jacket. "Agent Johnson. Officer ... down ... Terry Paulson ...." He hacked up blood.

"We'll find him," I said. "I know what he looks like."

"She ... she." Johnson fumbled for his jacket pocket, then lost consciousness.

I reached inside his jacket and pulled out a photo of a red-headed woman in a police uniform. "Terry Paulson's a woman?"

"*Was* a woman," Grayson said.

"I like redheads," Paulson's voice sounded behind us. "So sue me."

I jerked my head around. Paulson was standing with a semi-automatic weapon trained on Grayson.

My life flashed before my eyes. It didn't take long. I took a deep breath and went to my happy place. For a split second, Grandma Selma's sweet face replaced Paulson's angry one.

"Drop your guns," Paulson demanded.

"Do it," Grayson said.

I followed his lead, and bent down and laid my Glock on the floor beside his. As we started to rise, the blast of a gunshot sounded. I nearly fell to my knees. Then I realized it had come from outside the cabin.

Another blast sounded. The dim, yellow porch light shattered.

The room blinked out to black.

I dove behind the couch and crouched beside the fallen FBI agent. In the darkness, someone grabbed my hand and yanked it.

Hard.

I hoped it wasn't Paulson.

Whoever it was, he had the strength of a bear. I couldn't get free.

He pulled me across the room and we stumbled out the cabin door. In the faint starlight, I saw it was Grayson. Relief flooded through me. I finally knew who the good guy was.

"Let's get the hell out of here!" I whispered.

"You read my mind," Grayson quipped. "I knew you were talented, but really ...."

I punched his arm and giggled from sheer, scared-witless hysteria.

A twig snapped behind us. A shot ricocheted off a pine tree, showering us with splinters. Grayson grabbed my arm again, and we took off running for the car.

We were about thirty feet from the Mustang when another car's headlights came on, illuminating our backs and the road ahead of us.

"He's gotten to his car first," Grayson yelled. "We've got to get out of here fast."

"Who's driving?" I panted, out of breath.

"I call shotgun," Grayson answered, climbing into the passenger seat. "Get in, Drex, and drive like hell!"

I cranked the engine. When it caught on the first try, I wanted to kiss the dashboard. I slammed the Mustang into first and sideswiped the parked sedan as I made a wild attempt to turn it around on the narrow dirt road.

While I shifted and lurched, Grayson grabbed my phone and tried to call 9-1-1. There was no signal.

"I need to report that injured FBI agent," he said.

I shifted into reverse and made the last point on a ten-point turn. "Try again when we get nearer to Waldo. They've got better reception there."

"Right. But you may have to slow down when we find a signal. I'll need a minute to make the call."

I bit my lip and nodded, shifting into second gear. "I'll try to get some distance between us."

I stomped the gas pedal to the floor.

The tires spun dirt like a buzz-saw through soft pine all the way until we hit the pavement of US 301. I took the turn on two wheels. Soon, the blinking, pink-and-green neon sign of the Tropix Inn motel came into view. "Check your signal strength," I said, and let my foot off the gas.

"Three bars," he said, and punched 9-1-1. "FBI agent down at the Lake Alto Preserve," he shouted into the phone. "Send an ambulance, quick."

"Could you repeat that, sir?" I heard the operator say. I looked in the rearview mirror. Paulson's headlights were barreling toward us.

"FBI agent. Shot. Lake Alto Preserve," Grayson repeated as he flailed his arm at me to get going.

I hit the gas, but not soon enough. Paulson's blue Toyota slammed into the back of the Mustang with a sickening crunch.

I got a close-up look at the steering wheel, but avoided slamming my face into it. With my phone in his hand, Grayson didn't have time to brace for impact. He groaned as his already cracked clavicle hit the dashboard.

"You okay?" I asked as I stomped the gas.

"Yes. Cut the lights."

I did as instructed, and blew through the rest of Waldo in the dark, steering half blind.

As the forest and swamp retook both sides of the road, so did the darkness. Using the dim light of Paulson's headlights behind us and gut instinct, I managed to jerk the steering wheel sharply to the right and onto Obsidian Road.

I looked back. "Crap! Paulson's still behind us."

I'd hoped Paulson would miss the poorly marked turn, but the Mustang's back bumper had come loose and was dragging on the road, spewing a shower of sparks like a homing beacon for him to follow.

We were about three miles from Point Paradise when the Mustang coughed and skipped a beat. The tank was on empty.

I glanced in the rearview mirror. Paulson was about thirty yards away and gaining on us. I swore I could see his eyes glowing red behind the windshield like two evil reflectors.

The Mustang's engine sputtered and died.

"Crap!" I screamed as we began to roll silently along in the darkness. "We're out of gas!"

Grayson shot a glance in the side view mirror. "Oh, shit. Brace yourself—"

Paulson rammed the back of us again. The rear of the Mustang tilted up like a bucking bronco.

I tried to keep the car on the road, but with no power steering, the wheel locked down tight. The muscle car jackknifed, then rammed into the metal guardrail of the small bridge over Wimbly Creek.

Paulson's Toyota buzzed by us. Twenty yards past, his brakes squealed. His taillights flared.

He was coming back for us.

"We've gotta run for it!" I said.

"Excellent idea," Grayson said.

As I reached to unlock my seatbelt, a brilliant beam of white light shot out of the woods about eight feet off the ground. It honed in on us, blinding us as we sat in the Mustang.

I shook my head and squinted against the piercing glare.

Saved by alien abduction? Never saw that one coming.

I watched, dumbfounded, as the blazing white light split into two beams that bore down on us like huge, twin lasers. Unable to move my legs, I hazarded a glance down the road at Paulson. To my surprise, he'd turned his car around again and was hightailing it out of here.

Lucky him, I thought as his taillights flashed, then grew fainter against the powerful white lights engulfing and overpowering Grayson and me.

"What kind of aliens are they?" I asked Grayson. My sphincter puckered involuntarily in anticipation of being probed ....

"What in blue blazes are you two doing out here?" Earl's voice thundered from somewhere behind the twin laser beams.

The roof-mounted strobe lights on Bessie went out. In between the dark spots cratering my retinas, Earl and his gigantic black monster truck slowly came into view.

I never thought I'd be *that* glad to see my annoying cousin.

"You won't believe this," Grayson began.

I poked an elbow in his ribs to silence him. "We had a little car trouble, Earl," I said. "Give us a tow back home."

Earl gave the Mustang a once-over and whistled long and low. "Geez Louise. Looks like you backed over the Loch Ness Monster, Bobbie."

"Women drivers," Grayson said, leaving me with nothing to do but slap on a sheepish smile and save my payback for another day.

"Lemme hook her up. Good thing I was out coon hunting tonight." Earl climbed back in the truck, shifted gears, and began turning Bessie around.

While Earl hooked up the tow on the Mustang, I climbed into Bessie's cab beside Grayson and whispered, "Do me a favor. Keep quiet about this whole Mothman business. Earl already thinks I'm an idiot, and I just don't feel like getting into it with him tonight. We'll tell him everything tomorrow. Okay?"

"Tell who what?" Earl's head poked in the driver's side window. "Wait a minute." He shot us a sly grin. "Are y'all engaged?"

Grayson nearly snorted. "Well, it's a funny story ...."

"No!" I yelled. "We're not engaged. Are we ready to go?"

"Yes, ma'am. Party pooper." Earl got in, hit the gas, and pulled the Mustang out of the ditch. As we hobbled down the road dragging it behind us, I did my best to ignore Earl as he grilled us about our honeymoon plans.

We were about half a mile from home and an inch from me punching Earl in the face when we spotted taillights in the ditch off to the right side of the road.

"Look at that," Earl said, slowing Bessie to a crawl. "Another careless driver. Must be something in the air tonight."

From our vantage point six feet up in the air, we could see the undamaged back end of Paulson's vehicle. It was still running, but Paulson was nowhere to be seen.

"That looks like Paulson's car," Earl said. "Why in tarnation would he go off and leave his vehicle running like that?"

Before I could stop him, Grayson cracked, "Like I keep telling Drex here, Mothman doesn't need wheels. He prefers to fly."

I shot Grayson a dirty look. "I asked you not to mention 'the M-man.'"

"I think it's time Earl knew," Grayson said. "Because if my hunch is right, we haven't seen the last of the M-man tonight."

Chapter Fifty-Six

"YOU DON'T HAVE ANY proof that the guy pretending to be Paulson is the Mothman," I said to Grayson as Earl maneuvered Bessie around and backed the wrecked Mustang into the service bay.

"You don't have any proof he's *not*," Grayson argued.

"Is *that* what this is about?" Earl laughed. "I thought y'all was having a lover's quarrel." He waggled his eyebrows at me. "You afraid the little ol' Mothman's gonna get you, Bobbie?"

"Or maybe the Feds," Grayson said.

Earl winked at me. "The men in blue are after you!"

"Argh! You guys suck!" I clambered over Grayson's lap, yanked open the truck door, and tumbled onto my knees in the parking lot.

I got up and dusted myself off. "While you two joke around like a couple of jerks, whoever's after us could be hiding in the bushes getting ready to blow our heads off! The stupid Mothman has nothing to do with this!"

"But why'd the FBI show up if they wasn't chasing Mothman?" Earl asked.

I adjusted my wig. "The guy pretending to be Officer Paulson called them."

Earl climbed out of the cab. "But if Paulson's the killer, Bobbie, why would he call the FBI?"

Crap. He had me there. I scowled. "How the hell should I know?"

"The FBI doesn't usually get involved in simple homicide cases," Grayson said.

"I don't think ripping people's throats out is simple homicide," I argued. "But Earl's got a point. If this fake Paulson guy was guilty, why would he call the FBI? Why would he call *me* for backup?"

"Wait!" Earl's eyes grew wide—probably from the strain of using his noodle. "Maybe this *fake* Paulson's working undercover with the FBI, and he thinks one of *you* is the Mothman."

I rolled my eyes. "Then why would he shoot his own team?"

Grayson shut the cab door behind him. "Maybe this fake Paulson guy *didn't* call the FBI at all. He might've gotten a heads up somehow that the FBI was on the way, so he used it to his advantage. He could've been monitoring Terry Paulson's phone or radio or something. When he found out the FBI was coming, he played you along, Drex."

I grimaced. Grayson could be right. "He told me two prisoners escaped from Starke prison ten days ago."

"He might've known that because he was one of them," Grayson said.

I shook my head. "He didn't seem like the criminal type to me."

"Too good looking?" Grayson asked.

He struck a nerve. "No! The guy was *crying* at the scene of Vanderhoff's murder. He seemed genuinely unnerved. And he told me not to trust you, Grayson. Maybe when he saw us at his cabin, he thought you were holding me hostage. You *did* have a gun on me."

For once, Grayson finally lost his cool. "This guy's *an imposter*, Drex! He made us drop our weapons. He held us at gunpoint. He fired at us and tried to run us off the road! What more proof do you need that *he's* the bad guy here?"

I shrunk back. "Okay, okay. He's not who he says he is. I'll give you that. But that doesn't prove the guy's some ridiculous Mothman from outer space!"

I stomped my father's boots over to the office and flipped on the service bay lights for Earl. Grayson trailed after me.

"What about all those spider webs in his cabin?" Grayson argued. "They could've been the makings of a cocoon."

I made a sour face. "He doesn't clean up after himself. If that were a crime, every guy on the planet would be in jail."

"Okay. But if he's human, why did he abandon his vehicle? It was still running when we drove by."

I shrugged angrily. "Maybe he was afraid of being spotted, Grayson. He could've seen you on the phone. He might've thought you were calling the cops to report him."

Grayson grabbed my arm. "I don't think so, Drex. He left his car in the ditch because he didn't need it. He can fly."

I looked Grayson in the eye. "Don't you see how crazy that sounds?"

Grayson looked indignant. "No. Not really."

I shook my head. "Look. Whether Paulson's the Mothman or not, he's out there on the loose. We need to get inside and lock the doors. And call the Sheriff's Department!"

Grayson's face lost its tension. "You're right, Drex. He's nearby. And he's after us. We need to prepare ourselves."

A cold streak made my back arch. I suddenly became aware again of an uncomfortable dampness in my coveralls. For the second time since ditching diapers at age two, I'd peed my damned pants.

"Listen," I said. "I need a shower and a stiff drink. Stay here with Earl. He's exposed all alone out here in the service bay. When he's done unhooking the Mustang, both of you come upstairs and lock up behind you."

Grayson looked me over intently, as if trying to ascertain not only my plan, but my state of mind as well. Finally, he nodded. "Okay."

I turned and headed up the stairs to my apartment, each step harder and heavier than the last. Inside my bedroom, I kicked my father's burdensome old boots off into a corner. They seemed to stare at me accusingly as I unzipped my soiled coveralls. I dropped them on top of the boots and stared at the crumpled heap.

I peeled off my urine-soaked panties. Getting shot at had scared the piss out of me. Did that prove I wasn't fit to be a private eye? I added the wet panties to the heap in the corner, along with my sweaty bra. I put my wig on the bureau and padded to the bathroom, as bald and naked and vulnerable as a newborn chick.

As I stepped into the shower and the hot water trickled over my shaved head, I wondered how, in just under a week, my life could have gotten so far off track. One lousy, unlucky shot from some bike-thieving punk at the mall had changed the trajectory of my entire life.

A week ago, my daily routine had been simple. Mundane. Predictable. Now, it felt as if I'd been yanked out of line at Walmart and forced to star in a low-budget horror flick.

Mothman: The Redneck Years.

I stepped out of the shower, dried off, and wrapped myself in a towel. It was going to be a long night. I padded over to the closet to get a clean T-shirt. As I opened the closet door, my mouth fell open. My hairbrush dropped from my hand.

Staring at me, eyeball-to-eyeball, was the same creature I'd seen outside my bedroom window last night. The same hairy, human-like face. The same glowing, red eyes.

Mothman was finally coming out of the closet—and heading right for me!

I screamed. Mothman pounced on top of me. I guess I was going to die in Point Paradise after all.

Crap.

Chapter Fifty-Seven

I WAS IN A STRUGGLE for my life.

Mothman was real.

The creature came at me from its hiding place inside my closet. The sound of my own scream broke my paralytic shock. Running on instinct and adrenaline, I smashed my right fist into the monster's ugly, insectoid face.

He flew backward into my hanging clothes, then bounced back at me like a ricocheting bullet. I grimaced as his horrible, hairy face head-butted into mine.

His stiff, nasty whiskers scratched at my cheeks as I grabbed him by the torso and tried to throw him off balance. But I tripped on a flip-flop, lost my footing, and took him with me as I fell sideways onto the floor.

With the air nearly knocked out of me, I wrestled the creature on the shag carpet. Sometime during the struggle, Mothman ripped the towel from my body.

Naked as a jaybird, I scrambled on top of him, straddled his belly, and walloped him good with a one-two punch to the face. He tried to roll over onto his stomach, but I pinned him with my thighs. Then I set out delivering a set of kidneys jabs to his torso until he let out a weird, squeaky, fart-like sound.

Suddenly, the bedroom door flew open. Grayson burst in, holding Earl's shotgun. As he scrambled to my rescue, his face broke into a grin. Then the jerk burst out laughing.

I was ready to punch *him* in the face, too. "Uh ... a little help here?" I yelled.

Grayson shook his head. "What are you *doing*, Drex?"

I stared at Grayson, then down at my assailant. My adrenaline rush over, my thumping heart nearly stopped in my chest.

Mothman wasn't real.

He was a blow-up sex doll in a cheap monster mask.

I glared up at Grayson. My vision went red.

"Very funny, you smartass!" I shrieked. I yanked Grandma Selma's blanket off the inflatable doll's back and hastily covered myself with it.

Grayson pursed his lips in a poor attempt to hide his amusement. "Drex," he guffawed, "I promise, I had nothing to do with this."

"Sure you didn't!" I hissed. "Tell me, jackass. How'd you get that stupid thing to fly outside my bedroom window last night?"

"With one of them drones," Earl said, appearing in the doorway. He shot me a sadistic wink. "Ha ha, Bobbie! Looks like I got you good!"

Chapter Fifty-Eight

IT WAS NEARLY MIDNIGHT. The three of us were sitting vigil around the kitchen table, waiting for who-knew-what to come dragging up out of the darkness. I got up and poured Grayson and Earl some coffee, mainly because I didn't have any arsenic on hand.

"How could you do this to me?" I muttered angrily.

"Aww, don't take it so hard," Earl said. "Beth-Ann told me about how you and Grayson was gonna do a stakeout by the Stop & Shoppe. I figured I'd have me a little fun."

I shot Earl a scathing look. My whole life was nothing but a joke to him. "So Mothman was *you* the whole time."

Earl grinned proudly. "Yeppers."

"No." Grayson said, shaking his head. "It couldn't have been you in the woods the night of my accident. I didn't even know you then."

Earl looked over at Grayson. "What you talking about?"

"The night my RV broke down. I saw it. *Oculi rubere.*"

"The red octopus," Earl whispered, his eyes as big as plums.

"Red *eyes*," Grayson corrected. "The night I broke down, I saw glowing red eyes in the woods. I tried to roll up the window, then I felt this pain in my shoulder. I passed out. I couldn't remember anything else."

"That's when the Mothman bit you," Earl said.

"It was his seatbelt!" I yelled.

Grayson scooted his chair away from the table. "I can't say for sure if it was Mothman or not. But if it *was*, it wouldn't be the first time something like this has happened to me. I guess it's time I showed you two something."

"What?" Earl asked. "You got a tattoo of him?"

I thought Grayson was going to show us his two navels. But then he stood up and said, "Not here. Follow me."

We tromped down the stairs behind Grayson and out to the parking lot. Since we'd lost our guns at Alto Lake, Earl kept a wary watch for fake Paulson with his trusty Mossberg shotgun. After ascertaining the coast was clear, the three of us crossed the lot and climbed inside Grayson's RV.

"You might've noticed I've got padlocks on the cabinets and bedroom door," Grayson said as he pointed them out.

"Nope," Earl said. "Hadn't noticed at all."

I shot my cousin a dirty look.

"Well, there's a good reason for it." Grayson took out a jumble of keys and opened the padlock on one of the cabinets. It was full of brown bottles with eyedropper lids.

"You must really be into aromatherapy," I said dryly.

"Something like that." Grayson padlocked the cabinet again and shuffled down the small hallway, past the tiny bathroom to the bedroom. He unlocked deadbolt after deadbolt on the bedroom door. After unlocking the eighth one, he opened the door and stepped aside for Earl and me to have a look inside.

Cautiously, we peered into the room. The walls were padded with a thick, gray, quilted fabric that reminded me of the back of an insulated potholder. Heavy-gauge wire mesh covered the windows. It was the perfect lair for a psycho killer to keep his hostages.

Earl grunted. "Darn. I thought there was gonna be some kind a critter in here."

I turned to Grayson. "What is it?"

"It's an electromagnetic holding cell."

"Is that like a toaster oven?" Earl asked.

Grayson sighed. "In layman terms, it's a monster trap."

Earl's eyes lit up. "Woohoo!"

Grayson nodded. "And it's time we set this trap to catch the Mothman."

"You're kidding," I said.

Grayson shook his head. "No. I'm dead serious." His eyes scanned the ceiling of the RV above his head. "He's out there. I can feel him. But we're going to need the right bait."

Grayson shot a glance at Earl, raised an eyebrow, and tilted his head toward me.

Both men turned their heads, locked eyes with me, and smiled.

I scowled. "What?"

Then I figured out what, and ran for my life.

Chapter Fifty-Nine

"COME ON, DREX! WHAT do moths find irresistible?" Grayson's voice sounded muffled as he tried to reason with me from the other side of my locked bedroom door.

"I dunno," I yelled through the door. "You're the genius here. *Mothballs?*" I looked around for something to barricade the door.

"No. *Flames.*"

"So what? What's the pyro-maniacal leanings of a deranged insect got to do with *me?*"

"Think about it, Drex. I think he's attracted to your flaming red hair. He said he liked redheads, remember?"

I stopped shoving the chest of drawers toward the door. "That was fake Paulson, not Mothman."

"Po-*tay*-to, po-*tah*-to."

I groaned. "Okay. So what if he *does* like redheads? I'm bald, remember?"

"That's only a temporary setback. When he met you at the mall, you had all your hair, right?"

I frowned begrudgingly. "Yeah."

"Listen," Grayson said. "I think we have a chance of luring him into the RV if you could persuade him."

"Me? *Persuade* him? How?"

"With your feminine, redhead wiles."

My face puckered. "Right. And then what? Let him kill me in your rundown RV deathtrap? Uh...*no thanks!*" I tugged on the chest of drawers again.

"No. If I'm right about this, he'll be powerless around you."

I stopped and put an ear to the door. "What do you mean, powerless?"

"It's hard to explain. I'm going to have to show you. You're going to have to open the door."

I laughed bitterly. "No way, Grayson. I'm not falling for any more of you guys' stupid pranks."

"Don't you find it interesting that Mothman appeared to you in your Grandma's afghan? Your *security blanket?*"

I thought about it for a second. "No. That was Earl's doing."

"Oh. Right. Well, still, what if this Mothman creature feeds on your fears? What if he's able to lure his victims with a false sense of security?"

My brow furrowed. "What do you mean?"

"What if Mothman can somehow read minds, Drex? Know his victims' safe places? Then, he uses that knowledge to lure his victims. You know, make them feel like they have nothing to fear. It would explain how he's been able to overwhelm them without an apparent struggle."

"Or maybe he's just a smooth talker," I said through the door. "Like somebody else I know."

"What?" Grayson said.

Suddenly, I remembered something. "Grayson, in the cabin tonight, right before somebody shot out the lights, I saw an image of Grandma Selma's face over Paulson's. Was that a hallucination?"

"I don't think so, Drex. I think your vision was the work of the Mothman. He must be able to project images into your mind. He knew you wouldn't shoot your grandmother, right?"

My gut flopped at the thought.

"This creature knew your safe space," Grayson said. "It's your Grandma Selma, isn't it?"

I frowned. "Yes."

"He tricked you, if only for a moment. Now it's our job to figure out how to trick him back."

"How?"

"I'm going to need your wig."

I winced. "My wig? But I'll be bald! What do you need it for?"

"You'll see."

I cracked open my bedroom door and peeked out. Grayson was in the hall alone.

"Where's Earl?" I asked.

"He said he's making booby traps."

Aww, geez.

"You don't know him like I do," I said. "He shouldn't be left alone out there unsupervised."

Grayson nodded. "Okay. Then let's go back down to the service bay."

I grabbed Earl's Lucky Red ball cap to cover my bald head and handed over my *Woody Woodpecker* wig to Grayson. He and I tromped downstairs to the parking lot. While he walked over to his RV with my wig, I went into the service bay to see what Earl was up to.

As anticipated, I was neither surprised nor impressed by Earl's redneck ingenuity.

In a masterwork only he could have concocted, my brilliant cousin had taped together sections of cardboard boxes until they'd formed the basic size and shape of a refrigerator. Then he'd covered the whole Frankenstein mess with duct tape, sticky side out.

As usual, disaster had struck. Somehow the boy genius had managed to get the whole contraption stuck to his back. As I walked up, he was flailing around like Quasimodo stuck to a roach motel.

"Gimme a hand here, Bobbie!"

I smirked. "If I did, then I'd only have one left."

"Come on, Cuz."

"What *is* that thing, anyway?"

"What the heck's it look like?"

I smirked. "A redneck's worst nightmare?"

"It's a Mothman trap, you dingdong. Help me get it set up."

"How'd you get it stuck on your back?"

"I was gonna tote it out to the RV and ... uh ... I kinda forgot it was sticky."

I rolled my eyes and sighed. "Fabulous. Follow me."

"What's the plan?" I asked as Earl shuffled along behind me, hunched over with the trap stuck to his back.

"We make this thing look like a moth cocoon," Earl said as we made our way across the parking lot. "Grayson said that might be the creature's safe space."

Before I could come up with anything more stupid than that, Grayson emerged from his RV with a Windex bottle in one hand, my wig in the other.

"What's that?" I nodded at the Windex bottle half-full of brownish liquid.

Grayson beamed. "My proprietary blend of moth pheromones. I took the liberty of spraying your wig with them." He handed me the soggy mass of red hair. "Now, put it back on and I'll spray you down."

I stared at him. "Not in this lifetime."

Grayson blanched. "What? I've left the bedroom door in the RV unlocked. The plan is, you get all pheromoned up and wait for him in there. Earl and I will hide nearby. When Mothman goes inside, we'll run in and stick that cocoon thing over him."

Grayson took a glance at Earl's convoluted duct-tape trap and his confidence evaporated. "Earl, I told you to put the duct tape on the *inside*."

I stared at the two men. I was supposed to entrust my life to *these* two idiots? *Grizzly Adams* caught in his own moth trap, and Professor Pheromones with a Windex bottle full of happy hormone juice?

I don't think so.

"Hold on, gentlemen," I said. "I've got a better idea."

Chapter Sixty

TYPICAL ACADEMIC.

Grayson's moth-trap idea might've seemed good in theory, but it didn't translate in the real world—at least, not in *my* real world. If all went according to *my* plan, however, Mothman would soon be buzzing around us again, and into Grayson's monster trap.

I set my jaw to Wonder Woman mode and got to work.

I ripped Earl's sticky, cardboard box from the back of his flannel shirt and tossed it on the ground.

"Grab your duct tape and follow me," I commanded. "And you, Grayson. Spray down your monster trap bedroom with that pheromone stuff of yours. But be sure and save some for me. Come on, Earl."

My burly cousin shot me a look, but then tromped up the stairs behind me. He followed me into my apartment and down the hall to my bedroom.

I pointed at the floor. "Fix Mothman so he can fly again."

Earl grinned as he contemplated the deflated remains of his blow-up-doll creation. "Looks like he put up a good fight, Cuz."

"Get to work," I barked. "And don't use Grandma's afghan this time. Use *this* instead."

Earl caught what I threw at him and grinned. "Yes, boss man." He ripped off a piece of duct tape with his teeth, got down on his knees, and went to work.

While Earl doctored up the Mothman sex doll, I fished through my closet for the perfect outfit for our flying bait. I re-dressed the re-inflated body while Earl patched leaks and tested out the drone.

"Does it still work?" I asked.

"Ain't too much worse for wear, Bobbie. You never were good with a punch."

"Har har. Grab that stupid thing and let's roll."

When Earl and I emerged downstairs a few minutes later, the flying drone had been transformed. With the help of an old nightie of mine, fuzzy high-heeled slippers, and one of Grayson's pink T-shirts for a cape, Mothman had become Moth*woman*.

Grayson's jaw fell open.

"Spray her down, professor," I said. "Earl, tape that wig to her head, then let her fly."

"Yes, boss man."

"All right, men," I said, crossing my arms. "Let's get that pheromone scent up in the air, shall we?"

WITH EARL AT THE HELM of the remote control, Mothwoman worked like an insect's wet dream. She buzzed her way around the vicinity of the garage and bordering woods, advertising her wares like a mothy harlot.

Unfortunately, about ten minutes into it, things went a little off plan.

Earl emerged unexpectedly from the bushes and stepped under the light of a lamp post in the parking lot.

His hands were in the air.

Behind him was a man holding a gun to Earl's ribcage.

And it wasn't Paulson.

Chapter Sixty-One

"FBI SPECIAL AGENT TOM Hicks," the guy announced. "Come out now. And if you've got any weapons, lay them down."

Grayson and I glanced at each other from behind the RV. He nodded and laid Earl's Mossberg shotgun on the asphalt. I followed suit with my Daisy BB gun.

"What's going on here?" Hicks demanded.

"We're on your side, Agent Hicks," I called out from across the lot. "We're trying to apprehend Paulson ... I mean the guy who's pretending to be Terry Paulson."

The FBI agent poked his gun in Earl's ribs. "Is this him? I found him crouched in the bushes, giggling like a moron."

"No," I said, taking a cautious step toward them. "I know he looks abnormal, but he's just my cousin, Earl Shankles."

Suddenly, a large, pinkish, bird-like creature buzzed over us, mere feet from our heads. We all looked up.

"What the?" Agent Hicks yelled. He pointed his weapon toward the sky and fired twice.

Shards of plastic rained down on the parking lot. A moment later, Mothwoman smacked into the asphalt between us. She squealed and deflated with a long, flappy, whine.

I glanced up at Agent Hicks. His face was impossible to describe. He pointed his gun at Mothwoman, then Earl, then me; then just let it drop to his side. "Can somebody please explain what the hell is going on here?"

"It's a decoy," I said. "We're using it to lure Paulson in."

"With a flying blow-up doll?" Hicks eyed me like I was crazy. I couldn't blame him.

"It's a long story," I began, but Grayson cut me off.

"We don't have time for long explanations. Agent Hicks, whoever this guy is who shot your partner, he ditched his car nearby. He's out there somewhere ... he could be aiming a gun at us right now."

Agent Hicks nodded toward our Mothman trap. "Who's in the RV?"

Grayson fumbled. "Uh ... no one. It's part of the lure. I put on some soft music and lit a candle."

I smirked. "Nice touch."

Hicks jaw went tense. He pointed his gun at us again. "Shut up! I need some straight answers. Why is there a blow-up doll here wearing a monster mask and a red wig?"

I grimaced. "This Paulson imposter is ... uh ... partial to redheads."

"And monster ladies," Earl added, as if that explained everything else Agent Hicks needed to know.

I was preparing myself for being cuffed and led to a psych ward when Grayson stepped forward.

"Agent Hicks, I'm Nick Grayson, Private Investigator." He flashed his badge. "I'm working on a case for Chief Warren Engles."

Agent Hicks' eyes grew wide. But not as wide as mine.

"I'm here investigating reports of Mothman sightings in the vicinity. The apparatus you shot down was, as my assistant said, a pheromone decoy."

Agent Hicks appeared incredulous. "I thought Mothman was just an urban legend."

"That's what I'm here trying to determine."

Agent Hicks shook his head. "I've heard some ridiculous crap in my day, but this takes the prize." He chewed his lip for a moment, blew out a breath, and looked Grayson in the eye. "Okay. What's the plan?"

Grayson turned my way. All of a sudden, all eyes were on me.

Again.

Chapter Sixty-Two

"TERRY PAULSON WAS REPORTED missing by her family five days ago," Agent Hicks said as the four of us crammed into the small banquet in Grayson's RV. "I ran the plates on the Corolla in the ditch. They were stolen. The number's registered to a Mandy Vanderhoff."

I wanted to kick myself in the head. The blue Corolla. There were millions of them out there. Mandy drove one. I hadn't made the connection.

"This guy must've abducted Mandy," I said. "She has red hair. Terry Paulson has red hair. I've got ... I shot a glance around at the men's faces. I *had* red hair."

Agent Hicks nodded. "Interesting observation. Officially, Terry Paulson was last seen ten days ago, when she left Starke prison driving a police transport vehicle. Her passenger was a murder suspect named Eugene Hollister."

I gasped. "The guy pretending to be Terry Paulson must be Eugene Hollister! The dead body in the woods ... with the orange jumpsuit. Hollister killed her and switched clothes. He messed up her face, so no one could identify her."

"You could be right, young lady," Agent Hicks said. "Yesterday, we found Terry Paulson's body in a shallow grave about two and a half miles south of here."

"I told Paulson—I mean Hollister that I'd found a body," I said. "He must've gone back and hid it, then made me go back to the scene to show me it wasn't there." I shook my head. "He wanted me to think I'd imagined it. Then he must've gone back later that day and buried it. The rain would've washed away his trail."

"But why hadn't anyone reported Ms. Paulson missing until now?" Grayson asked.

"Apparently, the guy assumed Terry Paulson's identity," Agent Hicks said. "She was filling in as interim officer for Jack Barker. Nobody knew her in Waldo. Hollister could've reported in to the Alachua Sherriff's Department online. Or used a device to change his voice to sound like a woman over the phone."

My back stiffened. "They make devices like that?"

"Sure," Grayson said. "Hollister might've been able to fool department employees with it, but he couldn't fool Terry Paulson's family."

I shook my head. "That's why he didn't want to go to Vanderhoff's himself. Paulson ... I mean Hollister. He gave me that assignment because he was afraid old lady Vanderhoff would recognize Mandy's car. She must've made the connection anyway, and so he had to kill her."

"What's this Hollister fella look like?" Earl asked.

Agent Hicks pulled out a photo. "Kind of like Paul Newman, some say. I, personally, don't see it. Reports say he's got a way with the ladies, though."

Earl and Grayson both shot me *told you so* looks. I grimaced. As Agent Hicks passed the photo to Earl, I snatched it from his grubby hand and stared into the handsome, irritatingly attractive face.

I didn't recognize it.

"That's not him," I said, shaking my head. "That's not the guy who was pretending to be Terry Paulson."

I handed the photo to Grayson. He agreed. "You're right. It's not."

Hicks stared at us both. "Then who the hell are you trying to catch?"

I bit down on my lip. Hard. "I guess we'd better reset that trap and find out."

Chapter Sixty-Three

PHASE TWO OF "OPERATION Moth Trap" was well underway.

The door to the RV's monster-trap bedroom was open for business. A few feet down the hall, Grayson and Agent Hicks were holed up inside the miniscule bathroom. I didn't even want to know how two grown men were making that work. The soft music was playing again, and because Grayson insisted, a candle was left burning on the kitchen table to offer Mothman a symbolic "flame."

Our comrade in arms, the dearly deflated Mothwoman, was duct-taped to the RV's open doorway. She was wearing my wig, my sexiest lingerie, and a nylon rope around her waist.

I was positioned upstairs in my bedroom above the garage. My role was to flick on a lighter if I saw anyone approach. The light would signal Earl. He was hiding inside a smelly trash can by the RV.

I smiled to myself. That had been my idea. Being in charge of the plan had its privileges.

Once I signaled Earl, his job was to pop up out of the trash can and tap on the bathroom window to alert Grayson and Hicks that our prey was approaching the RV door. They, in turn, would then tug on the rope and yank Mothwoman inside.

Once the perpetrator stepped inside the RV, Earl was supposed to run around and close the door, then make sure it stayed closed until Agent Hicks and Grayson gave the all clear.

I looked down at the RV in the parking lot and shook my head. I wasn't kidding myself. This was a foolish plan devised by foolish people. Still, as I stood by the window and kept watch, I prayed with all my might that God would keep his promise to take care of children and fools.

Because if this didn't work, Earl and Grayson would never let me live it down.

Never.

Chapter Sixty-Four

ABOUT A QUARTER PAST two, I was about to call the whole thing off when a shadowy figure appeared out of nowhere. I blinked, unsure if I was just seeing things. In a split second, the dark figure somehow managed to traverse the parking lot. He was nearly to the RV door.

"Damn!" I hissed, and fumbled with the lighter. It faltered.

I tried again. The lighter shot out a flame. I pressed my nose against the windowpane, trying to see if Earl had seen my signal. My breath fogged up the glass. When I wiped it with my sleeve, the figure was gone.

So was Mothwoman.

Suddenly, a loud ruckus arose from the RV. It began to rock to and fro like it was in a Cat-4 hurricane. I opened the window and stuck my head out for a better view. That's when I saw Earl run into the RV toting a baseball bat.

The door slammed closed. An electric buzz stung the frosty air. Suddenly, all the lights in the house and parking lot went out, plunging everything into pitch-black darkness.

My heart lurched in my chest. I stood still as a stone, waiting, grinding my teeth in the inky night.

What in the hell's going on in there?

After what seemed like an hour, one lone flashlight emerged from the RV. Whoever had a hold of it pointed it up to my darkened bedroom window. The glare blinded me instantly.

"Argh!" I fumbled backward as footsteps crunched across the parking lot toward my open window. I tiptoed back to the windowsill, and strained to see beyond the stars dancing in my eyes.

"Who is it?" I cried out, hoping Mothman wasn't going to fly through my window again.

I was about to need another change of underwear when a second flashlight appeared. Then a third.

Then Earl's voice rang out from the gloom.

"Woohoo! Bobbie! We caught us a Mothman!"

Chapter Sixty-Five

"SO, WHO'S IN THE TRAP?" I yelled down from the bedroom window.

All three men were huffing and puffing, leaning against the wall of the garage looking like they'd just survived Walmart's Black Friday doorbuster sale.

"Eugene ... Hollister," Agent Hicks said between gasping lungfuls of air.

Earl grabbed his side and wheezed, "Boy howdy, I sure could use me a beer."

Grayson looked up at me. "How about you, Drex?"

"Me?" I called down. "I sure could use me a new life."

I WENT DOWNSTAIRS, and after the guys finally caught their breath, the four of us crammed into Grayson's RV.

"I don't get it," I said as Agent Hicks squeezed into the banquette across from me. "Why would Hollister be after *us?*"

"You saw him out at Lake Alto. He shot a federal agent out there. My partner Rick Tomlinson."

"Is he okay?"

"I can't say for sure. I waited until the ambulance arrived. He was hit pretty bad, but still alive when I left. You can bet Hollister was trying to eliminate you all as witnesses."

I chewed my lip. "But it wasn't Hollister I saw at the cabin. It was the guy impersonating Paulson."

Hicks looked me in the eye. "You absolutely sure about that?"

"It was dark, Drex," Grayson said. "We only saw him for a second. Hollister and the guy impersonating Officer Paulson look a lot alike. It could've been Hollister who ambushed us in the cabin, then chased us back here with Vanderhoff's stolen car."

How could I argue with Grayson? I thought I'd seen Grandma Selma out at that cabin, too. What kind of reliable witness did *I* make? With that stupid gonad stuck in my brain, I couldn't be sure that *anything* I saw was real. There was a real possibility I could've gotten Hollister and the other guy mixed up.

I blew out a breath. "I guess you're right, Grayson. But even if Hollister *was* the shooter, this other guy pretending to be Paulson ... he has to be tangled up with Hollister somehow. Why else would they have both known about that cabin at Alto Lake?"

Earl whistled and shook his head. "Is that coffee ready yet? All this figurin' is starting to give me a headache."

Grayson leaned over and checked the pot of coffee perking on his propane stove. It was our only option for an early-morning cup of joe. It was only five-thirty. The Stop & Shoppe didn't open until eight o'clock, and I didn't have any electricity.

I'd checked the electric meter. Hollister hadn't cut off my power. The electric company had. They weren't likely to turn it on any time soon, either. I owed them more than my entire net worth.

"You may be right, Ms. Drex," Agent Hicks said. "The two men might be working together. But right now, *your* mystery man's not on our radar. In fact, we don't have any data on him whatsoever. As far as we're concerned, he doesn't exist. But you come up with picture or a name for him, and I'll be the first to help you out."

Grayson poured the coffee while we waited on the good folks of Alachua County Sheriff's Department to provide luxury armed transportation for Eugene Hollister back to whatever dark holding cell they had waiting for him. From the sounds emanating from the bedroom of the RV, Hollister was none too happy about it, either.

"What about Mandy and Mildred Vanderhoff?" I asked Agent Hicks. "Who'll be working on their cases?"

"The Sheriff's Department, I suspect. But right now, they're both missing persons. I hate to say it, but thousands of people go missing every day, Ms. Drex. Cases with bodies take precedent."

"But Vanderhoff ... she was killed in her house. Her body was there."

Hicks took a sip from his mug. "Did you see it?"

I shook my head. "No. I saw blood, but no body."

"Neither did anyone else." Hicks took a peek out the small window beside the banquette. "Looks like my ride is here. Thanks for helping me capture Hollister, but we'll need y'all to clear out of the RV while we get him loaded."

We tumbled out of the RV. Earl headed for the bathroom in the service bay. Grayson walked toward the woods that lined the parking lot. I followed him over there.

"You've been awfully quiet, Grayson."

He sighed. "There goes a cool million, easy. Nothing I can do to stop it, either."

"Wait. You *still* think Eugene Hollister's the Mothman?"

"Not *the* Mothman. *A* Mothman. I think there's more than one out there, Drex."

I grimaced. "Really?"

"The guy we knew as Paulson. Where is *he? Who* is he? I agree with you. He and Hollister were working together."

"Okay. But why?"

"Lots of species join forces for survival. Safety in numbers, you know. But they especially gather together during mating season."

My nose crinkled. "Mating season?"

"Consider this, Drex. What if our Paulson impersonator had chosen Mandy Vanderhoff as his mate, and you were supposed to be Hollister's?"

I nearly choked. "What! That's crazy, even for you, Grayson! And why me and Mandy?" I shot him a look. "And don't say it's because they like redheads."

Grayson's lip twisted. "Only half of one percent of all the people on the planet are redheads, Drex. Why would these guys have gone to all the trouble to find you and Mandy unless there was something about you two that set you apart? What if redheads possess certain unique genetic traits that allow Mothmen to produce offspring with them?"

"Geez! If that were true, why didn't they take Terry Paulson when they had the chance?"

Grayson shrugged. "Maybe they tried. She could've been killed in the struggle to abduct her. Maybe she was sterile. Or had a hysterectomy. Or maybe there were three Mothmen, not just two."

I shook my head in exasperation. "Or maybe there were none. You never give up, do you, Grayson?"

He smiled thoughtfully. "Now what would be the fun in that?"

Chapter Sixty-Six

AFTER GIVING OUR STATEMENTS to the Sheriff's Department officers on the scene, we were summoned by the deputy in charge of the transport detail.

"You must be Detective Drex," he said as I approached his vehicle. He laughed and shook his head. "Hicks said you were a looker."

Considering the bald dome I was sporting under Lucky Red, I didn't know if I'd just been complimented or insulted.

The man held up two Glocks. "Which one of these belongs to you?"

"The nineteen, thanks." I took my gun and stepped back from the window of his vehicle.

"And this one's yours, I presume, Detective Grayson. By the way, Chief Engles sends his regards."

"Thanks." Grayson grabbed his Glock and headed toward the garage. I followed, hot on his heels.

"What's this business with Chief Engles?" I called out behind him.

Grayson turned to face me. "That's on a need-to-know basis, Drex."

I bit down so hard the tendons in my neck stood out. "You know, Grayson, this Paulson imposter we've been chasing? He's not a Mothman. He's probably just like *you*—another weirdo chasing down imaginary monsters."

Grayson's face was unreadable. "Why would he pretend to be Terry Paulson?"

I gave him half an eye roll. "Don't try to tell me you've never pretended to be someone you're not."

Grayson smiled softly. "Fair enough. But for the record, I think you're wrong. I think he's another Mothman."

I grimaced. "But that would mean ...."

"He's still out there."

I thought of my happy place. Grandma Selma. Then something clicked in my mind.

Grandma Selma. At the cabin. Was Grayson right? Did Hollister project her image into my mind? If so, he could've easily done the same with the image of the man I knew as Paulson. Hollister could've been both *men.*

I cleared my throat. "Maybe he's *not*, Grayson. What if Eugene Hollister is actually a shapeshifter? What if he and the man who pretended to be Paulson are the same guy? Then there'd be only one Mothman, and he's in federal custody."

Grayson's right eyebrow ticked up. "Well, I didn't see *that one* coming from you, Drex." He rubbed his chin. "Huh. I suppose it's possible. If Hollister can turn into a moth and fly, putting on a different human face should be child's play."

The sun was just beginning to peek over the horizon, and I shivered as we walked together back to the service bay. Earl was busy surveying the RV for damages caused by our stakeout last night, and I was still searching for a normal, pedestrian answer to the bizarre events of the past week.

"Something still bugs me," I said to Grayson. "Those weird phone calls to Mildred Vanderhoff. What reason would a creature like the Mothman have for following her around and asking her dumb stuff like what year it was?"

"I think he went there to see if Vanderhoff would recognize him or his voice. You know, to see if he needed to eliminate her as a witness."

I frowned. "Maybe."

Grayson poked me in the ribs. "Or the phone calls could've been little green men pulling a couple of cosmic fast ones."

I stopped in my tracks. "Little green men? Gimme a break, Grayson! Why would beings from outer space dress in old-fashioned clothes? Or use outdated landline phones to communicate with us? It doesn't make any sense!"

Grayson raised an eyebrow playfully. "Who knows, Drex? Maybe they were using an outdated issue of *Travel Guide to the Galaxies*. Or maybe their time machine was on the fritz and screwed up the dates. Like you said, the guy *did* ask what year it was."

I shot Grayson a look that made him wince. "He was probably just trying to make Vanderhoff look crazy. Like he tried to do with me."

"That's one theory," Grayson conceded. "But how about this? Just suppose for a minute that we're dealing with a couple of juvenile delinquent aliens who stole daddy's flying saucer, and are out on a joy ride. Why not prank a few humans along the way? You know, like you did to Vanderhoff when you were a kid."

I shot him a scowl. "Ugh."

Grayson grinned. "Or, think about this. What if this whole thing was some superior beings' attempt to blow our squirrelly little minds and leave us to ponder the exact questions you're asking right now?"

I shook my head. "Come on, Grayson. There's got to be a logical explanation for this. What did that guy say happened? The one who wrote *The Mothman Prophecies*?"

Grayson smiled. "John Keel. He concluded his investigation by citing Socrates. 'The more I learn, the less I know.'"

"That's real helpful," I said sourly.

"In the end, Keel decided that the whole Mothman debacle had been some kind of game."

I scowled. "A *game?*"

"Yeah. Keel realized that as soon as he figured out some element of the game, the other side changed the rules. You know, you chase a red-eyed, flying creature, they replace it with lights in the sky. You chase the lights, they send strange men door-to-door asking inane questions."

"Who is *they?*"

"Superior intelligences. Perhaps even the universal mind itself."

I shook my head. "That's crazy."

Grayson shrugged. "Perhaps. But as my personal hero, Charles Fort, speculated, 'If there is a universal mind, must it be sane?'"

My jaw came unhinged. "Even if all this *has* all been a game, why Point Paradise? Why now?"

Grayson shrugged. "This kind of thing is nothing new, Drex. Or even that uncommon. Since recorded history, mankind has been plagued by the unexplained. Monsters, magical beings, visitors from the stars."

"That's true," Earl said, emerging from the RV. "I found a two-headed turtle in Wimbly Swamp last year. Remember, Bobbie?"

Grayson laughed. "A two-headed turtle here, a Wendigo there. A mermaid in the ocean. A reptilian humanoid in an underground tunnel. What if all of these things were sent here to shake us up? To boggle our minds? Simply for the amusement of some higher intelligence who gets off on making us squirm?"

I grimaced. "Geez. That's a dismal prospect."

Grayson grinned. "Or maybe they do it to spark our imaginations. To see what we're capable of as a species. To keep things interesting for them *and* us. Either way, I, for one, want to keep on playing."

I studied Grayson. "Why? It's a game for lunatics!"

Grayson straightened his shoulders. "Because one day, I want to win a round. How about you, Drex? Don't you want to play along?"

I pressed my molars together and sighed in contemplation.

Grayson and me versus the quite possibly insane cosmic consciousness.

I've played worse odds.

Chapter Sixty-Seven

THE LIGHTS BLINKED back on in my apartment. Grayson had placed a phone call half an hour ago. That's all he would tell me.

"You thinking what I'm thinking?" Grayson asked me.

I groaned. "God, I certainly hope not."

"*Tacos*, Drex. I think we need one more run to El Molino before I blow this Popsicle stand."

I smirked. "Point Paradise isn't big enough to have a Popsicle stand. But okay. I'll borrow Bessie from Earl. We need to pick up the last few parts for your RV anyway. I don't know how you got them delivered in two hours ... and right now, I don't want to know."

Grayson grinned. "You're learning. It's better not to ask."

"IT'S TIME TO FISH OR cut bait," Grayson said as he dragged a chip through a bowl of El Molino's famous salsa. "Are you going to join my little traveling sideshow or not?"

I winced with indecision. "I'm not sure."

"Well, what *are* you sure of in this little slice of heaven we call life?"

Really?

I shot Grayson some side-eye. "I know I don't want to stay in Point Paradise."

Grayson frowned. His voice took on an unfamiliar, serious, business-like tone. "Sorry, Drex. That's not a good enough reason to join me. I want a partner with a burning desire to explore the unknown. Not someone simply looking to escape their current circumstances."

My brow furrowed. "I understand. Can you give me another hour or two to think it over?"

The waitress delivered a huge plate of tacos. Grayson and I eyed them greedily. He reached for one and I grabbed his hand.

"Well? Can I have just a little more time to let you know?"

Grayson locked eyes with me. "Why? What's the hesitation?"

"I have obligations here."

Grayson nodded and grabbed a taco. "I tell you what. You can have until the first signs of indigestion kick in. Fair enough?"

I smiled faintly and nodded. "Fair enough."

AFTER THE HUMONGOUS amount of tacos Grayson and I put away, I knew my time was running short. Sure enough, as soon as the flashing yellow light that marked Point Paradise came into view, Grayson belched.

"Excuse me," he said. "Well, looks like your time's up. Are we going to be partners or not?"

From the driver's seat of my cousin's monster truck, I spotted Earl working away in the service bay. My Southern guilt took over.

"Listen. I want to, Grayson. But I can't leave Earl in this financial mess."

Grayson looked at me wistfully. "I understand."

As I maneuvered Bessie's huge tractor tires into the parking lot, Earl came out toting a paper bag.

I rolled down the window. "What's that?"

Earl grinned. "Your trade for the tacos."

My face scrunched warily. I handed my cousin his lunch, and grabbed the paper bag he offered in exchange. I opened it cautiously and took a peek inside. My nose was assaulted by the stench of half a dozen balls of poop.

"Argh!" I smashed the bag closed and looked over at Earl.

He grinned and laughed like a redneck hyena. "Hahaha! Gotcha, Bobbie!"

"Earl, for the last time, *you're fired!*"

"What is it?" Grayson asked. "What's in the bag?"

I shoved the paper sack across the bench seat at Grayson. "See for yourself."

Grayson opened it and yelped. "Where'd you get this, Earl?"

My cousin grinned. "Compliments of one Mr. Eugene Hollister."

Grayson stuck his nose in the bag and sniffed.

Yep. Total sicko. And to think I was seriously thinking about entrusting my life to this guy ....

Grayson let out a whoop of delight. "Earl, you're not fired. Drex! Get out and come with me."

"What for?"

Grayson didn't answer. He just made a beeline for the RV.

I climbed down out of the cab and followed him.

"What's going on?" I asked, watching Grayson fiddle with a piece of wood paneling on the wall above the RV's banquette. He peeled away a section of paneling. I nearly fainted. Row upon row of dollar bills were stacked between the joists in the wall like insulation. He grabbed a six-inch thick bundle and handed it to me.

"Is this enough to buy your freedom?"

I blanched. "What? Why would you do that for me?"

"I'm not doing anything *for* you, Drex. It's payday. You and Earl *earned* this money. You wouldn't believe how much Mothman scat goes for on the black market."

My mouth fell open. "You mean ... I could be free?"

"Sure. As long as money's the only thing holding you back."

I chewed my lip. "Well, I also need to get my full P.I. license."

Grayson grinned. "I think I can help with that. What do you say? You ready to play the game?"

"The game?"

"Yes. The game for lunatics, as you put it."

I smiled up at Grayson. "Yeah. I'm ready to play. But unlike you, I don't care about winning. I just want to find the jerks who're running the show and rip 'em a new one."

Grayson laughed. "Hey. To each his own."

AFTER THE SHOCK OF seeing more cash than I knew existed on Earth wore off and my legs were able to hold my weight again, Grayson and I emerged from the RV to find Earl pacing around the wrecked chassis of my father's vintage Mustang.

He wagged a finger at me. "You sure did a number on your dad's car, Bobbie. It's gonna take me ages to fix it."

I shot him a wry smile. "Yeah. You might want to check the air filter while you're at it."

Grayson laughed.

Earl opened his mouth to speak, but I cut him off.

"Listen, Earl. The parts to finish off the RV are on the front seat of Bessie. Grayson wants to leave tonight, so I suggest you work on his vehicle first."

"Yes, boss man." Earl surveyed the massive damage to the Mustang and let out a low whistle. "Looks like I'm gonna need me a bigger bag of Fritos, Bobbie."

I shrugged. "Is that so? Well, you're gonna have to go to the A&P all by yourself, Earl. I quit."

My cousin's eyes grew wide beneath his shaggy bangs. "What? You can't quit on me, Bobbie. You're the *boss man*."

"Watch me." I handed him a paper sack.

He took it absently. "But you're a born grease monkey, like me."

"No, Earl. I thought I was. But turns out, I am so totally *not*."

Earl pouted. "You just gonna up and leave me here all alone, holding this sack of poop?"

"Look inside, Earl."

He shot me a wary glance, then opened the sack. One peek inside and his face turned as green as the stacks of money filing the bag. He looked up at me, his mouth hanging open like a screen door off its hinges.

My heart pinged.

Man, I thought it would feel better to finally win a round with him.

I scowled. "Earl, just finish up the repairs on Grayson's RV. And you can have Dad's Mustang. I won't be needing it anymore. I'm going with Grayson."

Earl took a long look at Grayson, then at me. "You sure about this, Cuz?"

"Yeah. I'm sure. I'm a lousy mechanic. And a lousy boss. Dad was right to pick you over me. I'm going upstairs to finish up some stuff."

"But—"

I whirled around, suddenly angry as wet hen. "Don't you *get it* Earl? You *won*. You can have this whole stinking place!"

"Win?" Earl asked. "Wait, Bobbie. You got this all wrong. Your dad didn't pick *me* over *you*."

"Yes he did. Dad always wanted a son. I turned out to be a lousy girl. So he picked you instead."

Earl shook his head. "Your dad didn't kick you outta the garage because you were a *girl*, Bobbie. Don't you think he kinda figured that one out the day you were born?"

I scowled. "Then *why?* Why else would he turn his back on me the day I hit puberty?"

Earl scratched his head. "I thought you *knew* why."

"Because I turned into a girl."

"*No*, Bobbie. That ain't it at all. On your eleventh birthday, your mom got drunk as a skunk and finally told your dad the truth."

I frowned. "The truth?"

"That your daddy ain't your daddy. Your real dad's a man named David Applewhite."

Chapter Sixty-Eight

"YOU AIN'T NEVER COMING back, are you?" Earl asked as he handed me another tissue.

"Why should I? This whole place ... my whole *family* is nothing but a *lie*, Earl." I honked into a Kleenex.

"Not all of it, Bobbie. *I'm* still your cousin, blood or not."

I smiled. "You're right." I stood up and gave him a hug. "Never is a long time. I'll stay in touch. I promise."

Earl nodded. "Good. All right, then. I suggest you get your fat butt in gear before Grayson changes his mind."

I laughed. "Had to get the last zinger in, didn't you?"

Earl winked. "Who says it's the last?"

As I turned to head up the stairs, Earl called after me. "Hey Cuz, don't forget to turn out the lights when you leave. I'm the new boss man, you know."

"Right," I said, saluting. "I know."

AFTER CALLING BETH-Ann to give her the news, I glanced around the bedroom I'd inhabited for the past six months. Unlike the ghostly memories of my parents, I hadn't made enough of an impression for it to linger here after I was gone. And for that, I was glad.

On the nightstand, the picture of my unhappy family glared at me, frozen in a time better off forgotten.

I picked up the framed photo and studied it. Dad was still frowning in his shiny, new Mustang. Mom still offered up her dour, distant countenance. And Grandma Selma still held me in her arms, her eyes glazed-over with a faraway stare.

I blew out a breath. Then something caught my eye I hadn't noticed before.

Me.

The baby in the photo. Her lips were curled, ever so slightly. She was *smiling*.

Had the picture itself changed, or just the way I *perceived* it? I shook my head.

Grayson's crazy ideas must be contagious.

I set the photo back on the nightstand. From under the bed, I grabbed a duffle bag and stuffed in a few clothes. On top of them, I placed Grandma Selma's afghan.

I stripped off my father's shoes and mechanic coveralls for the last time. Carrying them across the room, I realized just how heavy they actually were.

Suddenly, a devious smile worked its way onto my lips. I marched across the room and flung the boots and coveralls out the window. As they hit the asphalt of the parking lot below, the thud made me grin.

Naked, I stepped into the shower, and let the warm, soapy water wash me clean.

IT WAS DUSK WHEN I climbed into the passenger seat next to Grayson. Earl waved at us from the service bay as the old RV rumbled out of the parking lot. I waved back at him.

"You're going to miss him, aren't you?" Grayson asked.

I smiled. "Yep. Every chance I get."

Grayson laughed and tipped his fedora to Earl.

I looked over at Grayson. "So, Mister Private Investigator, what now?"

Grayson shot me a thoughtful smile. "Mothman may be played out for now. I think it's time we look for a new game."

"Sounds good. Any ideas?"

"I've heard reports of something strange going on in Plant City."

I laughed. "What? A killer weevil infestation?"

"Close. Possible alien invasion."

"Huh. And it's not even strawberry-picking season yet."

Grayson grinned. He shifted gears and steered the RV out of the parking lot and into the southbound lane of Obsidian Road.

I reached over and touched Grayson's arm. "Wait. I forgot something."

Grayson hit the brakes. "What?"

"This."

I rolled down my window, pulled the Glock from my purse, aimed, and fired. The flashing yellow light between oblivion and nowhere shattered into a million pieces.

Grayson flinched. "What'd you do that for?"

I smiled and faced the road ahead. "Just putting out the lights, like the boss man said. Okay, Grayson. I'm ready. Let's roll."

THE END—OF THE BEGINNING ....

Get a Free Gift!

How did Grayson End up in Bobbie's World?

Don't miss another sneak preview, sale, or new release of *Freaky Florida Mystery Adventures!* Sign up for my newsletter and. I'll send you a free copy of the *Moth Busters Secret Prologue* as a welcome gift. It's the only way you can get the inside scoop on how Grayson ended up in Florida!

https://dl.bookfunnel.com/o9qdji7hji

I hope you enjoyed Moth Busters! If you did, it would be freaking fantastic if you would post a review on Amazon, Goodreads and/or BookBub. You'll be helping me keep the series going! Thanks in advance for being so awesome!

https://www.amazon.com/dp/B07RC7HVD2#customerReviews

Now, sit back and prepare yourself for Freaky Florida Mystery Book 2 –
Dr. Prepper!

Dr. Prepper

FREAKY FLORIDA MYSTERY Adventures, Book 2
By Margaret Lashley

Prologue

LAST WEEK, I GOT SHOT in the head.

The doctor said I didn't have brain damage. But the things I did afterward make me question whether I should've gotten a second opinion.

First, I let a complete stranger stay in my Grandma Selma's apartment.

Okay, that's not *so* crazy.

But then I spent a week with that same stranger, rambling around Alachua County chasing after Mothman.

Yes, Mothman.

When I finally realized the guy might be a raving lunatic, I did the only sensible thing I could think of.

I ditched my entire life, climbed into his dumpy RV, and headed off to Plant City to help him save the world from an alien invasion.

You're welcome.

Chapter One

I WOKE UP AND SMELLED the coffee.

I cracked open a crusty eye. What I saw in the dim light sent memories of yesterday slamming into my brain like a saltwater tsunami.

Less than twenty-four hours ago, my cousin Earl Shankles had hit me with a family secret that turned my life into a complete dumpster fire.

My father who'd died six months ago wasn't my father. And my mother had run off with Mr. Applewhite, the postman. According to Earl, 37 years ago, I was Mr. Applewhite's "special delivery."

Funny. I didn't feel special.

So, with no one around to point my bastard-child finger at, I did something that a mere week ago I'd have considered totally irrational.

Insane, even.

I ran off and joined the circus.

To be more specific, I joined a monster-chasing, freak-show of a circus led by a man I'd known for all of six days.

From what he'd told me, Nick Grayson was a private investigator, an amateur entomologist, an alternative healer, and a noted—albeit somewhat disgraced—physicist.

If *any* part of what he claimed was true, his credentials blew mine out of the water.

All I brought to the table was a bachelor's degree in art appreciation, a fairly limited knowledge of antiques, and a fairly *un*limited distrust of ... well, pretty much anything that talked.

But I could shoot a gun better than anyone I knew—including Grayson. I'd pinned my hopes on that being enough to convince him to keep me on as a PI intern.

Otherwise, I was totally screwed.

Last night, after leaving my cousin in charge of running my family's auto repair business, I'd jumped out of my old life and into Grayson's RV.

But I hadn't started my life over with a clean slate. Not even close. I'd climbed aboard toting enough baggage to significantly lower the guy's overall gas mileage.

As I lay curled up on the RV's sofa, I thought about my friend Beth-Ann. The last words she'd said to me blasted through my mind like a hurricane siren.

Are you outta your ever-loving gourd?

Maybe I was.

But it didn't matter. It was *way* too late to turn back now.

From the gentle rocking of the RV, I could tell it was rolling down the highway, full steam ahead. I closed my eyes again.

Screw it, I thought. *Life is for living.*

I was a carpetbagger in search of *carpe diem*.

Woohoo. Let the good times roll ....

Chapter Two

IT HAD BEEN WAY PAST midnight when Grayson pulled his vintage RV into the parking lot of a Walmart in Inverness, Florida. I'd woken when he stopped, and watched him pass by me silently on his way to his bedroom in the back of the RV.

Exhausted, I'd immediately fallen asleep again on the couch. When I woke up again, it was still dark.

Coffee was on the stove. Amy Winehouse was on the radio.

I fumbled for my cellphone. It was 7:03 a.m. and we were already rolling again.

Ugh.

I dragged myself to sitting and touched the scab in the middle of my forehead. It was almost healed. Not bad for being the target of a ricochet bullet a little over a week ago. I scratched the itchy stubble growing in where my long auburn locks used to be.

My new hairdo was a memento from the overzealous staff at the hospital in Gainesville. They'd shaved my head all the way to my ears, leaving me with a bald spot not even the most ambitious comb-over could hope to cover.

I scanned the RV's tiny kitchen/living room area for Lucky Red. It was the Redman chewing tobacco ball-cap my cousin Earl had lent me to cover my billiard-ball noggin. I spotted it at the end of the couch, perched atop the head of ET, the extraterrestrial. Or in this case, ET, the world's ugliest lamp.

Good one, Grayson.

I leaned over and snatched the cap off ET's gray plaster skull. Lucky Red was my fallback until I could procure another wig. My last one had met its fate at the hands of a frisky Mothman. But that's another story ....

I yawned and pulled the cap over my stubble. My body reminded me I was in dire need of a shower and at least a half a gallon of coffee.

Sitting on the couch, I could almost reach the coffee pot on the kitchen stove.

Almost.

I groaned and made a Herculean attempt, but the pot of life-inducing go-juice remained irritatingly out of reach.

I scowled at the stove.

Why couldn't I have gotten some useful skill out of getting shot between the eyes? Like The Incredibles' *stretchy arms, maybe. But no. All I got was the knowledge that I had my twin brother's gonad knocking around in my brain.*

And, like all men, he was not being particularly helpful.

I grunted, hauled myself off the couch, and poured myself a jittery mugful of coffee. After gulping half of it down, I refilled my mug and wormed my way up to the RV's cab.

A slim man dressed all in black tipped his vintage fedora at me, giving me a glimpse of his own shaved dome.

He shot me a sideways glance. "Morning, sunshine. Sleep well?"

Grayson's cheery, morning-person tone might as well have been fingernails on a chalkboard.

"Yeah," I said. "Like a balloon animal in a cactus garden."

I flopped into the passenger seat beside Grayson and rubbed my sore neck.

Grayson laughed. "I told you to take the bed."

"Chivalrous of you, but no thanks."

The bedroom in Grayson's RV moonlighted as an electromagnetic monster trap. Call me paranoid, but I wasn't keen on the idea of losing consciousness inside a strange man's small, padded, soundproofed bedroom that had enough locks on the door to restrain Godzilla. I already had enough trust issues, thank you very much.

I blew out a sigh. "What happened to Walmart? I was gonna buy a wig."

Grayson fiddled with the knobs on some electronic contraption mounted to the underside of the dash.

"I wanted to get an early start," Grayson said. "Last night I got an up-date on that incident in Plant City. And, as you country folks are fond of saying, 'Time's a-wastin.'"

I shot him some serious side-eye. "I've never heard *anybody* say that."

I blew out a breath and took another sip of coffee. "Use that awful country accent one more time and I can't be held responsible for where the contents of my coffee mug fling themselves."

Grayson smirked. "I see you're not a morning person. Duly noted."

I looked out the window and almost smiled. Despite the crick in my neck and the grayish weather, it felt good to see the distance widening between me and my dead-end life back in Point Paradise. I took another slurp of coffee. It was damned good. I'd give Grayson that much.

"What's so interesting in Plant City?" I asked.

Grayson shook his head. "Not so fast, intern. First order of business is to get the boss a refill." He handed me his empty coffee mug.

"Is this part of my P.I. training?"

Grayson shrugged. "Only if you want to *continue* your P.I. training."

I grinned. Grayson was only a few years older than me, but he was already a seasoned private investigator. I was just a P.I. wannabe with a brand-new intern license. I needed two years of on-the-job training to qualify for a full-fledged Class C license. Thanks to Grayson and his trav-eling investigator show, I only had 103 weeks to go.

I grabbed his coffee mug. "Pinch of salt, right?"

Grayson's eyebrow ticked up. "Gold star, cadet."

I tumbled back to the kitchen, threw a couple of Pop-Tarts in the toaster, and poured us both more coffee. After delivering the mugs to the cup holders on the dashboard, I grabbed the pastries and parked my rear back in the passenger seat.

"Here you go." I handed Grayson a blueberry Pop-Tart.

He raised a suspicious eyebrow. "Already brownnosing, eh?"

I shrugged. "Figured it couldn't hurt. So *now* will you tell me what's going on in Plant City?"

"I got a call from one of my sources."

"Your *sources?*"

Grayson nodded down at the weird-looking equipment installed under the dash. "That's a ham radio. I use it to operate an informal hotline on an obscure channel. People call in with information. If it sounds interesting, I follow up."

I took a bite of Pop-Tart. "What kind of information?"

"You know. Unidentifiable tracks. Weird lights in the sky. Mutilated corpses. That kind of thing."

I sucked the sticky frosting from my front teeth. "Sorry I asked. So what's in it for the informants?"

"*Operatives*," Grayson corrected. He shot me a grin and batted his eyes. "Why, my undying gratitude, of course." He turned back to face the road. "That, and cold, hard cash."

"So, exactly what kind of strange phenomenon are we looking into?"

"A fellow in Plant City overheard an unusual radio transmission two days ago. A guy named Lester Jenkins got on a frequency and starting screaming, 'They're here! They're here!'"

I took a sip of coffee. "Huh. Maybe his in-laws came into town."

Grayson shot me a sideways glance. "A cop found him dead a few hours later."

I smirked. "Like I said, maybe his in-laws—"

"His head covered in some kind of slime," Grayson said.

"Huh. You've obviously never dealt with in-laws, Grayson."

He snorted. "Shut up and eat your Pop-Tart."

My gut gurgled. "Hey, can we stop at the next rest stop?"

"I guess. Why?"

"Let's just say I've got something I want to get rid of."

"If you mean what I think you mean, the toilet works just fine while we're underway."

I frowned. "Thanks. But that's something I'm going to need a bit more time getting used to."

Grayson eyed me. "Claustrophobic?"

I shrugged and stared at the road ahead. "Sure. Let's go with that."

Chapter Three

DOWNTOWN PLANT CITY appeared to have been snatched directly from an episode of *Mayberry R.F.D.* Compared to my hometown of Point Paradise, the place looked like Camelot.

Grayson, on the other hand, wasn't quite so impressed. After a quick drive past the main street's quaint little collection of coffee shops, boutiques, antique shops and restaurants, he announced he'd seen enough, and turned the RV onto US 92.

A mile or so down the road, a touristy billboard for Parkesdale Market came into view. I whined like a brat until I convinced Grayson to stop for a "World Famous" strawberry shake.

When he spotted Parksdale's candy-cane striped awnings, he sneered, but grudgingly pulled in. We got the shakes to go, and I was sucking down the last slurp when Grayson stopped the RV on a rural backroad we'd turned onto a few miles back.

"This looks like it," he said.

I eyed him sideways. "Is this a joke?"

Ignoring me, Grayson maneuvered the shabby RV up to a ten-foot-high, chain-link gate spanning a dirt driveway. It appeared to be the only way in and out of a barbed-wire-topped compound encompassing a couple of acres of half-cleared Florida scrubland.

The place looked like a low-rent prison for blue-collar offenders.

"Are you sure this is the right place?" I asked Grayson.

"Yes. Positive."

I was afraid of that.

The compound was situated in the back forty of a rural suburb comprised mostly of similar properties—trailer homes on small clearings tucked in amongst native palmetto bushes and pine trees. Most of the other neighbors, however, hadn't put quite so much time and effort into creating such an impressive *un*welcome mat.

I rolled down the window and stuck my head out for a better view. Partially hidden by trees, overgrown bushes, and an assortment of rusty household appliances, I spotted the outline of an old trailer. Beside it stood a satellite dish big enough to impress NASA engineers.

I crinkled my nose. "Well, at least he's got *something* worth protecting."

Grayson mashed a button on a black metal box beside the gate. A robotic voice crackled from a speaker.

"Identify yourself."

Grayson glanced over at me. Not knowing him that well, I would've sworn he looked just the teensiest bit embarrassed. He tipped his black fedora to no one I could see and said, "Gray Hotline."

I bit my lip as we waited in silence for a reply, seesawing between the desire to burst out laughing and the urge to ditch everything and run for my life.

A voice came over the speaker, deciding my fate.

"Proceed."

The gate clicked open and swung slowly across the dirt driveway with a long, painful *creak*. It came to a stop as it hit the side of a rusted-out refrigerator.

Grayson maneuvered the RV into what I could only describe as the abandoned set of *Sanford and Son—The Final Years.* Our dilapidated RV fit right in.

Grayson cut the ignition.

I nodded toward the junk. "I'm curious, Fred. Does this make me Lamont?"

Grayson groaned. "That joke belongs on the pile with the rest of this garbage. Just keep your head low and follow my lead."

We climbed out of the RV and picked our way through the maze of discarded rubbish clogging the yard. After tripping twice over the same rusted bicycle carcass, I managed to make it with Grayson to the steps of a wooden deck. Attached to it was the yellowed, algae-covered husk of a doublewide trailer.

A poorly hand-painted sign hung on the front door. It read: "The Tooth is Out There."

It was my turn to groan.

Grayson rang the doorbell with the elbow of his jacket.

I shot him a look. "What are you doing?"

He leaned in and whispered, "These people can be a bit obsessive when it comes to fingerprints and DNA."

As my mind ticked off the walking distance between here and the highway, the door cracked open.

Standing in the doorframe was a thin, pasty guy, probably in his late twenties. He sported a long, blond mullet and the kind of muscle tone that only gets chicks at Comic Con conventions.

I smiled to myself. The guy reminded me of Garth on *Wayne's World*. Except this dude was nerdier. His hair was frizzier. And, like the sign on his door foretold, his front teeth were "out there." I'd never seen such a pair of buck teeth.

I'd bet good money he could floss those beauties with his lips closed.

The guy smiled, making me want to double down on my bet.

"It's the mysterious Mister Gray! Welcome!" the Garth lookalike said. He turned to me. "And his beautiful protégé, I presume?" He bowed slightly and made a sweeping gesture with his arm. "Please, come in!"

Grayson handed over a business card as we entered mullet-man's secret lair. One glance around the interior and my mind wrote "bleach" on an imaginary shopping list. Then I scratched that through and wrote "dynamite."

"Thank you for your call," Grayson said.

The young man squinted at Grayson's card through the thick lenses of his black-framed glasses. "Gray Hotline," he read aloud. "Like gray *aliens*, right?" He winked at Grayson.

Grayson gave him a quick nod. "As far as you know."

The man extended a hand. Grayson shook it. "Well, pleased to meet you, Mr. Gray. I'm—"

"No *real* names," Grayson said, cutting him off. "Pandora, assign this new operative a name."

I looked around for a moment for Pandora, then blanched, cleared my throat, and said, "Uh ... Garth Waynesworld."

"First names only," Grayson corrected.

I saluted. "Yes, Commander Beetlejuice."

Grayson winced, but otherwise didn't skip a beat. "Operative Garth," he said, clearing his throat, "for our casework, we'll need to record your entire statement. We will, of course, use a voice-scrambling device to protect your identity."

Garth nodded solemnly. "No prob. That'll be a hundred bucks."

I stifled a smirk. Grayson reached into his jacket and pulled out a crisp C-note. "I heard you have pictures, too."

"Yeah. You can look, but no touch. You want copies, that's extra."

Garth might not have fashion sense, but he's got merchandising down pat.

"Fair enough," Grayson said. "Let's get started."

While Grayson set up to record Garth's statement, I looked around for a place to sit. Given the options, I decided to stand. The two men settled into a pair of old recliners I wouldn't have let a pet rat use for an outhouse.

I leaned against the doorframe between the living room and kitchen and tried to keep disgust—as well as mold and mildew—from congregating on my face.

Suddenly, I heard heavy breathing behind me. My back bowed into a prickly arch. Against all my willing myself not to, I turned and traced the source of the noise.

It was coming from the corner of Garth's kitchen.

I craned my neck, then took a step backward for a peek.

Glaring at me from inside a heavy wire cage was a monstrous black hound. As I locked onto its yellow eyes, the dog erupted into a snarling fit. Then it then let out a long, low, continuous growl that turned my Pop-Tarts and coffee into bubbling sludge.

"I see you've met Tooth."

Garth's voice sounded mere inches to my right, startling me so badly I nearly screamed. I swallowed hard, and plastered on a smile while my heart played a drum solo in my chest.

"Yeah. Nice puppy," I managed.

Garth laughed. "I put him in his cage whenever I'm expecting company. As you can see, he doesn't care for people all that much. But look. I think he likes you."

I stared at the gleaming, inch-long incisors on Cujo Jr. and was thankful for the metal bars between us. I envisioned the dog patrolling Garth's junkyard and the joke finally hit home.

The Tooth is Out There.

Hilarious.

Chapter Four

"AND THAT'S WHEN I HEARD Jenkins hollering, 'They're here! They're here!'" Operative Garth said, and took another swig from a half-gallon plastic bottle of Mountain Dew.

"Just to be clear, we're talking about *Lester* Jenkins," I said. "The guy who was found dead?"

"The dude himself, yeah. Then T-Rex got on the horn and yelled, 'Jenkins! I told you to I.D. yourself!' Haha! He's totally retrograde, man!"

"T-Rex?" Grayson asked.

"Oh. Theodore Rexel. Old army vet. He's got the closest repeater to Jenkins' cabin."

"Repeater?" I asked.

Garth's face suddenly collapsed. He stared at me as if I'd zapped him with a stun gun, then he shifted his flabbergasted gaze to Grayson.

Grayson shrugged apologetically. "She's new."

Garth eyed me up and down, as if I might be a spy, while Grayson explained the terminology. "A repeater's a *tower*, Pandora. It's like an amplifier for ham radio operators. You can bounce your signal off it to gain distance and volume."

"Oh. Right," I said, and laughed. "I forgot."

Garth appeared bored with the tedium of having to deal with a newbie. He let out a huge sigh and addressed Grayson as if he were the only worthy audience member in the room.

"Anyway, like I was saying, Mr. Gray, old man Rexel was ragging on Jenkins to follow protocol and give out his call sign. Rexel's a real stickler for the rules. Throwback from his crew cuts and shiny shoes military days, I guess."

Garth turned to me and spoke slowly, as if addressing a toddler with unpromising potential. "So, Pandora, you're supposed to give your call sign when you ping somebody's repeater. It's common courtesy. But Lester Jenkins never did. And that pissed Rexel off big time."

"Right, thanks." I thought about asking Garth what a call sign was, but I didn't want to piss *him* off big time, either.

Garth gave me a curt nod, pushed his glasses up on his pug nose, and continued his story with Grayson.

"So while Rexel was bitching at Jenkins, I got off the channel and called my brother, Jimmy. He's on the force. He hightailed it out there to Jenkins' cabin. Took photos before any other donut slugs showed up."

Garth turned to me. "A donut slug is—"

I gave him a sharp nod. "I think I got it."

Grayson clapped his hands together. "Excellent, Operative Garth. Now, how about a look at those photos?"

Garth grinned. "You're in for a treat, Mr. Gray." He fired up his laptop, clicked a few buttons on his keypad, and a full-screen view of Lester Jenkins' remains flashed on the display.

I blanched.

Dressed in jeans and a flannel shirt, Lester Jenkins' body was lying face-up in a bed of pine straw. His hair and face were wet with a gooey-looking substance. And something was off with his body. It was too ... *narrow*. And too flat. It was as if he'd somehow *melted* inside his clothes. My nose crinkled in disgust.

"This is interesting," Grayson said, pointing at Jenkins' neck and face. Both were peppered with small, narrow gashes. "Strange pattern for teeth marks. Short. Needle-like. Definitely not a predator with large canines."

Garth nodded, eyes narrowed in contemplation. "I see your point. And what about that slime? My brother said Jenkins' head and neck were covered in it. What kind of being could do that?"

I smirked. "A Chihuahua with a bad cold?"

The two men shot me dirty looks. I shriveled and backtracked. "Sorry. It's just that ... the pictures are so gruesome. I was ... comic relief, anyone?"

I shut my babbling mouth. Grayson turned his attention back to Operative Garth. "Like I said, she's new. So what did your brother think was the cause of death?"

Garth shrugged. "Gettin' his guts squashed out."

Again, Grayson didn't miss a beat. "I mean, *what* did the squashing? Have there been any unusual phenomena noted in the area recently?"

"He could've been stomped by Bigfoot," Garth offered hopefully. "Does that count?"

"Absolutely. So, Operative Garth, do you know if Jenkins was into Ufology?"

"Well, yeah. He was always trying to contact aliens with his ham radio. But he couldn't even pull off an EME. Can you believe it? What a doofin' putz."

I opened my mouth to say something, but Grayson's face read, "Can it." So I did.

Grayson shot Garth an insider's smile. "Couldn't do an EME? What a newb."

Garth's face relaxed, as if Grayson had earned another level of trust. He leaned in closer to Grayson. "When I use EMEs to signal to aliens, I'm careful. Discrete, you know? I use a signal deflector. That way, if I make contact, they can't find me directly. Jenkins wasn't much for following protocol. If that's what he was doing, he could've led them right to him."

"So you actually knew Jenkins?" I asked.

Garth looked up at me as if he'd forgotten I was there. "I've talked to him a couple of times. At Blarney's Bar."

I nodded. "You sure the body in these pics is Lester Jenkins?"

Garth shrugged. "Pretty good likeness, if you ask me. Especially after he'd had a couple shots of Mr. Jack D."

"Who do you think he was referring to when he said, 'they're here,'" I asked.

Garth pushed his glasses up. "Like I said. It could've been animals. Or aliens. Or even trespassers on his property. Jenkins was a hothead. I'm pretty sure he'd shoot at any of them."

"So, how much for copies of the pics?" Grayson asked.

Garth shot him a buck-toothed grin. "Depends, Mr. Gray. How much you willing to pay?"

Chapter Five

"NICE DOING BUSINESS with you, Mr. Gray."

Garth folded the greenbacks, then tucked them safely among the pens stashed in the plastic pocket protector safeguarding his flannel shirt from ink stains. He patted the front of Grayson's RV, then hit a switch on a remote-control device.

The gate on the chain link fence slowly creaked open.

"Contact me any time," Grayson said out the rolled-down window. "You do excellent work, Operative Garth."

Garth's wimpy shoulders straightened. The lenses of his glasses flashed yellow-white in the midday sun, as did his bucktooth grin. He stood at attention and stayed that way until we'd backed down the drive and were pulling away.

I waved at him one last time, then shot Grayson a sideways glance. "You really seemed to make an impression on him. What are you, some kind of nerd superstar?"

Grayson shrugged. "I'm known in certain circles."

"Really? What kind? *Crop* circles?"

"Among others."

I rolled my eyes. "No offense, Grayson, but that guy got my spidey senses tingling."

Grayson's left eyebrow hitched up a notch. "Huh. I didn't picture him as your type."

"Argh!" I whacked Grayson on the bicep with the back of my hand. "That's not what I meant!"

His lip curled. "You hungry?"

I winced. "After *that*? Geez, Grayson! We just saw pictures of a guy smooshed to pudding!"

Grayson licked his lips. "Mmm. *Pudding*."

I snorted. "Okay. To tell you the truth, I'm starving."

"What say we find us a nice taco stand, Pandora? Then go check out what's swinging with T-Rex?"

I grinned and shook my head. "Oddly enough, that's the best offer I've heard all day, CB."

"CB?"

"Commander Beetlejuice."

GRAYSON PICKED CONSUELO'S from among the half-dozen greasy-looking mom-n-pop cooking trailers we passed along a three-mile stretch of US 92.

"Who knew Plant City was a taco-lover's paradise?" Grayson said after we placed our order through the screened window of the rusty white food truck. He waved away a fly. "No wonder people retire to Florida."

We'd barely placed our bottoms on the bench of a picnic table when a woman stuck her sweaty face out the window of the traveling taco stand.

"Beezelshoes!" she hollered.

I smirked. "Looks like you're up, boss."

Grayson shot me a look, then got up to retrieve our food. He returned with two greasy cardboard plates heaped with tacos, beans, and yellow rice.

My mouth watered despite the images still buzzing around in my head. "Those pictures of Jenkins were really gross," I said, then picked up a fish taco and crammed half of it into my mouth. "Poor guy."

"Should've kept up his gym membership," Grayson said, eyeing me for my reaction. "The slob really let himself get soft."

I nearly choked on a mixture of disgust and chopped cabbage. I rolled my eyes, but I had to admit, Grayson's gallows humor was growing on me. So were his looks.

Except for the cheesy moustache.

Given his lean build, his intense, indecipherable eyes, and his rakishly angled fedora, half a century ago, Grayson would've been typecast as the bad guy in any black-and-white movie. Lucky for him, the line between the good guys and the bad guys had long since blurred into a million shades of gray.

I chewed my mouthful of taco. "So, what's your goal?"

Grayson focused his green eyes on mine. "Goal?"

"Yeah. What do you want to try and accomplish here?"

Grayson's brow furrowed. "Collect hard evidence on whatever alien or cryptid is involved in this. I thought you knew that when you climbed aboard the good ship lollipop. Or, in your case, Tootsie Pop."

Grayson stared at me and rubbed the small, blue bruise just below his right eye. I'd given him the mark a few days back when I'd beaned him in the face with a slightly used sucker. In my defense, at the time I'd thought he was a psycho killer. In hindsight, I knew he was no killer. The psycho part, however, was still up for debate.

I shook my head. "*You're* the one collecting evidence of aliens or whatever. I'm just here for the P.I. training."

His eyes narrowed. "No, Drex. As my new partner, you signed up for both."

"Geez." I chewed my lip. "Seriously, Grayson. Do you think chasing monsters is a job for sensible adults?"

Grayson's back stiffened. "We don't chase monsters. We chase the *truth*. And in case you haven't noticed, Drex, being a so-called sensible adult isn't all it's cracked up to be. In fact, it's nothing but a trap."

I stopped sucking down my soda. "What are you talking about?"

Grayson studied me for a moment. "Unless you absolutely love it, a job is a gilded cage designed to keep you *just comfortable enough* so it can suck the life out of you, like you're doing to that bottle of pop."

I grimaced. "Geez. That's pretty dark."

Grayson's left eyebrow arched. "Is it? I think it's pretty enlightened. Think about it. Whether you're counting gold bricks or pushing a broom, no amount of cash can buy back the time you waste doing something you hate."

I crinkled my nose. "It's not *that* bad out there."

Grayson's green eyes locked on mine. "Don't tell me you're having second thoughts, Drex. Do you really want to go back to ordering mufflers for busted Buicks and wiping strangers' dipsticks? If so, I'll take you back to Point Paradise right now."

He stood.

I grabbed his arm. "No! That's not what I meant!"

I bit my lip. "I guess ... I'm just wondering ...." I stared at the table.

"What?" Grayson said. "Just say it, already."

I cautiously looked up into Grayson's eyes. "Why *me?*"

He stared at me for a moment. "What do you mean?"

"You *know* what I mean. Why did you pick *me* to be your partner? Be honest. If I didn't have this thing going on with my brain—the twin—would you have even considered me for the job?"

Grayson sat back down and sighed. "You're broken, Drex."

I winced. "What?"

"I chose you because you're *broken*."

My eyes narrowed. "What are you saying? That you felt *sorry* for me?"

Grayson laughed. "No. That's not what I meant at all. Just the opposite, in fact."

Grayson leaned across the table toward me. "You've been broken by the world, Drex. You played their game and lost. And now, if I'm right about you, you're ready to tell them all to go shove it where granny hides her gin-spiked Geritol."

I leaned back and chewed my lip. Grayson's analogy was dead-on. But I didn't want him to know it. I wasn't sure *I* wanted to know it.

Grayson tilted his head and looked me in the eyes. "Am I right?"

I shrugged. "How does chasing monsters tell the world to shove it?"

Grayson's face lit up with an almost sinister delight. "Don't you see? It's the ultimate color-outside-the-lines kiss-off. No one can discredit you from an already unaccredited career. Am I right?"

My lips curled into a tentative smile. "Yeah, I suppose. But Grayson, even *you've* got to admit that's a pretty low bar."

"Bar, shmar. This whole idea of goal setting is nothing more than a no-win scenario designed by society to prove we'll never live up to its expectations. Let it all go, Drex. Sit back, let go, and breathe in the freedom."

I sat back and sniffed the air. "Right now, freedom smells like sweat and burnt tortillas."

Grayson laughed. "And here's the best part. If we .... No. *When* we come up with hard, irrefutable evidence that one of these cryptid creatures exists, there's no banana cream pie big enough to cover the egg that'll be all over their faces."

I grinned. Grayson messed up his metaphors, just like my Grandma Selma used to when she was alive. It was the one thing about him I was totally onboard with.

Something deep inside me relaxed. I sighed and reached for a taco. "So what do you think really happened to Jenkins, anyway?"

"Too soon to tell. We'll need to examine the body first."

"Wha—?" A piece of taco tumbled from my gaping mouth.

Grayson eyed the mangled glob on the table. "Or at least get our hands on the autopsy report."

I wiped my mouth with a paper napkin. "Ugh. I was afraid you'd say that."

Grayson locked eyes with me again. "By the way, how are you feeling? You know, with the whole vestigial-twin gonad thing going on in your skull. Had any more weird hallucinations?"

"None that spring to mind."

Grayson's face grew serious. "We're partners, now, Drex. If you want me to help you master your gift, you're going to have to let me know whenever you see something weird."

"*Gift?*" I scowled at Grayson. "If this was really a *gift*, I could return it."

Grayson shook his head. "Women. Even *God* doesn't know what to get them."

I sneered and took a savage bite of taco. As I chewed, I glanced over at the slob seated across from us. I nearly choked.

The man appeared to have just survived an attack by giant moths. His T-shirt was peppered with gaping holes which offered innocent bystanders glimpses of his doughy side-rolls and curly armpit hair. A long, gray beard hung down from his face and spilled onto his impressive beer gut. His neck and arms bore enough tattoos to qualify him as a human sandwich board.

If God really knew what women wanted, that guy wouldn't exist.

I nodded my head in the man's direction. "We're in Florida, Grayson. When you ask whether I've seen something weird, you're gonna have to be a lot more specific.'"

Grayson's eyes shifted to the tattooed man, then back to me. "I see your point. How about this: Have you seen anything that *shouldn't* be there?"

I nodded toward the tattooed man. "Yes."

Grayson snorted. "Okay. Anything you *wish* wasn't there?"

I nodded toward the man again. "Too many to count."

Grayson grinned. "All right, Drex. Have you seen anything that makes you question your traditional concepts of reality?"

I sighed. "No. But that picture of Jenkins reduced to flesh pudding comes close."

Grayson nodded and glanced back at the food truck. "That reminds me. I want to see a dessert menu. Flan, perhaps?"

"Ugh! You're incorrigible!"

Grayson laughed and ogled a laminated menu.

"You said our next step is to talk to that vet guy. Rexel, right?" I asked.

"Yes. I gave him a call while you were in the ladies' room. He said he could meet us at two o'clock."

I glanced at my cellphone. "That's in like, twenty minutes."

"No problem. It's just around the corner."

"Around these parts, Grayson, nothing is just around the corner."

His eyebrow shot up. "No? In that case, I suggest we get going, cadet."

Our eyes simultaneously shifted down to the last remaining taco on the table, then back up.

We both grabbed for it.

Grayson was quicker.

He shot me a victory grin, took a huge bite from the taco, and handed me the rest.

I smiled and took it.

I guess partnering with Grayson has its privileges, after all.

Chapter Six

THE DERELICT RV SHIMMIED southbound along the Redman Parkway that divided Plant City—the strawberry capital of the world—in half. As we crossed over SR 60, the parkway turned into SR 39. Not that the change in numbers made any difference. Everything along that strip of highway was the same, ubiquitous shade of forgettable.

As we passed through the tiny town of Hopewell, I began to wonder just exactly what the hell the people around here were hoping for.

I looked down and squinted at the tiny map on Grayson's smartphone. "Swiney ... or is it Swilley Road? Anyway, it's supposed to be around here somewhere. On the right. Before you get to Keysville Road ... or is it Keystone?"

Grayson shook his head. "Grab a pair of glasses out of the glove compartment, would you? You look like a politically incorrect emoji. All you're missing are chopsticks and a pointy hat."

I scowled. "Do it yourself, then."

I shoved his phone back at him. Grayson refused it.

"Nothing doing. Driving while operating a cellphone is worse than playing Russian roulette. Over a quarter of all accidents are caused by cellphone usage."

I rolled my eyes. "You and your so-called facts. Why don't you just let me drive, then?"

"Uh ... *because you can't see?*"

I scowled again. "I can see well enough to shoot."

"You've got presbyopia, Drex. Your near vision is deteriorating. Welcome to the short-arm club."

I frowned. "But I'm not even forty."

Grayson smirked. "You're an overachiever. Congratulations. Now grab a pair of specs so you can read the display, already!"

"Ugh!" I jabbed the button on the glovebox. It dropped open. I picked out a pair of cheap, plastic eyeglasses and settled them on my nose. When I glanced back down at the phone, I nearly gasped at the amount of detail it displayed.

"There it is," Grayson said. "Swilley Road, right?"

I looked up. The blur from the lenses made me instantly nauseated. "Ugh. Yeah. Right."

I looked down at the phone again. Grayson hooked a sharp right, sending me lurching sideways.

"Geez, Grayson!"

He snorted. "Come on, grumpy. Where's your sense of adventure?"

"Where granny hides her Geritol, apparently."

I took off the glasses. "That Garth guy said Rexel is a stickler for protocol. I don't want to look like a dimwit again. What was that thing you two were talking about? An M and M?"

"EME. It's ham radio jargon for a moon bounce. That's when you use the moon as a passive reflector to establish a signal path. Earth-Moon-Earth equals EME."

"Right." I still didn't understand what the hell he was talking about. But did it really matter? When would that subject ever come up again in my lifetime? *Never.* "Hey, after Rexel, then what?"

Grayson came to a stop sign and looked both ways. "We'll check out Operative Garth's brother on the force. Jimmy Wells."

"I thought we didn't use real names. And how'd you find out *his*, anyway?"

"It was on the mailbox. They live together."

"Oh." *Two guys, no gal. Well, that explains the filth.*

"So much for anonymity," I quipped.

Grayson's eyebrow ticked up. "And so much for your observational skills."

I frowned. Grayson noticed.

"Listen," he said. "You're new at this. Everybody's got to start somewhere. So be a good intern, would you? Keep an eye out for a small tower. That'll be Rexel's repeater. He said we can't miss it."

I licked my wounds as we drove through a half-finished subdivision. The place appeared to have been abandoned by its developer decades ago. Like some wannabee Chernobyl, a smattering of houses dotted the crumbling asphalt lanes and empty cul-de-sacs. The rest of the lots lay vacant and weedy.

We turned a corner. Amongst a stand of pines, I spotted a crude metal structure that resembled the Eiffel Tower—if it had been built by a scrap metal salesman after downing a bottle of mescal.

I jabbed a finger at the windshield. "Is that it?"

"Yes. Good eye, cadet."

I perked up and I allowed myself the edges of a smile. "Turn there," I said.

Grayson made the turn and rumbled down the road to the end. He pulled the RV onto a tidy, crushed-shell driveway leading to a modest, well-kept block house covered in brick a shade too red to be real. The lawn, trees, and bushes bore the precision trim jobs of a seriously hardcore anal-retentive.

Grayson shifted into park. Before we could even open the doors, a short, wiry old man emerged from the house, checking his watch. His bald, liver-spotted head glistened in the sun. When he looked up, his face appeared frozen in a state of permanent condescension. He probably could've played General McArthur if he wasn't the height of George Castanza.

"You take the lead on this," Grayson said, smirking as he threw me under the bus. "Get one under your belt."

"Wha—?"

"Like I said, just follow my lead."

"You're a minute and thirty-eight seconds late," Rexel barked as we climbed out of the RV.

"I ... we're ..." I fumbled.

"Excuse our delay, Mr. Rexel," Grayson said. "My partner, Pandora here, was overcome with admiration for your magnificent repeater."

Rexel peered over his bifocals at me. His skeptical frown softened into a smile that seemed so foreign to his face I was afraid it might crack. "Why thank you, young lady."

"That's some repeater," I winged.

Rexel beamed. "Built it myself."

"You don't say!" I cooed. "Truly impressive. You ever do EMEs with it?"

Rexel's face went disconcertingly dreamy. "Been known to do an EME a time or two, young lady."

I looked over at Grayson just in time to see his eyes finish rolling. I turned back to Rexel. "Mr. Rexel, we're here investigating the sad demise of Mr. Lester Jenkins."

Rexel sneered. "Not *that* sad, if you ask me."

I blanched. "Why?"

The skinny little man's face twisted as if he'd sucked a lemon wedge. "Damned amateur. Jenkins barely knew what he was doing. Always skimming the guidebooks and skimping on the rules." Rexel shook his angry, turtle-like head and spat. "That lazy scumbag was always kerchunking on my repeater."

I shot Grayson a quick, wide-eyed glance.

He grinned, but offered me no lifeline.

I nodded at Rexel sympathetically. "I hate when that happens."

Rexel gave me a sharp nod, then continued his tirade.

"No matter how many times I told him, Jenkins never gave out his call sign when he keyed up his radio. Pinged off my repeater without even so much as a 'How do you do.' It was annoying as all get out, I tell you."

What the hell?

I shot Grayson a *Mayday* look. He finally took the lead.

"So, Mr. Rexel, how did you know it was Jenkins if he didn't give his call sign?"

Rexel turned to Grayson and doubled up on his sour expression. "He was at that disgrace of a shack he called a cabin near 'bout every Friday. He'd always ping my repeater around the same time. Quarter to six. Right before happy hour at Blarney's Bar. It was the only thing that sorry S-O-B ever did on a reliable basis."

"I see." Grayson rubbed his chin. "And what about his last transmission? You heard it, correct?"

"Yeah. The idiot was yelling, 'They're here. They're here.' Sounded like he'd already had a few. I asked for his call sign ... you know, to keep a decent level of protocol. The man didn't bother to reply. I'm telling you, Jenkins had no manners whatsoever."

I sighed. *He was probably too busy dying.*

Rexel snorted derisively. "Jerk never even bothered to get more than a Technician Class license. Me myself? I went all the way to Amateur Extra Class."

Wow. Where's that extra class now?

Grayson acknowledged Rexel with a nod. "Did Jenkins say anything after that?"

"Nope. Let me tell you, I gave him a piece of my mind over not using his call sign. But the jerk didn't give me so much as the courtesy of a reply to that, either. Typical Jenkins."

Grayson's brow furrowed. "How far away is Jenkins' cabin from here?"

"Half a mile, maybe. It's down there, at the end. Where the road cuts off." Rexel pointed down a paved road that appeared to lead to nowhere. "Jenkins would park his truck down there and follow the trail in the woods."

"What happened here?" I asked, glancing around at the vacant lots and weedy sidewalks. "Why didn't they finish the subdivision?"

Rexel's expression told me I'd hit a nerve. "They were supposed to build more houses, but then the EPA said the land's too swampy. Damned EPA cares more about the life of some stupid toad-frog than it does its own war veterans."

Grayson gave the old man a sympathetic look. "Mr. Rexel, who do you think Jenkins was referring to when he said, 'They're here.'?"

Rexel shrugged. "Those damned toads for all I know. Like I said, he was a real booze hound."

Grayson nodded. "Well, thank you for your time, sir."

"Sure. Always happy to help out a fellow ham radio operator."

I nearly snorted. *Right. Unless he's Lester Jenkins.*

I plastered on a smile and climbed into the RV. Rexel came up to my window and looked at me as if he expected something.

"Uh ... that really is a really nice tower you've built there, Mr. Rexel," I offered.

Rexel shot me a lascivious grin. "You really like my little elephant, don't you?"

Yuck. "Uh...sure." I rolled up the window and locked the door before Rexel climbed in and gave me a hug or something.

Grayson turned the ignition, and as he slowly backed down the drive, Rexel winked at me and waved.

I groaned. "I feel like I've been slimed."

"What?" Grayson asked. "You mean like Jenkins?"

"No. Worse."

Grayson's right eyebrow flat-lined. "What's going on?"

"What did Rexel mean with that crack about me liking his little elephant?"

Grayson opened his mouth to answer.

"Wait!" I blurted. "If it's gross, I don't want to know."

Grayson laughed. "He was referring to his tower, Drex. A repeater that can receive further than it can transmit. You know, big ears, small mouth. Like an elephant."

"I'd say Mr. Rexel has big ears *and* a big mouth."

Grayson shrugged. "He seems harmless enough. A man needs his hobbies, after all."

"I guess."

Grayson reached below the dash and fiddled with the knobs on his ham radio. It crackled to life.

As static filled the cab of the RV, I frowned. All that stupid radio jargon the men had used with each other. Who in their right minds would care about any of that crap?

"I don't get it," I said finally. "What's so great about this amateur radio stuff?"

"What?" Grayson nearly veered into the gutter. "It's only like the *original internet*, Drex. With a ham radio you can talk to folks all over the world. Even in outer space."

"Outer space? Gimme a break. Don't tell me you believe all that stuff Garth said about talking to aliens?"

"Well, I believe it's *possible*, sure," Grayson said defensively. "Ever since Russia launched Sputnik, amateur radio buffs have been monitoring the skies for space transmissions."

Grayson smiled wistfully at the windshield. "The Apollo missions were a dream come true. As a kid, I remember tuning in to the astronauts' live broadcasts from space. Good times." He turned to me. "*That* was possible. So, why shouldn't we be able to tune in to space alien's transmissions?"

I shook my head. "I guess. But what are the odds of that happening?"

"I'd say pretty good. You may not realize it Drex, but there are over three million amateur radio operators around the world. Tuning in to an alien life form on a subspace channel is bound to happen. It's just a matter of time."

I snorted. "Meanwhile, you know, while you guys are waiting for ET to phone home and all, what else do you do for fun? Swap Tang recipes with each other?"

"No. We ...." Grayson coughed. "We exchange weather updates and whatnot."

I smirked.

"Don't knock it until you've tried it." Grayson turned a knob on the ham radio. "You can also monitor police transmissions with this baby. And airline pilot chatter. There's even some spooky 'black channels' out there broadcasting encrypted messages twenty-four seven. I think you'd be surprised what ham radio operators can pick up."

"No offense, Grayson, but if they're all like Garth and gramps back there, I'd be surprised if they could *pick up* anything."

Chapter Seven

A FINGER OF DREAD RAN a cold, sharp nail down my spine as I inched behind Grayson, mimicking his movements along each zig and zag in the narrow trail that meandered through the boggy Florida scrubland.

The terrain was flat and sandy, covered in a thick carpet of waist-high palmetto bushes. Amid the sea of jagged, silver-green palmettos, patchwork islands of dwarf, moss-covered scrub oaks and towering, red-barked pines jutted out.

The only sounds were our footsteps and my own groaning complaints. In the distance, the shrill, laugh-like call of a pileated woodpecker rang out. I wondered whether he'd just told a joke at our expense.

"Two buffoons walk into a forest ...."

Not only wasn't I in the mood for tromping through the woods—I wasn't dressed for it, either. The thorny palmettos clawed snags in my sweater, and the boggy mud collected on the bottoms of my new, white tennis shoes, weighing them down like Frankenstein clodhoppers.

When Rexel pointed out we could access Lester Jenkins' cabin at the end of the lane, Grayson had put our plans to interview Officer Jimmy Wells on the backburner. We'd left Rexel's house and driven directly to the stub-end of the unfinished road where the trailhead started.

As we tromped down the switchback path leading to Jenkins' cabin, the postmortem pictures of Jenkins flashed in my mind anew.

I shuddered.

This trail is a maze designed by a madman. A dead *madman! I hope there's not any more out here ....*

My cellphone chirped, startling the crap out of me. I made a mental note to change my ringtone from the theme of *Psycho* and pulled my phone from my pocket.

It was a text from Beth-Ann. *You OK?*

I smiled. She was on speaking terms with me again. I texted back. *Yes. With Grayson. Can't talk now.*

She texted, *Hope UR not alone in woods w/him. Ha Ha.*

I swallowed a knot that cropped up in my throat. *Don't be silly. Call U later.*

I shoved the phone back in my pocket. Beth-Ann had ripped me a new one for taking off with a man I barely knew and whom she'd never met. Her concern had been well meaning, but I couldn't take on her fears, too. I already had enough of my own. I crossed my fingers and hoped her dire prediction that I'd be found murdered by Monday didn't pan out. I'd just begun to feel I could trust the man in the black fedora. Maybe I shouldn't ....

"Grayson." I tugged on the backpack strapped to his back. "I don't get it. Why all these random switchbacks in the trail? Wouldn't it have been easier to make a straight path between the pines?"

Grayson turned to face me. "Either Jenkins was trying to disguise the trail, or he had the worst sense of direction of all time."

"Or he was crazy."

Grayson nodded. "A third, viable option."

I chewed my lip. "I think Jenkins *was* trying to hide the trail. But why? And Garth with his prison compound guarded by a hound from hell. Who exactly are these guys worried is going to get them?"

Grayson's eyebrows lifted. "Who, or *what?* That's the sixty-four thousand dollar question, isn't it?"

My nose crinkled. "For that kind of money, I'd like to take a stab at an answer."

Grayson's shoulders broadened. "Fine. But first, you have to name the game."

"Game? What are you talking about?" *Murder me by Monday?*

"You know. The *game.* The universal mind is playing with us again. I can feel it. Didn't you hear it laughing at us?"

"That was a woodpecker."

"And who put it there?"

I scowled. Grayson had an infuriating way of being right and wrong at the same time.

He smiled deviously. "We're following the clues for the next game."

Right. And the challenge for this round is, which one of us is the bigger lunatic?

I shot him a hard stare. "You really think so?"

Grayson nodded. "Absolutely. Now that the game is afoot, what's your next move, cadet?"

Flop-sweat broke out on my forehead. I'd never been any good at being put on the spot. "I ... I have no idea, Grayson. I wouldn't know where to begin."

Grayson's face grew somber. "Sure you do. You already figured out the biggest clue."

"What?"

"I see it on your face. *Fear.*" He locked eyes with me. "Never forget that. The game is *always* about fear. Identify your fears, and you have a chance of conquering them."

"Thanks, Yoda." My confidence might've fled like a bad blind date, but I couldn't shake my sarcastic wit to save my soul.

The woodpecker's shrill laugh sounded again.

"That must be Obi-Wan," I quipped. "I've been told he's our only hope."

Grayson squelched a grin, then turned and continued down the narrow trail. I sighed and followed suit.

A few switchbacks later, his backpack caught on a palmetto frond. As it came free, the frond flew back like a slingshot, jettisoning a passenger—a cockroach the size of a mouse.

It spread its wings and flew right at my face.

"Aaargh!" I screamed.

Grayson whirled around, eyes wide. He saw me swatting wildly at my insectoid nemesis and laughed.

"Scared of a little bug, are we? Yet another irrational fear you need to tackle, Drex."

"What do you mean, *another?*" I stopped waving my arms. "For your information, palmetto bugs aren't *little*, Grayson. They're *disgusting*. And they carry diseases! So it's not irrational to be afraid of them."

Grayson's lips twitched with amusement. "Right. And here I thought you were a true-blue country gal. So tell me, what's a roach ever done to you?"

"I grew up in the *South*, Grayson. Not in a *dump*. Roaches are filthy!"

Grayson's right eyebrow shot up. "Really? Then why do roaches clean themselves after coming in contact with humans?"

I scowled. "You just made that up."

Grayson smirked. "Did I?"

A lizard scurried across the trail. It took a flying leap onto a twig and grabbed the roach in its mouth. I grimaced.

Grayson snorted. "Come on, Princess Leia. Let's go before Jabba the Lizard gets you."

Chapter Eight

AFTER ANOTHER TEN MINUTES or so of dodging insects and insults, Grayson and I came upon a clearing at the end of the zig-zagging trail through the pines and palmettos.

We came face-to-face with the dark, ominous husk of a falling-down log cabin. The shattered front window had been crudely sealed with cardboard and duct tape. A tattered, camouflage-patterned tarp sagged over its broken roof.

"Oh, look. The honeymoon suite," Grayson said.

"Yeah. In *Apocalypse Now*."

A torn strip of yellow crime-scene tape waved lazily at us from a post on the front porch. Grayson rubbed his chin. "I guess we're not the first to arrive."

My upper lip hooked skyward. "You're not thinking of actually *going in*, are you?"

Grayson shrugged. "The scene's already been compromised, so we can't do too much more damage." He swung the backpack from his back and unzipped a pocket. "Here. Put these on."

I stared at the surgical booties in his hand. "Are you serious?"

"Yes. Over your shoes. We don't need to add our biology to whatever's already in evidence."

I slipped the booties over my muddy tennis shoes. Grayson donned gloves and picked the lock on the dilapidated cabin door. It took him mere seconds. The man had skills, I'd give him that. Where he'd gotten them, I wasn't sure I wanted to know.

Grayson slipped his lock-picking tool back into his pocket and turned to me. "Here we go, cadet. Our first official crime scene investigation together." He held up his cellphone. "Want a picture for your scrapbook?"

"I'll pass."

"Your loss." He slipped the phone back into his pocket and motioned for me to step inside. "Come on, then. Ladies first."

I grimaced. "I think this is a case of ladies *not* going first."

"Have it your way. But keep close."

"The place is the size of an outhouse. Do I have any choice?"

Grayson disappeared into the cabin. I made a few reluctant steps, then gave up and followed him inside.

The stale air in the log cabin smelled vaguely of fish.

And turpentine.

And putrefying flesh.

Yuck.

"What's that?" I pointed toward a corner heaped with electronics.

"Jenkins' ham radio equipment."

"No. Above it."

I raised my finger up, toward a clothesline strung high along the back wall. Draped over the line hung ragged, reddish-brown slabs of what appeared to be drying flesh.

My heart began to thump so loudly I was sure Grayson could hear it echoing off the log walls. But I was wrong. He hadn't noticed.

"Huh," he said, and walked over to the hunks of flesh hanging from the clothesline like Dahmer's dirty laundry. "Not your typical cafeteria mystery meat," he said as he took a piece of flesh from the cord.

He sniffed it. Then—against every normal, human instinct I knew—he opened his mouth to take a nibble.

"Stop!" I screeched.

He looked up, giving me time to run over and slap the meat out of his hand.

"What?" Grayson said. "It's not *human*."

"Ugh!" I hissed. "It's *deer* meat, Grayson. Venison."

"Huh," he said, studying the meat in his hand. "How do you know that?"

"My cousin Earl hunts deer, remember? And if it were human flesh, I doubt the cops would've left it hanging here."

Grayson nodded, apparently approving of my reasoning. "So, you think Jenkins was making deer jerky in here?"

"Yeah." I nodded toward the crude kitchen in the corner. "And from the looks of that meat grinder clamped to the table over there, deer hamburgers and meatballs as well."

Grayson looked impressed. "So *that's* what that thing is. I thought it was a giant pencil sharpener."

"Kind of looks like one. But it's a vintage LF&C hand-crank meat grinder. The pioneering homemaker's friend. My Grandma Selma had one. They're made out of galvanized steel. Practically indestructible."

Grayson's lip twisted to the left. "I don't get it. Why would anyone want to grind their own meat? I'm pretty sure we passed at least one Wendy's and two McDonald's on our way to Rexel's."

I snorted. "You really *are* a city boy, aren't you? Well, Mr. Fancy Pants, outlasting the apocalypse with store-bought goods doesn't come cheap."

Grayson shot me a wide-eyed stare. "Who said anything about the apocalypse?"

I picked up a wrapper from the floor. "I think this guy Jenkins was a prepper."

"A prepper?"

"Yeah. A survivalist. He was 'prepping' for the imminent breakdown of society as we know it."

Grayson scratched his chin. "I thought that already happened. You know, when they made Sharknado II."

I smirked and walked over to a plastic container the size of a breadbox. It was lying on its side near a corner of the cabin. The lid was off, and the container was covered in small, dirty handprints.

"See these wrappers strewn all over the floor? This container had a good month's worth of food in it ... before the raccoons got to it."

Grayson's eyebrow ticked up. "A month's worth of food in that small cooler?"

"It's not a cooler. It's what preppers call a portable food storage kit. This thing was packed with freeze-dried meals."

I handed Grayson a shredded foil pouch.

His nose crinkled. "Freeze-dried tuna fish. Yum." He let the wrapper fall back to the ground and picked up a small, gray tin marked Therma-

Fuel. "Well, look at that. Who knew doomsday survival included fondue?"

I snorted. "That's diethylene glycol. Kind of like Sterno on steroids. But it's for *heating*, not cooking. A small can like that could warm up this place for the better part of a day."

"What about this?" Grayson held up a lumpy object roughly the size and shape of a small loaf of bread. It was ashy white. "Let me guess. Fire log? Wait. Petrified fruitcake?"

I shook my head. "I dunno. I've never seen one of those. But if it's fruitcake, that would explain why the raccoons haven't touch it."

Grayson grinned. "Only a true sadist would include fruitcake in somebody's survival gear. Could you imagine if this thing was your last meal on Earth?"

Grayson dropped the misshapen brick onto the floor. It landed with a thud that rattled loose a few shards from the broken window.

I smirked. "Thick as a brick. Just like the ones my Aunt Lucy used to make. We used 'em for doorstops. They're not pretty. But you've got to admit, that thing would certainly last you a while."

Grayson stared at the ashy clump on the floor. "True. I think our family re-gifted the same fruitcake for over twenty years. But ours never turned white."

I shrugged. "Maybe it's mold. Or some kind of protective coating. Anyway, it's gotta be survival rations."

Grayson crinkled his nose. "If that's surviving, count me out."

I laughed. "Coming from the man who got hungry staring at Jenkins' man-pudding photos, that's rich." I looked over at a stack of empty Dr Pepper cans. "Meat and sodas. How long can someone survive on that?"

Grayson held up a magazine. "As they say, man cannot live by bread alone. I suppose that's why Jenkins also hoarded these lovely issues of *Paranormal Underground*."

I lifted Lucky Red and scratched my scalp. "So he *was* a UFO freak after all."

Grayson set the magazine down and turned back toward the radio equipment. "Hey. At least he was aiming for the stars."

I was about to groan at Grayson's lousy joke when something erased the notion from my mind.

It was the unmistakable sound of a gun's trigger-hammer locking into place behind me.

I started to turn around, but something poked me hard in the spine.

A strange voice spat out words usually reserved for old Clint Eastwood movies.

"You two. Put your hands where I can see 'em. *Now!*"

Chapter Nine

"WHAT ARE YOU DOING in here?" the man behind me demanded.

He poked the hard, pointy thing against my spine again. I had a feeling it wasn't a churro. I stared ahead at Grayson, afraid to look back for fear it might compel the man to blast a bullet through my guts.

"We're private investigators," Grayson said. He shot me a quick glance he must've meant to be reassuring.

It wasn't.

Not even close.

Grayson reached slowly for his jacket pocket. "Here. Let me show you my credentials."

"Don't even think about it," the man barked. "P.I. or not, you're disturbing a crime scene."

Grayson displayed his open palms. "True. But the crime scene tape was already broken when we got here. And, technically, you're disturbing it, too."

"I'm a police officer."

Grayson eyed him skeptically, making me think the man holding the gun didn't fit the part.

"Where's your uniform?" Grayson asked.

"I'm on plain-clothes patrol."

"Oh." Grayson's face relaxed a notch. "Well, in that case, nice to meet you, Officer." Grayson extended his hand.

The man behind didn't reach for it. Instead, he jabbed his gun in my back again and said, "Show me some I.D."

As Grayson reached inside his jacket, I slowly turned my head and caught my first sideways glimpse of the man holding us at gunpoint.

He was white. Short haircut. Surprisingly young—maybe mid-twenties—and dressed in camouflage hunting fatigues. He could've been a military hero or the Unabomber.

I shot the man a weak smile. "We're working for Chief Warren Engles."

The young man eyed me sourly. "Yeah, well ain't that special. Shut it, ma'am. And assume the position."

The position? What am I supposed to do? Bend over and squeal like a pig?

"What do you mean?" I squeaked.

"Put your hands behind your back." He glanced at Grayson's I.D. "You, too, mister. I'm cuffing you both. Put your tin badge away. You can explain what you're doing here to my captain back at the station."

The man's gun stopped poking my back. A trickle of relief washed over the dread standing on my throat, making it hard to breathe. As ice-cold cuffs slid around my wrists, my old sidekick, cynicism, wasn't about to miss this golden opportunity.

Well, I guess I can mark "get arrested" off my bucket list.

A touch of hysteria made me giggle at the utter absurdity of the situation—a bad habit I just couldn't' seem to break.

"You think this is funny?" the man with the cuffs spat at me. "We'll see who gets the last laugh here." He slapped a second pair of cuffs on Grayson and shoved him toward the cabin door. "All right. Let's go. And no funny business."

Grayson shot the man an incredulous look. "Funny business? Officer, I wouldn't dream of it."

GRAYSON AND I STAGGERED, single file, ahead of the man claiming to be an out-of-uniform cop. He'd refused to show us any identification, and we weren't in a position to argue. Cuffed like fugitives, we formed a strange, stumbling, six-legged centipede as we zigged and zagged through the narrow, maze-like trail carved in the palmettoes.

About midway along the path, Grayson called out from in front of me. "Officer, couldn't we solve this whole situation with the help of my old friend, Ben Franklin?"

"Ben Franklin?" I asked. "What about Warren Engles?"

"Wait a minute," the man said. "You trying to bribe me, mister?"

Grayson coughed. "Uh. Not as far as you know."

"That's it!" the young man yelled angrily. "Hold it right there!"

Grayson and I froze in our tracks.

"Turn around," he demanded. "*Slowly*."

I shot Grayson a dirty look. Had his big mouth just cost us our lives? What if this guy was no cop? What if he was the one who'd killed Jenkins in the first place? I had to get us out of this mess!

I winced and turned my pleading eyes to the young man with the gun. "Sir, we're sorry." I studied his face for signs of mercy, then a niggling thought wormed its way into my brain.

I've seen this guy before.

"Let's see that P.I. badge of yours again," the man demanded of Grayson.

Grayson shrugged. "I'd love to oblige. But I can't. It's in my jacket pocket."

The hard-faced young man brushed past me and snatched Grayson's wallet from the breast pocket of his jacket. While the man examined Grayson's badge, I studied his face and racked my brain over his features. That square jaw. That dimpled chin. Those pale-blue eyes ....

Where have I seen him before? On TV? At Walmart? A wanted poster at the post office? Match.com? Come on, think!

The man looked up at Grayson and sneered. "Well, Mr. Nicholas Grayson, looks like you won't be needing this anymore." He waved the tin badge in the air. "Bribing a cop is pretty good grounds for suspension of your license. And I think my father, the Chief of Police, can make it stick. I'll be sure and let him know all about your friend Ben Franklin, though."

Grayson winced as if he'd been punched in the gut. "I didn't mean any harm."

"Save it. Let's get going."

As the young man sidled by me again, the angle of his face and curve of his lips set the final pieces of the puzzle into place.

"Wait a minute," I said. "You're Jimmy Wells, aren't you?"

He eyed me suspiciously, but said nothing.

"It's you, all right," I said. "I recognize you from a picture at your brother's place. You two looked mighty cute cozied up together with that giant bong."

The man's smug smile flew away from his face. "Crap."

I shot a glance at Grayson. He was grinning at me like a proud professor.

"Don't worry, Officer," he said. "I'm sure we can work something out."

Chapter Ten

"SO YOU MET MY BROTHER, Gary," Officer Wells said after releasing Grayson and me from the handcuffs he'd kept us in until we'd cleared the path in the woods.

"Yes. Grayson and I met him this morning." I rubbed my wrists and attempted an ingratiating smile. "And his little lapdog, Tooth."

Wells' eyes widened. "Wait a minute. You two. You're not ...?" He closed his eyes and blew out a breath. "Tell me you're not Mr. Gray and Pandora."

"The very same," Grayson said.

Wells shook his head. "I thought Gary was just making that whole thing up. It's hard to tell with him sometimes. Crap! What other family secrets did my brother spill?"

"Besides the bong?" I asked. "Well, he said you were the first to discover Jenkins' body. He showed us the pictures."

A vein began to throb in Wells' neck. "That little twit! I'm going to kill him!"

Grayson took off his backpack and tossed it onto the seat of the RV. "Where'd you find Jenkins, anyway? Inside the cabin?"

"No." Wells glanced around to see if anyone else was within earshot. "Look. I shouldn't be speaking with you about this."

"We're professionals," Grayson said. "We keep our sources confidential."

Wells' eyebrow shot up. "Like you did with my brother, Gary?"

Grayson grimaced. "Oops. Well, we'll keep the bong confidential. Scout's honor."

Wells looked as if he might throw up. He swallowed hard and said, "I found Jenkins in a clearing by the side of the cabin."

"Was he still alive when you found him?" I asked.

"I thought so, at first. He was lying there, eyes open, like he was gazing up at the stars. I thought he might be alive, but when I grabbed his arm, it felt soft ... kind of like mashed potatoes."

My nose scrunched involuntarily. "What do you think happened to him?"

"I dunno. I've never seen anything like it."

Grayson cleared his throat. "Garth ... uh ... *Gary* told us that Jenkins' head was covered in slime."

"Yes. Some kind of lubricant or something."

Grayson nodded. "Anything else unusual?"

Wells chewed his lip. "Well, this is kind of weird, but I found Jenkins' ammo belt and boots first. They were on the ground in front of the cabin steps. The boots were standing up in the middle of the ammo belt, still laced up—like Jenkins had been jerked from his gear by some enormous power."

Grayson's eyebrow rose a notch. "Power?"

Wells studied his shoes. "I didn't put this in my report, but I saw a strange ray of light in the sky. White, like a search beam, sort of. It was off in the distance, but it still gave me this creepy feeling."

"What do you mean?" I asked.

"It's just ... argh." Wells shook his head. "Nah. You'll think I'm crazy."

He looked up. Grayson locked eyes with the young man. "Believe me, Officer Wells, we're the last people who'd do that."

Wells pursed his lips and blew out a breath as if he'd given up on something. "It's just that ... this idea came over me that Jenkins had simply *vanished* from that exact spot. You know ... that the boots and ammo belt were left behind when he got ... uh ... beamed up in that ray of light."

Wells studied our faces. I wasn't sure what he was looking for, but he must have found it, because he continued talking.

"Like I said, I just got this major case of the creeps, you know? Like that feeling you get when you think something's watching you. Anyway, I freaked a little and started running back toward the trail. I wanted to get the hell out of there before I got zapped myself. But then I spotted Jenkins lying in the pine straw and realized he hadn't been beamed up after all."

"Why would Jenkins have been wearing an ammo belt?" I asked.

Wells shook his head. "I don't know. Maybe he'd seen a panther or something. They're pretty sneaky predators. Maybe that was what was watching me." He glanced back toward the woods. "I honestly couldn't tell you. But what I don't get is why he left his AK-47 behind. I found it on the floor inside the cabin."

"Interesting," Grayson said. "Did Jenkins have any other weapons on him?"

"Not that the crime-scene techs found in their search yesterday. He didn't need anything else. An AK-47 usually does an adequate job in most scenarios."

Grayson nodded. "In combat situations, sure. But why would Jenkins feel the need to have an automatic weapon and all that ammo out here in these woods? It seems to me like he was preparing for some kind of showdown."

Wells shrugged. "You'd be surprised how many wild animals are out here. Lots of things with fangs and claws. Alligators. Wildcats. Rattlesnakes. Brown bears."

"Is that how you got those scars on your neck?" I asked.

Wells reached up and absently touched the fine, white lines on his neck. "These? No. Tooth gave me these—when he was still a puppy. He's not too keen on strangers, in case you didn't notice."

I grimaced. "I noticed. So they're treating this as a crime scene?"

"Well, it sure wasn't suicide," Wells said sourly.

"Any suspects?" I asked.

"None at present."

"What about aliens?" Grayson asked.

The young cop blew out a breath. "You talkin' Mexicans or Martians?"

Grayson shrugged. "Either one. I'm flexible."

Wells shook his head. "I knew I shouldn't have mentioned the light beam. Don't tell anyone, okay?"

"Absolutely," Grayson said. "It's just that I noticed Jenkins had a stockpile of UFO magazines along with his ammo. And your brother Gary said he intercepted a ham radio signal where Jenkins was yelling

'They're here!' over and over again. Could he have meant space aliens? Like you said earlier, could Jenkins have been 'beamed up' and then spit back out?"

Wells kicked the jagged line of asphalt where the paved road disappeared into greyish-white sand. "Look. Lots of folks around here think they see UFOs. My brother Gary's the worst. He's always going on about it. It was probably all his jabber that put that crazy thought in my head in the first place. UFOs aren't real. Like all the other times, this'll turn out to be something stupid."

"All the other times?" Grayson and I asked in unison.

"Sure. People call into the station all the time about lights in the sky. They turn out to be emergency flares. Beacons on cellphone towers. Even lightning bugs. One time, I actually had a woman run up to me all freaked out about 'flying monsters.' Turned out to be dragonflies. *Dragonflies!* People can be downright nuts."

"How about Jenkins?" Grayson asked. "Was he what you'd call a nut?"

Wells shrugged. "No more than any of the other old drunks who come down here to spend their golden years turning us locals' lives to crap. Jenkins had a fondness for getting blasted at Blarney's Bar. From what Gary tells me, Jenkins would drink his fill of Jack Daniels and blabber on about the end of the world to anybody who'd listen."

"The end of the world?" I asked.

"You know. Alien invasions. A woman president. Eight-dollar gasoline. That sort of crap."

Grayson smirked. "Was Jenkins prone to hallucinations?"

"Not that I know of. But once at Blarney's, he did mistake some other gal for his wife, Arlene." Wells snickered. "I remember Gary coming home one night and telling me Jenkins thought Arlene had shown up at the bar ready to clobber him with a frying pan. Gary said Jenkins ducked under the counter and hightailed it out the back door. That old bastard might've talked a tough game, but I think his wife was one showdown he wasn't prepared to deal with."

Grayson shot Wells a man's-man smile. "Thank you, Officer Wells. You've been a great help."

The two men shook hands, but when it was time to release the grip, Grayson didn't let go.

"Just one more thing," Grayson said, holding firmly to the young cop's hand. "I'd like to have access to Jenkins' body, or at minimum the coroner's autopsy report."

Wells' eyes widened, then narrowed. "No way!" He jerked his hand free. "Our deal was *your* freedom for *my* bong. That's it. We're done here."

"Right. But what about these pictures?" Grayson took out his cellphone and flashed a picture of Jenkins doing his human Jell-O impersonation. "Who should I say is the source?"

Wells crumpled. "Look. I'll see what I can do. Okay?"

Grayson nodded. "I appreciate that. Is Jenkins going to be cremated?"

Wells shrugged. "I don't know. His wife Arlene hasn't claimed the body yet."

"Why not?"

The young cop pursed his lips and shrugged. "Probably because nobody's seen her since the night Jenkins died."

Chapter Eleven

"WHAT'S YOUR TAKE SO far?" I asked Grayson as he hooked a left out of the desolate subdivision Rexel and a few other residents had been swindled into calling home.

He stomped on the accelerator. "Don't buy swampland in Florida."

"Har har. I mean, what do you think is going on with Jenkins?"

Grayson shrugged. "Hard to say. Like I said before, we need to get a look at his body, or the autopsy report."

"What about his wife, Arlene? She might be missing. You think she could've met the same fate as her husband?"

"Beamed up by aliens?"

I blew out a breath. "No. I meant do you think she's dead somewhere in those woods back there?"

"I don't know. Wells mentioned panthers and bears as potential killers. But the terrain around here is also the perfect habitat for Sasquatch—or as you Floridians like to call him, the skunk ape." Grayson's lip twisted to one side. "Now that I think about it, the Boggy Creek monster would find this area to his liking, too."

"What?" I smirked. "No giant spider or scaly iguanodon?"

Grayson grinned and showed me the palmetto scratches on his knuckles. "Nah. Too many sharp objects."

"So, I take it then that you think it was an animal that turned Jenkins into baby food?"

Grayson smirked. "There you go again, making me hungry."

He turned the RV onto SR 39. "Let's pick out a restaurant for dinner. I'm suddenly in the mood for venison and mashed potatoes."

I crinkled my nose. "You're sick, Grayson."

"I prefer the term 'desensitized.'"

I snorted. "Yeah. You keep living *that* dream."

Grayson laughed. "You're in a good mood. How about an evening on the town? I hear you can't beat Blarney's Bar for cheap beer and disgruntled wives."

I smirked. "To be honest, I could use a drink. But first, I'm gonna need a wig. I'm not going into a bar wearing a Redman chewing tobacco cap. In a redneck town like this, I might be accused of crossdressing. How far is it to Walmart from here?"

"Look it up on your phone."

I scowled. "Why? You know the way."

"Come on. You look so cute when you do your Mrs. Magoo impersonation."

"Very funny."

I got out my cellphone and tried not to squint as I punched the Google mic on the display. "Address of nearest Walmart."

The voice spilled out the answer.

I turned to Grayson. "Got that?"

"Affirmative."

I sat back and watched the shabby little town of Hopewell fade in, then out of view.

"I'm curious, Grayson. Why didn't Wells care when I mentioned that we were working for Chief Warren Engles?"

Grayson's eyes met mine. "That only works for the FBI. And even then, only under certain circumstances."

"Why's that?"

Grayson turned his gaze back to the road. "Right now, cadet, you don't need to know."

AN OLD MAN STOPPED in his tracks and looked me up and down as I climbed out of the RV in front of Walmart. Apparently, my ball cap and buzz cut didn't jive with my boobs. The judgmental sneer on his face could've made Jesus weep.

"Promise me you're coming back," I said to Grayson through the RV window. "I'm not dressed for long-term survival here."

"Don't be silly. I'll be back in twenty minutes, tops. I'm just going to find a UPS store and mail something off for analysis."

"The Mothman scat from the last job?"

"Bingo. As with any treasure, the value lies in its authentication."

"I thought it was the lies about authentication that added value to the treasure."

Grayson shook his head. "Drex, Drex. Always the skeptic. Hey! Pick me up a bag of Cheetos while you're in there, would you?"

"Sure. See you in a bit."

As Grayson drove away, a sudden wave of insecurity caused my gut to flinch.

Am I crazy? What am I doing in this strange town with this strange man?

What did I really know about Nick Grayson?

Not even enough to be sure he was coming back.

I checked my purse for my lifeline. A ping of relief flooded through me as my fingers found my cellphone in the bottom of my bag. I tucked it back in my purse and headed into Walmart.

Like a confused nomad wandering into a strange oasis, I was no longer certain what part of my life was real, and what was a mirage.

But at least I had four bars.

And a full battery.

Chapter Twelve

FOR A GUY WHO WAS COMPLETELY OCD about keeping his RV spic-and-span, making a living selling cryptid crap seemed totally out of character for Grayson. But then again, the need to make a living could trump anything.

I knew that all too well.

After my father died, I'd wasted the better part of a year trying to prove to his ghost that I could run the family auto repair business. I'd failed him on all levels—even at being his biological daughter. As it turned out, my cousin Earl had been both the real mechanic *and* the real relation.

I'd spent twenty-five years blaming Earl for stealing my job and my father's affections, only to find out it wasn't his fault at all. I'd been a real jerk to my cousin. And good-old Southern guilt was telling me I needed to make it up to him.

As I wheeled my cranky Walmart shopping cart past a display of ball caps, I took it as a sign to give Earl a call. But as I dialed his number, I realized sarcasm makes a better master than a servant. Dropping my caustic, barb-slinging routine with him was going to take some serious effort.

"Hey, Earl," I said sweet enough to make me nearly gag.

"Hey, there, Bobbie. Still alive, I see."

The snide tone of Earl's voice sounded like ... *home.*

I smiled. "You run the family business into the ground yet?"

He laughed. "Gimme another day or two. You know I can't work that fast. Thanks for turning out the light, by the way."

I cringed. As I'd driven away from Point Paradise last night, I'd shot out the lousy hole-in-the-wall's only claim to fame—the flashing yellow light hanging over the intersection of nowhere and oblivion.

"You all right, Cuz?" Earl asked.

"Sure. Sorry about the light. It was kind of ... symbolic for me."

"I get it. I'd a done a lot worse if I'd just found out my pappy wasn't my pappy. How's it going with Grayson?"

"I survived the night. And we're on a new case in Plant City. Some prepper guy got killed at his cabin. Someone—or some*thing*—mooshed him into a human Slurpee."

"That don't sound too good Bobbie. Be careful. You still got Lucky Red to protect you?"

"Yes." I touched the cap atop my head. "Don't worry. Your precious cap is safe with me. I'm at Walmart now looking for another one. I need a wig, too. Thanks to Mothman and your duct tape, my last one was shot to hell. I'll grab a new cap here and mail Lucky Red back to you."

"No. You keep ol' Red for as long as you need him. You deserve some better luck, Bobbie." Earl laughed. "Hey, maybe you'll get lucky with Grayson."

I rolled my eyes. "Is that all you think about, Earl?"

"That and pistons. What's so bad about that?"

"Nothing, I guess. Be good. I've got to go."

"I'm always good," Earl quipped. "At least, that's what all the gals say."

I clicked off the phone and smiled. So much had been upended in my life over the past few days, it was nice to know one thing had remained the same. My cousin Earl would always be a wisecracking pain in my ass.

And for some reason, I loved him all the more for it.

Chapter Thirteen

I WAS STANDING AMID the towering eyeglass racks in Walmart trying on "cheater" specs. Amidst the jumble, I found a pair of 2.5 magnification lenses in pink frames. I tried them on, but when I looked through them, all I could see was colorful donuts dancing in the air.

Weird.

I looked down. Slices of pepperoni pizza wiggled in a bright yellow background above a pair of red, leopard-spotted tennis shoes.

This can't be right. Am I having another hallucination?

I took off the glasses and rubbed my eyes.

"You gonna keep those?" a man asked.

My eyes blinked open.

I blinked again.

It hadn't been a hallucination after all. Suddenly, I realized that having 20-20 vision wasn't always an asset.

A short, pudgy, sweaty man in his late thirties was eyeing the glasses in my hands, licking his lips. The fabric of his shirt was imprinted with life-sized donuts—his pants likewise with pizza slices.

I couldn't decide whether I felt hungry or nauseated.

"Well?" the man asked.

"Uh ... no." I held out the glasses. "You can have them. They're a bit too strong for me."

He grabbed them from my hand. "Thanks. You're lucky. My eyesight is terrible."

Well, that'd be one *explanation for that outfit.*

"It sucks getting older," I said, and reached for a pink pair with 1.5 magnification.

"I know that's right." The man looked in my cart. "I see you picked a wig from the new Lucy Goosy line. Good choice."

I suddenly lost confidence in my prospective coiffure selection. I eyed the wig dubiously as the man plucked a dozen pairs of glasses from the racks.

"Why all the eyeglasses?" I asked.

He shrugged, causing the donuts on his shirt to undulate. "Buy one, get one sale. If all hell breaks loose, there won't be any glasses anymore."

There won't be any donut shirts, either. At least, I hope not.

"Wait a minute," I said. "Are you a prepper?"

The man glanced around, then whispered, "Yes. You?"

"Yes."

He gave me the once-over. "I haven't seen you at any of the meetings."

"I'm new in town."

"Oh. Well, listen. A couple of us are meeting at Blarney's tonight. You know the place?"

"Sure do."

"Stop by. Introduce yourself. We'll be there around seven."

"Thanks. I appreciate that."

He smiled. "The guys will like you. They're always on the lookout for breeding stock."

My back stiffened. What was *that* supposed to mean?

I was about to give donut dude a piece of my breeding stock mind when Grayson walked up. He eyed my cart full of cheap clothes, toiletries, Tootsie Pops and Cheetos.

He grinned. "All that scat cash burning a hole in your pocket?"

I glared at donut man and pasted on a fake smile. "Awe, you know me, honey." I gave Grayson a peck on the cheek. Pizza man's hopeful face collapsed like punched dough.

"Well, I better get going," he said. "Nice chatting with you."

"Yes," I said, too enthusiastically. "See you tonight!"

As the guy wheeled his cart away, Grayson turned to me. "I had no idea you're such a tease, *honey*."

I dropped the girlfriend charade. "Tactical diversion. Pizza Pants invited us to a prepper meeting tonight."

Grayson snorted. "*He's* a prepper? What kind of camouflage is that? In case he's attacked by a horde of health-food zombies?"

I shook my head. "I just pray the fabric's not scratch-n-sniff."

Grayson guffawed. "Well, honey, looks like we've got ourselves a hot date tonight."

"Hot date?"

"A ménage á trois—with chocolate sprinkles."

"You have one sick sense of humor, Grayson."

He grinned. "You love it. Admit it, B.H."

"B.H.?"

"Breeding hips."

Crap. He'd heard our conversation after all.

Chapter Fourteen

ONE STEP INSIDE THE hotel room and my nostrils shriveled.

I turned to Grayson. "Ugh! This place reeks! I thought I told you to ask for a *non-smoking* room."

Grayson plopped a small duffle bag onto one of the saggy twin beds. "I *did*."

I followed the worn trail in the nicotine-colored carpeting to the bathroom. The cheap laminate countertop and bathtub rim were pockmarked with amber cigarette burns. I stomped back into the main room. "Then who's the chain-smoker? The maid?"

"Actually, I think she died of emphysema a while back." Grayson pulled back the comforter on one of the beds. The threadbare sheets were rumpled and dirty. "Nobody's changed these since the Nixon administration."

My mouth puckered. "Gross. And I thought Jenkins' cabin was bad. Listen. I'm gonna get a shower, but I'm not touching either of those beds."

"Suit yourself."

I thought about the small lizard Grayson kept in a terrarium on the windowsill above the RV's banquette table. "Don't even think about bringing poor Gizzard in here."

Grayson's nose wrinkled. "I wouldn't. I have too much respect for the reptilia phylum."

I cocked my head and shot him a side-eyed sneer. "But not too much respect for *me*, apparently."

"Your habitat isn't under threat by Cuban invaders."

"It is if you count Miami." I glanced back into the ratty room and got the willies.

No self-respecting cockroach would stay in this place.

I couldn't bring myself to shower in the RV. It just seemed too—*up close and personal.* After that romp in the woods, my deodorant had given up the ghost.

I clamped my molars, grabbed my duffle, and marched into the bathroom. Both the countertop and floor were too disgusting to set the bag down on, so I hung it on the doorknob.

After locking the door, I pulled back the shower curtain, revealing what could only be described as a laboratory experiment gone horribly awry. I blew out a sigh and unbuttoned my jeans. A thought made me quickly refastened them.

I jerked open the bathroom door and yelled at Grayson.

"Is this a setup to make me want to stay in the RV? There's not even any toilet paper in here, for crying out loud!"

Grayson grinned. He was lying atop a bath towel he'd laid over the dirty bedspread. "Hey. You want toilet paper, lady, you've got to pay more than sixty-eight bucks a night."

I chewed my lip. "What am I supposed to ... you know, take care of my business with? A pillowcase?"

Grayson nodded toward the other bed. "I think someone already beat you to that idea."

I tried not to look. Failing at that, I closed my disgusted eyes and sucked in a deep breath. On the exhale, something hit me square in the gut.

I gasped and opened my eyes just as Grayson's football-sized travel bag tumbled to the floor in front of me.

"My emergency kit," he said. "Never leave home without it."

With the weight of my biological emergency pressing down on my bladder, I didn't bother to complain about being used for target practice. "What's in there?"

"Spray bleach. Disinfectant wipes. Toilet tissue. Rubber booties."

"Booties? *Again?* What is it with you and booties?"

"Hey. You get off on toenail fungus, be my guest."

"Gawd, Grayson! What are we doing in this dump?"

"Trying to stay on budget. Now you know why I camp in RV parks and Walmart lots. The bathroom facilities are much nicer. And cleaner."

I did the math. Staying in decent hotels would cost over four grand a month.

"Fine." I skulked back into the bathroom with Grayson's emergency kit.

As I showered in booties amongst a live studio audience of assorted flora and fauna, my lousy couch-bed in the RV slowly transformed into the penthouse suite at the Ritz-Carlton.

Grayson was a diabolical genius.

Either that, or he was pathologically cheap.

"NICE JOB ON THE BATHROOM," Grayson said as he emerged showered and dressed in black jeans and booties.

I finished putting on lipstick in the vanity mirror while he pulled a black T-shirt over his muscular chest.

"Yeah. You owe me dinner for that one."

Grayson smiled and nodded. "Fair enough. Nice wig, by the way."

"Thanks." I adjusted the shoulder-length, bob-cut I'd bought at Wal-mart. I wasn't sure if the auburn color clashed with my new pink blouse or not, and I didn't care. It was better than looking like a redneck tranny.

I turned to face Grayson. "You ready to meet the preppers?"

Grayson glanced up from his phone. "It's just six. We've got time."

"Not if I'm going to get a drink in me first. And something to eat. I don't want to take the chance those prepper guys'll make me lose my appetite."

"Okay, Miss Early Bird Special. Just let me put on a belt and shoes."

I shot a glance at his feet. "You're not keeping the booties on?"

"No. They clash with my outfit."

I laughed. "Why do you wear black all the time, anyway?"

"I thought I just covered that. So I never have to worry about clashing."

"Right. You wouldn't want to mix your donut shirt with your pizza pants."

Grayson grinned. "Exactly."

Chapter Fifteen

GRAYSON SHIFTED THE RV into park in front of a wooden structure that appeared to have been constructed entirely from the remains of old moonshine still explosions.

He let out a low whistle. "So this is the infamous Blarney's Bar."

My nose crinkled. "I think I'm gonna need a bigger glass of vodka."

A car door closed nearby. I glanced over and spotted the eyeglasses hoarder from Walmart. He ambled toward the bar's entrance, still sporting his fast-food couture.

"Damn," I said. "There goes my head start—and my hankering for pepperoni pizza."

Grayson smirked. "Come on, Drex. A man has a right to make his own unique fashion statement."

"Yeah. His is, 'Kill me before I accessorize.'"

Grayson laughed and nodded toward Blarney's. "Hey, you think they serve tacos in there?"

I shrugged. "Why not? They obviously serve troglodytes. But earlier, didn't you tell me you wanted venison and mashed potatoes?"

"Can't a guy change his mind?"

"Sure. So long as a girl can, too."

Grayson studied me with his green eyes. "Fair enough. Let's go check out the locals, shall we?"

"I can't wait."

We climbed out of the RV and walked across the dirt lot to the falling-down front porch that served as the entrance to Blarney's. Once inside, I made a beeline for the bar. But even though I gave it my best shot, I wasn't fast enough.

"It's you!" the guy in the pizza pants called out. "You came! Come join us!"

As the pudgy pizza man approached, I gave him a weak smile. "That's okay. We were gonna get a bite to eat first."

He squinted through pink glasses and shook his head. "Nonsense! We already ordered enough chicken wings for everybody in the place."

"Does that include me?" Grayson asked.

"Uh ... sure."

Grayson eyed me playfully. "Then count us in."

I scrunched my nose. "You've never seen Grayson eat," I warned.

"You've never seen *me* eat, either," Pizza Pants rebutted.

I sighed. "No, I haven't. Lucky me. Looks like it's going to be a banner night."

The man grinned. "Follow me."

The colorful donuts on his shirt wobbled up, down, and sideways like a Fruit Loops acid flashback, rendering me slightly seasick by the time he led us to a dark corner booth in the rear of the bar. I was surprised to see the back of a blonde head poking up from the booth.

What do you know? Pizza Pants brought a date.

Then the head turned around.

"Pandora! Mr. Gray!"

Operative Garth stood up and pushed his black glasses higher on his nose. "Welcome!"

Pizza Pants' eyes were almost the size of the donuts on his shirt. "*The* Pandora and Mr. Gray?"

"One and the same," Garth said. "I see you've met my colleague, Dr. Freddy Crum."

"Doctor? As in Ph.D.?" I stuttered.

"General physician," Garth said.

My jaw went slack. "You're kidding."

Grayson elbowed me. I blushed and fumbled out an apology. "Sorry, Dr. Crum. You just ... it's just that ...."

"It's okay," Crum said. "I like to keep a low profile. These crazy scrubs are intentional."

"*Intentional?* What do you mean?"

Crum slid into the booth across from Garth. "They make me invisible."

My left eye ticked involuntarily—my built-in woo-woo alarm. "Uh ... pardon the pun," I said to Crum, but I just don't see it."

Crum laughed. "As a physician, I mean. People don't see me as a doctor when I dress like a clown."

I cocked my head. "I still don't get it."

Crum shrugged. "Ever had an old woman lift her shirt and show you her boob?"

"I have," Grayson said, raising his index finger.

I shot him a dirty look and turned back to Crum.

"You see, in this getup, people don't constantly pester me for medical advice while I'm out buying groceries, walking the dog, and generally trying to have a normal life."

"Oh." I smiled at the doctor. "That's actually kind of brilliant. But you have to admit, that's some really 'out there' camouflage."

"The fast-food combo is one of my personal favs," Garth said, and high-fived Crum across the table. "In that getup, nobody even asks us what *time* it is."

Crum grinned up at us, then he suddenly appeared startled. "Oh, my! Where are my manners? Please! Have a seat, you two."

Garth patted the open stretch of brown vinyl beside him. As I slid into the booth next to him, Garth said, "Mr. Gray, you can sit by Dr. Prepper."

"Dr. Prepper?" Grayson asked and stared at Crum. "So, you really *are* a prepper?"

Crum glanced around the room, then gave a quick nod. "That's me. Dr. Prepper."

Suddenly, Garth belted out an old advertising jingle, giving us an exhibition of his buck teeth as he sang, "He's a prepper, I'm a prepper, Rex's a prepper, they're a prepper. Wouldn't you like to be a prepper too?"

Crum groaned. "I told you never to do that again."

Garth's laugh sounded like a donkey's bray. "Come on. Nobody can resist Dr. Prepper!"

Crum groaned again and glanced at the end of the booth. "Speaking of Rexel, looks like we'll need to pull up a chair for him. He won't be too happy about that."

"It's *his* rule," Garth said. "Last one here has to sit on the end."

Crum looked concerned. "Strange. Rexel's almost always the first one here."

Garth sneered. "'Bout time he got a taste of his own protocol. He's the original Debbie Downer."

Crum sighed and nodded. Then his eyes lit up. He rubbed his pudgy fingers together and said, "Quick! Tell us about your adventures before Rexel gets here."

I shrugged. "Well, there's not much to tell—"

"We just captured Mothman," Grayson said.

Garth's eyes nearly popped out of his skull. "The creature from Point Pleasant?"

Grayson grinned proudly. "The very same. Well, either him or a near cousin."

Crum's eyes widened. "No way! That must've been super exciting!"

"Exciting?" Garth aimed the word at Crum, his chin nearly touching his neck. "More like *freaking amazing!* Didn't I tell you their lives rocked?"

"Sheesh," Crum said. "The most exciting thing I've done lately is lance a boil on a kid's buttocks. Are you two working on a case here in Plant City?"

Garth answered for us. "They're investigating Lester Jenkins' death. They think Grays did it."

"Grays?" Crum whispered. "As in *Gray aliens?*"

Grayson cleared his throat. "Well, yes. That's one possibility. However, we haven't come to any conclusions yet. Pandora told me this was a prepper meeting. Do you two know much about prepping?"

"Enough," Garth said, and nodded at Crum. "Freddy and I are on the same survivalist team. I'm security and communications."

Crum raised an index finger. "I'm in charge of medical and safety."

Grayson nodded. "Makes sense. And Rexel?"

Garth scowled. "He takes care of inventory and supplies."

"Was Lester Jenkins part of your team?" I asked.

The two men looked at each other and burst out laughing.

"Lester? No way," Garth said. "He was too much of a hot head."

"And unpredictable," Crum said. "And, I might add, a slob."

I smirked. *That's rich coming from a guy wearing his own grocery list.*

"I agree with you about his lack of fastidiousness," Grayson said. "His cabin was a wreck. You'd think Jenkins would've kept it in better repair, considering the whole upcoming apocalypse and all. There's a hole in the roof the size of a basketball."

"Maybe that's why he went there," I said. "To repair his cabin."

"More like to get away from his old lady," Garth said. "He was always pissing and moaning about her. Couldn't keep his mouth shut."

Crum nodded. "Shoot first and ask questions later. That applied to Jenkins' *gun* as well as his mouth."

The waitress arrived with enough chicken wings to permanently ground an entire migrating flock. My stomach gurgled in anticipation, but I didn't want to be the first to reach for one.

"Help yourself," Crum said, heaping his plate with the barbequed wings.

"Thanks." My fork at the ready, I stabbed at the wings while I aimed my conversation at Garth. "We uh ... ran into your brother, Jimmy, today. He told us he found Jenkins' ammo belt and boots outside by the front steps, about fifty feet from his body. Why would a prepper like Jenkins take his boots off? According to my weather app, it was nearly freezing that night."

Garth shrugged. "Maybe they got wet and he was drying them."

I mulled over the idea. "Why do you think he had so much ammo with him?"

Garth licked sauce from his lips. "Because Jenkins was a total doomsday prepper."

"Isn't *every* prepper?" Grayson asked.

"No," Crum said. "Some of us are simply hoping to outlast the food and power shortages inevitable with an economic collapse."

"What do you mean?" I asked.

"The reign of Retail Man is coming to an end," Crum explained. "We can't continue to spend our way out of dips and recessions. The national debt is like an iceberg getting ready to sink our economic boat."

"That'll never happen," Grayson said.

Crum snorted. "That's exactly what they said about the Titanic."

"If the economy doesn't get us, global warming will," Garth said.

My nose crinkled. "Can't we just outrun the tide?"

Garth shook his head. "Rising sea levels are just a minor symptom, Pandora. Global warming's gonna change the entire weather pattern. Probably even the flow of the Gulf Stream itself. When it does, we're talking killer tornados. Droughts. Ice storms all the way to Havana. Not to mention the ten or twenty million folks along the shorelines with nowhere to live except in a tent in our backyards."

"Don't forget earthquakes," Crum said.

"Like the San Andreas?" Grayson asked. "But they've been saying that thing's going to blow for the last two hundred years."

Crum set down the bony remains of a chicken wing. "No. I'm talking about the New Madrid fault line along the Mississippi River. Lots of folks think when it blows, it'll leave a two-hundred-mile-wide gap running north to south right down the middle of the US."

"So much for the *United* States," Garth quipped.

Grayson shook his head. "Hold on a moment. I'm trying to wrap my head around this. How was Jenkins—or any prepper for that matter—going to solve any of those issues with a bucket of freeze-dried deer meat and a loaded AK-47?"

"They're not," Garth said. "That's short-term thinking. But you gotta make it through the short term to get to the long term."

Grayson nodded, his eyes thoughtful. "Your brother Jimmy told us Jenkins shot out the window in his cabin. Then he left his gun behind and went outside carrying a fully loaded ammo belt. Have any idea why would he do that?"

Garth licked barbeque sauce from his buck teeth. "Maybe his gun jammed when he fired it. It would've been useless."

"So, *then* what?" Grayson asked. "He was going to beat his assailant to death with his ammo belt?"

Crum laughed derisively. "Don't discount that idea. Jenkins has had more than a few screws loose lately."

I looked Crum in the eye. "What do you mean by *lately?*"

"Sorry," Crum said. "Client-patient confidentiality. But I'll say this. Over the past few months, he's been acting more paranoid than usual."

"Any idea why?" Grayson asked.

"Yeah." Crum's lips twisted into a wry smile. "A little condition called 'life.'"

Grayson drummed his fingers on the table. "Could carbon monoxide make someone paranoid? We found some spent fuel canisters in the cabin."

"What kind?" Garth asked.

Grayson deferred to me.

"ThermaFuel," I answered.

Crum shook his head. "No. That wouldn't do it. That stuff's made of diethylene glycol. It's non-toxic. Doesn't even smoke. You can use it indoors or out without worrying about carbon monoxide poisoning."

Grayson's brow furrowed. "What else could've pushed Jenkins over the edge?"

"Besides his wife Arlene, you mean?" Garth quipped.

Grayson's eyes narrowed, as if he'd noted Garth's comment on some list inside his head. "The scene at Jenkins' cabin indicated he must've felt an imminent threat. That whatever he was afraid of was right outside the cabin door. What would—"

"Hey guys," a familiar voice sounded.

Engrossed in conversation, none of us had noticed Officer Jimmy Wells approach. The young cop stood beside the empty chair at the end of the booth. His expression made me think he was trying to piece together how Grayson and I'd managed to crash his private prepper party.

"Sit down," Garth said to his brother. "Looks like Rexel is a no show. Somebody should search Google to see if Hell's frozen over."

Garth and Crum laughed, but Wells' face remained stoic.

"I was afraid of that," Wells said. "I just heard over the police radio that his truck was found abandoned by the side of SR39 this afternoon. I thought maybe one of you had heard from him."

We all shook our heads.

Wells eyed Grayson and me suspiciously. "Weren't you two out there earlier today?"

"Yes," Grayson said. "But just to check out his repeater." He locked eyes with me. "My partner has a thing for little elephants."

Wells' jaw tightened. "Was he acting strangely?"

Grayson shrugged. "Impatient. Paranoid. Angry at the world."

"That's Rexel's normal," Garth said.

Wells blew out a sigh. "I know."

Chapter Sixteen

AS GRAYSON PULLED THE RV out of Blarney's parking lot, he gave his pathetic Southern accent another try. It was almost as painful as my heartburn from the chicken wings.

"Cryin' shame 'bout Rexel," he said. "But it sure was mighty neighborly of Garth and Dr. Prepper to invite us to join their friendly little, Sunday-go-to-meetin' survivalist clan."

I shot him some side-eye. "Where'd you pick up that shtick? *Hee Haw*? And don't flatter yourself, Grayson. They're just looking for someone to take over Rexel's job of handling their inventory."

Grayson smirked. "Given those breeding hips of yours, darlin', I suspected as much. So, just how good are you with 'handling inventory' anyway?"

"Ugh!" I squelched a grin. "Shut up!"

I whacked him one on the bicep. "And can the corn-pone accent. I've already warned you about it once."

"You breeders are all the same," Grayson muttered, shaking his head. "Well, I guess it's your choice, ma'am. Do we turn right and head to the Walmart parking lot? Or left and go back to our lovely hotel suite?"

I sneered. "Anything but that ashtray of a motel."

"Walmart, it is," he said, and hung a right.

I breathed a sigh of relief, then punctuated the end of it with a rather impressive burp.

"Nice one," Grayson said. "Practicing for the Guinness Book?"

My ears grew warm. "Excuse me. It's just that I haven't had that many chicken wings—or leers from creepy guys—since ... uh, let's see ... *ever*."

Grayson grinned, then his expression went introspective. We traveled along in silence for a few minutes, watching the lights from one unmemorable business after another flash by like uninspired background filler.

As he made the turn onto the Redman Parkway toward our super-center stop for the night, Grayson finally broke the silence.

"Relationships are hard."

Crap.

The mention of the word 'relationship' always made me squirrely. I glanced over at Grayson, unsure where he was going with his statement. Random thoughts began ping-ponging around inside my skull like a nuclear reactor gone haywire.

Was Grayson interested in me as more than a business partner? Were my breeding hips really that alluring? Geez. Why hadn't anyone told me earlier? Why did I waste all that money on a ThighMaster? Wait! Maybe he decided our partnership isn't working out.

I'm too flippant.

Too naïve.

Too ... *gassy!*

I cringed. *Is he going to* fire *me?*

Grayson turned his head to face me. "Let me ask you something."

I closed my eyes and braced for the worst. "Okay."

"Jenkins and his wife obviously didn't get along that great. What made them think they could survive the end of the world together in that rattrap of a cabin?"

Relief washed over me like a tsunami. It was quickly followed by a small wave of disappointment. Then, to my surprise, a trickle of anger.

"I don't know," I said, opening my eyes. "But I'll tell you *this*. If I was Jenkins' wife and he tried to drag me to that crappy cabin to ride out the apocalypse, he'd be the first casualty on my list."

"That's what I figured," Grayson said, and turned his eyes back to the road. "Rather than go willingly, she'd put up a fight, right?"

"In my book, yeah."

"But how much of a fight? Do you think Arlene would kill him?"

I shrugged. "Push comes to shove? Why not? If Jenkins was half the jerk those guys said he was, living with him would've already primed Arlene for the job."

Grayson whistled. "Granted, the guy was no husband of the year. But *murder?*"

"You forget, Grayson. From what we've been told, she's a survivalist, too."

Grayson blew out a breath. "Right. I guess you can't be squeamish about the whole kill-or-be-killed thing when the end of the world is breathing down your neck."

"Yeah." I smiled to myself, enjoying his botched metaphor.

Grayson pursed his lips. "You know, until tonight, I never really thought about how many ways it could happen."

"Murder?"

"No. The end of the world. Nuclear power-plant meltdowns. Polar icecap meltdowns. Economic meltdowns. Societal meltdowns. I gotta say, the sheer weight of worrying about all of that doomsday stuff is *insane*. I wouldn't be surprised if the stress caused Jenkins to have his own *personal* meltdown."

I shrugged. "Maybe. But honestly, obsessing about the end of the world isn't much different than watching the network news."

Grayson eyed me, then chewed his lip. "I guess you're right about that. The news is loaded with doom and gloom stories you can't do anything about."

"Exactly." I stifled another burp. It felt like it could've been a record-breaker. "What else can a person do in this crazy, cruel world but stock-pile a few creature comforts and hope for the best?"

Grayson smirked. "Thanks. I think I finally understand the whole twenty-four-seven Walmart thing."

I laughed.

Grayson pulled up to a stoplight and studied me. "So let me get this straight, Drex. Am I right in believing you think these prepper folks are just sensible people preparing for a future that, at the moment, isn't looking so bright?"

I shrugged. "I wouldn't go *that* Pollyanna. But look. All I'm saying is that maybe they're not *all* completely bonkers. Some of their fears are justifiable."

"Maybe you're right." Grayson pulled through the intersection. "But whatever happened to enjoying the moment? Maybe I'm wrong, but it seems like these prepper folks are so busy worrying about some post-apocalyptic *tomorrow* that they've forgotten to have a good time *today*."

"I dunno about that. Tonight, Garth and Dr. Prepper seemed pretty happy to me."

Grayson smirked. "True. Beer has that kind of magical power over men."

I laughed. "Chicken wings, too. Who could possibly be sad with a nice, big gutful of chicken wings?"

"Uh ... *the chickens?*"

I laughed again. "Okay. The chickens."

Grayson pulled into the Walmart parking lot. It was surprisingly empty. As he parked the RV at the back-end of the lot, I stared at the yellow, flower-shaped icon on the store's blue sign. Was it my new emblem for "home sweet home?"

"Home sweet home," Grayson said, as if on cue.

I didn't know whether to laugh or cry.

"You can have the bathroom first if you want," he said.

I shook my head. "Thanks, but I already brushed my teeth in the restaurant washroom. I'm good to go."

Grayson smiled. "Low maintenance. I like that."

While I pondered what to make of *that* remark, Grayson cut the ignition. I undid my seatbelt and started to stand, but Grayson gently put his hand over mine.

The feel of his fingers on mine was electric.

"You know, all this prepping stuff?" he said. "Say it actually worked. Say you survived whatever horrific meltdown scenario played out. *Then* what?"

"I dunno."

"Me either."

He pulled his hand away, sending my emotions colliding against each other all over again. Relief. Disappointment. Anger. I really did need to get a grip. I concentrated on his words, and let logic iron over my rumpled feelings.

"To be honest, I just don't get prepping," Grayson said. "Struggling every day simply to keep your belly fed and your heart beating. It just doesn't seem like much of a life to me."

"You forget, Grayson. For most of human history, that's the way it's been."

His lips curled into a slow, thoughtful smile. "Life before Netflix. I almost forgot."

I matched his smile. Grayson's face grew serious again. "Call me crazy, but I think I'd rather go on to my reward—whatever *that* may be—than to survive and be forced to scrounge like a rat for whatever scraps remained in our decimated world. Wouldn't you?"

I nodded. "Probably, yes. But honestly, until the crap actually hits the fan, I don't think anyone knows whether they'd choose to live or die. I guess preppers are simply trying to keep their options open."

"Like Garth said, short term for the long term."

"Yeah."

From the dim light of the streetlamp shining through the windshield, I could almost see the gears turning in Grayson's mind. Finally, he said, "Fair enough," and got up from the driver's seat.

I followed him into the main cabin of the RV. He continued on to his bedroom. I stayed in the living quarters and took the cushions off the couch to access the storage bin underneath.

As I pulled a set of sheets from the bin to make up the couch, Grayson came back into the room.

"You need any help?" he asked.

The tenuous look on his face made me wonder if he was debating whether or not to kiss me.

I nearly dropped the sheets.

"Uh ... no. I'm good."

He turned to go, then stopped and turned around again, causing my heart to beat like a jackhammer. He smiled at me wistfully.

"You know, I can't stop thinking about Jenkins holed up in that disgusting cabin, surrounded by rotting deer meat and ammo. What kind of life is that?"

Definitely not thinking about kissing me.

"I dunno," I said.

"And that AK-47 bugs me," he said. "Why did he leave it in the cabin? Why would he have it in the first place? I'm thinking something in those woods must've been spooking him for a while. Not just this past week. Whatever it was, it had to be something he saw as a major threat to himself, and possibly even to his wife, Arlene."

I fluffed a pillow absently, my thoughts and heartbeat slowly returning to their usual paces. "Grayson, do you think Dr. Prep—I mean Freddy Crum, or Garth ... or even *Rexel* for that matter .... Do you think any of those guys might've killed Lester and abducted Arlene?"

"Why?"

"You know. For ... breeding stock. None of them seemed to like him. And with her husband conveniently out of the picture ... well, it's possible, isn't it?"

Grayson grimaced as he thought about it. "Yes. I suppose. But I doubt it. Those guys didn't seem like they had enough wits about them to be able to keep a woman against her will."

A sudden chill made me shudder. *What kind of wits did it take?* "Maybe you're right."

Grayson studied me. "What about you, Drex? Are you ready for the end of the world?"

"You mean like *prepper* ready?"

"Like *any* kind of ready."

Grayson peeled off his black T-shirt as he waited for my answer. I couldn't help but notice his six pack, and the yellowish, almost healed bruise between his neck and shoulder. Whether he'd gotten the wound from his RV accident or a bite from the Mothman he'd been chasing would be, it seemed, forever up for debate.

"Yeah," I said. "I guess you could say I've got a plan for the end of the world in the back of my mind."

Grayson's green eyes lit up. "Really? What is it?"

"I'm going to head straight for ground zero. My plan is to run headlong into the abyss."

Grayson cocked his head. "Why?"

"Like you said. What's the point of scrounging like rats in a destroyed world? When the time comes, I think I want to be the first to go."

Grayson winked. "Right after Jenkins, you mean."

I smirked. "Hopefully not *that* soon."

Grayson laughed. He reached into a drawer and pulled out a foil pouch. He opened it and tossed Gizzard a couple of freeze-dried crickets. "Listen. I'm gonna hit the hay. Sleep well. I'll see you in the morning—that is, provided we survive any random, overnight apocalypse."

Grayson grinned, held up crossed fingers, then disappeared down the hall.

I slipped into a T-shirt and sweatpants and lay down on the couch. In the dim light, I could just make out my new shoulder-length auburn wig hanging sideways off the side of ET's ugly, square-shaped head.

I smiled to myself. I'd survived the first day of my new life—my first day as a P.I. intern, and my first day as Grayson's partner.

I sighed, settled my five-foot-four frame into the lumpy couch cushions, and listened to the blood coursing through my veins. For the first time since I could remember, I felt ... what was the word for it?

Alive.

I whispered into the darkness.

"Goodnight, Grayson."

A tingle ran down my spine when, to my surprise, he whispered back.

"Goodnight, Drex."

Chapter Seventeen

I WAS LYING ON MY BACK. I couldn't see my hands in front of my face—not even the emerald ring I always wore—the one Grandma Selma had left me when she passed away.

My fingers searched the inky darkness to my left. Then to my right. Above. Below. No matter which direction I tried, my fingertips collided with a rough, flat surface mere inches from my body.

OMG! I was trapped inside a box. No ... a coffin!

Somewhere close by, a dog howled mournfully. The coffin was too short. My head was jammed in sideways. I tried to move, but I was wedged in tight.

Either that, or I was paralyzed. Or was I already dead?

The howling grew louder. Closer.

Heavy, slobbering intakes of breath sounded in the darkness, drawing nearer ... nearer.

Suddenly, something began scratching at the coffin.

Someone was digging me out! Or—oh crap!—trying to get in!

My mind froze with terror as the coffin lid first cracked, then flew away as it were caught in a tornado. Above me, the fangs of a hellish hound flashed white against the pitch black night.

It was Garth's dog, Tooth!

The beast's yellow eyes locked on mine. He let out a low, sadistic snarl, and lunged for my throat. I grabbed for my neck.

Suddenly, Tooth farted. He covered his muzzle with his paw and laughed like Scooby Doo ....

I woke up drenched in sweat, my head crammed sideways against the armrest of the couch.

Ugh. Damned chicken wings.

Forced into an odd angle, my neck ached like a stab wound. Stars danced in my eyes as I sat up and rubbed my shoulder blades.

Suddenly, an unearthly yowling sounded close by.

Instantly, I was wide awake. My spine jerked ramrod straight. My eyes darted wildly as I tried to decipher from which direction the horrible sound was coming. A vertebrae in my neck popped as I honed in on the culprit.

Then a grin crept across my face.

It was Grayson. In the bathroom.

The guy was either dying, or he was in dire need of singing lessons.

I laughed. *Huh. Maybe Mr. Perfect isn't so perfect after all.*

I hauled myself up off the couch, grabbed my wig off ET's sickly gray head, tugged it on, and fumbled my way around the tiny kitchen, trying to get a pot of coffee on the make.

The lifespan of an entire generation of fruit flies ticked by as I waited for the coffee to finish brewing. With mug in hand, I was about to do the old carafe-cup switcheroo when Grayson's voice sounded behind me, startling me so badly I nearly dropped my cup.

"Morning, cadet. Coffee smells gold star."

I turned around to find him wearing nothing but a pair of black jeans. No booties this time.

"Thanks," I said. "It's almost ready."

"Good. I thought this morning we would—"

I mashed an index finger over Grayson's lips. "No coffee, no talkie."

Grayson grinned. "My mistake. I'll go finish dressing."

I nodded, and watched Grayson shuffled off to his bedroom. Mercifully, the coffee machine beeped, signaling it was done. I poured myself a mugful. After downing a life-resurrecting slurp, I placed the warm mug against the aching crick in my neck.

"How's it working out with the couch?" Grayson asked from behind me.

Unable to turn my neck, I crab-stepped my body around to face him. Grayson's head, shaved bald a little over a week ago, was now covered in dark stubble like a 1970s-era G.I. Joe.

"I'll get used to it," I said. "But the singing in the shower? That's another story. I gotta say, *Bad to the Bone* is your song, Grayson. And I mean that in more ways than one."

Grayson started to smirk, then stopped. "You could hear that? My apologies. Not used to having an audience."

"No prob." I poured him a cup of coffee and added a pinch of salt. "At least you didn't quit your day job."

"Well, in case you haven't noticed, I kind of *did*." Grayson took a sip of coffee. "Mmm. Good stuff."

It *was* good coffee. Less than one cup in and I already felt nearly completely coherent. "Why did you quit?"

Grayson cocked his head. "What do you mean?"

"You know. How'd you go from being some noted MIT physicist to rambling around in an old RV chasing monsters?"

Grayson's face fell an inch. "I'm gonna need a bigger cup of coffee if I have to spill *that* story."

He flopped into the booth of the small banquette. I put a couple of Pop-Tarts in the toaster, reinforced my coffee mug, and slid into the bench opposite him.

"So?" I asked.

"Well, it all started when—"

A knock on the RV door turned both our heads, but I was the only one who winced from the effort.

"You expecting anybody?" I asked, rubbing my neck.

Grayson shrugged. "No. You?"

I started to shake my head, but thought better of it. Instead, I got up and opened the door.

Officer Wells was standing at the bottom of the steps, holding a kite. I knew the kid was young, but *really?*

"Did someone tell you to go fly that?" I asked, unable to stop myself.

Wells' brow furrowed, then he smirked. "No, ma'am. It was tangled up on your antenna, flapping against your roof. Couldn't you hear it?"

Now that you mention it, yeah. But I thought it was Tooth scratching at my coffin.

"Want some coffee?" I asked.

"Maybe a quick cup. Is Mr. Grayson decent?"

"Sure. Why do you ask?"

His eyes darted up and down, then away. I suddenly realized I was still in my T-shirt and sweatpants, minus any lift and support. I cringed and folded my arms over my boobs. "Come on in."

"Morning, Officer Wells," Grayson said cheerily. "What's up?"

I poured the cop a cup of joe and scooted to the bedroom where my new Walmart clothes awaited. The pink jeans, pink long-sleeved button-down, and white, fringe-covered fake-leather jacket were stuffed into the closet next to Grayson's all-noir collection. There was plenty of room. The man's entire wardrobe consisted of two pairs of black jeans, three black T-shirts, a black suit, and two black dress shirts. He was prepared for any occasion—as long as it was a nighttime stakeout or a funeral.

Comparing the clothes side-by-side made me realize maybe I'd gone a touch overboard in the girly department. But after being mistaken for a boy most of my life, and posing as a garage grease monkey for the past six months, I guess the pendulum was bound to swing a tad too wide on the rebound.

As I donned my town-tramp couture, I kept the bedroom door open a crack and listened in on the guys' conversation.

"I can't stay," I heard Wells say. "I snuck Jenkins' autopsy report out of the file on my boss's desk. I've gotta get it back before he misses it."

"What does it say?" Grayson asked.

"Read it yourself. With the exception of his skull, nearly every major bone in Jenkins' body had been fractured."

"What could do that?"

"Hell if I know."

I hurriedly buttoned my blouse as I scurried out of the bedroom and down the hall. Forgetting that it only took a few steps, I nearly tripped on Wells' long leg extending out from the banquette like a grasshopper's.

He pulled it in and apologized. "Whoa. Sorry about that, ma'am."

"My bad," I said, and glanced at the photo of Jenkins doing his road-kill impression. "Have you ever seen a man crushed like that before?"

"No, ma'am. Only in cartoons—usually with a steamroller."

Grayson pursed his lips. "I'd say we can rule out Wile E. Coyote. I mean, how would he get a steamroller into the middle of a swamp?"

My eyebrows ticked up a notch. "*That's* your problem with that theory?"

Grayson scanned the report, ignoring me. He locked eyes with Wells. "What else could explain it?"

Wells cleared his throat. "Being dropped from a high altitude would do it."

"Like from an alien craft?" Grayson asked.

Wells sighed. "I was thinking more like from a skydiving plane. It happens every once in a while out near Zephyrhills. A skydiver's chute fails and they hit the ground like a sack of wet cement."

Grayson's eyebrow ticked up. He turned a photo toward Wells. "Did any of them look like this?"

Wells grimaced. "Not exactly. Plenty of broken bones, sure. And pretty much smashed to a pulp, too. But when you're dropped from that kind of height, your body usually busts open like a watermelon."

I crinkled my nose. "What's the minimum height you'd have to fall from to get Jenkins' kind of injuries?"

Wells shrugged. "Offhand, I couldn't say."

Grayson rubbed his chin. "He's right. It's impossible to accurately calculate falling injuries."

"Why's that?" I asked.

"Every case is different." Grayson took another sip of coffee. "People have fallen off horses and died. Then others fall thousands of feet and end up with just a few scratches and bruises."

"Well, Jenkins' body wasn't 'busted open like a watermelon,'" I said. "The only cuts were around his head and neck. What could cause that?"

Grayson bit his lip and looked up at Wells. "You've heard about cattle mutilations, right?"

Wells sat up a little straighter. "Uh ... sure."

"They say some of them have broken bones, like they've been dropped from an aerial vehicle."

Wells shook his head. "I'd say that's a stretch."

Grayson eyed the autopsy report and grunted. "Well, whatever did it, one thing's for sure."

"What's that?" I asked.

Grayson shot me a look. "It's still out there."

A cold streak ran down my back. I wanted to change the subject. "Officer Wells, has there been any news on Jenkins' wife?"

"No, ma'am. She's still missing. We checked the house with a fine-tooth comb. She's not there." Wells stood. "Thanks for the coffee. But I've got to get this report back before anyone notices it missing."

Grayson stood and held out the report. "Thank you for letting me take a look at it."

"Keep it. That's yours. I made a copy at Walmart, in case you weren't up yet." He looked Grayson hard in the eyes. "We're even now, right?"

"Absolutely."

Wells' face relaxed a notch. "Good. Now do me a favor. Stay away from Jenkins' cabin. I don't need to be cleaning up any more piles of potted meat."

Grayson nodded and dropped the report onto the banquette table. He got up and opened the RV door for Wells. "Thanks again, Officer."

"We're even," Wells repeated as he stepped out the door.

Grayson nodded. "As far as you know." He shut the door, leaving Wells staring up at him like a deer in the headlights.

I shook my head. "So, what now?"

"Eat your Pop-Tart and put on your pink boots, Dolly. We're going to Jenkins' place."

Chapter Eighteen

SLACK-JAWED, I STARED at Grayson as he took a casual sip of coffee. "You really think it's a good idea to go back to Jenkins' cabin after you just told Wells you wouldn't?"

"Tsk. Tsk." Grayson shook his head. "You should listen more carefully. I said no such thing."

"You're impossible, Grayson! And in case you're not keeping tabs on these things, a guy just got himself murdered out there!"

"Who says he was murdered? And besides, when I said Jenkins' place, I meant his *other* place. You know, where he used to play house with his wifey."

"Oh." I studied my Pop-Tart. "Why didn't you say so in the first place?"

"Do I have to spell out every little detail for you?"

Grayson blew out a breath, and I suddenly worried he was thinking I was more trouble than I was worth. I swallowed hard and tried to come up with the kind of intelligent questions a proper intern might ask. I couldn't think of squat.

Maybe he should *fire me.*

"So, what's the plan?" I asked sheepishly.

Grayson set down his coffee mug and pointed an index finger to the sky. "Find the motivation, find the killer. At least, that's what most investigators focus on. But the game we're playing isn't quite the same."

"What do you mean?"

"Everybody we've talked to says Jenkins was a jerk, right?"

I raised an eyebrow. "That's putting it kindly."

"Right. So there was ample reason to, shall we say, help speed the man along to his own personal doomsday."

"So you *do* think he was murdered. By an actual human, I mean."

Grayson shrugged. "Jenkins' death could be a simple case of ticking off the wrong person. He could've gone to Blarney's, inadvertently pissed off some clodhopper, and became the hottest new dance floor for a hillbilly stomp fest."

My eyes narrowed. "Or his wife did him in and ran off with said clodhopper hillbilly."

Grayson nodded thoughtfully. "Another fine possibility. But then again, what if our killer *wasn't* human? What would be the motivation then?"

I held up my half-eaten Pop-Tart. "Uh ... breakfast?"

Grayson smirked. "*Typically*, yes. But Jenkins' body wasn't eaten."

"Hmm." I pursed my lips. "What if he taunted the animal until it finally fought back and killed him just for sport?"

Grayson took a slug of coffee. "A reasonable theory. But what if the killer wasn't an animal at all, but something more otherworldly than that?"

I groaned. "Everything leads back to aliens with you. Don't tell me these 'superior beings' you're so fond of were able to navigate billions of miles to get here but couldn't find a better test subject to probe than Lester Jenkins' sorry old ass."

Grayson laughed, then his eyes flashed with seriousness. "That's a pretty good point, cadet." He sighed, got up, and rinsed his cup in the sink. "I hate to admit it, but I think you're right. I just don't see anything *that* out of the ordinary going on here."

I frowned. "What are you saying?"

"Simple. No monster, no paycheck."

"We're giving up?"

"Cutting our losses."

I frowned. "What about that whole radio transmission thing? Jenkins yelling 'They're here,' and all?"

Grayson shrugged. "Like Rexel said. He was probably drunk." He dried his mug with a dishtowel and hung it on a hook. "I say we hit the road."

My back stiffened. "Come on, Grayson. We're here. We might as well check out Jenkins' house like you planned. If we don't find anything there to support this alien invasion theory, *then* we can go."

Grayson's mouth curled into half a smile. "Now *there's* that scrappy intern I hired."

I gave him some side-eye, then laughed. "Okay. Suppose Jenkins *was* abducted by aliens. And these other-planetary beings dropped him back to Earth without the courtesy of a parachute. What could possibly be their motivation?"

"Easy," Grayson replied. "Entertainment."

Chapter Nineteen

GRAYSON TURNED OFF the ignition. The old RV shuddered wildly, giving my sore neck a pleasant little mini-massage. It was midmorning, and we were parked on the street in front of a remarkably uninspired single-story house.

To call it a crackerbox would've been an insult to Saltines.

Not much more than a concrete-block rectangle with a door and a couple of windows punched out of it, the house was one of a street-full of nearly identical homes, each somehow more unremarkable than the last.

I tipped my head and glanced over my sunglasses. My upper lip hooked skyward. "Geez. How would you ever find your house in the dark around here?"

Grayson snorted. "I doubt anyone around here stays up past sundown. Come on. Follow me."

I climbed out of the RV and tried my hand at the kind of P.I. stealth mode I'd seen in the movies—head down, eyes darting around for danger. I glanced over at Grayson to see if I was doing it right.

I nearly choked. He was high-stepping it straight up the driveway like the leader of a marching band.

I scrambled up the drive and caught up to him just as he rang the bell. "What the—?" I asked, staring at him as if he'd lost his mind.

"What?" He mashed the doorbell again. "Just making sure no black sheep relatives are here pilfering through the family jewels."

Grayson's screwed-up metaphor made my eyes itch to orbit around their sockets. He mashed the bell a third time. No one came to the door. I figured his next move would be to pick the lock. But he surprised me again. He merely shrugged and walked around to the side yard.

I shook my head as I trailed after him.

Either he's the worst P.I. in the world, or I am.

"What are you doing?" I hissed at his back as we edged our way across a lawn that hadn't seen a mower in at least a month.

He turned around. "*Think*, Drex. The cops already checked the house and known relatives. So what's left? Where could Arlene Jenkins be?"

"Uh ... the garden shed?" I nodded toward a rusty metal structure in the corner of the lot.

Grayson shrugged. "Worth a shot."

He turned, took a step, and fell face-first onto the ground, letting out a loud grunt. He was up and back on his feet before I could even bite my lip to keep from laughing.

"You okay, there?" I asked, trying to appear concerned instead of amused.

"Yes." Grayson shook himself out and picked up his fedora. "Sizeable hole in the ground there. Watch your step."

He placed his hat back on his head, dusted himself off, and switched his gait from a cavalier jaunt to cautious, creeping steps as he approached the metal shed.

I stood back as he yanked on the handle.

The rusty door squealed open. Something fluttered inside. Then, like something from a bad horror movie, a dozen or so bats came darting out of the shed right at us.

Grayson covered his face with his arms and screamed like a little girl. "Aaaahhhh!"

I nearly bit through my lip, but it didn't help. I burst out laughing anyway. "Don't tell me the great monster chaser is afraid of bats!"

Grayson's eyes scanned the sky with disgust. "Rats with wings. That's all they are."

I pouted. "Even poor Batman?"

Grayson shot me one of his unreadable expressions. But if I had to guess, I'd say I'd just stepped in bat crap. I squelched the giggles banging against my tonsils. It wouldn't do to get fired on my second day at work. I was still in awe that I'd survived day one.

"What now?" I asked.

Grayson took a deep breath and picked up as if nothing had happened. "Arlene's definitely not holed up in there. It's worse than their cabin."

I shook my head. "Gross. Don't remind me. No woman in her right mind would stay in that filthy, falling-down hole in the woods."

Grayson gave a quick nod. "So either Arlene's run off, or there's another place she and Lester were supposed to meet when the end of the world hit the fan."

I smirked. Grayson's messed-up metaphors were becoming part of his charm. Like the cute guy in high school I let get away with saying "supposably."

"But where else could she be?" I asked, glancing around the backyard. I waved my hand, and the thorn from a straggly rosebush pricked my skin. For some reason—maybe the pain—I thought of my mother.

The day after my father's funeral, she'd run off with a guy named David Applewhite, who, I found out a couple of days ago, was my biological father. Maybe she hadn't wanted to waste another second of her life with the wrong man.

Maybe the same thing held true for Arlene Jenkins.

"Maybe she really *did* run away," I said to Grayson. "You heard those guys at the bar last night. None of them wanted Lester Jenkins on their prepper team. Maybe his wife didn't, either."

Grayson mulled over the idea as he inspected a rusty bicycle half buried in weeds. "Why would she have stayed with him this long, then?"

"Two reasons," I said. "One, he was alive. Two, he owned an AK-47."

Grayson smirked. "Fair enough." He dusted his hands off. "I guess that marks the end of the line for this case."

I sighed. "I guess you're right," I said as I stepped up onto a raised, wooden deck. It was the only thing in the backyard that seemed in halfway decent repair.

The heels of my new boots made hollow tapping sounds as I crossed the boards. I thought I heard the sounds echo back.

Strange.

"Did you hear that?" I asked.

Grayson looked up from the garden gnome he was examining. "What?"

"I thought I heard tapping. Or something. I'm not sure."

Grayson's eyes locked on mine. He put an index finger to his lips to shush me, and scanned the yard. I walked across the deck toward him. The echoing taps sounded again.

"Listen!" I said. "Did you hear that? Like muffled banging. Maybe from behind the neighbor's fence?"

Grayson grabbed my arm. "I think it's coming from under your feet."

I shot him a look. "Well, duh, but I'm talking about—"

"No. I mean from under the deck."

My eyes widened. "What?"

Grayson tugged me off the deck and scanned its perimeter with the intensity of a cougar on the hunt. He grabbed a plank and pushed.

A sinister glee swept across his face. "Aha!"

Chapter Twenty

GRAYSON YANKED UPWARD, and half the deck behind Arlene Jenkins' house rose up like a cellar door. Underneath it was a concrete floor. In the center of the concrete was an oval, metal door I figured must've been salvaged from a submarine.

"What the hell is that?" I asked.

Grayson gave me a sideways glance. "Don't tell me you've never seen a bomb shelter before."

"Bomb shelter? In Florida? Dig too deep here and you hit water."

Grayson stared at the gunmetal gray door. "It's a fallout shelter, all right."

Grayson picked up an abandoned rake and banged it against the metal door. From inside, the same number of beats repeated.

My mouth went dry. "You think Lester locked his wife down there?"

Grayson shrugged. "Who else could it be?"

"Cripes, Grayson! The guy's an animal! Help me get this open!"

I knelt down and yanked on the industrial-sized combination padlock bolting the door closed. Whoever was inside banged out a few more beats. I looked up at Grayson. "We need a welding torch to cut through this thing."

"Hold up a second."

Grayson ran off down the side yard toward the front of the house. The faint banging resumed again.

"It's okay," I yelled at the bunker door. "We're here to help."

The banging stopped. Either whoever was down there had heard me, or they'd given up. I wrung my hands until Grayson finally reemerged from around the side of the house.

My jaw dropped open. Grayson had a stethoscope around his neck. In his hand he toted a grapefruit-sized, white crystal.

What the hell?

Caught between a weirdo above ground and one below, I wasn't sure what to do next. I eyed the crystal, then the stethoscope. "You gonna perform a séance or an EKG?"

Grayson shot me some side-eye. "I left my shrunken heads in my other RV. Now shut it and watch the master at work."

Grayson cracked his knuckles, knelt down, and laid the crystal on the ground beside him. He put on the stethoscope, then placed the end on the padlock. He twirled the dial on the combination lock to the right. His eyebrow ticked up. He turned the dial to the left. One more turn to the right and he looked up at me triumphantly.

"Voilà."

He yanked on the lock.

It didn't open.

I smirked as his victory face collapsed.

"Crap. Hold on a second."

Grayson tried the same routine again. Right, left, right. This time, the padlock released. He picked up the crystal and glanced my way. "Brace yourself. Here we go."

"What's the crystal for?" I asked.

"To cold-cock the sucker."

I swallowed hard, then held my breath.

With the crystal in his right hand, Grayson's left hand slid the lock's thick, metal pin from the latch. He glanced up at me, licked his lips, and curled his fist around the handle to yank open the door.

He never got the chance.

The portal door flew open as if kicked by a mule. It struck Grayson squarely under his chin. He sailed backward and landed flat on his back on the deck, knocked out cold.

"Grayson!" I screamed. But then a shadow caught my eye. I turned back toward the bunker. To my horror, something pale and hairy peered out from the opening like a giant, grotesque pupa hatching from an underground cocoon.

Recking of death and smeared with blood, the creature flashed its savage eyes at me.

I froze in place.

Paralyzed, I was helpless as it lunged at me—bloody teeth snapping—red claws flailing.

I heard a gunshot.

Something struck my head.

My knees hit the deck.

The rest of me quickly followed.

Chapter Twenty-One

SOMEONE SLAPPED MY face.

Not woman-gently. Man-gently.

In other words, not gently enough.

"Ow!" I yelped and opened an eye. A black silhouette stood over me, the midmorning sun burning a corona around its edges.

"Thank goodness," a man's voice said. "I thought I was going to have to take you to the hospital."

I squinted up at Officer Wells. The glare off his belt buckle burned holes into my eye sockets.

"No hospitals," I muttered.

He offered me a hand. I took it. As he pulled me to my feet, I couldn't help but notice blood smears all over his nice, crisp uniform.

"What happened to you?" I asked. Then it all came flooding back to me.

The bunker. The submarine door. The monster!

I grabbed Wells by the shoulders and nearly jumped into his arms. "Where is it?" I screeched. "What the hell *is* that thing?"

"Calm down," he said, patting me on the back. "You're okay. You found our missing person, Arlene Jenkins."

I felt woozy and sick to my stomach. "That ... *thing* ... in the bunker? That was *Arlene Jenkins?* But ... she looked like ... she ... she came at me like an *animal!*"

Wells took me by the arm, steadying me. "She was a bit on the wild side, I'll give you that. Tried to put out my lights with a socket wrench. I had to wrestle her all the way to the front yard." Wells shook his head. "Pinning her down wasn't easy. If you ask me, that woman could turn pro."

I rubbed the knot on my head. "She attacked you?"

"I wouldn't go so far as to call it an attack. The poor woman wasn't in her right mind. Freddy says she's hysterical. Who wouldn't be? She's been locked down in that bunker for God knows how long."

I shuddered at the thought. "Where is she now?"

"Inside. Freddy—I mean, *Dr. Crum*—is examining her right now."

"Here?"

Wells nodded and tipped his hat. "Yes ma'am. That's one of the perks of living in a small town. Doctors still make house calls."

"Where's Grayson?"

"*Now* you think of me," he called out. "I'm okay, by the way."

I turned to see him sprawled out in a deck chair. He waved at me weakly with the hand that wasn't busy holding a baggie of ice to his chin.

"Can you stand?" Office Wells asked him.

"Yeah."

"Come with us, then."

Wells held me up by my elbow and led me into the house. Grayson followed behind us, grousing the entire way to the kitchen.

I rubbed the knot on the side of my head, then examined my fingertips. No blood. I looked up at Wells. "I thought I heard a gunshot."

"You did. It was me." Wells patted his holstered gun. "I was responding to a call a couple doors down. Shot a four-foot rattlesnake curled up on Mrs. Dolan's welcome mat."

I grimaced. "Oh."

"Saw your RV and figured I'd stop and see what you two were up to." Wells shot us both sour looks. "You guys seem to have a penchant for trespassing on the Jenkins' private property."

I bit my lip and looked down.

"But seeing as how you found Arlene, I'll let this one go."

A flashback of the bloody monster coming at me made me flinch. "How'd you figure out that thing was Arlene?"

Wells shrugged. "Process of elimination. Not too many platinum blondes around here. Especially ones with inch-long red nails and gold front teeth."

Geez. I would certainly hope not.

Wells picked up a framed photo from the countertop. "See?"

I crinkled my nose at the photo of the bleach-bottle blonde smiling next to a dour-faced Lester Jenkins. She was flashing a set of grillz that would've given Urkel street cred. "What's with the gold teeth, anyway?"

Wells opened the refrigerator and pulled out two bottles of water. He handed me one. "Portable wealth."

I twisted open the cap. "Huh?"

"You know," Grayson said, then winced. "Like during World War I and II. Whenever the economy tanks, gold remains a valuable form of legal tender." Grayson wiggled his jaw from side to side like a snake, then pressed the baggie of ice back up against it.

"For real?" I asked Wells.

He nodded. "Pretty standard prepper protocol."

I grimaced and tried, unsuccessfully, not to think about how one actually conducted a transaction involving one's own teeth. An incisor for a sack of groceries? A molar for a tank of gas? Would Arlene have to knock out her teeth herself, or would her creditor do the deed? As a post-apocalyptic form of currency, it seemed to me that no one had actually thoroughly thought that plan through.

"Seems like a painful way to do business," I said. "Yanking out your own teeth."

"Grillz slip on over your teeth," Grayson said.

Huh. Maybe they did *think it through.*

Wells handed Grayson a bottle of water. "Y'all drink up. You need to stay hydrated. *And* stay put. I'm going to check on Dr. Crum and Mrs. Jenkins."

Wells disappeared down the hall. Grayson tapped me on the shoulder, making me jump. "Jittery, are we?"

I scowled. "Bats. Monsters. Rattlesnakes. What next? And don't say aliens!"

Grayson grinned, then winced. He pressed his baggie of ice into my hand. "Hold this. I wanna get a peek inside that bomb shelter."

"Grayson! Stop!"

But he was already at the sliding glass door. I held my breath as he opened it, scrambled across the deck, and disappeared into the underground bunker.

Great. How am I supposed to stall Officer Wells? Ask for more ice?

I slunk down the hallway and peeked inside the room I'd seen Wells go into. He was talking to Dr. Crum, who had somehow managed to find an outfit even more absurd than the donut shirt and pizza pants.

The doctor was wearing Birkenstocks and a burlap sack-dress tied at the waist with twine.

What the?

A moan drew my attention to Arlene Jenkins. She was lying in bed, her hands tied to the bedframe with what appeared to be strips of torn sheet. Her fingers were raw.

Double what the?

I stepped inside the room. "What's going on in here?"

Arlene's wild eyes locked on me. "Witch!" she hissed.

Both men's heads jerked in my direction.

Wells rushed over, grabbed my forearms, and pulled me out of the room while Arlene screamed her head off.

"Why is she tied down?" I asked angrily. "Her hands ... the blood. Is she injured?"

"Calm down," Wells said. "Nothing serious. She broke a few fingernails digging at the door trying to get out. We've got her restrained, but just until she calms down and comes to her senses."

Crum joined us in the hallway. "Keep it down. I just gave her a sedative."

I stared at the doctor. "She thought I was a witch."

Crum shrugged. "Don't take it personally. She thought I was a space alien trying to conduct experiments on her."

"Really?" I studied Crum's burlap ensemble. "From where? Planet Bedrock? What's with the potato sack?"

Crum sighed. "It's part of—"

Arlene screamed again.

Crum glanced at the door. "Listen, I'll explain later."

I frowned. "What's going to happen to her?"

Crum slapped on his soothing doctor face. "She'll calm down. She's just a bit panicked. Trauma from being trapped in that bunker. I'll stay here with her until she comes out of it."

I frowned. "Doesn't she have any relatives nearby? A sister, maybe?"

"No," Wells said. "But Lester has a half-brother. Hank Chambers. I've already called him. He's on his way."

Grayson came hobbling down the hallway toward us. He eyed Crum's sack-dress. "What's up, doc? Laundry day?"

Crum blew out a breath. "I was on my way to Dreadmore when Wells called me."

"Dreadmore?" I asked.

"It's a kind of Medieval-themed survivalist camp," Wells explained. "Preppers go out there to practice living off the land."

Grayson nodded at Crum. "I can definitely see the appeal. I mean, why wait around for some lousy apocalypse when you can live today like it already happened?"

Chapter Twenty-Two

"YOU SURE YOU'RE OKAY to drive?" I asked Grayson as we walked down the Jenkins' driveway. "You might have a slight concussion. And it looks like you've got an alien creature trying to hatch out of your chin."

Grayson shrugged. "I've lived through worse. How's your bean counter?"

I felt the lump on the side of my head. "Lived through worse."

We climbed into the RV. Grayson turned the ignition, hit the gas, and the Jenkins' rundown, cookie-cutter neighborhood slowly disappeared in the rearview mirror. I turned to Grayson. He appeared deep in thought.

"Let me guess. Dreaming of joining the Dreadmore clan?"

Grayson snorted. "Hardly. Just trying to wrap my head around this whole thing. Jenkins locking his wife in that bunker. What if we'd never found her? Makes me wonder how many preppers might've already met a similar fate."

I shuddered. "I don't want to think about it. Where are we headed now?"

"I say let's grab some lunch and get out of here. Lester Jenkins got his butt kicked by some disgruntled country boy. Arlene got locked in a fallout shelter by her husband. Preppers have a penchant for burlap and AK-47s. Case closed." He turned to me. "I've seen enough. Agreed?"

"No."

Grayson shot me a surprised glance. "Really?"

I shrugged. "Arlene thought Dr. Crum was an alien. That he wanted to do experiments on her. Doesn't that seem strange to you?"

"Meh. Not that strange."

"You're kidding, right?"

Grayson laughed. "Listen, Drex. Nobody's willing to admit it, but deep down inside, everybody fantasizes about being anally probed."

Total sicko.

"Grayson, the poor woman was trapped underground for days! She was traumatized! Hysterical!"

"Exactly my point. It was psychosis. Aliens had nothing to do with it. I'd be off my rocker, too, if I'd been buried in a tin can with nothing but deer jerky and a stack of old Chuck Norris DVDs."

My nose crinkled. "That's all that was down there?"

"That and a few freeze-dried pot pies."

"Gross." I reached into my purse and pulled out two Tootsie Pops. "You want one?"

"Sure."

I handed him a disgusting green one.

He smiled. "My favorite."

That totally figures.

Grayson stuck the sucker in his mouth. The bulge it made in his right cheek balanced out his swollen chin. Topped off with the fedora, he looked like the Monopoly banker on the get-out-of-jail-free card—*if* he'd just gotten out of jail, but not scot-free.

I smirked at him.

"What?" Grayson said.

I turned my gaze to the road. "Nothing."

"Right. Keep your eye out for a taco stand, cadet. Let's get some gas and blow this town."

I wasn't sure if that counted as another messed up metaphor or not. I was cooking up a snarky comeback when Grayson's cellphone chirped.

His green eyes glanced my way. "Get it, would you?"

"Sure." I grabbed the phone from his jacket pocket and hit speaker. Wells' voice came on the line.

"Grayson?"

"Speaking."

"Wells here. Can you meet me at McGreggor Funeral Parlor?"

Grayson shot me a curious glance. "What's up?"

"It's about Lester Jenkins."

"Oh," Grayson said, and smiled. "Don't worry. I'll destroy the autopsy report. I promise."

"No. That's not it."

"What then?"

"It's ... about ...." Wells let out a shaky-sounding exhale. "Jenkins' body is missing."

Grayson let his foot off the gas. "Missing? How?"

"That's what I'm hoping you can tell me. Because from where I'm standing right now, it looks like he just got up off the slab and climbed out the funeral home window."

Chapter Twenty-Three

WHEN WE REACHED MCGREGGOR Funeral Parlor, Officer Wells was leaning against his patrol car, his head hanging down as if he'd just lost his best hunting dog.

I rolled down the window. "You okay?"

The young cop looked up, his eyes bright and angry. "I'm a laughing-stock at the station now. If my father wasn't chief of police, I'd probably already be fired."

I blanched. "Why? It's not your fault Jenkins' body disappeared."

"That's not it. It's *why* ...." Wells slammed his palm on the hood of the patrol car. "My brother Gary told his friends I was working with you guys—'Mr. Gray and Pandora, the alien hunters.' Word got back to the station ...." He closed his eyes, grimaced, and blew out a breath. "I am *so* screwed."

I winced in empathy. I knew exactly what Wells was going through. I'd felt the same way not much more than a week ago, when I'd first met Grayson. Joining him in his lunatic pursuits had been a leap of faith.

Off a cliff.

Without a parachute.

In other words, the choice hadn't been an easy one to make. To most people, the gap between normal and abnormal was galactic. But like most things, the more familiar you got with something, the less gonzo it seemed. As it currently stood, I wasn't totally convinced whether I was a legitimate P.I intern helping establish new scientific frontiers—or I was a fool helping out on an even bigger fool's errand.

Like Officer Wells, slowly but surely, what constituted "normal" was becoming increasingly unclear in my mind. Was that enough to make someone bitch-slap a patrol car?

Absolutely.

"What can we do to help?" I asked Wells softly.

He studied the pavement for a moment, then struggled to explain. "It's hard to …. Ugh! I dunno. Maybe …. Aww, crap." He looked up at both of us. "Could you just follow me inside? I need to show you something."

I glanced over at Grayson. "Sure," he said.

Wells stared blankly at the ground while Grayson and I got out of the RV.

"Ready?" Wells asked.

"Absolutely," Grayson said. "Lead the way, officer."

Wells turned and slowly dragged his feet toward the entrance, as if he were about to attend his own funeral. Grayson and I exchanged glances, then followed him like a pair of indentured pallbearers.

As we entered McGreggor Funeral Parlor, an older gentleman in a charcoal suit spotted us. He ducked into an office and discretely closed the door. A placard on the wall read, Jeremiah Simpson, Funeral Director.

"This way," Wells said, his face red and sheepish. He led us past the director's office and down a long, narrow hallway filled with photographs of funerals. Happy customers, I supposed. But not too many repeaters, I'd bet.

At the end of the hallway, Wells opened a door. We followed him into a room that smelled worse than the time Grandma Selma tried to make dill pickles in an old laundry tub. My face puckered.

"Jenkins was being prepped for embalming in here," Wells said.

Grayson's nose crinkled. He waved his hand in front of his face. "Looks like Glade beat me to my idea for a fresh new scent."

Wells nodded toward a long metal table with a sink on one end. "Mr. Simpson told me that he and his assistant put Jenkins' corpse on that table by the window. According to him, they went out to lunch. When they returned, his body was gone."

"Did they leave the window open like it is now?" Grayson asked.

"Yes. Mr. Simpson told me that in cooler weather, it helps with the uh … smell." He pointed out two slashes in the window screen. "He said those weren't there when they left for lunch."

Grayson sniffed the screen, making me wince. "Is he sure?" he asked.

"Uh ... yeah," Wells said. "I asked him the same question. Mr. Simpson's pretty particular about his screens. You know, for keeping out ... you know ... the ... uh ...*flies.*"

"Hmm."

While Grayson rubbed his chin and pondered, Wells appeared to edge closer and closer to the verge of panic. After chewing off another fingernail, he blurted, "What do you think happened, Mr. Grayson? Have you ever seen anything like this before?"

Grayson frowned. "Not exactly."

Wells' brow furrowed with hope. "But something similar, right?"

Grayson nodded and exhaled. "Yes."

Wide-eyed, Wells asked, "What was it?"

"I'd say this is the work of your basic, run-of-the-mill body snatcher."

Wells' mouth fell agape. "Body snatcher?"

Grayson shrugged. "Either that or Jenkins got up and climbed out the window himself. Your pick."

"That's it?" The young cop's face twisted in anguish. "So you really don't think aliens had anything to do with this?"

Grayson shook his head. "Absolutely not. Aliens don't cut window screens. They just go right through them."

I stared at Grayson. Now *my* mouth was agape.

Really? Your answer to this whole crazy mess is that aliens don't carry pocketknives?

I shot Wells a sympathetic expression. Poor kid had dared to go out on a ledge and believe, just to be shot down by a stupid hole in a window screen.

"How can you be so certain," I asked Grayson. "What about the way Jenkins was crushed? What would a body snatcher want with a body pulverized like that?"

Grayson shrugged. "Meat popsicles?" He turned to Wells. "Sorry, Wells, but I think we're going to wrap this up and go—"

"Wait! You can't do that!" Wells grabbed Grayson by the shoulders. "Please! At least, not yet."

Grayson studied the cop's earnest, boyish face. "You got another reason for us to stick around, son?"

Wells let go of Grayson and took a step back. "I ... I just think you shouldn't be so quick to rule out the possibility Jenkins' death was due to some kind of ... you know ... *extraterrestrial* involvement."

Grayson sighed. "Sorry, Wells, but you're going to have to do better than that to pique my interest. That story of seeing lights in the sky and getting a creepy feeling won't cut it. If you're going to convince me, I need solid evidence. You got any of *that* handy?"

Wells slumped, bit his lip, and studied the floor.

"Thought so. Sorry, kid." Grayson patted Wells' shoulder and headed toward the embalming room door.

I grimaced with empathy. "Sorry." I turned to follow Grayson out the door, but a firm hand gripped my shoulder, stopping me.

"Hold on a second," Wells said.

I turned to find the young cop was no longer slumping or wheedling. Wells' jaw was set. His eyes flashed with determination. "Miss Drex, tell me the truth. Do you believe in all this alien stuff?"

I winced. "I *want* to believe. Does that count?"

"It's going to have to. Help me. *Please.*"

"How? What can *I* do?"

"Convince your partner to hear me out."

I shook my head. "Sorry. I want to help. I really do. But you've got to have something better than anecdotes and hearsay to make Grayson change his mind. We've already got that out the yin-yang."

Wells nodded. "I understand. And I think I do."

I trailed the young cop down the hallway and out into the parking lot. Grayson revved the RV engine and waved for me to get inside. As I walked up to the driver's side window, Grayson rolled it down.

"What's the holdup?"

"Just give the poor kid a second, would you?"

Grayson took off his fedora and let out a sigh that could've filled a hot air balloon. "Okay."

"Thanks."

We watched as Wells pulled a plastic bag out from under the front seat of his patrol car. He walked up to us.

"I found this in Jenkins' cabin." He held up a cheap spiral notebook. "I submitted it as evidence, but it was dismissed—along with the pile of UFO magazines it was in amongst. To be honest, I dismissed it, too, at first. I mean, who'd take something like this seriously?"

Wells thumbed through the notebook until he found what he was looking for. He flipped it around and showed us a centerfold spread. The pages were covered in grade-school doodles of aliens, most of them in compromising sexual positions.

Grayson shook his head. "Thanks for the intergalactic anatomy lesson, kid. But unless there's more in there than some lecher's sick Martian fantasies, you don't have a case."

Wells closed the notebook. "There's more. Trust me." He pulled a small cassette recorder from his jacket pocket. "If what's on here doesn't convince you, nothing will."

Grayson eyed the recorder and licked his lips.

"Okay, Wells. You've got yourself one hour. Let's go get some tacos and talk."

Chapter Twenty-Four

WE WERE SITTING IN a booth at a tiny, strip-mall restaurant called Tacos Locos. Officer Wells was making his last-chance pitch to Grayson. The young cop had to convince him that something *way* past normal was going on around Plant City, or we were hitting the road, pronto.

"Lester Jenkins could be a jerk, for sure," Wells said as he eyed Grayson's frosty mug of beer with envy. "But he just didn't seem like the kind of guy who would lock his wife up to die alone in that bunker."

"You sure about that?" Grayson said. "From what I hear, the guy was no Gandhi."

"Believe me," Wells said. "I've been called out to the Jenkins' to settle more than a few domestic disputes. But their fights were always about Lester drinking too much or Arlene spending too much. Never anything that would drive him crazy enough to bury her alive."

Grayson leaned back in the booth and eyed Wells. "But he *did* bury her alive. Didn't even leave her a cellphone. He wanted her dead."

Wells drummed a finger on the table absently. "No. I just don't believe that. I think he was trying to punish her somehow. I'm sure he planned on letting her out. He just never got the chance."

Grayson's lips twisted to one side. "Okay. Let's say you're right. That still doesn't answer the question of why he locked her up in the first place. There are easier ways to stop a shopaholic. Just take away her credit cards."

Wells acquiesced with a nod. "I know. That's what has me stuck. Jenkins must've had a really good reason."

"Maybe it was *Arlene* who wanted *Lester* dead," I offered. "So, he stuck her in there to protect himself."

Wells pursed his lips. "If she was trying to murder him, Jenkins didn't mention anything about it in his notebook."

"What *did* you find in that thing?" Grayson asked.

"Mostly ramblings about the end of the world. This may sound weird, but I think in his own way, Jenkins may have been trying to *protect* Arlene."

"From what?" I asked.

"Listen and decide for yourself." Wells set a small tape recorder on the table, then pulled a tiny cassette from his shirt pocket. "I only caught the beginning of this before I got the call about Jenkins' body disappearing."

"Then you don't know what's on the tape?" Grayson asked.

Wells hesitated. "Well, not exactly. No."

Grayson's eyes narrowed. "So you were bluffing."

Wells cringed. "Sort of. But I figured if it was anything like the notebook—"

Grayson grinned and nodded his head. "Well played, kid. You got me. Now don't waste any more of my time. Let's hear it."

"Yes, sir."

Wells mashed a button on the recorder. As it began to play, a waitress delivered a pile of tacos to the table. I started to reach for one, but the words on the cassette made me lose my train of thought.

"*static* ... don't know what to think. The metal casing is definitely extraterrestrial ... *static* ... the earth's atmosphere usually tears holes in a meteorite. This thing is smooth ... *static* ... cylindrical shape."

I locked eyes with Grayson. "Is this for real?"

Grayson's green eyes flashed. "Shhh!"

The recording played on. "Something's happening ... *static* ... end of the thing is beginning to ... *static*."

Grayson barked at Wells. "Turn it up a notch."

Another voice came over the recording. "She's moving ... *static* ... keep back, there! Keep back, I tell ... *static* ... it's red hot, they'll burn to a cinder! Keep back there. Keep those idiots back!"

A gong-like sound reverberated, as if a huge chunk of metal had collided with the ground. Grayson and I exchanged glances as the voice on the tape resumed.

"Someone's crawling out of the hollow top. Someone or . . . *something*."

Screams in the background overwhelmed the man's voice, making the next words barely audible. "Something's wriggling out of the shadow like a gray ... *static*."

The tape went silent. I stared at Grayson. "Was that last word 'gray'?"

"I think so."

I nearly choked. "Gray, as in *aliens?* Is it possible that Jenkins really could've been ... *you* know?" I looked up at the ceiling.

"Possibly," Grayson said. "It would fit the autopsy findings. Aliens beamed Jenkins up, then did experiments on him that left those weird cuts on his face."

My brow furrowed. "What about the fact that most of his bones were broken?"

Grayson sat back in the booth and sucked his teeth. "Let's think about this. According to most reports, Grays are small creatures. If they used a transport tube designed for *their* anatomy, Jenkins would be too big for it. He would've been crushed when they tried to suck him up."

Grayson stopped for a moment. His eyes flashed, then he resumed his analysis. "Or, if the Grays used a transport beam, maybe it malfunctioned and Jenkins' DNA got scrambled into goo. In either scenario, Jenkins would be in no condition for anal probing, so they must've decided to jettison his carcass. It fell back to Earth and splat—Jenkins-flavored man-pudding."

I shot a glance across the table at Wells. The poor guy was slumped in his seat, his mouth hanging open wide enough to shove a doorknob into.

"You okay?" I asked.

My question broke Wells' stupor. His eyes flickered wildly, then he bolted out of his seat and yelled, "Are you *kidding* me? *Hell, no,* I'm not okay! Didn't you hear that tape? Earth is under attack by aliens!"

"But—"

Wells pulled his gun out of its holster and scrambled out of the restaurant like a madman on fire.

I stared at Grayson. "Is he right? Are we under attack?"

Grayson stopped chewing the side of his mouth. "It's a distinct possibility."

My gut flopped. "What are we going to do?"

"What we always do. *Investigate.*"

A shiver of dread ran down my spine. Grayson, on the other hand, seemed alarmingly unfazed. He sighed, grabbed a taco, and scooted out of the booth. I started to get up and follow him, but he stopped me.

"Sit tight, cadet. I've got this. But do me one favor."

"What?"

"Don't let the Grays eat all the tacos before I get back."

He shot me a wink, and a sudden wave of peace came over me. My body relaxed as if I'd been hit with a tranquilizing dart. As I watched Grayson sprint out the door, I realized that if Earth really *was* under attack by creatures from outer space, he was exactly the kind of calm-under-pressure leader I wanted by my side.

I only hoped for humanity's sake that the aliens didn't turn out to look like bats.

Chapter Twenty-Five

WHILE I WAITED IN THE restaurant booth for Grayson to talk Wells down off his alien-invasion ledge, I flipped through Lester Jenkins' bizarre notebook entries and wondered why any form of intelligent life would bother with our crazy asses in the first place.

On page 43, Sasquatch was doing it doggie style with a Gray. On the opposite page, a reptilian was putting his forked tongue to lascivious use on an insectoid's spread antennae .... *Ugh.* From every angle, humans—especially guys—were disgusting creatures, indeed.

I chewed my lip and wondered if perhaps Grayson was right. Maybe the only reason humans existed was to entertain the gods.

Maybe we're all merely fleas in the great cosmic flea circus of life ....

I glanced through a few more pages of Jenkins' sick drawings and lunatic ramblings, and found myself empathizing with the aliens.

I don't blame them. If I had a spaceship, I'd be soooo outta here.

"Stop ogling those poor, exploited aliens," Grayson's voice sounded above me.

Startled, my gaze shot upward. Grayson was standing at the end of the booth, his arm around poor Officer Wells' shell-shocked young shoulders. My ears burned.

I closed Jenkins' notebook full of home-drawn galactic porn and cleared my throat. "I was only reading it for the articles."

Grayson snorted.

Wells jerked away from his embrace. "How can you two laugh at a time like this?"

Because it's either that or start sucking my thumb, I thought.

"Look around, kid," Grayson said. "We're not under attack at the moment. And even if we were, this isn't a problem you can solve with a six-shooter. Jenkins had an AK-47, and look what it got *him.*"

Wells' lip quivered. Grayson put a hand on his shoulder.

"Sit down, Wells. Have a taco. Drink a beer. I think if an alien invasion were imminent, we'd have heard something about it on the news by now."

"Network news never tells the whole truth," Wells muttered.

Grayson nodded. "That's why I never watch it. Now sit down and eat. You're going to need your strength to kick all that alien butt later."

Wells gave in and plopped into the booth. I reached across the table to hand him back Jenkins' notebook. "Did you show this to your brother, Garth?"

Wells glanced at me with eyes more confused than ever. "You mean *Gary?*"

I cringed. "Yes. Sorry. We know him as Operative Garth. Has he seen the notebook or heard the tape?"

"No!" Wells shook his head. "That's all I need. Gary'd get on that stupid radio of his and the whole town would know in five minutes. I'd lose my job for sure!"

Wells slumped back in the booth and muttered to himself like a mental patient. "Not that it would matter, once the aliens take over."

Grayson munched on a taco. "Before we jump to any conclusions, I think we should go talk to your brother."

Wells glared at him, his eyes narrow slits. "Why?"

Grayson cocked his head. "You're a cop. You know why. Like you just said yourself, Garth's connected to the local underground communication channels. Don't you think we should gather some corroborating evidence before we call CNN and tell them the aliens are out to get us?"

Wells sighed. "I guess," he said sullenly. "But we can't right now. He's at work."

I tried to picture Garth at a place of employment. I liked to think I had a good imagination, but my brain couldn't stretch that far. Who on earth would hire him? Walmart? Taco Bell? An orthodontist?

"Where's he work?" I asked.

Wells' eyes shifted to the floor. "Dreadmore Village."

My eyebrows ticked up a notch. "That prepper place Dr. Crum was talking about?"

"Yes."

Grayson's lips took on a sadistic curl. "Well then, what are we waiting for?"

Chapter Twenty-Six

OFFICER WELLS' BATTERED old pickup bounced and swerved along the muddy, rut-scarred backroad like a sadistic carnival ride. I was on the bench seat, sandwiched between the young cop and Grayson. I hung onto the ashtray for dear life, wishing I had a mouth-guard to keep my teeth from chipping.

"This isn't a road," I said between bumps. "It's a collection of pot-holes."

As if on cue, the truck's right front tire sunk into a hole so deep it sent me lurching toward Grayson. He grabbed me to keep me from flying out the window. I ended up in his arms, both of us pinned against the side of the cab.

I'd have thought up another complaint if I hadn't been distracted by the feel of Grayson's skin against mine.

It was electric.

Heat shot through every part of me that made contact with his taut, muscular body. If Grayson felt the same buzz from my somewhat less slim and less muscular body, he didn't let on. Instead, he pushed me back upright and asked, "How much farther?"

"Another quarter mile or so," Wells said.

"Great," I groaned.

Wells shot me a sideways glance. "Dreadmore's a prepper colony, not the Holiday Inn."

"Cheery name," Grayson quipped. "How'd they come by it?"

"It's an intentional community with an intentional name," Wells said defensively. "It's designed to discourage unwanted visitors."

"Oh. Kind of like Cockroach Bay," I said. "Not high on the tourist list, but one of the prettiest places in Florida."

"Exactly," Wells said. "Keeps the gawkers away."

"So, are you a member of Dreadmore?" Grayson asked.

Wells blew out a breath. "I asked not to be listed on the official books. But yeah, I do my share of helping out. Security mostly. They're not a bad bunch of folks. Just looking to survive when the storm hits."

"So, Wells," Grayson asked. "Just exactly what kind of storm are you all planning for?"

Wells shrugged and shifted into low gear. The pickup bucked forward like a branded bronco.

"Varies," he said. "Some prep for a mega hurricane. Others a massive EMP. But most are worried about economic collapse. If China sells off its US currency, a wheelbarrow full of dollars won't buy a lima bean."

"What's an EMP?" I asked.

"Electro-magnetic pulse," Grayson said. "A solar flare."

"A big enough one could fry every electronic circuit on the continent," Wells said.

Grayson waved his hand across the windshield. "Picture it, Drex. No TV. No cellphones. No computers. We'd be back to the stone age before sundown."

"Exactly," Wells said. "That's what Dreadmore's about. Figuring out how to survive without electricity or commercial food supplies."

"Sounds like a hardscrabble existence," I said.

Wells shrugged. "Electricity and indoor plumbing are luxuries, Miss Drex. They've only been around for a few generations. Most of our grandparents grew up using outhouses and wood-burning stoves."

I chewed my lip. "Still, I mean, what's the likelihood of one of these EMP's hitting, anyway? A trillion to one?"

"More like a twelve percent chance in the next ten years," Wells said. "Or whenever the military decides to drop another one."

I nearly choked on my tonsils. "*Another* one?"

"In '62, they detonated an EMP over the Pacific," Wells said. "It fried electrical circuits all the way to Hawaii—over nine hundred miles away."

The old truck lurched forward, sending me careening into its dented metal dashboard. "Geez! That wasn't a pothole. It was a meteor crater!"

"Good call on vehicles," Grayson said. "My RV would've never made it."

Another pothole sent my knee banging into the dashboard. I shot Wells a sour look. "It would've been nice if you'd sprung for some shock absorbers. What year is this truck, anyway? Or would you have to check the fossil record? I guess being a cop doesn't pay well enough for you to have a decent vehicle."

Wells shot me some side-eye. "You done?"

I pouted. "Yes."

"I can afford a new truck, ma'am. But I prefer this one. No electronics."

"So it's EMP proof," Grayson said.

"Right. No circuits to fry, no engine will die." Wells hit the brakes. "We're here."

I glanced up at the dusty windshield. Through a stand of pines, I made out a collection of thatch-roofed huts and rough-hewn, wood-framed buildings, none bigger than a two-car garage. The sharp, acrid smell of a campfire hinted at my nostrils.

"Stay in the truck," Wells said. "I need to get clearance before you can enter. People around here don't take kindly to snoopers. Like I said earlier, our goal is to keep this place off the radar."

Wells climbed out of the truck and headed toward the shantytown. I turned to Grayson.

"What are you *really* hoping to get out of talking to Garth?"

Grayson tipped his fedora up a notch. "A second opinion on that radio transmission, for one. You heard it. It's hard to deny it sounds pretty authentic—as far as alien invasions go."

My eyebrows shot up in shock and surprise. "You weren't joking? This may actually be *real*?"

Grayson shrugged. "We'll see."

I reached in my purse and pulled out a Tootsie Pop to calm my nerves. I stuck it in my mouth, then turned to Grayson. "Want one?"

"Sure. Green if you've got it."

"No problem. I save those just for you."

Chapter Twenty-Seven

"IS IT THE TOOTSIE POP?" I asked.

All the burly men dressed in burlap sacks appeared to be staring at me.

"Probably the pink jeans," Grayson said.

Officer Wells shook his head. "More likely the fact that you're a girl. And your hips are wide. Good breeding stock."

Geez! Not this breeding stock crap again! I never thought I'd miss those damned work coveralls I left behind in Point Paradise.

I gritted my teeth, stuck my head down, and, ironically, wished I looked more like a guy. But there was nothing I could do to make my hips less "shapely." If there had been, I'd have figured it out years ago and sold my idea for a gazillion dollars.

A leer from a tattooed dude sent a creepy feeling wrapping around the back of my neck. I switched places with Grayson, putting myself in the middle between him and Wells. I thought about holding Grayson's hand, but I didn't want to give *yet another* guy the wrong idea.

As the three of us walked along the dirt path cutting through Dreadmore Village, we passed sights I never thought possible outside a low-budget caveman movie.

To our right was a makeshift clothesline—a length of rope strung between two hand-hewn posts. On it hung half a dozen stiff, raw deer hides. Next to that, a sweaty guy wearing one of the hides for a shirt pounded on a red-hot metal rod, then stuck it back into a pile of molten coals.

A grubby, nearly toothless man riding bareback on a donkey leered at me. As his burro trotted by, I saw it was pulling a small wooden cart stacked with rolls of barbed wire.

This is like a medieval fair—without the fun.

A few yards down to our left, we passed an open shack, its ceiling strung with upside-down bouquets of drying herbs. Next to the shack, a man was pumping water from a hand well into an animal-skin bag.

Just past the pump, Officer Wells stopped in front of a faded wooden shed. Its old tin roof was covered with more patches than one of Grandma Selma's quilts.

"Gary should be in there," Wells said. "I've got a couple of things I've gotta do. Go on in. I'll be back soon."

Wells opened the shed door and motioned for us to enter. I followed Grayson inside, glad to leave the set of *Grogg vs the Deerosaur.*

After everything I'd just seen, I didn't know what I'd expected to find inside the shack. I only knew that what I saw was definitely *not* one of the possibilities.

The room was glowing neon green.

I took a quick glance around. A hodge-podge of metal shelving units lined the wooden walls of the shed. Stacked on the shelves were thirty or so brightly lit aquariums. I didn't see any fish. Instead, each tank seemed to glow emerald-green from the filmy water contained within it.

My lip snarled in disgust. I pulled the red Tootsie Pop from my mouth and waved it at Grayson. "I'm not a hundred percent sure about this, but I think this may be where green flavoring comes from."

"Actually, spirulina is virtually flavorless," a voice sounded behind us.

I whirled around to see Operative Garth emerging from between the dirty, opaque-plastic flaps hanging over the back entryway.

"Spiro Agnew?" I asked.

"Spirulina," Garth said. "Edible algae."

I grimaced. "Uh ... I'm no scientist, Garth, but I don't think *any* algae is edible."

Grayson laughed. "People pay good money for it in health food stores, *Pandora.*"

Garth gave a quick nod. "That's right, Mr. Gray. But we don't plan on selling it. Spirulina's part of our alternative renewable foods program. ARF, for short."

I glanced around at the slimy aquariums. The thought of that gunk in my mouth made me want to ARF, all right.

"Interesting idea," Grayson said. "But why bother?"

"Excellent question," Garth said in a tone reminiscent of an evil genius. "Did you know that Florida's got the fourth biggest population of all the states? If the food supply chain collapsed today, grocery store shelves would be empty within days. Hours, maybe. That's why we're working on growing our own renewable supply."

I sneered. "And you have the added bonus of never having to worry about thieves."

Grayson shot me a look, then turned to Garth. "I thought you were in charge of *communications*."

"I am. But since Rexel went missing, I got stuck taking over his projects."

Grayson glanced around. He looked impressed. "So, Rexel set all this up?"

Garth nodded. "Yeah. I help him out sometimes. Keeping the tanks in balance is a lot of work. I didn't want to see his latest batch go bad."

If it did, how could you tell?

I slapped on a smile and tried to look less disgusted than I felt. "So, why algae, Garth?"

Garth beamed. "Another excellent question, Pandora. Compared to growing crops, spirulina is a lot less labor intensive. And you don't have to worry about GMO cross-pollination. Or the toxins and radioactive fallout that can happen with field crops."

I took a close look at one of the tanks and swallowed hard. "But ... I mean, how much of this stuff would you have to eat to survive?"

Garth grinned proudly. "That's the beauty of it. One and a half tablespoons of spirulina delivers all your daily vitamin needs."

Grayson nodded. "Impressive. But what about protein?"

"Got that covered, too, Mr. Gray." Garth grinned, then gestured like a snooty butler. "This way, if you please."

I followed the two men through the nasty plastic flaps of the back entryway. We emerged into an outdoor area sheltered from the sun by a loose, flappy roof made of white plastic draped over tall, wooden posts.

A breeze caused the sheets of plastic to flap like dingy ghosts above a jumbled row of narrow, wooden boxes. The boxes themselves were all up on raised platforms constructed of chain-link fencing that had been laid out horizontally and nailed to meter-high sections of tree trunks.

What the hell is in those boxes?

As if reading my mind, Grayson eyed the makeshift operation and plucked the Tootsie Pop from his mouth.

He turned to Garth. "So. What's for dinner?"

Garth licked his lips. "Let me show you."

He opened the wooden lid on one of the boxes and stuck a hand inside. When he pulled it out, his fist was covered in dirt as black and fine as coffee grounds. Between his fingers, a mass of reddish-pink creatures wriggled like spaghetti on LSD.

"Earthworms," Garth said with more enthusiasm than the word deserved. His blond eyebrows waggled above the dark frames of his glasses. "Six of these babies a day is all the protein you need."

My gut dropped four inches. "You're kidding."

Garth grinned. "Nope. Algae and earthworms. Rexel says after the apocalypse, they'll be the new pesto and pasta."

Forget Calgon. Chef Boyardee, take me away.

I sucked hard on my Tootsie Pop, hoping to abate the heaving feeling rising up from my gut. I didn't *want* to know, but couldn't stop myself. I *had* to know.

"How do they taste?" I asked. "I mean, *really?*"

Garth shrugged. "Not that bad with a little A-1 Sauce. Here. Try one." He plucked a squirming worm from his fist and held it toward me.

"Uh ... no thanks."

I'd rather eat the soles of my shoes—after walking through a dog park.

My stomach turned as Grayson plucked the worm from Garth's hand and popped it into his mouth. He chewed it enthusiastically for a second, then his face puckered into a wince.

"I hope you stockpiled a ton of A-1," he coughed.

I'd have laughed if I hadn't been overcome by disgust. I turned to Garth. "*That's* what you're going to live on? Worms and algae?"

Garth shook his head. "Of course not. You also need a bit of roughage. You know, to keep the system moving. Leaves, roots, bark. Anything non-poisonous will do the trick."

The look on my face snuffed out Garth's glow of confidence. He toed the ground with his army boot. "If you don't like that, there's plenty of other choices."

I eyed him suspiciously. "Like what?"

"Well, I don't know all the specifics. Rexel was our entomophagy expert."

"Ento *what?*"

Grayson elbowed me. "Expert on edible insects."

My skin squirmed with imaginary—and hopefully inedible—creepy crawlies. I whispered to Grayson out of the side of my mouth. "Do me a favor. If you ever hear of an impending apocalypse, just shoot me."

Grayson smirked. "Gladly."

I shot him some side-eye. Grayson cocked his head playfully. "What's wrong with bugs, Drex? Insects are a nutritious, highly replenishable food source. Am I right, Garth?"

"Absolutely, Mr. Gray. Algae, insects, and worms. They're all part of a healthy, balanced diet."

I nearly retched. "Yeah. If you're a gecko. Thanks anyway, Garth. But I think I'll go eat double-bacon cheeseburgers until I keel over."

Grayson laughed out loud, catching the attention of a man walking by Dreadmore's Earthworm Emporium. Garth saw him and ducked behind Grayson.

"Who you talking to, Gary?" the man in burlap asked.

Gary, aka Garth, sighed and said snippily, "They've already been approved by security, Jake. Don't bother—"

"Who approved them?" Jake demanded, barging into our circle. "Wait. Don't tell me," he scoffed. "Your brother Jimmy, right? And why aren't you in uniform?"

Garth looked down at his jeans. "Burlap makes me itch."

Jake studied Grayson and me as if he were sizing us up for his freezer. He was thin, wiry, and had the hard, sinewy face of a man who ate only for survival. From the sound of his tone, he took no pleasure in people, either.

"This is Jake," Garth said, then blew out a breath. "He's Rexel's ARF partner. He specializes in wild renewables like—"

"Lots of folks foolishly think they can rely on wild game," Jake said, talking over Garth. "But animals like deer and hogs'll be decimated within a year of the big one. Smart folks'll be eatin' rapid-producing animals. They're the only truly sustainable meat."

"Rapid producing?" Grayson asked. "You mean *re*producing? Like rabbits?"

"Rabbits," Jake hissed. "What a newb." He scoffed again and shook his leathery head. "I'm talking *field mice*, man."

I nearly choked on my Tootsie Pop. "You've got to be joking."

"Don't knock it until you've tried it," Jake said. "That sucker in your mouth? It has nearly the same calories as a field mouse. But candy's all carbs. With field mice you get fats, proteins, and essential minerals."

Garth sneered. "Along with tapeworms, parasites, and salmonella."

Jake glared at Garth as if he were a Cossack. "That's why you *cook 'em*, genius. Mice taste a hell of a lot better than them worms you're growin'."

"Says who?" Garth argued. "You'd have to eat like what—a couple dozen mice to get enough calories to last a single day?"

"*Seventeen*," Jake growled.

Garth shook his head. "That's a lot of rodent roulette with your gut, man. No thanks. I'll take my chances with earthworms."

I swallowed hard. "If those are the only two options, I think I'll take my chances with Tootsie Pops."

Jake stared at me in a way that made me wish my hips were smaller. "Gimme that," he snorted, and grabbed the sucker from my mouth.

"Hey! Watch it! You could've chipped my tooth!"

"Who needs teeth when you're dead?" Jake sneered. "You know this thing is lethal, right?"

I pouted defensively. "The FDA hasn't definitively linked red dye number—"

"That ain't what I mean."

Jake slapped the sticky head of the Tootsie Pop into his palm and closed his fist around it. The stick-end protruded between his knuckles. He shook his fist at me like an angry, homeless caveman. "See this here? Makes a pretty decent puncture weapon. Just aim for the soft tissue areas."

Grayson glanced at an imaginary watch on his wrist, then over at Garth. "Well, look at the time. Speaking of *areas*, could we find a private one to continue our conversation?"

Garth's face melted with relief. "Absolutely, Mr. Gray. You and Pandora follow me."

We left Jake and his deadly sucker-fist standing by the worm boxes and went back into the wooden shack full of aquariums. Officer Wells was inside, listening to the tape again. He hit a button on the recorder. The garbled buzz of the tape rewinding echoed like ghostly babble off the glass tanks lining the shed's walls.

"So what's going on?" Garth asked.

"We've got a tape we want you to hear," Wells said. "I want you to listen carefully, little brother. This could be the end of the world as we know it."

Garth's eyebrows met his mullet. "Good thing the spirulina's almost ready. Let's hear it, bro."

Chapter Twenty-Eight

OFFICER WELLS PURSED his lips and hit the play button on the tiny recorder. The eerie green glow of the aquariums provided the perfect backdrop to the otherworldly words emanating from the small device.

"*static* ... don't know what to think. The metal casing is definitely extraterrestrial ... *static* ... the earth's atmosphere usually tears holes in a meteorite. This thing is smooth ... *static* ... cylindrical shape."

I glanced over at Garth. To my surprise, he didn't seem very impressed.

"Something's happening ... *static* ... end of the thing is beginning to ... *static*. She's moving ... *static* ... keep back, there! Keep back, I tell ... *static* ... it's red hot, they'll burn to a cinder! Keep back there. Keep those idiots back!"

Garth started laughing. "Is this some kind of joke?"

Wells jabbed a finger at the recorder, silencing it. "No! Why the hell would you say that?"

Garth shrugged. "That's *War of the Worlds*, man. Orson Welles."

I shot a glance at Grayson. His index finger was pressed against his lips, and he was nodding as if he expected just such a logical explanation—or maybe even confirmation of something he'd suspected all along.

As for Officer Wells, he seemed as stunned as I was.

Wells stared at his brother. "Who?"

Garth snorted. "Orson Welles, bro. That famous broadcaster dude? Did that big radio prank back in the '30s?"

Wells' face exploded into an undecipherable jumble of emotions. "But ... but ... *that doesn't make any sense!* Jenkins recorded this over his ham radio. You can hear him breathing in the background. I thought ... I mean *Jenkins* thought ...."

"That it was real?" Garth asked. He snickered. "You and Jenkins and a ton of other boobs." Garth shot a look at my chest, then his eyes moved to my face. "No offence."

Wells' brow furrowed. "But how is that possible? And *why?*" He shook his head. "Rexel ... could he have pranked Jenkins to get back at him for being rude on the radio?"

"Perhaps," Grayson said. He chewed his lip, then shifted his gaze to Garth. "But I'm thinking the culprit is more likely a Cassini bounce."

Garth's eyes lit up. "Yeah. Of course, Mr. Gray!"

As usual, I was at a loss. "What are you guys talking about now?"

"I got this one," Garth said, and turned to face me. "Long story short, in 2004, the Cassini spacecraft buzzed around Saturn. When it did, it recorded a human radio signal bouncing around the planet's rings."

Grayson nodded. "Thus, the Cassini bounce."

"I still don't get it," Officer Wells said, saving me the trouble.

"Don't you see?" Garth said. "Radio signals never die. They just bounce around the solar system like pinballs. They're called skywave transmissions."

I finally got it—sort of. "Okay, let me get this straight. You think Jenkins just happened to randomly pick up the original broadcast of *War of the Worlds* on his radio?" I shook my head. "That just seems so ... *improbable.*"

Grayson nodded. "Yeah. You'd think so. But it happens."

Garth bobbed his mullet. "Mr. Gray's right. In 2014, some guy named Palboya was testing his radio equipment and picked up the skywave transmission of the Hindenburg disaster. It was broadcast back in the 1930s, too."

Wells' face was an unsolved puzzle. "The Hindenburg disaster?"

Garth crinkled his nose. "Come on, bro. From history class? That Zeppelin that caught fire? You know. That reporter guy yelling, 'Oh, the humanity!'"

Oh, the humanity, indeed.

"Ahem." Grayson cleared his throat. "Well, I guess that solves our little alien invasion problem, men. Looks like our work here in Plant City is officially completed."

"Wait!" Garth said. He turned to his brother. "What about Rexel? Is he still missing?"

"Yes," Wells said.

"So, don't you see?" Garth said. "You can't leave yet, Mr. Gray."

Grayson shook his head. "People go missing all the—"

"Yeah, I get that," Garth interrupted. "But what about Jenkins' body *disappearing?* I mean, how'd a dead guy get out a window? There's *gotta* be something funky about *that.*"

Jimmy Wells joined his brother's campaign. "Gary's right. This morning, I noticed something weird on one of Jenkins' autopsy photos." He took a picture from his front pocket and handed it to Grayson. "See those marks on Jenkins' neck?"

Grayson peered at the photo. "Where?"

Wells pointed a finger at the picture. "The two triangular marks. Here."

Grayson squinted at the photo.

"Here. Use these," I said, and pulled my pink cheater glasses from my purse. I handed them to Grayson. He didn't appear particularly grateful, but he put them on anyway.

"Do they look like alien implants to you?" Wells asked.

Grayson studied the photo. "More like something stomped on Jenkins with its cloven hoof."

Garth took a step back, his eyes as big as saucers. "You talking *Satan,* Mr. Gray?"

Grayson glanced at me. His eyes danced with amusement. "Uh ... I'm afraid that would be a *no.*"

I stifled a grin.

"What then?" Wells asked. "You think Jenkins might've been attacked by a wild boar?"

Grayson shrugged and bit his lip. "Maybe. Or a deer." He turned to Wells. "Do deer attack people?"

"Not usually," Wells said. "Unless Jenkins covered himself in pheromones and a randy buck took a shine to him. But it's not even rutting season."

"So, what could it be?" I asked.

"Something outside the normal range of possibilities?" Garth asked hopefully. "Something paranormal?"

"There is this one other possibility," Grayson said, and rubbed his chin. "A half-goat, half-man with a mean urge to stomp."

"A chupacabra!" Garth blurted. "Oh! That would be so cool, man!"

Grayson shook his head. "No. As fun as that would be, I don't think so. No sucking injuries."

Garth's face collapsed.

"So, what made those weird marks then?" I asked.

"I was just speculating," Grayson said. "But now I'm thinking maybe it *could* be him."

"Who?" Wells asked.

Grayson chewed his lip as we all waited anxiously for him to speak. Finally, he said one word.

"Pan."

"Pan?" Garth, Wells, and I said in unison.

"Yes. Pan."

"Who the hell is Pan?" Wells asked.

"Oh. Sorry," Grayson said. "Pan's a mythical creature. A Greek legend. He has the legs and horns of a goat, but walks upright like a man. The horns would explain the marks on Jenkins' face. And, well, because Pan is bipedal, that could explain how he was able to stomp Jenkins flat with his cloven-hooved feet."

Wells' face sagged. "Now I've heard everything."

Garth nodded as he mulled over Grayson's theory. "Interesting concept, Mr. Gray. But what would a Greek goat-man be doing down here in Florida?"

Grayson shrugged. "The same as everyone else, I suppose. Just looking for a place to ride out his golden years."

Chapter Twenty-Nine

"SORRY GRAYSON, BUT I don't buy your Pan theory."

Grayson poured maple syrup over a steaming pile of blueberry flap-jacks. "What? You don't like panpipes?"

"I *love* pancakes."

He shook his head. "For a P.I. trainee, you don't listen worth a crap, Drex. I said pan*pipes*. It's a musical instrument. Pan invented it. Thus, panpipes."

"Okay, I *get* it," I said sourly. "Pan*pipes*. So what else did this Pan creature do?"

"Well, legend has it he was the original Fred Astaire."

"Dancing? Let me guess. His favorite move was the stomp. And he liked to get his groove on with old white guys."

Grayson's upper lip hooked into a snarl. "Please! I'm *eating* here."

"I meant that he liked to stomp on—. Wait. *That* bothers you? Aren't you the guy who just ate a freaking *earthworm*, for crying out loud?"

Grayson shrugged. "And your point is?"

My eyes made a trip around the top of their sockets. "Okay, let's put a pin in Pan for the moment."

Grayson winced. His forkful of pancakes paused midway to his mouth. He started to say something, but didn't. Instead, he stuffed the pancakes into his mouth and mumbled, "Proceed."

"Jenkins didn't mention anything about a goat man in his notebook," I said. "But he did blather on and on about strange lights in the sky. And, of course, there's always the possibility he got more than one of those Luke Skywalker things you were talking about."

Grayson's head cocked to one side. He took a sip of coffee to wash down his pancakes. "*Star Wars?*"

"Those bouncing radio signals—you know, off Saturn's rings and all."

"Oh. Skywave transmissions."

"Yeah. Those thingamajigs. Well, what if that happened, but kind of in reverse?"

"What do you mean?"

"What if aliens picked up one of our old transmissions, and thought *they* were under attack?"

Grayson's left eyebrow flew up. He chewed on the idea along with a bite of bacon. "Huh. We've been broadcasting radio signals into space for over a hundred years. I guess one of them is bound to be intercepted and misunderstood at some point."

I tapped a finger on the rim of my coffee cup. "But what I don't get is, if that's what happened, why would aliens hone in on Jenkins as their first point of contact? I mean, what could be so compelling about the ramblings of some drunk old coot in a falling-down shack?"

Grayson's eyebrows met above his furrowed brow. "Lots of people who've changed the world came from humble beginnings, Drex. In fact, I'm of the opinion that the creator of the universe actually *prefers* an underdog."

I shook my head. "Then why crush him like a cracker?"

Grayson sighed and set down his coffee cup. "Good point. But wait a minute. As I recall, didn't God like to smite folks now and again?"

"Smite?"

"Yeah. That's what they called it when ...." Grayson's face shifted. His green eyes twinkled. "Hey. Maybe that's it."

"*What's* it?"

"What happened to Jenkins. Maybe that's what *smiting* is. You know, getting pulverized into pudding. Huh. No wonder you don't hear the term used much nowadays."

I fought a sneer and lost. "Yeah. I heard smiting went the way of verily and thee." I shook my head. "Earth to Grayson. In case you haven't noticed, God doesn't make house calls anymore. Or should I say, *cabin* calls."

Grayson smirked. "Right. Not since he farmed all his smiting out to the Grays."

I laughed despite myself. "Come on, Grayson. If little green men are running all over the cosmos, why haven't they tried to contact us? I mean, besides the smiting, of course."

Grayson locked eyes with me. "Who says they haven't?"

"Well ... duh! Only *everybody*. Except UFO nuts. Like you're always saying, where's the proof?"

"Oh ye of little faith. The proof is everywhere, if your eyes and mind are open enough to see."

"You're right, Jehoshaphat. My bad. I should've never let my subscription to the *National Enquirer* lapse."

Grayson snorted. "Okay, you want proof? How about this? When Nicola Tesla sent out his *very first* radio communication, he reported making contact with beings from outside our planet. Do you consider *him* a crackpot?"

"No. But you have to admit, he was a tad eccentric."

Grayson nodded. "Fair enough. Here's one. In 1977, a news broadcast in the UK was taken over by a being claiming to be Vrillon of the Ashtar Galactic Command."

"You're making that up."

"Nope. All across the UK, TV sets went blank, and this weird, inhuman voice droned on for something like twenty minutes. Vrillon said he was part of an alien race making first contact with us, and that they came in peace."

"That's ridiculous."

Grayson shrugged. "You can listen to it yourself on the internet. So far, no one's been able to satisfactorily debunk it."

"I can. It was *the Brits*, for crying out loud."

Grayson eyed me. "Tough crowd today. Okay. How about this? In 1974, the Voyager—a good-old *American* space probe—was launched into the cosmos. Onboard, it carried a pictographic image of the human body and our DNA helix. Flash forward twenty-seven years to 2001. A crop circle in England bore the *identical* basic format as the Voyager pictograph, only the body shape and DNA helix had been altered to reflect alien anatomy and genetics."

I picked up my coffee mug. "This crop circle. Was it in wheat or barley? I've heard you should never trust barley."

Grayson sat back in his seat and sighed. "See? That's the basic problem with humanity. Nobody wants to stick their neck out to believe. Everything's a hoax, no matter how good the evidence."

He threw up his hands in mock despair. "I mean, gimme a break. Take that Patterson film of Bigfoot. What more do you want? Nobody's willing to believe anything's real until we kill it and parade its head around town on a stick. We're still just dumb animals, Drex. Animals with cellphones and nothing worth saying."

An idea sparked in my brain. "Maybe that's *it*, Grayson."

"What do you mean?"

"Why alien life doesn't bother trying to contact us anymore. Maybe we're just too primitive. We're simply not worth talking to. Either that, or our technology is too inferior. Think about it. To an advanced civilization, even our cellphones might seem like two tin cans and a string."

"Maybe," Grayson conceded. "Or it could be that we've been forever shunned by the IWW for our bad manners."

My eyebrows inched closer together. "The IWW?"

"Intergalactic Welcome Wagon."

"What are you talking about?"

Grayson leaned toward me. "Remember the 'WOW signal'? You know, that radio signal Ohio State University got back in '77? It was the first and only signal their radio array ever detected that had all the hallmarks of extraterrestrial communication."

"Yeah. I've heard of it. But it was just a blip. The signal never repeated."

"Correct. And you know why?"

"No."

"Because we were rude."

My eyebrows shot up. "What?"

Grayson shook his head. "We didn't answer back right away. In fact, *nobody even noticed the signal for two solid days.*" He sat back and sighed. "By the time they tried to respond, it was too late. We failed a basic manners test, Drex. And quite possibly blew our chance at ever meeting that alien race or being invited to their next cosmic cocktail party."

I bit my lip. "Geez. Maybe you're right. I know I've dropped guys I was dating for less."

We both sat in silence for a moment, watching my over-easy eggs congeal on my plate.

"Grayson, if there *is* a cosmic consciousness out there trying to communicate with us, how can we tune in to it? Like your ham radio gizmo—do you think there might be a 'God frequency' out there somewhere? Could it be that we have built-in receivers in our brains, but forgot how to use them?"

Grayson studied me. "Big questions, Drex. And to be honest, I don't have all the answers. It's a massive universe out there. And it's full of unlimited possibilities. What's a mere mortal to do? Hell, I can't even decide what to watch on Hulu."

I smiled, but I wasn't ready to drop the topic. "I'm serious, Grayson. How do you think this so-called creator of the universe communicates with us?"

Grayson shrugged. "Lots of ways. Dreams. Thoughts. Visions. Feelings. Experiences. Insights."

"Keep going with that list and there won't be anything that's *not* a communication from God."

Grayson grinned. "Bingo, cadet."

I frowned. "You're nuts, Grayson. But at least we have one thing in common."

"What?"

"We like breakfast for dinner."

Grayson smiled. "Well, there you go. That's the one thing we've got."

I grinned. "So, is it time to head back to our home-sweet-home, the Walmart parking lot?"

"Not tonight. It's not polite to stay more than two nights in a row at the same Walmart, and that's one universal force I don't want to have to reckon with."

My eyebrow shot up. "So, what are we gonna do? Not another sleazy motel, please."

"No. Tonight we have an invitation to camp out."

"Where?"

"It's a surprise."

My nose crinkled. "I don't like surprises."

Grayson grinned like a fox. "Where's your sense of adventure?"

"I left it in my other jeans."

"But those cute pink ones make your breeding-stock hips look so hot."

I closed my eyes and blew out a breath. "Oh, geez. Please tell me we're not going back to Dreadmore."

Grayson laughed. I opened my eyes. He was grinning at me.

"We're not, are we?" I pleaded.

"Nope."

I blew out a breath. "Good. So where, then?"

Grayson motioned to the waitress for the check. "Someplace I know you're going to like even more."

Chapter Thirty

TAP. TAP. TAPPITY-TAP.

I cracked open one eye the narrowest slit humanly possible, then scanned my surroundings.

I was in the RV.

Good.

My pink jeans were still on my breeding-stock hips.

Also good.

At least I had *those* two things going for me.

Tap. Tap.

Through the tiny slit, my eye searched the room for the source of the ear-splitting, brain-crunching sound. It was coming from Grayson. He was at the stove, tapping scoops of coffee into a filter. I closed my eye and prayed that I might lapse into a coma.

But instead, I farted.

"Good morning to *you*, too," Grayson replied.

I clamped my jaw shut.

Don't laugh, Bobbie. Don't laugh. I'm telling you, girl, don't you dare freaking laugh!

I laughed. Then I opened my eyes to half-mast. Grayson was grinning at me.

"Sorry," I croaked.

Grayson shrugged. "Farts happen. You up for a cup of coffee?"

"Depends. Do I have to actually be *up* to get one?"

"Rough night, cadet? Oh. Silly question." He shot me a smirk. "Remind me to never leave you unchaperoned with Jose Cuervo again. Nice Mexican hat dance, by the way. If Pan was watching, I'm sure he was impressed."

I slowly peeled the side of my face off the vinyl couch. "Oh, crap. I thought I'd only dreamt that."

"You wish."

I shot Grayson a sheepish smile with the half of my face that was functioning. I sat up. A millisecond later, my brain followed my body's upward trajectory and slammed into my skull with a thud that ached all the way to my toenails.

Ouch.

I rubbed my forehead. Grayson handed me a mugful of coffee and studied me as I took a greedy gulp. The scalding heat of the bitter liquid on my tongue felt better than the jackhammer assaulting my brain. I groaned from both the pain and the relief.

Grayson shook his head and laughed softly. "Who knew you were such a party animal?"

I scowled. "What are you talking about?"

"You were the life of the campfire last night. Don't you remember?"

"Not exactly."

"I must say, that was the most unusual act I've ever seen performed with a corndog and a tequila bottle."

"Hardy har har." I looked over at ET, the intergalactic lighting fixture. He was bald. My hand went to my head. Nothing but stubble. "Where's my new wig?"

"If memory serves, you said, 'I don't need no stinkin' wig,' and threw it into the fire."

I felt my eyes pop halfway out of my skull. "I did not!"

Grayson grinned. "You did. And I'm sure most would agree it was the highlight of the evening."

I cringed. "*Most?* Who all was there?"

"Oh, pretty much everybody we've met since we blew into town. Plus an old friend."

"Huh?"

"Your cousin Earl. He showed up last night."

I'd have slapped my forehead if I thought I could survive the impact. "Ugh. Great."

The rumbling of a massive diesel engine rattled the RV windows. I knew the sound. It was Bessie, Earl's monster truck.

Grayson looked up. "That must be him now."

He padded over to the RV's side door and opened it. From the glimpse I caught of the rusted-out Buick chassis outside, I deduced we'd spent the night in the Wells brothers' junkyard compound.

Ugh. This just keeps getting better and better.

"Good morning, Earl," Grayson said. "Come on in."

Earl slowly stuck his shaggy head in the door like a cautious sloth. He winked at me, then turned to Grayson. "She had her coffee yet?"

Grayson laughed. "She's working on it."

"Whew! Good. Everybody knows she's just plain evil till she's had a cup."

I scowled at Earl as he squeezed the rest of his bear-like, six-foot-four frame into the RV's tiny main cabin.

"Howdy cuz," he said. "Nice floorshow last night. Or was it a dirt show? You know, on account a there wasn't no real floor?"

"Don't start," I groaned.

"I guess it's too early to argue semantics," Grayson said.

Earl nodded. "Yep. Grandma Selma always told us don't talk religion before breakfast. Speaking of which, look what I got." Earl opened a grocery sack and pulled out a box of donuts.

My eyes lit up. It was only the second time in my life I felt like kissing Earl Shankles on the mouth.

"Did you get me a banana crème?" I asked.

"'Course I did. And this little beauty, too. Thank the lord for twenty-four-hour Walmarts."

Earl pulled out what looked like a life-size Barbie scalp. He shook the platinum-blonde hooker wig at me and made googly eyes. It was only the millionth time in my life I felt like kicking Earl Shankles in the nuts.

"Put the wig on ET," I grumbled. "I still need to get a shower."

"ET?" Earl stared at me like I was crazy.

Garth poked his head inside the RV.

Awesome. It's a full-on party. Again, apparently.

"Morning!" Garth said. "I thought I smelled donuts. Got a spare to share?"

"Only glazed and crème filled," I answered sourly. "They were fresh out of spirulina-flavored."

"Spiro what?" Earl asked, staring at Garth's mullet as he reached for a donut. "You get that wig at Walmarts?"

Garth turned to face him. "Hey, have any of you seen Tooth?"

Earl blanched as his confusion grew. "You looking for a missing tooth?"

"Tooth's a canine," Grayson said.

Earl scratched his head. "Have I done had a stroke? ET and spirals and missing teeth. I don't understand a darn thing what's goin' on up in here."

I smirked and took a noisy slurp of coffee. "Welcome to the funhouse, cuz."

Chapter Thirty-One

I POURED EARL ANOTHER cup of coffee and topped off my mug. Then I set the empty carafe back on the burner and slid into the banquette opposite my burly cousin.

From the shower, Grayson's strangled-cat rendition of the Bee Gees' *Stayin' Alive* seemed a fitting background for Earl's and my equally off-key conversation.

Earl winced and tried to clean out his ear with his index finger. "Lordy! Somewheres a Gibb brother's gettin' a hernia operation."

I gave him half a smile. "I don't mean to sound ungrateful or anything, but what the hell are you doing here, Earl?"

"Checking up on you." He looked down at his coffee mug. "A feller can worry, can't he?"

"I've only been gone less than three days."

"I know." Earl locked eyes with me. "But we both know a lot can happen in a short time."

Like finding out your father's not your real father. And that your mother ran off with the guy who is. Or that you have the vestiges of a twin brother's nuts banging against your brainstem.

Or was that just the tequila?

"True enough," I said, and rubbed my aching head.

Earl laughed "You keep sowing your wild oats like you done last night and you're gonna run out of thread."

"Thanks for the life tip, coach." I blew out a breath. "So how're things going at the garage?"

Earl shrugged. "Slow, but okay, I guess. Since you took off, the only person left to talk to is Beth-Ann. And she don't even live in Point Paradise."

Oh, crap. I need to call Beth-Ann.

Earl slurped his coffee. "What with Artie shuttin' down the Stop & Shoppe for the weekend to fumigate for rats, I thought I'd take me a drive out to see you."

I cocked my head. It still thumped, but not as badly. "Is that your way of saying you miss me?"

Earl grinned. "Nah. But I *do* miss getting fired by you."

We laughed for a moment, then Earl's face grew somber.

"You really doing okay here with Grayson? He treatin' you okay and all?"

As I thought about Earl's question for a second, despite the hangover, an unexpected lightness of being took me by surprise. I smiled. "Yeah. I guess I've been too busy with our case to think about much of anything else. But, yeah, it's going okay."

Earl's eyes lit up. "You said on the phone you was investigatin' some feller that got hisself squashed, right?"

"Yeah. A guy named Lester Jenkins was found dead five days ago. Nearly every bone in his body was broken."

"Poor feller. What done it?"

"That's what we're still trying to figure out. We thought at first he'd stumbled onto a secret alien invasion. But that turned out to be a skywave transmission."

Earl's face crinkled in confusion. "Hold up a sec. You sayin' you think an alien's transmission fell out of the sky and flattened that feller?"

"No. It's ... ugh." I heaved a sigh. "Listen. The thing is, *how* Jenkins died isn't even the biggest mystery anymore."

Earl's left eyebrow flattened out. "Well, then what in the world is?"

"Where his body went. Jenkins was about to get embalmed when his body disappeared."

Earl sucked in a breath. "Alien abduction!"

"Of a corpse?" I snorted, sending a dull shockwave of pain pulsing through my skull.

"Hmmm," Earl said, his lips twisted to one side. His gaze shifted from the ceiling onto me. "I know! Bigfoot nabbed him!"

I shook my head. "No tracks."

"Then what's left?"

"Grayson thinks it may be some half-goat man named Pan."

"What would this Pan feller want with a dead guy?"

"No. Grayson thinks Pan may have *killed* Jenkins. But wait. You're right. What would *anyone* want with a dead guy?"

"That may be a moot point," Grayson said. He'd emerged from the bathroom wearing his signature black jeans and six-pack abs.

I tried not to stare. "What do you mean?"

"I just got off the phone with Officer Wells. Someone called in a report yesterday about a man sneaking out the back window of McGregor Funeral Parlor. According to the eyewitness description, it was Lester Jenkins himself."

I nearly dropped my coffee mug. "He's *alive?* How? And why are we just hearing about this now?"

Grayson slipped a black T-shirt on over his head. "The operator who took the call thought it was a prank and dismissed it. Then she saw the report in the newspaper this morning about the body going missing and—"

"Wait a minute," I said. "Come on! Jenkins was as dead as you can get. He couldn't have crawled out the window. It had to be someone else."

Grayson held up his hands as if proclaiming his innocence. "Look. All I know is that Wells told me the physical description fit Jenkins. And when he ran the tag number in the report, it was a match to Jenkins' truck."

"But that don't make no sense," Earl said.

Grayson grinned. "I know." He shifted his attention to me. "So, you know what that means, right?"

My nose crinkled. "What?"

"We're back in the game."

Chapter Thirty-Two

BESSIE'S HUMONGOUS tractor tires whined as we sped down the highway toward our date with a dead guy on the lam.

Either Lester Jenkins had come back to life and crawled out a funeral-home window, or, well, I didn't want to think about what the other options might be. Careening down the road in a pimped-out monster truck, I already had enough troubles on my mind.

To my left, in the driver's seat, sat my cousin, Earl. An unsophisticated, barrel-chested, straight-talking, country boy—he represented everything good *and* bad about my past. To my right sat my future. Grayson. A mysterious, wiry, enigmatic smooth talker who, at the moment, was chewing on a plastic straw like a deranged Pekingese.

It was times like these I wished I didn't think so much.

"Turn right here," Grayson yelled over the buzz of the tires. "Wells said he spotted Jenkins on Harney Road."

Earl yanked the steering wheel, sending me lurching sideways into an impromptu lap dance with Grayson. As I struggled to get back to the center of the seat, Grayson yelled. "That's them!"

Off to the side of the road ahead, a police car's lights flashed. As we drew nearer, the vehicle in front of it—an old red pickup truck—came into view.

Earl shifted into low gear and maneuvered Bessie into the grass behind Wells' patrol car. As soon as he hit the brakes, we opened the doors and tumbled from the monster truck like discarded beer cans.

Grayson and Earl took off toward the vehicles. Hindered by a blowout in my cheap flip flops, I was the last to arrive at the scene. When I did, I took my place in line beside Earl and Grayson, who were staring, open-mouthed, at Lester Jenkins. He was slumped behind the steering wheel of the red pickup like a sack of old potatoes.

I stood, dumbfounded, as Officer Wells questioned Jenkins through the driver's side window.

Earl elbowed me out of my stupor. "Pee-yew! That feller Jenkins might've come back to life like you said, Bobbie. But lord help. He brought the dead stank with him."

Grayson crinkled his nose. "Somebody needs to invent dead-guy cologne."

I was too stunned to even shake my head. "I don't understand," I mumbled. "How is Jenkins alive again?"

Officer Wells lowered his notepad and turned to face us. "He's not. This is Hank Chambers. Lester Jenkins' half-brother."

Chambers looked over at us and shrugged. "People say we look alike."

"What's that smell?" I asked.

Chambers' eyes narrowed, then his face went sheepish. "Oh. Sorry about that. My wife cooked up a pot of collard greens for me to take to Lester's wife, Arlene."

Earl whistled. "That'll do it, all right."

Wells adjusted his stance and glowered at us. "You three mind if I ask Mr. Chambers here a few more questions?"

Earl and I exchanged naughty-kid grimaces.

"Sorry, Officer," Grayson said. "Please. Proceed."

"Thank you." Wells turned back to Chambers. "Sir, when was the last time you talked to your brother, Lester?"

Chambers' mouth hitched up on one side. "Well, I guess that'd be the night he died. He buzzed me on the radio. Told me he was having wifey troubles again. I was supposed to meet him at Blarney's Bar, but he never showed."

Wells' right eyebrow shot up. "And you didn't think to go check on him?"

"Nah. You see, that wasn't the first time he's stood me up. Besides, he's a grown man. He can ... uh ... I mean, he *could* take care of himself, I thought." Chambers looked down. "Maybe I was wrong."

Wells scribbled on the notepad. "Why are you driving your brother's truck?"

"Mine's low on gas. Drove straight to Arlene's place when I got the news yesterday. Nearly didn't make it." He held up a five-gallon gas container. "I was just headed to the gas station to pick up some more go juice."

"Speaking of Mrs. Jenkins, do you know if she quarreled often with Lester?" Wells asked.

Chambers sighed. "Yessir."

Wells jotted a note. "How about you?"

"Me and Lester?" Chambers took off his ball cap and ran his hand through his unkempt, graying hair. "We had our share of brotherly squabbles. Nothing out of the ordinary."

Wells scribbled something on the notepad. "What about you and Arlene. Did you two get along?"

Chambers coughed. "Sure. Why? Did she say something?"

Wells shook his head. "No. But her doctor says she's been acting a little off since she came out of that bunker."

Chambers' face grew red. "Well, who wouldn't? Poor woman just lost her halibut."

"Halibut?" Wells asked.

"What?" Chambers said.

"You said she just lost her halibut."

"Clean out your ears, son. I said husband."

"My apologies," Wells said in a tone that negated his words. "There were reports that this vehicle was seen out at McGreggor Funeral Parlor yesterday."

Chambers' bulbous red nose twitched. "Well, I wouldn't know anything about that. I was with Arlene all day. Listen. Are we done here? I don't want to leave Arlene alone too long. Like that doctor said, she's mighty shook up."

"Uh ... sure," Wells said. "Thank you for your time. Here's my card."

Chambers took the card and tossed it onto the dashboard.

Wells took a step back from the truck. "We might need to examine this vehicle for evidence. I'll be in tou—"

Chambers hit the gas. The back tires spun gravel. Wells joined our gape-mouthed conga line.

"He sure was in a hurry," I said to Wells, then coughed at the dust.

He nodded. "There's definitely something off about him."

"Yeah," Earl said. "He got the haint stank."

"I'm going to tail him," Wells said, ignoring Earl. "Grayson, you're a private investigator. Could you drive over and keep an eye on Arlene Jenkins' place until I can get there?"

Grayson winced. "Well, we were going—"

"Oh! Oh! Can we? Can we?" Earl asked, jumping up and down like a kid.

Grayson shot me a look.

I shrugged. "Earl doesn't get out much."

Grayson sighed. "Sure, Officer Wells. We'd be happy to assist."

Chapter Thirty-Three

AFTER A QUICK RUN THROUGH the Taco Bell drive-thru, we settled into a spot in front of Arlene Jenkins' place behind a huge hydrangea bush. Earl thought it made the perfect hide.

"You think that bush is gonna cover this huge truck?" I asked, taking a taco from the bag. "That's like trying to smuggle an elephant behind a paper church fan."

Earl sneered. "Well, you got any better ideas Miss Smarty Pants? I'm—"

"Can it, kids," Grayson said, and nodded toward a white Chevy pickup parked at the Jenkins' residence. "That must be Chambers' truck in the driveway. The good thing is, Arlene doesn't know Earl or his truck. We can use that to our advantage."

Earl was about to take a bite out of his burrito, but stopped. "Hold up. What do you mean 'to our advantage'?"

Grayson's lips curled upward slightly. "We need to get a better assessment of the situation. You know, get inside the house."

Earl frowned. "How we gonna do that?"

Grayson lifted an eyebrow. "What you mean is, how are *you* going to do that."

"Huh?"

Grayson grinned like a mad scientist. "You wanted to play investigator, Earl. Now's your big chance. Go up and ring the bell. Ask Arlene for a glass of water or something."

Earl cringed. "Can I finish my burrito first?"

"Time waits for no beans."

Geez. Grayson has absolutely no grasp for metaphors whatsoever.

"Yes, sir," Earl said. He stuck his burrito on the dashboard and climbed out of the truck.

I elbowed Grayson and whispered. "Shouldn't you give him some kind of instructions?"

He locked eyes with me and raised an eyebrow. "Did that ever work for you at the garage?"

My face went limp. "Good point." I smiled to myself and settled in for the show as Earl slinked down the driveway like a hunchbacked crab.

"Earl's the kind of guy better off winging it, anyway," Grayson said.

"Sure," I said. "You keep telling yourself that. Admit it. You get your jollies throwing newbies to the wolves, don't you?" I shoved the last bite of a taco into my mouth.

"Don't *you?*" Grayson grinned and nodded toward the house. "See? He's doing fine."

I looked past Grayson's shoulder at Earl. He was at the door talking to Arlene. She smiled and let him in.

I nearly choked. "Well, I'll be."

I took a sip of Dr Pepper to clear my throat, then scrounged around the bottom of the Taco Bell bag. I pulled out a taco, wadded the empty sack, and tossed it onto the floorboard.

I glanced over at Grayson coyly. "I wonder what Earl said to win Arlene's confidence."

Grayson eyed the empty bag. "You gonna eat the last taco?"

I unwrapped it, took a bite, and smiled up at Grayson. "Nah. She would've never fallen for that line."

Chapter Thirty-Four

I'D BARELY HAD TIME to regret my lunch choice when Earl came flying out of Jenkins' house as if he were being chased by a gun-toting madman.

Correction: mad*woman*.

Arlene Jenkins was hot on Earl's heels, a pistol in one hand, a hammer in the other. If she hadn't tripped on a garden gnome and fallen face-first into a planter bed made from an old tire, I think she might've done Earl harm.

"That woman's plum crazy!" Earl hollered as he yanked open the driver's door. He heaved himself up into the cab, twisted the keys in the ignition, and stomped on the gas.

The G-force of Bessie's 540-horsepower Hemi engine sent my cheap wig flying off my head. It flopped like a platinum squid onto Earl's horrified face.

"What the?" He grabbed a handful of it and flung it out the window.

The sharp blast of a gunshot sounded behind us. I looked back just in time to see Arlene fire again. My poor wig flew apart like a dandelion in a hurricane.

Grayson hollered across me at Earl. "What the hell happened in there?"

"Damned if I know!" Earl punched the gas again. "Everything was going fine and dandy until she found out I wasn't the life insurance guy."

"Did she say how much she was expecting to get?" Grayson asked.

"All of it, I reckon. Call me a prude if you want, but I don't go for recently widowed women. Especially those of the lunatical variety."

My eyebrows met my hairline. "What? Are you saying Arlene Jenkins *came on* to you?"

Earl bit his lip and glanced in the rearview mirror. "Yeppers."

My nose crinkled. "Then she really *must* be nuts."

I turned around and stared out the back window of the cab. Arlene was smaller now, but I could still see her waving the pistol in the air. Earl hooked a right and the bleach-blonde, would-be assassin disappeared from view.

"That's not what I meant," Grayson said. "I was talking about the insurance policy. How much was Arlene expecting for a payout?"

Earl eased up on the accelerator and shrugged. "Told me she had a couple policies. The biggest was Mutual of Malaprop for seventy-five grand."

Grayson sighed. "Were any of these life insurance policies actually *real?*"

Earl's lips pooched out as he thought. "Pretty sure, yeah. She had a calculator, and papers spread out all over the dining room table."

"Hmm." Grayson rubbed his chin. "Anything else suspicious?"

"Well, now that you mention it, her house smelled like Clorox and Pine-Sol. I had her figured for the slobbenly type."

"*Sloven*—ugh!" I said. "You think she did a murder-scene clean-up?"

Earl's eyebrow shot up. "Huh. Well, that's a thought. But I tell you what. That place didn't smell like no collard greens to me. If that Hank feller brought her a mess of collards, you sure wouldn't know it by the stink. Unless a course, she done ate 'em all."

"Wait a minute," I said. "If Chambers brought Arlene the collards from *his* place, wouldn't *his* truck be the one that smelled, not Jenkins'?"

"Good point," Grayson said.

I gave myself an imaginary pat on the back. "And if he lied about that, Chambers could've also lied about the gas can. Maybe he's planning on burning Jenkins' body with gasoline."

Grayson looked at me funny. "A brother barbeque? Sick idea. But okay, I'll bite. Why would he do that?"

"To hide the evidence that he killed him. What else?"

"Nice idea, cadet, but Jenkins body's already been autopsied. What would be the point in destroying it now?"

I slumped back in my seat. Earl picked up the debate.

"Well, what about to hide a suicide? Them life insurance policies don't pay jack crap if you do yourself in."

Grayson smirked. "So you're saying Jenkins beat himself to a pulp for fun and profit?"

"Nah," Earl said. "I'm saying maybe somebody *else* did, after they found him already deader'n a doornail. They figured they'd cover up the suicide and get 'em some insurance money for their troubles."

Grayson sighed. "Like I said, the body's already been autopsied. I saw the report."

"What was the cause of death?" I asked.

"Indeterminable."

Earl laughed. "An insurance company ain't gonna settle for that. Not for a big payout anyhoo. I watch *Forensic Files*. Them fellers would exhume the body. Burnin' it to cinders would take care of that option."

I turned to Grayson. "I think Earl's on to something. But Arlene couldn't have taken the body. Crum had her sedated. Could Chambers have done it?"

Grayson said nothing, but I could almost see the gears in his mind turning.

"Well, look who we got here," Earl said, and hit the brakes.

Officer Wells' patrol car was approaching in the opposite lane. He stopped alongside us and rolled down his window.

"Chambers seems legit," the young cop said. "I followed him. He picked up the gas like he said he was going to. Then he stopped at Walmart. I figured I'd get over here and interview Arlene while she's alone. Anything to report on your end?"

"No sir." Earl waggled his eyebrows. "We got her all warmed up for you, Officer."

Wells' face went slack. "What are you talking about?"

Grayson leaned across me and yelled out Earl's window. "You might want to get Dr. Prepper to give her another sedative before you go in there."

A vein on Wells' neck popped out. "Aww, nuts. What did you all do now?"

Chapter Thirty-Five

I WAS DOING AN ENCORE of my man sandwich performance, this time between Earl and Grayson on the bench seat of Earl's monster truck. Officer Wells sat stewing in his patrol car beside us. We weren't exactly in what you'd call the cop's "good graces," but he didn't have much choice.

He needed us for what was about to go down.

The mission at hand was to capture and sedate a rather crazed and pissed off Arlene Jenkins. To that end, both vehicles were parked around the block from Arlene's place, waiting for the star of the show, Freddy Crum—aka Dr. Prepper—to arrive.

Earl was just about to get on my last nerve with his inane knock-knock jokes when finally, like manna from 1976, an orange Ford Fiesta sputtered into view. The driver, a pudgy guy wearing pink glasses and a green-and-orange pineapple shirt, waved at us as he drove by.

"That's him," I said.

Earl lifted an eyebrow. "Dr. Quack, M.D.?"

I jabbed him with my elbow. "It's a *cover*, okay?"

"Could a fooled me."

I rolled my eyes. "That's kind of the point."

Earl cranked the ignition on Bessie and we rolled in behind Wells' patrol car, forming a three-vehicle convoy with the Fiesta in the lead. We rounded the corner, then converged in front of Arlene Jenkins' house. Wells and Crum got out of their vehicles. We, like delinquent teenagers, were relegated to staying in the truck and awaiting further orders from Wells.

"It may take all of us to restrain her," Crum said, peering up at us from our high perch in the monster truck.

Wells frowned. "You sure we need them?"

"It pays to be on the safe side," Crum said.

Wells blew out a breath. "Okay. Here's the plan." His words were aimed at us, but his eyes stared at Jenkins' house as he spoke. "I'll ring the doorbell. You guys hide in the bushes by the house. You are *not to move* unless I tell you to."

"Got it," Grayson said.

Earl sucked his teeth. "If y'all don't mind, I think I'll wait this one out in the truck. I already done my round a hammer time with that crazy woman."

I winced. "Maybe I should wait with him."

Grayson shook his head. "Nothing doing, cadet. You want that P.I. license, you gotta learn to hang with the big boys."

I looked over at Earl. "You heard him."

My cousin grinned. "What? I never said nothin' about wanting to be no P.I."

"Come on," Grayson said, tugging my arm. "They're already almost to the front door."

I slid out of the seat, then Grayson and I ran across the front yard, skirting a virtual obstacle course of tire planters full of prickly-pear cacti. Crum lay in wait up against the wall beside the front door, a syringe full of happy juice at the ready. Grayson and I took position behind some overgrown hedges. Crum stuck out an arm and gave Wells the thumbs-up sign.

Wells nodded and rang the doorbell.

Nothing happened.

He rang it again.

As he reached over to make a third attempt, the door flew open. A wild-eyed, wild-haired Arlene Jenkins came barreling out, delivering an encore performance of her infamous Maxwell's Silver Hammer routine.

"Oh, crap!" Crum cried out.

Right before the hammer came down on Wells' head, he grabbed Arlene's striking arm. Crum seized the opportunity to jab her bicep with the syringe. He hit the plunger. A second later, Arlene dropped the hammer, then collapsed like a cardboard box in the middle of a monsoon.

"Help us get her inside!" Wells yelled at us.

Grayson and I scrambled to assist. Each of us grabbed an arm or a leg and hauled Arlene to the couch as she muttered crazily the whole way.

"Don't touch. Prickle people. Who are you?" she said as we carried her into the living room. Suddenly, Arlene's eyes flew open and she screamed. "Help! I'm gonna die in here!"

As we laid her on the sofa, Wells asked, "What's wrong with her, Freddy?"

"Post-traumatic hysteria," Crum said. "Here, this will help." Crum gave her another shot. "Arlene? It's me, Dr. Freddy."

She shot him a bleary glance. "Froggy?"

"Freddy." He smiled and reached toward her.

Arlene squirmed to avoid his touch, babbling like a sloppy drunk. "Stop prickling me, you fleak. Where shank. We die shank don't ... come bah." Her eyes rolled up in her head, then she passed out.

Crum shook his head. "I've been her doctor for years. This behavior—it's totally out of character. I've never known her to act so aggressively. She's definitely displaying signs of paranoia."

"Could she be ill? Poisoned, maybe?" Grayson asked.

Crum pursed his lips. "I suppose it's possible. I'll get some blood from her and run some tests."

"Hot in here," Arlene muttered, coming back to consciousness. "Kill you all." Her eyes closed again.

"That does it," Crum said. "I'm calling 9-1-1. Sorry, but it doesn't look like you're going to get any answers out of Arlene Jenkins today."

Chapter Thirty-Six

AS THE AMBULANCE DROVE away with a wigged-out Arlene Jenkins in tow, we sat in Earl's truck and debated whether the weirdness going on in Plant City had a down-to-earth explanation, or it originated from somewhere off-planet.

Earl was still an ardent proponent of alien implants. I was torn between poisoning and early-onset dementia. Grayson, apparently giving up on his buddy Pan, was insisting the whole thing could be chalked up to your basic, garden-variety domestic homicide.

"The only way life can be a bed of roses," he philosophized, "is if you're buried under one."

I shot Grayson a dour look. "I had no idea you were such a romantic."

"Let's ask the law," Earl said, nodding toward the house.

Officer Wells was coming down the driveway with Dr. Crum. If I didn't know better, I'd have suspected the doctor himself was under arrest. His expression was textbook nerdy bewilderment.

As they got close, Wells took a quick glance at us, then studied the ground a foot in front of his shoes. "Thanks for the backup. Things could've gotten way out of hand."

Crum shook his head. "I don't know what's gotten into Arlene. But I'm going to find out."

I dragged my gaze up from the hula-dancing pineapples on the doctor's shirt and locked eyes with him. "Dr. Crum, if Arlene was poisoned, could the same thing have happened to her husband, Lester?"

Crum raised his open palms. "I guess. But why would anyone want either one of them dead?"

"Insurance money," Grayson said. "Lester and Arlene didn't have any kids. With Lester out of the way, Arlene would be the sole beneficiary of his policies."

"But it *couldn't* be Arlene," I argued. "She has an—excuse the pun—*airtight* alibi. She was locked in that bunker when Lester was killed."

"That's not provable," Grayson said, slapping on that know-it-all professor expression I was beginning to loathe. "If she was, *who* locked her in there?"

"Lester," I said.

Grayson cocked an eyebrow. "You sure about that?"

I frowned. "Who else could it be?"

"How about Hank Chambers?"

"What?" I nearly gasped. "You think *Chambers* locked Arlene in there?"

"Yes."

"Why? As part of some evil plan to kill Lester and split the insurance payout?"

Grayson winked. "Bingo, cadet. She's got the alibi. He's got the girl."

"Nah," Earl said, shaking his head. "I don't buy it. Hank wouldn't do that to Lester. Them two brothers was tight. I seen pictures of 'em baggin' game together from all over the county. They was good hunting buddies."

Grayson snorted. "Two hombres alone in the woods together with dueling *pistolas*. What could possibly go wrong?"

"Listen," Wells interrupted. "The whole insurance angle doesn't hold water. I checked. The only life insurance on Lester was for five grand. Barely enough to bury him."

Grayson's lips twisted. "Well, if it wasn't for money, then it had to be for love."

"Hold up a minute," Wells said. "You think *Hank's* having an affair with Arlene?"

"I'd say it's a distinct possibility," Grayson said. "And it could've been going on for a long time. This scheme of theirs took a little planning."

I grimaced. "But Chambers is married!"

Earl laughed. "Since when's that stopped anyone from foolin' around?"

"That's also not accurate," Wells said. "Chambers' background check showed he's divorced, as of last month. Not too amicable, I might add.

His ex-wife threw him out of the house with nothing but a restraining order for company."

Grayson glanced at his cellphone. "Speaking of Chambers, where is he? Shouldn't he be back from Walmart by now?"

"You're right," Wells said.

Earl shrugged. "Well, it *is* the first of the month an' all."

Wells sighed. "I forgot about that."

The police radio on Wells' belt crackled. "Excuse me, I need to get this." He turned and walked away.

I glanced over at Dr. Crum. He was staring at the pavement, chewing his lip.

"What's wrong?" I asked.

Crum looked up, wide-eyed, as if I'd startled him. "Oh. Nothing. I just ... well, I'm kind of baffled by what's happening. First with Lester, and now Arlene."

"What do you mean, 'first with Lester'?"

"Well, I wasn't going to say anything because of patient confidentiality. But your question about poisoning got me to thinking. And, well, since he's dead, I guess Lester won't mind."

Crum looked at me in a way that made me think he was seeking my approval to continue. I gave it to him with a quick nod. "Right. Lester won't mind."

Crum shifted onto his other pink sneaker. "Lester came to see me a few weeks ago. He was having hot flashes and tingling in his hands. We'd made a joke out of it—that he was suffering from *men*opause."

He looked up at me. I gave him a weak smile.

"Anyway," Crum continued, "I didn't think that much of it until today. When I tried to touch Arlene. She told me to stop 'prickling' her."

"She was mumbling crazy talk," I said. "She could've been talking about the injections. Nobody likes needles."

Crum pursed his lips. "That's true. But she felt a bit warm to the touch, as if she had a slight fever."

"So you think instead of poisoning, she and Lester might've both contracted some kind of illness?"

Crum sighed. "Either one is possible. The flu's going around. And lots of things in the environment can cause adverse reactions. Food additives. Exposure to pesticides. Even the chemicals in cleaning products."

"You got any theories on which it might be?" Grayson asked.

Crum shook his head. "No. But I'll get on it as—"

"I'll catch you all later," Wells hollered, running by us and nearly bowling Crum over. "Got an emergency to get to," he yelled as he raced toward his patrol car.

"What's happening?" Grayson called after him.

Wells yanked open the car door. "Not sure yet, but I think we might've found Rexel."

"Where?" I yelled.

"Climbing the giant strawberry," he hollered, and took off with the lights flashing.

Chapter Thirty-Seven

"WHAT THE HECK?" I ASKED. "Giant strawberry? Did I hear that right?"

Crum nodded, his face drawn with concern. "Wells must mean the city water tower. It's painted like a strawberry."

"I got to see me that," Earl said, and fired up Bessie's massive diesel engine. "How do we get there, Doc?"

Crum sighed. "Take I-4 to Park Street. Head south. Can't miss it. Believe me."

"Thanks," I said. "You coming?"

Crum shook his head. "No. I've seen enough crazy for one day. And I need to get to the lab."

"Let's go," Grayson said. "Keep us informed on what you find out, Dr. Crum."

Crum nodded, but his eyes were studying some faraway corner of the sky. I figured he was either deep in thought or was trying to avoid seeing his own shirt.

Grayson strapped on his seatbelt and said, "Punch it, Earl."

My cousin obliged. He mashed the pedal to the floor, and we took off like a tractor out of hell. I tumbled into the side of Grayson, causing him to grunt.

Earl laughed. "You two just can't keep your hands off each other, can you?"

My ears burned. When I pushed myself off Grayson, I saw his cheeks were pink, too.

"THE FUN NEVER ENDS around here," Grayson said as Earl took the corner of Wilder Road on two wheels. Straight ahead, the massive water

tower loomed at us like the villain in a low-budget horror flick—*Attack of the Man-Eating Fruit Mutant.*

"Turn here, Earl," I said. "Onto Cherry Street."

Earl's face twisted into a lopsided grin. "Really? You sure we ain't looking for *Strawberry* Street?"

Grayson snorted and nodded toward the tower. "From the looks of it, we're already on *Sesame* Street."

Below the giant berry-shaped tower, a group of elementary-school-aged children were running wild, threading in and out of the growing throng of gawkers. Three patrol cars were already on the scene, their lights flashing. They looked like toys compared to the humongous strawberry.

"There!" Grayson said, pointing to an empty space on the side of the road.

Earl squeezed Bessie in between a faded blue church bus and an old ice cream truck. Grayson opened the door. The tune *It's a Small World* filled our ears as it crackled from the ice cream truck's audio system. The speakers sounded like they'd been shot since the early '70s.

"Somebody needs their xylophone tuned," Grayson said as we piled out of the truck.

"Hey, he's got creamsicles!" Earl hollered.

"No time." Grayson nodded toward the tower. "Look."

I stared up at the tower and blinked. I blinked again, thinking it might have been another twin-induced hallucination, but the view didn't change.

About a hundred feet up the stem of the colossal strawberry, a naked old white man was hollering and shaking his fist at the crowd like an angry maggot. Blue and red lights flashed alternately in my eyes. *It's a Small World* plinked at my ears like a toy piano hammered on by a chimpanzee.

This must be what it's like to have an acid flashback.

"You think that's Rexel?" Grayson asked.

I cringed. "Yeah. I recognize the liver spots on that shiny bald head even without my cheater glasses."

Earl elbowed me. "You sure that's *all* you recognize?"

I punched Earl in the gut. After a round of retaliatory sparing, we settled down and joined Grayson. He was staring up at an enormous yellow crane. It lurched in fits and starts toward the monstrous strawberry like a ten-story-tall praying mantis.

Mantris vs Strawzilla. It's got a nice ring to it.

Once the crane got within range, it extended a long, pendulous arm toward poor old Rexel, who was still flailing his fist like an angry, albino fruit-fly larva. Some guy dressed like a shortstop grabbed him by the torso, then yanked Rexel, kicking and screaming, into the basket of the cherry picker.

The crowd erupted into cheers, then half of them made a beeline for the ice cream truck.

"Well, I'll be," Earl said, succinctly summing up the event.

"Rexel was such a stickler for the rules," Grayson said. "What the hell's gotten into him?"

"Probably the same thing that got into Lester and Arlene," I said.

Earl's eyes grew wide. "You talkin' demon possession?"

I shot my cousin some side-eye. "Absolutely. And on a Sunday, no less."

Earl swallowed hard. "What do we do now?"

A man's voice sounded behind us. "I'd say dinner and a movie, but how're you ever gonna top *that* show?"

I turned to find Garth, the mullet-boy-wonder, grinning at us. "What are *you* doing here?" I asked.

"Same as you," he said. "Gawking. I heard about it on my ham radio." He laughed. "For us local operators, this is the event of the season. Maybe even the *decade*."

I frowned. "Why do you say that?"

Garth grinned. "Old T-Rexel, of course. The guy's always on our butts to follow protocol, then he gets naked and climbs the water tower like a geriatric King Kong. You can't make that kind of crap up."

"What you think got into the poor feller?" Earl asked.

Garth shrugged. "I dunno. But Rexel's definitely off his regular feed. Nobody's heard from him for days, and then last night he kerchunked my repeater."

Earl grimaced. "Listen here, Garth. It's better for ever'body if you keep your personal life to yourself."

"Wha—?" Garth gave everyone a good look at his buck teeth, then cringed. "Oh! No, man. It's not—ugh. Look, all I can say is, something's totally up with that old dude."

The flash of red and blue lights made us turn and stare. A police car drove slowly by. Rexel's face and palms were plastered to the rear side-window like a kid forced to leave the carnival too soon.

"There he goes," Earl said.

"Yep," Garth nodded. "Looks like the show's over. Where you guys crashing tonight?"

Grayson shrugged. "No particular plans."

Garth shot me a grin. "Well, you're welcome to camp at my place again. Pandora, your sombrero act last night put Rexel's puny deal here to shame."

I cringed inside. "Uh ... thanks, but—"

"We'd love to," Grayson butted in. He turned to me and winked a green eye. "But not too heavy on the booze tonight, honey. We've got a big day tomorrow."

Chapter Thirty-Eight

AGAINST ALL MY WILL and most of my better judgment, I'd ridden with Earl and Grayson back to Garth's chain-linked junkyard of a compound.

Earl was excited about the idea of camping out again with the guys in his monster truck. I, on the other hand, was trying my best to convince Grayson not to spend another night there.

"Come on, Grayson," I said as we climbed down out of Bessie. "We might as well head down the road and find a new case. There's nothing out of the ordinary going on here."

"You sure about that?" He studied me with those unreadable eyes of his. "It seems like only yesterday *you* were the one hell-bent on staying. Wait. It *was* yesterday."

My face flushed pink. I attempted to cover it with a white lie. "I changed my mind. You were right. This is just an ordinary case of domestic homicide."

Grayson's eyebrow ticked up a good inch. "I'm *right*?" He grinned and shook his head. "Come on, Drex. What's *really* going on here?"

Crap. It's like the guy can see right through me.

The truth was, at the moment, I didn't give a flip whether the folks around here were being driven wackadoodle by malaria-infested mosquitoes or sadistic, Southern-fried poltergeists.

I just wanted to get the hell out of Garth's compound.

If we stayed, I'd be facing a humiliating ribbing from the guys about last night. I could've probably handled the jokes if I'd known what to expect—but the fact was, I couldn't remember squat about what I'd done after that third shot of tequila.

I blew out an angry breath. "*Nothing's* going on."

It was a childish rebuttal, but the best I could come up with given the shaky state of my defense.

Grayson smirked. "So, what's the harm in staying another night then?" He turned to my cousin. "You in, Earl?"

Earl grinned. "You bet."

I scowled at my cousin. "What about the garage? Who's going to run it?"

Earl hooked his thumbs in his armpits and rocked back on his heels. "Seeing as how you can't fire me no more, I'm taking the liberty of a well-earned vacation day."

Grayson's lip curled up on one side. "Besides, we haven't entirely ruled out Pan as the perpetrator."

My molars clenched hard enough to crush rocks.

"Fine," I hissed. "We'll stay."

WITH MY ESCAPE PLAN foiled, I sat by the campfire and awaited my fate, armed with a marshmallow stabbed onto the end of a stick. I figured if anybody got me too riled, I could jab them in the eye with it.

I poked my jousting weapon into the flames and watched the marshmallow on the end swell, then begin to turn golden-brown on the edges.

"Nothing like cooking over an open fire," Earl said. He sat beside me and stuck a skewered hotdog over the flame.

Garth nodded. "It's probably the thing I look forward to the most when the apocalypse hits."

The most?

"I don't get it, Garth," I said. "Why are you a member of that Dreadmore camp when you've already got this place?"

Garth smiled, making me wonder how long it had been since I'd seen a dentist.

"Backup," he said. "Every smart prepper has a secondary bugout location. You know, in case the first one gets raided or blown off the map. Only a fool like Jenkins thinks they can survive alone in some old World War II bunker."

"He had the cabin as a secondary," I said.

Garth snorted derisively. "That rundown cabin wouldn't save him from a mosquito invasion."

"I *heard* that," Earl said, and swatted his forearm.

Garth shook his head. "The dude thought he could go it alone with his wife. But what if one of them gets sick or dies? No way, man. A real prepper knows there's safety in numbers. You need reinforcements in case you lose a crucial member. You know, like—"

"Rexel?" Earl asked.

Garth shrugged. "I was gonna say Tooth, but yeah, Rexel, too."

I cringed. "That lunatic's still missing?"

"Yeah."

Earl cocked his head. "But I thought they found him climbing that monstrositous strawberry."

I sighed. "I meant Tooth."

"Oh." Earl shifted his gaze across the small campfire toward Garth's brother, Jimmy. Dressed in jeans and a flannel shirt, the young cop could've been mistaken for a teenager at a Southern Baptist boot camp. Earl yelled to him across the blaze. "What's gonna happen to him, Officer Wells?"

Red flames reflected in Wells' eyes as he glanced up from his hotdog on a stick. "Tooth or Rexel?"

"Rexel!" I rolled my eyes in exasperation, and caught sight of my marshmallow. It had burst into flames and was dripping molten goo onto the red-hot coals. "Dang it!" I jerked my stick out of the fire, but it was too late. My marshmallow was nothing but charred remains.

"You never *could* cook worth a darn," Earl quipped.

"Shut it or this thing's going in your mouth." I looked over at Wells. "So, what about Rexel?"

Wells shrugged. "I don't know. He's at the hospital under twenty-four-hour observation. We're waiting on the psych evaluation to see if we can release him on his own recognizance."

"T-Rex's always been wound up pretty tight," Garth said. "It was just a matter of time before a spring broke."

I flicked the crispy black remains of my burnt marshmallow into the fire like I was casting a fishing rod. I stuck another one on the stick. "Any idea yet if what's going on with Rexel is related to the Jenkins' case?"

"If you ask me, I think their brains are being altered by alien implants," Earl said, then shoved half a hotdog in his mouth.

I jabbed him with the marshmallow on the end of my stick. "I wasn't asking *you*. And would you can it already with the alien implants?"

Earl's back stiffened. He mumbled at me with a mouthful of wiener. "Geez, Bobbie. Open that mind a yours to the possibilities. You didn't believe in Mothman, neither. And look where that got you."

I shot my cousin a dirty look. "What are you implying?"

Earl smirked, then glanced up and nearly choked on his hotdog. I followed his line of sight across the fire pit. Crum was standing there wearing his donut shirt, pizza pants, and the kind of facial expression I'd only seen on soap opera doctors—usually after unsuccessful brain transplants.

Earl rose to his feet. "What's up, Doc?"

Grayson, who'd been working away feverishly on his laptop, glanced up and said, "Whatever it is, it doesn't look good."

Chapter Thirty-Nine

INSIDE GARTH'S PREPPER compound, all eyes switched from the campfire to Dr. Crum.

He cleared his throat as flop sweat poured from his temples and dripped onto his donut shirt.

"Let me start by saying that what I'm about to tell you is, at this point, purely hypothetical," Crum said, wobbling as if he might faint.

I waved my marshmallow-on-a-stick at him like a magic wand. "I think you should sit down, Doctor."

Crum nodded. "Yes. I think we all should."

Eyebrows ticked up around the campfire. Each of us grabbed a lawn chair and dragged it toward Crum. We formed a tight circle next to the fire pit, and waited expectantly for the doctor to speak.

Crum wiped his brow with a paper napkin. It was so quiet all I could hear was the fire crackling. As the doctor nervously cleared his throat again, I shot a glance at Grayson. His eyes were shining like a kid let loose in a candy-store free-for-all. I could almost envision his hands rubbing together maniacally.

That weirdo lives *for this stuff.*

"I spoke to a friend of mine at the CDC," Crum coughed out like a confession. "According to Dr. Easterly, a new form of transmissible spongiform encephalopathy is affecting free-ranging deer, elk, and moose."

"Transpo *what?*" Earl asked.

Crum shot him a worried glance. "Trans—never mind. In layman's terms, it's called chronic wasting disease, or CWD for short. Anyway, the disease causes abnormal proteins to collect in brain and spinal cord tissues. They eventually burst and cause microscopic empty spaces, basically turning the animal's normal brain tissue into a sponge-like material."

"You mean like Spongebob Squarepants?" Earl looked around and laughed at his own joke. No one laughed back. He pouted and sat back in his lawn chair.

Crum chewed his lip. "No. I'm afraid this is no joke. The infected animals really suffer."

"What happens to them?" Grayson asked.

"It's subtle at first. Weight loss, drooling, droopy ears. Then a general wasting away of their health. So far, the disease has only been reported in western states."

"How many?" Grayson asked.

"Twenty-four."

Grayson whistled.

"I ain't followin' y'all," Earl said. "What's a sponge-headed deer got to do with anything?"

"I'm *getting* to that," Crum said. "You see, in the final stages of CWD, these animals lose their fear of people, and can get aggressive."

"Are you saying you think an infected deer attacked Lester Jenkins?" Grayson asked.

"Possibly. But it could be worse than that. A lot worse." Crum took a deep breath and steadied himself. "Lester and Arlene Jenkins—and perhaps even Rexel—could have contracted CWD themselves."

Garth flew up out of his chair, knocking it over. "Are you saying this CWD crap is *contagious?*"

Crum cleared his throat. "Yes. I mean, no. Not contagious like you might think. And right now, like I said, this is just a theory. As far as we know, the disease is only affecting deer. But according to Easterly, it's likely that human cases *will* show up."

"But if it's not contagious, how do humans get it?" Garth asked.

Crum locked eyes with Garth. "From eating the meat of contaminated animals."

Garth's mouth dropped open. "You're kidding me."

Crum shook his head. "I wish I were. The disease has already proven to be transmittable to other animals, including primates, our closest relatives. Easterly thinks it's not a matter of *if*, but *when* CWD will transfer to humans."

I cringed. "Geez! If it does, would the symptoms be like what happened to Arlene and Rexel?"

Crum shook his head. "We can only speculate at this point. But they would probably be very similar to Mad Cow Disease. First, a tingling and burning sensation in the face and extremities. In later stages, most likely dementia and psychotic behavior."

"That would certainly explain a few things," Grayson said.

Crum nodded. "That's what I was thinking. The symptoms Arlene is displaying would fit the profile to a T."

"If you're right, what will happen to her now?" I asked.

Crum shook his head. "Nothing good. This isn't nicknamed zombie deer disease for nothing."

"It turns deer into zombies?" Earl asked. "If people eat the zombie deer, do they turn into zombies too?"

Crum blew out an exhausted breath. "Basically, yes."

Grayson whistled long and low. "How many people are we talking about here, Doc?"

"Who knows? Easterly told me around fifteen thousand infected animals get eaten every year in the US. If a diseased animal got into a meat processing plant ... well, I'd hate to think about the consequences."

Wells rubbed his chin. "You said this disease is only affecting deer out West. If that's true, how'd Lester Jenkins get infected?"

"Oh! Oh! I think I know that one!" Earl said, bouncing up and down in his lawn chair.

I could almost hear a collective groan.

"And what would that be?" Wells asked tiredly.

Earl beamed. "I seen pictures of him and his brother, Hank huntin' out West. They must've brought some infected deer meat back with 'em."

"Huh. That actually makes sense," Wells said. "But what about Rexel? He didn't go out west, and he wasn't a hunter."

Garth shrugged. "He's old. He could've just gone off his rocker naturally."

"Or Rexel could've taken some infected meat from Jenkins' cabin," I offered. "It's just a short walk from his house."

"All he'd need was a nibble," Crum said.

I shot Grayson an "I told you so" stare. From the expression on his face, I didn't need to remind him how I'd slapped that hunk of deer meat from his hand a millisecond before he'd taken a bite.

"Awe, crap!" Garth said, and let out a groan so loud we all turned and stared at him.

"What's wrong?" I asked.

Garth cringed. "Rexel was in charge of alternative food procurement. He might've bartered with Jenkins for venison. If he did, he could've infected everybody at Dreadmore!"

I blanched. "You mean we could be looking at a whole army of zombies out there?"

"Not just zombies," Grayson said. "*Prepper* zombies."

We all stared at Garth. He shrunk back in his lawn chair. "Don't look at *me*. Except for chicken wings, I'm a vegetarian!"

Suddenly, an unearthly howl rang out from the darkness beyond the campfire.

The hair on the back of my neck stood on end. I joined the circle of anxious eyes darting back and forth, exchanging panicked glances.

In the dumbstruck silence came the sound of footsteps ...

fast and furious ...

crashing through the bushes toward us.

I shot a glance at my cousin. Earl's eyes were as big as boiled eggs. He jerked his body to standing and bellowed.

"Run everybody! It's the zombie apocalypsc!"

Chapter Forty

I KNEW I'D NEVER BE able to haul my breeder hips up into Earl's monster truck in time to save them, so I scrambled for the RV instead. Grayson was hot on my heels.

"What the hell's going on?" I yelled as we crashed into each other in front of the RV's side door.

"You think *I* know?" Grayson yelled. "Get in!"

I yanked open the door and scrambled inside, assisted by a less-than-helpful push from behind. Grayson climbed in nearly on top of me, slammed the door behind him, and set the lock.

I cringed. "I hope Earl's all right."

Grayson grimaced. "I hope he's all *wrong*. I'm not ready for a freaking zombie apocalypse."

I chewed my lip anxiously. "I'm gonna go turn on the headlights and see what's going on."

Grayson grabbed my arm. "I don't think that's a good idea. The lights may set them off."

I locked eyes with Grayson. "Then what are we gonna do?"

His green eyes flickered a shade darker. "Ride it out, I guess."

A sickening thought hit me. "Are the cab doors locked?"

Grayson's eyes locked onto mine. "Crap!"

"Out of my way!" I yelled.

We both bolted for the front of the RV. Our heads collided, then our bodies crammed together in the narrow passage leading to the driver's cab. Neither of us was going anywhere unless one of us budged.

Grayson grunted, tried to squeeze past me, then his chest went limp against mine. "Look," he said. "You do the passenger seat, I'll get the driver's side."

"Deal."

He stepped back enough for me to break free. I burst into the cab and nearly ran headlong into the windshield. I caught myself with both hands on the dashboard.

Through the glass, I saw something flit by in the darkness.

Panic shot through me afresh. I dove for the passenger seat. My hand flew up, ready to slam down on the door lock. But right before I made contact, I heard the sickening click of the door handle.

The door swung open.

"Grayson!" I screamed, and jumped a foot when his arms wrapped around me from behind. He held me tight as I stared out the open door, straining to see what I didn't want to see.

Two inhuman red eyes bore down on us from the darkness. A low, menacing howl pierced the night again. White fangs flashed in the moonlight.

With no better option coming to my scared-witless mind, I closed my eyes and screamed bloody murder.

Chapter Forty-One

AS I WAITED FOR THE zombies to eat my brain, I heard Grayson exhale a nervous laugh.

I opened my eyes.

Garth was standing outside the open passenger door, staring at me with a sheepish grin. "Look who came home for supper. Must've smelled the hotdogs." He glanced down at his furry, black companion. "Tooth, you're a bad doggy."

Grayson gave me a bear-hug squeeze and burst out laughing. I wriggled free from his arms and shot him a glance that made him nearly swallow his tongue.

I turned my anxious rage on Garth. "Your dog scared the bejeebers out of us!"

Garth grimaced. "Sorry, Miss Pandora." He patted Tooth's huge head. The dog whimpered. "He didn't mean any harm."

"Argh!" I bit down and took a deep breath to regain my composure.

The two men looked at me expectantly. What they were expecting, I had no idea. I took another deep breath and said, "Well, at least he's okay. We're *all* okay, right?"

"Except for Crum," Garth said. "His favorite pizza pants got ruined."

I winced. "Did Tooth bite Doc in the butt?"

Garth rubbed Tooth's head. "Nah. Don't tell anybody, but Tooth here's a wimp. He just talks a big game."

Earl came lumbering up. "Y'all okay in there?"

"Yeah," I said, relieved to see him. "But what happened to Crum?"

"Ol' Doc?" Earl laughed. "He'll be all right. He's just cleaning up a little special sauce he let loose in his pizza pants."

Chapter Forty-Two

AFTER DOING A QUICK headcount, it was confirmed that we'd all survived the zombie-free Tooth apocalypse. Granted, some of us a little better than others.

"Come with me," Wells said to Crum. "I think I've got a clean pair of sweats that'll fit you."

Too wired for sleep, the rest of us followed the men into the Wells brothers' trailer. Jimmy led Crum to the bathroom. Garth lured Tooth into his crate with a bone smeared with peanut butter and CBD oil—some kind of cannabis-based sedative, according to Garth.

"You want a squirt?" he asked me, holding the eyedropper.

"No. But I wouldn't mind a cup of coffee."

"Make that two," Grayson said.

"Coming right up." Garth put the coffee on, then reached into the cupboard and pulled out dainty china cups and saucers adorned with a delicate pink rose pattern.

"Nice dishes," I said. "Family heirloom?"

"No," Garth said. "I just like 'em. Have a seat."

I looked around and grimaced. From the state of the place, the maid hadn't been here since our last visit. I tried not to think about it, and joined Earl and Grayson on the couch. A moment later, Wells came back down the hall and sat down in a chair across from us.

Maybe it was the adrenaline crash, the dreadful deer disease, or the shock of still being alive, but none of us seemed to have much to say. Garth handed each of us a cup, and we drank our coffee in silence, waiting on Crum to finish wiping up his pizza sauce.

It took longer than any of us had anticipated.

It was Earl who finally broke the silence. He nodded at the crate, then addressed Garth. "You don't think that there hound of yours is going zombie, do you?"

Garth shook his head. "No. Tooth just suffers from separation anxiety. He's been like that since he was a pup. Jimmy's got the scars to prove it."

Wells nodded and touched his neck absently.

"So, where do we go from here, Mr. Gray?" Garth asked.

Grayson set down his china cup. "Good question. Let's see. So far, we've got one dead guy—"

"*Missing* dead guy," I said.

Grayson eyed me. "One *missing* dead guy, presumably murdered, and two people who appear to have lost their marbles eating zombie deer meat. Not exactly the storyline for a Hallmark movie."

"We don't know for sure it's zombie deer disease," Wells said, shooting Grayson a perturbed look. "There's no point in getting everybody all worked up about that. I think Arlene Jenkins is most likely suffering from hysteria brought on by Lester's death and being locked in that bunker."

"But what about Lester and Rexel?" I asked. "They don't have those excuses. Whether this deer disease thing turns out to be real or not, I'm thinking the cases still have to be related somehow."

"I agree," Grayson said. "When you look at it, Rexel and Jenkins shared several commonalities. They both were preppers. And ham radio enthusiasts." He turned to Wells. "Was Jenkins ever in the military?"

Wells shook his head. "I don't recall that from his background check. But they were both transplants to Florida."

Earl laughed. "Who ain't?"

Wells pursed his lips. "Jenkins' cabin was close to Rexel's house. There could be some environmental factor at play there."

"You mean besides the sponge-brain thing?" Earl asked.

Wells sighed. "Yes. It could be some toxin in the soil or water, or—"

"That still wouldn't explain his crushed bones," Grayson said. "Or the slimy substance you said was on his head."

"Halibut," Earl said.

We all turned and stared at my cousin.

Earl chewed the side of his cheek. "That Hank Chambers guy. He said halibut instead of husband."

"Are you saying you think he might be infected, too?" I asked.

Earl grinned. "All I'm saying is there's something mighty *fishy* going on. Get it?"

Wells shot Earl some side-eye. "I don't think—"

"Excuse me," Crum interrupted. He'd emerged from the bathroom wearing dark-blue sweatpants. They coordinated well with his donut shirt, which, unfortunately, appeared no worse for wear. "Sorry that took so long."

"Dr. Crum," I said. "You told us this chronic wasting disease can make animals lose their fear of humans and get aggressive. Do you think a deer is capable of crushing Jenkins' bones like the autopsy report showed?"

The doctor shrugged. "I guess it's possible."

"That would be some major overkill," Wells said. "I don't see why a deer would waste the energy."

"What about Rexel's bizarre behavior?" I asked. "Could chronic wasting disease make a man strip naked and climb a water tower?"

Crum thought about my question for a moment. "Yes, I suppose. But here's the thing. He and the others would've had to have eaten infected meat four or five months ago, maybe longer."

"Why's that?" I asked.

"Assuming it's like Mad Cow Disease, that's how long it took for advanced psychotic behavior to begin to manifest."

Earl opened his mouth to speak. Wells gave him a glare that would shut a normal person down. Earl, of course, didn't pay him any mind.

"Them hunting pictures I saw at their house. Looked to me like Lester and Hank bagged 'em a deer out West in spring or early summer. The grass was fresh and green."

Wells' hard expression softened. He shifted his attention from Earl to Crum. "If they *are* infected, how can we prove it?"

Crum chewed his lip. "I'll need to take another look at Jenkins' brain biopsy."

"What do I tell the folks at Dreadmore?" Garth asked.

"Nothing, for now," Crum said. "There's no point in stirring up hysteria until—" Crum stopped midsentence. "I need to get samples of that deer meat for testing. Where can we get some?"

"There may still be some in Jenkins' cabin," I said.

"Or in the bunker behind their house," Grayson said.

"Or Dreadmore," Garth said.

"That's a lot of places," Crum said, grimacing softly.

I winced. "If this does turn out to be CWD, can it be treated?"

Crum shook his head. "I'm afraid not. If it's anything like Mad Cow Disease, every victim will be dead within a year."

"Oh."

Crum sighed. "Seeing as it's nearly midnight, I suggest we all get some sleep and get cracking on this first thing in the morning."

"Right," Wells said. "I'll check out the Jenkins' bunker at daybreak. Should I take any special precautions when handling the meat?"

"Absolutely," Crum said. "If I were you, I'd wear thick gloves and put the samples in evidence bags. If you have a cut or scrape on your skin, well, I don't know if that would be enough to transmit the disease or not."

"Thanks," Wells said. "Okay, everybody, you heard the doctor. Let's reconvene in the morning."

AS WE HEADED BACK TO the RV, I turned to Grayson. "Do you still think this is just another domestic homicide?"

"No."

"What changed your mind?"

"The pieces don't fit. A deer—even a crazed one—wouldn't stomp a man until every major bone in his body was broken. Wells is right. Animals don't waste energy on revenge."

"What would, then?"

Grayson kicked a stone out of the path. "Someone playing a game."

"Pan?" I scoffed.

"Maybe. Or one of his friends."

I opened the RV door. "What are you talking about?"

"Lester Jenkins was less than what you might consider a stellar representative of the human race."

I climbed the first step. "Yeah. So?"

"Maybe the folks upstairs decided to crush Jenkins for his own repugnance."

I turned and looked Grayson in the eye. "That's pretty brutal."

He shrugged. "No worse than you stepping on a cockroach."

Huh. I guess he had me there.

Chapter Forty-Three

I WAS IN DREADMORE Village.

And they were after me.

Hordes of rigor-mortis-faced zombies with earthworms and green goo dripping from their mouths.

Struggling for breath, I stumbled as I ran from their eerie, Frankenstein shuffling. Frantic, I scanned the falling-down hovels for a refuge. My eyes fell upon a familiar one. I ducked inside the tin-roofed shack. My eyes darted around at the glowing green tanks of spirulina.

In a dark corner to my left, something moved. My knees knocked together audibly. To my horror, old man T-Rex lunged at me, naked. He jabbed a tablespoon of green slime at my face. I bolted past him through the dirty plastic flaps and into the compost area.

I climbed inside one of the wooden boxes to hide. As I sank into the dark, crumbly dirt, worms began to wriggle up and down my body. I wanted to scream, but the gurgling, snore-like breathing of nearby zombies made me hold my breath instead.

I closed my eyes and prepared to die.

Something tapped me on the shoulder. I turned and saw Grandma Selma. She was inside the box with me, stirring a pot of black goo. She lifted a spoon from the pot and offered me a taste. It looked and smelled like sh—"

"You okay there, Drex?"

I blinked. I was sitting in the RV banquette, a mug of coffee in front of me. "Uh ... yeah."

"Where were you? Didn't you feel me tapping you on the shoulder?"

"I ... oh. Yeah. I felt it. I guess I was just having a daydream."

"About what?"

I cringed. "Dreadmore. Everyone there was a zombie."

"I hope it was a dream and not a premonition," Grayson said as he sat down across from me. "I hate to say it, but this zombie deer disease is a real powder keg. If it goes ...." He shook his head. "We could be looking at the tip of the iceberg, Drex—at a whole new ball game."

"What do you mean?"

"These preppers. They're waiting on the apocalypse, right?"

"Yeah."

"But what if they *are* the apocalypse?"

Grayson sat back and laughed bitterly. "It all fits. I should've seen it before. It's a classic ploy from the universe's twisted mind."

I stared at Grayson. "What are you talking about?"

He blew out a breath. "The universe has a history of turning goons with guns into mindless assassins."

"Okay."

"While you were toasting marshmallows last night, I did some research. Do you know that *sixty-eight million* Americans own survival gear?" He shook his head. "There are over four million hardcore preppers out there, Drex. All sitting around waiting in fear of the total collapse of society. But what if it's a self-fulfilling prophecy? What if, by preparing for the end of the world as we know it, they bring it on themselves?"

I swallowed hard. "You mean by becoming zombies?"

Grayson smiled wryly. "You have to admit, it would be the ultimate irony. And you know how the universe loves irony."

"But what about—"

A knock sounded on the side door. I sprung from my seat to answer it, glad for the distraction.

Officer Wells was at the door. "I just came back from checking the bunker at Jenkins' house. If there was any deer meat in there, it's long gone now. Somebody left the bunker door open."

I sighed. "Great. So, now we might be looking at an army of zombie raccoons and possums, too. Come on in."

Wells grimaced at the prospect and stepped inside.

"I'd say at the moment, that's the least of our worries," Grayson said. "So, where next? Jenkins' cabin?"

"I was just heading over there," Wells said. "You guys mind giving me some backup?"

"Be happy to," Earl's voice sounded from the open door.

Wells' boyish face drooped like a soggy piñata. "Great."

AS WE DROVE PAST REXEL'S house on the way to Jenkins' cabin, I noticed his military-precision lawn had gone to pot like the rest of the abandoned subdivision.

"I hope the poor guy doesn't have mad deer disease," I said.

"Maybe he's just off his meds," Earl said. "Which way?"

"Follow Wells," Grayson said.

"Can't. He stopped back yonder."

I glanced in the rearview mirror. Wells' patrol car was pulled to the side of the road in front of one of the dozens of vacant lots. He was waving for us to go on ahead.

"It's just straight up there at the end of the road," I said to Earl. "We'll stop there and wait for him."

Earl pulled Bessie up to where the abandoned road disappeared abruptly into swampy pine forest and palmettos. The three of us climbed out of the monster truck and fed a few mosquitoes while we waited for Wells to catch up.

"How far back in them woods is it?" Earl asked, swatting the back of his neck.

I envisioned the zigzagging trail and wondered if its erratic design was intentional, or if it was a sign that Lester Jenkins had been losing his mind for some time now.

"As the crow flies, I'd say a tenth of a mile," I said. "As the possum trots, a good half mile, minimum."

Grayson shot me an amused grin. "Possum trots?"

"Here he comes," Earl said.

Wells pulled his patrol car alongside us and climbed out slowly. His face was as pale as talcum powder.

"What's happened?" Grayson asked.

"You're not going to believe this," Wells said. He shook his head. "*I* don't believe this."

"What?" I asked.

"I just got a call from dispatch. Someone reported finding a pile of coffins dumped along the road to Dreadmore."

"That's weird," I said.

"That's not the weird part," Wells said. "According to dispatch, the person who called in the report said that two of the coffins contained dead bodies."

"Well, they *are* coffins," Grayson said.

Wells shook his head. "That's not the weird part, either. The dispatcher said he was on the line with the caller when the guy screamed, 'They're coming back to life!' Then the connection went dead."

Chapter Forty-Four

THE SEARCH FOR INFECTED deer meat in Jenkins' cabin would have to wait. If Wells' police report about people in coffins coming back to life was true, that meant Earl had been right, too. A zombie apocalypse was well underway—and ground zero was Dreadmore Village.

"Climb in, Officer Wells," Earl hollered. "From what Bobbie told me, that puny little patrol car of yours'll never make it down the road to Dreadmore."

Wells took half a second to concede Earl's point and yelled back, "I call shotgun."

We scrambled up into Earl's monster truck and wedged ourselves in for the ride. Grayson and I were the ham and cheese between two slices of American white bread—one at the wheel and the other barking directions out the window.

"Take a left," Wells said. "Then a straight shot down SR39."

Earl hit the gas, then eased off. "Hold up. You think this might be a trick?"

"A trick?" I asked as we coasted down the road.

"You know. By all them zombies. Think they're just trying to lure us out to Dreadmore so's they can eat our brains out?"

"The one that got you would starve to death," I said. "You think maybe we should stop by Walmart and pick up some torches and pitchforks?"

Earl shook his head. "Some monster hunter you are, Bobbie. Everybody knows you got to shoot a zombie in the noggin to kill it."

I glanced over at Wells. Good thing he was by the window. He looked as green as a dill pickle. "Let's get going," he said. "I'm the only cop responding."

"Why?" Grayson asked.

The tendons in Wells' neck tightened. "Thanks to my brother and you guys, I'm the department's official 'Monster Boy.'"

Grayson stifled a grin. "In that case, better step on it, Earl. If lore is correct, you're right. The only way to stop a zombie is with a bullet to the head."

My mind flashed back to my daydream, premonition—whatever it was—of zombies run amok in Dreadmore. I'd said I'd wanted to be at ground zero when the apocalypse happened. God had finally answered one of my prayers.

Gee. Thanks, God.

I grabbed my purse and scrounged for my Glock. I found the pink carrying case under a stack of coupons for Glade air freshener, which I kept forgetting to buy. I pulled out the gun case and yelled, "If this is it, I hope everybody's packing plenty of ammo!"

"THAT'S IT, COMING UP on the left," Wells said.

He pointed to a road that wasn't much more than two orange clay strips worn into the knee-high grass of an abandoned cattle pasture. "Turn here, and try to stay in the ruts."

Earl hooked a left and Bessie's fat tractor tires started mowing down grass on either side of the overgrown road. The first quarter mile wasn't too bad. But when the pasture gave way to palmettos and the ground turned marshy, even Bessie began to struggle.

"Last night's rain didn't help matters," Wells said. "We may have to get out and push."

"Bessie don't like people touching her rear end," Earl said, and punched the gas.

After flinging enough red mud to plaster a Zeppelin, Bessie maneuvered through an acre of swamp glop all the way to the base of a small hill. Earl shifted to low gear, stuck his tongue out for assistance, and steered the monster truck toward the top of the mound.

"Woohoo! Thank heaven for Bessie!" he hollered as we reached the top.

We all sighed with relief—until we rounded a corner and another patch of pasture came into view.

Earl slammed on the brakes. But this time, the terrain wasn't the problem.

A black pickup truck was angled sideways across the lane. Behind it, scattered along the side of the road, lay a jumble of cheap wooden coffins, most of them broken open. Amongst them, three men were busy beating the life out of one another.

A fourth man was already face down on the ground.

"I'm confused," Earl said. "Are they fighting to get *inside* them coffins, or out of 'em?"

I cringed. "What the hell's going on?"

"Zombies," Grayson muttered.

"Which ones?" I asked.

Given that all four men had bloody faces, torn clothes and stunk to high heaven, it was a fair question.

"Only one way to find out," Grayson said.

"How?" Wells asked.

Grayson answered his question, but I wasn't listening.

I didn't want to know.

Chapter Forty-Five

"YOU KNOW HOW TO DRIVE this thing?" Grayson asked me.

I tore my eyes away from the wrestling zombies. "Bessie? Yes."

"Good. You stay here. Keep the engine idling. We may need to make a quick getaway."

Wells and Earl were already out of the truck and getting a feel for their weapons. Earl had his trusty Mossberg shotgun aimed at the zombies. Wells had his service revolver aimed at the ground.

"You got your Glock?" I asked Grayson.

He gave a quick nod. "Always."

"Be careful," I said, and scooted into the driver's seat. I watched through the windshield as the three men took cautious steps toward the brawling trio.

"Break it up!" Wells yelled.

The three zombies looked up, surprised at the intrusion. I recognized one of the brawlers as Jake, the hard-faced survivalist who thought bugs and field mice were perfect dinnertime snacks. Another one was Lester Jenkins' half-brother, Hank Chambers. The third guy I'd never seen before.

"What's going on here?" Wells demanded.

"He did it!" Chambers yelled.

"I did not!" Jake yelled back.

"Did too!" the third man screamed.

The three men went at each other again like bullies in a graveyard playground.

Men. Even when they're zombies, nothing changes.

"Hold it right there," Wells said, "or I'll shoot all your kneecaps out."

The zombie-men stopped strangling and punching each other, and slowly turned toward Wells. Their faces, bruised and bloody, appeared, for lack of a better word, *hungry.*

I swallowed hard. *Now what?*

"Any of you armed?" Wells asked.

"Only if you count treachery," Chambers said.

"Takes one to know one, Judas!" Jake hissed.

"Shut up!" Wells said. "Which one of you called this in?"

The unknown man took a step forward. Wells, Grayson, and Earl trained their guns on him like a vigilante firing squad.

"Don't shoot!" the man said. "I'm the one who called!"

"What's your name?" Wells barked.

"Samuel Simpson."

Wells grunted. "Come forward. *Slowly.*"

Jake and Chambers took a step forward along with Simpson. Earl and Grayson shifted their weapons in their direction, stopping the two men in their tracks.

Wells nodded at Simpson. "Just you."

Simpson resumed his slow shuffle toward Wells. When he got within six feet, the young officer held up his hand.

"Hold it right there," Wells demanded. "Show me some I.D."

"I'm truly sorry about all of this," Simpson said, fishing a hand in his back pocket. He pulled out a wallet and held up a driver's license.

Wells took it. "What's going on here?"

"You won't believe it if I told you," Simpson said.

"I *might.*" Wells glanced over at Grayson. "I've recently been working on expanding my belief system."

Simpson shot Wells a confused look. Wells tossed him back his wallet.

"All right, Mr. Simpson. Why don't we start with you telling me whose body that is over there taking a dirt nap?"

"It's Lester Jenkins, Officer."

While Earl held Chambers and mouse-munching Jake under armed guard with his Mossberg, Grayson made his way toward the coffins. He toed the dead guy's head and called out, "Yeah. It's Lester Jenkins."

Wells eyed Simpson. "So, you weren't lying about *that.*"

"No, sir."

Wells escorted Simpson up to the passenger-side window of Earl's monster truck. "Here," he said to me, and reached through the window.

I leaned across the bench seat and took what he handed me. It was the tiny tape player Lester Jenkins had used to record the skywave transmission of *War of the Worlds*.

"I want you to get this on tape," Wells said.

My brow furrowed. "What about—"

"Just do it."

"Yes, sir."

I scooted across the seat to the passenger window, hit the record button, and positioned the device on the window's edge to document the men's conversation. For the record, I wasn't too keen on the idea. I was worried we would tape over crucial evidence that no one in their right mind would believe without hearing it for themselves.

But as it turned out, it was worth it.

The story Samuel Simpson spilled was so bizarre it made the whole zombie apocalypse thing sound like a children's nursery rhyme.

Chapter Forty-Six

"LOOK, OFFICER, I'M just a lowly coffin delivery guy," was the line Simpson opened with.

I bit back against innate revulsion.

Simpson definitely had the right look for his profession. Pasty. Sweaty. Bony. Insectoid features topped with a greasy gray comb-over not even a mother could love. With any luck, the gash Simpson got on his chin during his scuffle with the other non-zombies would leave a scar. Then his face might have a feature worth remembering.

"That's my vehicle over there." Simpson pointed toward the battered black pickup. "It's not my usual delivery vehicle, but the road here is rough. And I was working ... sort of ... *off the books.*"

Wells' eyes flashed. "Explain 'off the books.'"

"I work for a company called Ash 200." Simpson paused and grinned like a coffin salesman. "Perhaps you've heard of it?"

Wells ground his teeth. "Not that I recall."

"No? Well, we help those of modest means with their *transition.*"

"You sell cheap coffins to poor people," I translated.

Simpson shot me some side-eye. "That's an uncharitable interpretation, Miss. But, yes."

"So you were transporting coffins to Dreadmore," Wells said.

"Yes."

"Why?"

"You see, Officer, occasionally, we have damaged or defective coffins that don't meet our high standards for customer quality. I have an ... uh ... arrangement with Dreadmore. They purchase them."

"What for?" Wells asked.

One of Simpson's thin, gray eyebrows shot up. "I never asked."

Wells' eyes narrowed at Simpson. "And the dead bodies? Did Dreadmore 'purchase' them, too?"

Simpson's eyes bulged. "No, sir! You must believe me. I knew nothing about them. That is, not until the accident. It was terrible, I tell you. I hit a pothole and the tailgate unlatched. The coffins ... well, you can see for yourself what happened."

Wells glanced over at the splintered coffins strewn along the road. He turned back to Simpson. "How could you not be aware there were bodies in the coffins?"

"I didn't load them. Just transported them."

"Who did, then?"

"Load them? Why, my assistant of course."

"Your assistant?"

"Yes. He works part-time for me and my brother, Jeremiah Simpson. You might know Jeremiah? He's the director at McGreggor Funeral Parlor." Simpson smiled broadly and reached for a card. "Perhaps you've heard of it?"

Wells sighed. "I've heard of it."

"Excellent! My brother and I like to keep the death business all in the family."

My nose crinkled. *I bet your family reunions are a real blast.*

Wells cleared his throat. "So, Mr. Simpson, do you have any idea how Lester Jenkins' body ended up in one of your defective coffins, and why your assistant loaded him in the back of your truck?"

"I'm afraid you'll have to ask *him* that. I was as surprised as you were when I found Jenkins' body lying in the dirt. And then to hear that banging."

"Banging?"

"Yes. From inside one of the coffins."

Wells' eyes grew wide along with mine. "From *inside?*"

Simpson cocked his head at Wells. "Well, yes. That's why I called the police, of course. You know. Because I found that man over there alive inside one of the coffins."

Simpson pointed toward the men being guarded by Grayson and Earl.

"Which one?" Wells asked.

Simpson sneered. "The unattractive older gentleman with the distended belly."

Wells blanched. "Hank Chambers?"

Simpson shrugged. "I don't know his name. All I know is when I got the lid off, he came at me like a crazy man. He's the one who started this whole unfortunate fracas."

"Wait a minute," I said. "You say you don't know Hank Chambers, but you knew who his brother Lester Jenkins was?"

Simpson's pasty features scrunched together, making me think of Templeton the rat. "Well, of course."

"How? From the funeral home?" I asked.

His face relaxed a notch. "Yes. That's it."

"So, how do we get in touch with this assistant of yours?" Wells asked.

Simpson's lips curled upward, but I wouldn't call it a smile.

"Easy," he said. "He's standing right next to your Mr. Chambers. His name is Jake Hinson."

Chapter Forty-Seven

"HIT RECORD AGAIN," Wells said to me.

His interview with Samuel Simpson was over. Simpson's assistant, Dreadmore's very own "Emeril of insects," Jake Hinson, was next in the hot seat. With no lips and a skeletal face, Jake looked like Fire Marshal Bill after a particularly nasty arson case.

"I know my rights," Jake hissed through his slit of a mouth. "I don't have to answer your questions without my attorney."

Wells' face registered surprise. "You have an *attorney*, Jake?"

"No."

"Then why bust my—" Wells glanced over at the recorder, then back to his fellow Dreadmore member. "I just have a couple of quick questions. Okay, Jake?"

Jake gave a quick nod and grunted his consent.

"You're a member of Dreadmore, correct?" Wells asked.

"You know I am, Jimmy. Why you wasting my time?"

"It's for the *record*," Wells said. "Do you really work part-time with Mr. Simpson at McGreggor?"

"Yeah."

Wells' nose crinkled. "That's kind of gross, even for you."

Jake sneered. "I just started a couple a months ago. Just to pick up some extra cash during the winter rush. Snowbirds don't always outlast the snow, you know."

What a sentimental sweetheart.

Wells nodded. "Okay. So Simpson says you loaded the coffins onto his truck. Is that right?"

"Yeah."

"Why?"

Jake scowled. "Because they told me to."

"Did you know what was in them?"

"No. Only thing they told me was that your brother ordered 'em."

Wells nearly choked. "*Gary* ordered the coffins?"

"Yeah. For the worm farm. Simpson told me he has some kind of deal going with old man Rexel to drop off defective coffins." Jake laughed. "But turns out this time Rexel was too busy doing a strip tease on the water tower, so your brother took the delivery. Or, at least he was supposed to."

A vein pulsed on Wells' neck. "But when you loaded the coffins, you'd have to have noticed two of them were pretty heavy."

Jake's tanned-leather face twisted into a sour sneer. "Listen, I don't want nobody snooping in my business, and I return the favor by doing likewise."

Wells sighed. "I get that, Jake. But I'm trying to help you out here. Who had access to the coffins before you loaded them?"

Jake shrugged. "Just about anybody, Jimmy. They were in a heap out in back of the funeral home."

"Okay," Wells said. "So you had no idea what was in the coffins?"

"I figured they were stiffs. But at least they were going to a good cause."

"What do you mean?"

"For the *ALF* program. Hey, we all end up as worm food in the end."

I cringed and almost ALF-ed.

"Okay, Jake. You're free to go for now. But stick around."

Jake nodded. "Much obliged, man."

The two men shook hands. Jake turned to leave. Wells called after him. "Oh, and Jake?"

Jake turned around. "Yeah?"

"Do you guys have any deer meat in the ALF program?"

Jake shook his head. "Like I told you, Jimmy. Deer ain't sustainable."

Wells nodded. "Good. I mean, no. Deer isn't sustainable. So do me a favor. If you run across any, don't eat it."

Jake eyed him suspiciously. "Why?"

"Just a friendly heads up. You mind your business, I'll mind mine."

Jake nodded. "As it should be."

Jake headed on foot back toward Dreadmore. I clicked off the recorder and shook my head. "Now what, Officer Wells?"

"Time to figure out who's lying."

Wells nodded over at Hank Chambers, who was busy trying to stay out of the sights of Earl's shotgun.

"I'm thinking Chambers should have the answer. If he doesn't know who nailed him into that coffin, then we may have a real twister of an investigation on our hands."

Chapter Forty-Eight

"ALL I KNOW IS, I FELL asleep on Arlene's couch and woke up in a coffin," Hank Chambers said. He pointed over at Samuel Simpson. "That ghoul over there was standing over me. I freaked and came out swinging. I mean, what else was I supposed to do? Look at his face! I thought I'd died and gone to Hell."

Wells and I glanced over at Simpson, then at each other. We could see Chambers' point.

"Why do you stink to high heaven?" Wells asked. "And don't say collard greens."

Chambers grimaced and brushed dirt off his sleeves. "I think the coffin was used."

Wells cringed, but not as much as I did.

"What were you doing at Arlene's?" he asked.

"You *know* what, Wells. You called me yourself when you found Arlene in that bunker. I was watching over her place while she was ... you know ... in the hospital recovering."

"Right," Wells said. "Do you know anything about that guy?"

"Who?"

"The ghoul," I said.

Wells shot me a dirty look. "Samuel Simpson."

Chambers glanced at Simpson. His face twisted with disgust. "No."

Wells glanced over at me. "Hit stop."

I mashed the button on the recorder.

Wells sighed. "Okay, Mr. Chambers, you're free to go for now."

Chambers nodded, took a step to leave, and stopped. He eyed both of us. "How the hell am I supposed to get home?"

"SO LET ME GET THIS straight," Earl said from the driver's seat of his truck. "*None* of those fellers was zombies?"

"For the last time, *no*," Wells said. "And please, do me a favor and drive slower. We don't want to tip our cargo."

Earl shifted gears, and I flinched as his humongous elbow came at my face like a side of beef. The four of us were wedged into the cab like human sardines, rocking and swaying in unison as Earl pivoted his muddy black monster truck forward, then backward, four times until he'd turned the massive vehicle around on the rutted old country road.

Compared to Bessie, Simpson's battered black pickup looked like the loser in a bar fight as it wobbled down the road in the opposite direction, carrying its load of empty, damaged coffins to Dreadmore Village.

I, personally, was overjoyed at the prospect of not having to see Dreadmore again. Or Simpson, for that matter. As far as I was concerned, the guy was up to no good.

"I can't believe you let Simpson go," I said to Wells.

"Being creepy isn't a crime," he replied.

Grayson eyed me playfully and pressed his palms together as if in prayer. "And for that, I am truly thankful."

I smirked and elbowed Grayson in the ribs. Then I shot a glance in the rearview mirror at Bessie's payload.

Hank Chambers sat in the back left corner of the truck bed, his longish gray hair flapping in the breeze. His weathered face was tilted toward the sun, and his arms rested atop the truck bed's side and tailgate.

On the other side of the truck bed lay a broken coffin containing the pulverized remains of Lester Jenkins. Seeing as how both men smelled like "eau de dead guy," we'd voted unanimously for them to make the trip together alfresco.

"What's going to happen to poor old Lester?" Earl asked. "He can't seem to get no rest."

"I guess that'll be up to Arlene," Wells said.

"I say ixnay on an open casket," Grayson quipped.

Earl, Wells, and I groaned in unison.

Distracted, Earl hit a pothole so deep it sent our butts rising off the bench seat.

"Watch it!" Chambers called out from the back.

Earl rolled down the window. "Sorry 'bout that."

All four of our faces puckered.

"Whoo-wee!" Earl hollered, rolling up the window. "Smells like polecat stew!"

"And weed," Wells said. "Anybody else smell pot?"

Grayson and I exchanged quick glances, then we knocked heads trying to catch a glimpse through the rearview mirror. Grayson reached up and adjusted the mirror to his advantage. He took a peek and laughed. I grabbed the mirror and angled it for a peek of my own.

Chambers was sitting on Jenkins' coffin—smoking a fat number.

"Maybe it's medicinal," Grayson said to Wells.

The young cop blew out a sigh. "At this point, I honestly don't give a rat's ass."

Grayson grinned. "So what do you think's going on with this whole 'coffin-whack-a-mole' business?"

"I have no idea," Wells said. "I just hope things don't get any weirder."

"Hate to break it to you, Officer," Earl said. "But I think they just did."

He nodded toward the back of the truck. We all turned and stared.

Chambers was yammering away, a joint in one hand, and Lester Jenkins' rotting skull in the other.

I nearly swallowed my tongue and then puked it back up.

"Alas, poor Yorick," Grayson said.

I stared at him, incredulous.

He shot me a snobby look. "What? Not a Hamlet fan?"

Chapter Forty-Nine

"I TOLD YOU HE WAS ACTING fishy," Earl said, winking at me. "You ought to listen to me more, Bobbie. Just for the halibut."

"We need to get him to a hospital," Wells said.

"Exactly what I was thinking," I said, glaring at Earl.

Earl's grin melted. He blew out a breath and climbed out of the truck. We all piled out after him and scurried to the back to get a better look at Chambers. He was still in the truck bed, engrossed in a riveting conversation with his half-brother's rotting head.

"Chambers? You okay, buddy?" Wells asked.

Chambers' wild, dilated eyes darted from his brother's skull to us. His expression was one of a man who'd never seen us before, and wasn't sure he liked what he saw.

"Go away. I don't want any!" he growled.

Grayson elbowed me. "Either that was some killer ganja, or he's been bogarting the venison."

"Chambers, we need to get you to a hospital," Wells said.

"Hospital?" Chambers asked. His gaze returned to his brother's rotting head. "I thought we were going to the Poconos."

"I think we'd better hurry," I said. "He doesn't look too good."

Earl opened his mouth, but I shut it with a dirty look.

"You're right," Wells said. "Earl, once we get to the highway, step on it. I'll call Freddy—uh, Dr. Crum, and have him meet us at County Memorial."

Chapter Fifty

DR. CRUM WAS STANDING outside the ER when we arrived. Dressed in blue scrubs and a white coat, I almost didn't recognize him.

He scurried over to the truck, took a gander at Hank Chambers' Shakespearean sonata, and went as pale as his lab coat.

"Holy mother of pearl," he muttered.

"What's wrong with him, Doc?" Earl asked.

"Looks like advanced stages of Mad Cow," Crum said. "I'm still waiting on Arlene's results before I call the CDC, but Chambers here pretty much confirms my worst fears."

"What should we do with him?" Wells asked.

"I already called for a stretcher," Crum said. "I'm going to admit him, then run some tests."

Earl crinkled his nose. "Might want to hose him off, first."

Crum ignored him. "Jimmy, did you get the samples of deer meat I asked for?"

"Not yet," Wells said. "So far, we've checked the Jenkins' bunker, but came up with nothing. We've still got Jenkins' cabin and Dreadmore to search."

Crum nodded, his brow furrowed. "Well, I suggest you get on it. And hurry."

"Dr. Crum!" a woman's voice shrieked.

We turned to see a nurse running toward us. She grabbed Crum by the shoulders, nearly slamming into him. "Dr. Crum!" she panted. "Arlene Jenkins ... she's missing from her room!"

Crum's face went slack. "Oh, crap."

"It's an angel!" Chambers hollered at the nurse. He dropped Lester's skull. It rolled down the pavement and came to rest at the nurse's feet. She took one look at it and collapsed in a heap.

"Oh, crap," Crum repeated absently.

"What should we do?" I asked.

Grayson cleared his throat. "First, might I suggest—"

"Shut it. I'll take it from here," Wells said, his jaw set like a vice.

A couple of orderlies arrived with a stretcher. "You, men," Wells barked at them. "Help me load this man, then get a wheelchair for the nurse."

The orderlies looked over at Crum. He nodded. "You heard the man."

Wells turned to Grayson, Earl, and me. "I'm going to search the hospital for Arlene. You guys go back to Jenkins' cabin and see if you can find any of that contaminated venison. The sooner we get a sample, the sooner we'll have some answers."

"Yes, sir," Earl said, and saluted.

"What should we do with the rest of Lester?" Grayson asked.

"I'll call for a body bag," Crum said.

Earl sniffed the air and winced. "Better double bag him, Doc."

For once in my life, I thought Earl had a valid point.

Chapter Fifty-One

"SO HERE WE ARE, BACK at the scene of the crime," Grayson said.

Earl shifted into park. The three of us stared through the truck's windshield into the ocean of palmettos and pines that stood between us and Lester Jenkins' cabin.

An eerie feeling came over me. I felt as if the woods had been waiting for this moment all along, patiently biding its time. Something told me that the second we stepped off the crumbling asphalt, we'd be crossing into enemy territory.

Mother Nature's declaration of war.

I swallowed hard. "You got the baggies?"

Grayson nodded. "Right here in the trusty Walmart bag."

"Barbeque tongs?" I asked.

"Roger." Grayson pulled out the tongs and clapped their ends together like a pair of castanets.

"What? No barbeque sauce?" Earl quipped.

I shot my cousin a sour look. "All right, guys. Remember, nobody touch anything that even *looks* like meat. And that means you, too, Earl."

Earl laughed and opened the door. But as he climbed down out of the truck, his demeanor changed. "I hope we don't run across no zombie deers out here."

I touched Grayson's arm. "I hope we don't run across any zombie *anything*."

WE WERE ABOUT HALFWAY down the switchback trail. Earl had the machete and was in the lead, chopping at the palmettos, which seemed hell-bent on scratching raw every inch of exposed skin they could reach.

Suddenly, Earl stopped short. I nearly ran into the back of him.

"What?" I asked impatiently.

"Look at that."

Earl pointed to a scraggly vine with hairy, serrated leaves. A half-dozen yellow fruits hung from it, each roughly the size and shape of a small egg. Bands of tiny spikes, about half an inch apart, ran lengthwise down the odd fruits. One of the pods had split open, revealing a stash of shiny, pea-sized seeds, each bright red with a black spot in the center.

"What is that?" Earl asked. "Looks like Seymour ate a bunch'a eyeballs."

"Momordica charantia," Grayson said. "Genus Cucurbitaceae. Class one invasive."

"Huh?" Earl asked, touching one of the fruits.

"It's some kind of cucumber, and it's not native," I translated.

Grayson eyed me. "Pretty close. It's also known as bitter melon, bitter pear, and balsam apple."

"Can you eat it?" Earl asked.

"Sure," Grayson said.

Earl plucked the fruit and opened his mouth.

"But only when it's green and cooked," Grayson said. "Ripe like that, it can cause you to rapidly lose fluids out both ends, and quite possibly expire."

"Huh?" Earl glanced over at me, the fruit almost on his tongue.

I reached over and swatted it out of his hand.

"It's poisonous!" I hissed. "Geez, Grayson. You've got to dumb things down in situations involving imminent death!"

"Pardon me," Grayson said. "Earl, for future reference, red and yellow are nature's warning colors. Didn't Ronald McDonald teach you anything?"

Earl took a sideways look at the thorny, poisonous fruits, then smiled at me. "Thanks for having my back, Bobbie."

"Yeah. Okay. Now get going, already!"

We trudged on through a dozen more zigs and zags in the trail. I was about to get seasick when we finally spotted the small clearing in front of Jenkins' cabin.

The broken front door was half ajar. On the weathered posts holding up the front porch, a second strand of yellow police tape, torn like the first, fluttered below it in the light breeze.

"It seems nobody bothers to heed the rules out here," I said.

Earl sucked his teeth. "Now what?"

"Let's go collect some zombie meat," Grayson said. "Some for Dr. Crum, and some for me."

I eyed Grayson. "What do *you* want with it?"

His right eyebrow raised an inch. "Have I taught you *nothing?*"

I winced. "Sorry. Of course. What was I thinking?" I ambled forward, but truth be told, I didn't have a clue what Grayson was talking about.

Rain had pooled in depressions in the camouflage tarp that covered the cabin's broken-down roof. I climbed the damp, rickety stairs and crossed the front porch. Earl took hold of the doorknob and forced the warped door open, nearly taking it off its hinges.

Inside the ramshackle dwelling, the section of tarp covering the large hole in the roof had filled with rainwater like a balloon. It sagged down between the joists like a washtub-sized hernia.

"Who's the Jenkins' new designer?" Grayson quipped. "Andy Warthog?"

"Earl, don't touch that!" I shouted.

My cousin was reaching for a ragged hunk of deer meat still clinging to the clothesline. He pulled his hand back as if he'd touched a hot stove.

"Geez, Earl! Use the tongs!"

"Actually, let me do it," Grayson said. "I prefer to collect my own specimens."

Earl grimaced at the moldy meat. "Knock yourself out, Mr. G."

While Grayson whipped out the baggies and went to work, Earl and I quickly surveyed the rest of the one-room cabin. The radio equipment was gone. However, the empty wrappers from the prepper meals were still strewn about the place.

On the floor by the window, I spied the white brick Grayson and I had discovered on our first visit. Though the deer meat showed signs of being gnawed on, nothing had touched the ugly, square-shaped lump.

"What *is* that thing, Earl?" I asked, pointing to it. "Grayson thought it was a fire log. I'm thinking it's a fruitcake."

Earl scrunched his face as he studied the thing. "Well, nothing's touched it, so I'm thinking fruitcake."

I shot him half a smile. "What's with the white stuff?"

"Lemme see." Earl leaned over and picked up the bumpy, ashy brick. He grinned and shook his head. "Maybe old Jenkins was into pottery."

I snorted. "If he was, that's one butt-ugly ashtray."

Earl held the lumpy brick up to the broken out window for a better look. He took a sniff. "Whew! Kinda pungent, even for a—"

Suddenly, an arm wielding a board shot through the window and whacked Earl over the head with it. My big, bear of a cousin keeled over onto the floorboards like a felled redneck pine tree.

Chapter Fifty-Two

"WHAT THE HELL?" GRAYSON yelled and dropped one of his baggies.

"Someone's out there!" I squealed. I knelt by Earl's side. He had a nasty gash above his right eye, but he was still breathing.

Grayson dropped his other baggie and reached for his Glock, but he didn't make it. A man burst through the open cabin door and aimed a rifle at his head.

"Put your hands up!" the guy demanded.

Hidden behind a full beard, moustache, sunglasses, and a cowboy hat, it was impossible to make out the man's face.

"What do you want?" I hissed.

"You!" a woman's voice shrieked.

For a second, I thought the voice had come from the gunman. Then I caught a movement in the doorway behind him.

"I *knew* you were cheating with my Lester!"

I stared into the wild eyes of a wigged-out Arlene Jenkins.

She might've been going slowly insane, but she still had the presence of mind to get herself to a hairdresser. Her platinum blonde hairdo looked fabulous. Her AK-47, not so much.

"Tie 'em up," she barked at the man.

"Hold on," Grayson said. "We just came to collect samples. See?" He started to reach for a baggie on the floor.

"Hands behind your back or your head comes off," the man said.

Grayson obliged. The man searched around for something to tie us up with. He spied the bloody clothesline drooping with deer meat. He cut it down and stripped the dried venison from it.

"Please, not that," I said.

"Shut up!" Arlene hissed. "Make it good and tight."

From the grunts Grayson was making, the man knew how to follow orders. He finished with Grayson and looked over at me. I started to stand.

"Stay down," he demanded. He knelt beside me. I put my hands behind my back and felt the jagged specks of dried meat on the twine saw into my wrists.

Not good.

"What about *him?*" the man asked Arlene. He stood up and toed Earl's body with his boot.

"He's dying," I said. "Look, this is all some kind of misunderstanding. All we wanted was—"

"Liars!" Arlene yelled. "You came to steal Lester's gold!"

"Gold?" Grayson and I asked.

"Don't play dumb with me, tramp," Arlene hissed. "Lester told you all about his secret stash, didn't he? Two-timing jerk! Well, where is it?"

I locked eyes with Grayson, looking for a clue. His face read, "Play along."

I blew out a breath. "Okay. You got me, Arlene. Untie Grayson and he'll show you where the gold is."

"You think we're idiots?" the man asked.

You really want to know the answer to that?

"Of course not. You see, it's just that you have to walk the site off in *paces*," I said, winging it.

"*Man*-size paces," Grayson said, picking up my lead. "I've got the treasure map. Untie me and I'll show you."

"They're lying," Arlene said, and raised her AK-47. "I say we put some bullets in both of 'em."

"Hold on!" the man said. "Without the gold, we don't have enough money to get to Georgia, much less the Poconos."

"I said let's kill 'em!" Arlene shrieked.

She aimed her gun at Grayson and pulled the trigger. My mouth fell open in horror as the AK-47 blasted out ... a round of hollow clicks.

"What the hell?" Arlene screamed.

The man snatched the AK-47 from her hand. "You really think I'd trust you with a loaded gun?"

Arlene grabbed for the man's rifle. "Now you listen to me, you two-bit coffin stealer!"

"Why should I? You three-timing, dime-store floozy!"

Arlene screeched and jumped onto the man's back. As she dug her red nails into his face, he collapsed to his knees, discharging his gun as he fell.

A spray of yellow water squirted from the herniated tarp as the bullet pierced it. A second later, it ripped open and a deluge of rancid rainwater sloshed down over the pair. The unexpected cold shower halted their wrestling match for half a second, then they went right back at it, yanking hair and throwing punches.

Amidst the chaos, I heard Earl snort. I tapped him with my foot. "You okay?"

He didn't answer.

I glanced over at Grayson. He was struggling with the rope that had him tied to a post.

"What do we do now?" I whispered.

He yanked on the twine around his wrists. "Hope the man wins." He gave me a hopeful glance, then his eyes darted up and past me.

His mouth fell open.

I was tied up facing the opposite direction. I couldn't see what Grayson was looking at. But something told me things were about to get a whole lot worse.

Chapter Fifty-Three

"WHAT IS IT, GRAYSON?" I whimpered, not wanting to know.

He didn't answer. He just stared, mouth agape, at something moving behind me. I winced, set my jaw to determined, and craned my head slowly to the right.

A mere three feet away stood the most hideous creature I'd ever seen. Its eyes bobbled and pulsed in its toad-spotted skull.

It was old man Rexel.

High as a kite.

And naked.

Again.

"Where be the fine wench?" he asked, drool dripping from his leering mouth.

A thin strip of leather crossed his boney, hairless chest. It supported a quiver of arrows, their pointy heads poking up from behind his back. In his right hand was an archery bow.

"Rexel!" I yelled.

He looked my way, his eyes spinning like whirligigs.

"Hurry! Untie us!" I nodded toward the soggy pair still wrangling around amongst the foil wrappers and filth littering the floor. "They think we know where Jenkins kept his gold. Help us before they kill us!"

Rexel's eyebrow shot up, along with something else I wish I hadn't seen.

"Do ye now?" Rexel said.

"Yes, m' lord," Grayson answered.

I turned toward Grayson. His face was dead serious. He shot me a subtle wink and nodded toward Rexel. I turned my head back toward the naked avenger, just in time to see him bend over and pick up the rifle.

Ugh. Shoot me now.

Rexel aimed the gun at Arlene and the mystery man. I closed my eyes, for a myriad of reasons.

"Enough of your tomfoolery," I heard Rexel say. "Untie them, you scoundrels!"

I opened my eyes. Arlene and her accomplice were sitting on the floor, arms crossed, glaring at each other like pissed-off brats. Arlene's hairdo was in ruins. So was the man's disguise. Minus his sunglasses and false beard, I recognized him right away. It was rat-faced Samuel Simpson, the coffin peddler with the black pickup truck.

"Hold it right there," a man's groggy voice sounded. Earl had come to. He had the AK-47 trained on Rexel.

Rexel laughed like a deranged schoolgirl. He thrust out his boney, bare chest and said, "Go ahead, ye puny human! Take your best shot. You can't kill me. I'm immortal!"

Rexel swiveled the shotgun toward Earl. Earl ducked, then squeezed the trigger on the AK-47. A series of rapid, hollow clicks rattled through the cabin.

Earl's eyes doubled. "Good golly! You really *are* immortal!"

"See?" Rexel laughed maniacally. "Told you!"

He dropped his bow and danced around like a frog on a hot stove. During his performance, a gold coin fell from somewhere on his person. I didn't want to know where. It hit the floor with a *plink* and rolled to my feet.

"Well, now," Rexel said, "I'm really sorry you all had to go and see that."

"What? The dancing or the coin?" Grayson asked.

He nodded over at Earl. "You. Chewbacca. Tie up those two."

"Why?" Earl asked.

"'Cause I *said* so. You've seen my lucky coin. I can't have you knowing the secret to my charms! Nope. Looks like you're gonna have to go on a little rampage and eliminate the witnesses! Then commit suicide. Now get busy."

Rexel kept the rifle aimed at Earl as my cousin tied up an endlessly babbling Arlene Jenkins and her creepy, comb-over sidekick, Samuel Simpson.

"Why are you doing this?" I asked.

Rexel's face registered sanity for a moment. "You ever try to live on Social Security?"

"I thought you had a military pension," Grayson said.

Good one, Grayson. As if that might bring Rexel to his senses.

"War don't pay like it used to," Rexel said, scratching his naked butt cheek as his eyes glazed over again.

"Now *you*," Rexel said to Earl. "Get over there by the stove. One false move out of you and I'll fire my gun into that propane canister. Send the bulk of us to Timbuktu."

Rexel laughed as if he'd made a joke, then he tied Earl to the stove. He stripped off his quiver and walked over to the cabin door. Using the rifle for support, he bent over and reached for something.

I shook my head.

Rexel's scrawny butt is the last thing I'll ever see. Good one, universe.

"Looky what I found." Rexel straightened up and turned to face us. He grinned and waved a loaded AK-47 clip.

We all stared, slack-jawed. But it wasn't the scrawny, naked man who'd made our jaws drop. It was the creature behind him.

The one lurking in the doorway.

It struck like a blur of lightning.

Rexel fired the rifle, but by then it was already a pointless gesture.

He didn't stand a chance.

Chapter Fifty-Four

WE WATCHED IN HORROR as, in one quick strike, Rexel's leathery bald head was entirely engulfed in the mouth of the biggest damned snake I'd ever laid eyes on.

Tied to the cabin's posts with bloody twine, we were a captive audience to the grotesque drama playing out before us. With Rexel's head firmly in its jaws, the snake slowly wound its thick, thigh-sized body around Rexel's scrawny torso.

Rexel's body twitched at first, then gave up. The sickening crunch of his bones as they crushed made me nearly lose my lunch.

Arlene screamed. I closed my eyes and turned away. Unfortunately, Earl kept me up to date with a blow-by-blow account, right up until the snake had swallowed Rexel whole and slithered off into the woods.

"How's that possible?" Earl asked.

"Rexel was a small man," Grayson said. "There've been reports—"

"No," Earl said, shaking his head. "That man was immortal. That's why I didn't fight back. So how is it that snake was able to kill him?"

My face went slack. Good thing my hands were tied, or I'd have throttled Earl to death myself.

Grayson stared out the cabin door. "I hope somebody finds us before that thing comes back for dessert."

"Dessert!" Earl said. "The fruitcake!"

I cringed. "How can you think about food at a time like this?"

Grayson sneered. "Especially *fruitcake*."

"Nah!" Earl said. "That log thing on the floor over there." He nodded toward the ashy brick. "That ain't no fruitcake."

"What is it, then?" I asked.

"It's *snake* poop! I got a friend who's a herpes a'tologist. You wouldn't think it, but when them big old snakes take a dump, it can come out all square like a brick."

"Well, that solves that mystery," I said.

"It certainly does," Grayson said. "I always wondered where fruit-cakes came from."

Chapter Fifty-Five

IT WAS NEARLY DUSK when we heard Officer Wells and his brother, Gary, aka Operative Garth, calling our names.

"Mr. Gray! Pandora!"

"In here!" Grayson yelled back.

The brothers' silhouettes appeared in the doorway of the cabin.

"You're okay!" Garth said with a happy, buck-toothed grin.

His brother didn't look quite so cheerful. Pale and sweaty, it appeared as if Jimmy Wells might faint. "Thank goodness," he whispered breathlessly.

The brothers looked us over for a moment. "Sheesh. Who all's in here?" Wells asked. "Is everybody all right?"

"Yes. Pardon us if we don't give you a hug," Grayson said.

Wells blanched. "Oh. Sorry. Gary, don't just stand there. Help me untie them." He nodded over at Arlene and Simpson. "But save those two for last."

"Use gloves if you've got them," Grayson said. "The twine is covered in deer blood. It might be infected."

Wells glanced at Grayson's raw wrists. "Crap." He handed his brother some rubber gloves. Garth attended to Grayson. Wells knelt by my side.

"Can you explain to me how *all* of you ended up tied to posts?" he asked.

"It's a long story," I said. "But it all ends with Rexel."

Wells' eyebrow shot up. "You found Rexel? Where is he?"

"In the belly of the beast," Grayson said.

"A ginormous snake came and swallowed him up whole," Earl said, filling in the details.

Wells shook his head. "Not again."

"*Again?*" we said in unison.

Wells pursed his lips. "Well, nothing's been confirmed yet, but more than a few free-ranging pets have gone missing around the area. And animal control just caught an eighteen-foot python in a sewer drain yesterday."

I cringed. "You mean there's more than one of those things slithering around?"

Grayson sighed. "Invasive species are called *invasive* for a reason, Drex."

OUR SEVEN-PERSON CHAIN gang wound its way through Jenkins' crazy maze of a trail, hopefully for the last time. Garth was in the lead, followed by Simpson, Earl, Arlene, and me, with Grayson and Officer Wells bringing up the rear.

"Keep your eye out for snakes," Wells called to Garth.

"Roger that," Garth called back. He squinted through his thick lenses and swung a machete at a palmetto leaf.

"I don't get it," I said to Grayson. "Why did the snake eat Rexel, but not Lester Jenkins?"

"Maybe it got disturbed," Grayson said. "When stressed, snakes have been known to regurgitate their food. But I think he may have just been too big to swallow."

"Swallow *this*," Arlene whined, and stuck out her butt. "I'm hungry!"

Hands cuffed behind her back, Arlene's mouth was open wide as she bobbed for a pendulous yellow fruit hanging from a hairy-leaved vine.

"Stop!" I yelled, and slapped the side of her head. Hard.

She glared at me, her eyes still wild. "You! You're after my Lester, you two-timing—"

"Yadda, yadda, yadda," I said. "Save it for your statement."

"Get going up there, Jenkins," Wells barked. Arlene scowled, turned back around, and trudged down the trail.

Grayson grabbed my arm and whispered in my ear. "You're no hero. You just wanted to slap her, didn't you?"

I didn't dignify his query with an answer. But damned, it was uncanny how well that man could see right into my soul.

Chapter Fifty-Six

I WAS SHOWERING IN the RV, getting ready for a farewell meeting with the preppers at Blarney's Bar, when I noticed the small cuts on my wrists. They were red and swollen.

The bar of soap I'd been holding landed in the shower pan with a thud.

"You okay in there?" Grayson called through the door.

"I don't know. I need to show you something."

Grayson opened the bathroom door and was at the shower curtain before I could even yell, "stop."

"I didn't mean this second!" I said.

"Oh. Sorry." Grayson turned to go.

"Wait. Look at this." I stuck my arm out from behind the shower curtain. "Do you think I got infected by the deer zombie disease?"

Grayson's hand wormed its way into the shower. His wrist had the same swollen cuts.

"If you did, so did I."

All of a sudden, I felt punched in the gut. My knees buckled, and I let out a cry. Grayson stepped into the shower, clothes and all. He wrapped his arms around me.

"Are we gonna die, Grayson?"

"I don't know. But look on the bright side, Drex. Worst case scenario, we can be zombie buds together."

Chapter Fifty-Seven

I STARED AT THE MOUNTAIN of Blarney's chicken wings, but somehow they'd lost their appeal. I wasn't the only one. Grayson eyed them with disgust and sipped his beer instead. Earl, however, dug right in.

I supposed ignorance truly *was* bliss.

I figured I'd let my cousin stay uninformed of the possibility he'd been infected with mad deer disease. Ignorance suited him. Besides, there was nothing we could do to change the fact that we could, quite possibly, be dead within the year.

"Officer Wells," Grayson said, greeting the young man walking toward our booth.

"Howdy, Officer," Earl said. "Sit down and help me out with these wings. Them two love birds are off their chicken feed."

Wells studied our faces. "Why's that?"

Earl shrugged and grabbed another wing off the pile. "Beats me."

"So, what've you found out?" Grayson asked.

"We'll know more when Freddy—Dr. Crum gets here. But for now, I think I've figured out the motive."

"For Lester's murder?" Earl asked.

Wells brow furrowed. "No. I think the snake solved that. What I'm talking about is why his corpse was taken."

"Right. The old disappearing corpse act," Grayson said. "Do tell. Was it love or money?"

"As it turns out, a bit of both."

Garth joined us. "Oh goody," he said. "Pandora, you wore those pink jeans again."

I rolled my eyes and scooted over for him to join me in the booth.

"Did Jimmy tell you yet?" Garth asked. "It was a love triangle."

"More like a love *quadrangle*," Wells said.

Earl sneered. "Can't you fellers see I'm trying to eat? Keep that kinky sex talk for after dinner."

I blew out a breath. "Okay, so what are we talking about here?"

Garth started to speak, but Wells stopped him. He answered my question himself. "Long story short, it turns out that Hank Chambers, Jake Hinson, and both Jeramiah and Samuel Simpson were all after the same woman."

"Arlene Jenkins?" I asked, incredulous.

"Yeah," Wells said.

My upper lip snarled. "Why?"

Garth's grin made me want to go take another shower. "You should know why, Pandora. They were all after her sexy breeding hips."

My nose crinkled. "I thought they wanted Lester's gold."

"Gold?" Wells asked.

"Yeah. I gave you the coin that fell out of his ... uh ... that Rexel had, you know, somewhere on his person."

Wells cocked his head. "That thing? It was a commemorative coin from last year's Strawberry Festival. Worth exactly squat."

"Then why was Rexel ready to kill for it?" I asked.

Earl laughed. "Why'd he think he was Cupid? That's what *I* wanna know."

Wells stifled an eye roll at Earl. "I ran some background on him. Turns out Rexel was discharged from the military for failing a psychiatric evaluation back in 1978."

"Okay, so that's Rexel covered," Grayson said. "He was one brick shy of a load. But what about the whole body-in-a-coffin shell game?"

Wells nodded. "From what I could piece together, after Lester Jenkins died Arlene found out he'd let all his life insurance policies lapse except for one—the five thousand dollars to bury him. I think we could all agree that could righteously piss a woman off."

We all nodded.

Wells chewed his cheek. "I think Arlene decided not to waste the money burying Lester. She and Hank Chambers decided to get rid of his body on the cheap. The trouble was, he'd already been delivered to Mc-Greggor Funeral Parlor. So Chambers had to bust him out."

"It's a dirty job, but somebody's got to do it," Earl quipped.

Wells shook his head. "So Chambers is pulling Lester out the window at McGreggor's when he gets caught by one or more of Arlene's other suitors. Either Jeremiah or Samuel Simpson, or both. Maybe even Jake Hinson, their assistant."

"That's when the crap really hit the fan," Grayson said.

"Exactly how I see it," Wells said. "Chambers tries to explain the predicament—that he and Arlene needed the money to run off to the Poconos to get married—and the jig is up because Arlene had promised *every one of those guys* the same thing."

I snorted. "And she said *I* was the two-timing floozy!"

"So how did Chambers end up in a coffin?" Grayson asked.

"That part's still not totally clear," Wells said. "I think the three spurned lovers—Jake and the Simpsons—conspired together to get rid of their main rival. They had the motive and means to seal Chambers in a coffin and haul him out to Dreadmore with his brother, Lester."

"Dispose of both of them in the back forty of a prepper compound," Grayson said. "That's two birdbrains buried with one stone."

"Right," Wells said. "But Samuel's accident with the truck foiled those plans. When the coffins dumped and broke apart, he and Jake weren't able to subdue Chambers. He came out of the box swinging. Chambers was beating those two to a pulp. That's why Samuel called the police for help."

"But Chambers said the last thing he remembered was being at Arlene's," I argued.

"And them three scrawny old men would a had a heck of a time gettin' Hank Chambers to go willingly into a pine box," Earl said.

"Arlene had to be involved," Grayson said. "I think she saved a sedative syringe from Dr. Crum and pumped it into Chambers when he wasn't looking."

I chewed my lip. "Why?"

"Chambers had just divorced," Wells said. "He was actually planning on marrying Arlene. He'd already changed the beneficiary on his life insurance policy to her."

"That meant Chambers had to die for her to collect," I said.

"Right." Wells took a sip of water and continued. "Arlene met Samuel Simpson when she called around for cheap ways to bury Lester's body. Samuel and she worked out some kind of deal, for love, money, whatever. But then Jake got involved and wanted his cut. Again, for love or money, I'm not sure at this point."

My nose crinkled. "But back at the cabin, Arlene was arguing with Samuel Simpson as if she hated him."

Grayson snorted. "Maybe because she figured he would end up being just like Lester, only with worse breath."

"Maybe," I said. "Or maybe she just wanted to break free of the whole prepper scene."

"Why?" Wells asked.

I shrugged. "Think about it from Arlene's perspective. What would be the use of surviving in a world with no gel nails or peroxide?"

"Or cosmetic procedures," Crum said, walking up to the table.

"What's up, Doc?" Earl said. "Thanks for the staples." He lifted his bangs to reveal his Frankenstein starter set.

Crum was eyeing me and Grayson. The look on his face made my gut flop. He didn't appear to be the bearer of good news.

"What have you been able to find out?" I asked as he took a seat in the chair at the end of the booth. I could barely see him over the mountain of chicken bones on the table.

A waitress came over. "One more order of wings," Dr. Crum said, "and a beer. A *big* beer."

I glanced over at Grayson. His eyes met mine. He pursed his lips.

"Let me start with the good news first," Crum said. "Jenkins' brain biopsy showed no signs of transmissible spongiform encephalopathy." He glanced over at Earl. "That means no zombie deer disease."

I shot Grayson a small, hopeful smile.

"But it's too soon to tell about Arlene," Crum said.

"It's got to be zombie deer disease," Garth said. "What else could make those dingbats start living the *la vida loca?*"

"You of all people should know the answer to that," Crum said, staring at him sourly.

Garth frowned. "What are you talking about, Doc?"

"You smoke weed," Crum said. "Hank Chambers came to the hospital higher than a kite on Mars."

Garth blanched. "I've been known to inhale, sure. But I never stripped naked and climbed a water tower."

"I know," Crum said. "And that got me to thinking, what would make someone do that?"

"Zombie deer meat," Earl said.

"Thanks for that suggestion," Crum said tiredly. "However, I may have another explanation."

"What?" I asked.

"Embalming fluid."

"What?" I asked again, nearly choking on my iced tea.

Crum blew out a breath. "You see, when Chambers' blood tested positive for marijuana, I searched his clothes and tested the stub I found in his pocket. It came back positive for methanol, formaldehyde, and ethanol. Embalming fluid."

"So?" I asked.

"Those are the same basic ingredients in the street drug, PCP."

"Would that explain his crazy behavior?" Wells asked. "The man was talking to a *skull*."

"Yes, it would," Crum said. "Typical effects include both visual and auditory hallucinations. So, more than likely, in Chambers' mind, Lester's severed head was talking back to him."

"I'd loved to have heard *that* conversation," Grayson said.

"What about climbing a water tower?" Wells asked.

"Actually, it makes perfect sense, now that I think about it," Crum said. "People under the influence of PCP report feelings of invincibility, euphoria, and an overwhelming desire to disrobe."

"What about archery?" Earl asked.

Crum ignored him and turned to Garth. "It also gives some people a strong distaste for meat. Didn't you say you're a vegetarian?"

Garth nearly choked on his beer. "Sometimes. But you just saw me eat a chicken wing!" He shot a glance at his brother. "I swear, Jimmy. I've got nothing to do with this. I didn't even sell them a brownie!"

Wells frowned. "I believe you. And I guess we can all think of a few people who might be able to get their hands on some embalming fluid."

Chapter Fifty-Eight

IT WAS TUESDAY MORNING, and we'd survived another night at the Wells' friendly neighborhood doomsday compound.

"You know, I think I'm going to miss all this junk," Grayson said.

I peered out the window of the RV at the rusted hull of a harvest-gold washing machine. A small tree had sprouted in its drum.

My eyebrows furrowed to a point. "Why would you miss camping in a junkyard?"

Grayson set his coffee mug on the counter. "Think about it. It's the perfect camouflage."

Given the condition of the RV's exterior, Grayson's statement was one of the few that had made real sense in the past couple of days.

A knock on the door saved me from having to reply. I opened it to find Officer Wells nodding at me.

"Morning. Coffee?" I asked.

Wells shot me a grateful smile. "Sure. I could drink a cup."

"Come in. Have a seat," Grayson called out.

Wells ambled inside and slid into the banquette. I handed him a steaming cup of coffee.

"What's up?" I asked.

The young cop shifted in his seat. "Before you two left, I wanted to let you know that Crum called me. The meat from Jenkins' cabin tested negative for chronic wasting disease."

I gasped. "So ... we're in the clear?"

"Looks like," Wells said.

"That's great!" I patted Wells on the shoulder and smiled at Grayson. He winked and gave me a subtle nod.

"From what I've been able to gather, Samuel Simpson and Arlene are the masterminds of this whole mess," Wells said.

"What's going to happen to them?" I asked.

"Simpson confessed to tripping out Arlene with embalming fluid-laced joints. But we're still not sure whose idea it was to bury Hank Chambers alive."

"Maybe you can get that snake to squeeze the truth out of 'em," Earl said, emerging from the bathroom.

Wells shook his head. "Since Chambers is still alive, and you three decided not to press charges for false imprisonment, Arlene might get to take that trip to the Poconos after all—with Chambers, one of the Simpsons, or whoever."

I shook my head. *Now that's what you call spoiled for choice. Not.*

Wells' police radio crackled.

"I better take this," he said and got up from the table. He shook hands with Grayson and me. "It's been weird, but I have to say, it's still been a pleasure meeting you all."

"We feel the same," Grayson said. "Take care and be safe."

"You, too." Wells smiled, then disappeared out the door.

"I guess I better be takin' off directly myself," Earl said. He turned to Grayson. "Before I do, can you answer me something, EB?"

Grayson shot him a look. "EB? You think I'm an extraterrestrial being?"

"Huh?" Earl's eyebrows converging below his staple line. "Well, there's a thought. But nah. I meant Encyclopedia Britannica. On account a you got all that crazy knowledge up in your brain."

"Oh." Grayson's enigmatic smile faded a notch. "What do you want to know?"

"All these prepper fellers we got tangled up with. They called themselves mercenaries. But as far as I could tell, there weren't 'nary a mercy among 'em. Would you say that's ironical or apropos?"

Grayson's right eyebrow shot up. He gave me a weird glance, then stood up and patted Earl on the shoulder. "Some questions just don't have any clear-cut answers, Earl." He nodded toward the restroom. "You done in there?"

"Yeah."

"Take care. Hope to see you soon, as far as you know."

Earl smiled. "You, too."

I looked up at my bear of a cousin. "Thanks for coming. You really helped us out."

"I dunno about that, Bobbie. I think I might a just got in the way. You had to save my hide more'n once."

I grinned. "You saved mine back."

Earl smiled. "Bobbie, I think you might a found where you belong."

I frowned. "You mean with Grayson? For the umpteenth time, Earl, we're just friends."

"That's not what Grandma Selma said."

My eyes bulged. "Don't tell me you're seeing ghosts!"

"Nah. I'm talking about that dream you told me about. You know, where she was in the coffin with you, stirring that pot of poop."

"Are you saying I'm stirring up crap?"

Earl blanched. "What? Heck, no!"

"What then?"

"In your dream, Granny offered you a spoonful, didn't she?"

"Yeah."

"I think she's tellin' you not to poop where you eat."

My jaw flexed. "Ugh! Earl, Grayson and I are just business partners!"

Earl nodded at me skeptically. "Well, it might be good to keep it that way. 'Cause, like I said, I think you're damned good."

I cringed and stared at the floor. "At messing things up? Yeah, I'm good at that all right."

"No, Bobbie." Earl took my chin in his huge hand and gently tugged my face upward until my eyes met his. "You're good at being an investigator. It's your calling. I can just feel it."

"Really?" My eyes filled with tears. "Like yours is to be a mechanic?"

Earl shrugged. "Yeah. For now. But life don't stay the same forever. You know that, cuz"

I smiled. "I know. Keep the garage afloat for me, will you?"

Earl nodded. "You know I will."

I thought Earl would turn and go. But he just stood there, staring at me expectantly. Finally, he winked and said, "Come on. Say it."

"Say what?"

He grinned. "You know what."

I laughed. "Earl, you're fired."

He snorted. "Ahh, now *that's* what I been missin'."

I smiled. "Speaking of missing, I want to give you back Lucky Red."

Earl frowned. "You sure?"

"Yeah." I grabbed the ball cap from atop the ugly alien lamp. "My hair's growing in, and ET doesn't like being affiliated with the tobacco industry."

Earl shot me a look. "Ok. Whatever that means. You take care now, Bobbie."

"You, too, Earl."

As he stepped out the door, Earl turned and waved to the little green lizard in the terrarium. "Bye, Gizzard." He winked at me, then squeezed his big frame out the door. Right before he closed it, I heard him say, "Bye, Garth!"

A moment later, the door opened again. A beaver with a blond mullet stuck his head in and grinned at me.

"Just came by to say goodbye," Garth said. "It's been a pleasure, Pandora. Where's Mr. Gray?"

I nodded toward the bathroom. "Indisposed."

Garth smiled and shook his head wistfully. "They say even the great ones do it. Tell him goodbye for me, will you?"

"Sure."

"I'll miss you most of all," Garth said, looking down at my breeding-stock hips.

"Right," I said, and closed the door.

With Grayson in the shower, I finally had a moment to text Beth-Ann. I picked up my cell phone and looked at the date. I smiled. I'd survived beyond the expiration date she'd predicted. I tapped a message into the phone.

It's Tuesday and I'm still alive.

A few seconds later, my phone chirped with her reply.

Glad to hear it. Now call me today or I'm going to track you down and kill you myself.

I grinned and gave her a call.

Chapter Fifty Nine

"BREEDER HIPS," I SAID to Grayson as he came out of the bathroom. "All of this craze about breeder hips. I just don't understand preppers."

"You and Arlene have that in common. Embrace your similarities."

I gave Grayson a dirty look. "I've got nothing in common with Arlene Jenkins or *any* of those other guys."

"I wouldn't be so sure. From the stories I heard, you and Lester appeared to have shared a certain propensity for getting drunk and—"

I slapped a hand over Grayson's mouth. "If what you're about to say has anything to do with that night at the campfire, please don't tell me."

Grayson grinned. "Have it your way. What say we have one more cup of coffee and hit the road. You ready?"

"Am I *ever*."

THE CHAIN LINK GATE swung open with a high-pitched *squeal*. "Thank you for your hospitality, Operative Garth," Grayson said into the intercom. "We'll be in touch."

"That would be awesome cool," Garth's voice crackled over the speaker.

Grayson hit the gas, and we sputtered down the dirt driveway in reverse. As he maneuvered the RV onto the paved road, I looked over at him and grinned mischievously.

"What?" he asked, shifting into first gear.

I stifled a smirk. "Sorry your theory about a half-goat, half-man didn't *pan* out."

Grayson shook his head and groaned.

I laughed. "Come on, Grayson. You *had* to have seen that one coming."

Grayson sighed. "I wasn't expecting a sneak attack from my own partner."

Partner. I like the sound of that.

I sat back and watched through the window as the occasional trailer peeked out from amongst the palmettos and pine trees. We rode on in silence until the sign for the interstate loomed ahead.

"So, where to now?" I asked.

Grayson grinned and waggled his eyebrows. "Well, seeing as how we're both still practically bald, it would be the perfect time to join the Hari Krishnas."

I laughed. "You're aware that I now know how to kill you with a Tootsie Pop, right?"

He smirked. "You got any left?"

I fished in my purse and handed him a green sucker. I unwrapped a blue one, stuck it in my mouth, and tossed the wrapper onto the floorboard. Grayson neatly folded his wrapper and tucked it in the ashtray.

OCD freak.

Grayson shifted the Tootsie Pop to his left cheek. "Okay, now I've got something for you."

"What?"

Grayson reached into his shirt pocket and pulled out a silver badge. "Here," he said, handing it to me. "I think you've earned it."

I grinned and grabbed the badge. My smile faded. "This says *Official Donut V.I.P.*"

Grayson shrugged. "Hey, you've got to start somewhere."

I blew out a sigh. Becoming a private eye was a lot harder than I thought it would be. But it had its perks. According the badge, I was now an official V.I.P.

"You ready for your next assignment?" Grayson asked.

"Sure. What is it?" I asked, pinning the badge to my purse.

"Your pick. At the moment, I've got reports about vanishing vets in New Port Richey, or a killer tomato in Ruskin."

I looked up at the fluffy clouds in the sky for an answer.

Hey. You up there. I need a sign.

In the distant blue horizon loomed a behemoth strawberry—Plant City's world-famous water tower. I smiled and turned to Grayson.

"Is a tomato a fruit or a vegetable?"

Grayson shot me a curious glance. "A fruit. Why?"

"I've dealt with enough fruits for the time being. Let's go find some missing vets."

"East it is," Grayson said, and turned right toward I-275.

The End

I HOPE YOU ENJOYED Dr. Prepper. If you did, it would be freaking fantastic if you would post a review on Amazon, Goodreads and/or Book-Bub. You'll be helping me keep the series going! Thanks in advance for being so awesome!

https://www.amazon.com/dp/194998902X#customerReviews

Where do Drex and Grayson go from here?

Find out in Oral Robbers!

Oral Robbers

FREAKY FLORIDA MYSTERY Adventures, Book 2
By Margaret Lashley

Prologue

I MADE IT THROUGH MY first official "investigation" with Nick Grayson without getting fired or taking an extended dirt nap.

In other words, I accomplished two of the three goals I'd set out for myself. The third—not falling for the guy—well, that one's still a little sketchy.

Traveling with Grayson in his ratty old Winnebago means he's always close.

Irritatingly close.

And every time we bump into each other, I get this weird, electric feeling.

Is it love? Is it hate? Is it an ungrounded electrical socket?

I really can't say for sure. But I read somewhere that love and hate sit side-by-side on the emotional scale—and that the true opposite of love is *indifference.*

Indifference is definitely *not* what I feel for Grayson.

Maybe the right word is *grateful*—albeit, begrudgingly so.

Grayson snatched me, kicking and screaming, out of my dead-end life as a second-rate mall cop. Then he shoved me, head-first, into his crazy, disco world of monster a-go-go.

Investigating reports of the unexplained with Grayson can be bizarre.

Dangerous, even.

But boring? No.

I *totally* give him that much.

Chapter One

"HOLD STILL, DREX. AND take that Tootsie Pop out of your mouth."

"Why?"

I glared into the eyes of Nick Grayson. He was my boss, private-eye instructor, and current owner of the world's cheesiest moustache.

We were in a sleazy motel off US 19, just outside New Port Richey. I was in bed, propped up on mysteriously lumpy pillows. Grayson, a physicist turned conspiracy-theory nut, was hovering over me, pasting electrodes onto my scalp.

His eyes gleamed maniacally as he hooked me up to his electroencephalogram machine. His plan was to scare whatever miniscule amount of wits I had left right out of my half-shaved noggin.

Fun times.

The last time Grayson strapped me to his EEG contraption, he'd shocked me to the core with a video of gray-skinned aliens being ambushed by military-style Rambos. After the mysterious militia freed three kids from glass holding tubes, they'd freed the aliens of their oversized heads.

Not pretty. Not pretty at all.

As I lay there, I still had no idea whether that bizarre video was real or not. I wasn't sure Grayson knew, either. And, for the time being, it didn't matter. Half an hour ago, I'd experienced something that had scared the bejeebers out of me even more—and it hadn't come from Grayson's test program.

I sat up in bed and frowned at Grayson. "Why can't I keep the Tootsie Pop?"

Grayson glanced up from fiddling with a knob on the EEG monitor. "You might choke on it. Besides, it's a crutch, Drex."

I scowled. "A crutch?"

Grayson locked his mesmerizing green eyes on mine. Dressed all in black, the wiry, fortyish man with the washboard abs had a mysterious hold on me. At times, I wanted to kiss him. Other times, I wanted to run from him—screaming. But most times, I felt compelled to follow his lead, glued to his side by my own twisted curiosity.

"An oral fixation," he said, studying me like I was his favorite new lab rat. "Like smoking. Or chewing gum. Typically brought on by insufficient breastfeeding during infancy."

My eyes narrowed. "Are you saying I have *mommy* issues?"

He smirked. "If the sucker fits ...."

I shot Grayson some side-eye. "That's rich coming from a guy with two navels. As far as *I* know, *you* came out of a test tube."

Grayson's eyebrows wagged below his stubble-covered head, which was usually covered by a black fedora. "An excellent argument for why I *don't* have mommy issues, I'd say. Now lose the Tootsie Pop and lay down."

I plucked the sucker from my mouth and put it in an ashtray on the nightstand. Cringing with disgust, I cautiously laid back onto the mystery-stain pillows. "Satisfied?"

"Yes." Grayson glanced at the used red Tootsie Pop. "But if *you* were, you wouldn't need *that* thing."

I scowled. "Just fire up your gross-out program before I change my mind."

Grayson's right cheek dimpled, a sure sign that a deviant smile lurked beneath his bushy black moustache. He snatched my Tootsie Pop from the ashtray and stuck it in his mouth.

Gross.

His right cheek bulged as he clicked a key on his laptop computer, then handed it to me. The screen blinked to life in my hands. On it, a yellow emoji face grinned above the words, "Welcome to My World!"

The ludicrous cliché was so on target I nearly laughed out loud. Grayson certainly lived in another world, all right. And, like some sort of pseudo-Stockholm Syndrome victim, I was slowly becoming part of it.

I'd just finished the first two weeks of my internship with Grayson. It had been a crazy ride—akin to costarring in a low-budget remake of *The X-Files*.

In redneck Florida.

In a rundown RV.

Let's just say, I wasn't expecting a call from Hollywood anytime soon.

"Okay. Here we go," Grayson said.

I glanced over at him. Something about his expression triggered my fight-or-flight response.

But it was way too late to make a run for it now.

Besides, it wasn't exactly like my life was brimming with other possibilities. Who else but Grayson would've taken on a reluctant, wet-behind-the-ears private-eye wannabe like me?

I'd been under the influence of vodka when I'd ordered a detective correspondence course from a late-night infomercial. And I'd been so angry I couldn't see straight when I'd handed over my family's auto repair business to my cousin Earl.

Suffice it to say, at 37, I was a tad behind schedule on my plan to retire at 45. Broke, angry, and recovering from being shot in the head, I'd been headed for a meltdown.

Instead, a meltdown found me.

Grayson's arrival at my auto-repair shop in his busted Winnebago had been the catalyst that had spawned the perfect storm—a tornado of emotions powerful enough to blow the remnants of my old life to smithereens. When he'd offered to provide the two years of training I needed to become a real private investigator, I'd jumped at the chance—and into his RV.

And now, here I was, in a sleazy hotel room, my shaved scalp glued by electrodes to a mind-altering machine invented by, quite possibly, a madman.

But, in all honesty, nobody had forced me to drink Grayson's crazy Kool-Aid. I'd made my very own pitcherful, spiked it with vodka, and willingly downed every last drop.

I blew out a sigh, slapped on a determined face, and gave Grayson a thumb's up. He nodded, then turned his attention back to the display panel on the EEG machine.

I glanced down at the computer in my lap and braced for impact. My job was to observe the macabre images that would soon be popping up on its screen. Grayson's task was to monitor my alpha brainwave activity during the test. The more alpha waves I produced, the more relaxed my nervous system was.

The concept behind Grayson's self-designed program was to help him—and now *me*—gain control over the physical reactions any sane person instinctively experienced when encountering the weird, the freaky, and the blatantly bizarre.

As Grayson had so artfully enumerated, "Screaming, pissing one's pants, fainting, and/or running for one's life aren't particularly helpful tactics when it comes to investigating unexplained phenomena."

He was right. Thanks to his tutelage, I'd already gained first-hand experience with all of the above. As a result, I was now eager to up my game.

"I'm ready," I said. "Let her rip."

Grayson nodded. "Okay. Here we go."

The screen on the laptop blinked. The yellow smiley face disappeared. In its place came the image of a cute, golden-haired little girl prancing in a field of daisies.

"Good. The baseline's set," Grayson said.

The next image appeared. It was the little girl again. This time, her mouth morphed into an evil grin, complete with a set of blood-dripping Dracula fangs.

My pulse quickened. I glanced up at Grayson.

He was staring at the monitor. His eye ticked like he was experiencing the early stages of Tourette's.

My alpha waves must've taken a hit.

I took a deep breath to calm myself. A moment later, the screen changed to a vintage, black-and-white video clip of *Nosferatu,* rising straight up from his coffin like the world's creepiest post-mortem erection.

Geez. Nosferatu doesn't mean "hideously ugly vampire" for nothing.

My heart skipped a beat. I breathed through it.

"Good," Grayson said, his eyes glued to the EEG display.

The image on the screen switched back to full color. A green-skinned, yellow-eyed vampire lunged toward me, snapping his bloody fangs at me like a ravenous piranha.

Breathe deep. It isn't real.

"You're not telling yourself it isn't real again, are you?" Grayson asked.

I flinched. "Why would you say that?"

"Because your alpha waves are remaining unusually high. Either you're mastering this, or you're still in denial."

I bit my lip. "What's so wrong with denial?"

Grayson eyed me. "Well, for one thing, in the case of a *real* encounter, it could get you killed."

I rolled my eyes at the ceiling. "I mean *besides* that."

Grayson frowned. "Don't you value your life?"

Maybe I would if I actually had one.

I shrugged. "Sure."

"Humph," Grayson grunted, and turned back to the EEG monitor.

In a way, I envied Grayson. The man had a distinct mission in life. He was absolutely certain that unknown creatures were hiding out in the nooks and crannies of rural Florida, and that, one day, we would be the ones to prove it.

In the past two weeks, we'd definitely shared some undeniably odd experiences. But whether what we'd encountered had been real or merely hoaxes, hallucinations, or the residual effects of brain damage, was still up for debate as far as I was concerned.

I'd yet to come across anything I could, with absolute certainty, say was "the real deal."

But then again, my life to date had presented me with very few "real deals." Instead, I'd honed my cynical chops on dead-end jobs, cheating boyfriends, and a mother who'd scammed me out of knowing my real father.

And now, here I was, hitching my wagon to a man who got his jollies searching for freaks of nature.

The irony made me nearly laugh out loud.

Was *I* Grayson's latest freak, or was *he* mine?

Chapter Two

LIKE MOST OF MY LIFE to date, things were going more than a tiny bit off-plan. But this time, for once, the misdirection was in my favor.

By now, Grayson and I should've been in Ruskin, Florida, investigating a story about killer tomatoes.

But this morning, as we'd watched Plant City's humongous strawberry water tower disappear in the rearview mirror, my P.I. mentor had given me the choice between the Ruskin tomato gig and checking out some sketchy dealings going on in a nursing home in New Port Richey.

Having been to Ruskin before, choosing the nursing home had been a no-brainer. Grayson, on the other hand, had apparently had his heart set on the homicidal fruit.

In an effort to maintain what he called, "a professional level of democratic decision-making," Grayson had challenged me to a thumb-wrestling match. Winner take all.

He'd failed to inform me of his secret weapon. The double-jointed jerk won best two out of three in no time flat.

Deadly tomatoes, it seemed, had been about to become an imminent part of my future. I'd been contemplating asking Grayson for a rematch when a call buzzed in on the old ham radio mounted under the Winnebago's dashboard.

Someone was calling Grayson's nutter hotline.

Little did we know then that our destiny was about to be changed by a bucktoothed weirdo with a blond mullet hairdo and a giant wimp of a dog named Tooth.

What he told Grayson and me would soon have us seeing red—but tomatoes would have nothing to do with it.

Chapter Three

I WAS RUBBING MY SORE wrestling thumb when the unexpected transmission crackled over the ham radio, sending an electric buzz through the cab of the vintage RV.

"Oh gee double-oh seven to Mr. Gray. Come in, Mr. Gray. Over."

I recognized the squeaky voice instantly. It belonged to one of our new conspiracy-chasing allies—a *Wayne's World* wannabe we'd dubbed "Operative Garth."

The thought of the skinny, bucktoothed redneck and his secret junk-yard compound made me smile. All in all, Garth was a good egg, as far as cracked ova went.

"Double oh seven?" I laughed and shot Grayson a look. "Is that prepper code for geek or nerd?"

Grayson's lips curled slightly as he reached under the dashboard for the radio. He unhooked the microphone and held it to his lips. "Gray here. Over."

"News flash," Operative Garth said. "Caught more buzz this morning about Banner Hill. Another vet reported missing this morning. Over."

"So, it's not an anomaly after all. Thanks for the intel, OG." Grayson replied in a tone that was serious, yet somehow mocking. I suddenly suspected I might be the foil in a new Leslie Nielsen movie.

Naked Nerd 33 1/3.

"My honor, Mr. Gray," Garth squeaked. "Over."

"Same MO?" Grayson asked. "Over."

"Yeah. Disappeared without a trace. Over."

"Any speculation on causation? Over."

"Money's on organ reapers," Garth responded. "Or body snatchers. Any theories? Over."

Grayson's right eyebrow flat-lined. "Too soon to speculate. But a third victim definitely thickens the plot. Keep in contact OG. Reward if tip pans out. Over."

"Cool!" Garth blurted. A moment later, he hastily added, "Over."

I imagined Garth grinning like a donkey, pushing his thick, black-framed glasses up on his pug nose.

"So, what gives?" I asked as Grayson hung up the mic. "I thought we were going to Ruskin."

"That's three veterans in less than a week. Vanished like Draino down a dump hole. Something's definitely up."

I eyed him skeptically. "Why? Is three some kind of magic number?"

Grayson kept his eye on the road. "Three drops the probability of random coincidence to near zero."

My brow furrowed. "But who in their right mind would kidnap veterans from a nursing home?"

"Exactly," Grayson said, nodding thoughtfully. "No one. Unless they had a good use for them."

A good use for old men? Now there's *a probability of near zero.*

"What about body snatchers?" I asked. "You know, like Garth said."

Grayson shook his head. "Not likely. As far as we know, they were still alive when they were taken."

My nose crinkled at the thought. "Organ reapers?"

"Doubtful. These guys are too old to be of any use for organ transplants."

I lifted my ball cap and scratched the auburn stubble growing in atop my shaved head. I knew Grayson wouldn't be satisfied until there was some screwball angle to the chase. I, on the other hand, just wanted to hang on for another 102 weeks to complete my P.I. internship.

"What about ritual sacrifice?" I offered. "To satiate demonic lust?"

"Hmm. A buffet of human organs." Grayson rubbed his chin as he pondered the idea. "You hungry?" He turned to me and smirked. "How about liver and onions for lunch?"

I shook my head.

Only you, Grayson. Only you.

Chapter Four

LIKE ASTEROIDS COLLIDING in space, Operative Garth's intel had sent Grayson and me careening off on another trajectory. After a quick stop for gas, we'd shifted gears and direction, setting Ruskin and its murderous crop of tomatoes aside for another season.

The disappearance of a third veteran from a New Port Richey nursing home had piqued Grayson's curiosity. With his weird-o-meter recalibrated, for once the universe had redirected us in my favor.

Our new destination required us to head west, toward the Gulf coast. I-4 would've been the most direct route, but definitely not the most reliable.

It was late November. Tourist season was in full swing.

We both knew all too well that I-4 would be clogged with Thanksgiving holiday traffic. With millions of white knuckles wrapped around fake-leather steering wheels, this time of year the only blessing from God that Floridians could count on was a rental-car invasion of biblical proportions.

Given the annual plague of travelers hell-bent on getting to Disney World for a relaxing family vacation, one tiny fender-bender could set off a road-warrior-style apocalypse.

So we took SR 39 north instead, and headed toward Zephyrhills.

After driving by cow pastures, rundown rural churches, and an ugly stretch of sprawl missing its urban, we hung a left on CR 54 and headed west, where we were treated to yet another string of trailer parks, strip malls, housing developments, and dollar stores littering the landscape like hurled garbage.

It was the side of Florida never featured on a postcard.

By the time we reached the outskirts of Zephyrhills, both of us were mesmerized by monotony, and hungry as all get-out. Thankfully, it was my turn to pick a place to eat.

When I spied Sargent Pizza, I practically yelled in Grayson's ear.

"Stop here!" I jabbed a finger at the low-rent pizza joint. Its checkered past as a failed convenience store was as obvious as a girdle on a goose.

Grayson frowned. "Why there?"

"I'm in the mood for pepperoni," I said. But that was a lie. I'd have chomped down on a lawn-clipping sandwich at Katie's House of Kale if that's what it would've taken to ensure liver and onions wasn't on the menu.

THE INTERIOR OF SARGENT Pizza appeared to have been fitted out entirely with furniture stolen from somebody's dead grandma.

Grayson sat across a scarred oak table from me, sipping coffee and waiting on his anchovy pizza. The only other patron in the place was some lady languishing in a corner booth. Judging by her outfit, she was either a hooker or she was blind and had been dressed by one.

"How much further to New Port Richey?" Grayson asked, adjusting the floral cushion tied to his chair by a dirty bow.

I knew his question was just a ploy to make me practice using my smart phone. But after perusing Sargent Pizza's menu and finding no organ meats on offer, I was feeling smugly generous.

I pulled my cellphone from my purse and punched a few buttons, trying not to let my fear of technology set my teeth to grinding. To my surprise, with very little prompting, a map with several routes and timeframes popped up on the screen.

Huh. Maybe Google Maps wasn't designed explicitly to spy on me in my underwear, after all.

I showed the routes to Grayson. "Looks like maybe another hour or two, give or take traffic."

Grayson gave me a quick nod, then removed his fedora and rubbed the stubble growing in on his head. Like me, we were both sporting a buzz cut. Mine, hidden under a ball cap, was courtesy of an over-exuberant ER staff when I'd been struck in the forehead by a ricochet bullet a few weeks ago.

Grayson's shaved head was self-inflicted—an attempt to achieve more accurate results from his EEG contraption. Or, at least, that was the story he'd told me. And, so far, he was sticking to it.

Grayson opened his laptop, but before he could click the power button, the pizza arrived. It was delivered to our table by a short, roundish man in his late fifties. Shockingly, the guy was sporting a moustache bushy enough to give Grayson's a run for its money.

I secretly found myself worrying that the close proximity of two Freddie Mercury-style moustaches might set off some kind of planetary disturbance that could end the world as we knew it. Then I secretly worried why in the world I would think such a thing ....

I've either sustained serious brain damage, or Grayson and his conspiracy theories are turning my mind to mush.

"Enjoy," the waiter said, leaning closer to Grayson as he set down the pizza.

I cringed and held my breath as the moustaches grew nearer and nearer to each other—just in case my theory had any merit ....

But then, as suddenly as he'd appeared, the waiter turned and left. No black hole appeared. No rift in the time-space continuum occurred. The guy didn't even leave a greasy skid mark.

I breathed a sigh of relief—and caught a whiff of cheese and freshly baked crust.

Maybe the heavenly aroma somehow counteracted The Moustache Effect. Or maybe I've officially gone insane ....

I glanced down at the pizza. It was as big around as a bicycle tire, and took up most of our table. Half the pie was garnished with pepperoni. The other half was rendered inedible by blackish-gray strips of dead fish.

Anchovies. Yuck.

"Looks good," Grayson said, and folded his laptop closed, oblivious to how close we'd come to planetary annihilation.

I shot him a look. "At least *my* half does."

"What've you got against anchovies?"

"Nothing. Just a rule my Grandma Selma taught me. Never order fish from a roadside restaurant that used to be a 7-11."

Grayson shrugged. "Suit yourself." He took a bite from an anchovy slice. His face went slack.

"Something wrong?" I asked.

"No." He forced a smile and another chew.

I smirked and picked up a slice from the pepperoni side. The melted mozzarella stretched like rubber all the way from the pan to my mouth.

Grayson discretely spit his mouthful into a napkin. "Trade you a slice."

I smirked. "Not a chance."

"Come on. What's it worth to you?"

I took another bite. "Mmm. This is *delicious.*"

His eyes fixated on my side of the pizza. "One slice. I'll let you pick the radio station."

I licked my lips and stared him square in the eye. "Let me drive the RV."

Grayson nearly choked on his own air supply. "What? Not a chance!"

I might've had mommy issues, but Grayson was totally OCD. And when it came to driving his RV?

Total. Bloody. Control. Freak.

"Why not?" I argued. "We're traveling backroads. Come on. Let me drive. That way, you can ... you can work on your computer."

I watched Grayson mull it over as he stared at my pizza. I knew his hesitation. It wasn't because the ratty old RV itself was worth much. The outside of the 1967 Winnebago looked like a traveling algae farm that had somehow survived a Cat 4 hurricane.

No. His concern was about what was on the *inside*.

Grayson had spent lord-knows-how-much money converting the RV's small bedroom into an electromagnetic monster trap, complete with steel walls, caged windows, and eight massive deadbolts on the door. He'd also crammed the cabinets in the Minnie Winnie with all kinds of spy equipment and secret potions and stuff. To Grayson, that junk was probably irreplaceable. Not to mention, the hoarder had stashed stacks of cash behind the paneling in the walls.

I smiled and chewed my pizza patiently. For once, I had the upper hand on Grayson. I met his mesmerizing green eyes with calm, serene clarity.

Grayson, you're obsessive-compulsive, a control freak, and a hoarder.

The thought made me stop chewing.

Huh. That makes three *things. According to Grayson's own logic, that means the random probability that he isn't a neurotic whack-job is officially zero.*

I studied Grayson as he considered taking another bite of anchovy pizza. The cheese hanging off his moustache wasn't helping his case regarding my whack-job theory.

I took a sip of Dr Pepper and smirked. "I have a valid Florida driver's license, in case you're wondering."

Grayson crinkled his nose. "I know."

"Then what's the problem? Just let me drive your crappy old RV, already."

He shook his head. "No can do."

"What's it gonna take?" I asked, reaching for another slice of pepperoni pizza.

"Three slices," he said.

I jerked my hand back. That was the rest of my half of the pizza.

What do I care? I won!

"Done!" I said.

Grayson flinched. "And you have to call me Mr. Gray."

One side of my mouth hooked skyward. "Like one of your nerdy operatives? No way."

"Yes, way. For a week."

I sneered. "One day."

He frowned. "Five days."

"Once," I said. "Final offer."

Grayson smiled in a way that made me feel as if I'd somehow managed to come out on the short end of this wager.

"Okay, then. Let's hear it," he said, and reached for a slice. "Call me Mr. Gray."

THE RV'S TRANSMISSION crunched like a handful of nails thrown into a garbage disposal.

I winced. Like an idiot, I'd turned the key in the ignition after the motor was already running.

I glanced over at Grayson. He was grimacing as if he'd been shot in the heart.

"Sorry," I said. "Stop hovering! You're making me nervous!"

I shifted into reverse, and slowly, carefully, inch by inch, backed the hulking old RV out of the parking space and into a lamp post.

Grayson closed his eyes and groaned.

"It was just a light tap," I said, trying to believe it myself. "I've never driven a rig this big before."

Grayson let out a painful-sounding sigh. "It's only twenty-four feet long, Drex."

"I'm used to driving the Mustang," I said. "This thing's got no visibility."

Grayson closed his eyes and took a deep breath. "I guess you have to start somewhere. But have mercy on me and the poor girl." He thumped a fist on his chest. "Any more screw-ups and I'm gonna refund your pizza."

I bit my lip, then carefully steered the RV out of Sargent Pizza's parking lot. I took a right, heading east on CR54.

"Geez," Grayson said. "I thought you said you knew how to drive. We need to go *west*. You should've turned *left*."

I kept my eyes on the road. "I know. I just want to make one quick detour. For supplies."

Grayson's right eyebrow flat-lined. "Twenty feet down the road and already I'm regretting this, big-time."

"Relax, Mr. OCD. I've got this."

Grayson's brow furrowed. "I don't have obsessive-compulsive disorder."

Rich, coming from a man who folds his Tootsie-Pop wrappers before putting them in the trash.

"Who said anything about obsessive-compulsive disorder?" I lied. "OCD stands for Officer, Commander and Detective."

Grayson's lips twisted to one side. "Sure it does. What kind of fool do you take me for?"

I gave him a sweet smile.

With that moustache? How about Borat?

Chapter Five

"SEE? THAT WASN'T SO bad," I said to Grayson as we hauled our shopping bags out of the Walmart supercenter on Gall Boulevard. Given the hordes milling about the place, I surmised we'd stumbled upon the cultural epicenter of Zephyrhills.

Grayson munched a handful of Cheetos he'd plucked from a bag as big as his torso. "Pardon me, lady. Do I know you?"

"You *wish*." I laughed and tousled the brand-new wig atop my head—an auburn, shoulder-length bob.

The burgundy-hued polyester flop-top wasn't the finest wig in the world, but compared to a ball cap or being bald, it made me feel like Sophia Loren. And, given my track record, there wasn't any point in sinking too much money into a quality hairpiece, anyway. The first two hadn't survived much more than a day each, thanks to Grayson's penchant for "unconventional fieldwork."

My first wig had been snarled into a sticky, duct-taped rat's nest during a scheme to entrap Mothman with the womanly wiles of seduction. The second one had been blown to bits by a stoned doomsday prepper sporting a kewl set of grillz.

As I strutted along in the Walmart lot, I hoped this third wig would stick around awhile—at least long enough for me to outgrow looking like a stunt double for *G.I. Jane*.

"You know, that hairstyle really does suit you," Grayson said. He took my hand and pirouetted me around in the middle of the asphalt parking lot.

As I spun, I felt it again. That odd, electric buzz I got in my gut every time Grayson touched me.

Unnerved, I broke free of his grasp.

"Thanks," I said. "Appearances are important. That's why you should lose that cheesy moustache, Grayson. You look like you got lost in Kazakhstan on your way to meet The Village People."

"Ouch." Grayson winced and pressed a hand over his heart as if he'd just taken a bullet. "So much for unconditional love."

"You're such a jerk," I said, pretending to laugh off his comment.

But it wasn't all that funny. In my heart the strange bedfellows of elation and terror were taking turns short-sheeting each other.

I couldn't decide which scared me worse—Grayson's electric touch, or the fact he seemed utterly content to throw away his life chasing imaginary monsters.

But then again, maybe that's what we all do ....

I yanked the RV's passenger door open. "Get in, Groucho," I quipped. "I'm taking you to Elfers."

One of Grayson's bushy eyebrows rose a notch. "Elfers?"

"Yes." I rattled one of my shopping bags. "And if you're a good boy, I'll even give you a green Tootsie Pop for the ride."

WHILE I DROVE WEST on CR 54, Grayson disappeared into the back of the RV with his Walmart purchases. One of them was a pouch of live mealy worms for Gizzard, the pet lizard he kept in a terrarium on the banquette table. We were just outside Zephyrhills when he came climbing back into the cab.

"You know what mealy worms taste like?" he asked as he flopped into the passenger seat.

I grimaced. "No. And I don't want to know."

"Suit yourself. But I find your lack of curiosity disconcerting." He fished his laptop from the floorboard, powered it up, and kept his eyes glued to it all the way to the next town.

Smart choice, since it was pretty much like the last one.

Sadly, like so much of "new" Florida, the once-quaint town of Westley Chapel had bourgeoned into yet another soulless collection of strip malls, dollar stores, and chain restaurants that spread outward, like a fungal infection, from where its original heart had been cut in half by I-75.

Still, despite its lack of planning or originality, compared to my tiny home town, Westley Chapel sparkled as glam as a Vegas showgirl—complete with fancy traffic lights and a genuine KFC!

As we passed a drive-thru convenience store, I thought of big fat Artie plopped in his chair at the Stop & Shoppe back home in Point Paradise. A wave of nostalgia passed through me like gas from a bad bean burrito.

Being born and raised in Florida, I guess so-called progress would always be a mixed bag.

I set my jaw to sullen resignation and drove onward. A mile or two later, the terrain went feral. I breathed a sigh of relief. Ahead lay miles of flat, unbroken scrubland—a hodgepodge of oaks, pines, palmettos and tangled underbrush.

Now *that* felt like real Florida to me.

I GLANCED OVER AT GRAYSON. He was happily tapping away on his laptop. He'd barely glanced up as we passed through the tiny towns of Odessa and Seven Springs. I wondered what he was working on, but decided not to disturb him.

Eventually, we wound our way toward the gulf coast and the promised land known as Elfers.

"We're here," I said as we passed a small roadside placard announcing our arrival.

Grayson looked up. His face collapsed with disappointment. "This is it?"

"What were you expecting? A fairyland village?"

Grayson shot me an earnest look. "Is that so wrong, Drex?"

Uh...yeah.

"Ghosts of a bygone era," Grayson said as we buzzed by a gray, wooden shack. "According to my Google search, Elfers is home to 13,612 residents and zero registered sex offenders."

"Really?" I asked. "How many *un*registered ones?"

Grayson grinned. "Good one. But I guess you can't believe every-thing on the internet. It also says the median home sales price here is ze-ro."

I smirked. "So people either never leave, or they give away their homes and flee."

"Perhaps. Or maybe elves never die, and therefore, never have to sell."

"Huh?"

"Oh! Pull in over there," Grayson said, and pointed across the street to a strip center called Elfers Square.

I shot him a look. "You serious?"

He shrugged. "We're here. Might as well see what the Elfer buzz is all about. I created this survey, see?" He shoved his laptop screen at me.

Elfer buzz? Survey? Shoot me now.

I shook my head. But from the childlike excitement on Grayson's face, I knew there was no point in trying to argue with the man. If I'd learned anything in my 37 years, it was that idiocy trumped reason every time.

I sighed, pulled into the strip center, and spent the next hour pissing and moaning like a spoiled brat while Grayson interviewed prospective Winn Dixie shoppers about their encounters with elves.

Yes, my life was just that fabulous.

Chapter Six

I WAS HIDING OUT BEHIND a stack of Winn-Dixie brand pork-n-beans, trying to distance myself from any affiliation with Grayson. I took another furtive peek around the tin cans. He was around ten feet away, standing by a barrel of cantaloupes.

Clad in black jeans, black shoes, a black shirt, black moustache and black fedora, Grayson looked like Mr. Peanut's evil twin hawking a dubious, new product.

Planters' dark-roasted nutcase.

Grayson glanced my way. I flinched.

He held up his little recorder for my perusal. The gleam in his eye made me question my own sanity.

Interviewing grocery shoppers about elves?

But then I got a look at the person he was talking to and felt relatively sane—comparatively speaking. The first victim in Grayson's inane interview scheme was an elderly man wearing a straw hat and overalls, without the courtesy of an undershirt.

So that's what happened to Tom Sawyer.

"I done lived here all my life," the old man informed Grayson proudly. "But I ain't never laid no eyes on no elf." He scratched his armpit hair and explained to Grayson that, "Elves wouldn't care nothin' for this town no how, seeing as how short they is."

"Can you elaborate?" Grayson asked.

"I don't rightly know," the old man said. "Is that some kind of dance?"

I nearly groaned out loud.

"Never mind," Grayson said. "Just tell me more about the elves."

"Well now," the man said, "you see, a goodly portion of Elfers floods ever' time the Anclote River swells up with rain."

After a pause, Grayson prompted the man. "Yes?"

"Well, it's purty obvious, ain't it? Any elves livin' in this here vicinity would've surely drownded by now."

I shot Grayson a sideways smirk.

Sounds perfectly logical to me.

With the calm, cheerful attitude of a true professional, Grayson thanked the old redneck. He shook his hand, wished him a pleasant day, and proceeded to stick his recorder in the face of an elderly woman in a faded, flour-sack dress.

She blinked at him behind pink, cat-eye glasses wedged tightly onto her doughy, Cabbage-Patch-Kid face.

"How are you today, lovely lady?" Grayson asked.

"Fair to midl'in," the old woman answered.

"May I have a moment of your time?"

"I guess. Long as it don't cost nothin.'"

Grayson shot me a thumbs up.

I rolled my eyes and ducked back behind the stack of bean cans. After making a full orbit around their sockets, my eyes landed on a display of kosher dill pickles. I studied them for a moment, carefully considering which size jar—half-pint, pint, or quart—would do the most effective job of knocking Grayson unconscious.

I decided on quart-sized.

I picked up a jar, tested its weight in my hand, and glanced around the pork-n-beans at my dubious P.I. partner. He was still talking to the old woman.

"Madame," he said, "I wonder if you might help me solve the mystery of Elfers' moniker."

The old woman squeezed a cantaloupe and eyed Grayson as if she suspected he might be missing a chromosome. I could totally relate.

"Now you listen here, sonny," the woman said, wagging a crooked finger at him. "Elfers weren't named after some nonsensical creature. It was named after my first cousin's grandfather's wife's favorite uncle."

"What?" Grayson leaned in closer. "Are you saying you're related to elves?"

Good grief! The man must be some kind of idiot savant—minus the savant part.

"No!" the old lady hollered. Her puffy face turned nearly as pink as her glasses. "I ain't no elf, you weirdo!" she yelled, and reared back and walloped Grayson in the chest with her giant vinyl purse.

The impact sent him reeling back into a stack of grapefruits.

"Now git!" she yelled as Grayson scrambled to regain his footing. "And shave that sorry old moustache of yours!"

If I hadn't been doubled over in laughter, I'd have surely peed my pants. As I gasped for breath, a grocery clerk went whizzing by me in Grayson's direction.

I instantly sobered up. Like a professional, I assessed the situation. Carefully and calmly, I returned the jar of pickles to the shelf.

Then, I bolted for the door like my wig was on fire.

I cleared the exit in under four seconds, then hauled ass for the RV. Grayson came flying out a few seconds later, looking as if he'd just robbed the place. He ran up to the driver's side and grabbed for the door handle.

"Scoot over!" he yelled through the closed window.

I smiled and pressed the lock on the door. "No way."

Grayson yanked the handle once, shot me a look, and scrambled for the passenger door.

I smirked as he climbed inside. I was in command of the driver's seat *and* the keys. And even Grayson had to admit, possession was nine-tenths of the law.

"Smooth move, Ex-Lax," I said.

"Just shut up and drive."

AN HOUR OR SO AFTER our hasty getaway from Elfers, I was still grinning from ear to ear. I'd bested Grayson. Again.

Even better, I hadn't hit a lamppost peeling out of the strip mall parking lot. But best of all, I'd MacGyver'ed a new use for a quart-sized jar of dill pickles.

Yeah. All in all, I was feeling pretty good about myself.

But I should've known better than to gloat.

Like my Grandma Selma always said, "Crowing over victories can send the pendulum of life swinging back to wallop you upside the head."

I wish I'd heeded Grandma's words. Or, at the very least, learned how to duck.

Chapter Seven

WE WERE CRUISING ALONG US 19 just a few miles shy of New Port Richey when it happened.

One moment I was staring at a huge circus tent with a banner for the Baptist Evangelical Resurrection Path Seekers. The next thing I knew, I was staring into a dark, empty void.

In the blink of an eye, the windshield—and everything else—had gone pitch black.

My entire world had been swallowed up by darkness, as if someone had slapped duct tape over my eyes and covered my head with a sack.

I gasped.

I'm blind!

Then I remembered I was driving and nearly swallowed my tongue.

I'm driving blind!

A horn sounded to my left. I jerked the steering wheel and screamed, "Grayson!"

My fingers clamped down on the steering wheel. Somewhere to my left, another horn blared out a passing warning.

"I can't see!" I screamed as brakes squealed to my left.

"What'd you say?" I heard Grayson ask to my right.

"I said I can't *see!*"

"Wha?!"

Suddenly, a mild electric shock went up my arms as Grayson's hands settled over mine on the steering wheel. His voice, calm and steady, whispered instructions into my ear.

"Listen carefully, Drex. Everything's fine. Let up on your grip. I'll steer from here on out."

Panic scrambled my brain.

Should I trust my life to a man who believes in elves?

Elves!

"Are you sure?" I squeaked.

"Yes. Let up on the gas, Drex."

Grayson's words felt warm and comforting against my neck. I eased up a bit on the gas pedal.

"Good," he whispered. "That's it. I've got the wheel now. You can let go."

"Are you sure?"

"Yes, I'm sure."

Reluctantly, I surrendered my grip on the steering wheel. A moment later, I bounced blindly along to the staccato joggle of the RV as it ran over a dozen or so roadway reflectors.

Slowly but surely, our velocity was slowing. I breathed a tiny sigh of relief.

Suddenly, the RV bounced. Another horn blared from the darkness on my left.

I grabbed for the steering wheel and screamed, "Grayson!"

"Gently on the brake now," he coaxed calmly. "Bring us to a stop. Easy does it."

I stomped the brake with all my might. My chest collided with Grayson's arms on the steering wheel.

"Ung," he grunted. "It's okay. We're safe. Good job."

He cut the ignition.

As the RV sputtered out, my body collapsed inward.

"Th ... thank you," I stuttered.

"What happened?" Grayson asked.

"I ... I'm not sure," I said, blinking wildly.

"Another vision?"

"No. Everything just went ... black."

I felt Grayson's hands gently cup my face. "Can you see me?"

"No." Fresh panic shot through me.

"Ease up, Drex. Stop trying so hard."

I blinked my wide-open, straining eyes. Nothing.

"Sit back," he said soothingly. "Close your eyes. Breathe."

I did as Grayson instructed, hanging onto his every word. His voice was the only familiar anchor I had left in the world.

Is this it for me? Has that stupid vestigial twin in my brain taken my sight for good? Crap! What am I going to do?

I was about to burst into tears when I felt Grayson's hand on my shoulder.

"It's a good thing you're not German, Drex," he said.

"What?" I whispered into the darkness. "Why?"

"Because then you'd be a not-see."

I groaned. Then I swallowed hard. Then I laughed despite myself.

"Let's just sit here for a while, cadet," Grayson said, and took my hand.

I concentrated on the warm, mild current of his touch. Slowly, my racing pulse returned to normal. Black turned to dark gray, then to a bluish haze, as if I were looking through a Vaseline-smeared lens.

As my vision cleared further, the first thing I made out was Grayson's blurry moustache in front of me.

I'd never seen anything so beautiful.

His face was inches from mine, watching my every move.

"You had a vision, didn't you?" he asked.

I shook my head. "No. It was more like ... I dunno ... a flavor."

His bushy eyebrows drew closer together. "A *flavor?*"

"Yeah. A ... *taste.*"

I made a sour face, then raked my teeth over my tongue. I rolled down the RV window and spit the foul taste from my mouth.

Grayson leaned forward in the passenger seat. "*That's* a new one. What exactly do you think you 'tasted'?"

"I'm not sure." I grimaced from the lingering, unsavory film in my mouth. "I think it was ... the flavor of *evil.*"

Grayson's left eyebrow arched. "Intriguing. And what, pray tell, does evil taste like?"

I shrugged. "I dunno. Tingly. Metallic. Like sucking on an old battery."

"Stick out your tongue," Grayson said.

"Why?"

He leaned forward, reached into the glove compartment, and pulled out a baggie of what looked like Q-Tips in vials.

My nose crinkled. "What are you doing?"

"Collecting samples, of course. Now stick out your tongue."

I blew out a breath. Grayson had gone from caring to clinical in two seconds flat. "Honest to God. I don't get paid enough for this."

Grayson stared at me, an incredulous look on his face. "You don't think I'm going to miss the opportunity to gather empirical evidence on evil itself, do you? Think about it, Drex. If I can proffer actual physical evidence of the physiological changes brought about by ectoplasmic enc—"

"Just shut up and do it," I said, and stuck out my tongue.

Chapter Eight

"I SUPPOSE WE CAN RULE out Viagra," Grayson said. "How about pregnancy?"

I stared at him blankly as we switched places and he climbed into the driver's seat of the battered old RV. "What are you talking about?"

"The cause of your temporary blindness," he said. He turned and shot me a look. "What did you *think* I was talking about?"

"With you, there's no telling," I muttered, then studied the windshield. "But to answer your question, no, I'm not pregnant. And I didn't take Viagra."

"Any other drugs or chemical stimulants?" he asked, cranking the engine and pulling back onto the road.

I plucked a blue sucker out of my mouth. "Only if you count Tootsie Pops."

"Sugar *is* a gateway drug. But as yet, it's not been proven to directly induce blindness, as far as we've been told. Unless, of course, you count diabetic retinopathy."

"No way," I said, and I chewed my lip from concern. "What else do you think could've caused me to lose my sight?"

Grayson pursed his lips. "Ocular migraine, perhaps. Did you experience any numbness or tingling?"

"Only on my tongue."

"Hmm." Grayson drove on for a minute. The ugly urban sprawl better known as New Port Richey came into view. "Amaurosis Fugax."

I glared at Grayson. "Did you just insult me?"

"What? No. Amaurosis Fugax is a sudden reduction in blood flow to the eyes."

My brow furrowed. "You mean like a stroke?"

"Similar, but no. Not technically. Did you have any loss of feeling on one side? Any trouble speaking?"

"No. You were *there*, Grayson. You heard me yelling."

"Right." Grayson shot me a smirk. "How could I forget *that?*"

"Har har har."

"Okay, okay." Grayson pulled up to a red light. "So, no stroke. Let's go back to the bad taste in your mouth. Could you describe it in more detail?"

I sighed. "I don't know. Like I said before. Tingly. Bitter. Metallic. Like a mouthful of old pennies."

"Pennies." Grayson lolled the word around on his tongue. "Exposure to mercury or lead could cause that, but it seems unlikely."

"Why?"

Grayson studied me for a moment. "Because I'd probably have experienced the same exposure."

I frowned. "Maybe you did. Maybe you're about to go blind, too." I looked down at the steering wheel.

Grayson smirked. "Nice try, but you're not driving again."

The light turned green. Grayson stomped the gas. The g-force sent me slumping back into my chair.

"You brush your teeth regularly?" Grayson asked, shifting into second gear.

"I beg your pardon?"

"Poor oral hygiene could account for the bad taste. Interesting side factoid. Did you know that when you brush your teeth, it's the only time you clean part of your skeletal system?"

I closed my eyes and shook my head. "No." And I didn't want to know.

"Okay, so you brushed your teeth," Grayson continued. "Dementia could also cause changes in taste perception. You're not holding anything back on me, are you?"

I shot him a sour look. "If I had dementia, how would I know?"

Grayson laughed. "I guess that leaves illicit drugs or vitamin supplements."

My back stiffened. "Vitamins?"

Grayson glanced my way. "Yes. Some supplements contain heavy metals like copper, zinc, chromium, and whatnot."

"Oh." I reached into my purse and pulled out a bottle. "Like these?"

"Flintstone vitamins with extra iron," Grayson said, grabbing the bottle from my hand and reading the label out loud. "Well, what do you know? Yabba, dabba do."

Chapter Nine

"COULD VITAMINS REALLY be the cause of whatever happened to me?" I asked as Grayson pulled the RV into a low-rent motel off US 19 called the Dilly Dally Motor Court.

"The metallic taste in your mouth, yes," he said, pulling up to the motel office. He parked and cut the ignition. "Loss of eyesight, I don't think so."

He unfastened his seatbelt and studied me with his piercing green eyes. "But there *is* one thing that could cause both."

"What?" I asked, not entirely sure I wanted to know.

"Pregnancy. Are you sure there's no chance you've got a hot-cross bun in the oven?"

I scowled. "Not unless I'm the Immaculate Conception, 2.0."

Grayson laughed. He rattled the jar of vitamins at me. "When's the last time you had one of these babies?"

"Right after lunch."

"Which one did you take? Barney, Fred, Wilma or Pebbles?"

"I don't remember." I chewed my lip, then realized Grayson was having a laugh on me. "You can be a real turd, you know that?"

Grayson smirked. "Just trying to make you smile. After all, laughter is the best medicine, they say."

I sneered. "Not when it's delivered by a quack."

Grayson snorted, then mocked offence. "The ingratitude!" he huffed, then flung open the RV door.

The thought of being left alone panicked me. What if I went blind again? "Where are you going?" I asked.

"To get a room. I think it's time to put that faulty noggin of yours through its paces."

I cringed. "Not more *Mystery Science Theater 3000!*"

"No. Something way better."

Grayson waggled his eyebrows like Groucho Marx, and suddenly I knew what "something way better" meant.

"Wait!" I said.

But it was too late. Grayson hopped out and slammed the RV door behind him.

As he disappeared into the motel office, I noticed he'd left the keys dangling in the ignition. I contemplated the odds of me going blind again if I stole the rundown Winnebago and made a mad dash for Poughkeepsie.

Probably considerably less than the odds of me being pregnant by immaculate conception. But then again, you never know....

Before I could make up my mind, Grayson reemerged from the motel office with a key chained to a wooden paddle. The look in his eye made me instantly curse my own indecisiveness.

In less than ten minutes, I would find myself lying in a lumpy bed in a sleazy hotel room with electrodes pasted to my head—the hapless Guinea pig of a slightly mad physicist with a pimped-out EEG machine.

Ain't life grand?

Chapter Ten

THE GREEN-SKINNED DEMON in Grayson's computer program snapped its bloody fangs at me again, then the laptop screen blinked out with a static buzz.

As the horrific image faded, it was replaced by the silly, smiling face of the cartoon vampire, Count Chocula. Above the breakfast-cereal icon's head, a conversation bubble read, "Have a chocolaty scrumptious day!"

I let out a sigh. Another of Grayson's bizarre desensitization training sessions had come to an end.

"So, we're done?" I asked, suddenly craving cereal. I sat up in bed and felt the tug of the dozen electrodes pasted to my head like a Medusa starter kit.

Grayson looked up from the EEG machine's display monitor. "Yes. You did well, considering."

"Considering what?"

"Your incident today. I don't see any brain anomalies on the printout. At least, no *new* ones."

I scowled. "Is that some kind of crack?"

He stared at me quizzically, like an emotionless Spock. "Is *what* some kind of crack?"

"The brain anomaly thing."

"You *do* have the vestiges of a twin lodged near your pineal gland, re-member?"

I flinched. I remembered, all right. "Do you think that's what caused me to go blind?"

Grayson shrugged. "It's a possibility. But, I'm curious. Why *now?* And why only *temporarily?* The mass on your brain might be partially re-sponsible, but I find your ingestion of vitamins intriguing."

I sneered. "*That's* what you find intriguing about me?"

Grayson continued his analytical monologue, seemingly oblivious to my comment. "Some element—or elements—of the supplement must've acted as a catalyst, precipitating interaction between otherwise inert substances."

My upper lip hooked toward the ceiling. "What?"

Grayson glanced over at me and held up the jar of vitamins.

"Pebbles go bam-bam on your brainstem."

"Oh." I sat up and tugged off an electrode pasted to my right temple. "Grayson?"

"What?"

"Thanks for being so cool during my ... uh, *incident*. While I was driving, I mean. I know you didn't want me to. I shouldn't have .... Anyway, you saved us. I could've gotten us both killed."

"All in the line of duty," he said softly, then grinned at me like the Cheshire Cat who ate the LSD canary. "Besides, the risk was worth it."

"What do you mean?" I asked sourly.

He wagged his eyebrows. "Now I never have to let you drive again."

I scowled. Grayson chuckled and went back to studying my test results. I pulled off a few more electrodes, then I blew out a breath.

"Nosferatu. Dracula. Count Chocula. What's up with the vampire theme?"

"One ghoul at a time," Grayson replied, his attention still on the EEG monitor.

I rolled my eyes. "Grayson, if I ever got a straight answer from you, I think I'd faint."

He glanced over at me. "Good thing you're in bed, then."

"Ugh!" I pulled off another electrode. "What've you got planned for your next program? Mummies?"

Grayson winked and tutted at me. "Come now, Drex. Mummies are for sissies. Everybody knows that."

I got up and headed to the bathroom for a hot shower and to scrub my stubbly head clean of electrode paste. I turned back toward Grayson. "So, what now?"

"I think you should call it a day." He grabbed the RV's keys from the cheap nightstand beside his threadbare twin bed. "I'll go pick up some dinner. What are you in the mood for, battery breath? Oh! I know. How about a fried Energizer bunny—and an 'alkali-ic' drink to go with it?"

I stared at him blankly. "I bet you've been waiting your entire life to say that to somebody, haven't you?"

Chapter Eleven

QUICK TRAVEL TIP: IF you ever go in search of the nostalgic high-lights of old Central Florida, sunrise over the parking lot at the Dilly-Dally Motor Court in New Port Richey is one that should by all means be *avoided*. Unless, of course, the alternative is to be trapped in one of their grungy rooms with a travel companion who sings in the shower like Barry Gibb with his nuts in a vice ....

I hauled my butt off the cold, concrete curb and stared at the artless still-life before me.

Cigarette butts on asphalt at dawn. A post-apocalyptic abstract.

I checked my cellphone. I figured I still had around five or six min-utes before Grayson finished his earsplitting aria. I shoved my phone back into my pocket and shuffled across the motor court parking lot to the dreary lobby. Inside, I downed a cup of crappy coffee and perused the giant rack of gleaming tourist-trap flyers.

One in particular caught my eye.

It had a Sasquatch on it.

I picked up the flyer and began pondering three of the great myster-ies of life.

Who knew the headquarters for skunk ape research was in Ochopee, Florida? Who knew there was a town on Earth called Ochopee? Who knew what Ochopee stood for? Eight Spanish urinations?

I let a few minutes tick by as I reflected on these burning questions. I was about to leave when another one of Grandma Selma's sayings popped into my mind.

"An ounce of prevention is worth a pound of government cheese."

I got up and hid the Skunk Ape Research brochures behind the mini-fridge, just in case Grayson wandered in later. Then I poured a couple of fresh cups of stale coffee, and joggled my way across the parking lot and back to the motel room.

I set the coffees on the ground beside the door and reached for the wooden paddle I'd stuck in the back waistband of my pants. The room key was fastened to the paddle like a ball and chain on an old-time convict.

I shook my head. Who would want to steal a key so they could return to this place was beyond my current mental capacity.

I opened the door and tentatively poked my head inside our cigarette-scented room. Mercifully, Pavarotti had finished his morning sonata. I bent down to pick up the coffees and blanched.

A lizard was using one of the coffees as a heated swimming pool.

Correction. A lizard was using Grayson's coffee as a heated swimming pool.

I plucked the little reptile out of his brown bubble bath and set him on the sidewalk to dry off. Then I slipped inside and parked my keister in the vinyl chair that had the smallest split in its seat.

I fired up Grayson's laptop and was slurping stale coffee and perusing local nursing-home websites when he emerged from the bathroom wearing his signature black jeans and blue hospital booties.

Yep. Livin' the glam life, all right.

"What was the name of that nursing home Garth mentioned?" I asked. "Bunker Hill?"

"Banner Hill." Grayson rubbed his chin. "I wonder if any more vets went missing last night."

I glanced at Grayson's killer abs and smooth, muscular chest and felt something inside me stir. Then I remembered the guy had swabbed my tongue for evil and interviewed hillbillies about elves. My swizzle-stick went limp.

"I didn't see anything about it on CNN," I quipped.

Grayson nodded. "Good one, considering you haven't had any coffee this morning."

I lifted my paper cup. "What do you call this?"

"That's not coffee, Drex. That's brown water."

I stared at the weak brew and crinkled my nose. "That's an insult to brown water."

"Hopefully the coffee's better at Banner Hill."

I looked up at him. "We're going there?"

"Yes."

"Right *now?*"

"Of course not. I need to put on a shirt and shoes first."

"Fine," I said, picking up the other coffee cup. "But first, you've gotta try this. It's really not that bad."

Chapter Twelve

"THAT LOOKS LIKE THE place," I said.

Grayson whistled long and low. "You sure?"

"Yeah. I recognize it from the website."

Grayson pulled the RV to a stop in front of a single-story, red-brick building. White, concrete-block additions had been cobbled onto both sides of the main structure. A string of small outbuildings sprouted like toadstools over a half-acre campus of asphalt parking lots and intermittent strips of patchy, threadbare lawn.

A huge oak tree shaded Banner Hill's front yard. Under it, a few droopy-seated park benches languished in the shade. Overall, the place reminded me of a third-world elementary school that had fallen from the sky onto a post-war parking lot.

A couple of old guys in wheelchairs were lined up along the brick wall outside the front door, smoking and squinting like geriatric peeping-Toms, the mid-morning sun filtering through the oak tree's thick branches.

"I don't think Banner Hill is gonna make the cover of *Architectural Digest* anytime soon," I quipped.

When Grayson didn't reply, I turned to face him. He hadn't cut the ignition. Instead, he was staring at the steering wheel, chewing his bottom lip.

"What's up?" I asked.

He shook his head and glanced over at the building. "Something doesn't feel right."

"Why? Were you expecting a welcome committee?"

"Not exactly." Grayson studied me for a moment with his unreadable green eyes. "Where are the reporters, Drex? Three vets missing, and not a single media van, cop car, nosy neighbor, nothing."

I cringed. Grayson had yet again had to point out the obvious to me.

"Maybe nobody reported them missing," I said, mostly in an attempt to save face.

"Hmm. I suppose that's possible." His eyes shifted back to the building. "But why?"

"Where did Garth get his intel about guys going missing?" I asked.

"From the guy who cuts his hair."

I nearly choked. "We're here based on the ramblings of a barber who thinks mullets are still a valid fashion statement?"

Grayson pursed his lips. "Not exactly. The barber's grandfather is living here. His name is Melvin Haplets."

"Oh."

"According to Melvin, the men here are slowly fading away."

I glanced at three old men lined up in wheelchairs by the front door. "Uh ... isn't that the whole point of this place?"

"Disappearing without a trace isn't." Grayson's gaze fell back on me.

"No. You're right," I said, ditching my snarky attitude. "Do you have any working theories?"

"One." Grayson held out two fingers, forming a V.

"Victory?" I asked.

"No."

"Veterans?"

"No."

"Vanishing?"

"No."

"Okay, Grayson, I give up. What, then?"

"Vampires."

I nearly choked. "Vampires? Get real!"

"Don't be so quick to discount vampirism," Grayson said. "Florida has a rich history of believers."

"Yeah? Name one."

Grayson smiled. "Okay, if you insist."

Oh, crap. Here we go again. Another of Grayson's drive-by "factings."

"Back in 2000, a guy from Tampa calling himself 'The Impaler' ran for the senate. He also made a bid for president of the United States in

2004 and 2008, telling reporters he wanted to become the first vampire president."

I cringed. "You're making that up."

"Nope. I listened to the TV interview myself. I've got to say, The Impaler had some well-thought-out opinions on capital punishment and veterans issues. Must've brushed up on things when he served on the Executive Committee of the Hillsborough County Republican Party. You know, before he went over to 'the V-side.'"

"One lone case," I said.

"Hardly," Grayson laughed. "Nowadays, people say they see vampires everywhere. Not long ago, a guy in Cape Coral was caught on video climbing atop a police cruiser and gyrating to the sweet tunes of *Rich Girl.*"

I frowned. "Are you saying all Hall & Oates are vampires?"

"Hmm. I never thought about that."

"Ugh! So, what's your point, Grayson?"

"Well, after the guy finished his dance number atop the cruiser, he tore off the windshield wipers for good measure. Then he jumped down, grabbed an American flag, and waved it around until he was taken into custody. According to the Lee County police affidavit, the man's solo act was inspired by 'a woman with fangs.' The man claimed she'd threatened him and scared him out of his home. He was absolutely convinced a human sacrifice involving vampires was about to occur."

"That didn't really happen, did it?"

"Sure did. The Lee County Sheriff's Office released the video. I saw it myself."

"Geez. Did they find out why he got on top of the police car?"

"Yes. He said he was 'looking for the Sheriff of Nottingham to help him stop the slaughter of small children.'"

I cringed. "There couldn't be any truth to that, could there?"

Grayson shrugged. "Who knows? They never caught the vampire woman who was allegedly harassing him."

"Or the meth lab that sold him the drugs." I shook my head. "Okay. Two totally isolated instances. That doesn't mean Florida's overrun with vampires."

"Then how do you explain the old guy in Daytona Beach who burned down his own house after screaming vampires were going to get him?"

"What?"

Grayson nodded. "It happened. And the guy was probably the same age as the old men sitting over there."

Grayson pointed back to the old guys smoking on the front porch of the nursing home.

"Really?" I asked.

"Absolutely."

"What happened?"

"The old guy went berserk. He broke out a few windows with his cane, then threw some ceiling insulation on the stove to really get the party started. Once the place was going up in flames, he grabbed a knife and started shouting, 'The vampires are going to defend themselves.'"

I shook my head. "That really happened?"

"Yes. And from what I hear, the house was a total loss. But on the bright side, nobody got hurt. And, he avoided being Baker-Acted because they couldn't prove he was incompetent."

"So ... the old man was sane?"

"Apparently so. So, do you need any more proof vampires are alive and well? I've got plenty more examples."

"No. That's enough." I frowned and shook my head. "Geez. What's the world coming to?"

"The same as always," Grayson said. "The world's always had its prophets, Drex. Some go down in history as heroes. Others just go down."

"So, what do we do now?" I asked. "Should we go interview Melvin Haplets?"

"That's the idea. But I doubt they'll let us just wander in." Grayson put his hand on the door handle. "I've got a plan. Leave your Glock behind and follow my lead."

Grayson pushed open his door, hopped out of the RV, and slammed the door behind him.

"Wait!" I said, fishing through my purse for my gun. I shoved it under my seat and scrambled after him. "What plan?" I called out.

"We're brother and sister," he said as I sprinted to catch up with him as he marched up the sidewalk. "We're looking for a new home for granny."

"Okay, we're siblings," I said to his back. "But what if they don't have any rooms?"

Grayson spun on his heels and eyed me as if I'd just confessed I was made of cream cheese. "According to my calculations, Drex, they should have at least *three* fairly recent openings."

My shoulders sagged. "Oh. Yeah."

He turned back toward the facility. "Keep up, and keep sharp."

"Yes, sir," I said, then mentally kicked myself in the ass.

Elf surveys and bathroom booties be damned. Nick Grayson might've been a kook about some things, but when it came to detective skills, he had me beat by a redneck mile.

Chapter Thirteen

GRAYSON SALUTED AS he passed the clot of old men congregated in wheelchairs outside the main entrance to Banner Hill. I offered them a weak smile as I passed by. One smiled back. The others stared, zombie-like, at some point of interest apparently only they could envision.

Just inside the entryway, a middle-aged woman with a mousy brown helmet of hair sat stoically, entrenched at her station in the cheap office chair behind the reception desk. Her tired face, beige polyester dress, and dreary disposition matched the nursing home's decor so perfectly that for a second I wondered if she'd been delivered in a box along with the rest of the uninspired furnishings.

"Hello. Ms. Draper?" Grayson asked, and flashed a charming smile.

"Ms. Draper's the owner," the woman said in a tone that mirrored none of Grayson's cheerfulness, whether it was fake or not. "I'm Ms. Gable. What can I do for you?"

"Oh. My mistake." Grayson smiled. "Forgive me. You have the air of ownership about you. An elegant pride, if you will."

The plump, frazzled woman sized Grayson up as if he were selling baby seal meat and she was head of Greenpeace. "Uh-huh. What do you want?"

Grayson smiled brightly and glanced over at me. "We have an appointment to tour the facilities. My sister Ginger and I are thinking of placing our granny here at Banner Hill."

"We only take men," Gable said bluntly.

Her red lips curled into a petty-tyrant smile. Mighty Casey was striking out. I stepped up to bat.

"Excuse me, Fred," I said, pushing Grayson aside.

He shot me a weird look. I knew why. For some reason, whenever I poured on the charm, it always came with a syrupy Southern accent. Don't ask me why.

I cleared my throat, moved a cheap vase of plastic flowers out of my face, and smiled sheepishly at Ms. Gable. "Yes. Well, Fred here would never admit it, but 'granny' is what our dear old granddad wants to be called nowadays. You know how it is. Dementia can be such an unpredictable thing."

Gable's face softened a notch. "Yes, it can. But at Banner Hill, we prefer veterans."

"Grandpa served in Vietnam, ma'am," I said. "By the way, I think it's super great that you want to honor those who've served our fine country."

"And their VA benefits guarantee payment," Grayson said.

I stepped on Grayson's foot, then leaned over the reception desk. "Yes, that's truly a blessing for everyone."

Gable eyed us both. "Now, this grandfather of yours. Is he ambulatory? This isn't a lockdown unit. We don't take wanderers."

I shook my head. "No. The poor thing can barely walk."

"He uses a cane," Grayson said.

Gable frowned.

"But mostly a wheelchair," I offered.

That cheered her up. Gable smiled and said, "Well, we do have a recent opening. Ms. Draper isn't here right now. Let me show you around."

"THIS WAY," GABLE SAID as she waddled down the facility's main corridor in shoes that appeared to have been constructed from road-killed marshmallows. The bleak hallway's sole decorative touches were metal grab bars and a smattering of cheap artwork in even cheaper frames.

Grayson and I trailed behind Gable like baby ducks. She stopped in front of a door with a small window in it.

"Have a look," she said, opening the door. "This is the rec room."

The room smelled of disinfectant, but was otherwise pleasant enough, given its overall clinical setting. On one side of the room, a couple of plastic-lined couches and lounge chairs had been grouped around a large-screen TV. On the other side, a half-dozen small tables were set up with checkers, chess, and other board games. In one corner, an old guy was passed out in a chair snoring, a book open on his lap.

Gable smiled. "One day, Mr. Green might just finish that book of his. He usually reads in his room, but he's taken to sitting in that chair since his roommate went mi—*ahem*—passed away three days ago."

"Oh," I said. "What happened?"

Gable looked at me funny. "He *died*. Follow me."

Gable turned and led us further down the hall to the kitchen to inspect the food preparation facilities.

"We're mighty proud of our food service here," she said, and opened a locked, metal door.

Inside, two rotund women in white scrubs and hairnets eyed us cautiously before giving us friendly, possibly even sincere smiles. I suddenly felt like a seventh grader standing in the cafeteria line staring at the lunchroom ladies, worrying that a double portion of French fries might give me more pimples.

"Very good," Grayson said to the pair, as if he were performing a military inspection. "Carry on, ladies."

"Wait," I said. I pointed at a metal tray. It was heaped with yellow clumps of glop dotted with suspicious red chunks—like a fake vomit omelet. "What's that?" I asked one of the women.

"Breakfast leftovers," she said. "Powdered scrambled eggs and Spam. You want some?"

"Oh. Sounds tasty," I said, with less enthusiasm than I'd meant to muster. "But I already ate."

"Why powdered eggs?" Grayson asked Gable.

Gable smirked as if she'd just told a private joke. "Like I said, most of the men we serve here are veterans. A majority have mental health issues. Most of the time, they think they're back in their military units. So we try to accommodate them by recreating G.I. rations. They eat 'em up, don't they, girls?"

The two women laughed. "Yes ma'am."

One woman with red curls peeking out of her chef's cap said, "Today's the first day in ages we've had any leftovers. Probably because of all the recent d—"

"*Ahem*," Gable growled forcefully, silencing the woman with a scathing look. "Ms. Frasier, I'll remind you that here at Banner Hill, we keep our clientele's business confidential."

Frasier looked puzzled. "But I didn't—"

Another glare from Gable sealed Frasier's lips for good.

"This way," Gable said to Grayson and me. "I'll show you what I mean about hearty appetites."

After taking another quick gander at the vomit omelet, I was skeptical. But when we stepped into the cafeteria, sure enough, the old guys inside were gumming their green Jell-O like there was no tomorrow.

"What unit you in?" one old man asked Grayson as we passed his table.

"Eighty-third," he said. "You?"

"Sixty, you piss-ant," he said, then shoveled another spoonful of gelatin into his toothless maw.

"See what I mean?" Gable said. "All they think about is war times. How about some coffee and cookies?"

My stomach gurgled. "Sounds delightful." I was starved. Grayson was so eager to get here that he hadn't even let us stop for donuts on the way.

Who in their right mind could forget about food?

We sat down at one of the worn, laminate-topped tables while Gable went to fetch coffee across the room.

"Spam. That could be significant," Grayson said under his breath.

"What do you mean?" I whispered.

Before he had a chance to reply, Gable returned with three cups of coffee and a plate stacked with vanilla sandwich cookies. She handed me a cup.

I took a sip. The coffee was so weak I almost longed for the crap at the Dilly Dally Motor Court.

Gable noticed my reaction. "Some of the men here drink coffee all day, so we water it down," she said.

"Ah," Grayson said.

I took a bite of cookie and could practically taste the expiration date. I tucked the rest of it into my napkin and tried to warn Grayson, but I wasn't quick enough. He popped a whole one into his mouth and nearly choked.

"So, Ms. Gable, what's your availability?" he asked, then proceeded to have a small coughing fit.

"Availability?" Gable asked.

Grayson took a slurp of coffee, swallowed hard, then glanced over at me. "Yes. Ginger and I'd like to bring gramps in for a tour, but we don't want to get his hopes up if there's no room at the inn."

"Tell you what," Gable said. "Fax me a copy of his military ID and monthly pension check, and I'll hold a space for him for twenty-four hours."

"That's mighty gracious of you," I said sweetly.

"It certainly is," Grayson said. "But I hope to return with him this afternoon, if that's amenable. He's quite anxious to find his new forever home."

"Certainly," Gable said. "Does four o'clock work for you?"

Grayson beamed. "Perfect."

"What's your grandfather's name?" Gable asked.

Before I could reply, Grayson blurted, "George Burns."

I closed my eyes so no one could see them roll.

Awesome, Grayson. I'm Ginger. You're Fred. Gramps is George Burns. Now all we need is Gracie and we've got our very own tragic variety show.

Chapter Fourteen

BACK AT THE RECEPTION desk, we thanked Ms. Gable and promised to return with Grandpa Burns for an interview for possible admission to Banner Hill. As the exit door closed behind us, I grabbed Grayson by the arm.

"Geez, Grayson, I thought we were here to *find* missing war veterans, not to create more out of thin air!"

"Basic investigative tactic," Grayson said. "If we're going to track down the cryptid turning vets into Captain Crunch, we need to familiarize ourselves with the layout and players. Did you notice? None of the vets wore nametags."

"No. I didn't notice."

Grayson frowned. "That's going to make it harder to find Melvin Haplets." He motioned with his chin.

I turned to see the same three old smokers in wheelchairs who'd been staring at us when we'd walked in earlier that morning.

"Hello, fellows," I said. "Would one of you happen to be Melvin Haplets?"

They all exchanged glances with each other. "No. We don't associate with him," said the man in the middle.

"Why not?" I asked.

"He's a fuddy-duddy," the same spokesman said, initiating a round of dry, cough-like laughter from the trio of geezers.

"Yes," I said. "Nobody likes a fuddy-duddy." I turned to Grayson, my eyes pleading for direction. I was at a lost for what to say or do next.

Grayson grabbed me by the arm. "Have a nice day, gentlemen," he said, and tugged me down the sidewalk.

"Don't stir the pot on Melvin," he whispered. "It might make him the next target."

"Target?"

"Yes. Every night for the past three nights, a resident vet has gone MIA. I think we're going to need eyes on the place overnight if we're going to catch the illicit action."

"Illicit action?" I said. "Look at those guys. They can't even *walk* and *they're* the *cool* guys."

"Exactly, Drex. They're sitting ducks, and it looks like somebody's got a taste for Vietnamese gamecock."

"What?"

Grayson turned and walked briskly toward the RV. He only had three steps on me, but given his long legs, I had to sprint to catch up with him.

"What are you saying?" I asked, jogging to keep up. "That vampires prefer Asian cuisine?"

"No. And don't forget. Vampires are just one of the working theories at the moment. Did you know that Spam is a favorite food in Papua New Guinea?"

Wha??? Either I missed something or Grayson is insane.

"Grayson, what are you talking about?"

"*Spam*, Drex." Grayson stopped beside the RV.

"Spam?" I asked, leaning up against the door so he couldn't open it.

"Yes. The breakfast omelet they served had Spam in it," he said, using his fingers to put air quotes around the word Spam.

I shook my head. "Maybe I need some real coffee, Grayson, but I'm just not following you."

He cocked his head to one side. "In Papua New Guinea, the Korowai tribe believes it's necessary to kill and eat any person they believe to have been possessed by a khakua demon."

My face went slack. "Oh. Well, of course. How silly of me not to make the connection."

Grayson shrugged. "It happens." He reached for the handle to the driver's door. I slapped it away.

"Grayson, I was being facetious! What are you saying? That the spirit of a khakua arrived at Banner Hill in a Spam can?"

Grayson's eyebrow rose a notch. "Well, not exactly. But I have to say, that's an interesting theory. Did you ever see that movie about—"

"Grayson! Just tell me what *your* theory is, okay?"

"I thought I did already."

I shot him some side eye. "Humor me."

"Fine. Up until the 1970s, the Korowai still practiced cannibalism. Then they were introduced to Spam. They said it tasted like long pig."

"Long pig?"

"Yes. Human flesh. You see, Drex, Spam is the modern-day cannibal's equivalent to cold cuts. It's 'Man in a Can,' if you will."

My stomach flopped. "What?"

"Someone at Banner Hill enjoys the taste of human flesh."

I cringed. "You've got to be kidding!"

"Negatory."

"Okay. Say that's true. Why start killing vets? Why not just keep buying Spam?"

"Perhaps someone's got a hankering for the real thing. Or, maybe they're just trying to stretch the old food budget. You know, kill two old birds with one stone."

"That's crazy."

"Crazy like a khakua." Grayson grinned and opened the RV door. "So, let's go find us a gramps, shall we?"

"What? Where? At the Gramps-R-Us store?"

Grayson smiled. "If only. By the way, good save in there. Turning granny into grandpa. 'Dementia is an unpredictable thing.' I'm going to have to remember that one."

I climbed into the passenger seat. "It's true. My Aunt Betty had dementia. She used to put her socks in her soup."

Grayson's right eyebrow arched. "You don't say."

I sighed. "You know, the whole cannibalism thing aside, in cases like Aunt Betty's, I guess Banner Hill wouldn't be the worst place to spend the rest of your life."

Grayson shrugged. "Are you kidding? They've got no icky guy in there."

My nose crinkled. "Are you blind? No offense to those poor vets, but I saw plenty of icky guys in there."

Grayson shook his head and turned the key in the ignition. "No. *Ikigai*. It's a Japanese term. It means 'a reason to get up in the morning.' In Okinawa they live past a hundred because of ikigai."

I smirked. "Or, maybe with all the icky guys around, it just *seems* like a hundred years."

Grayson groaned, then looked past me through the passenger window. "Who's that?"

A man's muffled voice sounded to my right. "Hey, man. You guys really shouldn't park here."

I turned to see the wide chest and shoulders of a well-built black man in short-sleeved beige scrubs. He bent down until his head came into view. An open, friendly smile crowned his lips. Dreadlocks poked out from the beige bandana on his head.

I rolled down the window. "Excuse me?"

He poked a thumb over his shoulder. "The folks there ... across the street from Banner Hill. Well, let's just say this is a bad place to park. Tires have been known to ... you know ... *disappear.*"

I followed the trajectory of the man's thumb over to the low-budget, Section Eight housing across the street from Banner Hill. The small, concrete hovels bore the unmistakable, dusty pallor of desperation.

Dirt yards. Faded paint. Dismal future.

"I lost a few tires myself," the man said, then laughed. "Then my whole car. Then my bike. Now I just take an Uber to work."

"You work here? At Banner Hill?" I asked.

"Yes. Just getting off shift."

"Hmm," Grayson said. "You need a lift?"

The man's face lit up. "Really? You sure?"

"Absolutely. I'm Nick Grayson. This is Bobbie Drex."

"I'm Stanley Johnson," the man said. "But I got to warn you, I live about ten miles from here."

"Climb in, Stanley," Grayson said. "Point us in the direction of the best taco stand in town, and your fare is paid in full."

I grinned and opened the door to let Stanley in, then crawled out of my seat and took a hunched-over position in the narrow passage leading to the main cabin of the RV.

"Tacos, huh?" Stanley said. "Well, let me tell you. You haven't lived until you've tried Topless Tacos."

My smile evaporated into a tight, white line.

Great. And here I'd thought I'd just left all the icky guys behind.

Chapter Fifteen

I KEPT MY MOUTH SHUT and tried to be a grown-ass woman about the fact that I was going to a topless taco joint with two strange men, both of whom were—to my great irritation—attractive enough to keep my feelings about them seesawing in perpetual conflict.

Why is it handsome jerks seem to have that mysterious power over women? Or is it just me?

I'd relinquished my seat to Stanley, so I scooted back to the main cabin of the RV. I plopped onto the couch and conducted an extended test of how much pressure per square inch the enamel on my molars could take before cracking.

After a while, curiosity overpowered my anger. I leaned forward and craned my ear to listen in on the conversation Stanley and Grayson were having up in the front cab.

"How long have you worked at Banner Hill?" Grayson asked.

"Not long. Six weeks or so." Stanley's deep voice danced with the lyrical lilt of the Caribbean. "What brings you two to Banner Hill?"

"We're looking for a place to put gramps."

"*Your* daddy or the missus'?"

"What?" Grayson asked. "Oh. We're not married."

I sat up straight and scowled. Had Grayson sounded *relieved* we weren't married?

The nerve!

Stanley laughed. "Brother and sister, then?"

"Not a chance," Grayson said. "We're partners."

Not a chance? What's that *supposed to mean?*

"Uh-huh," Stanley said. "So, in other words, you two living in sin, huh?"

"No. Not in sin," Grayson quipped. "In *an RV.*"

Stanley chuckled. "You're a funny guy, Grayson. I like you. This is a nice little rig you got, too. I had one kind of like it in Haiti."

"Haiti?" Grayson said. "Tough place."

"It can be."

"So, you're here on a green card?" Grayson asked.

"Sort of. Workin' on it, you know? Sometimes you got to pretend. Fake it till you make it, am I right?"

Grayson laughed.

"Hey man, do you mind if I slip out of these scrubs? I got a change of clothes in my duffle here."

"Not at all," Grayson said. "But it might be easier in the back."

"I heard that. Pretty tight up here."

Before I could scoot back on the couch, Stanley's head popped into the main cabin. My ears burned from being caught eavesdropping.

"Hey, sister. Just going to get into my civvies." Stanley held up his duffle bag.

"No problem," I said. "I'll just—"

Stanley flopped down on the couch beside me. I watched, open mouthed, as he wriggled out of his drawstring scrub pants and tugged them free over his white leather tennis shoes.

He stood. I gawked at his gorgeous glutes as he yanked his shirt off over his head, revealing bulging biceps and washboard abs that erased Grayson's six pack right out of my spinning noggin.

Stanley caught me staring and smiled shyly. "Oh. Sorry, Miss Drex. I hope you don't mind. I'm so used to—"

"No worries," I whispered, barely able to speak.

I knew it was rude, but I couldn't tear my eyes from the man's physique. I'd never seen a male specimen so suave he could actually rock an outfit of leopard-print underpants and white shoes and socks. Like a rabid pro-wrestling fan, not even one little part of me wanted to snicker at Jungle Jock.

"I'll be quick," Stanley said, and unzipped his duffle. He tugged out a pair of jeans and a red pullover sweater.

I watched in awe as his muscular legs, arms and chest disappeared underneath the denim and knit. Then, like some sexy cologne commercial,

Stanley untied the beige bandana on his head and shook loose his dread-locks so they could swing wild and free.

"Hand me those?" he said.

"Huh? Oh!" I unfroze, closed my drooling mouth, and handed Stan-ley the scrubs he'd tossed onto the couch.

"Thanks." He shot me that shy, sexy smile again.

As Stanley stuffed the scrubs into the duffle bag, something fell to the floor. I reached down and picked it up. It was a little leather bag tied with leather strapping—about the right size to hold a handful of pills, or maybe a nickel bag of pot.

"What's this?" I asked, handing it back to him.

"Oh, shit," he said. "Don't tell nobody, okay?"

"Tell who what?" I shot him a look I hoped was stern but still cool and sexy. "Are you doing drugs?"

Stanley's eyes widened. "No!" He tucked the little bag away in his jeans pocket. Then he glanced around and leaned over to whisper in my ear. "It's voodoo."

My left eyebrow raised an inch. "Voodoo?"

"Yeah. For protection."

My eyes grew wide. "Protection from *what?*"

Stanley glanced out the little window above the couch at the scenery whizzing by. He bit his lip and gave me a tight, close-lipped smile.

"Looks like we're almost there," he said. "I better go give your man Grayson some directions."

Then, before I could reply, Stanley and his duffle bag disappeared in-to the front of the RV.

Chapter Sixteen

"TURN HERE," STANLEY'S voice emanated from the front cab of the RV.

My fingers curled around the couch's armrest. A second later, I lurched sideways as Grayson hooked a hasty left. Once both of my butt cheeks were back on the couch, I turned and stood with my knees on the cushions. I glanced out the window above the couch. A sign for One Mile Stretch Road whizzed by.

A moment later, the RV came to a halt in front of a low-slung, concrete-block building. It was painted gunmetal gray. A dark-blue awning proclaiming TOPLESS TACOS hung over the front of the building like the Neanderthal brow-ridges of every caveman jerk who patronized the place.

I sneered.

So this is what a topless place looks like. Figures.

I clamped my jaw shut and stomped over to the side door of the RV. Stanley and Grayson were waiting for me in the parking lot. As I climbed out, Stanley shot me a tight-lipped smile. His eyes seemed to plead, "Let's keep this whole voodoo thing our little secret, okay?"

I scowled at him.

Why do all the good-looking guys have to be pervs?

Stanley flinched at my angry expression, then quickly recovered his smile. "You two are in for a treat," he said. "Follow me."

I prepared my women's rights speech in my head as he led us inside the building. But when I looked around, I was surprised to find that inside, the place actually looked like a legitimate restaurant.

I stared at the gleaming, red tabletops wondering where the dance poles were. The only tempting pictures on the walls featured empanadas and nachos. Not a scantily-clad bimbo in sight.

A cute, young woman in rather modest attire for a strip club came up to us carrying four menus.

Can't count to three, huh, honey?

"Sit anywhere you'd like," she said brightly. "I'll be right back to take care of you."

I bet you will.

I plopped down in a chair and glared at the menu like The Church Lady in an SNL skit. Then I read something that made me want to belt out a chorus of *Amazing Grace*.

"Oh, *look*, Grayson," I said cheerily. "TOPLESS stands for tomatoes, onions, peppers, lettuce, extra cheese, salsa and sour cream. Isn't that *clever?*" I shot him my best *stick that in your face and suck it* grin.

Grayson's wandering eyes settled on the menu. "Oh."

"What's good here," I asked my new best friend, Stanley.

He shot me the kind of tentative smile reserved for people with severe mood disorders. "Um ... the tofu tostadas are super yum."

"Hmm," Grayson grunted.

I smiled to myself. The disappointed look on Grayson's face would keep me grinning for at least the next three months.

AFTER TAKING A BITE of his Mahi taco, Grayson finally let go of his grudge and gave Topless Tacos the thumbs up. He washed down his mouthful with a sip of ginger beer and said, "Solid recommendation, Stanley. And, like I promised, lunch is on me."

Stanley let out a tinkling laugh. "Glad you like it, man."

The door to the restaurant opened, snuffing out Stanley's good humor like a paper match in a hurricane. Our new friend stared blankly at the man coming through the door.

It was a uniformed police officer.

The cop glanced our way and nodded at Stanley. "Johnson," the policeman said curtly, then headed to the cash register to pick up his takeout order.

I studied Stanley's face. The casual air about him was gone. In its place was a quiet, almost secretive determination. The best way to explain it was that Stanley had the look of a man who knew there was no such thing as a free lunch, but had decided to take his chances anyway—and lost.

The cop picked up his food and headed for the exit. He opened the door, then, when he was halfway out, said aloud to no one in particular, "Be careful of the company you keep." Then he disappeared out the door.

I glanced over at Grayson, wondering if the cop's remark had been meant as a joke, random advice, or a not-so-subtle warning. And who had he intended it for? Stanley? Grayson? Me?

"What's up with that?" Grayson asked Stanley.

"Officer Holbrook," Stanley said. "He's the cop who took down all my reports when my stuff got stolen outside of Banner Hill. I get the feeling he thinks I'm a liar."

"That's bull-crap," I said. "If he's not treating you right, why don't you report him?"

Stanley sighed. "Don't pay to stir up troubled waters when you got no piss-pot to bail your boat out with."

Geez. This guy mixes up metaphors worse than Grayson.

"I understand perfectly," Grayson said.

Of course you do.

I felt an eye roll coming on, but stopped it when Grayson locked his green eyes on mine.

"You can't look to the law for help when you're not exactly abiding it yourself, am I right Stanley?"

I shifted my gaze over to Stanley. He was nodding his dreadlocks. "Exactly, man."

Wait a minute. Is mixing metaphors an actual language? A kind of secret, male-to-male communication? If so, these two guys could be code-talkers.

"Well, you don't need to confess your sins to us," Grayson said to Stanley. "We operate outside normal parameters, ourselves."

Stanley's head cocked to one side. "Really?"

"Yeah," I said. "We're parano—"

Grayson kicked my shin. "We're paranoid about getting gramps into a good nursing home."

Stanley chewed on that information while I rubbed my shin. Finally, he said, "You look like good folks. Take my advice. Find another place for gramps. I wouldn't put my Pop Pop in Banner Hill. No way."

"Because of the *voodoo* problem?" I asked, my eyes darting to catch Grayson's reaction to my insider knowledge.

Stanley shot me a *what the hell are you talking about* look. Grayson followed suit.

I scowled. So much for winning one for the Gipper.

"Voodoo?" Grayson asked.

Stanley glanced around, then hunched his head down closer to his shoulders. "Something weird going down over there at the Banner, man."

"What do you mean, weird?" Grayson asked. "Have they been serving Spam more often?"

Stanley eyed Grayson like he was either a genius or a fool. I knew the look. I had it down pat myself.

"No. The men folk we been taking care of...." Stanley sighed. "It's like something's sappin' the life juices out of 'em."

"So your voodoo charm isn't working?" I asked, keeping my eyes on Grayson. My partner stared at me as if I might be crazy.

So that's how it is? You're not gonna give me one ounce *of credit for knowing about the voodoo?*

"Voodoo charm?" Grayson asked, turning to Stanley. "Are you worried about the khakua?"

Stanley frowned. "No, man. Voodoo don't work like that. They called a plumber. The toilets were all fixed last week."

I would've laughed if it hadn't been for the tragic fact that less than an hour ago, I'd actually considered these guys to be among the most attractive and intelligent I'd come across in years.

Years!

Stanley pulled the tiny leather pouch from his pocket and showed it to Grayson.

Grayson eyed it skeptically. "So, what's the voodoo bag for?"

Stanley's eyes darted around the restaurant, then he leaned in across the table. "For the haint," he whispered.

Grayson's brow furrowed. "Who's 'the haint'?"

Stanley shot me an incredulous look. I shrugged and said, "He's from up north."

Grayson turned to me, a confused look on his face.

The man knows about a New Guinea khakua demon but not Southern haints? Ugh!

I groaned. "He means the place is *haunted,* Grayson."

Stanley licked his lips and rubbed the little leather bag between his thumb and forefinger. "She's right," he whispered. "There's some kind of spirit roaming the halls of Banner Hill, and it's out for blood."

Chapter Seventeen

"A MALEVOLENT SPIRIT is loose at Banner Hill?" Grayson's green eyes lit up like twin traffic lights. "Tell me more."

Stanley glanced around, checking to see if anyone else was listening. Topless Tacos was empty except for us and another couple across the room. From the way they were shoveling nachos into their maws, I figured they couldn't hear us over the sound of crunching tortilla chips.

Stanley must've surmised the same. He leaned in over the table. His dark-brown eyes shifted from mine to Grayson's, then back again. "I seen her myself. That's why I gots me this protection amulet."

"What's inside it?" I asked, nodding at the little leather pouch.

"Don't know." Stanley shook his head. "If you look inside, you break faith. The voodoo spell won't work."

"Come on. That's bull," I said.

"Faith is the basis of *all* belief systems," Grayson said.

I opened my mouth to argue the point, then shut it. Maybe he was right.

"I probably don't need this thing, anyway," Stanley said, twirling the pouch by its leather string. "Old Mildred don't worry me too much. After all, it was her who gots me my job in the first place."

"Old Mildred hired you?" Grayson asked. "Are you referring to Ms. Draper or Ms. Gable?"

"Neither," I said. "Old Mildred's the haint, right Stanley?"

Stanley smiled at me. "That's right."

"So you're saying a spirit got you your job at Banner Hill?" Grayson asked.

"Round about, yeah." Stanley nodded. "Nina, a friend of mine, told me about the job opening at Banner Hill. She said they were looking for a *male* nurse, on account of Old Mildred."

"I don't follow you," Grayson said.

Stanley smiled slyly. "Old Mildred's a green-eyed devil, like you Grayson."

"Me? I'm no devil."

"He means she's the *jealous* sort," I said, translating for Grayson again. He might've been book smart, but Grayson didn't know his idioms or colloquialisms worth a crap.

"That's right," Stanley said. "Old Mildred's jealous as the day is long. She don't like no other women hangin' around. She done run off the last three women they hired at Banner Hill. That's why they took a chance on me. I was the only guy who applied."

"No way," Grayson said.

Stanley's eyebrow went up. "Look around for yourself. All the night nurses and orderlies there are men folk."

Huh. And here I thought that was because of the icky guy requirement.

"What about the manager, Ms. Gable?" Grayson asked.

"She don't work nights. Flies out of there at dusk like a bat out of hell."

"Have you actually *seen* Old Mildred?" I asked Stanley.

"Yeah. Seen her plain as I'm seeing you right now."

A shiver crawled up my spine. "It doesn't scare you—working with a ghost lurking around in the building? What if Old Mildred decides to take you next?"

Stanley studied me for a moment, then shrugged. "She won't. We got us an arrangement."

"What sort of arrangement?" Grayson asked.

"The Schultz, man."

Grayson nodded. "I see."

"The Schultz?" I asked.

"I know nothing, I see nothing," Grayson said. "Like that sergeant on *Hogan's Heroes.*"

Somehow, I managed not to roll my eyes. "Oh. Right."

Stanley nodded. "I let Old Mildred do her thing, she lets me do mine. I set that right with her my first night on the job."

"How?" I asked. "What happened?"

Stanley glanced around the restaurant again. It was empty except for us and the trail of nacho crumbs that had fallen from the laps of the couple who'd just left.

"On my very first shift, I was walkin' down the hall in the middle of the night and felt something coming up behind me. I turned around and that's when I seen her. Old Mildred. She was all hunched over by the exit door, starin' at me."

"How do you know she was a spirit?" Grayson asked.

"She was all fuzzy-like," Stanley said. He raised his hands and spread them out before him like a fan. "She was surrounded in this dim, purplish light. I knew right then and there I had to choose."

"Choose whether she was a ghost or not?" I asked.

"No, man." Stanley shook his head. "Choose whether or not I wanted to keep my apartment. The rent was due in a week. I needed the paycheck. I decided on the spot to make my peace with Old Mildred."

Grayson leaned in closer. "How'd you do that?"

Stanley smiled slyly. "I give the old gal a compliment. She *is a woman*, after all."

Grayson's cheek dimpled. "What'd you say to her?"

Stanley grinned. "I said, 'Hey, you gots a nice glow about you.'"

Grayson nodded. "Well played."

Stanley picked up the tiny voodoo bag. "Yeah. But next morning, I went and got me this here amulet anyway. Women can be a tricky folk. It don't hurt to have a little something extra backing you up. You know what I mean?"

I nudged Stanley on the arm. "What did Mildred do when you complimented her?"

"She showed me her teeth. What she had left, anyway." Stanley chewed his lip. "Pretty sure it was a smile."

"Then what happened?" Grayson asked. "Did she dematerialize?"

"Nope. She turned around and headed the other way. That's when I seen the poor woman was a *jorobada*."

I nearly spewed my mouthful of iced tea. "A chupacabra?"

"No," Stanley said. "Jorobada. What you call it? A lump-back. You know. Like the whale."

"Humpback?" Grayson asked. "Did you see her flukes?"

"I think he means hunchback," I said.

"That's it!" Stanley said. "Hunchback."

"I see," Grayson said. "Tell me. Was Mildred more the *Quasimodo* type, or the *Igor* type?"

Stanley shot Grayson a sideways glance, then stared at me. I was powerless to help him. It was taking all the strength I had not to flee the scene myself.

"I get the feeling you two gots some strange business going on," Stanley said finally. "You ain't really here to put your old pop-pop in a home, are you?"

Grayson shook his head. "No. We're more interested in your friend Mildred."

Stanley's mouth twitched. "What you want with Old Mildred? She's a harmless old soul."

Grayson's eyebrow flat-lined. "I thought you said she was out for blood."

Stanley shrugged. "Well, it might be blood. I can't say for sure. The men's been disappearing. And Old Mildred's definitely looking for something. Could be they gots something to do with each other, or maybe not."

"Could Old Mildred be draining their vital juices?" Grayson asked.

Vital juices?

"All right," I said, clearing my throat. "Could we get serious here? Vets could be being kidnapped. We need to figure out who—or *what's*—responsible."

Stanley nodded. "Yeah. But how you gonna do that?"

"Via surreptitious surveillance, tracking, and evidence collection," Grayson said.

Translation: Lure them in Grayson's bedroom and collect samples of their scat.

"Hold up a minute," Stanley said, his back straightening. "Are you guys cops? FBI?"

"No," Grayson said. "Private investigators. We specialize in the unexplained."

"Unexplained?" Stanley asked.

"Yes, unexplained," I said sourly, shooting Grayson a smirk. "You know. Zombies. Vampires. Mothmen. That sort of thing."

Stanley's mouth fell open. "No shit."

"No shit," Grayson said, wagging his bushy eyebrows.

"Well, in that case, I got a story for you," Stanley said. "But you got to promise not to tell no police."

Chapter Eighteen

"LAST NIGHT, I WAS MINDING my own business. You know, rearranging the supply closet," Stanley said, then crammed his mouth full of mango-tofu cheesecake.

"So, you were smoking a number," Grayson said, then slurped his coffee.

"Huh?" I grunted during the pregnant pause between the men's mouthfuls.

I was supposed to be typing notes on Grayson's laptop while he interviewed Stanley. But the two may as well have been man'splainin rocket science to a chimpanzee. Either that, or I was way less cool than I liked to think I was.

"How do you get 'smoking pot' out of 'rearranging the supply closet'?" I asked.

Grayson shot me a sideways glance, then locked eyes with Stanley. "Guess she's never worked retail."

Stanley laughed and gave me one of his shy, gleaming-white smiles. "Not much else to do at two in the mornin'."

Grayson nodded. "Go on."

Stanley licked cheesecake from his bottom lip. "Anyway, I just took my third toke when I started hearing voices."

"That must've been some good stuff," I said, trying to sound hip.

Grayson shut me down with a glance, then turned to Stanley. "Continue."

Stanley's eyebrows inched nearer to each other. "That's when I overheard two people talking out in the hall. Somebody said, '*We need another one.*'"

"Another what?" I asked.

Grayson locked eyes with me and shook his head. I scowled and looked down at the keyboard.

"Go on," he said to Stanley. "What did they say next?"

Stanley chewed his lip. "Something like, 'I can't take another one so soon. It'd be too suspicious.'"

"Were the voices men or women?" Grayson asked.

Stanley frowned. "Couldn't say for sure. It was mostly whispering."

Grayson nodded. "What else?"

Stanley sighed. "I slipped my roach back in my pocket and cracked the door open. You know, to get a peek—"

"Wait," I said. "Don't they drug test you guys?"

Stanley shrugged. "Sure. But grass don't count no more. If it did, they couldn't find nobody to work nowhere."

"Go on," Grayson said. "You were opening the door."

"Oh, yeah." Stanley exhaled. "But first, I waited until the smoke cleared—"

"Nice pun," I said.

"Pun?" Stanley asked.

Grayson stared me down, then ran a finger across his throat. I shut the hell up.

"What did you see?" Grayson asked.

"I thought I saw the shadow of Old Mildred on the wall, man. But then that damned roach started burning a hole my leg. Thought it was out."

I stopped typing and looked up at Grayson. He chewed his lip, then said, "Anything else?"

Stanley shook his head. Then, suddenly, he sat up straight in his chair. "Wait. I just remembered. I heard this strange sound. *Scree. Scree.* You know, like a squeaky wheel."

Grayson rubbed his chin. "Hmmm. A squeaky wheel gathers no moss."

Stanley nodded slowly. "*Exactly*, man."

I typed the words, *Really, God?* then backspaced over them.

"So then what happened?" Grayson asked.

"I snuck down the hall, following that freaky sound, man. Then I heard another noise. Sounded like the click the metal bars on the exit doors make. I peeked around the corner, but wasn't nobody there. Only an empty wheelchair sitting beside the glass doors."

"Hmm," Grayson said. "Is that unusual?"

"Kind of. Most guys at Banner Hill don't go nowhere without their chairs."

"Did you see anyone milling around outside? Staff members? Strangers?"

"No. But it was dark, so I didn't want to open the door, you know? But the wheelchair belonged to Charlie Perkins in 3F."

"How'd you know it was Charlie's chair?" Grayson asked.

"Because of that weird sound it made. I think one of the bearings is froze up on it."

Grayson nodded. "Proceed."

"Well, I wheeled Charlie's chair back to his room to check on him. He was gone. Like the others. Just vanished."

"Did you tell anyone?" I asked.

Stanley shook his head. "No. Not right away. I took the chair back to the exit doors. I figured I'd wait a bit. See if Charlie had just slipped out for a smoke or something."

My nose crinkled. "How could Charlie leave if he didn't have his wheelchair?"

"Not everybody in a wheelchair can't walk," Stanley said. "Some's just pure lazybones."

"Did you see anything else suspicious that night?" Grayson asked.

Stanley nodded. "Yeah. One thing."

My fingers poised with anticipation over the laptop keyboard.

"What?" Grayson asked.

Stanley chewed his lip thoughtfully. "Old man Windham's mole on his left cheek. I think that thing's turning color, you know?"

My fingers went limp.

"Did you report the incident the following morning?" Grayson asked.

Stanley shook his head. "No. I thought I'd monitor it for changes, first. See if it gets any bigger."

A tendon appeared in Grayson's neck. "I meant the disappearance of Charlie Perkins."

Stanley grimaced. "No way, man. You know how it is. Whoever smelt it dealt it. Am I right?"

Grayson sighed. "The law of the land."

My brow furrowed. "What?"

Grayson stared at me as if I were clueless, which, at that moment, I totally was.

"People who report crimes to the police often end up on the top of the suspect list," Grayson said.

"Exactly." Stanley bobbed his headful of dreadlocks. "That's why you got to promise you never heard any of this from *me*, okay?"

"If you're innocent, what does it matter?" I asked.

"Can't take the chance, man. I can't go back to Haiti."

My eyes grew wide. "Why? Are you a fugitive?"

Stanley's brown eyes stared at me pleadingly. "No, man. I just can't stand the sound of steel drums no more."

"Totally understandable," Grayson said, nodding thoughtfully. "Besides the abandoned wheelchair, did you see any strange lights, odd footprints, or whatnot?"

Stanley's left eyebrow rose. "You know, now that you mention it, I saw a strange, purple glow outside the door. The same kind I seen around Old Mildred."

"Interesting," Grayson said.

"Hold up," Stanley said. His eyes doubled in size. "You don't think these guys are gettin' beamed up by purple aliens or something, do you?"

Grayson pursed his lips. "Well, Stanley, that's what we're here to find out. So, any chance you know where we could rent a grandpa for the night?"

"You serious?" Stanley eyed Grayson and me. "What kind a kink you two into, man?"

"No kink," Grayson said. "We need gramps for bait."

Chapter Nineteen

"SO, EXACTLY HOW DO you spell Balsijet?" Grayson asked the derelict gumming grits across the booth from us at a local diner called, quite aptly, Johnny Grits.

About a half an hour ago, we'd dropped Stanley off at his apartment. Then, following our new operative's advice, we'd headed straight for the nearest plasma donation center in search of "grandpa bait" for our Banner Hill stakeout scheme.

After sizing up the unseemly selection of pale, toothless, ne'er-do-wells milling about the place, Grayson had lured an old man into his RV with a Jim Beam miniature and the promise of "more where that came from, mister."

I, in turn, had been assigned the lovely task of keeping gramps from escaping out the back of the RV while Grayson drove around searching for a good spot to conduct an interview to ascertain the old guy's mental capacity for the job.

Under my watch, the nearly toothless geezer had sat on the couch across from the banquette and downed three miniature whiskeys in under three minutes.

I was down to the last one and about to panic when Grayson pulled into a parking spot. Instead of handing the tiny whiskey bottle to guzzling Gus, I'd pocketed it. I'd had a sneaking suspicion I was going to need it myself.

With phase one of our scheme complete—procure "old guy"—we'd moved on to phase two. This involved getting "old guy" inside Johnny Grits and sitting upright in a booth without him puking on my shoes or feeling me up. Mission accomplished, phase three had commenced—interview and assess "old guy" to see if he was fit for duty.

We'd ordered breakfast for our new companion, and a bottomless pot of coffee for ourselves. Thankfully, the heavenly aroma of dark-roasted java was masking most of the un-heavenly aroma emanating from our new dining companion.

Wedged in the booth beside me, Grayson was attempting to elicit enough information out of the half-coherent old goat to fill in the blanks on the admissions paperwork for Banner Hill. So far, so good, as we'd yet been asked to leave the premises, despite the fact that the old guy was gassier than the Hindenburg.

"What?" the old man yammered, slinging a mouthful of hominy grits back onto his plateful of congealing fried eggs.

"How do you spell your last name, Mr. Ballsijet?" Grayson repeated.

While Grayson wheedled the details out of gasman, I was to fill out the application and try to keep the grease stains off the paperwork. Easier said than done when the interviewee was a toothless stutterer with a mouthful of grits.

"B-A-L-L-S-ijet," the old man slobbered.

"What was that last part again?" Grayson asked.

Hunched over, covering the admissions application with my arm like the class nerd during a pop quiz, the answer suddenly came to me. I looked up and smirked.

"I got it, Grayson."

B-A-L-L-S, idiot.

"Do you have any identification on you, Mr. Balls?" I asked with utmost cordiality.

Balls grinned, proudly displaying his one remaining tooth. "Right 'cheer." He reached into the breast pocket of his threadbare Hawaiian shirt and produced a pink wallet covered in tiny unicorns jumping over rainbows.

Right. As if this isn't surreal enough already.

Unicorn man opened a flap in his wallet and handed me a laminated card with his picture on it. It was the kind of ID card Florida required of residents in order to claim Social Security checks, food stamps, and/or avoid being picked up for vagrancy. Based on the wear around the edges, Mr. Balls had put the card to good use on all counts.

"Albert Balls," I read aloud, then glanced around for some hand sanitizer.

"That's me," Balls said, and stuck a boney thumb at his boney chest.

"Were you ever in the military, Mr. Balls?" Grayson asked.

"Yep. Army. Gulf War."

Grayson's left eyebrow formed an angular arch. "Pardon me, but you look rather old to have participated in that particular skirmish."

"According to his ID, he's only forty-nine," I said.

"Hmm," Grayson said. "So, Mr. Balls, what precipitated your accelerated physical deterioration? Radioactive fallout?"

"Huh?" Balls' eyes narrowed. "This ain't another one a them government experiment gigs, is it?"

"No, sir," I said cheerfully. "We simply want you to spend the night somewhere and report back to us what happened."

Balls eyed me suspiciously. "I ain't fallin' for that one again."

"What do you mean?" Grayson asked.

I kicked him under the table. "This is nothing like the last time," I said, smiling sweetly at Balls. "I think you'll like this gig. It comes with free Jell-O and Netflix."

"Humph," Balls said, licking grits from his livery lips. "What flavor Jell-O?"

Chapter Twenty

GRAYSON HAD BEEN GONE so long our waitress had left—without even saying goodbye. The woman who took over her shift was giving me and Mr. Balls the evil eye for the umpteenth time.

I could barely blame her.

Not only had we gone through over a gallon of free coffee refills, the body odor emanating from Balls had caused a no-fly zone that now encompassed the poor waitress's entire combat station. Every customer she tried to seat within twenty feet of us had waived a white napkin of surrender and fled.

I, however, had no such option. I'd been assigned KBFE duty—Keep Balls From Escaping—until Grayson got back.

I drummed my nails on the table and watched a glistening string of drool drip from Balls' lips onto his plate.

Come on, Grayson. How long does it take to find a place to fax a damned application?

My pinkie landed in something gooey. I glanced down.

Grits shrapnel. *Ugh.*

I reached for a napkin and cringed in pity for our replacement waitress. Our table looked like a herd of grits-shitting mole-rats had plowed through it after a drunken orgy in a mud pit.

I glanced around, then slunk lower into the booth. What else could I do? I couldn't take Balls out to the parking lot. That would've required me waking him up. As it currently stood, Balls was unconscious, facedown in a slice of apple pie á la mode. Monitoring his breathing seemed a hell of a lot easier than holding him hostage—or, heaven forbid—carrying on a conversation with him.

I shot the Johnny Grits waitress a sympathetic smile and waved a twenty-dollar bill at her. She took a deep breath and sidled over to the booth.

"He ain't dead, is he?" she asked, pocketing the twenty.

I glanced at Balls. He made a few more bubbles in his melted ice cream.

"Sorry about all this," I said. "Poor gramps is on his last legs." I glanced at her nametag. "We're waiting on the paperwork to get him into a nursing home, Wanda."

"Oh," Wanda said, trying not to inhale. "How much longer you gonna be here? I think my boss is getting ready to call the cops."

She nodded to her left. I glanced over at a red-faced man in a dirty apron. He was glaring at me as if I'd brought a herd of drunken, grits-shitting mole-rats into his fine establishment.

"I ... uh ...," I stuttered. Then I caught sight of Grayson coming through the front door. I nearly fainted with relief. "Oh! Wait! Here's my brother now!"

Grayson came strolling up to the booth in his all-black attire. He tipped his fedora at Wanda and me.

"He ain't dead yet," Wanda said.

"Dead?" Grayson asked.

Wanda nodded. "Ain't you the undertaker?"

"I assure you, Miss, I'm not taking anyone 'under' any time soon." Grayson flopped into the booth. "Could you warm up my coffee, please?"

Wanda scowled and wandered off behind the waitress station. I hoped for Grayson's sake she didn't keep a stash of arsenic on hand.

"Good news. Ms. Gable approved the paperwork I faxed over," Grayson said, wagging his bushy eyebrows at me. "Balls' admission is just pending an on-site interview. Our appointment's in an hour."

"An hour?" I glanced over at Balls. "He's gonna need a shower and clean clothes first."

Grayson sniffed the air. "Maybe we should rent a pressure washer."

"Your coffee, sir," Wanda said. She set the mug on the table in front of him and lingered there a moment. I thought I saw her lips curl slightly before she turned and swaggered away.

I chewed my lip. As a veteran of "the restaurant wars" myself, I'd have bet a solid hundred Grayson's java contained a side of "special sauce."

As Grayson's fingers curled around his coffee mug, I debated whether to warn him of his possible imminent demise via passive aggression. But then again, the guy was being pretty lackadaisical considering we now had less than an hour to get Balls prepped and ready for our mission.

"We're gonna need clean clothes for Balls," I repeated. "Walmart trip?"

Grayson raised the mug to his lips, then set it back down without taking a sip. He studied Balls for a moment. "No. In his state, Walmart might prove to be too much stimulus. Could incite a panic attack."

Grayson had a point. The Walmart in New Port Richey was, after all, a supercenter.

"Where we gonna find him a new outfit, then?" I asked.

Grayson picked up his coffee mug again. "Salvation Army donation box."

I frowned. For a beggar, Balls had turned out to be quite the little chooser. Before he'd fallen face first in it, he'd insisted on *two* scoops of ice cream with his apple pie á la mode.

"Balls might not go for hand-me-down clothes," I said.

Grayson laughed. "Believe me, he's not that particular. When you were in the ladies room earlier, he ate a dead fly on a dollar dare."

Chapter Twenty-One

"WHEW!" GRAYSON SAID, emerging from the tiny bathroom in the RV. "I've got to hand it to Mr. Balls. He certainly lives up to his name."

I gagged on the red Tootsie Pop in my mouth. "For the love of God, please don't elaborate."

Balls stepped out of the bathroom wearing nothing but Smurf underpants and a toothless grin. I looked down. Pappa Smurf appeared to have a bad case of the mumps. I died a little inside.

"Whelp, there she went," Balls said, and held up his hand.

Still cringing from my Papa Smurf sighting, an overwhelming force I couldn't understand made me open one eye. There, between Balls' thumb and forefinger, he held what appeared to be an un-popped kernel of corn.

"My last tooth," he said, displaying it as proudly as if he'd just found a gold nugget.

"That'll certainly cut down on the dental bills," Grayson said, then looked my way. "Your turn now, cadet. Get Mr. Balls dressed for his debut."

"Me?" I cringed. "Why *me?*"

"Because *I* just gave him a bath."

"So? Isn't that why you get paid the big bucks?"

"Yes. And that's why I get to make the executive decisions, too. Now, if you want to earn your P.I. merit badge, I suggest you get busy, girl scout."

I WIPED THE SWEAT FROM my brow, my hand trembling from exhaustion. Getting old man Balls dressed had been a feat akin to trying to cram a feral cat inside a garbage bag full of yapping Chihuahuas. *And* I'd had to do it while Grayson drove the RV like a bat out of hell.

"Good job, cadet," Grayson said as I flopped into the passenger seat next to him.

"How much longer to Banner Hill?" I asked.

"Almost there. How'd you manage it?"

"Please," I said, staring blankly at the windshield. "Just let the memory fade."

I reached into my pocket and pulled out the tiny Jim Beam bottle I'd stashed away earlier. I twisted off the cap and guzzled it down.

MY THROAT HAD ALMOST stopped burning when I heard a grunting sound coming from the back of the RV.

Grayson shot me a look. "What's up with Balls?"

I swiveled in my chair and leaned forward, trying to catch a glimpse of Balls without having to get up. He was lying on the sofa, sucking down a tiny bottle of whiskey like a baby goat. I stared at the empty miniature in my hand.

Dear God. That could be me *in twenty years.*

Horror hackled the hairs on the back of my neck. "Why do you buy booze in miniatures?" I asked Grayson angrily. "They cost a hell of a lot more than buying it by the quart."

Grayson shrugged. "I like the tiny little bottles. They're cute. And they're just the right size to mix vitamin water for Gizzard."

"Hey, what's with the lizard?" Balls' voice bellowed from behind us.

"Gizzard isn't a lizard," Grayson yelled back. He hit the brakes. I looked up and realized we'd arrived at Banner Hill.

As Grayson maneuvered the RV into a parking space along the street in front of the nursing home, he said, "Technically, Mr. Balls, Gizzard is an anole."

"Aww. Don't be talking trash about this here poor lizard," Balls yelled back. "She ain't so assholey."

"Not assholey," Grayson said. He cut the ignition. "Anole. *Anolis carolinensis,* to be precise."

I unbuckled my seatbelt. The whiskey had me feeling loose and sassy. I glanced over at Grayson. "You and your stupid phylum fixation. Lizard. Anole. What's the difference?"

"You're kidding," Grayson said, looking somewhat aghast as he stood and pocketed the keys. "A lizard is a reptile of the squamata order."

I scowled.

I'd like to squamata your order.

Instead, I hauled my butt out of the chair and followed Grayson into the main cabin of the RV.

"Anoles are part of the iguana family," Grayson said, picking up the terrarium from the banquette table.

"You don't say," Balls said, then stuck his tongue inside one of the empty whiskey bottles littering the sofa around him like a hobo nest.

Due to the slim pickings available at the Salvation Army drop box, Balls was dressed in a hot-pink Backstreet Boys T-shirt, white size-zero girls' jeans, black-and-white checked sneakers, and Gizzard-green socks.

Grayson studied him for a moment, then turned to me and whispered, "I don't think even an army could salvage that outfit. Let's hope Ms. Gable is colorblind, or our mission is doomed."

Balls half-rolled himself off the couch and stumbled toward us. He swayed gently up to the terrarium.

"Where we at, little lizard boy?" he asked Gizzard. His breath steamed up the glass.

"Like I said, Gizzard is a green *anole*," Grayson said, turning sideways to buffer the terrarium from Balls' deadly breath zone. "And she's female. You can spot the males by their brightly colored dewlaps."

I sighed audibly. Grayson was on another of his useless-fact tirades, and, as usual, at the worst possible moment.

Grayson, if you had a dewlap, I'd sooo be slapping it until it was brightly colored.

"Anoles belong to the chameleon family," Grayson went on, tucking the terrarium under his arm and safely out of Balls' reach. "This lucky girl can change color at will, disappearing into the background to avoid detection."

I glanced at Balls, then Grayson. Suddenly, I found myself jealous of a five-inch long, mealy worm-eating varmint.

Disappearing would come in sooo handy right now ....

"Whatever," Balls said, then peeked out the tiny window above the sofa. "Hey. Why'd we stop here?"

"For your assignment," Grayson said. He handed Balls a twenty-dollar bill. "Get us what we need and there's more where that came from, mister."

"Humph," Balls grunted, staring at the twenty.

"Stay right here for a moment," Grayson said. "I just need to get something from the glove compartment." Grayson turned and discretely nudged me on the shoulder. "Follow me," he whispered under his breath.

I trailed Grayson back into the front cab of the RV, hoping by some miracle he was going to tell me he was calling the whole thing off. Instead, he reached into the glove compartment and pulled out a black writing pen.

"See this?" he said.

"A pen?" I asked. "What're you gonna have Balls do? Hand out autographs?"

Grayson shot me a look. "It's a *spy* pen, Drex. Once activated, this little baby can deliver up to four hours of uninterrupted video and audio."

"Oh." I crinkled my nose at the innocuous looking writing instrument, then made a mental note to never accept another free pen from anybody. Ever. Again.

"Hopefully, this will catch some of the action going on in the nursing home overnight," Grayson said.

I cringed. "Like what? Bedpan races? Or Balls scratching his, you know—"

"That's a calculated a risk we have to take," Grayson said. "However, now that you mention it, to minimize that possibility I'm going to tuck the pen inside Balls' front pocket and aim it outward, like this."

He stuck the pen in his own pocket to demonstrate. "Now you do it to Balls."

We went back into the cabin. I stuck the pen in the pocket of Ball's pink Backstreet Boys T-shirt.

"What's this?" Balls asked, looking down at his shirt.

"A popular boy band," I said, hoping to deflect his attention from the pen.

"A monitoring device," Grayson said, negating my attempt at stealth. "So you can—"

"*Can*," Balls said, cutting him off. "I gotta go to the *can*."

"Right," Grayson said. "It's just right there."

We both stared at Balls.

"A little privacy, please," the old man said.

"Huh?" Grayson grunted.

I grabbed Grayson's arm. "I know exactly how you feel, Mr. Balls. Come on, Grayson. We'll be up front in the driver's cab."

"OUR APPOINTMENT'S IN five minutes," Grayson said, checking the time on his cellphone. "Think he'll be a while?"

"Like *I* would know?"

Grayson rolled down the driver's side window and shrugged. "Just in case, you know."

I knew. And I didn't want to think about it.

We sat in our seats and twiddled our thumbs. A few minutes later, from the back of the RV, a door slammed so hard the whole motorhome shook.

"Mr. Balls?" Grayson called out. "Are you okay?"

Suddenly, something flew through the driver's side window, hitting Grayson square on the side of his head. As it fell to his lap, I realized it was a wadded up twenty-dollar bill.

"I ain't crazy, you know!" Balls yelled.

"What?" I scrambled out of my seat and leaned across Grayson, craning for a view out the driver's side window.

Balls was standing in the parking lot about twenty feet away, hopping from foot to foot in his checkered slip-on tennis shoes. Suddenly, he began to belt out a loose, sing-song rap.

"You can put me in a war zone. You can put me in a disaster zone. Hell, you can put me in a cyclone! But ain't *nobody* puttin' me in no *nursing home!*"

"Wait!" Grayson yelled.

But, apparently, Balls wasn't in the mood for following orders. He took off in his tight white jeans and pink top like a love-struck teenybopper who'd just spotted Jonathan Knight.

"Crap," Grayson said. "There goes fifty-nine bucks for the spy pen."

"Sorry," I said, climbing off him and handing him the wadded-up twenty.

Grayson looked me up and down. "Well, cadet. Looks like it's time for plan B."

Chapter Twenty-Two

"PLAN B?" I ASKED.

The words left a taste in my mouth worse than pure evil had.

"Yes," Grayson said. "Congratulations. The Balls is in your court."

I sighed. "Grayson, the expression is, 'The *ball* is in my court.'"

"No. *Balls.*" Grayson clapped a hand on my shoulder. "As in, *you're* the new Balls."

My stomach dropped four inches. "What?! But .... I *can't!*"

Grayson raised an eyebrow. "Why not?"

"Well, I ... I'm *a woman*, for one thing!"

Grayson snatched the auburn wig off my head. "Could've fooled me."

I ran my hand across the red fuzz growing back from my hospital buzz cut. My mind raced like a rabid squirrel, trying to chase down another excuse.

"What about these?" I said, sticking out my chest. "Balls doesn't have boobs."

Grayson's lips twisted into a sadistic grin. "You're forgetting, cadet. You *yourself* told Gable that our dear old grandpa wanted to be a *granny*. Who says he hasn't had a bit of reconstructive surgery?"

My chest fell. "But ... but ...."

Grayson smiled. "Your quick thinking saved the day with that one."

I scowled. "Saved *your* day, maybe."

"But this is your reward," Grayson said.

"*Reward?* Posing as a geriatric tranny-granny? Come on, Grayson. You can't be serious!"

"Think of it this way," he said. "Now's your big chance, Drex. You get to go *undercover*. This is *real*, honest-to-God P.I. training."

My shoulders slumped.

Crap.

I glanced down at the discarded Salvation Army clothes piled up in the corner like the aftermath of a hobo three-way. I groaned. I knew full well my butt would never fit in any of those pants.

I launched into my own plan B—Begging.

"Can't we find someone else?" I whined.

"There's no time." Grayson glanced at his cellphone. "Our meeting with Gable is in three minutes."

I chewed my lip. "Can't we reschedule?"

"And lose another night? No." Grayson shook his head. "Who knows how many vets' lives could be at stake here?"

"But what about the surveillance pen? Balls ran off with it!"

Grayson grinned. "No worries on that count. I've got a whole case of them."

I sighed and watched my last hope fly out the RV window like Balls' golden tooth. I glared at Grayson. "You can't remember to buy toilet paper, but you've got a whole case of spy pens?"

Grayson shrugged. "Different folks have different priorities." He handed me a pair of purple leotards. "Now, how about trying these on for size?"

Chapter Twenty-Three

"IT'S SHOOOW-TIME," Grayson announced as he wrestled the folding wheelchair out of the RV and onto the street in front of Banner Hill. "Are you nervous about your first stakeout?"

I was. But I felt more angry than nervous. I glared at the wheelchair, wanting to kick myself. It'd been my idea to take the damned thing in the first place. I'd spotted it abandoned behind some bushes by the Salvation Army collection box where we'd filched the clothes for Balls.

Grayson unfolded the wheelchair and patted the seat. "You ready, Grampa Drex?"

I scowled and plopped my butt down in the chair. "Just push me, already," I demanded, and stuck a Tootsie Pop in my mouth.

Grayson heaved the chair, grunting from the effort. "Get out. Let me get the wheels up over the curb first."

"Nope." I crossed my arms and smiled. "Not a chance."

"How am I supposed to get you onto the sidewalk?"

"You're the investigative genius. Figure it out."

Grayson tugged until I thought he might blow a gasket. Still, I didn't budge.

I might've been more obliging if I'd had on a decent outfit. But as it stood, there was no way I was going to stand up and be seen in public dressed in smiley-face boxer shorts and purple leotards. Not in this lifetime.

"You wanted me on this stakeout, you gotta pull your weight," I said.

"I am," Grayson argued, tugging at the wheelchair. "I just wasn't expecting to have to pull *yours*, too."

He yanked the chair a final time. One wheel went up onto the curb. The chair skittered sideways, nearly dumping me out on my head.

"Careful!" someone yelled from across the parking lot. "You need a hand?"

"No!" Grayson called back. "It's all under control now."

Yeah, right.

"Geez, Grayson, I almost ate a dirt sandwich," I grumbled as he maneuvered the wheelchair onto the walkway. As he wheeled me toward the nursing home entrance, I checked my cellphone. "We're late for our appointment."

Grayson leaned over and whispered into my ear. "Give me your cellphone."

The hair on the back of my neck pricked up. "*No way* am I going in there without this, Grayson. What if somebody goes mental in there? How am I gonna call for help?"

"That's why they have those little call buttons by the beds," he whispered. "Now hand it over."

"Not happening." I tucked my cellphone into my leotard.

Grayson glanced around and sighed. "Fine."

"Fine," I hissed back, and punched the big red button marked *For Handicapped Access* with my fist.

The double glass doors slid open automatically. Grayson shoved the wheelchair over the threshold.

"Take it easy with the merchandise," I grumbled. Then I spotted Gable and lowered my voice an octave. "There she is."

I nodded toward the reception desk, where a smooth, helmet of hair was rising like a brown moon from behind the laminate countertop. It was quickly followed by Ms. Gable's glowering face and stout torso.

"You're five minutes late," she barked when she spotted us. "I just put your paperwork in the trash."

"Oh! So sorry about that," Grayson said, pouring on the charm. "Gramps was so excited, he couldn't decide what to wear. See?"

Gable looked at me and flinched.

"By the way, may I say you're looking lovely today?" Grayson added.

Gable didn't look too convinced. She gave me the once-over and said, "*That's* your grandfather?"

"Yes." Grayson reached down and adjusted the collar on the black button-down shirt I'd stolen from his closet after he tried to get me to wear a Looney Tunes hoodie. There was no way that was happening. It was too on the mark.

"Try to suck in your boobs," he whispered.

"What?" Gable asked.

Grayson whipped around to face her. "I told gramps he shouldn't suck those things."

"Agreed," Gable said. "Nasty habit. Choking hazard."

Grayson shot me a look. "I keep telling him that."

"Where's your sister?" Gable asked.

"She's um ... indisposed," Grayson said.

"Indisposed?"

"You know. Getting a high colonic. She ate a bad burrito. Her hemorrhoid cushion blew out and—"

I kicked Grayson's knee out. He nearly fell to the floor. He turned and shot me *what was that for* glare.

"Gramps gets feisty when he doesn't get his Geritol." Grayson held out his hand. "Hand over the lollipop."

I plucked the Tootsie Pop from my mouth and plopped the sticky sucker end into Grayson's palm.

Gable's eyes narrowed in her plump cheeks. "The paperwork you faxed over is for Albert Balls. I thought your grandfather's name was George Burns."

"Uh ... you mean *Georgie* Burns," Grayson said, spinning around to face her. "That's his ... I mean *her* stage name." Grayson sidled up to the reception counter and whispered, "Remember? We told you about his little ... *transition.*"

Gable scowled. "I remember."

Grayson grinned like a used insurance salesman. "So, you see, the thing is, now he—I mean *she*—won't answer to anything but Georgie."

Gable eyed me like I was a fake freak-show exhibit—The Person with No Discernable Reason to Live.

"Humph," Gable grunted. She skirted around the reception desk and addressed me. "Albert?"

I didn't react.

"George?" she asked as she reached my wheelchair.

I stuck my nose in the air.

"Georgie?" she said.

I glanced up at her and smiled. "Hi."

Gable frowned. "It says on your application he's got no teeth."

"Of course," Grayson said. "Those are dentures."

Gable nodded in admiration. "Huh. Pretty nice set." She turned to Grayson. "But they'll have to come out before bedtime."

Grayson nodded. "No problem."

No problem? I see a problem!

"He ... I mean *she* won't put up a fuss?" Gable asked.

"Georgie? No. No fuss at all. Right, Georgie?"

I glared at him.

"If she ever *does* get upset, just do this." Grayson reached over and snatched off my ball cap. Then, with the palm of his hand, he rubbed the red fuzz growing in on my head. He locked eyes with me. "See? She *really likes it* when you do that."

I forced a smile, and Grayson stopped. But when he pulled his hand away, I snapped at it like a rabid Pekinese.

Gable gasped. "She's a biter?"

"Only at me," he said. "Otherwise, Georgie's quite tame, aren't you, sweetie?"

I nodded and smiled sweetly.

Gable's face softened a notch. She went back to the reception desk and did an encore of her brown sunset impersonation. When she re-arose, she had our application in her hand.

She studied it for a moment, then looked over at me. "Remarkable family resemblance," she said. She glanced over at Grayson. "You look just like your grandpa."

I heard another gasp. I wasn't sure if it was from me or Grayson.

Gable picked up a big rubber stamp and pounded the application with a resounding thud.

"Okay, Georgie," she said, smiling at me. "Welcome to Banner Hill. You're just in time for dinner."

My mouth fell open. It was only 4:30.

"What's on the menu?" Grayson asked.

"A Friday-night favorite," Gable said.

"Fish and chips?" I asked.

"Nope," Gable said. "Liver and onions!"

Chapter Twenty-Four

"I GOTTA SAY, FOR NURSING home fare, the food wasn't half bad," Grayson said as he wheeled me toward my room.

"It wasn't *half* bad, Grayson. It was *all* bad," I hissed.

The main hallway now reeked of liver and onions, making me nostalgic for the homey smell of disinfectant and stale urine.

"Come on, Georgie, where's your sense of adventure?" Grayson asked as he shoved me down the hallway, jockeying for position along with the other wheelchair-bound residents.

What is this? A high-stakes race to see who can make it to the toilet in time?

"Adventure?" I asked.

"Enjoying local cuisine is an important part of the experience," he said.

I scowled. "You've got to be kidding. The only thing worse than liver and onions is chicken potpie."

"Potpie?" a frail voice said beside me.

I glanced to my right and caught a glimpse of a thin, black woman pushing a pasty old man slumped into a wheelchair.

"Don't be silly, Melvin," the woman in scrubs said. "You just ate. But don't worry. Tomorrow's Saturday. You'll have potpie for dinner then."

I groaned. Could this get any worse?

Then, as if to prove it could, Grayson leaned down and whispered in my ear. "That must be Melvin Haplets. You know. The grandfather of the guy who called in the reports. I want to talk to him."

Before I could protest, Grayson spoke up cheerily. "Melvin, do you mind if we visit for a few minutes? I want to introduce you to my grandpa. He needs to make new friends. It's his first night here."

The nurse smiled. "Of course. Melvin loves company, don't you Melvin?"

The old man stared up at her blankly from beneath his massive, snow-white comb-over.

She turned her head and shot me a kindly smile. "What room are you in—?"

"Georgie," Grayson said. "Room 3F."

"Perfect. It's just across the hall from Melvin in 4F." She put a hand on Melvin's shoulder. "How about I get you settled in your chair and you can have a nice chat with Georgie?"

Melvin drooled.

"That looks like a yes," she said, beaming at us. "I'm nurse Nina. Follow me."

Nina settled Melvin into a brown, plastic-lined Barcalounger, then aimed him at the TV mounted high on the wall.

"I've got your channel all set," she said to Melvin, and switched on the TV. Suddenly, we were blasted with five million decibels of static.

"Oops," Nina said, lowering the volume. "I better get going. My shift ends in an hour. I've still got rounds to make." She handed the half-comatose old man the remote. "Bye, Melvin. Have a good evening."

Melvin drooled and stared blankly ahead as she exited the door.

I elbowed Grayson in the stomach through the vinyl back of my wheelchair. "The guy's a turnip. We're not gonna get any information out of him."

"You're right," Grayson conceded. He shot Melvin a quick nod. "Enjoy your evening, sir."

As Grayson began a three-point turn to get us out of Melvin's room, the volume on the TV began to rise. Barely audible above it, someone said, "What kind of information youse guys lookin' for?"

Grayson stopped mid-turn. We both turned and stared at Melvin. He was still drooling, but his eyes had taken on a slightly more focused, semi-coherent glow.

"Khakua demon possession," Grayson whispered. "I knew it!"

"What?" I said, squirming in my chair. "That accent doesn't sound like New Guinea to me."

"Hush. Stay still." Grayson held me down by my shoulders. "The khakua has him in a psychic trance."

Grayson spoke directly to Melvin. "Great spirit of the Khakua, what is your purpose here?"

Melvin stared at us blankly.

"We mean you no harm," Grayson continued. "We're here to save you and your friends."

Suddenly, Melvin's eyes began to dart around wildly. I gripped the arms of my wheelchair and watched in horror as Melvin's hand reached out ... and grabbed a tissue from a box by his armchair.

Slowly, Melvin wiped drool from his chin, then locked eyes with Grayson. His mouth opened. Words began to form on his lips ....

"Listen, Bozo. My grandson send you, or what?"

I nearly fell out of my chair—not over Melvin's human veggie act, but from his Brooklyn wise-guy accent.

"As far as you know, yes," Grayson said, not missing a beat. "What's with the miraculous recovery from senility?"

Melvin sighed and rolled his eyes. "It's a ruse."

"A ruse?" I asked. "Why?"

Melvin shrugged. "I used to be an accountant. Everybody's always asking me for tax advice. If you're not careful, the idiots in here will talk your ears off. What do I care about their stupid reverse mortgages or their hippie-dippie grandkids' trust funds?"

"Perfectly understandable," Grayson said. "And, might I add, well played."

Melvin offered up half a smile. "Thanks. So what's *your* scam?"

"Scam?" Grayson asked, taken aback.

Melvin eyed me up and down. "I may be old, but I still know a *broad* when I see one."

"And I know an *antique* when *I* see one," I quipped.

"Grandpa Georgie has gender identity issues," Grayson said.

"Yeah." Melvin smirked. "Whatever. But lemme tell you, sonny, if you care about your dear old 'gramps' there, you won't leave her here overnight."

"Why not?" I asked, beating Grayson to the punch.

"Sounds like you already *know* why," Melvin said.

Grayson nodded. "The missing vets, yes. But we only know part of the story. We need you to fill us in." He sidled up to Melvin and clicked the black spy pen in his hand. "Tell us about the suspicious activities you've witnessed."

"Okay." Melvin glanced around, cleared his throat, then leaned in and whispered into the pen, "That was the *third* time this week they've served liver and onions."

Grayson's face fell like a drop-kicked soufflé. He clicked the pen again. "Well, thanks very much for the intel, Mel."

"No," Melvin said, grabbing him by the arm. "You don't get it. The Army always fed us liver to strengthen our blood. You know. So we could donate to the wounded."

"The guy's delusional," I whispered to Grayson. "He thinks he's still in the army." I gave Melvin a sappy smile. "We're at a *nursing home*, Melvin."

Melvin shot me a sour look. "No shit, Sherlocksky. But I know a battle zone when I'm knee deep in one."

Grayson chewed his lip. "What do you mean? Facilities like this are supposed to be the safest place for seniors such as yourself."

"Oh yeah? Tell that to Charlie," Melvin said. "Or Harry and Larry. Guys are disappearing around here faster than the stale cookies at teatime."

"Charlie Perkins?" Grayson asked.

Melvin glanced around, then upped the volume on the TV. "Yeah. He's the latest. He disappeared from 3F last night."

I grimaced. "*My* room?"

"What do you know about it?" Grayson asked.

Melvin hunkered down and turned up the volume on the TV even higher. He chewed his lip for a moment, then said, "All this past week, Charlie and the other guys kept disappearing for a couple of hours after breakfast. When they came back, they were all pale and weak, like somebody'd nearly sucked the life out of 'em."

"Maybe it was the liver and onions," I said.

"Or maybe *they* were the liver and onions." Melvin said.

"Huh?" I asked.

Melvin's eyes shone like a mafia madman's. "Don't you see? They *feed* our blood, then they *feed* on us!"

"Spam," Grayson said absently.

"What?" My eyes darted from Charlie to Grayson and back again. "Are you saying Charlie was *eaten?*"

Worst liver and onions EVER!

Melvin nodded. "Yeah, that's *exactly* what I'm saying. It's the only thing that makes any sense. They did something to Charlie and the other guys for a couple of days, then took them away for good in the middle of the night."

"What do you think 'they' did to the men during the days before they disappeared?" Grayson asked.

Melvin scowled. "Season 'em with A-1 Sauce? Sprinkle 'em with meat tenderizer? How the hell should *I* know?"

"Okay," Grayson said. "Do you recall exactly when Charlie disappeared last night?"

"Yeah. I'd just switched off *America's Got Talent*. That's when I heard his wheelchair squeaking down the hall in the middle of the night."

"Did you note the time?" Grayson asked.

"No. But it had to be nearly nine o'clock."

"That's the middle of the night?" I asked.

Melvin made a sour face. "It is around here, dick-chick."

Grayson nodded. "Did you *see* Charlie?"

"Naw."

"Then how did you know it was him?"

Melvin sighed. "Listen, bub. I was a mechanic in the Army. I used to be able to tell a Ford engine from a Chevy half-drunk and blindfolded at a hundred paces. It was Charlie's wheelchair all right. I could tell by the squeak of its wheels."

"Right," Grayson said. "Was Charlie alone? Did you hear any voices?"

"No. Just his wheelchair squeaking. Then he didn't show up for breakfast this morning."

"What do you think happened?" Grayson asked.

Melvin turned up the volume on the TV so high I thought his Miracle Ear might explode. "Aren't you listening? They *took* him." His fist pounded the arm of his Barcalounger. "The bastards sucked the blood out of Charlie, marinated him in mustard sauce, then served him for dinner!"

I blanched in horror and disgust.

Melvin leaned over toward me. "A little tip, Missy. Whatever you do, don't eat the potpie."

I shot Grayson a pleading look and mouthed the words, "Can we go now?"

Grayson cleared his throat. "Melvin, the nights that the other men disappeared. Were the circumstances similar?"

"Identical," Melvin said. "That's why I got me this." He reached over and opened a drawer on the nightstand.

I gripped the wheels on my chair, in case Melvin was packing a machete and I needed to burn rubber. I glanced over at Grayson. He was reaching for his Glock.

"Never go to bed without it," Melvin said, and pulled out a whole head of raw garlic. He peeled off a clove and popped it into his mouth.

"Garlic?" I asked.

"Yep," Melvin said between gnashing his dentures. "They don't cook with garlic around here. Say it gives the old guys the farts."

"And it keeps the vampires away," I deadpanned.

"That's just a myth," Grayson said.

"The garlic farts or the vampires?" I quipped sourly.

"Better to have garlic breath than end up a garlic pot roast!" Melvin said. He leaned forward and grabbed my arm. I nearly jumped out of my wheelchair. "You know what? If you like, you can call me Shrimpy."

I grimaced. "Uh ... no thanks."

"You got some nice choppers there," Melvin said, staring at my teeth. "Better hold on to 'em tight."

I cringed and yanked my arm away. "Why?"

"They ought to call this place Scammer Hill," Melvin said. "It's crawling with kleptomaniacs." He glanced up at the TV. "Listen, you two better get out of here, on the double."

"Before they get suspicious?" I asked.

"No. Before my TV show comes on."

"Matlock?" Grayson asked.

Melvin shook his head. "No. It's time for Hannibal."

Chapter Twenty-Five

"WHAT DO YOU THINK—VAMPIRES, cannibals or khakua?" Grayson asked as he wheeled me to my room across the hall from Brooklyn Mel.

"Dementia," I answered. "Melvin got all those crazy ideas from watching reruns of Hannibal Lecter."

"I disagree. Hannibal never drained his victims of blood. At least, not over a prolonged period of days."

"*That's* your problem with this?" I asked, shaking my head. "Grayson, I'm telling you, nobody's getting killed by vampires around here. And nobody's being served up for dinner, either. They're all merely the delusions of a lonely old man."

"But the *disappearances* aren't a delusion," Grayson argued, wheeling me into my room. "How do you explain the missing men?"

I got up out of the wheelchair and closed the door to my room. "Here's a concept. Maybe they all *died of old age.*"

Grayson frowned skeptically. "But why hide it?"

"Duh! Maybe the staff here didn't want to upset the other residents?"

Grayson laughed. "That's what I like about you, Drex. I can always count on you to come up with some ridiculous alternative solution."

"Wha—" I threw my hands in the air. "Wow. Look at the time. I better get ready for bed. It's almost six thirty. Surely visiting hours are over, aren't they?"

I glared at my unwanted houseguest as I unbuttoned the black shirt I'd stolen from his closet. Underneath, I was wearing a Dead Head T-shirt so tight it doubled as a corset and a bra. I untucked the T-Shirt from my purple leotard and smiley boxer shorts, and looked around for the duffle bag with my stuff in it.

Suddenly, the door to my room popped open. A familiar face surrounded by dreadlocks poked in.

"How's our new resident settling in?" Stanley asked, and shot Grayson a wink. Then he glanced over at me. His eyes doubled in size. "What are *you* doing here?"

"Balls flew the coop," Grayson said.

"And I'm plan B," I said.

"Geez!" Stanley stepped inside and closed the door behind him. "Are you serious?"

"Afraid so," I said.

Stanley eyed me up and down. "You can't wear that to bed. Let me get you a gown."

"A nightgown?" I said. "I'm trying to look like a *man*, remember?"

"I meant a *hospital* gown." Stanley stepped out into the hallway and returned pushing a small laundry cart. "I've got a fresh one here somewhere." He fished around in a pile of folded clothes. "Aha. Here we go." He handed me a mint-green gown that tied in the back.

I scowled. "My favorite designer. Louis Butt-out."

Grayson helped himself to a white lab coat from the cart and stuffed it into the duffle bag containing my "personal effects."

"I did *not* just see that," Stanley said.

"What do you want with the lab coat?" I asked Grayson.

"I plan to conduct a review of the missing guys' charts tonight," he said. "How about a little help, Stanley?"

Stanley closed his eyes and stuck his fingers in his ears. "I see nothing. I know nothing." He opened one eye and shook his head at Grayson. "Sorry, man. That's all the help I can give you."

Grayson clapped a hand on Stanley's back. "All I'm asking for is a little night watchman service. Keep an eye out while I peruse some files. Easy-peasey."

Stanley shook his head so hard his dreadlocks began to sway. "No way, man. I need this job."

"Fair enough," Grayson said. "Thanks for the doctor duds."

"You didn't get those from me," Stanley said, checking off something on a clipboard.

I picked up the glass of water by my bedside and held it up to the light. "This water looks bluish. Is it safe to drink?"

"That isn't for drinking," Stanley said. "It's for your teeth."

"My teeth?" I asked.

"Yeah. The ones that go into the glass."

My nose crinkled. "Oh. But I don't have dentures."

"You don't?" Stanley glanced down at the clipboard, then back at me. "According to this, you better get some quick. Before the count comes."

"Count?" Grayson asked. "As in ... *Dracula?*"

Stanley shot him a look. "No. As in *bed* count. It's lights out, dentures out at seven-fifteen, sharp."

"Sharp," Grayson said, nodding slyly. "Is that some kind of code?"

Stanley eyed Grayson. "Code?"

"For vampires. Sharp teeth and whatnot."

I shot Stanley an apologetic look. "Anything else I should know before we call it a night, Stanley?"

"Yeah. Don't listen to Melvin across the hall. He's crazy."

I smirked. "Ditto for Grayson."

AT FIVE MINUTES PAST seven, Grayson waltzed back into my room and tossed a small brown bag on my lap.

"What's this?" I asked, sitting up in my bed. The crunch of the plastic liner on the mattress made me cringe with disgust.

"It's your get-out-of-the-dentist-free card," he quipped.

I opened the bag and pulled out a pair of cheap, plastic vampire teeth. "What the?"

He shrugged. "Best I could do on short notice. Walmart doesn't sell choppers off the shelf."

As I plopped the fanged dentures into the glass of blue water on the nightstand, the door opened. An orderly I hadn't seen before glanced first at me, then at the teeth in the glass. He scribbled something on a clipboard and said, "Visiting hours are over in ten minutes. You need a bedpan, Georgie?"

"No. sir."

"Very good." The orderly disappeared, closing the door behind him. Grayson pulled a black pen from his jacket pocket.

"Here's your granny cam," he said, and hooked it to the sleeve of my thin, cotton gown. "Just tap here to start recording."

"Okay. When should I activate it?"

"Whenever you see something suspicious. Or you feel like you're going to pass out. Whichever comes first."

"Pass out? Why would I ...? Never mind."

"You gonna eat that pudding?" Grayson asked, nodding at a plastic container sweating condensation on my nightstand tray.

"Maybe."

"I was thinking it could be porphyria."

I crinkled my nose at the container. "I thought it was tapioca."

"I meant what's going on here," Grayson said. "Porphyria's a blood disorder, Drex. One of the treatments for it used to be the drinking of human blood."

There goes my appetite.

I handed Grayson my pudding cup. He peeled off the top and dug into it with a plastic spoon. "Mmm."

"Eat fast and then beat it," I said, folding my arms across my chest. "You've got one minute, then I'm pressing my alarm button."

Chapter Twenty-Six

AT EXACTLY 7:15 P.M., I saw the hall lights blink out through the crack under the door. I stretched out in my nursing home bed and yawned. After two weeks of sleeping in either sleazy hotels or the lumpy sofa in Grayson's RV, I felt like I'd won a free night in P. Diddy's retirement crib.

I was living large with my own full-sized bed, full-sized TV, and full-sized bathroom—one that, by the way, would *not* come with Grayson screeching *Bat Out of Hell* at the top of his lungs tomorrow morning at the crack of dawn.

Yeah. A girl could get used to this ....

I clicked off the lamp beside my bed and snuggled under the sheets. In the eerie green glow of the bathroom nightlight, I giggled like a naughty teenager as I fished around in the covers for my contraband cellphone. I pressed speed dial and called the only person I knew who wouldn't ask too many questions—or be freaked out by my answers.

"Hey, Beth-Ann," I whispered to my geeky, Goth girlfriend back home in Point Paradise.

"Bobbie. You're still alive," she deadpanned. "I was beginning to wonder."

"Yeah. Still got all my fingers and toes. How's the beauty-shop biz?"

"Slow. All the old ladies are saving up their cash for next week."

"Next week? Somebody's funeral?"

"No. Thanksgiving. It's the calm before the wash-n-set storm. Come next Tuesday, I'll be a madwoman, curling and teasing every old biddy's silver-blue do from Waldo to Fairbanks."

I snorted. "Why in the world do they bother?"

"I dunno. I guess they all wanna look better than their relatives. Or, at least better than the stuffed turkey they're sitting next to."

I grinned. "Speaking of turkeys, have you heard from my cousin Earl lately?"

"No. Why?"

"I was just wondering. You think he's actually trying to run the auto shop, or is he letting our family business fall to pieces?"

"I thought that already happened years ago."

I winced. "Ha ha."

"Listen. If you want, I can drive by the garage and snoop around. Tell Earl I've got transmission trouble or something."

"No." I sighed. "You're busy. Let's save that idea for a future emergency. Right now, I've got a different one on my hands."

"Don't tell me. You're pregnant!"

"Geez! No!"

"Sorry," Beth-Ann said. "At least tell me you've gone to bed with Grayson by now. I need some juicy gossip, stat."

"I'm in bed. But not with Grayson."

"Ooo la la! With who, then?"

"Not *who*. *Where*. I'm doing my first private eye stakeout!"

"Where? In a brothel?"

My nose crinkled. "No. A nursing home."

"Nursing home?" Beth-Ann laughed. "Why? Somebody steal gramps' Geritol?"

"No. They stole gramps himself."

"What?"

"I'm not kidding. People keep disappearing from here."

"New Port Richey? Of course they do, Bobbie. Anybody with brain cells and bus fare."

"I'm serious, Beth-Ann. Grayson thinks something really odd is going on."

"So do I. Why haven't you two hooked up yet?"

I shook my head. "Good grief, girl. Is that all you think about?"

"That and hair dryers."

I blew out a breath. "Look at us. Just like old times. Friday night and neither one of us has a date."

Beth-Ann laughed. "Sad, but true. At least your odds are better than mine."

"How so?"

"You're surrounded by beds full of men."

"Yeah. All old enough to have voted for Barney Rubble for president."

Beth-Ann giggled. "We *are* a pair, aren't we? I got stuck with all the old ladies. You got stuck with all the old men."

"Yeah. Lucky us."

"Eeew."

"What?" I asked.

"I just had a thought."

"About what?"

"Watch yourself, Bobbie. Old men can still get it up, you know."

"Eeew."

"Exactly. Hey! You know how you can tell which ones still can?"

I grimaced. "No."

"Depends."

"Depends?"

"Yeah," Beth-Ann said. "Depends on the bulge in their pants—if it's in the front or the back."

Chapter Twenty-Seven

BROOKLYN MEL WAS IN my room.

He was dancing around in a diaper.

It was bulging on the least favorable side.

"Rock and roll is the Devil's music," he said, then pirouetted toward a bookshelf like Doris Day on speed. "I prefer easy listening, myself."

He flipped the switch on a portable radio. Michael Franks' Popsicle Toes began to play. He sidled over to my bed and slipped a cold hand under my covers. He grabbed ahold of my left foot and lifted it toward his open mouth.

He wasn't wearing his dentures.

"Stop!" I yelled. I reared back my leg, preparing to kick Mel and his denture-less mug all the way to Denver.

Suddenly, Quasimodo burst into the room and bonked Melvin over the head with a bedpan.

I closed my eyes and hoped against hope that the pan was empty ....

I AWOKE WITH A SNORT, twisted up in the sheets like a pretzel. My naked butt was hanging off the left side of the bed.

The door cracked open. I squirmed to cover myself.

"Sleep well?" Stanley asked, poking his head in the door. "I just thought I'd check in on you before breakfast."

I jerked the covers over my derriere. "What time is it?"

"Five-twenty."

"A.m. or p.m.?"

Stanley grinned. "So, I take it you slept well."

"I was out like a broken taillight." I sat up in bed. "Do they put drugs in the water around here or what?"

Stanley shrugged. "Don't ask, don't tell. That's my policy."

"Right. I forgot."

"So, you're okay?"

"Yes. No body parts missing. Thanks for checking. Have you seen Grayson?"

"Not this morning. But breakfast is at six. Invite him, if you want. I'll come back and wheel you down."

"That'd be great. Thanks."

Stanley left without mentioning my embarrassing Southern exposure. I laid back in bed and counted my blessings. At least it hadn't been my smartass cousin who'd seen me. Mercifully, Earl didn't know anything about this stakeout. And he never would. I'd sworn Beth-Ann to secrecy over the phone last night.

I sucked in a deep breath and sighed. Then I stretched out on the bed like a stray cat on vacation. I hadn't slept this well since the time I drank eight margaritas and slashed all four tires on my cheating boyfriend Blanders' moving van.

Ahh. Precious memories ....

AS PROMISED, STANLEY returned to fetch me for breakfast. As he pushed my wheelchair around the corner and into the breakfast room, I nearly gasped. I'd expected Grayson. The other hairy, ape-like creature sitting beside him, not so much.

"What are you doing here?" I hissed.

"Hiya, Cuz," Earl said, swiping his shaggy black bangs from his eyes. "You didn't think I was gonna miss *this* did you?"

I shot Grayson a look that could've curdled the milk inside a Billy goat. He shrugged. "With you indisposed, I needed the backup."

Earl snickered at me in my wheelchair. "You got a bedpan under there, Bobbie?"

I sneered. "If I did, I'd have already beaned you upside the head with it."

"Well," Stanley said, "I'll leave you to your happy family reunion. I've got to go get Melvin, anyway."

As he turned to go, the skinny nurse from yesterday came running into the breakfast room.

"Stanley!" she gasped, nearly out of breath.

"What's wrong, Nina?"

Nina saw us staring, and lowered her voice. "I ... I just came from Melvin's room. He's not there. No one's seen him this morning!"

Chapter Twenty-Eight

AFTER SAMPLING A SPOONFUL of slimy porridge from his Banner Hill breakfast tray, Grayson had suggested we dine out. I'd darn-near left skid-marks on the terrazzo burning rubber with my wheelchair.

We were back at Johnny Grits, but I wasn't worried about getting thrown out, this time. Disguised as an old man in a wheelchair, I figured no one would recognize me without my sidekick, Balls. As for Grayson? He was on his own.

"So another poor old geezer flew over the cuckoo's nest?" Earl mumbled through a mouthful of bacon. "What's that make? Four now?"

"Yes," I said, eyeing Grayson sullenly. "How could you leave me in that place alone last night? *I* could've been the one who ended up buying it!"

"Buying what?" Earl asked. "I thought they didn't allow no solicitors."

Grayson eyed the tendons poking from my neck. "I had your back," he said to me. "I was camped out in the RV in the parking lot the entire night. All you had to do was ring me."

"Right," I said sourly. "And just how did you plan on getting in?"

"Stanley."

I slunk back in the booth. "Oh."

"That dude who wheeled you in for breakfast?" Earl asked. He wagged his eyebrows at me and laughed. "He your new boyfriend, Bobbie?"

I shot my annoying cousin my best evil grin. "I've got a scalding cup of coffee here, Earl, and I'm not afraid to use it."

Earl shrunk back in his seat. "Feisty this mornin', ain't ya."

Grayson took a bite of hash browns. "Let me see your pen, Drex."

Crap.

"I uh...I forgot to activate it last night."

Grayson eyed me blankly for a moment as he chewed his hash browns. He swallowed. "Did you see anything unusual last night?"

I winced. "Do dreams count?"

Grayson perked up. "Absolutely."

"I ...." I glanced over at my cousin, then leaned in and whispered something into Grayson's ear.

"What? I can't hear you," he said.

I scowled. "I said, I dreamed Melvin was dancing around in a diaper. Then he tried to suck my toes."

Earl laughed so hard he blew coffee through his nose.

I glared at him. "If you need the Heimlich, don't come crawling to me."

"Did you take a shower this morning?" Grayson asked.

I surreptitiously tried to smell my armpit. "No. Why?"

"Good. I need to swab your toes for saliva."

Earl hooted so loudly the waitress came running over.

"Is everything all right?" she asked, her eyes as big as the poached eggs she was carrying.

"Sorry 'bout that," Earl said, sopping up coffee with his toast. "Looks like I'm gonna need me some extra napkins."

I closed my eyes and smiled, secure in the knowledge that if I survived this moment, there was *no way* my life could ever get any worse. I opened my eyes. Grayson was holding a Q-tip in my face.

Well, there went that pipe dream.

"Can the swabbing wait until after breakfast?" I asked.

Grayson shrugged. "Sure. I guess so." He put away the baggie of cotton swabs.

While Earl was busy dabbing at his head-to-lap coffee stains with the extra napkins dumped off by the waitress, I leaned across the table and spoke to Grayson through gritted teeth.

"I still don't see why you had to tell Earl about our case."

"Like I said, I needed the backup." Grayson stirred a pinch of salt into his coffee refill. "And when I found out he was already in town, well, how could I resist?"

"Already in town?" I turned and scowled at my soggy, flannel-shirted cousin. "Are you *stalking* me, Earl?"

He laughed. "You *wish*, Cuz. I'm in town for the revival."

"The revival of what?" I asked. "Your dead brain cells? Too late for that."

"Faith," Earl said reverently, then patted his coffee-stained chin demurely with a paper napkin. "You remember the Baptist Evangelical Resurrection Path Seekers, don't ya, Bobbie?"

My nose crinkled "The *who?*"

"The BERPS," Earl said. "They came through Point Paradise about ten years back?"

I stared at him blankly. "I got nothin'."

Earl cocked his head at me as if I were a five-legged frog. "Come on, now. Reverend Bertie? He performed that miracle, remember? He healed that boil on Artie's butt."

I grimaced at the unearthing of a memory I'd worked hard to bury. "Oh, yeah."

"That doesn't sound like much of a miracle to me," Grayson said.

"Well, you didn't see the boil," Earl said.

I sighed. "Or the butt."

"Hmm," Grayson said. "Why is it I've never heard of these BERPS?"

"Luck?" I said.

"Oh, man! Mr. G, you're in for a treat!" Earl grinned and slapped Grayson on the back. "Nothing beats The Bertie in action! I'd bet good money that feller could even raise the dead!"

"Hmm," Grayson said. "If so, Bertie may be just the guy we're looking for."

Chapter Twenty-Nine

"Melvin was dancing around in a diaper. Then he tried to suck my toes."

My mouth fell open. I'd just heard my own voice—but I hadn't uttered a word. I scooted my wheelchair up toward the front of the RV.

"What's going on up there?" I asked.

No one answered.

Confined to my role as a wheelchair-bound vet, I'd been relegated to the back of the RV. I'd rolled the wheelchair up to the narrow passage leading to the front cab, but it was too wide to fit through.

I banged the wheels against the walls a few times, then I remembered that I could walk. I got up out of the wheelchair and poked my head into the driver's cab. Grayson was driving. Earl was in the passenger seat, fiddling with Grayson's laptop.

"Hey, Bobbie!" Earl said. He grinned at me and started dancing a jig with his upper torso, working the black spy pen like a majorette's baton. "Waahoo! It worked!"

"What worked?" I grumbled.

"This here spy pen! Looky here!"

Earl pushed a couple of keys on Grayson's laptop. A video of me came on the screen.

I flinched. I recognized the booth at Johnny Grits, but not the close-up shot of the face on the screen. Whoever it was looked like Lucille Ball trapped in a lice-infested internment camp.

My mouth fell open as I watched my face filled the screen like a hostage selfie. Then my video image said, *"Melvin was dancing around in a diaper. Then he tried to suck my toes."*

Earl had struck blackmail gold.

"Ha Ha! Got you good, Bobbie!" my cousin said, twirling the spy pen between his huge fingers. "Boy howdy, I want me one of these babies!"

I snatched the pen away from him. "Grayson's got a whole case full of 'em. If he gives you one, will you go away?" I glared over at Grayson. His eyes were on the road, but his cheek was dimpled.

Jerk!

"Well now, that ain't very charitable of you," Earl said, "seeing as how I come all this way to help you out."

"You came to see Reverend Reflux," I said.

"Bertie and the BERPS," Earl corrected haughtily.

"Whatever!"

"I'm pulling over to get gas," Grayson said. "Drex, go sit on the couch and take your shoes off."

"Yeah. Cool your heels," Earl said. "Good idea, Mr. G."

"What?" I hissed.

"I'm not taking sides," Grayson said. "Actually, Earl just reminded me that I forgot to swab your toes."

"It was just a *dream*," I said.

Grayson maneuvered the RV onto an exit ramp. "You never know. The khakua is a tricky demon."

"That's right," Earl said. "Why you think they sell so much Ex-Lax?"

Something inside me gave up. I surrendered, blew out a huge sigh, and went back and flopped onto the couch.

GRAYSON FINISHED SWABBING my toes, then dropped the Q-tip into a vial. "If it tests positive for saliva, I'm going to need samples to compare it with," he said as I inched my feet back into my cheap, black, nursing-home issue slippers. "Next time you're in the cafeteria, I want you to swab the cups and glasses. I'll also need samples from the staff."

I shot Grayson a look. "I've got a better idea. Why don't *you* play gramps tonight and swab people yourself?"

He grinned. "I would, but Gable would recognize me."

I grinned back. "It's *Saturday*. She doesn't work weekends."

"Hmm." Grayson chewed his bottom lip. "That gives me an idea."

I groaned. *Not another one.*

"Let's all go to the plasma center. See if we can spot Balls."

"Pardon me, Mr. G," Earl said, chewing his lip. "But ain't that illegal?"

My eyes rolled involuntarily. "Balls is the name of the guy who was supposed to be spying for us last night."

"Oh," Earl said. "How would we spot him?"

I deferred to Grayson.

He looked to his left and said, "Well, for one thing, the guy's especially well-endowed."

"WHY DID THIS BALLS feller run away in the first place?" Earl asked as we drove toward the plasma center after the gas-up and swab-down.

Because he has even more brains than he's got balls.

"Some people just can't be caged," Grayson waxed philosophically.

"Ain't that illegal?" Earl asked.

I closed my eyes and laid back on the couch.

Apparently, I've died and am now in some kind of psychotic purgatory. It's the only thing that makes any sense.

"Here we are," Grayson said, pulling up to the curb. He slammed on the brakes. I nearly fell off the sofa.

"There he is!" Grayson yelled.

"Balls?" I called back.

"Yes," Grayson said. "I'd know those Smurf underpants anywhere!"

Yep. Psychotic purgatory it is.

"He's taking off," Grayson said, bursting into the main cabin. "Let's go. We've got to catch him!"

"Sorry," I said, lying back on the couch. "I can't run in these stupid nursing home slippers."

Grayson eyed the black, plastic shoes. "Okay, Earl. It looks like it's you and me, bud."

Earl nodded. "You can count on me, Mr. G."

The two scrambled out the side door. As it slammed behind them, I laid back on the couch and smirked.

Two boobs against four balls.
May the odds be ever in my favor.

Chapter Thirty

I WAS UP IN THE FRONT cab, contemplating stealing the RV and never looking back, when I spied Earl and Grayson stumbling around the corner of the plasma center. Each was holding tight to the arm of some naked guy who was squirming like a dog about to get dunked in a vat of flea dip.

I leaned closer to the windshield for a better look. The guy wasn't naked. He had on Smurf underwear. As my eyes moved upward to scan his face, I realized it wasn't Balls. I poked my head out window.

"Let him go," I yelled. "That's not Balls."

"You sure?" Earl hollered. "How can you tell?"

I blew out a sigh, hoping to erase the image of Papa Smurf seared into my brain. "Believe me. A woman knows these things."

"I know he's not Balls," Grayson said, wrestling with the guy's arm like it was a python. "But he's got on his underwear. I detained him for questioning, and I need you to take down his testimony."

Lucky me.

"I demand that you unhand me at once," the man said. For being dressed solely in boy-sized Smurf underpants, the guy managed to pull off a fairly dignified huff.

"Where'd you get the Underoos?" Grayson asked.

The man bucked like an angry burro. "I found them by the trash cans over there."

"He was carrying this," Grayson said, and handed me Balls' pink unicorn wallet.

Crap! Where's the Purell?

"Where'd you get the wallet?" I asked, holding it between the pinch of my thumb and forefinger.

He shrugged and shot me a sullen stare. "Came with the underpants."

I grimaced, totally jonesing for some industrial-strength sanitizer. "What happened to the rest of your clothes?"

The guy stopped squirming. "Look, I didn't know she was a cop, okay?"

"Who?" I asked.

"Right," he said sourly. "Just read me my Mirandas and get it over with."

A speck of his spittle landed on my forearm. I wanted to jump into a vat of bleach. "Look, perv, we're not after *you*. We're after the guy who was wearing those Smurfs before you. Do you know him?"

"No."

"Did you see him drop them?"

His nose crinkled. "No way. I don't swing that way."

"Well, did you—"

"You ask a lot of questions for a man with boobs," he said, shooting me a cocky stare.

My neck muscles tightened. I held up the spy pen I'd swiped back from Earl. "Look. You didn't happen to see a pen like this one, did you?"

"Well, yeah," he said.

I nearly fell over. "Uh ... okay. Hand it over."

"I don't have it."

"Why not?" Grayson asked.

The guy shrugged. "I didn't want it."

Earl gulped like an unclogging drain. "You didn't *want* it?"

The guy scowled. "What for? It's not like I need to write a rent check to Rockefeller." He nodded his greasy head to the left. "It's over there. By the garbage cans."

Earl let go of the guy's arm and sprinted toward the trash bins.

"Where is everybody?" Grayson asked captain underpants. "The plasma center's usually swarming with people."

He shrugged. "Down at the revival, I guess. Some guy came up in a van and announced they had free food over there. I was nearly trampled in the stampede."

"BERPS?" I asked.

"Sorry," he said. "Mushrooms always give me gas."

"Found it!" Earl hollered from behind me.

Grayson and I turned to look. Captain underpants seized the opportunity to escape. He jerked free of Grayson's grasp and ran for it.

"Dang! Should I chase him down?" Earl hollered.

"No. Let him go," Grayson said. He took the pen from Earl and slapped him on the back. "Good job."

"Huh," Grayson said, studying the spy pen.

"What?" I asked.

"It appears to have been activated. It could contain valuable information."

I sneered. "Or E.coli."

Grayson stuck the pen in his shirt pocket. "I think this calls for a celebration, team! How about some topless tacos?"

Earl looked at him sideways. "Sorry, Mr. G. But ain't that illegal?"

Chapter Thirty-One

WHILE EARL AND I MUNCHED on topless tacos, Grayson pulled Balls' spy pen in half, revealing the USB stick hidden inside. He stuck it into a port on his laptop and, after wiping his fingers with a wet-nap, grabbed a tortilla chip, crammed it into his mouth, and punched a few keys.

The computer screen blinked to life. "Showtime," Grayson said, wagging his eyebrows like Groucho Marx.

Earl and I scooted our chairs around the table for a better view of the video. But we needn't have. The audio crackled with static, and the video remained totally black.

"Maybe he was wearing an eye mask," Earl said.

Grayson and I exchanged glances, then looked back at the screen. "The pen must've been inside Balls' pocket," Grayson said.

"I *hope* it was his pocket," I said, then took another bite of taco before I lost my appetite.

"Come on, I'll give you a dollar for it," Balls' voice suddenly emanated from the laptop speakers.

I paused mid-bite. We all leaned closer to the screen.

"You ain't got no dollar," a woman's voice said.

"Do, too."

Grayson paused the video and whispered, "I bet that's the dollar I gave Balls for eating a dead fly."

Earl's nose crinkled. "Ain't that illeg—"

I slapped my hand over Earl's mouth. "Shhh!"

Grayson tapped a button to resume the video, which continued on in pitch blackness.

"See here?" Balls' voice asked.

"Huh. Where'd you get the condom?" the woman asked.

"Came with the wallet."

"All right. Have a swig."

A *glug-glug* sound—like a bottle being poured down a drain—emanated from the speaker.

"Hey! That's more than a swig!" the woman screeched.

Balls grunted, then the sound of him panting hard and heavy filled the speakers.

"Gross. What's he doing now?" I asked, not wanting to know.

"Running, I think," Grayson said.

"Ungh! Ow!" Balls grunted.

"That would be him falling down," Grayson said.

"No!" Balls screamed.

Suddenly, a video image blinked onto the screen. It was a side view of one of Balls' checkered tennis shoes, his foot still in it.

"He must've dropped the pen," Grayson whispered.

"Or it fell out of his pants," Earl said.

A weird, helicopter-like whooshing sound overtook the audio. Leaves and garbage lifted up and began swirling around Balls' feet. A strange, purple glow shone on the white squares of his tennis shoes.

"This is your last chance," an unearthly voice said in a strange accent.

"Romanian?" Grayson asked.

"No thanks," Earl said.

Suddenly, Balls' checkered sneaker pivoted on its heel. He was turning, possibly to flee. The pen must've rolled slightly, as a brief image of Balls' terrified face flashed onto the screen. Then everything blinked out to black. Both the video and audio cut out.

"Crap," Grayson said. "He must've stepped on the pen and turned it off."

I glanced over at my cousin. His eyes were the size of globe grapes.

"What just happened?" Earl whispered. "Did outer space critters get Balls?"

"Inconclusive," Grayson said. He sat back in his chair and rubbed his chin. "Stanley mentioned that Old Mildred emitted a purple glow. He also said he saw a strange purple light outside the nursing home the night Charlie Perkins disappeared."

"And now, here the lights are again," I said.

Earl grabbed my arm. "You think it could be an attack of the Purple People Eaters?"

I jerked my arm free. "Get serious!"

"What?" Earl balked. "They're *real*, Bobbie. They made a song about 'em and everything."

I looked to Grayson for support. To my surprise, he appeared to be mulling the idea over.

Great.

I shot him a dirty look.

"What?" Grayson asked. "Many folk legends and ballads are based on real events."

Earl smirked. "Told ya so, Cuz."

I lifted my butt cheeks one at a time and sat on my hands. It was the only way I could stop myself from slapping someone.

Chapter Thirty-Two

GRAYSON WAS DEEP IN thought as he drove us back to Banner Hill. I was in the passenger seat beside him, fake disability be damned. I'd called shotgun right before we left Topless Tacos, and now Earl was in the back cabin, trying his best to pop a wheelie in my wheelchair without landing on his fat head.

I tapped Grayson on the shoulder. "What else could cause a purple glow?" I half-whispered, hoping Earl wouldn't overhear.

"Ionizing radiation, for one," Grayson said.

I flinched. "Radiation?"

Grayson nodded. "Radium, in particular. Sufficient quantities of radioactive radium or polonium can create an eerie purple glow, if the conditions are right."

"What kind of conditions are necessary?"

"Well, being at sea level, for one."

"Okay. We've got that one covered. What else?"

"A critical accident in a particle accelerator."

My gut slumped. "You mean like a nuclear meltdown?"

"Precisely."

I ground my teeth in frustration. Still, an atomic explosion seemed more plausible than Purple People Eaters. "Crystal River nuclear plant is only fifty miles from here."

"Hmm." Grayson shifted his eyes from the road toward me. "Any reports of recent mushroom cloud activity in the area?"

I returned his stare, dead on. "No. I think we'd have heard something about it on the radio or something."

"Humph. Too bad." Grayson turned back to face the road. "That would've explained the sudden wind gust quite nicely."

We drove along US 19 for a few minutes in silence, taking in the sights of the city—mainly factory-outlet carpet stores and used automobile sales lots.

"Wait," Grayson said. "There *is* another possibility."

I tore my eyes from a late-model Buick with a windshield sticker marked down to $649.99. "What?"

Grayson hesitated. "Nah. You'll think it's silly."

I glanced back at Earl sitting in my wheelchair making gorilla faces into a hand mirror. "Try me."

"Well, certain types of mushrooms glow with purple bioluminescence."

I smirked. "Before or *after* you eat them?"

Grayson's cheek dimpled. "Take the order Agaricales. It's indigenous to temperate and tropical climates, and includes over seventy-five species of bioluminescent fungi."

"What are y'all talkin' about?" Earl asked, poking his shaggy skunk-ape head into the cab.

"Bioluminescent fruit bodies," Grayson said. "And their cousins, incandescent mycelium."

"Huh?" Earl said.

I blew out a sigh. "Glowing mushrooms."

"Y'all think purple toadstools got old Mr. Balls?" Earl asked. "That's crazy."

I nearly gasped. For once, I was in total agreement with my cousin. I shot Grayson a smug glance and folded my arms over my chest.

"Get real," Earl said. "Ever'body knows toadstools wouldn't hurt nobody."

"Why not?" Grayson asked.

Earl snickered. "'Cause they're *fun-guys*. Get it?"

And there goes that *brief alliance.*

I whacked Earl on the arm. "Get back in the wheelchair or you're gonna need that thing for real."

"Party pooper," he grumbled, then disappeared along with his taco breath.

I looked back at the road. Grayson was exiting the highway too soon. "Grayson, Banner Hill is the *next* exit."

"I know." He smiled and shifted gears. "Just thought we'd do one little stop on the way."

Chapter Thirty-Three

"AWE, GEEZ. NOT THIS place," I groused when I caught sight of the huge circus tent.

The monstrous pyramid of fabric was set up in one of those vacant lots used to sell pumpkins during Halloween and fireworks in July. Currently, it was mid-November and they were selling salvation—at least until the Christmas trees arrived.

"I couldn't help myself," Grayson said, pulling up to the massive, white tent. "I felt something stirring in my soul."

I shot him a dirty look. "I told you to stop at four tacos."

Grayson grinned. Suddenly, banging and grunting sounded from the back cabin.

I turned to see Earl slamming the wheelchair into the wall at the end of the passageway that lead to the front cabin.

"You gotta get out of the chair first," I said. "What a dope."

AFTER EARL FINALLY got out of the wheelchair, I'd revived my role as disabled vet. Grayson was pushing me in my Salvation Army wheelchair across the dirt parking lot toward the entry flap of the biggest damned revival tent I'd ever seen.

I scowled at my cousin shuffling along beside us. All of this was his fault. During lunch, he'd talked non-stop about Bertie and his magic healing powers until he'd piqued Grayson's curiosity.

As a result, I'd ended up, yet again, the victim of another of Grayson's hastily planned "field research" tactics.

I was to fake an illness in order to try and get Bertie to "lay hands on me." While I was being felt up, Grayson was going to surreptitiously scan Bertie's electromagnetic field with a detector, or some stupid crap like that.

Whatever.

"Salvation is at hand," Grayson said, raising a hand toward the tent.

"Well, 'salvation' had better keep his hands to himself," I grumbled. I frowned up at the huge, glittery banner draped over the entryway.

Reverend Bertie & the Baptist Evangelical Resurrection Path Seekers!

Below that spangled banner, a smaller, hand-painted one read; *Hurry! November 17-23 Only!*

"Get your miracle while it's hot," I quipped.

Then, suddenly, everything went black. My sight had blinked out again like a porch light in a horror movie.

"I can't see," I said.

"Oh! Are you here for a healing?" I heard a woman's voice say.

"Yes, we are, fine lady," Grayson said from a point above and behind me.

I elbowed him through the back of the chair. "Grayson, I can't see!"

"She's blind?" the woman asked.

"Yes," Grayson said. "Since birth."

"Only Bertie can save her!" Earl sobbed.

"Well please, come this way. We're not open yet, but I'll see if Bertie has time for a true believer."

"We're believers, all right," Earl said. "I been a BERPSer for over twenty years."

"Well, isn't that something," the woman said. "In that case, follow me."

My wheelchair started to roll. Behind me, I heard Earl snicker. "You got some actin' chops, Cuz. Blind. Ha ha! You nearly fooled me!"

THE ROOM WAS STILL and quiet, except for the noisy inhaling and exhaling to my left. I recognized it and the Frito breath as belonging to my cousin, Earl.

"Lettuce pray," a semi-effeminate man's voice rang out.

I felt a hand on my shoulder, then an overwhelming whiff of Old Spice cologne.

"Brother, are you ready to see again?" the voice asked. He was so near I could feel the heat of his breath.

The hand shook my shoulder. "Are you ready?"

"Uh. Oh...yes," I fumbled into the dark void. I turned my head sharply. Something stuck me in the eye.

"Ow!" I cried out.

"Sorry, brother," the man said. "I was just making sure you weren't faking it."

"By poking my eye out?" I grumbled, rubbing my eye.

"Silence," the man said. "Peace be with you. Let the miracle begin."

I felt my ball cap lift off, then a cold, sweaty palm landed on my forehead like a giant tree frog.

"Jeeezus!" the man said, nearly startling me out of my chair. "Jeeezus! We call upon you now to heal our dear brother!"

His hand pushed off my forehead, sending my head craning back. I heard a vertebra in my neck pop. Then a shadow passed over me. I blinked. The world had gone from black to gray. I blinked again.

My vision had been restored!

Hovering over me was a sweaty little man with beady black eyes. He was staring at me from beneath the worst toupee I'd ever laid eyes on.

"Can you see me, brother?" Bertie asked.

"I can see you!" Earl cried out.

I stared at Earl, then back at Bertie. I was too dumbfounded to even be annoyed at Earl.

Geez. Maybe the guy can *perform miracles.*

"Claim your healing!" Bertie said.

"I claim it," I blurted, before Earl could beat me to it. "Brother Bertie, I can see!"

Chapter Thirty-Four

AFTER TIPPING THE TOUPEE-topped faith healer a twenty, I'd insisted that Grayson and Earl wheel me out of the revival tent rather than walking out on my own two legs.

I'd told them it was in order to avoid suspicion and maintain the ruse of me being an old nursing home vet. But the truth was, I was getting a real blast out of making those two haul my butt around like they were my personal *Dumb and Dumber*.

"Ugh," Earl grunted as he lifted me through the side door of the RV and tossed me onto the sofa like a sack of potatoes. "Maybe next time you can get Bertie to heal your *legs*, too."

"One miracle was quite enough," I said, trying to make a joke of it. But inside, I squirmed with unease.

Had it all been a coincidence, or had Bertie actually cured me of my blind spells?

"I told you Bertie was the real deal," Earl said.

"He's *real* all right," Grayson said, hauling the wheelchair through the side door of the RV. "But exactly what kind of *deal* has yet to be determined."

I shot Grayson a *WTH* look. "Wait. You believe in a cannibal *khakua* demon, but not faith healing?"

Grayson shrugged. "No. I believe in faith, to a certain extent. But you're forgetting one important fact, Drex. You faked being blind. Therefore, uh ... no miracle."

"Oh, yeah," Earl said, then frowned.

I sat up on the couch. "But that's just it. I *wasn't*. Faking it, I mean. I ... I had another one of those blind spells."

"What?" Grayson's face registered so much concern it scared me. "Why didn't you tell me?"

I winced. "I did! You just didn't believe me."

Earl shook his head and tutted, "Oh, ye of little faith."

"When did the blind spell come on?" Grayson asked, ignoring Earl. He locked his mesmerizing green eyes onto my dark-brown ones.

I sat up and chewed my lip. "Well, I was reading the tent banner, and—" I gasped. "Just like last time! Oh my God. You don't think my blind spells are related to Bertie, do you? That he has some kind of weird, psycho-kinetic powers?"

"Perhaps," Grayson said, studying me. "But it's more likely hysterical blindness."

"Hysterical!" I yelled. "Who's hysterical?"

"No one, as far as you know," Grayson said. "It could also be triggered by traumatic memories."

I frowned. "But the first time it happened, I didn't even know Earl was coming yet."

Grayson's cheek dimpled. "Back further than that, Drex. Were your parents carneys, perhaps? Were you ever traumatized at a carnival?"

"Not that I can recall. But I *do* have a weird aversion to clowns."

"It'd be abnormal not to," Grayson said. "What about the bad taste in your mouth? Did you experience that again, too?"

Earl snickered. I shot him some side-eye.

"Well, now that you mention it, yes," I said.

"Did you take another Fred Flintstone?" Grayson asked.

"No."

Earl raised his hand. I clenched my molars together. "What, Earl? This is *important*."

"Uh, could a kale smoothie make your mouth taste bad?"

I sneered. "Ha. Ha. I didn't have—"

"Uh, yeah you did." Earl shrugged sheepishly. "When we were at Topless Tacos, I might've dumped that little sample cup they were hand-ing out into your iced tea."

I closed my eyes to keep them from burning a hole through Earl's skull.

"Any tingling like before?" Grayson asked.

I thought about it for a moment and opened my eyes. "No."

Grayson nodded. "What did it feel like when Bertie touched you?"

"Like ikigai."

Grayson's eyebrows raised a notch. "Bertie's touch infused you with a reason to live?"

"No. *Icky guy*. As in his clammy hands gave me the creeps."

Earl gasped. "How could you talk bad about brother Bertie? He's no creep! He's been around for ages!"

Grayson shifted his gaze to Earl. "How *many* ages?"

Earl shrugged. "I dunno. But Granny Selma once told me that when she was a teenager, Bertie rubbed her warts clean off her."

Eew!

"Hmm. I've heard of such accounts," Grayson said. "Never underestimate the power of suggestion. How old is Bertie?"

"Don't rightly know," Earl said. "But Granny was eighty-one when she died four years ago. Bertie would'a had to be at least that old."

Grayson rubbed his chin. "Interesting. He doesn't look a day past fifty."

"Maybe he's related to George Hamilton," Earl said.

"Or Nosferatu," Grayson said.

Earl's eyebrow ticked up. "Nose hair who?"

I scowled. "Bertie, a vampire? Come on, Grayson."

Earl gasped. His eyes grew wide. "Lordy, lordy! That's why Bertie's always in that tent. He don't wanna come out in the daylight for fear a burnin' up!"

"That's a common myth," Grayson said.

"Tents?" Earl asked.

"No. That vampires are sensitive to daylight."

"How do you know all this stuff, Mr. G?" Earl asked, and sat down next to me on the sofa.

I sensed one of Grayson's conspiracy theories coming on, and groaned. I figured I might as well have some refreshments to go along with the show. I scrounged through my purse for a Tootsie Pop and struck gold. A red one. My favorite.

Grayson unfolded the wheelchair and took a seat close in front of us, like a disabled Army recruiter. "Bram Stoker was the first to bring vampires to mainstream attention."

"Wow," Earl said. "Was he some kind a monster hunter like you are, Mr. G?"

"Hardly. He was a business manager for a theater in London. He got paid so badly he had to supplement his income by writing sensational pulp novels."

Earl's eyes grew wide. "How sensational were they?"

Grayson's left eyebrow rose a notch. "The most famous was the one he wrote in 1897, about Dracula."

"That dude from Transylvania!" Earl whispered breathlessly.

Grayson sighed. "Actually, Romania. Stoker based Dracula on Vlad III, a Romanian royal. He was also known as Vlad Tepes, which, roughly translated, means Vlad the Impaler."

"Did this Vlad feller sleep in a coffin?" Earl asked.

"No. Murnau made that up."

Earl's head cocked sideways like a confused puppy. "Murman?"

"No. *Murnau*," Grayson said. "The German guy who wrote the silent film about Nosferatu in 1922. He also invented the idea that vampires disintegrate in daylight."

Earl scowled. "Why would he go and do that?"

"For the same reason all writers embellish their stories."

"To make 'em better?"

Grayson laughed. "No. To keep from getting sued for plagiarism."

Earl nodded thoughtfully. "What about the whole drinking blood part?"

"Yeah. About that ...." Grayson took off his fedora. "Old Vlady boy liked to run people through with spikes for his dinner-time amusement. That's how he ended up being called The Impaler. But, as far as we know, he never drank any of his victims' blood. Stoker made that up."

Earl's nose crinkled. "So that's all malarkey, too?"

"'Fraid so."

"But what about all the vampire cults?" I asked. "People all over the world believe in vampires. If there's nothing to it, why would the legend persist?"

"In a nutshell? Bad timing," Grayson said.

"Huh?" Earl and I said in unison.

Grayson gripped the wheels on the wheelchair like he was contemplating doing a wheelie.

What is it with guys and wheelies?

"The year Stoker's Dracula novel debuted, the world was in the grips of a plague of tuberculosis," Grayson said, apparently giving up on the idea. "Back then, it was called consumption. People afflicted with it would cough up blood. And their bodies would waste away until they look like the walking dead."

"That must've been horrible," I said. "But I still don't get the connection."

"The victims looked like bloody-mouthed ghouls," Grayson said. "Add a pinch of superstition and a dollop of hysteria, and you've got a whole new diagnosis—being 'caught in the vampire grasp.'"

I blanched. "What?"

"That's what they called having tuberculosis back then."

I scowled. "You're making that up!"

"I am not. Look it up for yourself. A man named Simon Whipple Aldrich died of it. His gravestone in Rhode Island says, 'consumption's vampire grasp seized his mortal frame.'"

Earl shot up off the couch. "Mr. Whipple was a vampire?"

"Yeah," I said. "That's why he was always squeezing the Charmin."

"Joke if you want," Grayson said. "But people were dropping like flies from the disease. Then a foreign doctor from Eastern Europe arrived in Illinois with a cure."

"Thank goodness!" Earl said.

"Not so much," Grayson said. "His cure was to dig up the first known victim, cut out her heart, burn it, and feed it to her infected brother."

"Did it work?" Earl asked.

I bopped him on the arm.

"No," Grayson said. "Because tuberculosis isn't caused by vampires. In truth, there's only been one verified account of a death related to vampires."

"Shannon Dougherty?" Earl asked.

"No. It was a guy who put cloves of garlic in his mouth to ward vampires off. One got lodged in his throat while he was sleeping and he choked to death."

I shot Grayson a *gimme a break* look. "Any relation to Melvin?"

"So the garlic thing's real?" Earl asked.

"About as real as clinical vampirism," Grayson said.

Earl's eyes grew wide. "I *knew* that clinic I went to took more blood samples than they needed!"

I smirked. Grayson was getting a dose of the medicine I'd been enduring from "Dr. Earl" for nearly four decades. I hope it cured him of ever inviting him along on our investigations again.

"Well, at least we're in agreement about doctors," Grayson said. "Those blood suckers aside, *clinical* vampirism is real enough—at least to those who suffer from it. They truly believe they need to drink human blood in order to survive."

"Where would they get a crazy idea like that?" Earl asked.

Grayson sighed and stood up from the wheelchair. "I thought we just covered that. Books and movies."

I couldn't believe my ears. I grabbed Grayson's arm. "Wait a second. Let me get this straight. Are you saying that *vampires aren't real?*"

Grayson shot me an incredulous look. "No. They're real all right. They just don't drink blood."

I scowled. "Then what the hell was the point of that desensitization program you made me watch? Why put me through all that for nothing?"

"It wasn't for nothing," Grayson said. "It was to help you to conquer your own self-generated fears."

"What about the mirror thing?" Earl asked, making a face into a hand mirror. "Vampires ain't got no reflection, or is that just a myth, too?"

I grinned. The strained look on Grayson's face made enduring the vampire video worth every second.

Grayson sighed. "Look, Earl—"

A loud knock on the side door of the RV silenced Grayson mid-sentence.

"Hey!" a man's voice called out. "You guys okay in there?"

Chapter Thirty-Five

GRAYSON, EARL AND I exchanged glances. We were in the RV, parked beside the BERPS revival tent, and someone was pounding on the side door.

"Who could that be?" I asked, flinching at the reverberating knocks. "Didn't I pay Bertie enough?"

"Anybody in there?" a man's gravelly voice called out.

"Quick. Get in the wheelchair," Grayson said, pushing it toward me. I hustled my butt into it and reached for the doorknob. "Try to act natural," he whispered at Earl, who was thumb-wrestling with himself. "Or, well, just do the best you can."

Grayson snatched open the door. I rolled my wheelchair next to him, nearly running over his foot.

A wiry, muscle-bound guy was standing right next to the door. Half of him was covered in black leather, the other half in tattoos. "You got engine trouble?" he asked.

"No. We're fine," Grayson asked. "Why?"

"You've just been parked out here for a while." The man adjusted the red do-rag on his head and tried to peek inside.

"My friend here just had a healing by Bertie," Grayson said. "We were just discussing him."

"We were?" Earl asked, looking up from his thumbs.

I shot him a gonad-withering glare.

"Yes," Grayson said. "We were just wondering how old the miracle man is."

"Bertie's ninety-nine," the biker wannabe said. "He turns a hundred on Monday. We're having a big celebration."

"A hundred years old," Grayson said. "Interesting. How long have you been working for him?"

"Been with Bertie for forty years. He stopped me from squandering my life on drugs, sex, and rock-n-roll. I've been working for him ever since."

"Doing what?" Grayson asked.

"I drive that van over there."

The man pointed to a white panel van. The back end was covered in bumper stickers. The side of the van was sported an oversized mural of Bertie dressed in white, holding his hands up below a rainbow. "I pick up people and take 'em to and from the revivals."

"Nice gig," Grayson said. "And a nice rig, too." He held out his hand. "I'm Grayson."

"Rocko," the man said.

I bit my lip.

Rocko. Of course your name's Rocko.

"Nice to meet you," Grayson said. "Bertie looks darn good for a centenarian."

Earl leaned over and tapped Grayson on the arm. "Mr. G," he whispered, "Bertie's a *Baptist.*"

"What's the secret to his exceptional longevity?" Grayson asked Rocko, turning his back to Earl.

"Faith," Rocko said. "And daily flossing."

"Makes sense," Grayson said, nodding in agreement. "Flossing's included as one of the critical factors in the *Living to 100 Life Expectancy Calculator.*"

Rocko smiled, revealing a nice set of pearly whites. "That's exactly right." He tipped his head to Grayson. "Nice to meet a fellow believer, brother. See you at the revival tonight?"

Grayson grinned. "Sure thing. We wouldn't miss it for the world, Rocko."

Chapter Thirty-Six

I WAS BACK IN MY WHEELCHAIR, and the three of us were back on the road, speeding down US 19 toward Banner Hill and my date with a potpie dinner.

Fun times.

"I can't believe Bertie's gonna be a hundred in two days," Earl said, then glanced back at me from the passenger seat. "Bobbie, you got more wrinkles than Bertie does."

I bumped the wheelchair against the narrow passage leading to the driver's cab. "Shut up, Earl. At least my wig looks real."

Earl chewed a toothpick and grinned. "Yeah, you keep on livin' that dream, Cuz."

"Grayson, what do you think Bertie's secret is?" I asked, ignoring Earl.

"Well, it isn't bathing in the blood of virgins," he replied. "Elizabeth Bathory proved that ineffective back in the 16th century."

"Of course," I said, hoping that agreeing with Grayson would prevent him from elaborating. "So what else could keep Bertie looking so young?"

Grayson adjusted the rearview mirror and locked eyes with my reflection. "I believe Bertie maintains his vitality by sucking the life from his hosts."

My nose crinkled. "What?"

"You know," Earl said. "Like that old lady back in Point Paradise who's always trying to get you to host a Tupperware party."

I looked around for a flyswatter to whack Earl.

"I believe there may be more to Bertie than meets the eye," Grayson said.

I sneered. "Like what? You think he's hiding a tin-foil hat underneath that awful toupee?"

"No." Grayson pursed his lips. "I'm serious. There's definitely something in this faith-healing gig for Bertie. And it's not money. Otherwise, like you said, he'd have a better toupee."

"I *heard* that," Earl said.

While I scrounged around in my purse for a Tootsie Pop, Grayson steered off the exit ramp. He stopped at a red light and stared absently out the windshield. "I have to say, Bertie and his followers' interest in good dental hygiene is intriguing."

My lip hooked skyward. "Earth to Grayson. What the hell are you talking about *now?*"

"Good teeth," he said. "Eternal youth. Regeneration by taking the life forces of others." Grayson pulled a small electronic device out of his breast pocket. "Results from this indicate definite signs of abnormal behavior."

I pulled the blue sucker from my mouth. "A TV remote? What's your addiction to *The X-Files* got to do with this?"

"Nothing." Grayson shot me a glance in the rearview mirror, then readjusted it and steered the RV through the intersection. "I suspect Bertie could be a psychic vampire."

"You mean that feller can read what your blood's thinkin'?" Earl asked.

Where's a damned flyswatter when you need one?

"Not exactly," Grayson said, not missing a beat. "Accounts of psychic vampires have been recorded throughout time. They appear in the religious and occult texts of numerous cultures."

"Really?" Earl asked.

"Yes. The term psychic vampire denotes any person thought to be feeding off the life forces of others, leaving them feeling exhausted or drained of energy."

I glared at Earl. "I thought the term for that was *relatives.*"

"This is no joking matter," Grayson said. "If I'm right about this, we need to act fast."

"Act fast?" I asked. "Why?"

Grayson pulled up to the street in front of Banner Hill and shoved the transmission into park. He turned back to face me, his green eyes deadly serious. "Because, in less than two days, we could be facing a psychic vampire apocalypse."

Chapter Thirty-Seven

"VAMPIRE APOCALYPSE?" I asked, nearly choking on my Tootsie Pop. "What are you talking about?"

Grayson cut the ignition and the old RV sputtered out on the street in front of Banner Hill. "We could be looking at a killer vampire cult that's about to go mainstream."

"That sounds bad," Earl said.

"Very bad." Grayson waved the TV remote gismo at me. "See this?"

"Yes. I'm not *blind*." Then I added sheepishly, "At least, not right now."

"What is that, Mr. G? Some kind a vampire zapper?" Earl asked.

"No. A vampire *detector*," Grayson said.

I sighed.

I'm already in a leotard and a wheelchair. What the hell. I'll bite.

"How does it work?" I asked.

"Good question, cadet." Grayson turned the device until a I could see a little window-like gauge on its face. It looked a bit like a miniature bathroom scale.

"This is an electromagnetic field detector," he said. "We all emit our own electromagnetism."

"You mean like Magneto Man?" Earl asked.

Grayson's eyes made a ninety-degree orbit around their sockets, then stopped. "Well, actually, yes." He jabbed a finger at the small window in the device. "This gauge here detects fluctuations in electromagnetic fields."

"And that detects vampires *how?*" I asked.

"Not just any kind of vampires," Grayson said. "*Psychic* vampires. Electromagnetic field detectors like this one have provided undeniable proof of psychic vampires affecting the electromagnetic fields of their victims while feeding off their energy."

My brow furrowed. "Really?"

"Really. In fact, I detected electromagnetic anomalies when Bertie laid his hands on you. It could explain what Melvin said about the missing vets being gone for a few hours, then coming back looking drained. And it's a bit too coincidental that those veterans started disappearing the exact same week Bertie and the BERPS rolled into town."

I chewed my lip. "Okay. But this energy feeding isn't fatal, is it?"

"No."

"Then how do you account for the fact that four vets have gone missing?"

"Maybe old Bertie sucked their batteries dry," Earl said.

I whacked him in the bicep. "Get real."

"Earl may have a point," Grayson said. "Being older and possibly rendered fragile from combat, it's likely Larry, Harry and Charlie were already in a weakened state. Perhaps Bertie devoured too much of their energy and they died unexpectedly."

"That's impossible," I said.

"Is not," Earl argued. "If Bertie's got Magneto Man's powers, he can make the ocean start swirlin' up. Zapping a few old coots would be child's play."

"Magnetokinesis," Grayson said, rubbing his chin. "Interesting idea. Electromagnetic pulses have been known to cause blackouts, and even silence crickets."

If one will silence this conversation, come on, electromagnetic pulse ....

"Listen," I said, "Say Bertie *is* capable of all that mumbo jumbo. How did our wheelchair-bound victims manage to get from Banner hill to Bertie's BERPS tent?"

A horn beeped. I glanced out the windshield.

A white van emblazoned with Bertie's smiling, graven image pulled into the parking spot in front of the RV. Rocko got out and waved a tattooed arm at us. Then he opened the side door, activated a lift, and lowered an old man in a wheelchair down to the ground.

The old man was the missing Melvin Haplets.

What do you know. Two mysteries solved with one old stoner.

Chapter Thirty-Eight

THE THREE OF US STARED out the windshield as Rocko pushed Melvin in his wheelchair toward the entrance to Banner Hill.

"Well, that solves the mystery of how the vets got to Bertie," I said. "And where Melvin Haplets disappeared to, as well."

"Interesting," Grayson said. "I need to talk to Melvin." He reached for the door handle.

"Hold on!" I said. "First, explain this business about a killer vampire apocalypse, and why do you think it's going to happen in two days."

"Bad timing," Grayson said.

"I don't care," I said. "We can talk to Melvin in a few minutes."

"No," Grayson said. "I meant that's why I think there's going to be another apocalyptic event similar to the one that happened in the late 1800s."

I frowned. "Don't tell me tuberculosis is making a comeback."

Grayson shrugged. "Okay, I won't. But do you know what the difference is between a cult and a mainstream religion?"

"Uh ...."

"About a hundred years."

My eyebrow ticked up involuntarily. "What?"

"Ten little decades," Grayson said.

Earl scratched his head. "I thought you said a hundred years."

Grayson closed his eyes for a moment, then laid the electromagnetic field detector on the dashboard and turned to face me. "Think about it, Drex. Back in its early days, Christianity was considered a cult by the Jews and Romans. Jesus was worshipped, feared, and misunderstood by millions—as were all prophets in their early days."

Earl appeared stunned to silence by the news. I prayed Grayson would keep talking.

"Go on," I said.

"After Christianity went mainstream, Protestants, Quakers and Baptists were considered cults by early Christians. Actually, come to think of it, some people still consider Southern Baptists a cult, what with the snake handling and whatnot."

"Snake handlin' is *real*," Earl said. "I seen it myself."

"I'm not saying it isn't real, Earl," Grayson said. "What I'm saying is it hasn't been *accepted by the mainstream*. Not yet, anyway."

"Oh." Earl's brow furrowed. "What about that Jim Jones dude, and that Wacko guy? Were they religions or cults, Mr. G?"

"Excellent question." Grayson nodded like a pleased professor. "That's exactly the point I'm trying to make. We call those cults, because *they didn't last*."

I sneered. "Yeah. I guess it's hard to keep the ball rolling when you advocate mass suicide."

"Exactly," Grayson said. "They didn't survive long enough to become anything but a cult."

Earl's brow furrowed. "So, you're sayin' any old crazy thing can be a religion if it sticks around long enough?"

"Well, that's just it. If it's too crazy, it *won't*. Time has a way of uncovering the flaws in an idea, Earl. Anything too weird will eventually self-destruct. But if an idea can hold water long enough, then it has a chance of gaining a foothold ... of going mainstream."

"So, basically, what you're saying is religion is whatever belief passes the test of time?" I asked.

Grayson shrugged. "More or less."

I shook my head. "I'm not buying that."

"Think about it, Drex. Every religion was a cult when it first began."

I frowned. "Maybe a long time ago."

"What do you consider a long time?" Grayson asked. "Less than two hundred years ago, a guy named Joe Smith said an angel named Moroni told him to dig up some gold tablets buried in a hill near his house in New York. Smith translated them into the book of Mormon—and now it's a mainstream religion with over twelve million followers."

I scowled. "Are you mocking religion?"

Grayson looked aghast. "Not at all. I'm just saying that everybody's got to start somewhere."

"So how long we talkin' about, Mr. G, before a cult turns religious?"

"Another excellent question, grasshopper. It's been said that if an idea can outlast its founder for a few generations or so, then it tends to get a green light by society. But even then, if it's too out there, believers have to whittle off some of the crazier edges to survive. You can't get a job at Walmart if you go around wearing a beard and a flowing white robe."

I smirked. "You sure about that?"

Grayson's cheek dimpled. "Okay. I'll concede the point."

"Wait," I said. "You still haven't explained why you think there's going to be an apocalypse *in two days*."

"The hundred year mark," Grayson said. "Bertie's about to turn a century old."

"So?"

"If history repeats itself, that means he's got at least three generations of believers. His 'teachings' could be about to become the next mainstream religion."

"So?"

Grayson blew out an exasperated sigh. "What if Bertie's 'teachings' aren't about saving people, but harvesting their energy instead? What if he's a master of magneto-kinesis, and is teaching his disciples how to drain bodies' electromagnetic systems until they're dead?"

Earl gasped. "Ol' Magneto Man harnessed up the Earth's electromagnetic field and used it to get mountains to tumble down. He beat the tar out of a whole army of folks."

"That's absurd!" I said. "It was just a comic book!"

Grayson stared me down. "If ye had but the faith of a mustard seed, you could move mountains."

My mouth fell open. Could Grayson actually be right?

"Rocko said they were planning some kind of celebration for Bertie's birthday on Monday," Grayson went on. "It could be to announce the launch of a whole army of psychic vampires who've been trained as natural executioners."

"But ... but ...." I stuttered.

"Exactly," Grayson said. "No one believes they're capable of such a thing. It's genius, really. They've been free to travel from town to town, recruiting members and harvesting just enough lives to stay off the radar screen. It's the perfect crime."

"And them bastards get the added bonus of no wrinkles," Earl said.

I couldn't wrap my head around it. "Why in the world would Bertie choose New Port Richey to kick off his cult of doom?"

Grayson shot me a know-it-all smile. "You may not be aware of this, but New Port Richey has been the hub for many a high-stakes political campaign. Why, Ronald Reagan himself spoke at Southgate Shopping Center when he campaigned for the presidency in 1976. George W. Bush stood on his soapbox at the community college during his bid in 2000, and came back for more in 2004, making Sims Park one of his re-election campaign stops. Dan Quayle, Joe Biden and even Sara Palin followed in his footsteps, making stops at Sims Park on their marches toward the White House.

I shook my head in disbelief. "Grayson, even if what you say is true, and Bertie's ready to announce to the world he's got a psychic vampire army, how in the world could we ever hope to stop them?"

Grayson grabbed me by the shoulders. "By feeding them junk food, Drex."

"What?"

"Listen closely and follow along. Psychic vampires feed off the life energy of others, right?"

"Uh ... okay."

"Let's assume they *must* take in the vital life forces of others or they'll grow weak and die."

"I'm with ya," Earl said.

Grayson nodded. "Good. So, according to reports, the best victims for psychic vampires are those who are compassionate, empathetic and generous."

I rolled my eyes. "All right."

Grayson looked me square in the eye. "That could explain why *you* weren't affected by Bertie."

I sat up in my wheelchair. "Excuse me?"

"If we're going to expose these psychic energy suckers, we're going to need to trap them with a nice, juicy victim," Grayson said. "A real happy-go-lucky sap."

If Earl had had a tail, it would've been wagging. "Sounds like a Jim Dandy plan to me, Mr. G.," he said. "Where we gonna find us one of those?"

Chapter Thirty-Nine

"HOW WAS THE POTPIE?" Stanley asked, popping his head into my room at Banner Hill.

"All I can say is, good thing I brought a pile of these." I pulled a Tootsie Pop out of my purse.

Stanley laughed. "Those'll rot your teeth out, you know."

I nodded toward the glass of blue water by my nightstand. "Tell it to the dentures."

"Uh, that's why I stopped by. I just wanted to give you a heads up that the tooth fairy is about to make a house call. Better hide the contraband."

"What?"

Stanley glanced down the hallway, then back at me. "Lose the lollipop, pronto. And get your fake teeth into the glass."

"Oh. Right." I scrounged in my purse and pulled out the plastic vampire choppers.

"Here he comes," Stanley said. He wrapped his lips over his teeth and shot me a gummy-looking smile.

The door opened wider. The same guy with the clipboard from yesterday walked in. I plopped the choppers into the glass and mimicked Stanley's toothless grin.

"Good work, Georgie," clipboard man said. "You're fitting in here nicely." He waved a bandaged hand at me. "Not everybody does." He shot Stanley a warning glance. "Watch out for Melvin across the hall. He's a biter."

"Thanks for the heads up," Stanley said.

The tooth fairy left. I stuck the Tootsie Pop back in my mouth and crawled into bed. "I saw Melvin came back this afternoon. Is everything all right with him?"

Stanley's face softened with relief. "Yes. The little man caused us quite a stir this morning. But turns out, he just went a little AWOL. He left this morning without signing out."

"How's that possible?" I asked as Stanley tucked me in with his rippling biceps.

Yeah, I could get used to this, all right.

"This isn't exactly a lockdown unit," Stanley said. "People are free to go in and out from 6 a.m. to 7 p.m. Otherwise, the old chimney smokers around here would stage a mutiny on the Banner."

I smiled. "Oh. Right."

A knock sounded at the door. To be on the safe side, I performed an encore of my gummy smile. "Come in!"

A doctor in scrubs and a surgical mask strolled into my room. Stanley's eyes widened. "Is there another flu epidemic going on, doctor?"

"No," the doctor mumbled through his mask. "I just came in to give Georgie the results of the test we conducted earlier."

"What test?" I asked.

The doctor pulled down his mask, revealing the worst moustache in the Western Hemisphere.

"Grayson," Stanley said. "What are you doing here?"

He nodded toward me. "I needed to let our patient know her toe swabs tested negative for saliva."

Stanley's face puckered. "Huh?"

"Never mind, Stanley," I said. "Long story."

"I also want to talk to Melvin across the hall," Grayson said. "Okay if I pop over there?"

"No can do," Stanley said, shaking his head. "Little man came home this afternoon totally whipped. He went to bed without even eating dinner. And potpie is his favorite."

"Whipped, you say?" Grayson's eyebrows met in the middle of his forehead.

Another knock sounded on the door.

"That would be my associate," Grayson said, and yanked open the door. Earl bumbled into the room looking like Sasquatch in beige scrubs.

"Howdy, y'all."

"What do you need an associate for?" Stanley asked.

Grayson shrugged. "With lights out at 7:15, I figured he and I'd have plenty of time to check out the records of the missing men. I know you don't want to get involved, so I brought Earl to be my lookout. You can count on us to be discreet. Just get us into the file room. We'll blend in like staff. No one will even notice."

Stanley chewed his lip as he thought it over.

"Hey, what's this button do?" Earl asked, and mashed a shiny red button on my bedside.

The wail of an alarm nearly blasted me out of bed.

"Shit!" Stanley hollered. He scrambled to my bed and whacked a button, silencing the alarm.

"Oops," Earl said. "My bad."

Stanley jogged back to the door, glanced up and down the hallway, and then came back in and closed it behind him.

"Look, man," he said, his eyes trained on the door like he was expecting a SWAT team to burst in any second. "Wait here. I'll go get the records. Don't touch anything, okay?"

He took a step toward the door, then eyed Earl suspiciously. "On second thought, Earl, you come with me."

Earl glanced at Grayson. He gave him the nod.

"Be right back," Stanley said. "Larry Meeks, Harry Donovan and Charlie Perkins, right?"

Grayson nodded. "Correct."

Stanley turned to go, then whipped back around on his heels again. "*Please*, don't touch anything while I'm gone!"

"You have our word," Grayson said.

Stanley's mouth pursed with regret. He grabbed Earl by the bicep and led him into the hallway. As the door closed behind them, Grayson turned to me.

"Okay, quick. We need to concoct a plan for exposing Bertie at the revival tomorrow."

I sat up in bed. "Shouldn't we wait until Earl comes back?"

"No."

"Why not?"

"Basic strategy 101, Drex. When you don't know who the patsy in a card game is, it's you."

Chapter Forty

GRAYSON WAS EATING the sweaty little tub of tapioca by my bedside when the door cracked open. Rasta Stanley and his skunk ape sidekick snuck back inside.

Stanley handed over three files. "Here you go, man. What you hopin' to find in them, anyway?"

"Some kind of connection," Grayson said.

Stanley's brow furrowed. "Connection? You mean to Old Mildred?"

"As far as you know, yes," Grayson said. "We need to figure out why these three men in particular were targeted. Was it their blood type, toothpaste brand, electromagnetic energy, or whatnot."

"What was that last one?" Stanley asked.

"Whatnot?" Grayson asked.

"No. The thing before that."

"Ah. Electromagnetic energy." Grayson nodded. "It's quite possible that Larry, Harry and Charlie could've been emitting energy fields that were particularly tasty to psychic vampires."

Stanley's face dropped two inches. "Psychic vampires?"

"Yes."

Stanley stared, dumbfounded, at the man impersonating a doctor, licking tapioca from his overgrown moustache. Then his eyes shifted to the hairy, itchy-eyed man ogling the controls on my bed like a Ritalin-deprived toddler.

Finally, Stanley turned to me, his eyes pleading for an anchor in the vortex of insanity swirling around him. But given the fact I was posing as an old tranny vet with vampire teeth for dentures, I wasn't exactly the most reliable port in the storm.

Stanley let out a big sigh. "I know nothing, I see nothing," he said, and slowly backed his way out the door.

AFTER STANLEY DID HIS Schultz routine and fled, Grayson and I sat Earl down in the recliner by my bed and hooked him up with headphones and a TV remote set on *Pimp My Ride*.

With Earl floating around in redneck heaven, Grayson and I were free to peruse the files of the three missing veterans without his annoying interference. Even so, we had to be quick. Visiting hours were over in eight minutes.

"Did Larry have hemorrhoids?" Grayson asked, flipping through Harry's file.

"Uh ... yeah," I said.

"So that makes three things so far," he said, scribbling in a notebook.

"Three?"

"Yes," Grayson said, counting on his fingers. "All three men served in Vietnam, they all showed signs of borderline anemia, and they all used Preparation H."

"What does that mean?" I asked.

"Either we've got a Vietnamese khakua with a penchant for cabooses, or we need to do more research."

I grimaced at the unwanted imagery flashing across my mind. "What happened to your psychic vampire theory?"

Grayson looked up from the file. "Who says it can't be both?"

I closed my eyes and sighed.

Awesome. Here we are, Larry, Moe and Curly, searching for Larry, Harry and Charlie. Maybe, if I pray hard enough, the evil twin inside my brain will do a voodoo dance and I'll lapse blissfully into a coma overnight.

Chapter Forty-One

"RISE AND SHINE," A demonic voice whispered in my ear.

I shot up in bed so fast I knocked heads with my human alarm clock.

"Oww!" I yelled. "Grayson, how did you get in here?"

"It's quarter after six, sleepy head. Banner Hill's been open for business for fifteen minutes."

"Well, *I'm* not." I scowled and pulled the covers up to my neck.

"Nice knot on your noggin," Grayson said, rubbing his own forehead. "How'd you get it?"

I touched the lump above my right eye. My gut went slack. "I ... I don't know. I dreamed I got whacked on the head by Old Mildred last night. I mean ... I thought it was a dream ...."

"Interesting," Grayson said, leaning in for a better look. "Do you bruise easily?"

"Not that I'm aware of."

"What do you remember about last night?"

"Aw, geez," I moaned. "Could I at least have some coffee before the interrogation?"

"It's on the nightstand."

I spied the steaming cup. Relief washed over me. I grabbed it and took a big gulp while Grayson studied me like a lab experiment.

"Anything else you remember?" he asked.

I took another slurp and felt the caffeine kick in like heroin. "I remember that after you and Earl left last night, I was reading over the files and—" I shot up in bed. "Where *is* Earl?"

"Don't worry. I sent him to pick up donuts."

I sighed again and took another slurp of coffee.

"So, you were reading the files," Grayson prompted.

"Yes. And ... that's all I remember. I guess I fell asleep."

"Can't blame you there. Those case files weren't the most riveting reading material I've ever run across." Grayson took a sip of coffee, then locked his green eyes on mine. "So, you said you dreamed of Old Mildred again?"

"Yes."

I closed my eyes and tried to recall the dream, but it flitted out of my grasp, like my last boyfriend. I opened my eyes.

"All I remember is that Mildred had a huge hunchback. Then you woke me up." I shivered. "And I feel sweaty, too. All the way to my toes."

Grayson's left eyebrow ticked up. "Interesting. Let's swab 'em."

He pulled out something that looked like a small medicine vial, then screwed off the top. The lid had some kind of applicator thing on it, like a jar of rubber cement.

"Show me the tootsies," he said.

I didn't bother to put up a fight. I stuck my foot out from under the covers. "Go ahead. Knock yourself out."

I'D JUST FINISHED DRESSING and jonesing for a crème-filled donut when Grayson returned with Earl in tow.

"Where'd you get that knot on your noggin?" Earl asked, tossing the bag of donuts to me. "Wrestlin' with your inner demons again?"

"Or *outer* ones," Grayson said. "This could be the work of Old Mildred."

"That hunchbacked old soul sucker?" Earl asked.

Grayson stared at him for a moment, then glanced down at my feet. "Of course," he said, shaking his head softly. "It's been staring me in the face the whole time."

"What has?" I asked.

"Incubus and succubus."

"Inky and sucky *who*?" Earl asked.

"Incubus and succubus," Grayson repeated. "Sex demons."

Earl crinkled his nose. "After Bobbie? I ain't buyin' that."

I closed my eyes and blew out a sigh.

"Incubus appears to sleeping women at night," Grayson explained. "He lies on top of them, trapping them into sex."

"But Bobbie ain't no woman," Earl argued.

"No, but she's pretending—" Grayson shook his head as if to clear it. He gave me a sheepish smile. "Yes, she *is*. A woman, that is."

I supposed I should've been grateful for the acknowledgement, but I just wasn't feeling it. "Grayson, what's this got to do with the men who've gone missing?"

"The succubus is the female version," Grayson said. "She comes to men at night and lures them into salacious behavior. Repeated sexual activity with either kind of demon is thought to result in deterioration of the victim's health, both mental and physical. It can even lead to death."

Earl's eyes grew wide. "You sayin' Old Mildred could be one of these succubus critters?"

"That's exactly what I'm saying."

"But why would she suck my *toes?*" I asked.

Earl laughed. "'Cause, Bobbie. You ain't got what she's *really* lookin' for."

Gross.

"Give me your spy pen," Grayson said. "Maybe we caught the succubus in action."

"Okay."

As I scrounged around in my bedclothes for the pen, someone knocked on my door.

"Come in," I said.

Stanley side-stepped into the room. His face looked grave. "Good. You're all here," he said.

"The pen's missing," I said, glancing over at the nightstand. My gut flopped. "So are the files!"

Stanley shook his head slowly. "And so are two more resident vets."

Chapter Forty-Two

"TWO MORE VETS DISAPPEARED?" I gasped. I grabbed a paper napkin and wiped the vanilla crème donut from my lips. "How did it happen?"

"Nobody knows," Stanley said. "They just vanished, like the others."

"Dang!" Earl handed Stanley the bag of donuts. "Sounds like that succubus critter sure had her a busy night last night. Donut?"

"Succubus?" Stanley asked, turning to me. His eyes widened in surprise. "How'd you get that bump on your head?"

"I hit it on the bed railing," I blurted, before Earl could say anything.

"Actually, I think it could be the work of Old Mildred," Grayson said, popping the rest of a powdered donut into his mouth. "The old gal may have attacked Drex in her sleep last night."

Stanley's eyes grew wide. "You were attacked by Old Mildred?"

I cringed. "Maybe. Things are kind of blurry. I dreamed about her, then woke up with this knot on my forehead."

"I was afraid this would happen," Stanley said, staring absently at the chocolate glazed donut in his hand. "I told you Old Mildred doesn't care for other women hangin' around."

I wiped my hands on a napkin and reached in my purse for a Tootsie Pop to calm my nerves. "I know this sounds weird, but I think Old Mildred took my spy pen—and the files on the other missing guys you brought us last night."

Stanley shook his head. "But why? What would an old ghost want with those things?"

"Good question," Grayson said, pulling out the little testing vial he'd swabbed my toes with earlier. He held it up to the light. "But one thing's for sure, Drex. You weren't dreaming. There's definitely saliva on your toes."

A shiver of disgust ran down my spine. On the one hand, at least I wasn't crazy. On the other hand, *someone sucked my toes last night!*

"Hmm," Grayson said, studying the vial. "I wasn't expecting that."

"What?" I asked.

"According to the test results, Old Mildred is a pothead."

"LET ME GET THIS STRAIGHT," Stanley said after I told him my recurring dream and Grayson showed him the test vial results. "Someone's actually been sucking your toes while you're asleep?"

"Yep. A succubus," Earl said. "Wait a minute, y'all. Wouldn't a succubus suck a *bus?*"

I winced to stop an eye roll. "Ignore him, Stanley. Those two vets who went missing last night—was Melvin one of them?"

"No." Stanley helped me into the wheelchair. "Why? You don't think *he's* the one sucking your toes, do you?"

The thought of the pasty, Brooklyn comb-over champ gumming my big toe made me nearly dry heave. "Ugh! I hope not!"

"There's no way to tell who the culprit is from this," Grayson said, pocketing the test vial. "I only used a six-panel preliminary saliva test. I'll need another sample in order to conduct a DNA match."

I winced. "*Another* sample?"

"Listen, man," Stanley said, "I get what you're trying to do here. But I can't be part of it."

"Too late for that," Grayson said. He opened the door to my room, stuck his head out, and glanced up and down the hallway. "I really need to talk to Melvin," he said, turning back to face us. "I need to find out what he knows about the BERPS, and if he saw or heard anything last night."

"You can't man," Stanley said, pushing me out into the hall. "Melvin got up early and left with some tattooed guy."

"Don't touch that!" I hollered.

Stanley and Grayson's heads swung my way. Earl jerked his hand away from my bedside as if he'd been shocked with 10,000 volts.

"Sheez," I growled at my cousin. "Keep your mitts off the buttons!"

I returned my attention to Stanley. "Why was Melvin in such a hurry to leave this morning? Did you see what kind of vehicle the guy was driving?"

"No. But I think we should make an appearance before anyone comes looking for us, too."

Stanley took the reins on my wheelchair ushered me into the main hall toward the breakfast room. There wasn't another person in sight.

"Where is everybody?" Grayson asked.

"It's Sunday morning," Stanley said. "Around here, that means you either get in a van to go to church, or you head to the rec room there for an exercise class."

Earl peeked into the rec room and laughed. "Anybody wanna work up a sweat to old Regis & Cathy Lee DVDs?"

"In leotards or not?" Grayson asked.

"Ugh!" I grumbled. Someone needed to take charge of this lame operation. From the looks of it, it was going to have to be me.

"Stanley, you go grab the files on the other two missing men and meet us at the RV," I demanded. "Grayson, you take the helm on my wheelchair. And Earl? For the millionth time, stop touching that!"

Chapter Forty-Three

"WHAT'S THE PLAN, MR. G?" Earl asked as Grayson rolled me down the sidewalk in front of Banner Hill, toward the RV parked on the street.

"Nothing's set in stone, as far as you know," Grayson said. "But with two more vets missing this morning, we need to act fast."

"Agreed," I said in my best commanding tone. "We need to put our heads together on this."

Earl picked up a fallen oak branch, stuck an end in his armpit and shot it like it was an Uzi. "You can count on me!"

My eyes had just completed their orbit in my sockets when we reached the RV. Stanley came trotting up, holding his duffle bag.

"You got the files?" I asked.

"Yeah, man. But I think the tooth fairy is getting suspicious."

"Tooth fairy?" Grayson asked, looking intrigued.

"The guy who checks the dentures at night," I said.

Earl laughed. "Woo, boy, I love me some spy talk! Can I have a secret code name, too?"

"Sure," I said. "Ignoramus."

I looked up at Stanley from my wheelchair. "You in? We could really use whatever insider info you might have about Banner Hill and the guys who've gone missing."

Stanley winced and bit his lip. "Uh ... geez."

"Please," I said, touching his arm. "We may be the only hope these guys have."

Stanley's board-straight posture went limp. "Okay. But can you drop me off at home afterward?"

I nodded. "Absolutely. Now, let's load up."

"Where are we going?" Stanley asked.

I glanced around and noticed everyone was staring at me with expectant looks on their faces.

Crap. Am I really in charge now? What have I done?

"Uh ...." My gut gurgled. "We need protein. You know, to fuel our brains. Those donuts didn't cut it. I say we hold a strategy meeting at Topless Tacos. Everybody in?"

"Yeah, sure," Stanley said. "I could eat."

"Tacos sound good," Earl said. "What time do they open?"

"Eleven," Grayson said.

I glanced at my cellphone. It was 9:38. "Oh. Well, if you drive slow, Grayson, we should get there just as they open."

Grayson snorted. "If I drive *that* slow, we'll be pulled over for causing a public hazard."

"Uh, looks like we got a problem, Houston," Earl said.

"Ugh! What now, Earl?" I grumbled.

He nodded toward the back of the RV. "Looks like somebody done stole the back tire, Mr. G."

Our eyes shifted to the gaping dark hole under the chassis where the back left tire used to be.

"Great," I said. "What do we do now?"

Earl grinned. "Not to worry. Sit tight. I got us a plan."

BEFORE I COULD OBJECT, Earl had disappeared, off on a self-described "secret mission" to obtain a new tire for Grayson's RV.

Knowing Earl's penchant for both auto mechanics and James Bond films, I gave him about a fifty-fifty chance he'd return alive.

Meanwhile, Grayson, Stanley and I sat around on a bench outside Banner Hill, looking like time travelers who'd arrived thirty years too early to our retirement party.

"I don't understand it," I said to Stanley. "Why has nobody reported any of these vets missing?"

"They *have* been reported missing," Stanley said.

"To who?"

"To Ms. Gable. From what I hear, she's got Officer Holbrook investigating."

"That cop we saw at Topless Tacos?" Grayson asked.

Stanley nodded and fiddled with the end of one of his dreadlocks. "Yeah."

"What do you know about Rocko?" I asked.

Stanley's brow furrowed. "Who?"

"The tattooed man who drives that Bertie and the BERPS van. He's the one who dropped Melvin off here yesterday afternoon."

"Oh. That guy." Stanley shrugged. "Nothing, really. He just started turning up this week to take people to that revival thing."

"Doesn't anybody monitor their comings and goings?" I asked.

Stanley shrugged. "Hey, if it's church related, it kind of gets the green light around here. No questions asked."

Grayson shot me an *I told you so* look. I pursed my lips.

"The tattooed guy's name is Rocko," I said to Stanley. "It seems awfully suspicious that he began showing up the same time the vets started going missing, isn't it?"

Stanley opened his mouth to answer. The roar of a loud muffler appeared to come out. It pierced the sleepy, mid-morning slumber surrounding Banner Hill, and was quickly followed by the blast of a horn tooting out the musical notes to the first line of *Dixie*.

I suddenly wished I was in the land of anywhere but here.

"Who's that?" Stanley asked.

"Earl," I said. "That's his truck, Bessie."

Earl parked the massive, black monster truck on the street in front of Grayson's RV. Comparing them side by side, the two vehicles were almost the same size. However, Bessie came equipped with a 540-horsepower Hemi engine and tractor tires taller than me. With enough rope tied to its trailer hitch, that truck could yank the teeth out of King Kong.

Earl hoped out of the cab and waved to us. Then he bounced a new tire out of Bessie's tail gate and disappeared with it on the other side of the RV.

"Okay, start from the beginning," I said to Stanley. "When did the vets first go missing?"

Stanley glanced around, then lowered his voice. "First I heard of it was Wednesday morning, four days ago. That's when Larry Meeks disappeared from room 2G. But whatever happened to him went down on Tuesday night."

"Why do you say that?" Grayson asked.

"Wednesday morning, his bed was made up."

"So?"

"Larry *never* made up his bed. Said it hurt his arthritis."

"So, you're saying he never slept in his bed Tuesday night?"

Stanley nodded. "Which was weird, because the day before, I couldn't get him out of it. Said he was too tired to get up."

"I remember that from his file notes," I said. "You recommended a blood analysis. The results showed he had mild anemia."

"That's right."

"What about Harry Donovan?" Grayson asked.

"Pretty much the same routine. Harry ate dinner Wednesday night, and was still up when denture check rolled around."

Grayson cocked his head. "What's up with this whole tooth patrol thing, anyway?"

Stanley shrugged. "Draper insists on it. Anyway, Harry disappeared the next morning."

"Was his bed still made up?" I asked.

"No. I tucked Harry in that night myself. The guy was white as his sheets."

"And Charlie?" I asked.

Stanley stared at his hands. "Pretty much the same thing. Ate dinner Thursday evening, then disappeared overnight."

I glanced down at the files Stanley had pulled from his duffle bag. "These new guys, Tom Hallen and Joe Plank. Were they at dinner last night?"

"Sure. Nobody misses potpie night."

My gut gurgled involuntarily. I set my purse on the bench and scrounged around for a Tootsie Pop. Grayson took the opportunity and grabbed the files from my lap.

"These new guys. Did they have bloodwork done in the days preceding their disappearance?" he asked as he flipped through their records.

"Not that I know of," Stanley said.

I plucked the sucker from my mouth. "Wait, I just realized something."

"It's about time," Grayson said. "Tootsie Pops are a mental crutch, Drex."

I shot him some side eye. "No. These men. They're all *DNRs*."

"Democrats, Not Republicans?" Earl asked, wandering up.

"No!" I frowned. "They're all on their last legs, and they know it. They've all signed DNR forms—as in Do Not Resuscitate."

Chapter Forty-Four

WITH ALL FOUR OF US crammed into Bessie's front cab, we looked like hillbillies heading to a Sunday hootenanny. Stuck between Earl and Grayson, there was no escape.

"This is kind a like *The Expendables*," Earl said, shifting the monster truck into third, making me duck right to avoid his giant elbow.

Why do I always have to sit by the gear box?

"What are you talking about?" I asked, bracing my foot against the floorboard in case more evasive maneuvering was required.

"That movie," Earl said. "Them vet fellers that went missing. Maybe they knew they was probably gonna die."

Grayson took his nose out of the file he was reading. "Well, given that the youngest one of the bunch is seventy-two, that's pretty much a given."

Earl shook his head. "That ain't what I mean."

"What, then?" I asked.

"These fellers what disappeared from Banner Hill. What if they believed they was on a secret mission—one they wasn't likely to come back from?"

Like when you went out to get a tire for the RV?

"Hold on a second," Grayson said. "You may be onto something." He shuffled through the files. "Tom and Joe were in Vietnam at the same time. From 1960-62. So were Larry, Harry and Charlie."

I shot Grayson a look. He tapped a finger to his temple. "Eidetic memory, remember?"

My brow furrowed. "Is it possible they were all members of the same troop, fighting the Viet Kong together?"

"It's possible," Grayson said. "Now they could be banding together to fight a new enemy."

"*King* Kong?" Earl asked.

I elbowed him in the ribs. "What if they all have that Peoria thing, Grayson?"

Grayson's left eyebrow disappeared under his fedora. "Peoria?"

"You know. That blood disease. What did you call it?"

"Porphyria." He glanced at the files. "There was no mention of it in their paperwork."

"What if the enemy they were all fighting was Old Mildred?" Stanley asked. "What if she took them to some other world with her?"

"Hmm," Grayson said. "An intriguing possibility. There does seem to be some evidentiary commonality, what with the purple light you reported, Stanley. The light also appeared right as Balls was attacked, too."

Stanley flinched. "Something attacked someone's balls?"

"I knew it!" Earl said. "It's the Attack of the Purple Pe—"

I jabbed Earl in the ribs again. "Shut up and drive. We are *not* going down that road again."

THE CUTE WAITRESS AT Topless Tacos had already taken our orders. When I find something good, I tend to stick with it, so she already knew mine by heart—Mahi tacos and nacho salad.

While the four of us waited in hungry anticipation around the shiny red table in the corner, we discussed Bertie's potential as the leader of a new psychic vampire cult hell bent on world domination.

Well, at least it wasn't boring.

I took a slurp of Dr Pepper and looked up. Through the glass storefront, I saw a white van pull into the lot. As it parked, I was treated to the smiling face of Bertie and his rainbow BERPS.

"Uh-oh. We've got company," I said.

Earl whistled. "Speak of the devil."

"Not so fast," Grayson said. "That has yet to be scientifically proven."

Stanley's face twisted with worry. "What do we do now?"

Grayson leaned in across the table and whispered, "Improvise."

We all nodded uncertainly, then turned and stared out the plate glass window. Rocko climbed out of the van, clad in his customary black leather and full-sleeve tattoos. He put on a pair of sunglasses, adjusted his red do-rag, and swaggered across the parking lot up to the front door.

He flung it open and glanced around. The cocky confidence plastered on his face withered into disappointment.

"Where're all the topless chicks?" he asked, whipping off his sunglasses.

The feminist in me smirked.

"False advertising," Grayson said.

"Figures." Rocko's shoulders slumped. "Hey. I know you. Yesterday. Parking lot. You're the RVers, right?"

Grayson tipped his fedora. "Nice to see you again, Rocko. Please, join us if you like."

"Thanks. Let me just make a pit stop at the head, first."

Rocko ambled out of earshot. I leaned in close to Grayson. "What are you doing, inviting the enemy to the table? How are we going to discuss bringing Bertie down now?"

"Elementary," Grayson said. "We fight fire with fire."

"We're gonna burn the place down?" Earl asked. "Ain't that illegal?"

"Not arson," Grayson said. "To slay a *psychic* vampire requires a *psyche* approach."

My nose crinkled. "I don't get it."

"Just follow my lead." Grayson looked around the table at Earl and Stanley. "No mention of Bertie or psychic vampires, got it?"

"Got it," Earl said, and saluted.

"I didn't see nothin', I won't say nothin'," Stanley said.

"Shh. Here he comes," Grayson whispered. He motioned for Rocko to sit beside him.

"Tough day at the office?" Grayson asked the former biker turned van driver.

I suddenly felt a migraine coming on.

"Last day of a revival is always the hardest," Rocko said. "I could use a beer."

"Let me buy you one," Grayson said.

Rocko shook his head. "No. I gave all that up for the BERPS."

"Me, too," Stanley said. "Wine is a whole lot less gassy."

Grayson shot Stanley a quick *can it* look. "What?" he asked, holding up his hands. "It's true."

"So, Rocko," Grayson said, turning on the charm, "What do you like most about your life on the road with Bertie?"

What is this? An interrogation or a date?

"The opportunity to travel, I guess," Rocko said. "Meet new people."

"Nice." Grayson slapped on a grin. "Sounds like you're a religious man and a free spirit."

"Yeah, I guess." Rocko broke into a smile. "I like to think so."

"Perhaps you can help us, then," Grayson said. "My friends and I were just discussing the difference between a religion and a cult."

Grayson glanced our way. We all smiled and nodded like idiotic bobble-heads.

"Cults are bad," Rocko said.

"That's right," Grayson said. "You know how you can spot the difference?"

Rocko bit his lip. "Uh ... cults serve Kool-Aid?"

"Well, yes," Grayson conceded. "That, and the fact that cult leaders are bullies. They're always acting better than everybody else. You know, like they've got some special powers nobody else has."

Rocko nodded. "Uh-huh."

Grayson scooted his chair closer. "Cults don't like you to think for yourself, either. If you don't follow the rules, or if you say something bad about the group, a cult leader will tell you you're a disbeliever, and that you're going to burn in hell."

Rocko's face reddened. He shifted in his seat. "Really?"

"Absolutely. Cult leaders are slick," Grayson said. "And they're total control freaks. You see, they keep members under their thumbs by telling them that all kinds of horrible things might happen if they even *think* about leaving the cult."

Rocko chewed his lip. "Bertie's always telling me I should get my tattoos removed."

"What?" Grayson gasped. "These beautiful works of art?"

"Is that one supposed to be Woody Woodpecker or Miss Piggy?" Earl asked, nodding at Rocko's forearm.

Grayson shot my cousin a *shut it* glare, then turned back to Rocko. "Cult leaders are also cheapskates. The skinflints don't even want their workers to be able to have a place of their own."

The veins in Rocko's temples looked like tree roots. "I been workin' for Bertie for forty years. All I got to my name is a sleeping bag stowed in the back of the van."

"That's not fair," Grayson said. "Cult leaders also—"

"Wait a minute," Rocko said. "Are you saying *brother Bertie* is a cult leader?"

"Me?" Grayson gasped, then shot us a surreptitious wink. "How would I know, brother?" He put a hand on Rocko's shoulder. "All I'm saying is, that if the shoe fits, somebody's likely to get kicked in the ass with it. I just don't want it to be *you*."

Chapter Forty-Five

"WELL, LOOKS LIKE IT'S all over but the cryin'," Earl said, and nudged me on the elbow. We stared across the table at Rocko. Grayson had reduced him to rubble.

"I gave Bertie the best years of my life," Rocko sobbed. "And for what?" He grabbed Grayson's bottle of beer and glugged half of it down.

Grayson wrapped an arm around Rocko's shoulder. "Don't beat yourself up, brother. We've all been there."

"That's right," Earl said. "I used to believe in Bertie, too. I sent him a pile of emails about poor Sally, but he never even bothered to write back."

"Sally?" Rocko asked, sniffing back a tear.

Earl nodded. "The two-headed turtle I found in Wimbly swamp last year. She's a red-eared—"

"Amen, brother," Grayson said loudly. He shifted his eyes to me and nodded once. "What about you?"

I flinched. "Uh ... I found out my father isn't my father."

"Amen. Everybody's got troubles," Grayson said.

Stanley glanced over at me, his eyes wild with stage fright.

"Brother Stanley?" Grayson prompted.

Stanley licked his lips. "Uh ... I can't go to Jamaica without somebody sticking a joint in my mouth."

Grayson nodded. "That happens to everybody, son."

"Amen, brother," Rocko said. "Kingstown. Those were the good old days."

"All right, men. One for all, and all for me. We've got work to do." Grayson straightened his shoulders and puffed out his chest, morphing from mentalist to Army man in half a second flat.

Impressive.

"Five men have gone missing from Banner Hill," Grayson said as if he were laying out the tactical maneuvers for an impending war. I could almost see the American flag flying behind his head as he spoke.

"These heroic veterans fought on foreign soil so we could be free. Now, it's up to us to return the favor. We need to find out what happened to them, and set our MIAs free—if they're still alive. Can I get an amen?"

"Amen!" Earl and Rocko cheered.

Stanley and I glanced at each other, then chimed in lamely. "Amen."

"We'll fight our enemies wherever we find them," Grayson preached.

"Amen!" Rocko and Earl cheered.

"Amen," Stanley and I muttered.

"If Bertie's the bad guy, we'll shut him down. Amen?" Grayson crooned.

"Amen!" Rocko and Earl roared.

"Amen," Stanley and I said.

Grayson shot Rocko a determined, tight-jawed stare. "No man should have to do another's bidding, brother."

Rocko nodded his tear-stained face. "Yes, sir."

Grayson leaned in across the table. "Now, listen closely, everyone, and do exactly as I say ...."

Chapter Forty-Six

"YOU ALL IN, BROTHER?" Grayson asked Stanley, as Rocko loaded me and my wheelchair into the back of his rainbow Bertie van.

"I gotta go see the voodoo priestess first," Stanley said, chewing his lip. "Bertie's some bad juju. I'm gonna need a spirit animal or something for backup."

"Good idea," Grayson said. "Best to cover all the bases. This is the Bible Belt, after all, and a lot of people around here know how to use it."

I cringed.

Worst mixed-metaphor ever.

I sighed and resigned myself to my fate. I was half-bald, and half-heartedly on a half-baked mission with a pile of half-wits, headed for a showdown with Bertie and his half-assed toupee.

What more could a girl ask for?

After loading me into the back, Rocko and Grayson climbed into the front of the van. Grayson turned to face me from the passenger seat. "You got the EFD?"

I patted the electromagnetic field detector duct-taped to my waist underneath my shirt. "Tucked and ready."

"Got your vest?"

I winced. "Bullet proof vest? I didn't think—"

"No. Wool," Grayson said. "It's supposed to get cold tonight."

"Oh. Yes, Dad."

"Good. You know the plan?"

"I know it." I squirmed in my wheelchair and pulled out the Tootsie Pop I'd stashed in a side pocket. I pointed it at Grayson like a toy gun. "You can count on me, Sarge."

"Wow," Rocko said. He turned the ignition and the van shuddered to life. "Sounds like we're preparing for war."

"In a way, we are," Grayson said. "You said it yourself, Rocko, 'Cults are bad.' We can't let this go unchallenged."

"Right." Rocko backed the van out of the parking lot of Topless Tacos. I could tell by the reflection of his face in the rearview mirror that Grayson's Kool-Aid was kicking in, big-time.

I waved to Earl and Stanley, who were sitting in Bessie, ready and waiting to tail us to the revival tent.

"Did you know that most major foreign wars were fought over religious intolerance?" Grayson asked Rocko.

"No, sir," Rocko said, pulling out into traffic.

Grayson patted him on the shoulder. "That's what makes America so great, brother. We don't fight over theological differences. We fight over socioeconomic ones. Economics is our religion."

"Huh?" Rocko grunted.

I let out a jaded laugh. "If that's true, then why do so many people go to church, Grayson?"

Grayson shrugged. "To live longer, of course."

I plucked the sucker from my mouth. "Are you saying you believe in eternal life?"

Grayson turned his head to face me again. "Studies show that regular church attendance increases life expectancy. Frequent attendees live an average of 83 years. Non-attendees about 75."

I frowned. "Maybe. But they spend all those extra years in church, so it's a wash."

A dimple formed in Grayson's cheek. "Fair enough. Now ditch the Tootsie Pop, cadet, and get ready to rumble."

Chapter Forty-Seven

THE INSIDE OF BERTIE'S revival tent was a fire-hazard waiting to happen. Packed to capacity, people had squeezed into every folding chair in the place, then lined the fabric walls two- and three-people deep.

The electric buzz of the pulsing crowd was palpable. And, for the first time, I began to think Grayson's theory about Bertie being a psychic vampire might actually be plausible. If Bertie really could feed off the energy of others, tonight would be an all-he-could-eat buffet.

With Bertie's van-man Rocko with us, we were quickly ushered up to the front row. I have to say, it was cool getting the red carpet treatment. But the envious stares we garnered as Rocko parted the sea of humanity in the tent made me seriously question some folks' charitable intentions.

Once we reached the front row, Grayson parked me at the end of a long line of other folks in wheelchairs. The swell of anticipation was contagious. I even felt my own pulse quicken as I watched people shift nervously in their seats, putting on or pulling off the jackets and hats they'd worn to fend off the chill of the cold front that had blown in that afternoon.

Above the constant, murmuring hum of the throng behind me, a belch blasted out. I craned my neck around to give the impossible ingrate some side-eye. It was Earl, grinning at me like the cat who ate the canary carbonara.

"Just making a joyful noise unto the Lord, Cuz," he said.

"Earl, you're such a cretin!" I shouted.

As the words left my lips, the tent grew silent as a grave.

My last word, "cretin," echoed through the sudden hush like the call of an angry cricket. I shrunk back into my wheelchair, mortified.

I had no idea my voice sounded that shrill when I screamed!

Like a mortified turtle, I slowly stuck my head up and glanced around. The room was still silent. But nobody was paying any attention to me. All eyes were on the stage directly in the front me. I turned to look, too.

A man was walking across the raised wooden platform. He stopped at the microphone set up center-stage. He tapped it three times, sending staccato sound bites blasting through the tent.

"Brothers and sisters, are you ready for a miracle?" he yelled.

"Yes!" the crowd roared back like thunder. Then the chanting started. "Bertie! Bertie! Bertie!"

A moment later, Bertie stepped out onto the stage in a suit I'd seen somewhere before.

On Colonel Sanders.

The hordes went wild.

Bertie smiled, raised his right hand, and pranced around the stage like a rock star. Then, in a move that made my jaw drop, he did a reverse moon-walk, stepped up to the mic, and put his hands together.

The room went so quiet you could hear a pinhead drop.

"Lettuce pray," Bertie said, and bowed his head.

Grayson whispered in my ear. "Ready for your close up, cadet?"

I swallowed against the rising bile in my gut. "As ready as I'll ever be."

TEN MINUTES LATER, a sing-along with Bertie had whipped the crowd into a hypnotic frenzy. Bertie was playing to the believers, pointing here and there yelling, "Be healed!"

Suddenly, a plus-sized woman in a small-sized tank top and rainbow-striped leggings stood up and yelled, "Halleluiah!" She plowed down the aisle of believers behind us, then ran toward the stage.

Right as she passed by Grayson and me, she doubled over, as if some invisible force had punched her in the gut. She convulsed, babbled incoherently, and fell to the floor in front of me, writhing and rolling around like she was trying to put out a fire.

"Bertie's got her in his energy-sucking grasp!" Grayson said. "We've got to do something!"

Before I could stop him, Grayson scooted around the back of my wheelchair and knelt by the woman's side. He looked up at me. "Hurry, Call nine—"

I kicked him in the buttock. "Shh! Leave her be. She's just fallen out in the spirit."

The woman grunted and kicked out wildly. Grayson jerked to standing, his face scarlet. He lowered his eyes and scurried back to his position behind my chair.

"Shouldn't somebody at least cover her up?" he whispered into my ear. "Her spirit isn't the only thing that's fallen out."

I didn't want to look.

My spirit was willing, but my flesh was weak. I got an eyeful that will haunt me until I reach the Pearly Gates.

I shivered with disgust, then looked up and saw something even more horrifying.

Up on stage, a line of people was forming to be healed by Bertie. The person at the very front of the que was as big as a bear—and his name was Earl Shankles.

I closed my eyes, willing this all to be a nightmare I'd wake up from soon.

"What's he doing up there?" Grayson asked.

"I don't know," I said, shaking my head. "As far as I can tell, Earl's gone rogue."

Chapter Forty-Eight

THE CROWD WAS SWAYING to the beat of *I'm a Believer*. Earl was inching his way toward Bertie, who was standing center-stage. Earl's eyes appeared glazed over, as if he were hypnotized, or in some kind of trance. But then again, they often did ....

"Come, brother," Bertie coaxed.

Earl took a few more zombie-like steps, the stopped two feet in front of Bertie.

"What's your name, brother?" Bertie asked.

"E ... Earl."

"And what brings you to seek a miracle tonight?"

"I'm not here for me," Earl said.

The crowd oohed and aahed.

"What faith from this kind and generous spirit!" Bertie said, offering a giant grin to the hordes. He turned back to Earl. "Pray, son, then who are you here for?"

"Sally," Earl said.

Bertie's face fell like an anvil off a cliff.

"You!" he squealed, scrambling away from Earl. "Security!" he shrieked. "Get him! It's that freak with the two-headed turtle!"

Two burly biker-men rushed the stage and grabbed Earl by the arms. I could tell by the bad forearm tattoo that one of the men was Rocko.

I started to get up. Grayson's hands pressed down on my shoulders. "Don't blow your cover," he said. "Earl will be all right."

I stared up at the stage, helpless to do anything.

"But Bertie, you're Sally's only hope!" Earl yelled as they hauled him away.

Grayson's hand squeezed my shoulder. "Time for Plan B," he whispered in my ear, then shoved me forward so fast I nearly fell out of the wheelchair.

"I bear testament to Bertie's powers!" Grayson yelled.

Bertie's panicked eyes landed on us. Seeds of recognition set in. He pulled himself together and straightened his bolero tie. "Brothers!" he cried out. "So good to see you again! Come up here where everyone can see you!"

As Grayson wheeled me up the disability ramp toward the stage, Bertie told the throng of believers our backstory.

"Brothers and sisters," he said, "these two came to see me yesterday, on a mission to restore this poor soul to health."

The crowd murmured acknowledgements. Grayson wheeled me up to Bertie. He laid his clammy hand on my shoulder.

"Mind you, this poor crippled man didn't ask to be healed of lameness. You see, until yesterday, he was also blind, weren't you?" Bertie squeezed my shoulder. Hard.

"Yes!" I chirped. "I was blind, but now I see!"

The hordes erupted in cheers.

"Okay, calm down," Bertie said. "Now I'm going to lay hands on this man and he's going to *walk!*"

A second round of applause and yelling broke out.

Under the cover of the cacophony of cheers, Bertie leaned over, slapped his froggy palm on my forehead and said, "I don't know what your game is, but I know you're with that two-headed turtle freak. If you really can walk, I suggest you do it when I tell you to, or you're gonna need that wheelchair for real."

Bertie raised up, grinned, and waved at the crowd. "Be healed, brother! Get up and walk!"

I stood up. The crowd went wild.

"Walk!" Bertie said.

For the first time in my life, I was a believer. Stage fright was *real*. My mind was scrambled. My legs wobbled so badly I could hardly take a step. Half paralyzed with fear, a sudden thought made me nearly collapse back into the wheelchair.

Is it stage fright, or is Bertie sapping my psychic energy?

"Excellent," Bertie said in a tone that sent a shiver down my spine. "Take him to the recovery room."

A biker dude pushed me back into the wheelchair. I landed with a thud, then craned my neck around, trying to see Grayson.

I spotted him in a dark corner of the stage. Two security guards had him pinned down. I turned back to face the crowd. I zeroed in on a guy taking money from the collection plate. His face seemed familiar, but my mind was too scrambled to recall his name.

"Help," I said, half-heartedly. Knowing help was nowhere nearby.

"Make sure he doesn't get away," Bertie whispered to the bodyguard as he wheeled me away.

I had a bad feeling about this. And, even worse, I had a bad taste in my mouth.

Again.

Chapter Forty-Nine

I WAS BLIND. AGAIN.

But this time, I couldn't tell if I was having another spell of lost eyesight, or if it was because wherever I was being held against my will was as black as pitch.

It was cold, too. Like, meat-locker cold.

I shivered and felt the telltale tug of the ropes binding my wrists and ankles to the wheelchair. The goon who'd tied me up had warned me to keep quiet or he'd gag me, too. I'd obeyed. What other choice did I have?

After he secured my arms and legs to the chair, he'd put a hand over my eyes and rolled me down a passageway behind the stage. I heard the click of a door handle, then movement as he'd drug me backward into a cold, dark room. He'd spun my chair around so my back was to the door, then removed his hand from over my eyes.

"Don't make a sound," he'd demanded before he shut the door. As it closed, it clanged heavy and metallic.

Maybe it *was* a meat locker.

A sudden thought sent shivers down my spine.

Cripes! Maybe this is where they store the bodies!

Blind and alone, I fought against the rising panic in my throat. The goon hadn't gagged *or* blindfolded me. Was that a good sign or a bad sign? I strained my eyes open as wide as they would go. I still couldn't see squat. To top it off, my mouth tasted like Lincoln had come to life from a roll of pennies and taken a dump on my tongue—just like the other two times I'd gone blind.

I have to get out of here!

I tried scooting with my torso, hoping it would move the wheelchair. But it wouldn't budge. My mind swirled with panic. Were bodies hanging on hooks all around me, empty husks sucked dry of life-giving energy by Bertie and his believers?

I didn't want to wait around to find out.

"Help!" I yelled into the darkness.

"Help me!" Someone cried out from across the room.

"Oh my God!" I said. "They got you, too?"

"Yes! Save me!"

"Who's doing this to us?" I asked.

"Brother Bertie!"

My gut flopped. "Crap! I knew it!" I called back. I squirmed against the ropes binding me to the wheelchair.

"Help!"

"I'm trying, but I'm tied up!"

The rancid, metallic taste in my mouth intensified. I wanted to spit, but was worried it'd end up all over me. I didn't want to die like that.

Suddenly, I heard the door crack open behind me, then footsteps. Someone was approaching—*to kill me?*

"Who's there?" I squeaked.

"Bertie!" the other hostage called out.

"Shut up!" a man's voice yelled behind my back. A hand of unknown origin clamped onto my shoulder. If it had been Grayson, I would've felt the electricity of his touch. It if had been Earl, I'd have smelled his Frito breath.

A clammy hand landed on my forehead.

No doubt about it. It was dirty Bertie himself.

My mind scrambled. Had Bertie turned on the lights when he came in, and I was blind again? Or was he operating in the dark, hoping I wouldn't recognize him?

"What do you want with me?" I asked.

"The question is, what do *you* want with *me?*"

Suddenly, hands were all over me, patting me down. One hand stopped on the EFD gizmo taped to my side. The other hand stopped on my right boob.

I heard Bertie gasp. "Brother, when did you become a sister?"

"It's a long story," I said.

"What's this thing?" he asked, ripping off the EFD taped to my side. "Is this some kind of remote control recording device?"

"No," I said.

"A bomb?" The pitch in his voice rose. "Are you trying to blow me up?"

"No!" I pleaded into the dark. "I ... I just wanted to record your electromagnetic field disturbance."

"My *what?*"

"Your psychic energy fluctuations, okay?"

"Really?" he said. "How does this thing work?"

"The monitor detects electromagnetic changes," I offered hopefully.

"Is this the monitor?"

"I ... I don't know. I can't see. I'm having one of my blind spells again."

"So ... you haven't ... *seen* anything?" he asked.

"Uh ... no."

Bertie grabbed the wheelchair, spun me around and began shoving me forward.

"Are you going to kill me now?" I squealed.

"Kill you?" Bertie asked.

"Yes." I blinked back tears. Suddenly, the gray outline of the room came into view.

"Hell, no," Bertie said. "Just don't sue me, okay? I didn't know you had boobs!"

I glanced down at my lap. The EFD monitor lay between my knees, where he'd tossed it. The indicator was all the way past the red zone.

"Help me!" the voice called out to my left.

"Shut up!" Bertie shouted.

I hazarded a sideways glance and caught sight of a shiny, white, coffin-looking thing.

What the hell?

"You're ... you're going to let me go?" I stuttered.

"What?" Bertie said. "Of course. Why wouldn't I? I thought you were some kook out to discredit me."

"No way. I'm a believer," I lied, hoping it would save my skin.

As Bertie reached the door, my eyesight was hazy, but clearing. He stopped pushing the wheelchair, then scooted around it and flung open the door. Even with my limited sight, I could see he was red and sweaty from the ordeal.

"Sorry about this," he said as he pushed me toward the door. "I'll untie you in the hallway. This has all been just a silly misunderstanding."

"Sure," I giggled hysterically. "That works for me."

Suddenly, a dark shadow appeared in the open doorway.

Not another blind spell! I thought, and closed my eyes hoping to ward it off.

"And just where do you think you're goin'?" Earl's voice boomed into the room.

Aw, no!

My wheelchair came to a screeching halt, nearly catapulting me out of it. I flung open my eyes.

Earl's burly, bear-like silhouette blocked the oversized doorframe. I locked eyes with him, hoping to tell him we were in the clear, if he'd just—but then I realized he wasn't looking at me.

Earl was staring at a point near my right elbow.

I shifted my eyes in that direction. The shiny barrel of a pistol was pointing right at my cousin's beer gut.

Aw, shit!

"New game plan. Get in here and close the door behind you," Bertie barked.

I shook my head.

I could scarcely believe it.

It was just too bad to be true.

Chapter Fifty

THE METAL DOOR CLICKED solidly behind us. My vision had cleared enough to see that Bertie was holding us at gunpoint in a long, narrow room with metal walls.

The room was empty except for a shiny, white, pod-like contraption in the corner that appeared to be some kind of flash-freezing unit. Next to it was a rectangular object covered with a beige tarp. It was about the size and shape of a double-door freezer. If this *was* a meat locker, it was in need of fresh meat.

"Lord-a-mercy! Is that your *coffin?*" Earl asked, pointing at the long, cylindrical machine in the corner.

"No!" Bertie said. "It's not a coffin. It's a hyperbaric chamber."

"Oh! Like the one Michael Jackson and Bubbles slept in," Earl said.

Bertie's already red face went crimson. The tendons on his scrawny neck stuck out like a lizard's dewlap.

"See?" Bertie screeched. "This is why I can't have nice things! People think I'm a freak!" He aimed the gun at Earl's belly. "Now get over there. Get in the cage!"

"What cage?" Earl asked.

A vein in Bertie's temple began to pulsate as if it were about to erupt. "The one under the tarp over there. Now do it!"

Earl strolled over to investigate what was under the rectangular stretch of tarp.

As he bent over to pick up the edge of the fabric, someone cried out from underneath it.

"Help me!"

The woman I'd heard earlier!

"You got somebody else in there, too?" Earl asked. "That's illegal, you know."

"Shut up and get in!" Bertie said.

Earl lifted the tarp, revealing a huge, wrought-iron cage. Inside, half naked and frazzled, was the biggest damned parrot I'd ever seen.

"Dirty Bertie!" it squawked at an ear-splitting decibel.

"For the last time, shut up, Polly!" Bertie yelled. He blew out an angry sigh and muttered at me. "Gift from a grateful believer. Been the bane of my existence for nearly fifty years."

"Why are you doing this to us?" I asked.

"Because the last thing I need is more bad publicity," Bertie said. "Everybody thinks it's a miracle from God that I look this good at one hundred. If they find out that it's because of the chamber there, the mystery surrounding my persona will be ruined. I'll just be another blowhard hack."

"Just tell 'em you eat Kale," Earl said, stepping into the cage. "Like all them celebrities do."

Bertie thought it over. "But then, I'd have to eat kale."

"That's the down side," Earl said, closing the cage door behind him.

"Listen, I'm sorry about this," Bertie said. "But I can't have anyone knowing about the hyperbaric chamber. And I'm too damned old to start eating kale now. My colon would blow a gasket."

"I heard that," Earl said, rubbing his stomach. "If I had to choose between life and kale, I'd be hard pressed to decide myself."

"Thanks for understanding," Bertie said, locking the bird cage with a padlock. "I'll have to wait until the crowd's gone before we can dispose of you two."

"Dispose?" I asked.

"Mind if I eat the sunflower seeds while we wait?" Earl said, picking up the parrot's food cup.

Bertie shot him a look. "Eat the damned bird for all I care."

"Thanks." Earl smiled at Bertie, then glanced over at me. My exasperated expression made him blanch.

"What?" Earl asked, and popped a sunflower seed into his mouth.

I COULD SEE AGAIN, but it was mostly red.

I'd been tied to a wheelchair for what seemed like hours now, forced to watch Earl eat sunflower seeds and try to teach a half-buzzard parrot named Polly how to say, "two-headed turtle."

Oh, the humanity.

"How'd you find me?" I asked Earl, just to get him to stop saying two-headed turtle.

"Rocko," he answered, spitting out a seed hull. "He let me in the back door."

I chewed my lip. "I wonder what those other two bodyguards did with Grayson."

Earl shrugged. "Maybe they got him caged up with another parrot somewheres."

I shook my head. "If Grayson doesn't show up soon, our only hope is to talk Bertie into letting us go by swearing on our lives to be discrete. Can you do that?"

"Two-headed turtle," the parrot said.

I slumped back in my wheelchair. "You're right, Polly. It's hopeless."

Chapter Fifty-One

I'D ALMOST DOZED OFF, content in the fact my life would soon be over, and I'd never have to hear the words "two-headed turtle" ever again.

The door handle squeaked. I jerked back to full consciousness.

The door flew open. Bertie stepped inside, flanked by two of his bouncer goons.

"How about a nice ride in the country?" Bertie asked.

"That sounds cool," Earl said. "Can we stop for hamburgers on the way? I'm starvin'. Sunflower seeds just don't—"

"Shut up!" Bertie screeched. He nudged one of the men. "Put some duct tape over his mouth."

Right. Now *you shut him up.*

"Can't we work something out?" I asked as the two thugs took Earl from the cage, duct-taped his hands together, then plastered a strip over his mouth.

"Sorry," Bertie said. "Like I said before, I can't have anyone knowing I sleep in a hyperbaric chamber. They'll think I'm some kind of sideshow freak, like they did my father."

"You're not a first generation healer?" I asked.

"No. My father and grandfather were also what the old timers called 'electric people.'"

"Electric people?"

"Yeah. You know. People who stop watches if they wear 'em. Or make street lights go out when they walk by."

"But there's more to your gift than that," I said. "The device I brought with me. It says you're able to alter people's electromagnetic fields. Is that how you heal them?"

Bertie shrugged. "I don't know. I never questioned it. But maybe there's something to that. I remember folks used to call my grandfather the 'Magneto Man.'"

"We're ready, boss," one of the bodyguards said.

I looked up. The other tattooed muscle man was hauling Earl toward the door. My cousin glanced back and shot me what I figured he meant as a reassuring face—the part that wasn't covered in duct tape, anyway. I smiled and nodded back.

God speed, cousin.

"Let's go," Bertie said, and shoved my wheelchair out the oversized metal door. Only when we joggled over the threshold did I realize we'd been inside the metal trailer of a semi-truck. It'd been parked up against the raised walkway that led to the stage.

When we turned a corner and rolled out onto the stage, it was shocking to see how dramatically everything had changed. The crowds were gone, along with their kinetic energy. The tent was an empty hull. Only a few side lights and exit signs illuminated the stale, dull air within it.

"All this will be gone after our big celebration tomorrow," Bertie said.

"Your hundredth birthday," I half-whispered.

He gave me a sad smile. "That's right. Too bad you won't be around to see it. It's gonna be spectacular."

"The ushering in of a new vampire cult," I said.

Bertie's face shifted from mild empathy to not-so-mild anger. "What?"

"That's what my partner, the private investigator believes. He says you're a psychic vampire."

The two bodyguards turned and looked at me. I might not have known all the tricks Grayson did, but I was a fast learner. And, as a former mall cop, I knew what it was like to put your life on the line for barely over minimum wage.

"Be careful, guys," I warned. "That's *really* how Bertie stays so young. He doesn't heal people. He sucks the life energy out of them, instead."

The two goons exchanged glances. "Bullshit," the one closest to me said.

"Fine. But don't say I didn't try to warn you. That's what Bertie's planning to do with me and my cousin. We're his next energy meals, ready to eat."

The guys' faces registered a hint of skepticism. Whether it was about me or Bertie, I couldn't ascertain.

I turned to Bertie. "Why aren't you hauling us away in the big semi-truck?"

He frowned. "What do *you* care? It uses too much gas."

I nodded. "Oh, sure. I guess all that money you save goes to give these guys a good salary and benefits."

The goons frowned.

"Have you seen the cost of health care plans?" Bertie said. He looked over at the guys. "I'm working on it, I promise."

"Still?" I laughed. "You've had a hundred years already."

"Shut up!" Bertie yelped. He jabbed a gnarled finger at one of the guys. "You. Duct tape her mouth."

"We didn't bring the tape with us," the goon said.

"Ugh!" Bertie groaned. "Do I have to do *everything* myself, you half-w—"

The two men were glaring at Bertie.

The old man backtracked quicker than Bo Jangles.

"Don't get me wrong, fellas," Bertie said. "You guys do good work. Tell you what, I'll get the tape myself." Bertie took a step toward the side of the stage, then turned around. "On second thought, let's just go. Load 'em up in the van."

"I hope you're getting paid extra for homicide," I said to the guy pushing my chair.

"Time and a half," Bertie said.

"Oh. Sure. Just like San Quentin," I quipped.

Bertie's face twisted with rage. "Come on, you two. Let's go!"

BEHIND MY BRAVADO OF sarcasm, I was trembling like Jell-O in a 9.7-Richter earthquake.

When Bertie and his goons rolled me out into the dirt parking lot behind the massive revival tent, my teeth began to chatter. Whether it was from fear or the stark, chilly breeze, I couldn't say for sure. In the cloudy night sky above our heads, tree branches rustled like tissue-paper ghosts, swirling to the rhythm of the unseen wind.

"Keep moving," Bertie barked.

The guard who had Earl by the arm shoved him forward. My wheelchair lurched.

Ahead, in the distance, the white van glowed surreally in the light of an overcast moon. On its side, Bertie's larger-than-life image—once comical—now appeared sinister, like a ghoul beckoning us to our fate.

An icepick of fear stabbed me in the back.

I knew that once they loaded us on board, we were doomed.

I closed my eyes and prayed for a miracle.

Chapter Fifty-Two

EARL WAS BOUND AND gagged with duct tape, yet he didn't seem to sense the peril we were in. His trusting nature was the opposite of mine. Sometimes, I was envious of it. But not at this exact moment.

Bertie and his two bodyguards were taking us to his van to be "disposed of." Earl wasn't even putting up a struggle. He must've really believed it when Bertie had said we were going for "a ride in the country."

I opened my mouth to yell, "Run, Earl!" but I didn't get the words out. The guy pushing my wheelchair hit a muddy pothole. I lurched sideways with the chair and the armrest knocked the words right out of me.

"Ung," the goon pushing me grunted.

"What's wrong?" Bertie asked.

"Nothin'. Just stuck in a hole."

As the guy shoved at chair trying to get out of the hole, I pleaded with our captor. "It's not too late to call this off, Bertie."

"I'm afraid it is, sister," Bertie said. "I can't let anything jeopardize my big party tomorrow."

Suddenly, as if on cue, strange jungle drums began to echo in the darkness, just beyond the reach of the lamp posts' yellowish, conical beams of light.

Bertie's face creased with concern. "What the hell?"

Somewhere in the near distance, a voice broke into a tribal chant, filling the thick air like a portent from an old Tarzan movie.

"Hooga-shaka. Hooga-shaka."

"Stay away!" Bertie yelled. Clearly spooked, he grabbed his gun from his pocket and pointed it at me. "Stay away or the girl gets it!"

"Girl?" the goon pushing my wheelchair said. He stopped in his tracks.

"Bertie's crazy," I whispered.

"Hey Walter, I think the old man's losing it," he yelled to the other guard who had ahold of Earl. "Thinks this old buzzard here's a woman."

Walter looked me up and down, then stomped his feet. "I *knew* this would happen! I've still got three years on my car payments!"

"Hush!" Bertie screeched.

The three men clammed up momentarily. In the silent void that followed, a ghostly woman's voice echoed in the breeze. "Let them go-oooo, Bertie."

Bertie froze. "Is that ... is that you, Ma?"

"Uh," the voice fumbled. "Yes, Bertie. I am your mother. Let them go-ooo."

Bertie's face puckered. "I can't, Ma! They ... they think I'm a freak, like Dad!"

"Freaks need love, too, Bertie, baby," the woman cooed.

Bertie's eyes darted around wildly. "If that really *is* you, Ma, call me what you always called me when I was a kid."

"Uh ... can you give me a hint?" the voice asked softly.

Bertie winced. "BB. Remember?"

"Ah, yes. Beautiful Boy," the voice sang.

"No," Bertie whined. "Bastard Brat. I hate you, Mommy!"

Bertie raised his gun and fired into the darkness. The blast's recoil sent his frail frame tumbling onto the soggy ground beside me. As he fell, the front of his toupee flapped up and over, then clung to the back of his skull like a road-kill possum.

Bertie glanced up at me. His sinewy face registered sheer terror. He dropped the gun and scrambled to secure his toupee. As he knelt on the ground and folded his fake hair back onto his moon-like pate, the goon in charge of me hustled over and kicked the gun out of his reach.

"No guns, Bertie," he said.

Bernie looked up at him with the face of an angry child. "But—"

A man's deep voice echoed from the darkness to my right, silencing Bertie. "I call upon you, great animal spirit!"

All of us craned our heads in that direction and peered into the chilly, night air. Suddenly, an African warrior stepped into the ghostly light of the lamppost.

It was Stanley!

Dressed only in a bear-claw necklace and an animal skin, he waved his arms like an orchestra conductor and yelled, "Harness the wind, spirit animal! Defend the innocent!"

A sudden blast of arctic wind gusted across the parking lot like an invisible tsunami. Overhead, a tree limb cracked. I looked up. Above me, a five-foot long, horned beast was hurtling at us from the sky like a rogue asteroid.

I screamed and ducked.

A second later, I heard a sickening thud.

"Unkgh!" Bertie grunted, as the creature landed squarely atop his back. The impact knocked Bertie off his knees, flattening him in the dirt like a dehydrated belly-flop.

"Get thee off my behind, Satan!" Bertie screeched, clawing at the fork-tongued monster riding his spine. He glanced up at me, wild eyed, and yelled, "Help! Get it off me!"

Tied to the wheelchair, I couldn't exactly offer much assistance other than to cheer the beast on.

"What should we do?" I heard Walter yell. I looked over at Bertie's bodyguards just in time to see them exchange glances, then take off running—in the opposite direction.

Frozen in horror, I was fated to watch, helpless, as Bertie writhed on the ground beside me, wrestling in the mud with a monster every bit as ugly as the devil himself.

Chapter Fifty-Three

"SOMEBODY HELP!" I FINALLY managed to yell, my eyes still glued on Bertie and the beast wrestling in the mud beside my wheelchair.

Stanley, who'd been standing frozen with his mouth open, suddenly thawed. He ran over to Earl and ripped the duct tape from his mouth, then he sprinted up to me.

"You okay?" he asked. "What happened?"

"You didn't see?"

"No. I only heard a thud and—"

"Augh!" Bertie grunted.

Stanley and I turned and looked down at the ground, where my wheelchair had been blocking his view.

The reptilian creature had Bertie in a headlock. The old man's toupee was gone, a casualty of the melee.

"Dear lord, what *is* that?" I asked.

"An iguana," Stanley whispered, a stunned look on his face.

I looked up at him. Stanley's eyes grew wide. A proud grin popped onto his face. "My spirit animal. It came!"

Earl came hobbling over for a look.

"Lord-a-mercy!" he said, getting an eyeful of Bertie and the beast. "Them's the worst dang hair plugs I ever seen!"

HAVING BESTED BERTIE, the iguana slithered off into the night. As for Bertie, after his heavyweight match with Iguanodon Jr., he was so worn out he couldn't even sit up.

"I guess there's no need to restrain him," Stanley said as he untied me.

"Nope. That feller's spent his last dime," Earl said.

I glanced around. "Where's Grayson?"

"So *now* you ask about me," Grayson said, stepping out of the darkness. By his side was Nina, the skinny black nurse from Banner Hill.

I shot him an angry look. "Why didn't you help us escape from Bertie?"

"That's *my* fault," Stanley said. "In order to summon my spirit animal, Nina said someone had to play the bongos." Stanley shrugged. "I don't know how."

Grayson grinned and banged on the bongos strapped to his waist. "See? I told you I was multi-talented."

I gave Grayson a begrudging smile. "Where'd you get the spirit animal idea, Stanley?"

"From Nina." He nodded toward her. She's not just a nurse. She's also a voodoo priestess."

Nina folded her hands and bowed her turbaned head. The clatter from the bone necklaces around her neck made me shiver with awe.

"Wow," I said.

"And a powerful priestess she is," Stanley said. "She helped me summon the great spirit of the iguana."

"Actually, that was a zombiguana," Grayson said.

"You put a dead iguana in a trance?" I asked Nina. "That's amazing!"

"No," Grayson said. "Zombiguana is the term I invented to describe iguanas trapped in a metabolic stupor."

My nose crinkled. "What?"

"Iguanas aren't native to Florida," Grayson droned on, ruining the magic of the moment with his dry, boring facts. "Therefore, their bodies aren't adapted to cold temperatures. Anything approaching the forties causes iguanas to half-freeze. With a strong enough wind, they drop from their tree perches like overripe mangos."

"You're making that up," I said, shooting Stanley and Nina an apologetic smile.

Grayson shook his head. "When are you ever going to trust me, Drex? Zombiguanas are a real phenomenon. In fact, last year, the National Weather Service started issuing warnings about falling iguanas."

Bertie let out a moan. "Need ozzie ...."

We all turned and stared at our forgotten nemesis. The poor old geezer was lying face up in the dirt, weakly waving a hand at us.

"What are we going to do about him?" Stanley asked me. "You want to press charges? He *did* hold you at gunpoint."

"His mama didn't love him, and he can't wear a watch." Earl said. "Ain't that punishment enough?"

"It all depends on his involvement with the missing vets," Grayson said. "At this point, we've still got no proof he's guilty of anything but poor taste in head rugs. The only card we've got left is to wrangle a confession out of him."

A sadistic grin crept slowly onto my lips. "I think I've got an idea on how we can do just that."

Chapter Fifty-Four

THE DOOR TO BERTIE'S semi-trailer clicked closed behind me, trapping him inside.

The sadistic grin on my lips grew a little wider. "Give Bertie half an hour in there with Earl and that parrot, and he'll spill the beans, guaranteed."

AS IT TURNED OUT, BERTIE broke in under three minutes. Frantic banging from inside prompted Grayson to open the door.

"Please," Bertie groaned. "Can't ... can't—"

"Fine," Grayson said.

He walked over and knelt beside the old man. Bertie was leaning against the wall by the hyperbaric chamber, holding a pillow over his head like giant earmuffs.

"Ready to answer some questions?" Grayson asked as I walked up beside him.

Old Bertie must've been in bad shape. He didn't even react to the fact that I could walk. Instead, he stared at Grayson, wide-eyed as a strangled chicken.

"Please," Bertie panted. "Must ... chamber ...."

"Chamber?" Grayson asked. "You need a chamber pot, old man?"

I gasped. "I think he means he needs his hyperbaric chamber!"

Bertie nodded, his face turning the color of a blue Tootsie Pop. "In by nine ... or die," he gurgled, then slumped sideways. His torso collapsed to the floor.

I glanced at my cellphone. It was 8:56.

"Hurry!" I yelled. "Stanley, you get his feet. Grayson, you get his arms. We've got to get him into that hyperbaric chamber!"

"Dirty Birtie," the parrot squawked as we lifted Bertie into the chamber. Freed from its cage, Polly was promenading around like a penguin that'd barely survived Mardi Gras.

"I don't understand," I said to Earl. "Why didn't Bertie just climb into the chamber himself?"

"He tried to, but Polly wouldn't let him. She kept chasing him around, worryin' that old feller half to death."

"Why didn't *you* help him?"

Earl balked at the idea. "I thought he'd get all rejuvenated up in there then suck my vital juices!"

I turned and stared at Bertie. Inside the chamber, he looked like a long-distance space traveler whose cryonic capsule had sprung a leak.

"Anybody know how to operate this thing?" I asked.

"I think I can figure it out." Stanley studied the buttons for a minute. "Okay. I think I got it. Seal the lid."

"It may be too late," I said, and nodded at Bertie. His coloring had gone from blue-raspberry to grape.

Stanley grabbed Bertie's wrist. "Aw, man. No pulse. He's already gone."

My heart pinged with sadness for Bertie. Sure, he'd been a jerk. But I knew all too well what it was like to feel like a freak.

"Let's get him out of this thing and back to wherever he usually spends the night," I said. "I know he wouldn't want to be found here like this."

"First, let's say a prayer for his soul," Nina said.

"Say a prayer for yourselves!" a man's voice rang out.

We all whipped around to face the door—and found ourselves staring down the barrel of a sawed-off shotgun.

Chapter Fifty-Five

"YOU KILLED HIM!" ROCKO yelled.

He aimed his shotgun at us as we stood around the hyperbaric chamber, staring at Bertie's blue face.

A collective gasp echoed through the semi-trailer. We all simultaneously raised our hands and took a step back from Bertie—all except Grayson, that is.

"No, Rocko. Bertie killed himself," Grayson said, taking a step toward him.

"What?" Rocko's angry face softened a notch. "Bertie committed Suicide?"

Grayson pursed his lips. "Well, in a way, yes."

"I don't believe it," Rocko said, shaking his head.

Neither did I.

I shot Grayson a *what the hell* look. He opened his palms and took another step toward Rocko.

I blanched. Either Grayson was being heroic and trying to save us, or he was sealing our doom.

"Hear me out," Grayson said. "Brother Bertie believed he would die if he didn't get into that hyperbaric chamber by nine p.m. He didn't make it because he didn't make it."

"What?"

Rocko's face crinkled in confusion. The rest of us followed suit and stared at Grayson.

"His belief is what killed him," Grayson said. "Faith is a powerful, mystical thing that can't be quantified."

"Actually, he died at 8:59," Nina said.

All eyes shifted to the woman dressed in African voodoo garb.

"What? I'm a nurse," Nina said. "I noted his vitals on my watch. It's a habit of mine."

"Your watch could be wrong," Grayson said.

I tugged on Grayson's sleeve. "That's hardly the point to be arguing right now," I whispered, nodding toward Rocko.

The leather-clad ex-biker was standing in the doorway looking utterly shattered. He was blocking our only exit from the semi-truck trailer. He still held the shotgun, but at the moment, it hung limp in his hand, pointed at the ground.

"Lettuce pray," Earl said, breaking the silence. "Come on over, Rocko. Let's join hands in a circle."

I stared at Rocko, wondering who he would shoot first. Then, just like that, I got the miracle I'd prayed for. Rocko laid the sawed-off shotgun on the floor and ambled over to us.

Stunned, I joined the circle holding hands around Bertie's dirty body as it lay in state in his hyperbolic chamber.

We all stood as one, in silent reverence for the man who could've been a psychic vampire, a scam artist, a healer, or merely suffering from dementia.

I glanced around. Our group included one voodoo priestess, one dreadlocked warrior, one fake paraplegic, one tattooed biker, one fedora-topped physicist, and one bear-sized redneck. As different as we all were, we were united in one thing—paying our final respects to the hundred-year-old faith healer who, sadly, never figured out how to resurrect his own hair.

The irony that our circle looked like some kind of bizarre cult ritual wasn't lost on me. Earl's words only added to the surreal nature of the moment.

"Dear God, whoever and wherever you are, take our brother Bertie with you," Earl prayed, his eyes shut tight, his face pinched with sincerity. "Ol' Bertie tried hard to do what he thought was best. He couldn't heal old Sally, but Grandma Selma swore he got rid of her warts. Amen."

"Amen," we all echoed.

"Oh, and P.S., God?" Earl said, squeezing his eyes shut once more. "Is it all right with you if I keep Polly?"

Chapter Fifty-Six

BERTIE LOOKED AT PEACE tucked into his bed inside his cozy travel caravan. The guys had washed and dressed him in a fresh, white suit. Nina and I'd done our best to resurrect his mangled toupee.

I made the final adjustments, tugging the fake, silver-white cap of hair over the doll-like row of hair plugs dotting his pale forehead.

"There," I said. "He's ready."

Rocko came over and gazed sadly at Bertie. "I mean, the guy could be a tool sometimes. But why did he have to die?"

"Some things just are beyond our understanding," Grayson said.

"Like two-headed turtles?" Earl asked.

"Yes." I slipped an arm around my cousin's waist. "Like two-headed turtles."

"I guess we'll never know what happened to those missing vets now," Earl said.

I turned to Rocko. "Do you think Bertie could've been involved? Could he have used his semi-trailer to haul them away?"

"If he did, I never saw anything," Rocko said.

"I hear you," Stanley said, nodding his head. "Pleading the Schultz."

"No." Rocko let out a sigh. "The old guy had his secrets, but I really don't think he was a murderer."

"Dirty Bertie!" Polly screeched as Earl brought her in to pay her last respects.

"His untimely death was certainly inconvenient," Grayson said. "We may never know now if Bertie was a psychic vampire or not. However, we may still be able to clear his name about the missing veterans."

"How?" Rocko asked.

"By proving *you* did it," Grayson said. He reached for his Glock, but didn't pull it out.

"Me?" Rocko said.

"You had ample opportunity when you picked up the men in Bertie's van. Maybe you transported them to the revival, or maybe you took them for your own ulterior motives."

"Like what?" I asked.

Grayson studied Rocko's face. "Selling their body parts. Exacting revenge for their ex-wives over unpaid alimony. I can think of a dozen viable money-making reasons."

Rocko rolled his eyes. "If I had any money, you think I'd be living in the back of a van with Bertie's face on it?"

Grayson's brow furrowed. "Good point." He turned to Stanley. "There's still the possibility Old Mildred's ghost got the men. If she's responsible, Bertie would be innocent of any wrongdoing."

"Bertie!" Polly screeched. "Dirty Bertie!"

Rocko winced and twisted an index finger in his ear. He shot a sour face at Earl. "You sure you want that bird?"

"Me and Polly are friends now," Earl said. "We understand each other, don't we girl?"

Polly sidled up to Earl's leg and squawked, "Two-headed turtle."

Earl beamed like a proud papa. "Yep. I'm sure."

"Then she's yours." Rocko clapped a hand on Grayson's shoulder and nodded toward the caravan door. "Brother, I want you to go clear Bertie's name, if you can."

I glanced over at Bertie's corpse. "What about—"

"I'll notify Bertie's family," Rocko said. "You guys take off. If you hang around, it'll just stir up questions about vampires and stuff we don't need to get stuck having to answer."

Grayson nodded and shook Rocko's hand. "Thanks, brother. You can count on us. If Bertie's innocent, we'll prove it."

Rocko knelt beside Bertie. A tear slid down his cheek. "To think, he was so close to turning a hundred."

"He made it," Grayson said.

Bertie looked up at Grayson. "What do you mean?"

"Some Asian cultures mark the start of someone's life as the date of conception, not birth. In those terms, Bertie lived well past the century mark."

Rocko nodded and wiped his eyes. "Thanks for the reminder, brother."

Grayson smiled. "That life isn't the number of years you live, but the life you put into those years?"

"Well, sure," Rocko said. "That, and that Asian chicks are hot. After all this blows over, I'm moving to Thailand."

BESSIE'S ENGINE ROARED and the revival tent faded into the darkness. Relief washed over me.

It was extremely short-lived.

"We need to talk about our stakeout plan for Banner Hill tonight," Grayson said.

My gut flopped for the fourteenth time that day. "What?"

Wedged between Grayson and Earl in the front seat of his monster truck, there was no physical escape from the madness. I was going to have to talk my way out of it.

"It's too late," I argued, scrambling for excuses. "It's already past nine-thirty. That's midnight at Banner Hill. The doors are already locked!"

"I can get us in," Stanley said. He'd called shotgun and had a window seat to our human sardine act.

"Won't they suspect something?" I asked hopefully.

Stanley shook his head. "No. I told the other guys working tonight that I was taking you to see your brother. Said we might be back late tonight. They're expecting us."

"Well done," Grayson said.

"No way am I going back there tonight," I said, digging in my heels. "Haven't we had enough crazy for one night?"

Grayson took my hand, put his lips to my ear, and whispered the magical words I'd been longing to hear. "If we solve this case tonight, you don't have to spend another night in Banner Hill."

I blew out a sigh. "Fine. I'm in. What's the plan?"

Chapter Fifty-Seven

"WHERE YOU GUYS BEEN all evenin'?" Melvin asked after poking his head out of his room across the hall from mine.

"Sorry if we disturbed you," Stanley whispered, pausing my wheelchair in the hallway in front of my room. He leaned over and patted me on the shoulder. "I really need to grease the wheel on your chair, Georgie."

Stanley straightened his back and wagged a finger at Melvin. "And you, young man. You should be in bed. It's after ten o'clock."

"I was worried," Melvin said, giving his rumpled comb-over a swipe with his gnarled hand. "I thought maybe they'd come and got Georgie, too."

"Who?" Stanley asked.

Melvin glanced both ways down the hall. "The vampires," he whispered. "I heard y'all talking about 'em this morning. You want a clove?" He held up a head of garlic.

"There's no such thing as vampires," Stanley said. "Now get back in bed."

Melvin scowled. "Have it your way. But I ain't taking no chances." He popped a garlic clove in his mouth, then disappeared behind his door.

Stanley rolled me into my room. "See? I told you that old coot was crazy. Get ready for bed. I'll be back in a few minutes to set things up."

I WAS IN BED IN MY hospital gown, dunking my vampire teeth into the glass of blue water beside my bed, when I heard a light tap at my door. The door squeaked open. Stanley entered, pushing a laundry cart.

Operation "Get Old Mildred" was about to begin.

Stanley closed the door behind him, then laid his hands on a bag stuffed with dirty laundry. It began to squirm like an oversized larva. Stanley untied the drawstring. Grayson's head popped out like some tragic, not-meant-to-be-funny scene in a low-budget horror movie.

"Seen any toe-sucking parasites?" Grayson asked, inching the laundry bag down to his waist. He reached into it and pulled out his black fedora. He popped it atop his shaved head.

"No," I managed, stifling a laugh. "But Melvin across the hall asked about vampires again." I shook my head. "I just don't get it. What's up with everybody's infatuation with vampires?"

Grayson birthed himself from the bag, pulling its sides down to his knees, then kicking it free. He sat up on the cart and pulled a static-cling sock from the side of his black shirt. "Every culture since time immemorial has had some kind of legend about a blood-sucking monster."

"Yeah," Stanley said. "They're called politicians. Now keep it down, *please*. We don't want to disturb the other residents."

"Right." Grayson hopped off the cart.

"I'll be back in a few with the second load," Stanley whispered, pushing the cart and its deflated laundry bag out the door.

"Thanks, Stanley," I said. "We appreciate you helping us."

"I know nothing, I see nothing," he said, then smiled and shut the door behind him.

"The Egyptians had Sekhmet," Grayson said. "The Greeks, Ambrogio."

"What are you talking about?" I asked, adjusting my bed covers.

Grayson cocked his head at me. "Vampires, of course."

"Of course."

"If any of the old legends are true, the creatures mentioned in historic lore would have to be thousands of years old by now."

I fluffed my pillow. "And your point is?"

Grayson rubbed his chin. "Suppose this blood-sucking creature ran out of relatives to care for it? What better place for it to hide out than in a nursing home?"

"Huh?"

Grayson nodded his head. "It's ingenious, really. The perfect solution."

I sighed. "Again, Grayson. What in the world are you talking about?"

"Sticking elderly vampires in nursing homes, Drex. Think about it. Dinner is easy to catch—like sucking seniors in a barrel." Grayson smiled. "*Meals on wheelchairs*. Brilliant!"

I blew out another sigh and pulled the blanket at the end of the bed up and over my legs. "I thought you said Bram Stoker *invented* vampires."

"The modern version with capes and bad sideburns, yes. But we could be dealing with a much older creature from ancient mythology. A pre-vampire, yet nevertheless blood-sucking, parasitic being. As you might recall, most of the missing men suffered from anemia."

"Yeah. I remember." I sat up and chewed my lip. "This Ambrosia dude and Seek'em creature. What did they look like?"

"Sekhmet was a warrior goddess. Egyptians drew her as having the likeness of a lioness," Grayson said. "Ambrogio was actually a regular guy. An Italian mortal who Apollo turned into the first known human blood sucker."

"Why'd Apollo do that?"

"Because they both wanted the same chick, Selene."

"Ugh!" I groaned. "Guys!"

Grayson laughed. "Long legend short, Ambrogio was cursed by Apollo so the only way he could touch Selene was to drink her blood. Doing so also had the rather inconvenient side effect of killing her."

"Most contact with males usually does," I deadpanned.

Grayson's cheek dimpled. "Anyway, Selene died and legend says she became the Goddess of Moonlight. She now forever more shines down on the children who carry both Ambrogio's and her blood—their progeny of vampires."

I frowned. "Great. Let's hope Ambrogio wasn't too lucky with the ladies."

Grayson shrugged. "He *was* Italian."

"Ugh!" I groaned. "It's all just nonsense." I scrounged around in my purse for a Tootsie Pop to calm my nerves. Grayson's words had spooked me. It was going to be a long night.

"Remember the TV show *The Night Stalker?*" Grayson asked out of the blue.

"No."

"How about the *Twilight* saga? Or *Buffy the Vampire Slayer?*"

"Yeah." I stuck an orange Tootsie Pop in my mouth. "Want one?"

"Sure." Grayson took the green sucker I'd handed him. "It may seem trivial, but TV shows like those have kept the idea of vampirism alive."

"So what?"

"Just postulating, but what if our belief in vampires keeps the reality of them possible?"

My nose crinkled. "You mean like our thoughts turning random particles into real matter—that quantum physics stuff you're always talking about?"

Grayson's green eyes shone in a way I'd never seen before. "Precisely, cadet." He sighed, and his eyes dulled again. "But sadly, more and more, poor vampires are being dumbed down to cartoonish freaks, just like poor Bertie was."

"What do you mean, cartoonish freaks?"

"You know. The 'Count' on *Sesame Street*," Grayson said. "Count Chocula. Even *Spongebob Squarepants* has an episode with Nosferatu in it. The poor, mighty vampire was reduced to a hash-slinging slasher who made the lights flicker at the Krusty Krab whenever he showed up. You have to admit, that's a pathetic end for Murnau's fearsome creation."

Grayson stuck the Tootsie Pop in his mouth and tipped his fedora back on his shaved head. I smirked.

If Kojak and Super Mario had a baby ....

He glanced at his cellphone. "What's keeping them? It's well past ten o'clock. The unexplained phenomenon we're waiting on could appear any minute."

I grinned. "You talking about Earl or Old Mildred?"

Grayson laughed.

Suddenly, a weird *scree, scree* sound echoed down the hallway. The hair on my arms pricked up.

"That doesn't sound like the laundry cart," Grayson whispered.

"Oh my lord, Grayson! That's the sound Stanley described—the night Charlie Perkins disappeared!"

The sound stopped at my door. Grayson pulled his Glock, then sprinted over and hit the light switch, plunging the room into darkness.

"You're going to shoot at a ghost?" I whispered.

"Shhh!" Grayson hissed.

Slowly, the door creaked open.

In the dim glow of the hallway night lights, a gnarled, black, withered hand snaked its way inside. It clamped hold of the edge of the door.

I gasped.

A gravelly voice wafted into the darkness. It sounded like it said, "Old Mildred ...."

Chapter Fifty-Eight

I LURCHED UP IN BED and clawed around in my purse, desperately searching for something—anything—I could use to defend myself from the gnarly-handed ghoul creeping into my room.

Scree, scree.

The door creaked open wider ....

Scree, scree.

The hand reached out, revealing a boney arm ....

Scree, scree.

Then a shoulder ....

My fingers found purchase and wrapped themselves tightly around my makeshift weapon. I snatched it from my purse and hurled it toward the black silhouette skulking through the door.

At that exact moment, Grayson flicked on the lights.

I watched, in horror, as my bottle of Flintstones vitamins bounce squarely off the forehead of an old black man pushing a mop and bucket. The guy, dressed in blue janitor coveralls, crumpled to the ground like a heap of old clothes.

"Oh my God!" I squealed and scrambled out of bed. "I'm sorry, I'm sorry, I'm sorry!" I said as I ran over to him.

He gave no response.

Grayson knelt beside him and checked his neck for a pulse.

"Is he dead?" I squeaked.

"No. I think he'll live." Grayson locked his green eyes on mine. "Nice throw, DiMaggio. Now, help me get him up."

We pulled the old janitor to sitting, then lifted him into my wheelchair. He sat there limp as a ragdoll for a moment, then let out a groan.

"Are you okay?" I asked. "I'm so sorry!"

"I ... I think so," he said, rubbing the rising knot on his head. "What'd you go and do that for?"

I cringed. "I thought you were Old Mildred."

At the mention of her name, the old man's eyes grew wide. "You know about Old Mildred?"

"Yes."

"And it seems you do, too," Grayson said, studying him.

"That I do," the geriatric janitor said. "Been here near as long as she that runs the place."

"Gable?" Grayson asked.

"No." The old man chuckled. "Gable just a baby. I'm talkin' 'bout Ms. Draper, the owner. Mildred was her sister."

"Her sister?" I gasped, offering him a glass of water. He turned his nose up at it.

"Never touch the stuff." The old man perked up and smiled. "But I'll take one of them Tootsie Pops, if you got another."

"Sure. Hold on." I ran over and grabbed my purse off the bed.

"Old Mildred was somethin' special," the janitor said as I searched for a sucker amid the wrappers, coupons, and Walmart receipts crammed inside my pocketbook. "She lived here back in the '80s."

"What do you mean, 'something special'?" Grayson asked.

The old man shrugged and took the Tootsie Pop I offered, unwrapping it as he spoke. "She was a simple-minded gal, that Mildred. What folks back then called 'retarded.' Ms. Draper had her livin' here, amongst the old folks, until she up and died in 1988. Ever since then, ol' Draper wouldn't let no other woman stay here overnight, on account a what happened to Mildred."

"What happened?" I asked.

"Well, I don't like to be spreadin' no rumors."

The janitor popped the sucker in his mouth. Grayson and I exchanged glances.

"We're here on official—" Grayson began. I stepped on his toe.

"We won't tell anybody. We promise," I said.

"Well, all right then," the old man chuckled. "Legend has it, one night poor old Mildred bit off more'n she could chew. Found her dead in her bed, with somebody's big toe stuck in her throat. She been wandering these halls ever since."

"Wow. That's quite a story," Grayson said. "Have you ever seen Old Mildred yourself?"

The old man shrugged. "Sure. From time to time. She always partial to showin' up right around Thanksgivin'."

"Why do you think that is?" Grayson asked.

"Her anniversary, I guess. Mildred died here the day before Thanksgivin'."

"Oh." I frowned. "How sad."

The old man nodded. "Sure was. Draper never forgave herself. She was supposed to be watching her, you see? But she'd gone off to see some beau she was sweet on. That woman ain't never dated nobody since, as far as I know."

"Has Mildred ever ... uh ... killed anyone?" I asked. "Her ghost, I mean."

The old man's gray eyebrows rose and inch. "What? Why you askin' me that?"

"Five men have gone missing from here this week," I said.

"Huh," he grunted. "Well, I'll be."

"Does everyone here know about Old Mildred?" Grayson asked.

"Mostly," he said. "Word gets around, you know. But if 'n you asked, wouldn't nobody admit to it. You can't say word one around Ms. Draper about Old Mildred. She'll fire you faster 'n' double-aught buckshot."

"Have you heard any rumors about the men that've disappeared?" Grayson asked.

The old man shook his head. "Not that I recall."

Grayson pursed his lips. "Did you notice anything suspicious during any of your shifts this week? You see, each man went to dinner, but none of them made it to bed. When the staff went to get them for breakfast, they were gone. Their beds hadn't been slept in. They were still made up with military precision."

"Don't see how it could be Old Mildred," the janitor said. "When she was alive, she never made her bed. No, sir. She been haunting these halls for over thirty years. And ain't nobody just up and disappeared in the night before."

He stood and grabbed his mop. "Well, I best be gettin' back to my rounds. Thanks for the lollipop, Miss."

"You're welcome." I cringed out a smile. "Sorry again about ... well, you know."

"Don't you worry your head none about it." He tapped his boney knuckles on the thin, white tufts of hair atop of his skull. "Head's the hardest spot on old Sampson Jones."

Chapter Fifty-Nine

AFTER BIDDING SAMPSON and his poor head-knot farewell, I crawled back into bed while Grayson shuffled through the drawer on my nightstand.

"What are you looking for?" I asked.

"A spoon to eat your tapioca pudding cup."

"It's behind the glass with the fake dentures."

Geez. If a random stranger wandered in on this conversation, we'd be committed.

Grayson grabbed the spoon and held it up. "Got it!"

I leaned back in bed. "I wonder, does Draper know about the disappearance of the vets? If she does, you think she's covering it up? You know, to protect the memory of her sister Mildred?"

"Unlikely." Grayson shrugged and worked on peeling the lid off the pudding. "Why would she care about the reputation of a ghost?"

"What if she's protecting a *live* person, not a ghost?" I asked. "Sampson mentioned Draper had a boyfriend ...."

A sudden thought made me gasp. "Grayson! What if the 'beau' Draper snuck off to see the night Mildred died was *Bertie?*"

"Hmmm." Grayson frowned. "The timing's right. But what about—"

The door creaked open. Stanley entered, dragging Earl by the arm.

"I thought I told you to put him in a laundry bag," Grayson said.

Stanley shot Earl a look. "I couldn't get him to go in it."

Earl stuck his chin out and pouted. "I'm claustrophobic. Just like Polly."

Right. And you've also both got brains the size of walnuts.

"You didn't bring that stupid bird with you, did you?" I asked.

"No." Earl jerked free of Stanley's grasp. "*He* wouldn't let me."

"Thank goodness someone has some sense around here." I glanced back over at Grayson. "What were you—"

"No time left for talking," Grayson said setting the half-eaten pudding cup back on my nightstand. "We're already running behind. Okay, troops, take your positions. And keep alert."

Grayson stashed his fedora in my closet and donned the white lab coat hanging inside. "I'll check out the hallways with Stanley," he said. "Earl, you hide in the bathroom, like we planned. Be ready to spring into action if Old Mildred stops by for another round of digital digeridoo."

Earl's brow furrowed. "Of what?"

"Toe sucking," I said.

"Yes, sir," Earl saluted. "You can count on me."

Stanley and Grayson disappeared out the door. I laid back in bed and let out a sigh. "Great. Just what I need. Another night with ikigai."

Earl shot me a look. "You ain't no prize yourself, Cuz."

Chapter Sixty

SOMETIME IN THE NIGHT, I was startled awake by the sound of heavy breathing.

I flinched with panic, and clamped my eyes shut. Slowly, I cracked one open.

Where is the sound coming from?

The door leading to the hallway was closed. That meant the rasping sound was coming from ...

... inside my room!

At the foot of my bed!

Right where the eerie, green light to the .... My gut went limp.

Crap! You've got to be kidding me.

I jumped out of bed and padded to the bathroom. In the glow of the green night light by the sink, Earl was sitting sprawl-legged on the floor. His head was slumped over the toilet bowl. He looked like a drunk-ass gorilla after too many Halloween Jell-O shots.

The weird, rasping sound was being caused by Earl snoring into the toilet bowl. Like an echo chamber, it was sending them bouncing off the wall tiles.

I bit down on my molars. Hard.

It took every bit of willpower I had not to slam the lid and flush.

Instead, I took a deep breath, then jabbed my big lump of a cousin in the ribs with my big toe.

Earl sprang to life like a mummy in a movie. One of his meaty hands shot out and grabbed my foot.

"Aha! Gotcha, you toe-sucking pervert!" he yelled.

"Shhh!" I hissed. "It's just me, Bobbie."

"*You're* the toe-sucking perv—"

"Hush!" I whispered. "You fell asleep."

"Oh."

I leaned over and slapped his face. "There, that ought to help you stay awake."

He rubbed his cheek. "Thanks, Bobbie."

"Don't mention it." Guilty pleasure washed over me. I fought back a grin. "Now stay alert!"

"Yes, ma'am."

I crawled back in bed and pulled the covers over me. My fingers were still stinging from slapping Earl, but I didn't care. I was happy in the satisfaction that, no matter what else happened, this stupid stakeout hadn't been for nothing.

I'D BARELY GOTTEN MYSELF settled back in bed when I heard the knob on the hallway door begin to turn.

I held my breath.

The door cracked open.

If I hadn't taken Grayson's desensitization training, I'd probably have peed my pants.

A short, hunchbacked creature crept into my room.

This was no dress rehearsal. This was the real deal.

I LAY IN BED, FROZEN with fear, as the hideous creature entered and slowly closed the door behind it. The room was pitch black, save for the eerie green glow of the bathroom nightlight.

In the darkness, I heard what sounded like dragging footsteps as the hunchbacked ghoul made its way to the foot of my bed.

Heavy breathing filled the air, along with a horrid stench.

Then something so utterly crazy happened that I nearly blacked out from my mind not being able to process it.

Somewhere in the dark, Michael Franks' *Popsicle Toes* began to play.

Holy crap! The other two nights—they hadn't been dreams after all!

The covers lifted at the foot of my bed. A cold, clammy hand brushed my ankle.

Earl! Where are you? I screamed inside my head. *You're supposed to grab Old Mildred!*

My haywire brain raced in tempo with my heart. My pulse thrummed in my eardrums.

Should I yell for Earl or not? Would I be foiling his surprise attack?

Then I heard it.

That telltale, echoing rasp of breath.

Earl had fallen asleep with his head in the toilet.

Again.

Chapter Sixty-One

I WAS CAUGHT IN THE grips of the undead.

A shadowy entity had ahold of my left foot.

Paralyzed with fear, I lay helpless in bed as my leg rose in the air like Linda Blair's—under the control of some otherworldly demon.

Fear shot down my spine like a bullet of ice. Toxic vapors enveloped the room. A wave of nausea swept through me.

I blinked into the green-black darkness. The dark silhouette at the foot of my bed disappeared. Then, just as suddenly, reappeared.

A slimy sensation, like a cold-water slug, slithered across the bottom of my foot.

Then came a disgusting slurping sound.

I nearly dry-heaved.

It was Old Mildred, all right.

And she was sucking my big toe ....

Chapter Sixty-Two

"FORGIVE ME, JESUS," I heard a voice call out in the dark.

Ack! Old Mildred's fixing to kill me!

I lurched up in bed. A hollow, metallic sound gonged, then reverberated off the walls.

"What's happening?" I screeched.

Suddenly, the lights flipped on, searing my retinas with a blinding white flash.

I squinted through the stars in my eyes. I couldn't believe what I saw.

Earl standing at the end of my bed holding a dented bedpan.

A second later, Grayson and Stanley rushed into the room.

"What's going on?" Grayson yelled.

"I kilt Old Mildred," Earl whimpered.

Grayson and Stanley stared at the floor at the foot of my bed. I crawled across the covers for a look.

For the second time in ten seconds, I couldn't believe my eyes.

Crumpled on the floor, half buried by a Santa-sized laundry sack, were a pair of hairy, pasty legs clad only in white socks and the same cheap black slippers I'd been issued.

"Looks like Old Mildred wasn't a hunchback after all," Earl said.

"Or a shaver." Grayson heaved the sack from atop the body, revealing the open back of a hospital gown and a flabby, white, pimply bare ass.

Grayson groaned. "I may never eat tapioca pudding again."

"Who is it?" I asked.

"Only one way to find out."

Grayson squatted down and started to turn the body over. Suddenly, the door flew open as if it had been kicked by a mule.

"Hold it right there!" a man's voice yelled.

All eyes shifted from the body on the floor to the man at the door—then to the barrel of the gun in his hand.

"Don't move," he said.

I recognized the weapon as a Glock. I recognized the face as the man I'd seen at the revival ... the one stealing cash from the collection plate.

Where do I know him from?

His name was on the tip of my tongue ....

Chapter Sixty-Three

"HOLBROOK!" STANLEY said. "What are you doing here?"

The cop we'd seen at Topless Tacos rushed into the room and closed the door behind him. He waived the pistol at Earl and Grayson. "Hands on the walls. Now!"

Grayson cleared his throat. "I know this looks a bit odd, officer, but we were just—"

"Shut up!" Holbrook hissed. He glanced down at the mangled heap of legs and laundry lying on the floor. "What did you do to him?"

"Him?" Earl asked. "I thought Old Mildred was a woman."

"Shut up!" Holbrook said. "All of you. Get in the bathroom. Now!" He jabbed his gun in Grayson's ribs.

"Easy! Okay!" Grayson said. He held his hands up and marched into the bathroom. Earl and Stanley followed suit.

I started climbing out of bed to join them. Holbrook closed the bathroom door. He grabbed a chair and was dragging it across the floor when he turned and glanced at me.

"Not you, old man. You stay there."

My heart lurched in my throat.

Why? Am I the next one on your list of vets to "disappear?"

"I ... I ...." I stuttered.

"What?" Holbrook said, staring at me. He tucked the Glock into his waistband. "Stay in bed. Sorry about the disturbance."

As Holbrook turned his back on me and wedged the chair under the bathroom's doorknob, I realized he hadn't recognized me. No wonder. When he'd seen me at Topless Tacos, I'd been a woman with shoulder-length red hair.

"Go back to sleep," Holbrook said, dropping a pill into my water glass. The liquid turned blue. "Drink this. You won't remember a thing."

He handed me the glass. I smiled weakly and took a sip of the bitter brew.

"There you go," he said. Then he turned, bent down, and wrestled with the giant laundry sack on top of the guy with the hairy legs. "I'll be back in a minute for him," he said, heaving the sack onto his back. "Sorry about the toe thing. He's always been a bit funny that way."

Holbrook turned to leave. My mind raced. What was Holbrook going to do to my friends he had locked in the bathroom? Were *they* going to end up on his missing persons list?

I had to stop him! I reared back and heaved the water glass at Holbrook. It cracked against the side of his head.

"Ow!" he yelled as he stumbled. He slapped a hand against the wall for balance, then turned and glared at me.

"Take that, DiMaggio!" I yelled, standing up in my bed.

Holbrook's eyes doubled in size. He turned back toward the door, but it was too late. I leapt on top of him and his hunchback sack, slamming him sideways into the wall.

"Get off me, you crazy old man!" he yelled, trying to shake free of me.

I held on for all I was worth. "Stop!" I screeched as Holbrook regained his balance and lumbered, Frankenstein-like, out the door and into the main hallway of the nursing home.

"Get off!" he yelled again, and dropped the sack. He tried to claw at me, but I clung to his back like a super-glued turtle shell. I knew it was up to me alone to stop him. Everyone else in the place was either locked up or in a wheelchair.

"Why are you doing this?" I hollered, feeling the cold air on my backside as my hospital gown flapped in rhythm to Holbrook's lurching steps.

"I could ask you the same thing, old man!" Holbrook yelled back.

Then, suddenly, he froze.

I followed his blank stare down to the end of the hallway.

What I saw through the glass exit doors made me wish I had on clean underwear.

Or, at least, underwear.

Chapter Sixty-Four

AN EERIE PURPLE GLOW was emanating just outside the glass exit doors of Banner Hill. It was the strange, violet glow Stanley had warned about. The purple glow that made people disappear ....

Holbrook saw it, too. He stopped in his tracks, heaving to catch his breath. "Get off," he wheezed.

"Not happening," I said.

"Shit," he hissed, and began turning around, grunting with each awkward, jerky step.

I held tightly to his back. My plan was working. The burden of carrying me was wearing Holbrook out. I squeezed my thighs around his sides even tighter.

"Come on, old man!" he yelled. "You're killing me. Let go!"

Holbrook took a few steps down the hall, then turned right.

I knew what that meant. He was heading for the side exit. If he made it, I figured I was a goner. But what else could I do to stop him? If I let go of a hand to poke him in the eye, he'd surely sling me off. If I fell off, he's surely stomp me to death! I dug my nails deeper into his shoulders.

"Argh!" Holbrook yelled, then staggered determinedly down the short hall to the side exit door. He laid a hand on the push-bar and gasped. "You've got some grip for an old man."

"He takes Kung Fu lessons," a voice quipped behind me.

Grayson!

I craned my neck around. Grayson and Earl were standing right behind me. One was armed with a Glock. The other with ... a bedpan.

"How'd you get out of the bathroom?" I asked.

Grayson winked. "You're not the only one who knows Kung Fu."

"Ugh!" Holbrook groaned. He shoved open the exit door and lumbered off into the night, carrying me on his back like a worn out rodeo bull.

"Drop and roll, Drex!" Grayson called out.

I let go and tumbled into the grass. Holbrook took off. Grayson sped past me, leaping over me as he ran after him.

"You okay, Cuz?" Earl asked, holding out a hand to help me up.

"I think so." I did a quick survey of my body parts. "Yeah. I'm okay. Let's go!"

I ran in the direction Grayson had gone. Earl followed right behind me. Fifty yards out, in the dim haze of a lamp post, I saw Holbrook hobbling toward a Grand Safari stationwagon parked in the lot.

Its lights blinked on. Its engine roared to life.

Someone was there waiting for him.

Holbrook jumped in. The stationwagon took off, burning rubber.

"Over here," Grayson called out.

Earl and I ran over to the RV. Grayson was standing beside the passenger door, shaking his head.

"Let's go!" I yelled. "They're getting away!"

"No can do," Grayson said, and nodded toward the rear of the RV.

"Crap!" I yelled. "Who the hell keeps stealing our tires?"

"Looks like it's gonna be Bessie to the rescue," Earl hollered. "Follow me!"

"Where's Stanley?" I asked as we raced toward my cousin's monster truck.

"He stayed behind to check on your secret admirer," Earl quipped.

"Who was it?" I asked, not sure I wanted to know.

"We didn't have time to stick around and find out," Grayson said, opening the passenger-side door.

I started to climb in, then realized I was wearing a hospital gown—and not much else.

"You first," I said.

"I already called shotgun," Grayson said, offering me a hand up.

"But—"

"And I already saw your caboose." He waggled his eyebrows. "And might I say, *choo-choo.*"

I pinched the back of my gown together and climbed in. Once Grayson's butt hit the seat, Earl punched the gas pedal to the floor. The g-force could've made me lose my dentures—if I'd been wearing any.

As we tore through the parking lot, I realized I'd never been so embarrassed—or proud—in my entire life.

I was a real-life private-eye trainee—on a real-life, high-speed chase.

And Grayson thought I had a nice caboose.

Chapter Sixty-Five

AS IT TURNED OUT, TAILING the twenty-foot long stationwagon wasn't that hard. It had the turning radius of a small cruise ship.

"Not the best choice for a getaway vehicle," I said.

"I don't think it was chosen for that purpose," Grayson said.

"What do you mean?" Earl asked.

"Look at the thing. It's as big as a hearse."

"So why did they choose it?" I asked.

Grayson shot me a look. "I thought I just covered that. Because it's as big as a hearse. Nobody would suspect there were bodies inside."

I cringed with fear and disgust. Then I held on for dear life as Earl's monster truck chased Holbrook's sheet-metal land cruiser all the way into New Port Richey's old downtown strip.

As we sailed by a couple of blocks, the quaint, striped awnings and wrought-iron railings of the old buildings reminded me of New Orleans. Then I remembered we were chasing a guy who sawed people up for body parts.

"Hurry!" I said, staring at the road ahead.

The stationwagon's brake lights flashed in the distance about a quarter mile ahead of us. Earl stopped at an intersection.

"What are you doing?" I yelled.

"Looking both ways," Earl said. "You can't never can be too careful."

I glanced over at Grayson. He was preoccupied, staring out the window at a mural. It was hard to miss.

The drawing was nearly as large as the building itself, and depicted a crowd of people in brown, old-timey bathing suits taking a dip in a body of water—either a lake or the ocean.

Earl hit the gas. I lurched sideways into Grayson.

"Lucky them," I said as the mural disappeared from view. "Those old timers probably drowned before they had to live here."

"Don't be so fast to judge," Grayson said, pushing me back to my center position on the bench seat. "Back in the 1920s, New Port Richey used to be a magnet for the rich and famous. In fact, it was once dubbed 'The Hollywood of the East.'"

"Yeah, right. I guess now it's just part of "The Redneck Riviera.'"

Grayson shook his head. "Is this as fast as she'll go?" he hollered at Earl.

"Lord, no," Earl said. "I just didn't want to scare y'all." Earl punched the gas pedal and plastered us to the back of the seat. The tractor-sized tires hummed like a swarm of bees, and we made a city block in two seconds flat.

"We're gaining on them," I said.

"That's the point," Earl said.

We were maybe twenty yards behind them when the Grand Safari ran the stop sign at the intersection. Earl slammed on the brakes. I nearly hit my head on the windshield.

"What the?" I groused. "Earl, you can't stop at every—"

Hoooonnnk! A deafening horn blasted us from the left. A split second later, a huge semi-truck blew through the intersection.

I settled back in the seat. "Good call, Earl."

A second later, the taillights of the stationwagon lurched sideways. The sound of breaking glass and twisting metal filled the air.

"Lordy! They've done crashed," Earl said.

Earl drove us up to the scene. The stationwagon had clipped a corner, spun around, and crashed into a cigar shop. The store was decorated with a mural of a straw-hat sporting, stogie-chomping gator. Smoke billowed from the car's crumpled hood, lending the surreal effect that the gator's cigar had somehow come to life.

Someone groaned inside the car.

"I think it's time to call the police," I said.

Just then, behind us came the blip of a siren and the flash of blue lights.

"No need," Grayson said. "They're already here."

Chapter Sixty-Six

"WELL, TESTS DON'T LIE, but I can barely believe it," the patrol officer named Daniels said. "None of you tested positive for alcohol. Not even *you*, Holbrook."

Daniels had lined us all up against the wall opposite the now mangled mural of the cigar-smoking gator. He was shaking his head in wonderment that all of our breathalyzers came back clean.

"The tow truck is on its way," Daniels said. "Now, will somebody tell me what in the world is really going on here?"

Grayson and Holbrook exchanged glances. "I was doing an investigation at Banner Hill nursing home," Holbrook blurted. "This man is a lunatic. He's impersonating a doctor!"

"I'm the one conducting an investigation here," Grayson said, tugging the collar of his white hospital coat. "You've got a dirty cop there. In fact, I believe he's the mastermind behind a body-snatching ring."

Holbrook shot his fellow officer a *see what I mean* look.

The confused cop shifted his gaze over to the rest of us—Earl, me, and Ms. Gable, who'd been behind the wheel of the stationwagon.

"Somebody *else* want to help me out here?" Daniels said.

Another car pulled up beside us. Stanley got out, paid the driver, and tugged a giant laundry sack out of the back seat. Then he reached in and pulled out Melvin Haplets.

"What's *he* doing here?" I asked.

Stanley shrugged. "Turns out old Melvin may be Old Mildred instead."

"What?" I gasped.

Officer Daniels winced as if he'd just had an aneurism. "*Now* what?" He shook his head and pointed his weapon at the new arrivals. What've you got in the bag, bad Santa?"

"Uh ...." Stanley stuttered.

Grayson cleared his throat. "Excuse me, officer. If my theory is correct, that bag contains evidence of Holbrook's trafficking in human body parts."

Stanley dropped the sack like it was made of molten lava. "It *does?*"

"Looks like they got us," Melvin said to Holbrook. "The gig's up."

"Shut up!" Holbrook hissed. "Don't tell them anything!"

"Like what?" Melvin asked. "That you're my nephew?"

Holbrook's face crumpled. "Look," he said to Daniels. "It's not body parts."

"*What* isn't?" Daniels asked.

"What's in the bag," Holbrook said. "It's not body parts."

"What is it then?" Daniels demanded. He turned to Stanley. "You," he barked. "The guy who brought the bag. Open it."

"Me?" Stanley asked.

"Yes, you."

Stanley winced, then untied the drawstring. Resigned to his fate, he closed his eyes and cautiously reached a hand inside the bag. When he pulled it out, he had ahold of a tube of Preparation H and a brown prescription bottle.

"Medical supplies?" Daniels asked. "What are you doing with these?"

"*Me?* I know nothing!" Stanley said.

"Stealing them," Melvin said. "What else?"

I peeked inside the bag. The missing men's files were there, tucked among a mountain of pill bottles, bedpans, cotton swabs and tubes of denture cream. I stared at Melvin. "Why did you take all this stuff?"

Melvin shrugged. "To sell at the flea market. Have you seen what they want for a decent condo around here? Social Security don't cut it."

"How long has this been going on?" Daniels asked.

"Only a week," Melvin said, sounding disappointed.

"But Melvin," Gable said, "you've been at Banner Hill for years. Why start stealing now?"

"Ask *him*." Melvin nodding toward Holbrook. "Christmas is coming. He told me this girl he met on line wants him to buy her a boob job."

"What?" Gable screeched.

"It's a lie, honey," Holbrook said. "I ... I was conducting my own investigation into the missing office supplies."

From the look on her face, Gable wasn't buying a nickel's worth of Holbrook's BS. "No you weren't. I knew it! You're a two-timing fleabag!"

"Don't play dumb, Gable," I said. "You're in on it, too. I saw you waiting for him in the parking lot. You drove the getaway vehicle."

"I ... I didn't know anything about this, I swear!" Gable choked back a sob and glared at Holbrook. "You told me we were going on a romantic getaway!"

"We'd have made it, too," Holbrook said, "if you hadn't crashed the damned car. Why weren't you wearing your glasses?"

Gable pouted angrily. "You told me I looked sexier without them. And contacts bother my eyes. They make me squint." She demonstrated, giving us a spot-on impression of Miss Piggy—constipated on macaroni.

"I bet it was a lot easier to sneak supplies past her with her glasses off, eh?" I said to Holbrook.

Holbrook's shoulders slumped. "Look. I was just trying to cover for my crazy klepto uncle. Melvin kept stealing things. I didn't want him to lose his room at Banner Hill. I swear I didn't know what was in the bag."

"Then why did you take it with you?" I asked.

"Okay. Everybody just hold it," Daniels barked. "Without more evidence, it'll be hard to pin charges on *any* of you. My money's on Holbrook. Any of you have any other evidence against him?"

"Yes!" I cried out. "He tried to poison me!"

Daniels looked me up and down. Bald and in a hospital gown that barely covered my bottom, I couldn't blame him for being skeptical.

"Apparently, you survived," he said. "Got anything else?"

I did. But it was a long shot. "I saw Holbrook stealing money from the collection plate at Bertie's revival."

Daniels' face hardened like quick-setting plaster. He turned his angry eyes to Holbrook. "You dirty scum! Stealing from the Lord!" The cop marched over to Holbrook and slapped a pair of cuffs on him. "You're going to jail, you lowest-of-the-low!"

"If I may," Grayson said, raising a finger. "I still think theft is just the tip of the iceberg when it comes to Holbrook. Officer, we've got five vets missing from Banner Hill nursing home." He grabbed the prescription bottle from Stanley and rattled it. "This prescription is for Charlie Perkins. One of the missing men."

Daniels shook Holbrook by the collar. "What do you have to say for yourself now?"

Holbrook glared at Grayson. "I want an attorney."

"Actually, now that I think about it, Ms. Draper, the owner, has been missing for a week, too," Grayson said. "Holbrook might've done something with her, as well."

Gable spun around and slapped Holbrook hard across the face. "How could you? She's just a little old lady!"

"Look who's talking," Holbrook said. "You said she's the worst boss you ever had!"

"You work at Banner Hill?" Daniels asked Gable.

"Yes."

"Why didn't you report the disappearances?"

Gable winced. "Ms. Draper left on vacation with strict orders for me not to call unless the place was burning down, or she'd fire me. And I *did* report the missing men. I told Officer Holbrook."

Daniels shot Holbrook a disgusted look. "I think we can all figure out why *he* didn't report it." He shoved Holbrook toward his patrol car. "Didn't want anybody snooping around Banner Hill, did you, you disgrace to the uniform!"

Daniels shoved Holbrook into the back of his vehicle, slammed the door, and turned to face the rest of us. "All right, you bozos. Let's go."

"To the police station?" I asked.

"No. To Banner Hill. I want to see for myself what the hell's going on there."

Chapter Sixty-Seven

THE HORIZON WAS TINGING pink as we pulled up on the street in front of Banner Hill in the wee, pre-dawn hours. On the eastern side of the building, I thought I saw a flash of purple light shimmer, fairy-like, then disappear around the corner.

Could that be Old Mildred saying goodbye?

I shook my head to clear it. After a crazy night with no sleep, I figured I was so tired I was hallucinating. What I'd seen was merely a reflection coming from the lights atop the other patrol car officer Daniels had called in for backup.

I glanced in Bessie's rearview mirror. Holbrook and Melvin were cuffed in the back of Daniels' patrol car. Gable had ridden up front with Daniels. Her helmet of brown hair was in tatters.

As for me, Stanley, Grayson, and Earl, after threatening to call out the troops if we did anything suspicious, Daniels had followed behind us as Earl drove his monster truck back to the nursing home.

Earl shifted Bessie into park. A moment later, a pink Cadillac with vanity plates DRAPER1 pulled up in front of us. A scrawny little old lady in a pink knit suit and matching leather pumps climbed out of the driver's seat.

"What's going on?" she asked, smoothing her silver, salon-styled hair. She glanced over at the patrol car, still loaded with passengers. "Ms. Gable!" Draper screeched. "What are you doing in a police car? Are you under arrest? You're fired!"

"But!" Gable said, and scrambled out of the car.

"Now hold on," Officer Daniels said, coming around the car and taking Draper by the hand. "I don't believe there's any call for that. Ms. Gable is just helping me out in an investigation."

"Oh," Draper said. Then something clicked inside her brain. Her face puckered. "An *investigation?*"

"Yes," Daniels said. "Into five residents who've allegedly gone missing at your nursing home. We want to do a formal head count. Match up records with residents—and stolen medications."

"Someone's been stealing medical supplies?" Draper's face snarled like a psychotic Pekinese. She turned and glared at us as we climbed down out of Bessie. "Officer, I know everyone on staff. That man over there is no doctor. And that woman is no resident of Banner Hill!"

Gable cleared her throat and smiled sheepishly at her boss. "Well, Ms. Draper, while you were gone, I—"

"She assisted us in our investigation," Grayson said. He straightened his shoulders, stepped up to Draper, and showed her his tin P.I. badge.

"Oh," Draper said. Her snarl faded to a sneer. "I see. Well, thank you. But how did *you* get involved, Mr.—?"

"Grayson. Nick Grayson. Ironically, we were alerted to the disappearances by the nephew of one of your residents, Melvin Haplets."

I glanced over at the patrol car. Holbrook's face went white. "I'm gonna kill that nitwit," he muttered.

"Melvin Haplets?" Officer Daniels asked. "Isn't he one of the men I have cuffed?"

"Yes, sir," Gable said.

Stanley stuck an elbow in my ribs and whispered, "I *told* you Melvin was crazy."

"You, Stanley Johnson!" Draper barked, wiping the smirk off Stanley's face. "Stop horsing around with that man—woman—whatever it is! Get busy helping Officer Daniels. We're going to search Banner Hill from top to bottom. If we don't find those missing vets by nine am, I'll kick all your rotten heads in!"

Chapter Sixty-Eight

AN HOUR LATER, UNDER the eagle-eye command of Tyrannosaurus Draperi, all the residents' rooms at Banner Hill had been thoroughly searched.

During the raid, two things of note were found. One small cache of dirty magazines under a resident's mattress, and a tackle box hidden inside Melvin Haplets' closet. Inside it, he'd stashed away enough Viagra and Preparation H to, well, I really didn't want to think about it.

"I leave town for a week, and everything goes to hell," Draper said, shooting Gable some serious side-eye.

"I'm sorry," Gable said, looking as if she wanted to disappear behind the reception desk she was standing beside. "I was a fool for love. I didn't realize Holbrook was just using me for cheap rent and free medical supplies."

Draper nodded, then walked over and wrapped a scrawny arm around Gable's plump shoulders. "Aw. There, there, dearie. It happens to the best of us."

Draper's soft side took me by surprise. "You've been scammed before?" I asked.

She shot me a sour look, then turned and walked down the hallway.

"What a tyrant," I whispered to Gable and Grayson.

Halfway down the hall, Draper spun around on her pink heels. The look on her face turned my gut to ice-water. "I heard that!"

She took a step toward me. Gable and I both gasped. I expected to be beheaded, or at least court-martialed. But the old lady took a few steps and stopped, then leaned up against a doorframe, as if she'd lost her balance.

"Are you all right?" I called out, sprinting toward her. Grayson and Earl followed right behind me.

"Hush!" Draper hissed. She pressed her dangly old ear against the door and sniffed. "Humph!" she grunted, then stepped back and tried the handle. It was locked.

She turned and stared at the three of us like we were useless lumps. "Stanley!" she screeched. "Unlock this closet door at once!"

I realized Stanley was nowhere to be found—unless ....

Crap! Draper's caught Stanley "rearranging the supply closet!"

"Grayson, do something," I said, hoping my eyes conveyed what my lips could not.

"Allow me," Grayson said, ignoring me. He pulled a tool from his pocket and quickly picked the lock. "Step aside, ma'am. This may not be what you think it is."

Draper laughed cynically. "You think I was born yesterday?"

"No, ma'am," Earl said. "I'd say at least a good eighty or a hundred years ago."

Draper glared at Earl, then pushed Grayson out of the way. She flung open the door. "Aha! Just what I thought!" she said.

We all stuck our noses in for a peek. But what we saw wasn't just what *I'd* been thinking.

Not by a longshot.

Chapter Sixty-Nine

THROUGH A THIN VEIL of marijuana smoke, I made out the wild eyes, dirty faces, and singed hair of three half-starved old men. Dressed in filthy clothes, they must've been held prisoner in the supply closet for days—if not weeks!

"This is Stanley's work," Draper said. "It has to be. He had the key—and the stash."

"Stanley?" one of the three men asked, then laughed. "No, man, we're waitin' for Vlad."

Grayson's green eyes grew wide. "Vlad the Impaler?"

The three homeless-looking guys exchanged glances, then nearly rolled on the floor laughing.

"No, man. Vlad the *Inhaler*."

The three men broke into another round of giggles.

"Hey!" the third man called out. "You guys got any munchies? I'm starving!"

Officer Daniels came running up. He took one look in the closet and blanched. "What's going on here?"

"Looks like we found three of the missing men," Grayson said. "But two are still unaccounted for."

Daniels stared at the men. "Who did this to you? Who has a key to this room?"

"Oh! Oh!" one of the old men grunted and held up his hand. "I do! I do!"

TRYING TO INTERVIEW the three stoned old geezers was like trying to pop corn without a lid. New kernels of truth kept springing up when and where we least expected them.

After feeding the men spam omelets and plenty of weak coffee, their story began to emerge, bit by bit, like a dismembered corpse from a bog.

"Let me get this straight," Officer Daniels said. "Nobody did *anything* to you?"

"No, man," Larry Meeks said, scrambled eggs trapped in his scraggly beard. "We all went to Oldstock."

"Oldstock?" Daniels asked.

"Yeah," Harry Donovan said. His bloodshot eyes gleamed with fond memories. "It was *wild*."

"What's Oldstock?" I asked.

"Oh, oh!" Charlie Perkins grunted. "I know this one!"

Harry and Larry smiled and nodded. "You tell 'em, Charlie."

Charlie beamed at us with eyes so dilated they appeared solid black. "Oldstock was a dream," he said. "Every band from the '60s was there. Well, everybody that's still alive, that is."

"Oldstock," Earl said. "I heard of that. It's the remake of that hippy fest, Woodstock."

"Right," Larry said. "About the only thing that's changed is the price of admission. We had to sell our plasma to get enough money for tickets."

Grayson and I exchanged glances. That explained the anemia and sapped energy.

"Yeah, but it was worth it," Charlie said.

"Right on, man." Larry fist-pumped the air. "That was *our* music."

"Your music?" I asked.

"The music we all fought together with during Vietnam," Harry said.

"So you all served together?" Grayson asked.

"Yeah," Harry said. "Back in 1960 when we joined, there weren't even a thousand troops deployed in that blamed old second Indochina war." He sighed. "Even fewer came back. Those of us who did, well, we kept in touch over the years. As our wives died, we all moved to Florida and ended up here at Banner Hill."

"But where are the other two men?" Grayson asked. "Tom Hallen and Joe Plank?"

"Vlad's got Tommy," Larry said.

"Vlad. You mentioned him," Grayson said. "I thought you were joking."

"No. Vlad's real, man," Harry said. "He's our weed connection."

"He drove us to the Greyhound station so we could catch a bus to the concert," Larry said. "We got back early this morning. He could only hold three of us in his Smart car. We're waiting for him to drop off Tommy, now."

"Yeah," Harry said. "He's runnin' late, man."

Larry's Jitterbug phone rang. "Hey, that's Vlad now. Says he's at the front door with Tommy. Somebody should go get him."

"Oh! I will! I will!" Charlie said.

THE EERIE PURPLE LIGHT emanating from the dashboard of the Smart car proved that Vlad wasn't an alien or a ghost.

He was a Lyft driver.

As Tommy Hallen climbed out of the passenger seat, his buddies cheered and slapped him on the back. Grayson tapped on the driver's side window and waved a twenty at the man inside. He rolled down the pane of glass.

"I'm curious," Grayson said. "Why do people call you Vlad?"

"Because that's my name," he said in a thick, Eastern European accent. "Vladmir Popescu. I'm from Romania."

"Interesting," Grayson said. "Mind if I show you a video?"

"Sorry, man. I only drive."

"No. I mean, I want to find out if you ever gave this guy a ride."

Vlad shrugged. "Okay, fine."

Grayson opened his laptop and played Vlad the mysterious audio of Albert Balls arguing with a woman over too-big a swig of alcohol. Then of his feet in checkered tennis shoes.

"I recognize the voice," Vlad said. "That's Al, all right. I usually give him a ride when I pass by the plasma center. But that night, he wouldn't get in. I told him it was his last chance, but ...."

"Ah. Thanks," Grayson said. "That explains everything but the disappearance of—"

"Hold up a minute, Larry said, looking over Grayson's shoulder at his laptop. Grayson had paused the video on the last few seconds, when Balls' face had appeared. "That guy in the video. He's the jerk who stole my Viagra and took off with Joe and that chick from the band!"

The four old geezers exchanged teary eyed glances. "Good old Joe," Harry said.

"Good old Joe," the men repeated. Then they saluted and said in unison, "Another soldier who went down rockin.'"

Grayson's cheek dimpled. He turned to me and whispered, "I guess there are worse ways to go."

Chapter Seventy

AFTER TAKING OUR TESTIMONIES, Officer Daniels and his colleague released us on our own recognizance. Left to our own devices, we went straight to Topless Tacos for one last meal before we left town.

"Gros orteil," Grayson said out of nowhere, after we sat down at our favorite table.

We all looked up from our menus.

"Where?" Earl asked. "Is that somethin' new on the menu?"

Grayson's cheek dimpled. "In a way, yes." His eyes shifted to mine. "It's French for 'big toe.'"

"I don't get it," Earl said.

"That's what Draper's sister died from," I said, cutting Grayson off before he could say more. "Mildred choked to death on a big toe."

"I heard Old Mildred choked on a clove of garlic," Stanley said. "That's why Draper won't allow it in the kitchen."

"Huh," I grunted. "Either way, that could explains why Draper instigated the tooth fairy patrol."

"So, is Old Mildred real or not?" Earl asked.

"Doubtful," Grayson said.

"Then maybe I don't need this after all," Stanley said.

He pulled out the little voodoo pouch he kept in his hip pocket. He studied it for a moment, then looked up at me. "Where'd you hear that Mildred choked on a big toe?"

"From Sampson, the night janitor," I said.

Stanley's eyes grew wide. "I've heard of him. He used to work at Banner Hill."

"Used to?" I asked.

"Yeah," Stanley said. "Until he died last year."

Grayson and I locked eyes for a moment, then Grayson reached over and grabbed the amulet from Stanley's hand. He untied the string and emptied it onto the table.

A huge clove of garlic tumbled out.

"What does it mean?" I asked.

Grayson shrugged. "Hell if I know."

I looked over at Stanley. He shook his head. "I see nothing. I know nothing."

Earl picked up the clove of garlic and popped it into his mouth. He chomped down on it, then met our blank stares with a quizzical furrow of his brow. "What?"

AFTER THE LAST TACOS were devoured, Stanley left with a Lyft driver Grayson had ordered using his cellphone. We all waved as he disappeared with Vlad in his Smart car.

"Well, I guess I better get going myself," Earl said. "I'll give you two a lift back to Banner Hill."

"Sounds good," Grayson said.

Grayson's cellphone began vibrating on the table. "Must've left it on silent for the stakeout last night," he said. He picked it up and clicked the green answer button. "Hello?"

Grayson smiled and mouthed the words, "It's Rocko." He put the phone on speaker and set it in the center of the table.

"Brother Grayson!" Rocko's voice boomed over the phone.

"Yes, I'm here," Grayson said. "What can we do for—"

"Did you ... uh ..." Rocko stuttered. "Uh ... have you happened to see Brother Bertie around?"

"What?" Grayson said.

"I ... I got up this morning and ... the semi's gone, man. It's just ... *gone!* And so is Brother Bertie."

"Well, that's an interesting development," Grayson said, in the understatement of the century. "We'll keep you posted if we see anything."

"Thanks, man. But hey, if you do find him, you're on your own. My plane leaves for Thailand in three hours."

"I see. Well, good luck and God speed," Grayson said, and hung up.

"Bertie's disappeared?" I said.

Grayson shot me a look. "Brilliant deduction, cadet."

"You think old Bertie played possum?" Earl asked.

Grayson's left eyebrow flat-lined. "What's a marsupial got to do with any of this?"

"He meant did Bertie fake his own death," I said.

Grayson shrugged. "Huh. Who knows?"

Earl grimaced. "Dang it. Now I'm all worried."

"Why?" Grayson asked.

Earl pouted. "You think Bertie will want Polly back?"

I closed my eyes.

That's what you're worried about?

"I highly doubt it," Grayson said. "Where is that parrot, anyway?"

"In a box under the passenger seat." Earl glanced out the window toward his truck. "I guess I should probably let her out, huh?"

"Yes. You do that," Grayson said. "And then head on home. We can get a ride from here."

"WISE MOVE," I SAID as we watched Earl through the plate glass window of Topless Tacos. He'd climbed into the cab of his monster truck, and was now in the midst of what appeared to be a pillow fight gone horribly awry.

"He'll survive," Grayson said.

"I know. But what about Bertie?"

"That's who I was talking about."

I stared at Grayson. "You don't think Bertie's actually come back from the dead!"

"Resurrection," Grayson said, mulling the word over. "If you think about it, traveling prophets and con artists have been with us throughout history, Drex. Counterfeiters. Fake royals. Snake-oil salesmen. Amway distributors."

My brow furrowed. "Are you saying Bertie is the reincarnation of some historical crime figure?"

"Not necessarily. Maybe he played with a possum and never died in the first place."

I smiled to myself. Mixing up metaphors was becoming part of Grayson's charm.

He took off his fedora and rubbed the stubble growing back on his head. "A really good confidence man would never get caught in the first place," Grayson said. "Who knows how many scammers are out there were never detected?"

He rubbed his chin, then looked into my eyes. "Here's a thought, Drex. What if con artists are always the same people, just in different garb?"

"What do you mean? Like immortals?"

Grayson shrugged. "Maybe. What if Brother Bertie is part of some small band of alien creatures with incredible lifespans, masquerading on Earth, adapting to whatever scheme keeps them from being noticed?"

"I guess it's possible," I conceded. "Are you planning to go after him?"

Grayson smiled and shook his head. "No. I've got a feeling we've seen the last of Bertie and his crew of soul-sucking BERPS. They're probably already in hiding somewhere, planning their next reincarnation."

I blew out a sigh. "I still say somebody just stole his semi." I popped the last bite of taco in my mouth and nearly choked on a sudden thought.

"Grayson! That truck that blew through the intersection last night. I bet it was the thieves stealing Bertie's semi!"

"Okay. So how did Bertie himself disappear?"

I frowned and slumped back in my seat. "Maybe Rocko or some of Bertie's goons loaded him up in it to take him to a funeral home."

Grayson smirked. "Oh ye of little faith. So you no longer believe Bertie healed you of your blind spells?"

I sat up straight. "No. I've got a theory about that, too."

Grayson smiled. "What is it?"

I stared into Grayson's eyes. "Viagra."

Grayson nearly choked on his iced tea. "Okay," he hacked. "Let's hear it."

I leaned in over the table. "You said before that Viagra was one of the things that could've caused my temporary blindness."

"Yes, I did. But how—"

"Hear me out. Melvin and Holbrook were putting pills in the water glasses of their victims at Banner Hill, so they wouldn't remember them sneaking into their rooms to steal their stuff. What if Melvin spiked my water glass with Viagra to ...." I swallowed against the bile rising in my throat. "To try and put me in the mood."

Grayson's cheek dimpled. "Okay, but—"

"The dreams I had about Melvin *weren't* dreams. I think he slipped me Viagra every night I was in Banner Hill. Mystery solved."

Grayson folded his arms across his chest. "What about the first time it happened, on our drive to New Port Richey?"

I chewed my lip. "I thought about that. You remember that woman who was in the corner booth at Sargent's Pizza? The one who looked like a hooker?"

"No. I don't recall."

I rolled my eyes. "*Sure* you don't. Anyway, maybe our waiter was planning a little somethin'-somethin' with her. What if he spiked her drink—or his—and accidently delivered it to me instead?"

Grayson cocked his head and unfolded his arms. "I suppose it's possible. But more likely, he didn't wash the glasses very well and you caught somebody's second-hand mickey. That place was nothing but a pick-up joint, for sure."

"Why do you say that?"

"Because any respectable place would've had liver and onions on the menu."

"No. *That's* what explains the bad taste in my mouth."

Grayson smirked. "And here I was blaming poor Betty and Bam-Bam."

Chapter Seventy-One

WHILE WE WAITED ON the Lyft driver to come and take us to Banner Hill, Grayson paid the check, then tapped a few keys on his computer.

"Huh," he grunted. "Did you know that foot fetishism is the most common sexual fixation relating to body parts?"

I nearly choked on the Tootsie Pop in my mouth. "As opposed to what? Wait! Don't answer that."

"According to some sexpert at *Cosmo*, toe sucking is called *shrimping*." Grayson looked up at me. "It makes sense, if you think about it."

"I don't want to think about it!" A thought made me cringe. When I'd first met Melvin, he'd asked me to call him Shrimpy.

Ugh! There goes ever eating seafood again.

"Sucking toes is totally gross," I said.

Grayson looked up from his computer. "Why? Melvin's got his oral fixation, you've got yours."

I scowled. "What are you talking about?"

"Those Tootsie Pops of yours. Those who suck on straws shouldn't break a camel's back."

Ugh!

With a Tootsie Pop lodged in my mouth, it was difficult to defend my position. I settled for shooting Grayson a scowl instead.

He smiled. "But I suppose the ultimate oral fixators are incubus and succubus."

I raised a snide eyebrow. "Not vampires?"

Grayson shot me a look. "I think we just proved they don't exist, Drex."

I blew out a sigh. "Right. What was I thinking?"

WHEN WE GOT BACK TO Banner Hill, we were in for a rude surprise. We'd both forgotten about the RV's stolen back tires. Now all four were gone.

"I guess I'll call Earl," Grayson teased.

"No!"

"Triple A?"

"Better."

While Grayson dialed, I climbed into the back of the RV. Gizzard was waiting there in her terrarium.

I picked up one of the miniature Jim Beam bottles from the couch where Balls had emptied it. I rinsed it out, and fixed the anole some fresh vitamin water.

"Thanks, little Gizzard," I said as I filled her water dish.

"For what?" Grayson asked, coming in behind me.

"For being our spirit animal," I said. "If you think about it, one of her iguana relatives saved us. Even if it was a zombie."

Grayson smiled. "That, it did."

I plucked the sucker from my mouth and studied Grayson. "Do you really think I have an oral fixation?"

He shrugged. "Sometimes a Tootsie Pop is just a Tootsie Pop. And a taco is just a taco."

I smiled. "Now *that's* a belief I can get behind."

Grayson took a packet of mealy worms out of a cupboard and dropped a few into Gizzard's terrarium. "You know, I've been thinking about what you said, about vampirism being the ultimate oral fixation."

I groaned. "Please, can we give this whole vampire thing a rest?"

"I don't mean vampires as blood suckers or soul suckers. But as *oral robbers*."

My brow furrowed. "Oral robbers?"

"Yes. Those who steal with their mouths—not by way of fangs, but with words."

"I don't understand," I said.

Grayson turned his back on me and reached back into the cupboard. "What if I told you I was thinking of letting you go, Drex?"

My gut fell four inches. "What? Why? What did I do wrong?"

He turned back around. "Did you feel an internal shift?"

"Internal shift?" I said. "I feel *destroyed*. Like I want to throw up! Why are you doing this?"

"To prove my point."

"What point? That I'm no good?"

"No. That in a way, we're all oral robbers—*with our words*."

"Huh?" I whined.

Grayson studied me clinically. "All I did was utter some particular arrangement of tones through my vocal chords. You interpreted them as words, and applied your own meaning to them."

I was hurt. And on my last nerve with Grayson's stupid analogies. "Come on, Grayson! Just tell me. Am I fired, or what?"

Grayson locked his green eyes on mine. "My words formed images in your mind that sent chemical and hormonal secretions into your blood-stream, causing emotions that shifted your entire world view."

I glared at him. "Fine. I'll pack my bags and leave with the Triple A guy."

"See?" Grayson said. "Now you're insecure about your whole future, based on a couple of words that came out of my mouth."

"You'd be undone, too, if you just got fired and had to go back to Point Paradise and work with Earl!"

"That's just it," Grayson said. "You don't have to. I didn't fire you. I only asked you, 'What if I told you I was thinking of letting you go?' You did the rest yourself."

I blanched. "So ... I'm not fired?"

"No. Like I said before, it was all to prove my point. Every word we say is a psychic vampire, Drex, striking others with the power of sugges-tion that either drains or boosts the energy of its intended target."

"Oh," I said, feeling a wave of confused relief wash over me. "In other words, we all live and die by the thoughts and words we choose to be-lieve?"

"Exactly," Grayson said. "Unless coronary artery disease gets us first."

Chapter Seventy-Two

WITH FOUR NEW TIRES on the RV, we were finally ready to leave New Port Richey behind and head out on our next adventure.

I glanced over at Nick Grayson, the man in black. The man who murderized metaphors. The man with my future in his hands.

Why do I put my faith in this man? I wondered. Then I remembered. Because every time I think Grayson's nothing but a lunatic, he says something so profound it blows my mind.

I sat back and smiled. By my own admission, ours was a conflicted, ironic, and so far, platonic partnership. I might occasionally wish Grayson was dead, but something about that man made me feel alive.

Plus, for once, we'd finished a case with my wig still intact. I flipped down the visor and checked my shoulder-length auburn hair in the vanity mirror. I tugged the wig a tiny bit to the left.

Perfect.

"Ready to hit the road?" Grayson asked.

I nodded. "Ready. Where to next, chief?"

"Excellent question, cadet."

Grayson's cheek dimpled as he leaned over to open the glove compartment. His shoulder brushed mine, and a tingle of electricity passed through me.

If he felt it, too, he didn't let on. Instead, he pulled out a brochure and snapped the compartment shut.

"Look what I found at the Dilly Dally Motor Court," he said, handing me the brochure. "Someone stuck a bunch of these behind the refrigerator in the lobby."

I stared down at the brochure for the Skunk Ape Research Center in Ochopee, Florida.

"Do you think it's a sign from the universe, or a conspiracy?"

"Conspiracy?" I stuttered.

"Yes. You know, like someone doesn't want us to go there."

Grayson's calm, green eyes studied me, giving nothing away.

"I ... uh ...." A sharp hiss of static from the ham radio underneath the dashboard saved me from perjuring myself.

"Oh gee double-oh seven to Mr. Gray," the transmission crackled. "Come in, Mr. Gray. Over."

I smiled and shook my head softly as Grayson picked up the mic. Goofy, buck-toothed Operative Garth had either saved my bacon—or was about to throw me into the frying pan.

"Gray here," Grayson spoke into the mic. "Come in, oh gee double-oh seven. Over"

"Heard about Melvin and the bogus missing vets. Sorry about the bum lead. Over."

Grayson shrugged. "It happens. Anything new and interesting on the grapevine? Over."

"Yeah. Possible skunk ape encounter down in the Everglades. Over."

"Well, I'll be a monkey's uncle," Grayson said. He grinned and plucked the brochure from my hand. "A sign from the universe, it is."

The End

Ready for More *Freaky Florida Mystery Adventures?*
Find out where Bobbie and Grayson go from here in their next crazy adventure, *Ape Shift.*
Check out ***Ape Shift*** now on Amazon!
https://www.amazon.com/dp/B086ZVMKRK

Get a Free Gift!

Don't miss another sneak preview, sale, or new release of *Freaky Florida Mystery Adventures!* Sign up for my newsletter for insider news. I'll send

you a free copy of the hilarious *Chronicles of Florida Woman* as a welcome gift!

https://dl.bookfunnel.com/ikfes8er75

Or, if you prefer, follow me on Facebook, Amazon or BookBub. They'll
let you know when my next book is out!

Facebook:

https://www.facebook.com/valandpalspage/

Amazon:

https://www.amazon.com/-/e/B06XKJ3YD8

BookBub:

https://www.bookbub.com/search/authors?search=margaret%20lash-
ley

*I hope you enjoyed Oral Robbers! If you did, it would be freaking fantastic
if you would post a review on Amazon, Goodreads and/or BookBub. You'll
be helping me keep the series going! Thanks in advance for being so awesome!*

https://www.amazon.com/dp/B081VS4S77

More Freaky Florida Mysteries

by Margaret Lashley
Moth Busters
Dr. Prepper
Oral Robbers
Ape Shift
More to Come!

"I want to believe, but I mean ... really?"

Bobbie Drex

About the Author

WHY DO I LOVE UNDERDOGS? Well, it takes one to know one. Like the main characters in my novels, I haven't lead a life of wealth or luxury. In fact, as it stands now, I'm set to inherit a half-eaten jar of Cheez Whiz...if my siblings don't beat me to it.

During my illustrious career, I've been a roller-skating waitress, an actuarial assistant, an advertising copywriter, a real estate agent, a house flipper, an organic farmer, and a traveling vagabond/truth seeker. But no matter where I've gone or what I've done, I've always felt like a weirdo.

I've learned a heck of a lot in my life. But getting to know myself has been my greatest journey. Today, I know I'm smart. I'm direct. I'm jaded. I'm hopeful. I'm funny. I'm fierce. I'm a pushover. And I have a laugh that lures strangers over, wanting to join in the fun.

In other words, I'm a jumble of opposing talents and flaws and emotions. And it's all good.

I enjoy underdogs because we've got spunk. And hope. And secrets that drive us to be different from the rest.

So dare to be different. It's the only way to be!

Happy reading!